Players

PLAYERS

Nina Lambert

CENTURY · LONDON

First published in Great Britain in 1993 by
Random House UK Limited
20 Vauxhall Bridge Road, London SW1V 2SA

Random House South Africa (Pty) Ltd
PO Box 337, Bergvlei 2012, South Africa

Random House Australia Pty Ltd
20 Alfred Street, Milsons Point, Sydney, NSW 2061
Australia

Random House New Zealand Ltd
18 Poland Road, Glenfield, Auckland, New Zealand

The catalogue data record for this book is
available from the British Library

ISBN 0 7126 5569 7 (Paperback)
ISBN 0 7126 5901 3 (Hardback)

Photoset by Deltatype Ltd, Ellesmere Port, Cheshire
Printed in England by Clays Ltd, St Ives plc

For Mike, with love

Prologue

To die; to sleep;
No more; and by a sleep to say we end
The heart-ache and the thousand natural shocks
That flesh is heir to . . .

William Shakespeare – Hamlet

Act Three, Scene Four. The final performance. The last ten minutes of my career.

It's a full house tonight. Five hundred people sitting in the dark, watching us. Two women on a spotlit stage, playing two halves of the same person. But this time only one of us is acting. The other one's doing it for real.

We look alike, thanks to the wigs and make-up. One night we swapped parts in the second act for a lark and nobody out there noticed. Are we playing the same character, different roles? Or the same role, different characters? If there are two people inside everyone, that means there are four of us up here. And at the moment, it feels like three against one. I'm outnumbered, but I won't let that stop me.

You've only just come in? Never mind, you haven't missed much, the best bit is still to come. Eve One – that's me – is a creature of emotion and impulse. Eve Two – my alter ego – thinks and plans. We've spent the play telling each other what to do, joining forces, falling out, making a collective mess of our dual life, a life that's very nearly over, thank God. In this final scene, Eve One takes an overdose of sleeping pills. And not before time.

This will be the last time I die, or live, on stage, the last time I share the limelight with my rival, my best friend. In the heat of performance, she won't notice that the tablets are slightly smaller than usual. I swapped them for the dummy ones on the props

1

table, in the interval, when no one was looking. I'm a great believer in improvisation. Specially during a long run. It helps to keep things fresh.

It would be simpler, of course, to take them later, in private. But not easier. An audience forces you to overcome fear, a role gives you something to hide behind, the strength to do things your real self could never do. And besides, what more fitting exit for an actress than to make her final bow on stage?

The fight scene. Carefully rehearsed so that we don't really hurt each other. If only life could be choreographed as neatly. Kick, scratch, bite, throttle. And Eve Two is out for the count, leaving Eve One free to destroy herself, to quell the pain once and for all.

Mustn't take too many. Don't want them working too soon, don't want sirens and stomach pumps and shrinks and everyone saying it was just a cry for help, poor thing. No. A handful now, here on stage, as my fond farewell to the theatre. And a top-up once I'm safely in bed, ready to sleep for ever . . .

The phone rings. Suspense in the auditorium. Will Eve Two manage to answer it and summon aid in time? Then the twist in the tail, to keep you all guessing. Then the applause, the only send-off I need or want.

Soon it will all be over.

ACT ONE

January 1958–Autumn 1963

There are two tragedies in life. One is to lose your heart's desire. The other is to gain it.

Bernard Shaw – Man and Superman

1

January–December 1958

To lose one parent . . . may be regarded as a misfortune;
to lose both looks like carelessness.

Oscar Wilde – The Importance of Being Earnest

'This isn't a prison, remember,' said the gaoler, with a phoney professional smile. 'I want you to think of this as home.'

Paula wasn't fooled by this come-into-my-parlour pep talk. She'd heard it all before. There was all the difference in the world between a home, however unhomely, and a Home, and this place, like the last one, reeked of rules and restrictions. Not that she intended to stay here long.

The welcoming spiel over, Paula was escorted to a sludge-painted dormitory, smelling of lino and disinfectant, where she was allocated a bed and a locker and left in the care of a gap-toothed fifteen-year-old with terminal acne who offered her an illicit Woodbine and asked what she was in for, as one old lag to another.

'My father buggered off,' shrugged Paula, lighting up, 'and then my stepmother started knocking me about.' She chose not to mention the reason for Marje's attack, not that it would raise any eyebrows in a place like this.

'I've been here going on two years,' the girl told her chattily. 'My mum's ex came round one night and done her in with a hammer. My two little brothers are fostered,' she went on, picking at a juicy pimple on her chin. 'When I'm eighteen I'm going to go on list, get my own place. So we can be together again. As a family, like.'

Paula couldn't blame her for dreaming. She had done it herself often enough, nurtured the foolish hope that Dad would somehow turn up out of the blue, smelling of Brylcreem and booze and bellowing, 'Where's my sweetheart? Where's my favourite girl?'

5

And then she would remind herself that she hated Dad, that she would never forgive him for walking out on her, just as her mother had done before him. He had disappeared one night when Paula was eleven, leaving a note by her bed saying 'Sorry, love. You're not to blame.' Marje had soon convinced her otherwise. Not that Paula had needed much convincing. And besides, bad things were easier to bear if you deserved them. She had done her best to deserve them ever since.

She was well shot of Dad, and Marje. Well shot of Stan, Marje's soft-spoken lodger, with his warm, easy smile and empty promises. Well shot of –

No. She wouldn't think about that, wouldn't think about any of it, ever again. She would suppress every memory of her life to date and start again. But not here. Not here.

Paula stayed out of trouble, not without difficulty, until the Sunday night, when the weekly half-a-crown pocket money was doled out after supper, increasing her total assets to one pound two and fourpence. By then she had done a full recce and worked out her plan of escape.

As the clock on the landing struck five, Paula crept from the dormitory, carrying a ready-packed duffel bag, dressed at the double in the freezing washroom and made a perilous exit via its frosted glass window. Half way down the icy drainpipe she lost her grip and fell the last ten feet onto the frozen flowerbeds, jarring her bad ankle. For a moment she lay immobile, hissing with pain, thinking that she had broken it again, dreading sudden lights and noise and discovery. But the pain eased and the silence held. For once God was on her side. Retrieving her bag, Paula picked herself up and limped forward into the blackness.

The Home, a former lunatic asylum in rural Essex, was set well back from the road and surrounded by high railings. After several attempts, Paula managed to lasso one of the iron spikes with her dressing-gown cord, brought with her for the purpose, which she climbed like a rope, hoping that it wouldn't snap under her weight, until she was high enough to hoist herself over the top.

She landed heavily on the other side, jarring her ankle again, but this time she felt nothing but elation. Drunk with sweet, sudden freedom she ran towards the crossroads, half a mile away, where she thumbed the passing traffic, shivering with cold and excitement. After five minutes or so a lorry picked her up in its headlights and lumbered to a halt.

'You're out and about early,' bellowed the driver, a ruddy-faced middle-aged man with a Northern accent. He wasn't a local, thought Paula thankfully, he wouldn't know there was a council home nearby, wouldn't suspect her of absconding.

'Got to get to work in London by half eight,' said Paula chirpily. 'I've just been home for the weekend.'

'You're in luck. I'm delivering to the West End. Hop in.' Paula climbed aboard, all happy-go-lucky girlish smiles. 'So where-abouts do you work, love?'

'Selfridges, in Oxford Street.' Dad had promised to take her there, years ago, to visit Santa Claus in his grotto and see the Christmas lights. The visit had never come off, but she had enjoyed looking forward to it. The real thing would probably have been a disappointment. 'In Ladies' Fashions. I'm a trainee buyer.'

Paula was a good liar. A compulsive one, Marje would have said. On this occasion, it helped that she looked older than her years, thanks to her hastily applied make-up and a well-developed bust, a dubious fringe benefit of being fat. She could easily pass for sixteen.

They drove for a while without speaking, with Paula transfixed by the unopened tube of Rolos vibrating on the ledge above the dashboard. A sudden stop at traffic lights sent it hurtling to the floor; she bent to pick it up, hoping that he would offer her one. He did.

Bliss. The glutinous caramel coated her teeth like icing before dissolving and descending and settling, indestructibly, around her hips. Eating, especially sweet things, was a love-hate affair, a scourge and a comfort, an expression of defiance and despair. As always, it made her even hungrier. Luckily, they stopped at a transport caff for breakfast, where Paula allowed her chauffeur to buy her a fry-up and two slices and a pint mug of tea. He turned out to have a daughter 'about your age' who was a student nurse.

Paula duly admired a photo showing her scrubbed and smug in her uniform, hating her for having a father and a mother. She responded by inventing a cosy little family of her own, complete with a gran and a couple of siblings and a budgie, wondering all the while what it must feel like to be normal, to be a real, proper, paid-up person.

7

Fooled you, thought Paula, as he dropped her off outside Selfridges. His kindness should have been a good start to her adventure, but of course he wasn't being kind to her, Paula, only to the person she'd pretended to be. If he'd known what she really was he'd have turned her in at the nearest nick.

But he hadn't. The first, most important hurdle was past. There were millions of people in London, they would never find her here as long as she stayed out of trouble, instead of looking for it. That was the real challenge. Old habits died hard.

Intent on redeeming one of her lies, she hung around outside Selfridges till it opened and presented herself at the personnel department, where she was handed an application form requiring full details of her education and previous experience and the names of two referees. Paula left without filling it in.

After several abortive enquiries in smaller establishments, with her bravado fast fading, she found herself being quizzed by the rigidly corseted manageress of Estelle Modes, an outsize shop in the Edgware Road.

Paula answered her questions demurely. She changed her surname from Butcher to Baker and claimed to be living with an aunt in Stepney, quoting the address she had seen on her birth certificate, a slum that had long since been cleared. She was seventeen, she continued glibly, and had worked in two stores in Harlow, a bogus bridal outfitters (which had since closed down, she explained), and an equally fictitious dress shop (which had recently changed hands).

The truth was she had once held a Saturday job at Woolworth's, from which she had been sacked for swearing at a customer, and at Boots, where she had quickly fallen foul of her ratbag of a supervisor. But this time she would bow and scrape with the best of them. For the time being, anyway.

Fortunately, Estelle Modes had just lost their previous junior, who had left, it appeared, without giving notice. The pay was only four pounds a week plus commission but Paula was in no position to be fussy, and neither, it seemed, were they. At least there was no form to fill in and no demand for references, possibly because she would not be required – or permitted – to handle money, the till being manned by the boss woman and her heavyweight sidekick. Well conned, the manageress asked if she was free to start right away, further evidence that they were either desperate or too mean to advertise.

'We'll give you a week's trial,' said Mrs Sharp, a name which suited her beak-like nose and gimlet eyes, framed by extravagant winged spectacles. 'You go forward only when I or Mrs Norris are serving, or when we pass a customer to you.'

Paula spent her first day cleaning the glass counter and full-length mirrors with methylated spirit, sweeping the thinly carpeted floor with an ancient Ewbank, sewing loose hems and buttons in the back shop, and making tea, of which she was allowed to partake for sixpence a day, to be docked from her wages. She drank several cups, heavily sugared, to dull her appetite. In the busy midday period she managed to serve one customer, who tried on half a dozen hideous outfits and bought a pair of support hose for five and eleven.

Sharp went to lunch at eleven, Norris at two. Paula was given a choice between ten and three. She chose the latter, by which time breakfast was a distant memory, but resisting the lure of the nearby sandwich bars she made do with a tube of fruit gums to save money. She spent her break window-shopping in Oxford Street, dreaming of all the things she would buy when she was rich. Quite how she would get rich she hadn't decided yet, but one thing at a time.

On her way back she visited the Selfridges powder room, for a free wash. A young woman was in there, vainly trying to calm a fractious infant, whose angry tears proved to be catching. Choking back a sudden sob, Paula took refuge in a cubicle and wept jerkily into a soggy length of San Izal, cursing herself all the while for being pathetic and ruining her make-up.

Emerging dry-eyed a few minutes later, she dabbed Creme Puff over her pink, shiny cheeks and renewed her lipstick, hating the sight of her round, podgy face and short, straight, mousy hair and boring brown eyes. She had been quite skinny, as a child, with fair, almost platinum curls. Dad had always said she was beautiful, like her mother. He had never said a bad word against her mother, she was just a kid, he said, they'd got married far too young because of the war, in case he didn't come back.

Dad had never told her that her mother had died, or how. But Marje eventually had, after Dad had left, just as Marje

9

had told her the real reason her mother had abandoned her, providing proof, if proof were needed, that she was bad, unloved, unlovable . . .

Stan had loved her, so he said. Paula had almost believed him. Almost, but not quite. She was too good a liar herself to be that gullible. It hadn't been Stan who deceived her, but she, Paula, who had deceived herself. However much she tried to shift the blame, onto Dad, or her mother, or Marje, or Stan, it always came back to her, like a boomerang. She had messed up the first fourteen years of her life, but the next fourteen would be better. How could they be worse?

Sharp and Norris dismissed her at ten past six, with a reminder to clock in by quarter to nine next morning. It was raining hard, so Paula took shelter in Marble Arch tube station, watching wet people pour through the ticket barriers in the scramble to get home. Somebody had left an *Evening News* in a phone booth. Ignoring the photograph of General de Gaulle on the front page, Paula turned to the classified and began reading through the flats to let.

There were several bedsitters from £2 a week, described in tortuous abbreviations. They would probably want a month's rent in advance and key money. It wasn't worth wasting fourpence on a phone call, let alone the fare to go and view. She'd have to sleep rough for a while.

After an hour or so it stopped raining. Turning up the collar of her thin council-issue trench coat, Paula set off to explore. At the junction of Oxford Street and Tottenham Court Road her nostrils picked up the pungent odour of fried fish. Following it to its source she bought sixpence worth of chips, chewing each one to a pulp before she swallowed it and licking the greaseproof paper for the last vestiges of salt and vinegar. This feast stimulated her gastric juices, leaving her even more ravenous than before. Perhaps she'd have another bag later on, before she went to bed. Bed. That was a joke.

She kept walking for the next couple of hours, to keep warm, past pubs and shops and restaurants, weaving stories around the people she observed sitting at tables in the window, waiting for buses, hailing taxis, walking hand in hand. She knew that they probably led dull, uneventful lives, but she liked to imagine that

10

interesting things happened to them, the way they did to people in books. Paula had done a lot of reading in the last few months, to while away her imprisonment. Reading was less painful than thinking, fiction gloriously remote from her own experience, full of beauty and bravery and happy endings and comfortable, comforting lies.

Drawn towards Soho by cooking smells, she found herself in a red light area full of cinemas showing blue films, and strip joints with evil-looking bouncers hanging around outside. Tarts were parading up and down, dressed in tight leather skirts and high-heeled winklepickers, their faces vivid expressionless masks. Paula admired their nerve. If you had to be bad, you might as well do it in style.

But remembering her resolution to stay out of trouble she kept on the move, still none the wiser as to where she might spend the night. Anywhere official, like a Salvation Army hostel, carried the risk of discovery. Which left public places like railway stations and shop alleyways and the Embankment, no doubt patrolled by the police whom Paula was anxious to avoid, in case they were looking out for her. She walked on into Shaftesbury Avenue, lured, moth-like, by the bright lights of the theatres.

Paula had been to the theatre only once, as a child, to see *Dick Whittington*, who had come to London, like her, to seek his fortune. Dad had given her a bar of milk chocolate all to herself, one of the black market goods he had wheeled and dealed in before they came off ration. Paula remembered little of the performance, but she remembered the taste of the chocolate, remembered feeling happy, in an anxious kind of way, because she already knew from experience that happiness, like food, never lasted long. One minute Dad would be cuddling her and tucking her up, the next she would be alone and awake, cold and hungry and often wet, tied to the bedpost to stop her straying while he was out, knowing better than to cry. Even so, she had gobbled up the magic of the evening as greedily as the chocolate, as if knowing that it would be her one and only taste . . .

It was then that she noticed the neon proclamation: *Sir Adrian Mallory as King Lear. Edmund Kean Festival Theatre production. Limited season.* A hand-written placard announced, *House full. Some gallery seats available from 10 a.m. on day of performance*

11

only. It wasn't the play that interested her, but the queue that had formed outside the theatre.

A couple of dozen people were sitting on the pavement, wrapped in blankets and sleeping bags. They must be waiting, Paula realized, for the box office to open tomorrow morning. This was a godsend. If she joined the queue she could spend the night here, respectably, with no questions asked.

Relieved to have found safe harbour she sat down on her copy of the *Evening News*, next to an elderly woman swathed in a thick winter coat with a tartan rug over her knees. She looked sideways at Paula, taking in her thin mac and bare legs.

'You'll be frozen to death by morning,' she observed hoarsely. 'Didn't you bring anything to wrap up in?'

'I'm all right,' said Paula. 'I don't feel the cold.'

'Bully for you. I feel it something chronic, with this bloody chest of mine.'

Her choice of adjective predisposed Paula, who swore like a navvy, in her favour. As did the offer of a Du Maurier, which she dragged on hungrily.

'Rain always sets off this sodding cough,' continued her neighbour, hacking away into a handkerchief between puffs. 'Mind you, if the performance is good, it never gives me any trouble . . . Sod it. It's started again. Here, have a share of my brolly.' She erected a large black umbrella beneath which Paula huddled thankfully. At this point the old girl began spouting poetry at the top of her voice, oblivious to the odd looks she was getting from the rest of the queue, or perhaps even enjoying them.

> *'Poor naked wretches, wheresoe'er you are,*
> *That bide the pelting of this pitiless storm,*
> *How shall your houseless heads and unfed sides,*
> *Your looped and window'd raggedness, defend you*
> *From seasons such as these?'*

Paula didn't recognize the quote from the play, though the reference to pitiless storms and houseless heads and unfed sides seemed apt enough. The old girl was obviously a nutter.

'Must have seen this play a dozen times,' she continued. 'I've seen Wolfit and Redgrave and Gielgud. But they say Mallory's

12

pipped them all. Did you see him in *Tony and Cleo*, last year?'

'No,' said Paula.

'Bloody brilliant he was.' She drew breath to give another rendering, but mercifully her cough intervened.

Rashly, Paula proffered her last fruit gum but the old woman waved it aside and gave her the brolly to hold while she rooted in a wicker shopping basket for her Thermos. She poured some tea into the cap and knocked it back.

'Have some,' she said, refilling it and passing it to Paula. 'There's a drop of scotch in there. It'll warm you up.'

Paula took a big hot swallow. The drop had been added with a generous hand and the familiar smell of Dad was inescapably consoling.

'Thanks,' she said. And then, to humour her, 'Do you go to the theatre a lot, then?'

'Oh, I see everything. I don't usually pay, mind. I've worked most places, they all know me, and if there's a seat going spare they let me have it. Not for this, though. This was all sold out before it got to London. Besides, I quite like queuing. You meet some nice people in queues. What about you, darling? Seen anything good lately, have you?'

'Um . . .' Paula's abject ignorance robbed her of her powers of invention, forcing her to settle for a sullen 'No'.

The woman didn't seem surprised. She delved back into her basket and withdrew a brown paper bag.

'Fruit cake,' she said. 'Dig in.'

Paula took a thick slab and wolfed it down, provoking the question, 'You had your tea tonight, lovie?'

'Not yet,' said Paula, hoping to inspire further largesse.

'Finish it, then. Go on.' And then, catching her off guard, 'So are you here for the play, or just looking for a place to kip?'

It was difficult to lie with a face full of cake. 'Place to kip,' mumbled Paula, feeling as if the words 'in care' were branded on her forehead. Bugger it. Now the old bat would start ticking her off, perhaps even try to shop her. 'Any objections?' she added, preparing to move on.

'Free country,' she shrugged. 'All sorts latch on to these queues. Drunks, vagrants, you name it. Don't worry. The police won't bother you here.'

Her tone betrayed a scant regard for the guardians of the law. Reassured, Paula accepted another piece of cake.

'Beatrice Dorland,' said her companion, holding out a ring-encrusted hand. 'You can call me Bea. What about you?'

'Paula. Paula Bu – Baker.'

'Ran away from home myself,' said Bea, scraping a match against the pavement and setting fire to another fag, 'to go on the stage. Fifty-odd years ago, nearly. Very odd, some of them. Actors were still rogues and vagabonds then. As for actresses . . . I couldn't have gone back home after that, even if I'd wanted to. My family were respectable, you see. But I've no regrets. Even though I never found fame and fortune. Used to work as a dresser, between parts, till my chest got the better of me. Still, there's something to be said for being a lady of leisure. At least this way I'm free to pick and choose what I see of an evening. I always sit in the gallery if I'm paying. That's where the real theatre-lovers sit. You meet a nice class of people in the gods . . .'

She rattled on. The effect was strangely soothing. After another swig of fortified tea, Paula's head began to nod and she dozed off under a share of Bea's blanket. She dreamed that she was running, that they were catching up with her, unaware that she had cried out in her sleep until Bea murmured, 'Steady on, lovie. It's all right.' The gritty voice was gruff but gentle and soon she slept again, waking up with a start to a poke in the ribs.

'Get that inside you,' said Bea, handing her a warm bacon roll and a paper cup of sweet, frothy coffee. 'Another hour and a half to kill before they open up, lazy sods.'

'What time is it?'

'Half eight. You were out for the count. Must have been that drop of scotch.'

'Half eight? Oh shit.' She scrambled to her feet. 'I'll be late for work.' She took a gulp of coffee and stuffed the roll in her duffel bag. 'Thanks. How do I get back to Marble Arch?'

'Straight ahead to Piccadilly Circus and then the 6 or 12 bus,' said Bea, adding casually, 'I'll buy you a ticket for the play. See you back here at seven thirty tonight, okay? If you haven't got a bed for the night by then, you can bunk down on my settee.' And then, seeing the mistrust in Paula's eyes, 'If I was going to give you away, I'd have done it by now. Best of luck, darling. Here.' She

14

shoved a flat red Du Maurier packet in Paula's coat pocket, still shiny in its cellophane, and raised her paper cup in a valedictory toast. 'Chin chin.'

Paula ate the roll on the bus and made it to work with a minute to spare. The day followed the same pattern as before, with Sharp and Norris taking it in turns to swoop on customers, oozing false, fulsome compliments as large ladies draped themselves in shapeless garments.

'Oh, but that's just Modom's colour,' they would drool. Or 'It's the copy of a Paris design,' or 'Our seamstress will alter it for you, free of charge.' (Our seamstress was a wizened old piece-worker who hobbled in to deliver and collect.) Paula soon learned to mimic their patter, with some success, notching up her first sale just as Norris returned from lunch, while Sharp was busy cooing over another client.

Far from congratulating her, Norris seemed annoyed to have missed the sale herself. The customer was one of her regulars, she said – a claim which Paula could not dispute – so the commission would have to be split. Paula bit her tongue and managed a docile nod. If she got sacked now, she wouldn't get a penny out of them, she would have slaved all yesterday for free. And besides, all shops were the same. There would always be some old bag who had it in for her, no point in cutting off her nose to spite her face.

Bea wasn't an old bag, somehow, even though she must have been pushing seventy. There was something irreverent and rebellious about her that closed the generation gap. And true enough, she could have turned Paula in while she slept, but she hadn't done, which made Paula inclined to take her up on her offer of a bed, even if it meant sitting through *King Lear* and pretending to enjoy it.

She treated herself to a sit-down tea of chips and beans, washed down with a glass of Tizer, in a greasy spoon in Poland Street and arrived at the theatre at twenty past seven to find Bea waiting for her in the foyer, almost unrecognizable in a beaded black cocktail dress and fur stole, with a fox's head gaping glassily out of one end of it. This ensemble was set off by a long rope of pearls, half a dozen jingle-jangle bracelets and elbow-length black gloves. The heavy winter coat of last night had hidden a figure of skeletal thinness.

15

'So you came,' she said casually, puffing on her customary fag through a long tortoiseshell cigarette holder. 'I was all set to flog your ticket for at least a fiver. Let's have a drink in the Dress Circle Bar. You are eighteen, aren't you?' she added, winking, leading the way up the stairs. 'Harry!' she boomed, poking the programme-seller – a florid, middle-aged man in a dinner jacket – in the ribs. 'Good to see you.'

'Bea darling,' he greeted her, waving away her shilling. 'Haven't seen you for a while. Thought you were dead.'

'I'll outlive you, you old queen.' She moved on and elbowed her way towards the bar. 'What's yours?' she called over her shoulder.

'Whatever you're having,' said Paula, playing safe, and a moment later Bea returned with two Bloody Marys.

'Chin chin,' she said cheerily, downing hers in a couple of gulps. 'Know the story of *King Lear*, do you?'

'Not really,' said Paula, taking a judicious sip and enjoying the way the vodka hit the back of her head.

'Well, he's this vile-tempered old king with three daughters. Two of them grovel to him like mad because they're looking to inherit all his loot. But the third, Cordelia, can't bring herself to suck up to him, even though she's fond of the old sod. So naturally he cuts her off and hands his kingdom over to her two ugly sisters while he's still alive, stupid bugger. Well, what do you suppose happens then?'

'Dunno. Yes I do. Once they've got the money, they can't be bothered with him any more, right?'

'Right,' applauded Bea, before continuing her throwaway summary of the plot, adding that it might sound like a load of twaddle, but not to worry, it would all come alive on stage. As the warning bell sounded, Paula knocked back the rest of her drink, and followed Bea, somewhat unsteadily, out into the street and up several flights of stone stairs to the gallery, where they took their seats on the steeply tiered narrow benches giving a bird's eye view of the stage far below. For Paula, used to the cheap front stalls in the cinema, it seemed very grand to be looking down instead of up, neck craned towards the screen.

Not that she had been to the pictures very often. If she had any money to spare she would always rather spend it on something to eat. Marje didn't keep any food in the house – she got free meals at the pub where she worked – so if Paula wanted anything besides her free school dinner, she had to pay for it herself, out of her paper round money and Saturday jobs. She would never have spent three bob on a theatre seat, enough for half a dozen bars of chocolate. Still, it wasn't her money.

She yawned as the curtain rose, responding to the snake of vodka slithering sleepily through her veins. And what followed was a kind of sleep, or rather a trance, populated by vivid dreams, dreams that she didn't quite understand but which made their own perfect sense at the time, the way dreams do. It was like looking into a magic mirror, paralyzed into staring submission, captivated by the strange enchantment of a world which lay, tantalizingly, just beyond her reach, a world full of pain and pathos which provoked and purged her, leaving her dizzy and elated and confused.

In the interval Bea, who was gasping for a fag, went off to have a smoke, leaving Paula to queue for an ice cream which she barely tasted, though she wolfed it down eagerly enough. She sat staring at the safety curtain, onto which were projected ads for charcoal biscuits, Bear Brand nylons, and Clarks Start-Rite shoes, while her mind stayed numb, suspended, unwilling to return to dull reality.

She was relieved when the lights dimmed again, making her invisible, weightless, unconfined by flesh, able to spy, unseen, on lives larger and more important than her own, to suffer and exult in safety, by proxy, while others raged and wept and triumphed on her behalf. And then suddenly, too soon, it was all over. Bar the shouting.

There were thirteen curtain calls as the audience rose to its feet, bellowing approval. Bea roared a gravelly, full-throated bravo, which was echoed all round the gallery. Adrian Mallory, suddenly tall and vigorous, not hunched and frail, bowed again and again, holding his hands out either side of him to acknowledge his fellow-actors, his magnificent eyes, visible even from this distance, flying upwards to the gods where his loyalest, fiercest critics were assembled.

It was the best part of the evening, releasing the plug on all the pent-up passions of the last three hours, draining away some of the pent-up poisons of the last fourteen years. Paula clapped till her hands hurt, unaware that the tears were streaming down her face until Bea shoved a hanky at her with a gruff, ''Fraid it's a bit damp.'

Paula blew her nose, ashamed of herself, as the house lights went up, finally breaking the spell. As they filed out of the theatre she felt excluded by the knowledgeable chatter all around her, people twittering at each other in loud, posh-sounding voices. She had a hollow feeling of having been taken in. It was finished now, gone for ever, leaving her as empty as before.

'We'll never get a taxi at this rate,' muttered Bea as the crowds descended on an insufficiency of cabs. 'I'll have to pull one of my stunts. Take your cue from me.'

Grabbing Paula's hand she fought her way through the crush towards the edge of the kerb, where she suddenly let out a piercing cry and keeled over, clutching her chest.

'My pills,' she whimpered, as Paula crouched down beside her, momentarily alarmed. 'I left them . . . at home.'

Urged on by a robust wink, Paula jumped up.

'My gran's got a bad heart,' she informed the crowd of gaping onlookers. 'I've got to get her home right away. She forgot to bring her pills. If she doesn't take one quickly she could die!'

Amidst virtuoso whimpers from Bea, two public-spirited bystanders commandeered the nearest taxi and lifted her into the back of it, while Paula mumbled incoherent thanks, struggling not to laugh. Bea revived sufficiently to tell the driver her address while Paula covered her face with the damp handkerchief and began weeping anew, with mirth this time.

'Wish I did have a dicky heart,' confided Bea *sotto voce*. 'A nice quick way to go. No such luck.' Whereupon she collapsed into a fit of genuine coughing which lasted until the cab drew up outside a five-storey building in what Bea referred to as West Ken. Opening the heavy outer door, she handed her latchkey to Paula and told her to go on up to the top floor.

'These bloody stairs are a killer when I can't get my breath,' she croaked. 'I take them in easy stages.'

She had managed the stairs in the theatre well enough, but suddenly she seemed ill, old, exhausted, as if her little charade was about to come true.

'I'm all right,' she said irritably, rejecting Paula's supporting

18

arm. 'I'll get there in the end. Go in and get the kettle on, for Christ's sake. I'm parched.'

Paula ran on ahead and did as she was told. It took Bea a good five minutes to appear, which gave her time to look around, her footsteps dogged by a fat fluffy ginger cat. She peeked furtively into the fridge, mouth watering at the sight of a big lump of cheese, sliced ham, sausages, a bowl of tomatoes, a couple of pork pies and – oh temptation – a large wedge of chocolate cake topped with whipped cream and glacé cherries.

Stifling her hunger pangs, Paula peered into the bedroom, which was small with a sloping roof, housing a sagging, lumpy double bed, a vast mahogany wardrobe and a matching dressing table with a triple mirror, laden with perfume bottles and jars of cream. The living room was quite large with an air of tawdry, faded splendour, bathed in the dim pink glow of a tasselled standard lamp. There was a chaise longue by the window, upholstered in balding plum-coloured velvet, an old-fashioned writing desk with lots of little drawers, a drinks trolley stacked with bottles and glasses, a dark green chesterfield settee, its leather pitted and cracked, a rocking chair, a Chinese screen, and several occasional tables covered with framed photographs, as was the mantelpiece, dominated by a big black clock which chimed cheerily as if in greeting. The walls were covered in red flock paper, most of which was obscured by ancient theatre posters with curling edges. The gas fire was burning low, filling the room with welcoming warmth.

Paula moved on to the bathroom, where she used the wooden-seated lavatory, washed her hands with Pears' soap and dried them on a threadbare towel, admiring the stuffed parrot which sang soundlessly in the gilded cage suspended, chandelier-style, from the ceiling. Catching sight of herself in the mirrored cabinet above the washbasin, she opened it, dispelling her hated reflection, to find dozens of pill bottles, a length of black rubber tubing and, nestling in a metal tray, a hypodermic syringe.

She shut the cabinet hurriedly as she heard the front door slam and emerged to find Bea tilted almost horizontal in her rocking chair, with the fat ginger cat on her lap.

'Make the tea, will you darling?' she wheezed as the kettle shrieked. 'Nice and strong.'

19

Paula spooned tea into a china pot, found two blue-ringed cups, and dispensed milk and sugar.

'Bless you. I'll have it with a splash of scotch.' She indicated the bottle of Johnnie Walker on the drinks trolley. 'Help yourself.'

Paula did so, hoping that it would help recapture the sensations she had felt in the theatre. The newly familiar glow spread through her, sharing its strength.

'There's a phone in the hall,' said Bea, watching her over the rim of her cup, 'if you want to ring your parents.'

'Haven't got any parents,' said Paula sullenly. 'They both took off years ago. You want to be careful, taking in someone like me. Juvenile delinquent, I am.'

'Ah, well, it takes one to know one.' Bea hoisted herself to her feet. 'That tea's given me a second wind. I fancy a Welsh rarebit. With a nice big dollop of Pan-Yan pickle. Make the toast for me, will you, while I slice the cheese.'

Paula followed her into the kitchen.

'I always get peckish this time of night,' Bea went on. 'When I was on the stage, I could never eat a thing before I went on. But afterwards I'd have a good old gut-bash. So what did you think of the play?'

'Dunno,' said Paula, unable to put her feelings into words. 'Just as well you told me what was going on beforehand or I wouldn't have made head or tail. I was never much good at school.'

'They shouldn't be allowed to teach Shakespeare in school,' said Bea, sawing several thick slices off a big square loaf and passing them to Paula. 'Put people off it for life, they do.' She began carving a slab of orange cheese. 'Shakespeare wrote for the rabble, you know, as well as the nobs and snobs. I've met Adrian Mallory, of course. Knew him long before he was a Sir.'

'What's he like?'

'An absolute swine, darling. But the women adore him. God knows, there were enough of them, even though he had one of the made-in-heaven marriages. Leastways, that's what the public thought. Strung his poor wife along, he did, till he had his knighthood safely in the bag, and then dumped her for Davina Winter. The girl who played Cordelia tonight.'

'Cordelia? Isn't she an awful lot younger than him?'

'Only thirty years or so. He's not quite as old as he looks done

20

up as Lear. I'm not saying she can't act, mind, but he gave her a leg up, you can count on it. A leg over I should say, randy old git. Now Fay Burnett, the first Lady M, was a real lady. I was her dresser once, back in '47. You must have heard of her, surely?'

Paula shook her head.

'You haven't seen *Only a Rose*? Or *Samarkand*? Or *Dangerous Woman*? Bit before your time, I suppose. Made her name in Hollywood, playing plucky Englishwomen in those wartime propaganda films. She's more or less retired now. Remarried a rich American producer. Good for her, say I.'

The cheese was bubbling nicely under the grill. Paula withdrew the pan and Bea transferred the slices onto two pretty plates with scalloped edges, much too nice to eat off. She gave them to Paula to hold while she threw a checked tablecloth over the enamelled table and laid it with knives and forks, a jar of pickle and two wine glasses.

'Get stuck in while I open the plonk,' she said, rattling around for a corkscrew and then grunting briefly over a bottle. 'Red all right for you?'

'I suppose so. I've never drunk wine.'

'I shouldn't encourage you, I suppose. Corrupting your morals, I am.'

Morals, thought Paula. Tell that to Marje. She'd soon tell you what a little slag I am.

'Just one glass,' said Bea, with belated restraint, recorking the bottle and returning it to the cupboard. They clinked glasses and Paula took a mouthful. It tasted bitter, but it produced the same warm glow as the vodka and the whisky. As her hunger retreated and the wine loosened her tongue Paula found herself talking about Estelle Modes and doing an impromptu take-off of Sharp and Norris, eliciting a gratifying bark of laughter from Bea.

'Sharp isn't too bad,' Paula conceded, 'but Norris is a greedy bitch. She did me out of six bob in commission. I'd have told her to get stuffed if I hadn't needed the job. Another place might ask for references.'

'What time did you say Sharp went to lunch?'

'Eleven. Why?'

'If you see me tomorrow morning, you don't know me, okay?' Bea heaved herself to her feet. 'You'll find some linen and

21

blankets in the airing cupboard. Help yourself to tea and toast in the morning and anything else you fancy. You can stop here for a bit, if you like,' she added casually, 'till you find somewhere else.'

'Only if I pay for my keep,' said Paula quickly. That way she wouldn't have to feel grateful.

'Too right you will. One pound ten a week or you're out on your ear. Don't be late home tomorrow. We're due to see *Hedda Gabler* at eight.'

'Who's she?'

'She's a play. Goodnight then, darling. If I were you, I'd have a bath before you turn in. Have you got a change of clothes?'

'Yes. If I can iron them.'

'In the cupboard, in the hall.' Bea disappeared into the bathroom and emerged ten minutes later, looking glassy-eyed. Paula's mind flew back to the hypodermic in the medicine cabinet. Perhaps Bea was diabetic, she thought. But she couldn't very well ask about it without admitting that she'd had a snoop. Easy-going though Bea might seem, Paula was wary of falling foul of her, even though falling foul of people had been a point of honour until now.

She took the hint about the bath. It was a treat to have clean, hot, unscummy water that Marje hadn't used first, nice to be warm and private instead of shivering, fat and naked and miserable, in tepid communal showers. She couldn't have stomached such kindness from an ordinary person, she hated being pitied and patronized. But Bea was different. Bea was anything-goes, take-it-or-leave-it, Bea was couldn't-care-less. Bea smoked and drank and swore. Bea conned people into thinking she was dying just to jump a taxi queue. Bea was tough as old boots, a woman after her own heart.

Paula ironed her spare blouse and skirt for the morning and washed the old one in the bath with her smalls, hanging them up on the pulley in the kitchen. The chesterfield was hard and lumpy, so she settled for the chaise longue, which was marginally less so. After a night on the pavement, however, it felt like a feather bed. The cat had followed Bea into her bedroom, whence emanated reassuring snores. It couldn't last, but for the moment she was almost happy.

*

Next morning Paula made herself some toast, thickly spread with real butter – a great treat – and thick-cut marmalade. She washed up from the night before, taking pleasure in drying the pretty plates and putting them back in the cupboard. Replacing the milk jug in the fridge, she couldn't resist helping herself to just a little sliver of the wedge of chocolate cake. She was just licking the sticky crumbs off the knife when Bea appeared at the doorway, haggard in a faded blue candlewick dressing gown.

'I didn't mean to wake you,' began Paula, colouring.

'It wasn't you, it was this lousy shrinking bladder of mine.' Bea lit her first fag of the day, coughing all the while. 'I meant to tell you to take that piece of cake with you, for elevenses. All right for your tube fare, are you?'

Paula scowled.

'Yes. And I'm supposed to be on a diet,' she muttered, as Bea parked her cigarette in the corner of her mouth and wrapped the cake in a piece of greaseproof paper.

'Plenty of time for that. Puppy fat. You might as well have these.' She put the pork pies into a paper bag, adding a couple of tomatoes and an apple. And then, seeing Paula's mutinous expression, 'Well, what are you standing there for? Piss off or you'll be late.'

Clutching her bag of goodies, Paula fled, swallowing the treacherous lump in her throat, inventing ulterior motives for Bea's kindness. Perhaps she would turn out to be a lez with a fetish for fatties. Perhaps she needed the thirty bob a week to keep herself in fags and booze, or planned to use her as a live-in skivvy. Life had taught her not to trust, or rely on, anyone. No one else had ever cared a damn about her, why the hell should Bea?

Paula spent all morning cleaning the plate glass windows with the aid of a rickety stepladder. At eleven Sharp went to lunch, instructing her to assist Norris in her absence. Two minutes later a customer came in, wearing a striking purple wool suit and a matching picture hat festooned with ostrich feathers. It was Bea.

She silenced Paula's involuntary acknowledgement with a freezing glance and turned her attention to Norris, looking her up and down with aristocratic hauteur.

'Can I help you, modom?'

'I hope so. I'm Lady Briggs, of Dolphin Square. My niece is a regular customer here. You know her, of course? The Honourable Mrs Peregrine Brierly-Stone.'

'The Honourable Mrs Brierly-Stone?' warbled Norris, with a show of feigned delight. 'Oh yes indeed.'

'Poor gel hasn't been too well lately,' boomed Bea. 'So I thought I'd buy her a few things to cheer her up. Perhaps a dozen frocks, couple of blouses, skirts, oh, and a new tweed jacket, she's enormous across the bust these days, poor lamb. She must be about your size by now. Perhaps you'd try on that pink thing, over there, so I can see how it looks.'

She indicated a lobster-coloured two-piece.

'Modom would like me to . . . to model it?'

'Well, it's hardly likely to fit me, is it?' drawled Bea, looking magnificently bored and bony. 'And while you're at it, you can show me that blue evening dress, and what can you suggest for a Palace garden party in June?'

It was like the theatre, only better, because she, Paula, was part of it. While Norris disappeared in and out of the changing room and pirouetted grotesquely to order, Paula managed to serve three genuine customers and earn herself seventeen and six in commission. Sharp returned from lunch to find her colleague draped in turquoise georgette and Bea declaring, 'Perfect for Glyndebourne. Now, thinking ahead to Ascot . . .'

Paula, assisting her customer in the changing room, emerged to hear Sharp hissing at her colleague, 'What the hell's going on?'

'Lady Briggs is buying some new clothes,' lisped Norris, 'for her niece, a client of mine. The Honourable Mrs Brierly-Stone. We happen to be the same size.'

'Mrs Brierly-Stone? Isn't she one of my customers?'

'No, she's one of *my* customers . . .'

Slipping out into the shop, Paula whispered briefly to Bea in passing. A moment later Norris appeared swathed in a fussy floral print, closely followed by a grim-looking Sharp.

'I know you, don't I?' boomed Bea, to the latter. 'You served my niece, last time we were here.'

Norris's face fell down to her feet. Sharp beamed obsequiously.

'So sorry I missed you, Lady Briggs. Perhaps I can take over now.' Norris, her face fossilized with fury, stood rigid as a dummy while Bea scrutinized her critically.

24

'I'll take it,' she said at last, adding, 'I have a lunch appointment at the Ritz. I'll be back at three to choose the rest.' She swanned off, leaving Paula in an ecstasy of gleeful anticipation.

It was glorious. Sharp and Norris hissed and spat at each other between ensuing customers, Norris finally exploding with, 'You know bloody well we've never had an Honourable Mrs Brierly-Stone, or a Lady Briggs. She's wandered into the wrong place, for God's sake. I mean, why would someone like her shop in a dump like this?'

'I thought you said Brierly-Stone was one of your regulars?'

'Only because I knew you'd try to make out she was one of yours! I got to her first. I sold her fourteen new outfits!'

'So I'll split the commission with you on those. But when she comes back, the sales from then on are mine.'

'Bitch! No wonder nobody stays here long!'

'Mind who you're calling a bitch. I'm in charge here. One word to Mr Blick, and you'll get your cards.'

'Screw Mr Blick! Which is exactly what you've been doing, isn't it? More fool you. I know for a fact that he's knocking off Elsie Peters, at the Queensway branch. He even tried it on with me!'

'Liar! You're just jealous, that's what you are. You'd never have got this job if it wasn't for me putting in a word for you, after you were sacked from Gorringes . . .'

'I've had just about enough of this. I'm off to lunch and I'm not coming back!'

'Good bloody riddance! And hand over the key to the till right now or you'll be hearing from the police!'

Norris flung it at her and stormed out, bumping into an incoming customer. Sharp patted her hair and looked at her watch.

'You can take this one, dear,' she cooed at Paula. 'Lady Briggs will be back any minute. If you don't mind missing lunch today you can leave a little bit earlier tomorrow.'

Bea kept Sharp hard at it for the rest of the afternoon. Deciding that she was more her niece's size than Norris ('I realize now she's much slimmer than I thought') she demanded everything she had bought so far one size smaller, and required Sharp to model a dozen more outfits, playing up to her vanity with a stream of absurd flattery.

'Clothes hang so well on you, my dear,' said Bea as Sharp

paraded in a voluminous lime green duster coat. 'You should have been a model.'

Meanwhile Paula struck lucky with the customer Sharp had discarded and clocked up another three sales, bringing her commission for the day up to one pound seven and three. Obligingly, she assisted Sharp by wrapping all Bea's purchases.

'Well, thank you so much for all your help,' said Bea finally. 'How much does that come to?'

Sharp cleared her throat.

'Three hundred and forty-seven pounds, twelve and eight-pence,' she announced hoarsely, barely able to conceal the tremor in her voice.

'Is that all?' said Bea, rummaging in her handbag. 'Incredible. One wonders why one bothers to go to Hartnell. If only you sold things in my size.'

'Our seamstress . . .' began Sharp hopefully, but Bea interrupted her with a brisk 'Silly me. I've gawn and come out without my cheque book. Tell you what, I'll send my maid round to collect the packages in the morning and she can settle up with you then. I must fly. Goodnight, Mrs Blunt.'

'Goodnight, Lady Briggs,' twittered Sharp, seeing her to the door and jumping about like a dervish on the pavement till she managed to stop a cab. 'I hope I'll have the pleasure of serving you again soon.'

She returned to the shop, flushed with triumph.

'You can run off home now,' she said to Paula. And then, as if afraid that she would follow Norris's example, she added a munificent 'I've been very pleased with your work to date. While there are just the two of us, we'll put your money up to four pounds ten, all right?'

Paula couldn't wait to tell Bea that Norris had walked out. With luck, Sharp would have difficulty replacing her, and she, Paula, would have the chance to earn a bit of money. She ran up the stairs to find a plate of sausage and mash waiting for her, which Bea told her to eat quickly or they'd be late for the theatre. She dismissed Paula's praise for her performance with the words 'It was a straight lift from Edith Evans as Lady Bracknell. *Importance of Being Earnest.*' Paula looked blank. 'They're doing it in rep at Richmond next month, you'll like it.'

'Aren't you having anything to eat?'

'I had mine earlier. We'll have a snack when we get in. We're in the good seats tonight. Complimentaries. Haven't you got anything else to wear?'

'Only what I had on yesterday.'

Bea disappeared for a moment and returned with a black velvet opera cloak and a black silk turban.

'Try these.'

Uncertainly, Paula did so, her lank hair and lumpy figure disappearing into the disguise. Drawing the folds of the cloak around the drab navy skirt, skimpy pullover and cheap cotton blouse, she went to inspect herself in the full-length mirror in the hall.

'I look bloody ridiculous.'

'If you think that, don't wear it.'

Better to be laughed at than ignored, thought Paula, driven by her own exhibitionism. Attention was the next best thing to admiration.

Hedda Gabler, said Bea, as they waited for the tube ('No more taxis till I draw my pension on Thursday'), was a woman who married the wrong man, only to continue to fancy an old flame. Unable to tolerate the boredom of her life any longer, she ended up blowing her brains out. The lover, Bea explained, was being played by Neville Seaton, an up-and-coming young actor in whom she had a personal interest.

'I know his ma,' she bellowed, above the roar of the train. 'She and I toured together, back in 1925. We still send each other Christmas cards. Neville played Edmund to Mallory's Lear at the Kean last year but then he left the company, he and Sir A didn't hit it off. We'll go behind afterwards and see him.'

Bea sailed into the foyer, duchess-like, to claim her free seats and greeted the front-of-house manager, an old acquaintance of hers.

'How's business?'

'Grim. The house is all paper tonight. Tynan really laid into Moira. The notices are going up at the end of the week.'

'What did he mean?' asked Paula as they took their seats in the stalls.

'That they've given away a load of free tickets, to make the

27

place seem full, and the show's about to close. Tynan's a theatre critic, he panned it. Moira Ledbury's not really up to the part, she's really a light comedy actress, but she's the chief backer's current bit of stuff.'

The play was a lot easier to follow than *King Lear*. But there was no magic in it, despite a good performance by Neville Seaton. The leading actress was shrill and mannered, and Bea wasn't the only person who started coughing. This time Paula was happy to talk about it over her Bloody Mary in the interval.

'She deserved all she gets,' she said of Hedda, between puffs at her cigarette, taking care not to burn a hole in the velvet cloak. 'She's a cow. The sooner she does herself in the better.'

'You're hard on people, aren't you? Yourself included.'

'Well, it's better than being soft.'

'A better actress would have made you see her point of view. Hedda's trapped. In those days, remember, you were stuck with a husband for life. I wouldn't like to sit in judgment on anyone for marrying the wrong man. It took me three goes to get it right.'

'So were all your husbands in the theatre?'

'The first two were. Tom was killed at Vimy Ridge. Then I married Hugh, but he left me for another man.'

'A man?'

'These things happen in the theatre, dear. Then I met Jack. Jack was the love of my life. He died in '52. That was when I finally gave up on the business. I'd used up all my courage, I suppose. No one suffers like actors do. Terror, disappointment, humiliation, injustice, despair. God only knows why any of us do it. It's like a drug.'

A drug, thought Paula, like booze, like food, something that deadened pain.

The applause at the end was unenthusiastic. People began filing out before the curtain call was over.

'Let's go back now,' said Bea, 'and tell poor Neville it wasn't his fault.'

Bea's crony escorted them through the no-entry pass door which led backstage. Paula breathed in the smell of sawdust and varnish, overlaid with a sweet, stale scent, like talc mixed with sweat. She followed Bea up two flights of narrow metal stairs and along a dingy, twisting corridor where Bea knocked on a door marked 'N. Seaton' and bellowed, 'It's only me, Neville. Bea Dorland.'

The door opened. Neville Seaton was still wearing his stage make-up. It looked very obvious, close to, and Paula could see how the years had been painted on, making him look in his early forties, rather than late twenties. He had removed his brown wig and beard, revealing reddish-gold hair, and donned a pair of gold-rimmed spectacles. There were two other visitors in the room, a girl of about sixteen and a boy a few years older, both with a glass in their hand. By the look of them they were brother and sister, with the same vivid flame-coloured hair. Paula found herself staring at them. They were beautiful.

'Bea,' said Neville Seaton glumly, embracing her. 'Mother should have warned you not to bother. We're coming off any day.'

'And we all know why. You were wonderful, darling. This is my friend Paula.'

Paula drew her cloak tighter around her.

'You were . . . er . . . terrific,' she said, anxious, for once, not to show herself up.

'I stank,' said Neville Seaton shortly. 'Bea, have you met Isabel and Richard Mallory? Have some of Richard's champagne.' He picked up a bottle of Bollinger and filled two more glasses. Bea did a double take.

'You're never Fay's little ones, are you? But of course you are, you're both the image of her. Last time I saw you, you were just tots . . .'

So these were Adrian Mallory's children, thought Paula, with something like awe. Their provenance seemed to bathe them in a godly glow, as if they had not been conceived and born like ordinary mortals but descended, fully grown, from the flies.

'Bea was Fay's dresser, on *A Nightingale Sang*,' prompted Neville, jogging their memories.

'Of course!' Richard Mallory's greeny-grey eyes lit up in sudden, intensely flattering recognition. 'We came to a Saturday matinée and the nanny was late collecting us . . .'

'. . . and you did scrambled eggs on toast for us while Mummy had her nap,' finished his sister. She had a low, attractive voice and a ready, if slightly shy, smile.

'Imagine you remembering!' crowed Bea, glowing with

29

gratification. 'Good as gold, you both were. Sat all through the performance without a murmur. How's your ma these days?'

'She's very well, thank you,' said Isabel Mallory politely. 'She's living in Los Angeles now.'

'We went to see *Lear* last night,' said Bea. 'Paula here got through a whole box of Kleenex.'

Unused to theatrical hyperbole, Paula blushed, feeling foolish. Isabel reassured her with another radiant smile, while her brother said dryly, 'I never got round to catching it myself. Izzie's already done duty for both of us. She sat through it about six times at the Kean.'

'Three times,' Isabel corrected him, sighing.

'But then, Neville was playing Edmund at the Kean,' added Richard, shooting his sister a mocking look. Isabel flushed.

'And tell me, how's Helen?' went on Bea, either not picking up the innuendo or choosing to ignore it.

'Tired,' said Neville. 'She's due in March. And William's going through the monster phase.'

'We must introduce him to our dear little stepbrother, Toby,' drawled Richard. 'Davina believes in free expression. The only time the little beast gets a walloping is when I'm at home. The latest au pair is terrified of him. Almost as terrified as Izzie.'

'Richard,' remonstrated Isabel. 'You're being a bore. People don't want to hear about Toby. We really ought to go. Neville must be anxious to get home. Can we offer you a lift anywhere?' she added, turning to Bea.

'Well, that's very sweet of you, darling. West Ken. If you're sure it's not too much trouble. Where are you living these days? Not still in Chelsea, are you?'

'No, Windsor,' said Isabel, rather glumly. 'You're on our way, honestly. 'Bye, Neville.'

'Goodnight, Izzie. I'll try and catch your Titania next term.' He kissed her briefly on both cheeks.

'Don't. I shall be awful in it. You know how dire school productions are.'

'She's just fishing,' said Richard. 'She's all set to take FRIDA by storm, same as you did.'

'That seems like a long time ago,' said Neville. 'Good luck with *Godot* then, Richard.'

30

'Cheerio, old man. Hope the brat pops out with all its nuts and bolts in working order.'

''Bye, Neville darling,' said Bea, giving Neville a hug. 'Do you have anything to go to?'

'Just a telly. Bingley in a six-part *Pride and Prej.* I loathe the box, but the money's good.'

He shook Paula's hand and flashed her an automatic smile, but his eyes remained fastened over her shoulder, to where Isabel was standing by the doorway.

Paula was deeply impressed by Richard's car, a red sports two-seater. The two girls clambered into the back, where they perched on the parcel shelf with their knees up to their chins. Bea started asking Richard about Oxford, where he was reading English. Paula listened hard, still watching a play, not all of it comprehensible.

'So are you involved with the OUDS?' Bea was saying.

'Not any more. I've set up my own rival group, Renegade. We're kicking off with *Waiting for Godot* . . .'

'Are you still at school?' asked Isabel, of Paula, speaking across her brother.

'No,' said Paula, rather defensively. 'I've got a job.'

'Lucky you,' said Isabel. 'What do you do?'

'I'm a trainee buyer. In ladies' fashions.'

'So do you get lots of super clothes at a discount?'

'Er . . . yes.'

'I adore that cloak. And the hat.'

Paula squirmed, unused to compliments. She had never met anyone remotely like Isabel before.

'I like your coat,' she countered awkwardly, miserably aware of her lack of social graces. It was of plain dark green wool with a grey fur collar, left open to reveal a light blue jersey dress with a drawstring waist. Isabel looked elegant and expensive and warm and terribly clean.

'Thank you. So, are you and Bea neighbours?'

'I'm her lodger.'

'I do so envy you, being in town. We used to live in Radnor Walk, just off the King's Road, but the house was sold when our parents split up. Now we're simply miles out, half way between London and the Kean. When Richard comes down and I leave school, next summer, we're going to share a flat.'

31

Paula should have hated Isabel Mallory. She had everything. She was slim and beautiful, with two parents, albeit divorced, both of whom were rich and famous and successful. To make matters worse, she was nice. She was everything Paula wasn't, everything Paula would have liked to be. But she didn't hate her. She was captivated by her. If either one of them had been a man, it would have been love at first sight.

'Would you two like to come up for a tipple?' said Bea as the car drew up, all too soon, in Castletown Road.

'We'd love to,' said Richard, 'but we've got an early start. I'm driving Izzie back to school in Gloucester.'

'Well, remember me to dear Fay, won't you? Lovely to see you both. And thanks for the lift.'

'Goodbye, Paula,' said Isabel, as if they were old friends. 'Hope we meet again sometime.'

But they wouldn't, of course. Paula felt the same sense of loss as when the curtain had come down last night. Something brief and brilliant was already over.

She began quizzing Bea as soon as they were inside, following her slow progress up the stairs.

'Who's Freda?'

'F-R-I-D-A. The Foster Roberts Institute of Dramatic Art. Sir Adrian went there, so I expect Isabel will too.'

'Did you go to FRIDA, then?'

'Heavens no. I just latched myself onto a touring company as a dogsbody. Some people still start that way, but it's much harder than it used to be. The reps are closing down, you see. It's the bloody telly that's done it.'

She leaned against the door jamb, panting. 'Help yourself to some supper, darling, I'm going straight to bed.'

She disappeared into the bathroom and emerged some minutes later, in her dressing gown, her face relaxed and with the familiar glassy look in her eyes.

'Can I get you some tea? Or Bournvita?' asked Paula, hoping to lure Bea into further conversation and find out more about the Mallorys. It was as if she had arrived late for a performance and had to leave early, missing the vital beginning and ending of the play.

But Bea just smiled vaguely and said, 'No thank you, dear. I've had my nightcap. Sleep well.'

The seed was sown, the pattern set. From then on Paula went to the theatre three and four times a week – musicals, comedies, thrillers, straight plays, classics – anything Bea could wangle a comp for, followed, with luck, by a visit backstage. Her Sunday afternoons were spent in the one and nines in the local fleapit, and sometimes the evenings as well if the film was worth seeing again. Paula sat through two consecutive showings of *Cat on a Hot Tin Roof* and three of *Gigi*, wondering wistfully what it felt like to be as sexy as Elizabeth Taylor or as slim as Leslie Caron.

With Norris gone, Sharp seemed to mellow, and Paula soon learned to feed her ego and exploit her insecurities. An embittered divorcée, she was hopelessly enamoured of Mr Blick, the slimy proprietor of Estelle Modes, with its branches in Queensway, Clapham Junction, Hounsditch, New Malden and Chigwell. She lived in hope that he would one day leave his wife, who didn't understand him, and make her the new mistress of his empire. Wisely, Paula did not tell her of Mr Blick's attempt to feel her up in the stockroom, an advance which she had parried by accidentally dropping a pair of pinking shears on his foot.

After a month of screening potential rivals for her throne, Sharp had told Blick that none of the applicants were suitable and recommended that Paula be promoted to second in command. Not only because she would be cheaper to employ than another Norris, but because she displayed a natural flair for selling – Paula thought of her sales pitch as her lines, her customers as the audience – thereby increasing Sharp's override commission on total turnover. Paula was soon clearing eight pounds a week after tax, a fortune.

Paula insisted on buying all the food, because Bea herself hardly ate a thing. The local deli was an Aladdin's cave of new and irresistible tastes – rich, fatty salami, potato salad in thick mayonnaise, yard-long French bread, cream-stuffed continental gâteaux, and best of all, iced Polish doughnuts. Having stocked the fridge at her own expense, Paula felt entitled to raid it in the middle of the night. These furtive nocturnal feasts, while Bea snored, were drenched in excitement and guilt. Once she had gorged herself until she was physically sick. It occurred to her then, as she retched and heaved, that this was a way of eating as much as she liked without putting on any more weight.

But for once in her life, Paula's weight was an advantage. The customers of Estelle Modes liked to be served by someone of generous girth. Paula soon collected a clutch of regulars, enjoying the power she exerted over them, the income they earned for her. Over dinner she would recount her day to Bea, illustrating her narrative with ever more polished impersonations – of her clients, of Sharp, of Mr Blick, of the wisecracking Italian who ran the sandwich bar across the road, of the irascible Pole who owned the local deli, of Mr Vernon, the odious landlord's agent who called once a month to collect Bea's absurdly low controlled rent and to urge her to vacate the premises for 'a suitable consideration'.

Shortly after Paula's arrival, a speculator had acquired the freehold of the block with a view to disposing of the sitting tenants, modernizing their flats, and selling them off with vacant possession. Everyone had been served with a solicitor's letter requiring them to quit within the month upon pain of court action and damages. The ground-floor tenant had responded by having a heart attack on the spot before Bea, who knew her rights, called on her neighbours, told them the law, and advised them not to budge. Thanks to her, the widow who lived below her had been offered, and accepted, two hundred pounds as the price of moving out and had gone to live with a daughter. Not to be outdone, someone else had settled for five. Which left only Bea and one other recalcitrant tenant still in residence.

'Bugger his consideration,' Bea would splutter as she inhaled her evening meal. 'Where else am I going to get another place this cheap? I told him, I'm bloody well staying put till I croak. I know I look about a hundred and ten, but I'm only sixty-eight. Sixty, to him.'

Indeed, when Mr Vernon called round, on the first Saturday of every month, Bea made a point of 'fixing her face' and somehow contrived to control her cough, presenting him with a picture of stubborn, if skinny, good health. But as spring and summer gave way to a bitter winter, she went out less and less, and often didn't feel well enough to accompany Paula on her outings, always insisting, however, that she go on ahead, and staying up to demand a full and detailed critique of the play or film on her return.

On non-theatre nights they would read plays together, taking all the parts between them. Paula enjoyed these sessions even more than sitting passively in the audience. With every week that passed she became more informed, more impatient, more aware of how *she* would do it, how she would escape the confines of her body and lend it to the spirits that waited to inhabit her.

Christmas came. Bea bought a huge tree that was going cheap on Christmas Eve and induced the greengrocer's lad to carry it up the stairs for her. Paula arrived home from work to find it decked out with lights and tinsel.

'Not bad, is it?' wheezed Bea, admiring her handiwork. 'Put the frigging fairy on the top for me, will you darling? What's up? Something wrong?'

'No, nothing,' said Paula, blowing her nose. She stood on a chair, took the fairy and a piece of silver wire and attached it to the topmost branch, struggling against the tears. She wanted to throw her arms around Bea and tell her she loved her, but she couldn't, wouldn't do it. Because sooner or later, Bea would desert her too.

She knew now that Bea was dying, even though it was never spelt out, knew what that hypodermic in the bathroom cupboard was for, knew that once a month Bea visited a dubious doctor in Soho who did illegal abortions and purchased from him the means to make her life tolerable, rather than endure the indignities of legitimate and ultimately useless treatment.

'I'm like you,' she had said once. 'Don't like being bossed about by do-gooders. Catch me ending my days stuck full of bloody tubes and being kept alive when I'd rather be dead. I've lived by my own rules, and I'll sodding well die by them.'

The thought of Bea dying made her throat tighten and her eyes smart. She didn't know how she was going to bear it, even though she was used to bearing things. Everything Bea had given her – or rather lent her – was temporary, not least her friendship. Good things never lasted long.

Seeing the two brightly wrapped packages under the tree, Paula added the presents she had bought for Bea – two hundred Du Maurier and bottles of scotch and vodka. She picked up her own and felt them. They were both books.

'Go on,' urged Bea. 'Open them now if you like. I'm going to.' She ripped the paper off the vodka bottle without ceremony.

'Thanks, darling. Just what I wanted. Let's start without waiting for Santa, shall we? Tonic or tom?'

'Tonic, please,' said Paula, reluctant to remove the wrapping. She would have liked to savour her anticipation a little bit longer. She hadn't had a present in years, apart from the charity hand-out the Christmas before.

'Make a wish,' said Bea, returning with two bubbling glasses and a plate of mince pies.

Paula shut her eyes and wished very hard. It wouldn't come true, of course. It cost too much money. She had already made enquiries and been horrified at how high the fees were. And having run away, she couldn't apply for a grant without blowing her cover. And anyway, she was too fat, they wouldn't want her. What chance did she have against people like Isabel Mallory?

Perhaps, when Bea died, she'd do what she had done, find a rep to take her on as an ASM, toil away for a pittance, at everybody's beck and call, in the hope of a walk-on part one day as a maid. If she could face being poor and hungry again. If she could face the prospect, no, the certainty, of waiting in the wings, perhaps for ever, nursing impossible dreams.

'Well, go on,' said Bea. 'Open them.'

Paula did so, running her fingernail under the Sellotape and peeling it back, to preserve the pretty paper. She looked at the titles for a moment without speaking.

'I never said anything,' she said, going very red.

'You didn't have to.'

One of the books was *Selected Audition Speeches*. The other, by someone called Stanislavsky, was entitled *An Actor Prepares*.

2

Spring–Summer 1959

But be not afraid of greatness: some men are born great, some achieve greatness, and some have greatness thrust upon them.

William Shakespeare – Twelfth Night

Hearing the post plop through the letter box downstairs, Isabel made a speedy, if sleepy, descent before Toby the Terror beat her to it. Misappropriation of the Mallory mail was his latest fiendish fad, one which was indulged, like all his vices, with impunity. Sundry bills, cheques, letters, tax demands and appeals from theatrical charities had been gleefully flushed down the ground-floor loo, later to be retrieved by the plumber called in to unblock the sodden but still identifiable mass.

Davina had thought it wildly amusing and a sign of superior intelligence; Daddy had told Isabel, irritably, not to fuss. No matter that she had missed two anxiously awaited letters offering her places at RADA and the Central; as Daddy had been quick to point out, they were just fallback positions in the unlikely event of her failing to get into FRIDA, his alma mater, where she would, in due course, win the de Vere Medal, as he had done before her, the launching pad to a theatrical career almost (but not quite, of course) as brilliant as his own. A career which had been plotted while she was still in her cradle.

Unlike Richard's, which had been plotted against. Sometimes Isabel envied him that. Richard's early thespian leanings – parts in the inevitable school plays and a juvenile role in one of Fay's films – had been brutally straightened out by the kind of savage, destructive criticism which made Adrian Mallory as feared as a director as he was revered as an actor. Having well and truly lost his nerve, Richard had replaced it with profound contempt for the theatrical establishment, personified by his father, with its

37

cliquery, hypocrisy, snobbery, bitchery and arse-licking (both the metaphorical and literal kind).

'If you can't join it, beat it,' Richard was fond of saying. And beating it had eventually, inevitably, come to mean just that; he had 'beaten it' the previous Christmas vac, and since then he had kept his vow never to come home – for want of a better word – again.

Like Isabel, Richard would have preferred to remain with Fay rather than Adrian, but not at the cost of joining her in self-imposed exile. Having impregnated Davina, Adrian had asked for a divorce by long-distance telephone, while his wife was filming in Hollywood (a hack 'cameo' performance undertaken to meet a tax demand). Fay, with all the fury of a woman scorned, had not only granted his request but been quick to announce her own prospective remarriage. A piece of tit for tat which had effectively cost her her children – Richard, because he was half way through his A levels at the time and on course for Oxford, Isabel because she couldn't have borne to leave her brother behind.

Since then, both siblings had spent their summer vacations with Fay in California, stolidly enduring the hospitality of her new husband, Marty Bauer, a Hollywood producer, who shamed them by treating them as visiting VIPs and swamping them with an excess of generosity and goodwill. At least they had no such problems with their stepmother.

Isabel couldn't wait for the Easter holiday to finish. It was hateful being in this house without Richard as an ally. She despised herself for needing to compete with Davina, for wanting so badly to please her father and make him proud of her. But the alternative to his approval was icy indifference, of the type he displayed towards Richard. There was no middle ground. Perhaps it was just as well that his ambitions for her coincided so conveniently with her own.

'I would never encourage my children to go on the stage,' Daddy would tell journalists, with less than total honesty. 'I know how doubly hard it is to succeed when weighed down by the burden of a famous name.'

It was theatrical custom to stress the drawbacks and play down the glaringly obvious advantages of being born into the business – access to the right, influential people, the opportunity to call in favours granted by the powerful parent, the automatic media interest generated by the family name. Oh, you had to have talent, of course you did, but then thousands of people had talent and sank without trace. The Equity figures were dismal proof of that. At any one time eighty per cent of the profession were 'resting'; drama school graduates gave up acting after an average of seven years for men, four for women, female roles being ten times thinner on the ground than male. Talent was useless without the right breaks, and Isabel knew, despondently, that her career was ready-broken, like a horse, waiting only for her to step into the saddle and show that she could ride.

'Letter,' crowed Toby, reaching the mat seconds before her. Spotting the FRIDA logo on the envelope imprisoned between his chubby fingers, Isabel made a grab for it; Toby, a natural streetfighter, kicked her shin and escaped with his booty intact. Desperate to catch him before he locked himself in the loo, Isabel gave chase, causing him to trip and fall. Still gripping the letter he set up the most bloodcurdling ululations, loud enough to penetrate his mother's beauty sleep in the bedroom above.

'What's going on down there?' she called shrilly as Ingrid, the au pair, a slow-moving girl from Stockholm, abandoned a pan of half-scrambled eggs and tried to soothe his cries, getting a fist in the face for her pains. Davina descended on a cloud of coffee-coloured silk and gathered up her wailing offspring in a fierce embrace.

'Izzie hit me,' burbled Toby, the lying little brat.

'I didn't touch him,' began Isabel, but Davina, spying the envelope, interjected with an icy 'So that's what all the fuss is about. He would have given it to you if you'd asked him nicely, instead of bullying him. Give it to Mummy, darling.'

Toby, with a guile well beyond his four years, yielded up his plunder instantly. Davina tossed it contemptuously at her step-daughter.

'They're recalling you,' she said, as Isabel tore it open. 'Adrian phoned Julian Clavell yesterday. Don't worry, the second audition is just a formality in your case.'

Isabel muzzled a volley of counter-sarcasm, more out of bloody-mindedness than self-restraint. Davina was always trying to goad her into retaliatory action, which she could report, Toby-

39

style, all tears and injured innocence, to her husband. Any confrontation with Davina would lead to a gut-wrenching 'private talk' with Daddy.

'How can you do this to me, Izzie?' he would say, making her feel a perfect bitch. 'Davina's got no other family but us, remember. Can't you find it in your heart to be kind to her, for my sake?'

He would sit there like some melancholy, magnanimous god, bemoaning the petty rifts between his worshippers, stressing the all-encompassing nature of his love if only they would learn to share it. If Mummy had accepted the situation, surely Isabel could do the same?

Forget Mummy's well-hushed-up nervous breakdown and her stint in a high-class Californian clinic, supposedly for 'routine tests', having the electric-shock treatment which had left her more depressed than before. Forget her alopecia, her panic attacks, her continuing sessions with the shrink and her daily cocktails of mind-numbing pills. Just remember her public pride and her face-saving, highly lucrative remarriage to a man who worshipped her, a kind, boring, patient man without looks, class, culture or charm, just a genius for doing deals. A man as different from Daddy as he could possibly be. No wonder she didn't love him.

Isabel met her father on the landing on her way back upstairs, reeking of that ghastly aftershave Davina had bought him and wearing his rehearsal uniform of a louche black polo neck, blue jeans and a leather jacket. In recent years he had taken to dressing like an ageing bohemian, anxious to keep up with the new breed of angry young actors and directors. Adrian Mallory was a tall, broad-shouldered imposing man of enormous physical presence. At fifty-five he considered himself to be in the prime of life, revelling in the power and prestige of his position as artistic director of the Kean, and flaunting his young and beautiful new wife, the emblem of his undimmed sexual vigour.

'I gather you're through to the second round,' said Adrian, as if he had only just heard. 'Well done, darling.'

'It was a foregone conclusion in my case,' said Isabel bitterly, craving reassurance. 'So I'm told.'

'Of course it was,' said Daddy blandly. 'I mean to say, all these kids with stars in their eyes, ranting and raving away at the long-suffering panel, driving them to despair. Can you imagine what a huge relief it is when someone like you comes along? Two or three students a year, if they're lucky, have that special something. The rest are just taken on to make up the numbers. Drama schools need fees, remember. Would you like me to go through your pieces with you?'

'No thank you, Daddy. I don't want them to think you've been coaching me, I've got enough unfair advantages already. I won't come with you to rehearsals today, if you don't mind. I really ought to do some A-level revision.'

The Duchess of Malfi, with guess-who as the Duchess – was due to open at the Edmund Kean the following week. Isabel had been sitting in at rehearsals, not only because she found rehearsals compulsive viewing, but because she knew that her presence, however unobtrusive, put Davina off her stroke. But today she couldn't face people wishing her 'good luck' with Davina smirking and sniping behind her back.

Half an hour later Isabel reached the breakfast table just as Davina was preparing to leave it; Adrian was on the telephone, in the hall.

'Here's a thing,' said Davina casually, tossing *The Times* at her stepdaughter. Her dark hair was swept up in a tight topknot, emphasizing her long, sharp, prima ballerina features. 'Neville Seaton was in an accident last night.'

'What?' Isabel nearly knocked over her cup. 'Is he hurt?'

'Quite badly, it seems,' purred Davina.

Isabel scanned the one, bare paragraph, which was headed: *Actor in car crash.*

Neville Seaton, the actor, was undergoing emergency surgery at the Bristol Royal Infirmary last night following a collision on the A370 near Bristol, where Mr Seaton is currently appearing at the Old Vic. Mrs Seaton was treated for minor injuries. The other driver, as yet unnamed, was killed instantly.

'Oh God,' said Isabel, profoundly shocked.

'It's an ill wind,' commented Davina. 'At least his wife will know what bed to find him in, for a while.'

41

'That's great, coming from you,' countered Isabel, cursing herself even as she spoke for taking the bait.

'Are you casting aspersions on your father?' queried Davina, wide-eyed, pleased to have provoked her.

'You know very well who I'm casting aspersions on,' pursued Isabel recklessly. 'Everyone knows the real reason Neville left the company. It was nothing to do with "artistic differences" and everything to do with him refusing to go to bed with you.'

'I'm afraid it was the other way round,' said Davina calmly. 'As your father is very well aware. What everyone *does* know is that you have a pitiful schoolgirl crush on Neville. Or has it already got beyond that stage? No,' she answered herself, before Isabel could frame a denial, 'I think not. That's the whole problem, isn't it?'

And with this shaft of infuriating insight she swept out, leaving Isabel to repent of her hasty outburst at leisure. There was a gurgle of gooey bye-byes to Toby in the hall, a shout of "Bye, darling!' from her father, and the sound of the front door slamming and the car driving away.

As soon as they had gone Isabel rushed to the phone, but it rang before she reached it.

'Izzie? Have you heard about Neville?'

Isabel sat down on the floor. 'Yes. I was just about to ring you.' Having banished himself from his father's house, Richard was spending the vac at the Oxford house he shared with other third-year students. 'Is it worth ringing the hospital or will they only speak to relatives?'

'To hell with that. I'll tell them I'm his brother. I suppose Davina was crowing like a bloody vulture.'

'I hate her,' seethed Isabel, by way of confirmation. 'I hate her brat. I hate this house. I –'

'Then come up here for a couple of days,' said Richard, picking up the plea in her voice. 'There's a room empty at the moment. If you take the 11.20 from Paddington I'll meet you at the station. Meanwhile, I'll see what I can find out.'

Isabel packed an overnight case and left a note for her father, saying, 'Gone to stay with Richard for a couple of days. Back on Thursday. Love, Izzie.' By then the spat with Davina would be two days old, not that that would spare her another 'private talk' on her return, this time explaining, in pained, patient detail, how

Neville had pursued Davina without mercy, making it impossible for her to work with him. She could just about bear it as long as he didn't mention her 'schoolgirl crush'.

Was it that obvious? She had kidded herself that only Richard knew her secret. And possibly Neville as well, given that he had encouraged it, however indirectly, by coming to see her perform in the school *Dream* last summer, following it up with a six-page letter full of detailed, constructive criticism and suggestions, and cultivating his friendship with Richard, who, as a would-be impresario, was keen to 'collect' actors, writers and directors who shared his anti-establishment attitudes, particularly ones who had fallen foul of his father.

The journey passed in a trance of morbid thoughts. She kept visualizing the accident – the screech of tyres, the sudden impact, the mass of twisted metal, the siren as the ambulance approached, the broken bones and bleeding flesh. Her imagination was a curse at times like this, tormenting her with too much detail, as if she were thinking herself into a part rather than living through a real experience. It was an occupational hazard to lose sight of the dividing line between genuine emotion and a kind of self-induced hysteria.

Richard was waiting for her on the platform. She knew straight away that the news was bad. He didn't tell her what it was until they were seated in the privacy of the car.

'He was hit on the driver's side by a van that didn't stop at a junction. Helen escaped with cuts and bruises, but Neville's lost an arm.'

'Oh God,' said Isabel. She felt numb, exhausted, as if she had worn out her emotions too soon.

'He's being allowed visitors as from tomorrow. I thought I'd go and see him. Want to come with me?' Which was his way of saying that he didn't want to go alone.

'Do you think we should?'

'Yes. Not many people will. They'll be too embarrassed.'

So was Isabel. But she would hate Neville to know that.

'The place is a bit of a tip, I'm afraid,' said Richard, changing the subject, as he started up the engine. Undergraduates were forbidden to keep cars, one of the many rules Richard took a pride in flouting. 'Or rather it has been, since Patrick moved in. He's barely house-trained.'

'Patrick?' echoed Isabel vaguely, unable to remember which of her brother's numerous friends – or boyfriends – Patrick might be.

'He was Lucky in the *Godot* we did last year.'

'Oh, yes,' said Isabel, jolted out of her torpor. 'I remember.' How could she forget? 'He was good.' Hauntingly so. She recalled being introduced to him, briefly, after the performance, seconds before some girl had borne him off.

'He's good all right, when he can be bothered. And he's got brains too. But he's bone idle. At the rate he's going he'll be lucky to get a third. That's why he's stayed up for the vac, in the hope of making up for lost time. He's got some working-class complex about letting Ma and Da down.'

He parked outside the house in St John Street and led the way inside.

'Delaney!' he called. 'Have you taken the hint and gone out or are you still infecting the place with your putrid presence?'

A tall, dishevelled man with a shock of shaggy dark hair and a three-day stubble appeared at the top of the stairs. He was wearing a crumpled open-necked shirt, trousers that had long since lost their crease, and a boyish smile, all three rather the worse for wear.

'Isabel,' he said, descending, switching a pair of blue eyes on to full beam. He managed to invest the innocuous salutation with a wealth of hidden, if obscure, meaning, as if they had once been lovers.

'Hello, Patrick,' said Isabel, coolly returning his stare. 'I'm sorry to descend on you like this.'

'Pity it wasn't in happier circumstances. There's some tea in the pot, if you'd like some. Have you had your dinner yet? I mean lunch.'

The soft, warm, lazy, Irish voice seemed to mock her cultured Mallory vowels.

'I'm not hungry. And I'd rather have coffee, thanks.'

'Coming up.' He went off to fetch it.

'So how's the old bastard?' said Richard, preparing for a restorative sniping session.

'He's rigged a second audition for me at FRIDA. According to Davina, that is.'

'So tell them to poke it and take up the place at RADA instead.

It'll be good practice for turning down a job at the Kean in two years' time. Because by then I shall be wanting you for Renegade . . .'

Patrick returned at that moment with a tray, laid with a tarnished silver coffee pot pilfered from the Windsor house – Davina had hunted high and low for it – three chipped mugs, a leaking bag of sugar, half a packet of custard creams and a bottle of milk with a grimy bottom.

'Are you reading English as well?' said Isabel, well schooled in polite small talk.

'No. Greats.'

'Latin's his second language,' put in Richard. 'He started off wanting to be a priest. Can you imagine it?'

Patrick slid back in his chair with his hands behind his head.

'I was a big hit as an altar boy,' he explained. 'But the trouble is, the priest upstages you all the time. I'd always rather play the lead, so I set my sights on the seminary. And then I found out about girls.'

'But they lock up their daughters where he comes from so he came here instead. Don't worry, I warned him off you,' Richard added cheerfully, much to Isabel's mortification.

'Unfortunately,' sighed Patrick, flashing her another insolent, knowing smile. 'Richard tells me you're all set to go to drama school.'

'I'm hoping to, yes,' said Isabel shortly. Damn Richard for telling him anything at all, for saddling her with the role of little sister.

'I've been thinking I might give the acting game a whirl myself,' said Patrick. 'Better than working for a living. Richard's hoping to take the next Renegade production to the Edinburgh Festival. Who knows, perhaps I'll get discovered.'

Isabel chose not to comment on this fatuous possibility. Better than working for a living indeed.

'Izzie doesn't approve of jumped-up amateurs taking short cuts,' put in Richard. Isabel met Patrick's laughing blue eyes with a cool green stare.

'Thanks for the coffee,' she said briskly, draining her cup. 'I've got a bit of work to do, so if you'd show me my room, Richard, I'll leave you two in peace.'

45

Patrick shrugged good-naturedly, put his feet up on the coffee table, and fell to perusal of *The Sporting Life*. Richard led Isabel upstairs to a single room whose usual occupant had gone home for the vac.

'You're not going to sit and wallow all afternoon, are you?' he said, sighing. 'Time enough for that tomorrow.'

By way of an answer Isabel burst into tears. Richard took her hand and let her grizzle into his shoulder.

'Just pray that Neville doesn't feel the same way about you,' he said warningly. 'Then you'd really have something to cry about.'

They had put him in a private room, to stop him being plagued by fellow-patients who had seen him on the telly. Visitors were restricted to one at a time, so Richard went in first.

'He's doped up to the eyeballs,' he said, rejoining her. 'So he probably feels worse than he's letting on. Helen's already been discharged. She's back at home with the kids, he's not expecting her till this evening.'

Neville was nearly as white as the sheet. He stretched out his left hand and squeezed hers hard.

'Izzie,' he said. 'Good of you to come. I'm afraid it's a bit of a freak show,' he added, indicating the empty pyjama sleeve.

'I brought you some paperbacks,' said Isabel, putting them on the bedside table, adding inadequately, 'It gets so boring in hospital. When are they going to let you out?'

'They haven't said yet. I've got to have occupational therapy. Learn to tie my laces with one hand and all that.'

'How's Helen?'

'Pretty shaken up. It was worse for her, in a way. At least I can't remember anything about it. One minute I was driving along and the next I was . . . like this. Real Rip van Winkle stuff.'

He was making an effort to sound cheerful, for her benefit. She wished he didn't feel the need to.

'I suppose I was lucky,' he went on. 'Or so they keep telling me. Luckier than the other poor bastard, anyway. Apparently I can sue him, even though he's dead, his insurance will pay. Just as well. Don't suppose I'll be offered too many parts in future.' His voice cracked without any warning and his eyes spilled over. 'I'm sorry,' he said, ashamed. 'You'd better go.'

'It's all right,' said Izzie, taking out her handkerchief and stanching the flow. Impulsively, innocently, she bent forward and kissed his cheek, unprepared for his sudden, convulsive response as his arm went round her neck and he pulled her towards him, murmuring her name. And then she was aware of his lips on hers, and his tongue inside her mouth, and the taste of his tears, and a sense of being sucked down into a soft, deep, dark, sad, shared, private place. He's married, she told herself guiltily, but it didn't help. She didn't want to steal him, after all, just to borrow him . . .

He pulled away first.

'I'm sorry,' he repeated, irritably this time. 'I shouldn't have done that. It must be the drugs. Or loss of blood. I still feel a couple of pints short of a gallon. Not that that's any excuse. Please forget that ever happened.'

'Don't apologize,' said Isabel, bowing her head, hiding her blushes in the curtain of her hair. 'It was my fault.'

'You shouldn't have come. You might catch whatever it is I've got. God. I'm not being very brave, am I?'

Isabel didn't answer. She sat holding his hand, squeezing it, feeling the silent sobs shudder through him and vibrate all down his arm and into hers. They stayed like that for several minutes, without speaking, till a nurse came in and asked her to leave.

'Best of luck on Thursday,' said Neville, pulling himself together. 'Richard told me. I'm glad you're trying for FRIDA.' He spoke forcefully, with the brooding, gloomy passion that she loved. 'They've got the toughest programme and the highest drop-out rate. They'll stretch you to breaking point and that's what you'll respond to best.'

She had needed him to say that, needed the incentive. Doing her best for Daddy was capitulation. Doing it for Neville was a challenge.

FRIDA occupied three adjacent four-storey houses in Pimlico, one of which had been converted into a student theatre. Messrs Foster and Roberts, two stage-struck Victorian builders, had founded the school with a view to installing their shared mistress, Miss Nellie de Vere, a distinguished actress of advancing years, to run it.

47

Miss de Vere and her successors had prospered. FRIDA was now one of the top half dozen drama schools and took a pride in its reputation for long hours, army-style discipline, and summary dismissal of anyone who cut classes or otherwise failed to make the grade. For Isabel, used to a boarding school regime – every minute of the day accounted for and no time to get up to mischief – this was not in any way daunting; she had a monastic propensity for hard work.

Work was the driving force in the Mallory household. Both her parents had worked non-stop, Daddy for the glory, Mummy to pay the bills. From her cradle she had not seen them for weeks, months at a time, while they were away touring or filming, and striven to be extra specially good, whenever they were at home, in the hope that if she deserved them better she might be rewarded with more of their time and attention. Just as Richard, always a troubled, rebellious child, had misbehaved at every opportunity, no doubt with a similar end in view. Neither technique had borne fruit, merely setting a pattern of behaviour for both of them which had later proved impossible to break.

The premises were empty of students, it being the Easter holidays. Below street level a basement room with a barre and wall-to-wall mirrors was visible through the wide, tall windows. The main entrance was approached by a flight of stone steps; above the heavy double wooden doors was a gleaming brass plate inscribed: FOSTER ROBERTS INSTITUTE OF DRAMATIC ART EST. 1886. Isabel pressed the bell and was let in by an elderly doorman, indistinguishable from the ones who sat in a little cubbyhole and guarded the stage entrance at every theatre in London. He checked her name on a list and directed her down a long corridor towards a waiting room.

She walked quickly, ignoring the various rolls of honour on the walls either side, lettered in gold on curlicued panels and bearing the names of former graduates (including Daddy), winners of the de Vere Medal for the Most Promising Student (including Daddy), and those who had fallen on the field of battle. (A fate which Daddy had escaped, thanks to the flat feet which had debarred him from active service.)

There was one other person in the waiting room, a plump girl with peroxide-blonde hair.

'Hello,' said Isabel, sitting down beside her and picking up a distinct whiff of whisky underneath the cheap perfume. Evidently she wasn't the only one who was nervous. Isabel's appointment was for eleven o'clock, and it was still only quarter past ten. If she hadn't been a compulsively early person, she could have avoided having to make small talk with the preceding candidate.

'Don't you remember me?' said her companion. 'You're Isabel Mallory, aren't you? Sir Adrian's daughter?'

Much as it irked her to be described thus, Isabel smiled in affirmation. The girl looked vaguely familiar; perhaps she had seen her among the sea of faces at her first audition.

'I'm awfully sorry,' she said. 'I'm hopeless on names.'

'Paula Baker. We met in Neville Seaton's dressing room, after *Hedda Gabler*.' And then, seeing Isabel's surprise, 'I've changed my hair since then. And I've lost quite a bit of weight. Not enough, though.'

'You were wearing a hat,' said Isabel slowly, placing her. She prided herself on being observant, noticing little details, filing them all away. 'And a cloak. The hair suits you.' Privately she thought it tarty, but it suited her nonetheless.

'Ciggie?' offered Paula. Isabel shook her head. 'Did you hear about Neville? We saw it in the paper. Bea rang his mum. His arm was amputated.'

'I know,' said Isabel. And then quickly, not wanting to discuss it, 'What pieces are you doing?'

'Oh what a rogue and peasant slave, from *Hamlet*, and Jimmy Porter's anti-woman speech from *Look Back in Anger*.'

'Male parts?'

'There's nothing in the rules against it. It was Bea's idea. She said as men get all the best lines the rest of the time, I might as well pinch them while I can. I thought it might make them sit up and take notice, instead of just staring at my tits.' Nonetheless, she was wearing a tight red jumper, belted at the waist, as if to hedge her bets. 'I'm after the scholarship. A place isn't much good to me without it. And they only award the one, the mean bastards.'

'Can't you get a grant?'

'No point asking for one. I was expelled from one school, then I played truant mostly at the next one, then they took me into care, then I ran away. My name's mud where I come from. Bea would

49

help me out, but she's only got her pension. Besides, she's done enough for me. I'd have ended up on the streets if she hadn't taken me in. Must be nice not having to worry about money, like you.'

She said it without apparent rancour, with a kind of admiration. Isabel remembered Paula as a shy, puddingy girl, one whom she had felt compelled to be extra nice to, with some innate sense of *noblesse oblige*. But today she seemed talkative, self-assured, pushy – though perhaps that was just an act. Or Dutch courage.

'You're lucky, having your Dad to teach you,' Paula went on in the same matter-of-fact tone.

'He didn't. Not directly, I mean. You're not supposed to be coached.'

'Bugger that. Bea took me through my pieces line by line. She says you don't get anywhere in this business unless you're prepared to cheat, so I might as well start the way I mean to go on. Bea says . . .'

She faltered as a woman in a tweed suit appeared.

'Miss Baker? Mr Clavell will see you now.'

'Here goes,' said Paula, squinting into a plastic compact. 'I'll be in the pub on the corner afterwards, if you fancy a drink. Don't have to be at work till one.'

'All right,' said Isabel brightly, unable to think of an excuse. 'I'll see you there.'

As soon as she had gone Isabel made a dash for the cloakroom and was violently sick, not that there was anything in her stomach for her to eject; she hadn't been able to face breakfast. She wished she had Paula's chirpy, irreverent confidence, artificial or not, wished she'd thought to have a stiff drink to quell her nerves. What did she have to be nervous about? It was all a put-up job, after all. But that meant she had all the more to prove, to the panel if not to herself.

She felt a perverse envy of Paula. Her childhood sounded hideous, and yet it must have yielded a wealth of experience. Next to her she felt weak, flabby, naïve, a pampered child of privilege. What was it Neville had said? 'They'll stretch you to breaking point and that's what you'll respond to best.' He had meant that she was too used to cosseting, to praise, to being told how talented she was.

His six-page letter on her Titania had been a revelation. She had

50

cringed with shame at having been seduced by that worthless, ignorant applause, resorted to so many cheap effects, developed so many bad habits, been so untrue to herself. He had noticed every tiny flaw in her performance, displaying a total recall and merciless attention to detail that were far more precious than praise.

She rinsed out her mouth with water, patted her face with a wet handkerchief, and chewed stolidly on a peppermint to clean her breath. Then she paced around for a bit, chanting her lines. She kept it up until five to eleven, when she made her way back to the waiting room, just before the tweedy woman arrived to fetch her and lead her up two flights of stairs to a large, bare rehearsal room.

Julian Clavell, the principal of FRIDA, was a balding, fleshy man of about fifty, with thick lips, bright darting eyes peering over half-moon glasses, and a neatly trimmed grey goatee beard. He was sitting at a trestle table strewn with application forms and photographs, flanked by two cohorts, a thin, wispy-looking woman in ski pants and a foppish, thin-faced younger man wearing a paisley cravat, whom Isabel recognized as Peter Austell, an actor currently appearing in a long-running West End play.

'Take a seat, Miss Mallory,' said Clavell, his fruity voice echoing in the emptiness all around her. The last audition had taken place on a spotlit stage, in the school theatre, with invisible voices calling out at her from the darkness of the auditorium. It would be harder in broad daylight, doing it to faces she could see, more like a rehearsal than a performance.

'We'd like a preliminary chat before you give us your pieces,' he went on. 'This is Mrs Winston, who teaches movement, and Peter Austell, of course, needs no introduction. We're very fortunate to have him with us as a tutor during his London run.'

The interview was the real acting test, thought Isabel, as they began firing questions at her. An exercise in improvisation by any other name.

'Why do you want to act?' The standard trick question; whatever she said would sound wet. She had examined every possible response, ranging from the unthinkable 'Because my father expects it of me' to the hackneyed 'Because it's the only thing I can do'.

'The same reason as everyone else, I suppose, whether they admit it or not. I want to be loved.'

'You think actors, as a breed, are driven by some perceived lack of – or greed for – that commodity?'

'I think all artists are.'

'You regard yourself as an artist?'

'Not yet.'

'You think art can be taught?' put in the woman.

'I think it can be developed.'

'The last candidate answered the question rather less subtly,' said Clavell. 'She said, as I recall, that she wanted to be rich and famous. You don't share that ambition?'

'Not really. Fame and fortune are just trappings.'

'But surely they're an indicator of the public love you crave?' put in Peter Austell.

'There are plenty of good actors who aren't rich or famous. And plenty of rich and famous actors who aren't all that good.'

'And what is your definition of a good actor?'

'One who finds and expresses the truth, in the text and in himself.'

'In that case, what comments would you make on the performance you're about to give us?' Clavell again. 'What strengths and weaknesses should we expect of you?'

Isabel's hands began to sweat. She laid them face down on her skirt, to dry them off.

'I made sure I understood every line, and its context. I also think I have a flair for verse-speaking. On the minus side, I'm self-conscious and afraid to take risks. I hide behind superficial technique to cover over the cracks. I tend to want to lose myself in the character, rather than find the character within myself.' Thank God for Neville's letter.

'Very well, then.' Clavell seemed pleased. Perhaps he thought she was quoting Daddy. 'Now let's see if we agree, shall we? Go right to the back of the room and start in your own time.'

Isabel's forced self-praise and self-castigation spurred her to prove herself right and wrong. She discarded her carefully rehearsed nuances and let the words spurt, new-minted, from her mouth, tapping the well of feeling which she feared to draw on too deeply, never knowing what snails or sludge might be dredged up in the process. 'Acting is a bit like making love,' Neville had written, heedless of her ignorance on that subject. 'A fine balance between self-abandon and self-control.' Suddenly, if fleetingly, she understood what he meant.

'Thank you,' came Clavell's voice, bringing her back to earth. 'That's all for the moment. We'll be in touch.'

Limp from the ebb of adrenaline, Isabel had left the building – she had no memory of doing so – hailed a taxi – no memory of doing that either – and let it drive her half way to the station before she remembered her promise to meet Paula in the pub. After some hesitation she asked the cabbie to turn around, driven more by good manners than inclination. She expected to find Paula gone already, but she was standing with her elbows on the saloon bar, puffing on a cigarette and nursing an empty glass.

'How was it for you?' she greeted Isabel gloomily. 'They kept you long enough.'

'Hard to tell. Er . . . can I get you another one of those?'

'Thanks. Scotch and ginger. It's full of calories, but I'm past caring.'

'Shall we sit down?' suggested Isabel, ordering the scotch for Paula and a dry sherry for herself, just to be sociable. Paula laid claim to a small round table in an alcove and ground out her cigarette. 'How did you get on?'

'I fucked up,' said Paula succinctly.

'Oh, I'm sure you didn't.'

'I did too. I should have known better than to have a drink beforehand. I never normally touch it in the daytime. Bea would have my guts.'

'What happened? Did you forget your lines?'

Paula struck a match and lit another cigarette.

'No. It was that snooty woman that did for me. She asked why I couldn't get a grant, and I told them the truth, more or less, like I told you. So she said, what would I do if I didn't get the scholarship, and I said I'd have to get a night job, cleaning offices or working in a caff. And she said they didn't approve of students taking jobs, so I said . . . Oh Christ. How stupid can you get.'

'Go on,' prompted Isabel. 'What did you say?'

'I said in that case I'd go on the game, if I had to, as long as they gave me a place.' Isabel giggled delightedly. 'Go on, laugh,' growled Paula. 'I deserve it. I was all set to play Little Orphan Annie, so they'd feel sorry for me. I had it all planned. A real tear-jerker. But when it came to it I couldn't bring myself to do it. I hate bloody grovelling. Proves I'm not much of an actress, doesn't it?'

'Acting's about truth, not lies.'

'Oh, very clever. You should have seen her face. The bloke with the beard just smiled, but that toffee-nosed Peter Whatsisname looked like I smelled bad or something.'

'What about your pieces?'

'Oh, I'd nothing to lose by then, so I gave them everything I'd got. What the hell. I'd already blown it.'

'There are other drama schools.'

Paula glared. 'Yeah. And three of them have already turned me down. Bea said I wasn't really ready to go for auditions. Told me to join an amateur dramatic group, just to get a bit of experience behind me. But I wanted to get a place under my belt before she . . . the thing is, she's not very well.'

Her voice wavered and she blew her nose hastily into a handkerchief; Isabel realized belatedly that she was genuinely upset and trying hard not to show it. But she was spared the need to sympathize by Paula grabbing hold of her wrist and squinting at her watch.

'Bloody hell,' she muttered, finishing off her drink in one swallow. 'I'll be late for work at this rate. What a waste of half a day's pay. Not to mention the lousy audition fee. Talk about a rip-off. They must be creaming it in.'

Isabel thought of her monthly allowance from Daddy, the large money orders from America at Christmas and birthdays, and heard herself mumbling, 'If you get a place, but not the scholarship, I could give you a loan.'

Paula looked at her oddly.

'Why? You don't even know me.'

'Because I'd like to help.'

'Because you feel sorry for me,' corrected Paula. 'Because you feel guilty. I wouldn't, in your shoes. You want to be careful. People can spot a soft touch a mile off. Thanks for the drink.'

And with that she slung her bag over her shoulder and sauntered off, as if she didn't have a care in the world.

*

Isabel heard on Monday that she had been accepted. She felt no sense of triumph, just a dull relief, coupled with the same old doubts as always, and guilt that a place had fallen into her lap when Paula wanted, needed it so much more than she did.

After A levels came the school play – *Twelfth Night*, in which she was playing Viola. Daddy's schedule at the Kean prevented him attending, but Richard turned up for the last of the three performances, two days before the end of term, accompanied, disconcertingly, by Patrick. Isabel didn't realize they were in the audience until a message reached her, in the communal dressing room, that she had visitors.

Richard was still high on post-finals euphoria and the success of Renegade's summer production, a satirical revue entitled *Antidotage* which was on course for the Edinburgh Festival. Patrick looked as scruffy as ever, despite having donned an ill-fitting suit, an off-white shirt and a red silk tie which Isabel recognized as one of Richard's.

'You were great,' he said simply. His eyes were faintly mocking, as always; Isabel mocked them back.

'She was wonderful, darling,' Richard corrected him, in a camp theatrical drawl. 'Soooper performance. Seeing you all togged up as a boy made me feel positively incestuous. Come on. I got permission from the deputy head to take you home straight away. Told her our dear pater had been rushed to hospital.'

'Richard, you didn't!'

'One of my better performances, wasn't it, Patrick? I explained how he needed an emergency egoectomy to remove a malignant growth.'

'Didn't she realize you were pulling her leg?'

'I wasn't. I was deadly serious.'

'I'd like to meet your father,' remarked Patrick. 'See if he's as much of a monster as Richard paints him.'

'Then you'd be disappointed,' snapped Isabel, depriving herself of the joy of a good giggle.

'She simply adores me bitching about him when there's just the two of us,' said Richard. 'Eggs me on to say all the things she feels guilty even thinking. But not in front of a third party. With you here, it's Daddy right or wrong.'

'That's enough, Richard,' muttered Isabel, vexed to have this inadmissible truth shared with a stranger. Richard could never resist playing up to an audience. 'Anyway, what's all the rush? I'd rather stay here than go back to Windsor early.'

'You're not going back to Windsor. I've found us a flat. Elizabeth Street, near Sloane Square. Walking distance from FRIDA. I went to view it just after finals. Didn't want to tell you before in case anything went wrong.'

'Richard!' Isabel flung her arms around him in delight.

'We can move in right away. Only one catch. Patrick's staying with us for a day or two before heading back to the Emerald Oile.'

'If you've got no objection,' said Patrick.

'Why should I?' shrugged Isabel. 'I turned up on you.'

'They're going to pack your trunk for you,' said Richard, 'and send it on. Hurry up. We'll grab dinner somewhere on the way.'

Isabel threw some civvies into a suitcase and fled, anxious to avoid the misplaced sympathy of her classmates, most of whom were still partaking of post-performance refreshments. She leapt into the MG beside Richard, with Patrick doubled up in the back, and the car roared off towards freedom. A moment later Richard pulled up at a petrol station, leaving her briefly alone with Patrick.

'You really were very good,' he said.

'Thank you.'

'But you could have been better. You were too scared of showing up the rest of the cast. Waste of time. I bet they all hate you anyway. Even though you're the most popular girl in the school. Or rather, because you're the most popular girl in the school.'

'That's rather Irish, if you don't mind my saying so,' said Isabel, producing an emery board from her bag and attacking an already perfectly manicured nail.

'That's why you're always so nice, isn't it, to compensate for making other people feel inferior.'

'I'm not aware of doing any such thing,' said Isabel lightly, determined not to rise to the bait. 'But even if I did, I doubt if it would work on you,' she added sweetly.

'So don't be nice to me. Make me feel special.'

'That's an original chat-up line, I must say.'

'But I'm not trying to chat you up,' protested Patrick

56

innocently. 'I wouldn't dare.' And then, as Richard resumed his seat, 'Richard warned me that you pack quite a punch.'

Isabel flung her brother a how-could-you look, eliciting a sheepish smirk. That would teach her to confide in Richard in future.

'A cautionary tale,' said Richard unrepentantly. The tale concerned Craig Matheson, the Hollywood heart-throb she had dated the previous summer. No doubt he had slanted it in his sister's favour, but even so it did her little credit.

Matheson was ego-boostingly attractive, in a teeth, tan and biceps kind of way, and Isabel had enjoyed leading him on and letting him down, congratulating herself on being immune to his skin-deep charm and robotically expert push-button technique. In the end he had invited her to a party at his Mexican-style hacienda, at which she turned out to be the only guest, and made one final determined attempt to get her into bed before losing patience and resorting to brute force.

Isabel had narrowly averted rape by grabbing hold of a heavy glass ashtray in mid-struggle and crashing it against Matheson's temple with a strength born of blind panic. He had been too stunned to retaliate, giving her time to flee, reassured by the valedictory roar of 'Frigid bitch!' that she hadn't killed him. Frigid. Tell that to Neville. No wonder she hadn't heard from him since the day at the hospital. She must have well and truly frightened him off.

Richard stopped at a restaurant in Stroud just in time for last orders. He and Isabel shared a bottle of champagne while Patrick demanded a pint of draught Guinness in an almost impenetrable brogue, affecting not to understand its unavailability and forcing them to fetch it, in despair, from the nearest pub, just to shut him up. Unable to control her features, Isabel gave in and laughed, an involuntary olive branch which Patrick acknowledged with un-concealed triumph.

'So tell me about the flat,' said Isabel, over the soup.

'It's a twenty-five-year lease. Executor's sale. Auction. A bargain. Had to make a cash offer so I phoned Fay and she sent me lots of lovely dollars.'

It was typical of Richard to do things without consulting her. Isabel would have insisted on viewing and re-viewing dozens of places before finally making a choice.

'Have you bought any furniture?'

'Just what came with the flat. You can choose how you want it done up and I'll pay, Fay said she'd foot the bill. Or rather, Marty will. I'll have it all finished by the time you get back from the States.'

This was his sop for not coming with her this year, his excuse being that he had too much to do, finding backers for Renegade and setting things up in Edinburgh. Isabel's spirits sank again at the thought of a whole summer of Mummy's highs and lows without Richard there to share the burden.

'What time's your appointment tomorrow with this so-called agent?' Richard was saying to Patrick.

'Two o'clock. And less of the so-called.'

'Second-rate, then. The decent agents can afford to be fussy, they wouldn't want anything to do with a raw, untrained, inexperienced beginner like you. Mind you don't sign anything. Some of those crooked bastards sew you up for seven years at a time. And don't turn your back on him either. He might be after more than his ten per cent.'

'Belt up, for pity's sake. Nag, nag, nag.'

'I've grown up in this business. I know what goes on. Tell him, Izzie.'

'Richard's right. You ought to find out who else he's got on his books before you commit yourself. There are a lot of sharks out there. What's his name?'

'Rex Jordan. Don't tell me, you've never heard of him.'

'I've never heard of him,' said Isabel.

'Well, whatever happens,' said Richard, 'you're committed to Renegade for the Festival dates, remember.'

'Relax. I'm not one to let down a mate.'

'There you go again. Don't think of me as a mate. Think of me as a future impresario, who could be useful to your career. Start thinking like a pro.'

'A prostitute, would you mean?'

'A professional, you bog-Irish peasant. I'll tell you who else turned up to see the show,' he went on, turning to his sister. 'Neville Seaton.'

'Oh really?' said Isabel vaguely, inhibited by Patrick's presence. 'How was he?'

'Getting some radio work, he said. He and Helen are moving back to London. We went for a drink afterwards. Remember the old trout we met in his dressing room? Beatrice Dorland? He'd just been to her funeral.'

Isabel remembered Paula telling her that Bea had taken her in off the streets, and the catch in her voice when she mentioned her illness. She ought to look up her address in the phone book, drop her a line of condolence before she left for the States.

It was two a.m. by the time they arrived in London. The flat proved a big disappointment, dirty and smelling of stale linen and unneutered tom. Isabel, who was allergic to cats, began sneezing in response to the moulted hairs which covered every dusty surface.

'What about sheets?' asked Isabel in disgust, viewing the grubby mattresses, with their stack of old folded blankets.

'In there,' said Richard, pointing to a large parcel on the floor. 'Towels too. I got Peter Jones to deliver care of the estate agents, knowing how neurotic you are about germs.'

'Don't waste any of them on me,' said Patrick, yawning. 'I don't mind roughing it on the couch.' He helped himself to a blanket and made himself comfortable.

Still sniffing, Isabel selected a room on the ground floor. Like the rest of the flat, it was badly in need of redecoration and full of wartime utility furniture. Perhaps it was just as well she was off to the States. It would take weeks to bring the place up to standard. She would choose the decorations before she went and leave Richard to cope with all the noise and mess. Serve him right for leaving her to cope with Mummy on her own.

Next day she rang an agency who sent round a char to spring clean while she spent a busy day in Sanderson's and Harrods, poring endlessly over wallpapers, carpets and curtain fabrics before listing her final choices, all in plain, subtle shades of sky and smoke and ice. Richard, being colour blind, had absolutely no eye for decor.

She got back to the flat late that afternoon to find it restored to shabby cleanliness and smelling of Mansion polish. Richard was out, Patrick dozing on the ageing moquette settee which he had used for a bed. Isabel stared at him furtively for a moment, unobserved. The jacket of his suit, crumpled as ever, was slung across a chair back, and he had removed Richard's red tie, revealing the lack of a top button on his shirt. His abandoned posture, one arm flung above his head, the other hanging limp and long-fingered, brushing the floor, gave him the exposed, trusting babe-in-the-wood air of an innocent abroad in a wicked world.

The phone in the hall began ringing.

'It's me,' said Richard. 'Won't be home till late, if at all. Ran into some people who might be interested in backing Renegade. Tell Patrick for me, will you? We were supposed to be going to see *Five Finger Exercise* this evening.'

'I thought he was only staying one night?'

'He's been fixed up with an audition tomorrow morning. Rex Jordan's flattered him half to death, convinced him he's the new O'Toole. Must go.'

'Hello there,' came a sleepy voice behind her. Tousled and yawning, Patrick treated her to one of his tattered smiles. 'Did you have a nice time shopping?' He made it sound supremely trivial.

'Yes thank you. Richard just rang. He's tied up, won't be able to go to the play with you tonight.'

'Never mind. You can come with me instead.'

'I can't,' said Isabel automatically. And then, groping for an excuse, 'I'm just about to ring a girlfriend. We arranged to meet up.' She searched her mind for someone to try, but most of her London-based contemporaries wouldn't be back from school till later in the week. Remembering her resolution to contact Paula, she began leafing purposefully through the directory till she found a Dorland in Castletown Road. With Patrick watching her all the while, she dialled the number.

'Hello?' A radio was blaring out 'Volare' in the background.

'Paula?' said Isabel brightly, relieved to have got an answer. 'It's Isabel Mallory.'

'Oh,' said Paula. 'Just a minute.' She turned it off.

'I was terribly sorry to hear about Bea.'

'Thanks.'

'Er . . . How about supper, this evening?'

Paula didn't answer for a moment; Isabel assumed she was thinking of an excuse to say no, unaware that Paula was too surprised, momentarily, to respond.

'If you like.' She sounded flat, depressed. Oh God, thought

Isabel, she didn't get a place at FRIDA and I won't know what to say to her, and the whole thing will be hideously embarrassing and I wish I was going to the theatre with Patrick instead.

'Super,' enthused Isabel. 'Shall I come round to your place first?'

'Might as well. I'll see you later, then. 'Bye.'

Isabel turned to Patrick, avoiding his eyes. 'Richard tells me you're staying another night. I'll leave my key under the mat, and whichever one of us gets in first can put it back there for the other. If I don't see you again, good luck with your audition.'

'Oh, I'm only going along to keep Rex sweet. It's a touring production, for at least four months. It would clash with the Edinburgh Festival.'

'What's the play?'

'*The Long and the Short and the Tall*. Rex has put me up for Bamforth, the O'Toole part.'

'If you're offered it, take it,' Isabel felt bound to say. 'Richard will understand. He wouldn't expect you to turn down real work.'

'I'm not that keen, honestly. It would mean starting rehearsals right away and the thing is, the family are expecting me. I'm homesick and I feel like a break. And there will be other parts,' he added, with ingenuous complacency.

Isabel, reared on the Mallory work ethic, was appalled by such amateurish sentiments. No one put their personal life first if they wanted to succeed. And yet she couldn't help envying him his readiness to do so. Actors were like drug addicts, sacrificing everything to their habit – home, family, stability, love, health, sanity. The profession was littered with people broken on the rack of their obsession.

'Have a nice evening with your friend, then,' said Patrick casually, slinging on his crumpled jacket. And with that he went off to the theatre without her, leaving her feeling short-changed, cheated, with only herself to blame.

'Top floor!' yelled Paula, from above, when Isabel rang her doorbell, an hour later. A bunch of keys landed on the pavement at her feet. Paula was waiting for her at the top of the stairs.

'Hello,' panted Isabel. 'Heavens, I would hardly have

recognized you. You've lost an awful lot of weight.' Paula was wearing a dirndl skirt puffed up with stiff petticoats which made her waist seem terribly narrow.

'Not enough,' said Paula. 'Still another stone to go. Would you like a drink before we go? There's an Italian place that's quite cheap. Better be. I'm paying.'

'Oh no,' said Isabel. 'I invited you.'

'I'm flush at the moment, it's okay. Scotch, vodka, red wine?'

'Er . . . some wine would be nice.' Isabel sneezed a split second before she spotted a fat ginger cat.

'Bless you.' Paula opened a bottle and poured two glasses, filling them up to the rim. Isabel could tell by the smell that it would taste of stewed tea and take the coating off her teeth.

'I got that place at FRIDA, believe it or not,' said Paula, as if she didn't much care either way.

'Me too,' said Isabel, relieved. 'What about the scholarship?' She stifled another sneeze in her handkerchief.

'No joy. Tight-arsed buggers.'

'So you'll have to work at nights?'

'I was planning to, like I said. But Bea was worried about it. Said they worked the back off you at FRIDA and threw you out if they caught you slacking and had a down on people who took jobs. So she fixed things.'

'Aah-choo. Sorry. Hay fever. Fixed things?'

'Took a thousand quid off the landlord to move out. Left it all to me in her will. He didn't know she was dying, of course. Soon as the money was safely in the bank, she took an overdose. Riddled with cancer, Bea was. But she was terrified of hospitals.' She kept her voice light, matter-of-fact. 'There was a post mortem, it all came out at the inquest. The landlord realized he'd been conned and turned nasty, gave me twenty-four hours to move out. I told him I'd honour the agreement she signed and vacate at the end of the month and not before. No matter what she signed he can't get me out without a court order. Squatter's rights.'

'I'm sorry,' said Isabel, blowing her nose. 'About Bea I mean. And the flat.' Despite Paula's flippant tone, she could see the changes grief had wrought on her face. She looked older, some of her bounce had gone.

'Oh, I'm just being bloody-minded. I can pick up a bedsitter, no trouble. First time in my life I've ever had any money. If I'd known it was coming to me I wouldn't have asked FRIDA for their stinking charity. 'Nother drink?'

'No thanks,' said Isabel, eager to escape the cat. 'Shall we go and eat now? I'm starving.'

Paula led the way to a tatty little trattoria in the North End Road. Isabel ordered spaghetti bolognese with a green salad, Paula just the salad, without dressing.

'Is that all you're going to eat?'

'I had a big lunch. Chianti all right for you?'

Paula insisted that Isabel drink her share. Wine was seventy calories a glass, she said, she'd be doing her a favour. She became more talkative with every swallow, treating Isabel to a send-up of her failed auditions at RADA, LAMDA and the Webber-Douglas and giving hilarious impersonations of Julian Clavell, ski-pants and Peter Austell. She displayed an impressive knowledge of the theatre and turned out to be much more intelligent than she looked.

'I didn't rate your stepma in *The Duchess of Malfi*,' she commented, unwittingly making a friend for life. 'Wasn't worth the train fare to the sticks.'

'I only saw the rehearsals,' said Isabel. 'I won't be able to catch it till it comes to London in the autumn. I'm spending the summer with my mother, in America.'

'Lucky you. Has she got a posh place in Beverly Hills?'

'Um . . . yes. Her husband's a producer. The house is very nice, I suppose . . . if you like that kind of thing.'

'What kind of thing?'

'Well . . . a bit flashy.'

'Stinking rich, is he?'

'Yes. Just as well. She doesn't work any more, you see.'

'So, do you get to meet lots of film stars and such?'

'Sometimes.'

'Like who, for instance? You haven't met Paul Newman, have you?'

'No. But I dated Craig Matheson, last year,' said Isabel, slipping into Americanese. Paula looked suitably impressed.

'Wow. Did you go to bed with him?'

'No.'

63

'Why not? Is he queer?'

'No such luck,' said Isabel. And then, playing to the gallery, 'Actually, he tried to rape me.'

Paula demanded a blow-by-blow, ending up with a frank 'You didn't half ask for it, you know. Now if that had been me, *I'd* probably have raped *him*. But then, fat girls can't afford to be fussy.'

'You're not fat.'

'I still feel it. I'd love to be really slim like you.'

'I bet I weigh more than you. I'm eight stone ten.'

'I'm only eight-seven,' said Paula, pleased. And then, suspiciously, 'How tall are you?'

'Five seven.'

'There you go then,' said Paula glumly. 'I'm only five six and a half.'

'Oh, for heaven's sake. Let's have the *zuppa inglese* for pud. My treat this time.'

'Well . . . all right . . .'

They ended up having two helpings each and a couple of Sambucas with their coffee, both of them becoming tiddlier and gigglier by the minute. Eventually a yawning waiter, having swept the floor and put up the chairs, presented them with a bill they hadn't asked for and they had a cheerful squabble about how to split it, which Paula won.

'This is my new address and phone number,' said Isabel, as they rose to go, tearing a sheet from her diary. 'Give me a ring to tell me when you've moved. I'll be back on the seventh of September.'

They began walking towards the tube, saying their farewells at the corner of Castletown Road.

'Cheerio then,' said Paula, suddenly awkward and almost shy again. And then, looking into the distance over Isabel's shoulder, 'Christ almighty. The *bastards*.'

She began running. Isabel turned to see a pyramid of furniture on the pavement – a double bed, topped by an upturned settee, topped by a bureau with all its drawers hanging out; around this edifice lay chairs, tables, a chaise longue with a rent in its upholstery, kitchen stools, pictures, and a broken mirror. Clothes and books were strewn everywhere. Stumbling over the debris Paula opened the front door and raced up the stairs, with Isabel close behind.

She caught up with Paula to find the door of the flat boarded up, with the ginger cat scratching piteously at the rough, unfamiliar wood. Paula hammered at it furiously, screaming profanities, while Isabel tried in vain to comfort her, saying that it couldn't possibly be legal and they'd better go to the police straight away and ring a solicitor in the morning. Eventually Paula ran out of steam and sank to the floor, cradling the cat in her arms.

'No point,' she said. 'You can bet your life they've smashed the place up inside and cut off the water and the electric. Won't be liveable in. I wouldn't mind if they hadn't put her stuff out on the street. I was going to find an unfurnished place, where I could keep it. The flat's just a flat. But the things in it . . . they're all I had left of her. Shit. Shit, shit, shit.'

She was trembling, her eyes bright with unshed tears.

'It's all right,' Isabel heard herself saying. 'We'll pile everything we can in a taxi and take it round to my place. Then first thing in the morning we'll ring Pickford's and get them to collect the rest.'

'What?'

'We've got a spare room. There's masses of space. You can stay with us . . .' And then, remembering Richard, and wondering what on earth he would say '. . . until you find somewhere else.'

Paula stared at her for a moment.

'You mean it? You don't mind?'

'Why should I mind? I'm off to America in a couple of days, remember.' Another sneeze.

'Oh God,' said Paula faintly. 'First Bea, now you.' She began laughing, a cracked, high-pitched, hysterical sound. 'First Bea, now you. There's one born every minute.' Abruptly she collapsed into sobs, while Isabel sat on the floor with her arm around her, making hush-hush noises between sneezes.

After a couple of minutes Paula wrenched herself free and growled, 'I'm sorry. I haven't cried since she died.' And then, sending a shiver down Isabel's spine, 'Since I killed her, I mean. Still want me to stay with you, do you? Did you hear what I said? I killed her.'

'What are you talking about?'

'She begged me to do it. Said she didn't have the guts. Told me to wipe the hypodermic clean so it wouldn't have my prints on it. Told me just how much to put in it. Showed me the suicide note she'd written, so no one would think it was me. Then she told me about the money, and the will. Said that now she'd got everything fixed, she could die happy. She kept saying please. I knew the pain was bad. I knew how scared she was. So I did it. I killed her. Because I loved her.'

'It's all right,' murmured Isabel, hugging her. But Paula was stiff, unresponsive.

'I'll never love anyone again,' she hissed. 'You're my witness. I swear to God I'll never love anyone ever again.'

3

Summer–Autumn 1959

Men prize the thing ungain'd more than it is.

William Shakespeare – Troilus and Cressida

'I'm afraid we've already got a visitor,' said Isabel, in the taxi. 'A friend of my brother's. Richard likes the oddest people. But he'll be leaving tomorrow.'

Richard's odd friend had forgotten to put the latchkey back under the mat. It took a good two minutes of hammering on the door, leaning on the bell and shouting through the letter box before he finally appeared, wearing nothing but a pair of Y-fronts and a sleepy, sinful smile.

'For heaven's sake,' said Isabel crossly, like some doughty white huntress reproving an importunate tiger. 'People can see you. This is Paula . . . ah-choo . . . she's just been evicted. Put some clothes on and help us bring in all this stuff.'

The flat was oddly arranged. The front door at ground level by-passed it, serving the flat above, so you had to go down to a basement to get in and then up again, internally, to reach the bedrooms.

'Let me carry those for you,' said Richard's friend, reappearing, dressed, a moment later and relieving Paula of sundry items of luggage. He had blue eyes deep enough to swim in and a voice as soft and warm as a fur coat. 'What's her name?' he asked, as the cat began sniffing round his ankles.

'Brimstone.'

'Hello there, Brimstone, I'm Patrick. Come on in, both of you, and make yourself at home.'

Still in shock, Paula did little more than stand there, passively observing all the activity generated on her behalf. Patrick made repeated journeys in and out, up and down, while Isabel paid off the taxi and made up a bed for her. But she didn't thank either of them for their trouble. Thank you was even harder to say than sorry. Meekly obeying a sneezing Isabel, she fell into bed, with Brimstone at her feet, and retreated into a restless semi-sleep, endlessly re-enacting the moment when she had plunged that needle into Bea's arm and held her close, soothing her fear, until she slipped peacefully away.

The savage pain of it had obliterated her brief, heady triumph in getting that place at FRIDA. Bea had been so pleased for her. Wanting to give her that pleasure, before she died, had been the whole point of keeping at it, despite all the rejection and disappointment and despair. It had been Paula's way of thanking her and telling her how much she loved her. And now she was gone. Now she had no one to please but herself, nothing to spur her on but her own ambition. Ambition couldn't possibly hurt you as much as love.

She woke to the sound of Patrick splashing and singing in the bathroom next door. By Bea's watch it was seven fifteen, a veritable lie-in. For the last few weeks she had been getting up at dawn, wrenched prematurely from sleep by small-hours panic and unable to return to its restless embrace. But for once she lay idle, basking in the promising morning light leaking through the threadbare curtains and the cheerful noises on the other side of the wall, filled with the cautious well-being that follows a fever.

She waited for the sound of footsteps returning to the floor below before venturing out and washing away the night. Patrick had left a ring round the bath and spilt water on the floor; Paula cleaned up after him, fearful that Isabel would think she was the culprit. The front door slammed as she emerged; he must have gone straight out.

Sorry-glad to have missed him, she went downstairs with Brimstone in search of breakfast, not that she ate breakfast any more, just two cups of black, sugarless coffee. After filling a furry kettle and rooting around in cupboards full of chipped china, she found two inches of congealed Camp in the bottom of a greasy bottle. There was no milk for the cat; the fridge was empty, and smelled of bleach.

'All right, all right,' she told Brimstone, who was yowling her impatience, just as the front door clicked open, releasing a draught of morning air smelling of traffic and overnight rain.

'I managed to catch the milkman,' Patrick greeted her, ambling into the kitchen and handing her a bottle of gold top. He was wearing a very creased white shirt and a navy blue suit which had an uneasy air of Sunday best about it. While Paula found a saucer, he bent to pick up the cat, covering his jacket with ginger hairs. His own hair, which was thick and black and badly in need of a trim, was sticking up at the back where he had slept on it; he had cut himself shaving. 'Did you sleep all right?'

He embellished the question with a lazy, appraising smile, revealing very white teeth which were slightly crooked. They matched his nose, which was on the skew, as if it had once been broken. He shouldn't have been good-looking because his face was out of proportion, the forehead too high, the eyes too close together, the chin too pointed, the cheeks too gaunt, but the smile sort of evened everything up, shifting all the pieces into place, making them fit.

'On and off.'

'If you're looking for tea, there isn't any. Let's find a café, shall we?'

'Shouldn't we wait for Isabel?'

'Seems a pity to wake her. She can always ring Fortnums and have them send over some kedgeree.'

It seemed sneaky to share a joke at Isabel's expense, but she found it impossible not to return his conspiratorial grin, not to risk being late for work for the sake of his company. They found an Italian coffee bar nearby where Patrick drank several cups of tea with three sugars, saying he didn't much care for coffee, and tucked into two rounds of bacon sandwiches. Regretting the *zuppa inglese* of the previous evening, Paula made do with a double espresso and a cigarette.

For someone with an audition in two hours' time, he displayed a remarkable lack of nerves. He seemed much more concerned with going home as soon as it was over than landing the plum role of Private Bamforth, a role Paula herself would have killed for, had she been a man. *The Long and the Short and the Tall* was yet another hit play without a single female part, let alone a good one.

'It's my parents' golden wedding tomorrow,' he explained, with his mouth full. 'I have to be there. There's going to be a big family party.'

Big was an understatement. Paula affected an interest in his tribe of relations, just for the suspect pleasure of hearing that soft, sexy, lilting voice of his.

'I was a change-of-life baby,' he said. 'My two brothers, Sean and Michael, are both grandfathers already. They took over the family business when my dad retired. Roofing and scaffolding. My eldest sister, Maureen, is twenty years older than me. She's got three children, her husband's in second-hand cars. Then there's Kathleen, she's got two boys, married to a teacher. And Mary, she's got four. Her husband's a farmer in County Meath . . .'

Paula listened with half an ear, pitying these dreary-sounding women whose identities went no further than their husbands' occupations and the number of their progeny. She felt sorry for anyone who did roofing and scaffolding and farming and teaching and sold second-hand cars, anyone who wasn't an actor. And then he mentioned a girl called Teresa to whom he was 'sort of engaged'.

'So when are you getting married?' asked Paula, implying by her tone of voice that marriage was a bore and hoping she sounded older than not-quite-sixteen. She wished that she was a sophisticated eighteen-and-a-bit, like Isabel.

'Oh, we haven't set a date yet. In a few years, I expect.'

'Will she wait that long?'

'Girls do, where I come from.'

'And where exactly do you come from?'

'Kilmacross. That's about twenty miles outside Dublin. Do you know Dublin at all? It's a great place. Real people live there. Which is more than you can say for Oxford,' he added, with feeling.

'So if it's such a great place, why didn't you go to university there?'

'Too near home,' he said, as if it were perfectly logical. Paula began to get the picture. Dublin might be a great place but the family cramped his style.

She steered the conversation back to his career, if you could call three Renegade productions at Oxford a career. He'd been spotted in *Antidotage* by an agent – an agent! – hence this chance to read for a proper part. Paula echoed Isabel's astonishment that he planned to turn it down.

'Aren't you ambitious?'

'I'm not out to sell my soul, if that's what you mean. If I make it, it'll be on my own terms. I don't want to lose sight of who I really am.'

But who was he? It was as if there were two people sitting opposite her – a would-be rebel and a hidebound traditionalist, one pair of feet kicking over the traces and the other stuck knee-deep in a bog of convention.

Just as there were two people sitting opposite him. The old Paula and the new, still jockeying for position, one holding her back and one spurring her onward to let him know that she was interested and available. That didn't mean she was falling for him, of course. He was a challenge, that was all. He had no way of knowing that she was still fat inside.

After all these months of hibernation and starvation, she was ready to emerge from her chrysalis, no longer some defenceless grub at the mercy of the nearest predatory beak, but a creature with wings who could settle and sting and then fly away. Given half a chance she would alight on someone like him, take her pleasure, and move on. And then, reassured by her conquest, she would look in the mirror and finally see the slim blonde beauty she longed to be . . .

By the time she got back from work that night, Patrick had left for Dublin, straight from his audition, and Isabel had had Bea's remaining furniture delivered to the flat. Some, inevitably, had been nicked overnight, but most of it was too old to be worth stealing. Two days later Isabel flew off to Los Angeles, full of polite apologies for leaving her so soon and assurances that of course Richard didn't mind her being there, if he did he would have said so, Richard wasn't the tactful . . . ah-choo . . . type.

Richard, returning after a night spent with a friend, had greeted his unexpected guest with his customary nonchalance. Paula should have found him irritating, with his affected drawl and supercilious manner, but she felt oddly comfortable in his presence, knowing that he was queer, which she wouldn't have guessed but for Isabel's tactful, 'You don't have to worry about being alone in the house with Richard, by the way. He's homosexual.'

Paula was surprised at her openness on the subject, not to

71

mention Richard's own; you could get had up for it, after all. But as Bea had told her, things were different in the theatre. The theatre had its own laws.

As it happened, she had the flat more or less to herself. Richard was hardly ever in, forever meeting people and making contacts. He had a genius for PR, with the infant Renegade Productions getting mentions all over the place, including a large feature in *Plays and Players* headed 'The Angry Young Impresario', in which Richard declared his commitment to unknown playwrights, actors and directors, his passionate opposition to censorship, his determination to prove that experimental drama could be profitable and popular, and his loathing of the bureaucracy that went hand in hand with state subsidy. There was a photograph of him looking intense and intellectual and another of one of the sketches from *Antidotage*, the current Renegade revue, showing Patrick done up as Harold Macmillan.

'Till you find somewhere else,' Isabel had said, but Paula had insisted on paying rent to make it harder for them to ask her to leave. Living here, she was a member of the Mallory set, a circle she could never have hoped to join otherwise. And with Bea's furniture in the living room – much better than the stuff which was there already, which she managed to sell to a junk shop, with Richard's permission – it began to feel familiar, safe, her own.

But the best of it was that Richard obviously wanted and expected her to stay, otherwise he wouldn't have entrusted her with supervising the decorations in Isabel's absence, a project Paula thoroughly enjoyed, despite her initial qualms. And, Richard pointed out, Isabel was bloody lucky to have someone efficient like her there to organize everything. Paula made no bones about bawling out the workmen if things weren't done right; left to himself, Richard would have let them get away with murder.

Sharp, meanwhile, was deeply impressed by Paula's new posh address and high-class flatmates. She raised no objection to giving Paula time off to go up to Edinburgh for the first night of *Antidotage* and even offered to look after Brimstone for her while she was away. Richard, who had driven up a few days before, had arranged for Paula to have a room at the company's digs. It was the nearest thing to a holiday she had ever had, the ostensible reason for her ill-concealed excitement. The real reason was the prospect of seeing Patrick again.

She took the overnight train from King's Cross, sitting up all night to save the cost of a third-class sleeper. She didn't believe for a minute that Richard would be there to meet her as promised at six in the morning, and indeed he wasn't. But Patrick was, all scuffed shoes and shiny trousers, hands in pockets, hair uncombed, sharing some raucous joke with the ticket collector. The sight of him made her clothes feel uncomfortably tight, especially that over-optimistic 34-inch-hip pencil skirt.

'Richard's still in bed,' he told her, taking her case. 'The landlady's got a nice big bowl of porridge waiting for you. I told her you'd be hungry after your journey.'

'I'm not. I don't eat breakfast.'

'Away wi' ye, lassie. You'll fade away.'

'How do you do accents? Can't seem to lose mine.' Received pronunciation had so far defied Paula's powers of mimicry. Any attempt to doctor her vowels made her sound horribly mock-genteel, like Sharp.

'I don't know. I just do them. They're easy.'

'I'll bet everything is for you.' He shrugged, not denying it. 'So how was your summer?' she added, wincing as he crunched the gears of Richard's car.

'Oh, fine. I got an upper second.'

'By the skin of your teeth, Richard said.'

'Don't spoil it. The family thinks I'm a genius.'

'Are they coming to see you?'

'Tomorrow. They can't make it for the opening. One of my uncles died and the funeral's today. Should be there myself, really. But Richard wouldn't put off the first night. The show must go on and all the rest of it. If he wasn't a mate of mine I'd have told him to go to hell.'

'What about Teresa?' pumped Paula, appalled by his unprofessional attitude. Bea had gone on stage the night she had heard of her first husband's death at Vimy Ridge. That was what professionals were made of.

'Imagine you remembering her name. She's coming with my parents.'

'Richard told me you turned down that part.'

73

'Yes. They phoned me at home the next day. Unfortunately I was in plaster at the time. I'd just come off my motorbike.' He grinned. 'Even though I haven't got one, worse luck. In any case, Renegade's a better bet. Richard's been working his backside off finding backers and making sure the critics come and give us some good reviews. He's hoping to take *Antidotage* on tour, and on to London.' It was as if he had thought it all out in advance, thought Paula.

Antidotage, as a fringe production, was being staged in a draughty hall with minimal facilities. The Renegade company, all toffee-nosed Oxford types, comprised half a dozen actors, all male, and four backstage workers who covered stage management, lighting, costumes and props between them, with Richard in overall charge. None of them deigned to acknowledge Paula's existence, not even Patrick, once he got down to work. She was able to sit and watch the rehearsal unobserved, fascinated.

She had expected him to be a bit of a dilettante, easy-going and sloppy. But he proved to be temperamental, impatient, pernickety, and only too well aware of his own phenomenal talent. He had split-second comic timing, a chameleon-like gift for impersonation, no inhibitions and no compunction about stealing every scene. He was single-minded, ruthless and seemed to thrive on an atmosphere of conflict. In short, whatever he said, he was ambitious.

Patrick was evidently not well liked by the rest of the company, which was hardly surprising. Everyone else was replaceable, expendable; he was not. Without him there would be no show to speak of, and if the rest of them wanted their share of the glory they knew they had to put up with him.

'What did you think?' he asked Paula, after rehearsals were over, less than an hour before the curtain was due to rise. Suddenly he was all shambling charm again, guileless and apparently oblivious to the huffiness all around him.

'Not bad, for a one-man show. Remind me never to share a stage with you.'

'I was never any good at team sports,' he admitted cheerfully. 'Boxing's my game.'

'So I see. No wonder everybody hates your guts.'

'That's their problem, not mine.'

'Why do you let him get away with it?' she asked Richard.

But Richard just shrugged and said, 'It works in performance. The others rise to the challenge once there's an audience out there. He brings out the best in them. We'll come across tonight as one of those close-knit companies with wonderful, unselfish ensemble playing. All part of the illusion.'

Richard was right; it did work in performance. Triumphantly so. In the collective intoxication of laughter and applause and cheers and back-slapping, you would have thought that Patrick was genuinely popular among his fellow-players. And at the party afterwards, in the Caledonian Hotel, with Richard pouring champagne down the throats of his hand-picked first-night guests, Patrick came across as a diffident, unaffected chap, rather inarticulate without a script and embarrassed by all the gush.

'I've never met such a bunch of pseuds in all my life,' he hissed into Paula's ear. 'Let's get out of here.'

'You can't leave. You've got to impress these people. Some of them are potential backers –'

Ignoring her protests, Patrick took hold of her arm and inveigled her out of the room and past the doorman into Princes Street.

'Either they like the show or they don't,' he said. 'Either I can act or I can't. I can keep up that toadying for ten minutes or so, just for a laugh, but if I stay there I'll end up disgracing myself.'

'But –'

He caught her mouth in mid-speech, strangling her lecture at birth. Success was the ultimate aphrodisiac; fired by all that much-despised adulation, Patrick needed to discharge his surplus energy and contempt. And she was the nearest receptacle. Any woman would have done. This wasn't how she had planned it; she had wanted to seduce him. As it was he had beaten her to it, a little fat girl who was anybody's for a bit of attention. Suddenly she was scared. There had never been anyone else but Stan, who wasn't fussy, she didn't even know if she was any good at it . . .

'Let's go home,' said Patrick. 'Everyone's at the party, we'll have the place to ourselves.'

He took her acquiescence for granted. He dominated her in exactly the same way as he had dominated the other actors, by forcing her to compete. Far from retreating, she found herself running to keep up.

He made love the way he performed on stage. Selfishly, confidently, flamboyantly, exuding the same sense of threat, inspiring her to try harder, like a novice playing opposite a star. It reminded her of the time Dad had 'taught' her the quickstep, lifting her off her feet and whirling her round the floor in a weightless, breathless delusion of grace. And now Patrick spun her round and round in time to a different kind of music, making her giddy and glad. For a moment it was enough to blot out the past, to make her feel renewed and reborn. It was sweet and corrupting, like black-market chocolate, presaging the hunger to come.

Afterwards he kissed her hair absently and drew her into the crook of his arm and said, 'I'm sorry I was careless.'

'Catholics aren't allowed to be careful, are they?'

'No. Fornication's less of a sin if you manage to get the girl pregnant.'

There was just a hint of unease beneath the flippancy.

'Well, you didn't. It was safe. Otherwise I would have said. Catch me getting myself knocked up. I've got my career to think of. But you want to watch out. Sooner or later your luck'll run out.'

'Next time I'll take precautions. I promise.'

'Next time? I thought Teresa was arriving tomorrow.'

'Who said anything about tomorrow?' he said, disappearing under the bedclothes and burying his face between her legs.

He knew she was a greedy pig, knew she had no will power. She would regret this binge tomorrow but for the moment she would gorge herself, grab whatever was on offer while the going was good. It wasn't love, just gluttony. Tomorrow disgust at her own weakness would serve as an emotional emetic, cancel the whole experience out, leave her just as she was before.

'You're sweet,' he murmured sleepily, throwing an arm across her as if to prevent her escape. Sweet. Well so she should be. She felt like a bee sated with nectar, sinking under its own weight into the well it had drunk from, robbed of the power to fly away.

Having already made arrangements to stay a second night and been prevailed on by Richard to sell programmes, Paula had no choice but to stick it out. Mr and Mrs Delaney and Teresa duly arrived the next day at Mrs Sinclair's, where rooms had been reserved for them. Teresa was small, dark, shy and very pretty in an apple-cheeked, milkmaid kind of way. Patrick introduced her to Paula with perfect composure, his conscience clear. By his lights, he had done nothing wrong. Teresa was saving herself for her wedding night; he had told Paula so himself. In respecting her virginity, he gave himself the right to practise on other women rather than her, making a virtue out of it. And those other women were made well aware, in advance, that he was already spoken for, so that he could pride himself on being honest and avoid the danger of getting involved. He had a nice little system going, thought Paula. Life was so simple for men.

The parents, a devoted old couple in shabby clothes – dress sense obviously ran in the family – had clearly spoiled him rotten from birth. Paula could tell, watching them in the audience, that most of the undergraduate humour was lost on them, but they laughed and clapped nonetheless, despite the obscene innuendoes and breaches of good taste. Anything their broth of a boy appeared in was all right by them.

After they were all safely tucked up in bed, their broth of a boy crept down the corridor and knocked on Paula's door.

'Go away,' she hissed, well aware that Teresa was sleeping two rooms along.

'What's wrong?' he said in his normal voice. It sounded hideously loud.

'Be quiet! People will hear!'

'Well, let me in and they won't.'

She did so, glaring.

'How can you do this to her, you two-timing bastard?'

'How? I showed you that already. But since you insist, I'd be happy to show you again . . .'

'But she's . . . she's nice,' Paula heard herself saying, wriggling free of his embrace.

'I know. That's why I'm in your room and not hers.'

'Suppose I tell her?'

'She'll think you're a bitch. She'll cry and I'll comfort her. I'll say sorry and she'll forgive me. But you're not a bitch. So it's not going to happen.'

77

No, thought Paula, defeated, as he turned the key in her door. I'm not a bitch. But I will be one day. You'll see.

It had been a long summer. Isabel was fed up with premieres and pool parties and barbecues and the beach, fed up with the sunshine and smog. She looked forward to a grey, chilly London autumn, full of damp dead leaves and gunmetal skies and rain racing down the window panes, and the promise of a cold, crisp, cleansing winter.

But she went through the motions of being sorry to go, having politely declined Marty's ever-open offer of a screen test. She was cameragenic, he told her, a natural. Hardly surprising. She looked so like Fay it was embarrassing. People never stopped commenting on it.

How enticing this life must seem if you were on the outside looking in. All those thousands of pretty girls hanging around the studios, willing to sleep with anyone who might get them a walk-on part. Girls who had spent their lives reading movie magazines and dreaming of wealth and fame, who mistook success for happiness. Girls who reminded her of Paula.

Success, if you were fifty and female, like Mummy, was having quit while you were ahead, with a rich, ageing, doting husband like Marty to pick up the bills. Although Mummy would have passed for forty, thanks to a facelift which had sharpened her cheekbones, tautened her jaw, given her a waxen smoothness around the eyes.

Her good days were devoted to winning her brave, never-ending battle against mental and physical decay. There would be sessions with her therapist, her masseur and the visiting hairdresser who hid her baldness with glossy borrowed tresses. There would be visits to the beauty parlour for facials and manicures, figure-maintaining lengths of the pool and sessions at the gym, and indefatigable shopping expeditions. On good days she would be almost like her old self, energetic, volatile, endearingly full of caustic wit. She would bitch happily about Daddy and Davina and almost convince Isabel that she was getting better.

Her bad days – which were fast outnumbering the good – were spent entirely in her emperor-size bed with the curtains drawn,

78

barely coherent with depression. The doctor would be called, medication prescribed, tests scheduled. There was periodic talk of a hysterectomy as a cure for all her ills. Meanwhile she would lie there, doped and drowsy, rambling endlessly about Daddy.

'I was selfish,' she would lament. 'I put my career first, instead of my husband and children. I never wanted children. I was a terrible mother to you and poor Richard. I never looked after either of you, hardly ever saw you. I'm a wicked, wicked woman and I deserve to be all alone . . .'

Whatever the clinical diagnosis, Isabel was afraid that Mummy was going mad, like her own mother before her. A brilliant society beauty, she had been committed to a mental institution at the age of thirty and drowned herself, in a lavatory bowl, a year later. A fear which did nothing to assuage Isabel's guilt at leaving her mother in this state.

'Don't worry,' said Marty, the day before Isabel's departure. It had been a 'bad day' with a vengeance, the worst so far. 'I'll look after her for you. It's a pity you didn't decide to stay, but if you ever change your mind . . .' He took hold of her hand and squeezed it, fondling it rather more than the gesture required.

I'm imagining things, thought Isabel. It was Richard who had first put the doubt in her mind, last summer, warning her to be careful, Marty wasn't getting much at home these days and he knew a dirty old man when he saw one. But it was typical of Richard to think the worst of people. Dirty old man or not, Mummy was lucky to have him. Without Marty, what would become of her?

She arrived home to an empty flat, Richard being in Edinburgh, and Paula at work. Richard had assured her, the last time they had spoken, that she wouldn't recognize the place, Paula had done a marvellous job in keeping the workmen on their toes . . .

She stood for a moment in the hall, thinking that she had opened the wrong door. The walls were covered in a hideous rosebud-strewn paper and on the floor was a shiny, swirly, synthetic fitted carpet in variegated shades of dried blood. Appalled, Isabel toured the flat, upstairs and down. The dried-blood carpet had been laid throughout and the rampant floral effects were everywhere. Even the curtains needed pruning. And the woodwork and doors and ceilings were all in *pink*, or rather pinks, according to the ambient blooms. The whole flat reminded her of an overdressed, blowsy woman, the kind who had shoes and handbags dyed to match her hat and whose nails were precisely the same colour as her lipstick . . .

The flagrant snob who lurked inside Isabel, pretending she didn't exist, jumped out and shrieked aloud in horror. The cat, who was prowling round the place as if it owned it, miaoued at her in insolent response. Isabel let out an earth-shattering sneeze.

'Izzie?' She turned, eyes still blazing, to see Paula smirking at her. 'Welcome home! I left work early, specially.'

'Was it Richard?' accused Isabel, by way of greeting. 'Is this one of Richard's diabolical practical jokes?'

'Richard? What joke? He's still in Edinburgh. The show's had rave reviews. It's going on tour. They're hoping to bring it to London. Isn't it great?'

Her sunny expression did nothing to dispel Isabel's fury.

'What happened to the list I gave him?' she demanded. 'The list of the wallpapers and curtains and carpets I chose before I went away?'

'He lost it,' said Paula innocently. 'He didn't want to bother you, so he told me to go ahead and do what I thought best. What's the matter? Don't you like it?'

'Oh, it's terrific. All we need is a madam and a dozen tarts and we'll be in business. Bloody Richard. If I trust anything to him, anything at all . . . It's not enough to leave me to cope with Mummy all summer, he has to let you loose on my flat!' She was silenced by another sneeze, more thunderous than the first.

'It's Richard's flat too,' said Paula, aggrieved, flushing. 'And he likes it. So he said.'

Isabel ran abruptly out of steam. It wasn't fair to take it out on Paula. What a spoiled bitch she must sound . . .

'I'm sorry,' she said stiffly. 'I'm just tired. It was a long flight.' And an even longer summer. She sat down limply on the stairs. After a moment's hesitation, Paula sat down beside her, whereupon the cat jumped onto her lap and began purring extravagantly, as if taking her side in the argument.

'It's just that I loathe pink,' said Isabel apologetically. 'I only like flowers in gardens, and vases. It's not your fault. Richard set us both up. He's always played horrible . . . ah-choo . . . tricks on me, ever since we were kids.'

'It was having all those blank cheques to spend that did it,' said Paula. 'I suppose I got carried away. It was so nice to be the customer, for a change.'

'It's all right. I know you only meant to help.'

'No I didn't. I did it for me, not for you. I pretended it was my place, my money, I had the time of my life. Why can't you just lam into me for having bloody awful taste? Do you think I don't know that?'

'Taste is a personal thing,' began Isabel. 'I never meant to –'

'Offend me?' mocked Paula. 'You know, I had a choice. First of all, I thought I'd try to copy you. I'd give anything to be like you. And then I thought, no, because however hard I tried that's all I'd ever be. A copy. So I decided to be me. An original. If you're common, you might as well make a feature of it. I'm not apologizing for what I am. If you want me to move out, now you're back, just say so. I won't burst into tears or anything.'

It was a test, not an invitation.

'If I want you to move out, I'll say so,' muttered Isabel, forcing herself not to be too polite. She blew her nose to hide another sneeze.

'Hay fever still bad?'

Isabel drew breath to tell the truth, as Paula had enjoined her to do, only to meet the cat's gaze full on. As if reading her mind, it recoiled from her and burrowed deeper into its mistress's lap.

'What's the matter, Brimstone? This is Isabel, remember? She's your friend. Shake paws.' She picked one up and extended it. Feeling absurd, Isabel shook it, steeling herself to put up with smarting eyes and a streaming nose for the foreseeable future. Better than feeling as if she had deprived an underprivileged child of its only plaything. She'd shown herself up quite enough for one day.

'Must be all the pollen on the walls,' she muttered, as she sniffed back another nosequake. 'Look, I'm going to bed now. I've got to get some sleep.'

'Before I forget . . .' Paula fetched an envelope from behind the clock in the living room. 'Letter for you. Arrived today. I'll leave you to get some kip, then. I'm off to see Michael Redgrave in *The Aspern Papers*. Sleep tight.'

81

But she didn't, thanks to the letter.

6 September 1959

Dear Isabel
Welcome home. I hope you had a nice trip. It seems a long time
since we last talked. Can we meet for lunch? How about this
coming Tuesday? I'll ring you to confirm.

Yours, Neville

The writing was as bold and black as ever; she'd forgotten that he
was left-handed. Isabel lay down, shutting her eyes against the
beribboned posies on the opposite wall, one ear cocked for the
phone. Tuesday. And today was only Thursday. Lunch. Did he
have something to tell her? She began writing the script in her
head. *I love you. I've always loved you. And you love me too, don't*
bother to deny it. What a chestnut that line was. Why was it always
a woman's role to deny things, to be coaxed into admitting the
obvious?

Eventually she dozed off, only to spring to attention, instantly
alert, as the phone began ringing in the hall below. She nearly fell
downstairs in her haste to pick it up. There was the sound of
someone pressing button A.

'Paula, it's me,' said a voice, before she got the chance to
announce herself. 'Are you coming up this weekend?'

'Paula's out,' said Isabel rather crossly, disappointed that it
wasn't Neville. 'Can I give her a message?'

'Isabel? Well, hello there. It's Patrick. Richard wasn't expecting you back until tomorrow.'

'Richard's hopeless on dates. Is he there?'

'No, he's having dinner with someone or other. So, how are
you?' he continued, all cheerful telephonic charm. 'How was
Uncle Sam?'

'Very well, thank you. Congratulations, by the way. I hear
you've had a big success.'

'Yes, isn't it grand? Ask Paula to show you the scrapbook. She's
our honorary press secretary. Tell her I'll be there to meet her on
Saturday morning unless she rings me to say she's not coming.
Have to go. No more change. 'Bye.'

Isabel put the phone down, wondering.

Paula woke her next morning with a conciliatory tray of coffee and toast.

'Patrick rang,' yawned Isabel, sitting up on her elbows. 'He's going to meet you at the station on Saturday unless you ring to say you're not coming.'

'Bloody cheek. As if I'd waste the fare. If he rings again, don't let on. He needs taking down a peg.'

'You mean . . . it isn't to do with Renegade?' said Isabel, playing it dumb. 'He said you were their press secretary.'

'Oh, there's a scrapbook, if you'd like to see it. The critics all falling over themselves hailing Patrick as a major new talent. As if he wasn't big-headed enough already.'

'So you and Patrick . . .'

'I went up to Edinburgh for the first night and we ended up in bed together. With his po-faced fiancée two doors along. It was hysterical.'

'His fiancée?'

'Oh, you wouldn't believe the set-up back home. Thousands of brothers and sisters and nieces and nephews and a little old Irish mother and a virgin bride all lined up for him, good Catholic breeding stock. I feel sorry for her, honest I do.'

'So do I,' said Isabel, reaching for her coffee.

'It was just curiosity really,' shrugged Paula. 'I've had better than him.'

'Like who?' said Isabel ungrammatically, torn between prurient curiosity and a fear of Paula's superior knowledge.

'Oh, I've been around,' said Paula vaguely. 'That's how I ended up in care, they reckoned I was a nympho. For two pins I'd have him arrested. That'd learn him. I won't be sixteen till next week.'

'Sixteen? I thought you were the same age as me.'

'Actresses always lie about their age. Got to go, I'm running late for work. Only one more week, yippee. For a while, anyway. I promised Sharp I'd help her out during the sales. She reckons she'll be lost without me.' She turned to go. 'And you can stop worrying about Brimstone, by the way,' she added, as an afterthought. 'I'm taking her to work with me this morning and then Sharp's taking her home. The poor bitch needs something to love. Richard told me you were allergic to cats, the first day I was here.'

'It's all right,' began Isabel, mortified. 'You don't have to . . .'

'Yes I do,' said Paula, over her shoulder. 'I was getting too fond of her anyway.'

'Isabel.' Neville rose to his feet to greet her. His phone call had been brief to the point of abruptness, but his face lit up at the sight of her, flooding her with hope.

'Neville.' He was wearing a spotted blue bow tie that gave him a rakish air, and she noticed that the reddish gold of his hair was flecked, for the first time, with silver.

'You look wonderful. So tanned.' Isabel had worn a white sleeveless shirtwaister to show off her honey-bronze to maximum advantage. As a pale-skinned redhead, she never sat in the sun, which brought her out in freckles. The tan had come out of a fabulously expensive bottle.

A waitress appeared with two menus. He had suggested Schmidts in Charlotte Street and it was crowded and noisy as always; the perfect place for a private conversation.

'You heard that Richard's taking *Antidotage* on tour?' said Isabel brightly, to hide her nerves. 'They've been turning people away every night, apparently.'

'Yes. He seems to have pulled off quite a publicity coup. Every time I pick up a paper I seem to read something about Renegade. I gather this Patrick Delaney's quite a find.'

'So they say,' said Isabel. 'I must catch the show if it ever comes to London. So, how are you?'

'Short of money, pending the insurance claim. That's what I wanted to talk to you about. I thought it only fair to warn you beforehand. I've taken a teaching job. At FRIDA.'

Startling though the news should have been, it came as an anticlimax. So that was why he had asked her to lunch.

'I went to see Julian Clavell and he was too embarrassed by this' – he indicated the empty sleeve – 'to turn away a former student fallen on hard times. Those who can't, teach. I hope having me there as a tutor won't put you off.'

Isabel was spared the need to answer by the arrival of her schnitzel, garnished with egg and anchovies, with red cabbage on the side. She tried to summon up some appetite, anxious not to show her disappointment. How stupid of her to think, to hope, that he was going to make some theatrical declaration of love. Trust her to read too much into one ill-considered kiss. Did he really not feel anything for her? Or was he simply reluctant to take advantage of her? And now she would have to see him every day at FRIDA, making her torment worse.

They turned to shop talk, casting gossip, FRIDA's internal politics, the latest plays by Harold Pinter and Arnold Wesker, and how impossible it was to get seats for the film of *Ben Hur*, which Isabel had already seen in the States. Eventually Isabel forced herself to say, 'How's Helen?'

'She's been a tower of strength,' he said. 'As you can imagine, I've been perfectly bloody to live with lately. I'd never have got through all this without her. Whatever you do, don't marry an actor. They make the worst possible husbands.'

'I've no intentions of getting married,' said Isabel, truthfully. 'Not for years and years anyway. Not till I've done all the things I want to do.'

Hence the appeal of a man who was already married, she thought with sudden insight. She craved romance, not domesticity. She had no wish to keep house for him, no wish to bear his children or take him away from his noble, long-suffering wife. She just wanted a love affair. An actress ought to know first-hand what love felt like . . .

'Not hungry?' he said, as she abandoned her meal. He had ordered goulash and mashed potatoes, and left most of his as well.

'Not very. You know, it's always irritated me, in films and plays, how nobody ever finishes a meal, or a drink.'

'They hold up the action. And anyway, who wants to finish a double cold tea on the rocks or bread steaks soaked in gravy browning?' He reached across the table for her hand and said gently, taking her by surprise, 'Don't think I don't know how you feel. I encouraged it. I was flattered. It was terribly wrong of me. Helen and I . . . well, we've had our problems. But the accident brought us both up short. We had a long talk and agreed to try and make a go of things. I respect you and care about you far too much to contemplate a casual affair. I couldn't bear to hurt you, Izzie.'

'It's all right,' she said, too emphatically. 'I understand. I'm not a home-breaker, like Davina.' And then, yielding to a hectic impulse, 'What really happened between you and her?'

He hesitated for a moment before saying, 'We had a very brief affair, at her instigation and with my full co-operation. She's a very attractive woman. Helen had just had a baby and things were . . . difficult at home. Which isn't an excuse, just a reason. When I tried to end it, she threatened to tell my wife, so I told my wife instead. Davina retaliated by complaining to your father that I wouldn't leave her alone, and the rest, I think, you know.'

'Bitch,' muttered Isabel.

'Ah, well, it's always the woman's fault. Men can't help themselves, can they? Blame it on Davina, blame it on Helen, blame it on anyone but me.'

'I am blaming you. And Daddy. I don't know how he can be so blind.'

'He loves her, I suppose. Which is why I didn't bother to defend myself. It seemed kinder to leave him in ignorance. I hope you'll do the same.'

'Even if I told him the truth, he wouldn't believe me,' muttered Isabel, hoping nonetheless that one day her father would come to his senses. It would be bliss to see the back of Davina for good.

'I have to go,' she said, finally, after a second cup of coffee, unable to prolong the encounter any longer.

'See you at FRIDA, then. And don't worry about other people thinking you're the teacher's pet. I intend to be very hard on you.'

It would be his way of showing he cared. She would have to be content with that.

It was a mistake to look forward to things, thought Paula. She should have learned that by now. She had wanted to be an actress more than anything in the world, viewed FRIDA with all the awe of a pilgrim within sight of Mecca. For months she had lived in suspension, waiting, looking forward, planning, counting the days. And now that she was doing what she had dreamed of for so long, she was, quite incredibly, bored. Or perhaps it wasn't so incredible. She was back at school, after all.

She hadn't minded learning from Bea, who had a knack for making things seem easy. At FRIDA they made hard work of everything. You arrived thinking you could act a little – they'd given you a place, after all – only to be told that not only you couldn't act, you couldn't speak or move or even breathe without being taught again, from scratch, like a baby.

Isabel didn't seem to mind, but then Isabel was intelligent, educated. When you were ignorant and relatively thick, it didn't help to be reminded of it at every turn. Isabel thought nothing of lying on the floor for an hour at a time filling and evacuating her lungs to the chant of 'Hoo, ho, how, hee' or endless rolling her Rs. Now softly, in a stage whisper, now in a gallery-busting shout, while a shrill middle-aged matron in polka-dot trousers and plimsolls marched up and down the rows of prone bodies like a sergeant major in drag exhorting them to 'breathe in and attack'.

The first couple of lessons were a bit of a laugh. And having learned to say rrrr and ho and hee and breathe in and attack, Paula was keen to move on. But progress wasn't allowed. However hard you tried, you were never doing it quite right, so they made you do it every day, singly and collectively, till you wanted to scream with frustration. 'Fee, figh, foh, fuck!' Paula yelled one day, only to be told to go and stand in the corridor until the class was over, as if she were six years old. Nobody even laughed, except Isabel, and that wasn't till after they got home that night.

Movement was even worse, with Mrs Winston, ubiquitous in ski pants and ballet pumps, supervising sadistic contortions which would have taxed an acrobat, reminding Paula with every flash of her evil eye that she was fat and ungainly and slow. Sometimes her muscles would hurt so much from the day before that she could barely move; only pride kept her at it.

Isabel, of course, was horribly fit. She had learned ballet, she went skiing every winter, she was the school tennis champion, she held a life-saver's badge for swimming. There wasn't a movement which she couldn't execute with ease and without sweat. And yet, as if that wasn't quite enough reason to hate her, she was eternally self-critical, forever agonizing about the size of her feet and grumbling about her legs being too skinny. How could anyone's legs be too skinny? If she'd known the misery of fat ankles – it was impossible to lose weight off your ankles – she would have known when she was well off.

Then there was voice production, taught by Peter Austell, another old enemy from the interview panel.

'How many cigarettes a day does it take to produce a sound like that?' he demanded as Paula tried to project the lines,

Two voices are there; one is of the sea,
One of the mountains; each a mighty voice

to the back of the room, to repeated interruptions of 'I can't hear one voice, let alone two', and 'You're breathing in the wrong place', and, worst of all, 'Again!'

'I don't know. Ten.' Cigarettes were the mainstay of her diet. If she didn't smoke, she would eat.

'Sounds more like forty. Miss Mallory, show Miss Baker how it should be done, will you?'

It was like listening to a clarinet after a foghorn. Not that Izzie would dream of trying to show her up. She just couldn't help it, that's all. Couldn't help having inherited first-class lungs and vocal cords, couldn't help knowing how to use them – she had been lead contralto in the school choir – couldn't help an inbred, unlimited capacity for sheer hard work or the profound humility that made her eager to learn and learn and learn.

All of which showed, even though they hadn't even started acting yet, apart from pretending to be a leaf or a twig or some unlikely animal at the zoo, exercises which Paula regarded as a waste of time. The nearest they had got to real acting was mask work, a class taken by Neville Seaton. They started off with 'bland' masks that robbed you of all your features, forcing you to rely on movement to convey meaning. It was supposed to teach you 'economy'. Hidden and yet horribly exposed, you did improvisation exercises in front of the rest of the class, which got you used to making a complete idiot of yourself.

Paula felt as if she were trying to act in a sack. And yet Isabel managed to play the most eloquent silent music, reminding Paula, not that Paula needed reminding, that she would never, in a million years, be in the same league as Isabel, however hard she tried. Which didn't stop bloody Neville Seaton from accusing Isabel, easily the best student in the class, of being too mannered.

'We're not playing charades here,' he barked. 'There was far too much pretence and wasted energy there. Next time I want to see less effort, more effect.'

Isabel took it like a lamb. He never missed a thing, she claimed. And the better the student, thought Paula, the more critical he was. Which was perhaps why he tended to encourage Paula, rather than find fault with her. But the more she learned, the more uneasy and demoralized she became, the more obvious it seemed that the whole point of the FRIDA course was to put people off acting for life.

She wouldn't have been able to stick it without Isabel as an ally, but at the same time she resented having to share her with so many other people, false friends who hid their envy behind a show of goodwill. Everyone wanted to know Isabel, everyone was nice as pie to her face, but Paula had overheard them bitching about her behind her back, because she was a Mallory. They might have forgiven her her beauty and her talent, but they couldn't forgive her modesty, or rather they couldn't believe in it, couldn't accept that she wasn't as two-faced as they were.

What made Isabel so vulnerable, in Paula's view, was her crippling need to be liked. A failing Paula strove to avoid. Especially when a postcard arrived from Patrick, postmarked Oldham, with the note, 'Looking forward to getting together in London next month.' Smug bastard. Every time she thought of the times they had got together she felt consumed with fury, for fear of feeling something else. A something else which would have broken her golden rule never to become dependent on anyone. On the other hand, she was more than happy for Isabel to become dependent on *her*. Izzie needed someone to look out for her. Soft in the head, Izzie was.

But Isabel apart, Paula preferred making enemies to friends. Enemies kept you on your toes. She soon designated the scholarship-winner, Brenda Price, as the focus of her hostility. Price had evidently expected to be the star pupil and hadn't bargained for someone like Isabel Mallory stealing her thunder.

'Cast list has just gone up for next term's *The Country Wife*,' announced Price, joining Isabel and Paula in the college snack bar one lunch hour. 'Three guesses who's playing Margery Pinchwife.' A smile of smug delight.

'You?' said Isabel, apparently genuinely pleased.

89

'No, you,' said Price. 'Congratulations.'

Price had talent all right. She managed to invest the innocuous words with a very explicit sub-text.

'Oh. Thank you,' said Isabel. 'What part are you playing?'

'Mrs Squeamish. I must have all of fifty lines to learn. And you,' she said, turning to Paula, 'are Mrs Dainty Fidget. You've got nearly as many.'

'Well, it's not as if anyone's going to see it,' said Isabel. 'Apart from relatives, that is.' Outsiders were banned from first-year student productions, which were deemed unworthy of all but a token audience.

'Well, we couldn't expect Sir Adrian to come to a show just to see you playing a supporting role, could we?'

'Shut it,' said Paula, without ceremony. 'You're just jealous.'

'Absolutely not,' said Price. 'I know *exactly* how Izzie must be feeling. I'd *hate* to be in her position.'

'Well you're not,' Paula reassured her, 'so you can stop worrying about it.'

'Izzie's the one with the worries. I mean, my mum and dad wouldn't know if I was good or not. They'll clap themselves senseless anyway. But in *your* case . . . I suppose you must be *terrified* of letting your father down.' She assumed a look of earnest sympathy.

'Why don't you go and fuck yourself?' suggested Paula, blowing smoke in her face.

'Paula!'

'Nice friends you keep,' commented Price, pleased to have sparked a reaction. 'I expect you have trouble fending off the hangers-on. I've never gone in much for social climbing myself.'

At this Paula put down her cigarette, blew on both palms, leaned across the table and slapped Price hard across the face, making her squeal with shock and attracting astonished stares from the other students.

'Go on,' snarled Paula. 'Your turn. What's the matter? Scared of me, are you?'

Price stood up and took a step backwards.

'I'm going to report you for that,' she said, visibly shaken.

'Do what the hell you like. Now either hit me back or piss off.' She hoped she would hit back, certain of victory. Paula had learned to fight at an early age, with feet and fists and nails, and seeing Isabel sitting there, turning the other cheek as usual, was more than she could bear.

But disappointingly Price pissed off, choking back a sob. A horrified Isabel promptly ran after her. Paula relit her cigarette. All around her was deathly silence.

'Well, what are you all gaping at?' she said. 'The performance is over.' But she didn't mind them gaping. Not in the least. She had her audience, she had them riveted, and the feeling it gave her was better than sex.

Eventually Isabel returned.

'I wish you hadn't done that,' she said quietly, aware of the flapping ears all around them. 'I don't need you to protect me. I would have handled her remarks in my own way. By ignoring them.'

'Well, I handled them my way. By shutting her up. Not before time, either. She's been getting on my tits all term.'

'You can't go round hitting people. They'll throw you out.'

Paula gave a tough-guy shrug.

'So? It wouldn't be the first time I've been expelled. I don't sit by and watch a friend of mine being insulted.'

'And I don't sit by and see a friend of mine wreck her career. You can't keep behaving like some Bash Street Kid if you want to get on . . .'

'Miss Baker?' It was tweed-suit-and-glasses, Julian Clavell's secretary. 'The Principal would like to see you in his office. Right away, please.'

Ignoring Paula's protests, Isabel followed her into Clavell's office. He ignored them both for a moment while he took his time finishing some paperwork. Finally he put the cap back on his pen and fixed them with a piercing stare. Expression number ninety-three in the ham actor's handbook, thought Paula, swallowing an involuntary snort of nervous laughter.

'Miss Price has just been sent home,' he said, making the familiar steeple with his fingers. 'She proposes to see a doctor. She is also talking about pressing charges for assault. I take it you don't deny that you struck her?'

'She asked for it,' muttered Paula sullenly.

'It was my fault,' interjected Isabel. 'I handled things badly. I –'

'Miss Price has no complaint against you, Miss Mallory,' he barked. 'But you may as well listen to what I have to say, in the hope that you can persuade Miss Baker of the gravity of her position.'

He turned his attention back to Paula.

'Never in all my years at FRIDA have I encountered a physical assault by one female student on another.' Paula noted the use of female. It was all right for blokes to fight, of course. But then blokes didn't go squealing to the teacher.

'When we accepted you – you were a borderline case, I might add – we made generous allowances for the fact that you were less privileged, in terms of education and background, than the average applicant. But we did expect you to conform to certain standards of civilized behaviour. A student who cannot discipline herself in real life is unlikely to respond to the disciplines of her chosen profession. I must insist that you make a formal apology to Miss Price. Otherwise I will have no option but to suspend you and put your case up to the board of governors.'

It would happen, for sure, sooner or later. She'd never be able to keep her nose clean for the next five terms, she wasn't sure that she even wanted to. But if it happened now, like this, Isabel would be sure to blame herself . . .

To hell with that. She would eat humble pie, just this once, but not for Isabel's sake. That would be a sign of weakness. She would do it as a test of her acting ability. No need to be ashamed of that.

4

Summer 1960

We are not happy, nor can we be happy; we merely desire happiness.

Anton Chekhov – The Three Sisters

Following its long run in the West End, the satirical revue Antidotage *is hoping to repeat its success in New York. After try-outs in Boston, Newhaven, Washington and Philadelphia, the show plans to open off-Broadway at the end of September with the original London cast, notably Patrick Delaney, winner of* Plays & Players *Most Promising Newcomer award.*

All is not roses, however, for Renegade Productions, brainchild of Richard Mallory (son of Sir Adrian), whose last two ventures have flopped. Undaunted, Mallory is translating a play from the original Spanish, the work of a political prisoner languishing in one of General Franco's jails.

Says Mallory, 'The manuscript was smuggled out of Spain and although the playwright must remain anonymous, to protect him against reprisals, he is without doubt a major talent. The only problem will be in getting this play past the Lord Chamberlain, given our absurd and outdated censorship laws.'

The play, entitled Bondage, *features incest, rape, sodomy, nudity, explicit language and on-stage simulated sex. Mallory hopes to bring the play to London this autumn.*

Isabel tossed *The Observer* back at Richard across the breakfast table.

'You'll never get a licence, you realize.'

'That's the whole point!' said Richard. 'I'll refuse to make any cuts on grounds of artistic integrity and announce that we have no

93

choice but to play it under theatre club conditions. By which time everyone will know that it's obscene and offensive to public decency. That should get them applying for membership in droves.'

'And if the critics slate it?'

'Let the bastards have a field day. The key word is controversial. What we need is a few bring-'em-in quotes, like "Utterly revolting", and "An evening of unmitigated filth". Which it is.'

'I thought you said it was a work of genius.' She drowned a few more cornflakes with her spoon, watching them sink into a soggy mess at the bottom of the bowl. She felt physically sick with apprehension – not just about playing Irena that night in FRIDA's end-of-year *Three Sisters*, but because both Daddy and the Bitch would be in the audience. They had missed *The Country Wife*, thank God, because their own shows had to go on, but this time the one-and-only friends-and-family performance was being he'd, against normal practice, on a Sunday night – the result, Isabel was certain, of behind-the-scenes collusion between her father and Julian Clavell.

'It's more of a work of genius than you think,' said Richard. He picked up the breadknife and stretched it across the table towards her. '*Swear by my sword,*' he quoted solemnly, '*never to speak of this that you have seen.*' It was the most sacred of their childhood vows of silence, a relic from an early visit to *Hamlet*.

Isabel closed her fingers around the blade and parroted, '*Upon your sword, I swear.*' And then, seeing the satanic gleam in Richard's eye, 'Oh God. I should have guessed. You wrote it yourself, didn't you?'

Richard answered by way of a smirk.

'People are bound to realize,' said Isabel.

'You didn't. And you're about ten times brighter than the average critic, let alone the average theatregoer.'

'But if you want to write a play, why not write a good one?'

'Look what happened to the last one I wrote,' said Richard touchily, referring to the last Renegade flop. 'You thought that was good, as I remember. That didn't stop it being slaughtered at birth, just to punish me for being too successful.'

'Oh,' sighed Isabel, understanding. 'So this is your revenge.' Richard had taken his failure very hard.

'On the sheep-like public, on the wing-clipping critics, on the get-rich-quick backers who've lost their nerve, on the anti-Mallory snipers who say that *Antidotage* was a lucky fluke and that I'm a flaming nine-day wonder.'

'Marty won't cough up this time, you know. He'd think it was pornographic.'

'I won't be asking Marty for any hand-outs in future. I've found myself a business partner.'

'Oh Richard. Not another rich old queen who's going to sulk if you don't come across . . .'

'Absolutely not, darling. This is strictly business. Name's Vincent Parry. East End self-made type, fingers in all kinds of pies. Stage-struck and looking for a nice little tax loss on the side.'

'And how did you get to meet someone like that?'

'At a first-night party, for a play he'd backed. He has a reputation for picking winners. I've been trying to interest him in Renegade for ages, but this is the first time he's come across.'

'And of course you've told him this play's a fake?'

'No need. It was his idea. Vince is your original wide boy, knows a money-making racket when he sees one. Anyway, not a word to P or P. Neither of them is capable of keeping their big trap shut.'

They had long ago become P 'n' P, despite the on-off nature of the relationship. Paula broke things off roughly once a week, refusing to take Patrick's calls and forcing Isabel, as reluctant go-between, to paraphrase messages like 'tell that mick bastard to go fuck himself'. She made no secret of two-timing him at every opportunity, with Patrick responding in kind while remaining prophylactically 'engaged' to his girlfriend back home (who was more than welcome to him, Paula declared, repeating her claim to have 'had better than him').

As if to prove her point she was doggedly working her way round every hetero male student at FRIDA, whether she fancied him or not. It didn't seem to bother her that people called her a slut behind her back. But it bothered Isabel.

'Why do you do it?' she asked. 'To make him jealous? Or because you're jealous?'

'To please myself,' asserted Paula. 'You ought to try it some time. Hedge your bets instead of saving up all your pennies for that one-armed bandit of yours.'

The betting reference was Patrick's influence. He had a passion for horses, knew the form and ancestry of every runner in every race, and loved to indulge in hypothetical flutters and clock up imaginary winnings. Refusing to back his hunches with hard cash was part of his anti-money affectation.

'I might get rich,' he would say, 'and then I'd never know if people loved me for myself, now would I?'

'I suppose,' said Richard casually, 'you wouldn't be interested, would you, in the part of Serafina?'

Serafina, the heroine of *Bondage*, spent most of the play semi-naked, engaging in masturbation and sexually harassing her impotent elder brother.

'You must be joking,' said Isabel.

'Hmm. I thought you'd say that. Well, I felt obliged to give you first refusal. Remember you swore on my sword,' he added as two sets of footsteps were heard on the stairs.

'The top of the morning to you both,' Patrick hailed them in his joke-Irish voice. He had spent the last few nights with Paula, pending their next bust-up, and their noisy lovemaking had kept Isabel awake till dawn, not that she would have slept a wink anyway. 'What's up, Izzie? First-night nerves? Or should I say, only-night nerves,' he added, a seasoned pro talking down to a mere student.

Nerves wasn't the word for it. Every time she so much as imagined her first cue, her airways would start to close, her limbs to freeze, her sweat glands to drench her in the cold murk of fear. At the final rehearsal she had given a dreadful performance, and the worst of it was, Neville hadn't said a word about it, hadn't even noticed anything was wrong. But Daddy and Davina surely would. And so would Patrick, who would be there to watch Paula play Masha, to see Isabel make an idiot of herself.

'A bit nervous, yes,' said Isabel shortly. She despised herself for wanting his good opinion, for having sneaked in, unbeknown to him, to see *Antidotage* no less than four times. It was her habit to make repeated visits to anything she admired, to draw inspiration, learn, observe, absorb and steal. His style was big and bold and fearless, in sharp contrast to her own, which was full of minutely observed, understated detail; next to him she felt pedantic and timid. It didn't seem fair that Patrick could do all that without

96

anyone having taught him how. He was like a pianist who couldn't read music but played, instinctively, by ear, making up his own arrangements as he went along, never striking a wrong note, mocking all those hours of five-finger exercises practised by less gifted hands than his.

'You've no need to worry,' Patrick assured her, filling his cereal bowl up to the brim and spilling flakes all over the cloth. 'Paula tells me you're bloody good.'

'Shut up, Patrick,' said Paula. 'There's enough pressure on her to be good already.' She turned to Isabel. 'I've been telling him about Davina and how she's even less fussy than me. I thought it might be a lark if he seduced her.'

'What a splendid idea,' beamed Richard. 'Word is that she's been positively rabid since Adrian had his prostate out last year. I wasn't far off with that egoectomy, was I?'

'Just think,' continued Paula, helping herself to a cup of coffee to wash down her breakfast cigarette. 'We could fix things so your dad caught them on the job. Mind you,' she added, 'it wouldn't do Patrick's prospects a whole lot of good, now would it? Sir A isn't the sort of person a thrusting young actor should fall foul of.'

'Specially one as thrusting as Patrick,' muttered Isabel.

'Oh, isn't she in a filthy mood this morning?' tutted Richard. 'Paula darling, can you spare me a minute? There's some Renegade publicity bumph I want to show you.'

He bore her off to his study, leaving Patrick alone with Isabel, something she usually contrived to avoid.

'Patrick's panting to get his end away with you,' Paula had told her. 'But the poor lamb's got scruples about nice girls, so he says. Only goes for easy lays like me. If you ask me he's just scared of intelligent women and even more scared of rejection. Have a heart, Izzie. All he needs is a bit of encouragement. You'd be doing me a favour.'

A Nice Girl. What a damning phrase that was. She would much prefer to be a bad girl, like Paula. That commanded a different kind of respect. Nobody messed with Paula. If Paula were in love with Neville, she would have the guts to do something about it . . .

'Paula was only joking,' said Patrick, misinterpreting Isabel's grim expression.

'Oh, don't mind me. If you feel like playing Russian roulette with your career, that's up to you. My father can be very vindictive.'

'So I hear. Richard told me about him sacking Neville Seaton . . . would you pass the sugar, please?' And then, catching her eye as she did so, 'Paula says you're in love with him.'

Trust Paula to open her big mouth. Isabel wouldn't have told her but for the knowledge that if she didn't Richard would.

'Paula was just tormenting you,' said Isabel, hitting back with her choice of verb. 'Neville's a married man with two children.'

'Which is part of the attraction, isn't it? It gives you an excuse not to do anything about it. With you, everything happens inside your head. It's safer.'

'I don't see you taking many risks in that department,' countered Isabel. 'Make a play for Davina with my blessing. *She's* a sure thing.'

She dared him with her eyes to take a risk, there and then, but he didn't fall for it, knowing that she was itching to put him down.

'Excuse me,' she said, quitting while she was still ahead. 'I've got things to do.'

'Well, if I don't see you again before tonight, break a leg and all that.' He smiled that haphazard smile of his. Or rather one of a whole repertoire of carefully structured smiles, each one like a Chinese word-picture with a meaning all its own. This one somehow managed to negate her minor victory, claiming it for himself. She envied him his facial shorthand, his mastery of every feature, his sheer physical fluency. She felt suddenly wooden, heavy, lifeless, flat, a puppet without strings.

But his taunt had helped make up her wavering mind. Isabel left the flat quickly, before she lost her nerve, and made for the nearest telephone box, anxious not to be overheard. She fumbled in her purse for four pennies, fed them into the box and dialled Neville's home number, praying that he would answer and not his wife.

'Hello?' Relief. Terror.

'Neville, it's me, Izzie. I have to talk to you. I can't go on tonight. I can't.'

A short pause.

'Oh dear. Well, in that case I'd better come straight to FRIDA and sort things out or we won't have a show tonight. Thank you for letting me know. I'll be with you shortly.'

She hung up, trembling. His cryptic choice of language was a promise in itself. Otherwise he would have addressed her by name, reported to his wife, 'That was Isabel Mallory bleating that she can't go on. I'd better go and calm the poor child down.' But instead he was going to invent some technical crisis, proof that he felt guilty, that he couldn't trust himself to tell the truth.

FRIDA was only a short walk away. It being a Sunday, the building was all locked up. Isabel paced to and fro on the pavement outside, trying to keep her courage up. She couldn't carry on like this any longer. Couldn't bear being so close and so far apart, couldn't bear submitting to the fierce foreplay of his tuition without hope of consummation.

Neville was only a man. Men couldn't help themselves, he had said so himself, albeit in jest. All she had to do was make the first move. If she missed this chance she wouldn't see him again till next term, and besides, her period was due tomorrow, if anything happened she would be all right . . . She started as a taxi drew up and Neville got out.

'We'd better go in,' he said, producing a bunch of keys and opening the front door. Their footsteps echoed off the high ceilings as he walked ahead of her along the corridor and up the three flights of stairs that led to his office.

'Now what's all this nonsense about?' he said sternly, taking refuge behind his desk and gesturing at her to take a chair.

'I told you. I can't go on tonight.'

'Then you've no business being an actress. You go on come hell or high water. You don't need me to tell you that.'

'Davina will be there. She'll want me to be bad.'

'If you can't cope with ill-will, then bad is what you'd better be. If you want to be popular, then aim low, be mediocre, don't make anyone else feel inadequate. But if you want to be good, you've got to learn to deal with hostility, to see it as a barometer of your own worth.'

His voice was brisk, matter of fact, not sympathetic at all.

'It's not just Davina. It's Daddy. The last time he saw me I wasn't trained, he made allowances. But now . . .'

'But now he'll judge you more harshly and so he should. No one said it would be easy. No one said you wouldn't be scared. In any case, you like things to be difficult. You need to be scared. If you're not hopelessly hooked on adrenaline by now, then you may as well give up.'

'It's more than being scared . . .' He thought that she was bluffing, that this was just an act, an excuse to see him. And so it was, but the excuse was genuine, if that made sense. 'I feel ill with it. I've never been this way before. I know it sounds self-indulgent and hysterical. But you must have noticed how bad I was at the dress rehearsal. All I could think about was getting through the lines. I couldn't concentrate on anything else. I don't know what's wrong with me. It's never happened before.'

For a moment she forgot her ulterior motives, for a moment she must have seemed genuine, because he softened quite suddenly and said gently, 'Stage fright. Everyone gets it, from time to time. It strikes from nowhere but if you don't give in to it eventually it passes.' He got up and crossed to where she sat, standing over her. 'I'm sorry. I did notice something was wrong but I thought you were just attention seeking. You're becoming dangerously dependent on adverse criticism. So I decided to withhold it. I'm afraid I misjudged you, because I . . . Izzie . . . don't cry.'

Awkward now, he offered her a handkerchief and put his hand on her shoulder.

'I never cry in front of people,' she mumbled angrily. 'It makes me look so hideous.'

He squatted at her feet, looking up at her. 'You could never look hideous,' he said, reaching up to brush the hair out of her eyes. 'I'm sorry. If it had been anyone else but you, I'd have invited her in for a chat, dispensed wisdom and understanding and courage. But you . . . I've neglected you. It was wrong of me to take this job. I took it for selfish reasons and now we're both paying the price.'

'I don't mind paying,' muttered Isabel thickly. 'I just want what you're making me pay for. Every time I see you I pay and pay and pay for nothing! Nothing at all!'

Her voice rose in an explosion of fury and frustration, only for him to silence it, pulling her head down to meet his, pouring all the months of waiting into his kiss, reassuring her that he had wanted this as well, every bit as badly, that if she'd had the nerve this could have happened long ago though not, perhaps, with such intensity. Isabel sank forward onto her knees, sending the chair toppling

100

backwards. For a moment they remained locked together in an attitude of prayer, as if sanctifying their sin.

'Izzie, this can't mean –'

'I understand about Helen. I won't ask for more than this, I promise.'

'This isn't about being fair to Helen. It's about being fair to you. I kept hoping that the accident would put you off . . .'

'What do you take me for?' Though to be honest, the attraction had always been more spiritual than physical. It was his mind that she found seductive, not his body.

'A romantic. It's up to me to be realistic, for both of us –'

She kissed him again to shut him up, before he talked himself out of it. She could feel him weaken, feel herself getting stronger, overcome by a heady sense of power. With luck he wouldn't realize that she hadn't done this before, because she had done just about enough for her ignorance not to show, preparing for this moment with the same disciplined determination she applied to her work, hoping, against all the evidence, that it would be all right on the night, that when it happened for real it would be touched by magic.

The magic which could make the clumsiest move seem balletic, turn banalities into poetry, convert fastidious indifference into raging, shameless need. That little core of liberating truth that swept aside pretence, that transformed and glorified everything it touched. And now, at last, she could feel it happening. It was like one of those sudden, elusive moments in performance when everything worked, everything clicked, when you were in control and yet not in control, when something stronger than yourself took over and yet took nothing away . . .

It hardly hurt at all, but even if it had done she wouldn't have let it show. He rolled her on top of him, to make it more comfortable for her on the bare hard floor, throwing her into a panic. But everything seemed to come naturally, everything about it felt familiar, as if she had rehearsed it countless times in her dreams. For once she didn't worry about whether she was doing it right, for once she trusted to instinct, did whatever it was that Patrick did on stage . . .

'Slow down,' he whispered, as she raced on ahead, carried away with her own virtuosity. 'Izzie, please slow down or I'll –' And then she found herself uncoupled and felt the warm stickiness on her skin, while she continued to yearn deep inside like a damp shore deserted by the ebbing tide.

'I'm sorry, Izzie.'

'My fault,' said Isabel, mortified. Damn. What a stupid, ignorant mess she had made of things. And she had so wanted it to be perfect.

'The fault was entirely mine, in more ways than one. I'm afraid that wasn't the most reliable form of birth control.'

'It's all right. I'll take care of it in future.' She didn't want him to feel responsible for her. She wanted only to ease away the permanent frown between his brows, to lift the shadows that had settled on his face, to make herself necessary, no, essential to his well-being, most of all to please, to be selfish in the most thoroughly selfless way . . .

'I ought to tell you there isn't any future.' He ran his fingers through her heavy copper hair. 'Poor Izzie. I was the first, wasn't I?'

Isabel hung her head. Now he would feel guilty. She should have done it with someone else first, someone who didn't matter, just to get the hang of it, and yet she was glad she hadn't. She might have bungled the physical side, but emotionally it had felt right, touching the only erogenous zone that mattered, the one inside her heart.

'We'll have to be very discreet,' he said. 'If the college found out, it would invalidate my end-of-year assessment, jeopardize your diploma . . .' .

More to the point, he would get the sack, thought Isabel. Worse, his wife would get to hear of it. She couldn't bear to be responsible for that.

'Don't worry,' she said. 'I'll be very careful.' Now it was for real she wouldn't take any risks. She wouldn't even tell Paula.

'You were marvellous, darling,' gushed Davina, after the per-formance that night. All eyes turned to look at her as she swanned into FRIDA's tiny theatre bar, raven-haired and rampant in a tight red dress with her distinguished husband towering by her side. How Isabel envied Brenda Price her dull, provincial parents, so unobtrusive as to be almost invisible. She had been dreading this moment.

'Thank you,' she said wretchedly, returning Davina's false smile. Her father took both her hands.

'A beautiful Irena,' he said quietly, but loud enough for everyone to hear, well aware that he was the real star of the show. He could project the merest whisper to the back of the largest auditorium. 'Subtle, understated, seething with undercurrents. You've come on amazingly in the last year. Congratulations, Izzie darling.'

'And you too, Paula,' put in Davina. 'I thought you gave Masha a wonderfully *earthbound* quality.'

'You're too kind,' purred Paula in her new posh accent. It was Patrick who had painstakingly transformed the flower girl into a duchess, succeeding where Peter Austell and others had failed. 'Can I introduce Patrick Delaney?'

Patrick produced his most inoffensive smile.

'I'm honoured to meet you, sir,' he said. 'And Lady Mallory. I'm your biggest fan.'

'You're in Richard's revue, aren't you?' trilled Davina, looking Patrick up and down with predatory interest. 'We keep meaning to catch it. Such a pity those other two plays closed so quickly,' she added, turning up the volume as her stepson approached.

'Richard,' acknowledged Adrian heavily, without extending his hand.

'Daddy, darling,' cooed Richard, in his campest voice, blackening his father's frown. 'Long time no see.'

They hadn't met in well over a year. Isabel occasionally visited for Sunday lunch, taking Paula with her for moral support, but Richard had kept to his vow to stay away.

'All these doting parents are frightfully am-dram, don't you think?' drawled Richard, kissing Isabel effusively on both cheeks. 'Still, it was a soooper show, thanks to my two best girls. And Neville, of course. He's just been promoted to number one on my list of must-have directors.'

The mention of the name produced a very loud silence, interrupted by Patrick with a blatantly deferential, 'Actors always make the best directors. I was lucky enough to see Sir Adrian's *Three Sisters* at the Kean, in '56. With Lady Mallory as Natasha. I'm afraid it spoilt me for any other production.'

Paula listened cynically while Patrick poured forth a stream of the purest blarney, exhibiting total recall of every nuance of interpretation, every innovative bit of business, every stylistic quirk of the allegedly definitive Mallory version of the play. She knew he was being a bloody hypocrite, that he had thought it mannered and heavy, that he firmly believed, as Neville did, that Chekhov should be played at a cracking pace, lightly and deftly, not done in lugubrious slow motion and milked for every meaningful pause. But he sounded quite disgustingly sincere.

Isabel, meanwhile, took longer than she should have done to realize what Patrick was playing at. She had almost forgotten the plot they had discussed at breakfast that morning. It seemed so long ago. He was well into his stride now, comparing the unfortunate Brenda Price's Natasha with Lady Mallory's own immortal portrayal of the sly, trivial intruder who takes over the household by marriage. Perfect typecasting, thought Isabel sourly, while Lady Mallory lapped up every last droplet of flattery.

Isabel had to force herself not to look at Neville, who was on the other side of the room, pinned up against a wall by Brenda Price's parents. The thought of spending all summer with Mummy, away from him, didn't bear thinking about. This year she would have to find some excuse to stay at home . . .

'Shall we go, then, darling?' boomed Adrian, who was taking Isabel and Paula out to dinner.

'I'll go and find Paula.'

'Richard's just taken her home,' said her father. 'She said something about a bad headache.' They must have sloped off to the pub, thought Isabel. Fortunately Daddy sounded more relieved than affronted. He had never been able to make Paula out; she hovered between respect for him as an actor and an irreverence towards him as a person that bordered on the insolent. 'But Patrick's going to join us instead.'

Patrick caught her eye behind Adrian's back and winked. God, thought Isabel, he doesn't waste much time.

Adrian had booked his regular table at the Ivy, where his arrival, as always, provoked an obsequious welcome. This time Patrick didn't ask for draught Guinness, choosing a more subtle form of comedy in the shape of earnest but nicely underpolished good manners and intelligent but not too informed conversation, striking just the right balance between keeping his end up and knowing his place. He was too clever to make a play for Davina direct, under her husband's nose; much more effectively, he made a play for Isabel instead, shooting smouldering looks in her direction at every opportunity, simultaneously throwing Sir Adrian off the scent and spurring Davina to upstage her supposed rival at the first opportunity she got.

Isabel found herself going along with it. It was like one of those improvisation exercises they gave you at FRIDA; every time Patrick threw the ball in her direction, professional pride demanded that she catch it.

'I hear that you're off to America next month,' said Adrian, over the saddle of lamb. 'No problems with American Equity?' he fished, no doubt suspecting that Marty had had a hand in fixing things.

'Oh, I wouldn't know,' said Patrick guilelessly. 'I leave all that kind of thing to Richard. To be perfectly frank with you, Sir Adrian, I'm not looking forward to it one bit. I dread another long run and that's the truth.'

'English humour very rarely works in the States,' put in Davina reassuringly. 'And the system over there is quite barbaric. A bad review from the *New York Times* and you close the same night. Horrendous.'

'So I've heard. As Richard keeps saying, I owe everything to Renegade. But my agent has other ideas. He's gone and fixed up this audition at Stratford . . .'

Had he? wondered Isabel. He was so convincing it was hard to know what was real and what was an act.

'. . . And one at the Bristol Old Vic,' continued Patrick. He shrugged modestly. 'I think he tends to oversell me. But whatever happens,' he added, with a soulful shake of the head, 'I couldn't leave Richard in the lurch.'

Whereupon Daddy began talking at interminable length about the new season at the Kean, its recently enhanced Arts Council grant, and his plans to expand the company and establish a permanent London base. He sounded like a salesman touting his wares. Oh God, thought Isabel, he *wouldn't*.

Of course he would. He was quite capable of poaching Patrick just to spite Richard, whether or not he really wanted him in the company . . .

'Strange your agent didn't put you up for the Kean,' said Daddy, confirming her suspicions. 'Especially as we're casting for the new season.'

'Oh, I suppose he thought I didn't stand a chance,' said Patrick, with a self-deprecating shrug. 'Everyone knows you get first pick.' Isabel winced at the exaggeration, but Daddy, well used to sycophants, took it at face value.

'Well, it's true that we're choosier than Stratford. I'm not making any promises, but given that you're a friend of Izzie's . . . Give me the name of your agent.'

Feigning excitement – if Patrick was really excited he wouldn't show it, reasoned Isabel – Patrick wrote it down.

'Rex Jordan? Don't know him.'

'He's not a big name. Richard kept telling me not to sign with him.' Isabel watched as Rex Jordan went up several notches in Daddy's estimation. 'But the way I look at it, a beginner like me is lucky to have an agent at all.'

Apropos of nothing, he shot Isabel another come-to-bed look which she returned in kind, just to annoy Davina, who was becoming more frustrated by the minute.

'Perhaps we'll try to catch your Thursday matinée,' purred Davina. 'We don't have a performance that afternoon. Or is the house already full?'

'Oh, we always have room for royalty. I'll have them put two best seats aside for you.'

'Excellent,' said Sir Adrian. 'It'll give me some idea of what you can do. Well, time we went home. Can I drop you off anywhere, Patrick?'

'Patrick's staying with us at the moment,' said Isabel wickedly. Davina's eyes narrowed.

'Richard offered me the settee,' said Patrick gallantly, managing to sound like a bad liar. 'I've been having a few problems with my landlord.'

Patrick didn't in fact have a landlord. He had spent the last nine months living out of one suitcase, sleeping on floors and flitting from one borrowed – or shared – bed to another. Isabel couldn't help admiring his indifference to creature comforts. To her the flat was a sanctuary, now redecorated to her own austere taste (except for Paula's room), filled with stark Scandinavian furniture from

106

Heals, and kept spotlessly clean by a surly char of whom Isabel was terrified but whom Paula kept effortlessly in line.

'Won't you come in for some coffee, Daddy?' said Isabel, as he dropped them off. Davina had very kindly yielded the front seat to Isabel, knowing that she was prone to car-sickness. 'You still haven't seen the flat.'

'Another time,' said her father, seeing Richard's MG parked outside. 'Ring me tomorrow, will you, darling? I've got a suggestion to make. Goodnight both.'

'That was some performance you put on tonight,' said Isabel as they watched the Daimler drive away. 'I never thought anyone could crawl so much without the use of hands and knees.'

'I wasn't bad, was I?' acknowledged Patrick modestly.

'Daddy's only using you to get at Richard, you realize. He knows *Antidotage* doesn't stand a chance in New York without you.' Damn. That sounded like a compliment. 'You made a big hit with Davina,' she added dryly. 'Paula would have been proud of you.'

'And of you.' His eyes shone extra blue in the darkness. 'The way you were looking at me back there, you almost had me fooled . . .'

Isabel cut him short by inserting her key in the lock and shouting a cheery 'Hello, you two! We're home!'

'Come and have a drink!' called Richard from the living room, where he and Paula were half way through their second bottle of champagne.

'A toast,' Paula greeted them. She was more than a little drunk. 'To my first starring role.'

'Would you believe it,' said Patrick, 'two curtain calls at FRIDA and fame has gone to her head.'

'Fuck FRIDA. And fuck the three snotty sisters.' She raised her glass aloft. 'I'm playing the lead in *Bondage*.'

Isabel looked at Richard.

'You're not serious.'

'Don't sulk,' said Richard. 'I did offer it to you first. And on my sword we swore, remember?'

'On your what?' hiccupped Paula. 'Sounds filthy.'

'Julian Clavell won't give permission,' put in Isabel. 'Not for a play like that.'

'Then I won't ask for it.'

'Then they'll kick you out.'

'Let them. Patrick never went to drama school and he's doing all right.'

'Understand one thing,' said Patrick, turning to Richard. 'This had better be a joke. Because over my dead body is Paula playing Serafina.'

'Why shouldn't I?' demanded Paula.

'Richard knows what I think of that bloody play. I'm not letting him exploit you.'

'I always knew you were a prude at heart,' mocked Richard. 'It's your Catholic upbringing coming out.'

'If she wanted to pose for a porno mag,' said Patrick, 'I'd say go ahead, at least it doesn't pretend to be anything else. But *Bondage* is pseudo-intellectual shit and you know it.'

'Well, what if it is?' said Richard coolly. 'As long as it generates lots of lovely publicity, who cares?'

'I care, about her!'

'Liar!' spat Paula. 'You don't care about anyone except Patrick-the-big-I-am-Delaney!'

'You're pissed. Let's go to bed and we'll talk about it in the morning.'

'You can go to bed if you like. As long as it's not mine. Trust you to try and spoil everything! Why don't you just bugger off?'

She stomped unsteadily out of the room and up the stairs, with Isabel close behind.

'I'll show him,' she muttered. 'I'm fed up with that big-headed bastard telling me what to do.' She fell onto the still rumpled bed and began tearing an empty Durex wrapper into tiny pieces.

'I hate to agree with Patrick,' Isabel felt bound to say, 'but I think you're making a big mistake.'

'Whose side are you on? It's all very well for you. You like it at FRIDA. I hate it. I feel as if they're squashing all the life out of me, as if they're trying to turn me into something I'm not.'

'The first year always feels like that. It's like hoeing, digging, weeding, sowing. Next year things will start to grow. And you were so good as Masha tonight.'

'Oh, yes. Earthbound.'

'You know better than to worry what that vixen says.'

'I've learned all I'm going to learn at FRIDA. I don't want the same things as you. And the things I do want I want soon, now. Richard knows that. He's the only one of the three of you who takes me seriously. He could easily find someone else to play Serafina. But he's taking a chance on me, because he wants to help me. Because he believes in me. Because he knows I'll give it everything I've got.'

Isabel battled briefly with her conscience, settling for a feeble 'Look, I hate to say this, but I'm dreadfully afraid that . . . that Richard is the victim of a hoax. It wouldn't surprise me if this play had been written by some sick practical joker.'

It didn't work.

'So? I don't care. All I care about is getting noticed. Think ahead, to when we graduate. You'll get the de Vere Medal, I'll be one of the also-rans. Statistically, three or four of our year will be in work five years from now. This is my chance to be one jump ahead of the rest of them. And anyway, I can't afford to stay on.'

'But I thought Bea had left you enough to –'

'I went to this quack in Harley Street and he's fixed up for me to have a nose job. It'll leave me pretty well skint.'

Isabel stared.

'But there's nothing wrong with your nose!'

'Have a look at these.' She rummaged in a drawer and produced some glossy studio photographs. 'I had them done to send out with my résumé, to reps and agents and people. They cost me a packet, and all for nothing. Haven't shown them to anyone else. Looks ten times worse than it does in the mirror, doesn't it? I never realized how bloody ugly I was.'

The camera was as unkind to Paula as it was generous to Isabel. True enough, Paula's nose wasn't photogenic, dominating her face at the expense of her other features.

'What chance have I got with a conk like that in *Spotlight*? I'd have to file as a character actress to have any chance of work at all. And can you imagine if I ever did a screen test? A scream test more like.' She reached for her cigarettes. 'I'm having it done next week and that's that. They're going to whip out my adenoids at the same time, they say it'll do wonders for my voice. Cheap at the price. So spare me the lecture. I get enough of that from *him*.'

'Perhaps he actually cares about you.'

'He just wants to control me, that's all. Don't be taken in by the laughing-boy charm, he's just a rotten bully on the quiet. He can't bear to think I'm not dying for love of him, like all the other stupid cows he gives it to. No wonder he's engaged to that country bumpkin back home. She's no threat. She thinks he's God's gift. She thinks she was put on this earth to darn his smelly socks.'

There was a crashing noise from below and the sound of the front door slamming. A moment later, Richard tapped at the door. He was bleeding from the corner of his mouth.

'Did he do that to you?' wailed Paula, throwing her arms around him.

'I think he was trying to defend your honour,' said Richard, sitting down on the bed. 'Accused me of being a raging pervert and sleaze-merchant. Look, darling, I never realized he'd go off the deep end like that. I mean to say, he hardly sets the highest moral tone himself. If you want to back out, no hard feelings. I don't want to come between you two lovebirds.'

Isabel went to fetch cotton wool and TCP and began dabbing at Richard's split lip. Despite Patrick's passion for boxing she had never heard of him hitting anyone in anger.

'You've done me a favour,' sniffed Paula. 'I've told him a million times he doesn't own me. I can get screwed any time I like without any help from him. Good bloody riddance.'

Isabel found herself thinking of Paula's cat. 'I was getting too fond of her anyway,' she had said, and the same applied to Patrick. Richard's play, like Isabel's allergy, was as good an excuse as any to make the break.

Isabel felt as if she had just cancelled a dental appointment. Unfortunately that was no cure for toothache.

'You're not coming at all?' Fay had said faintly. Or perhaps the line was just bad.

'I'm sorry to let you down, Mummy. But Daddy's got permission from FRIDA for me to understudy at the Kean, over the vac. There are three new plays going into rehearsal, which is a wonderful chance for me to learn.'

It was true, after all, a heaven-sent excuse to stay at home.

'What parts are you covering?'

110

'Just tiny ones. But it's the experience that counts.'

'Oh darling. I'm so disappointed. But of course I understand . . .' Mummy had always understood the importance of work. Isabel hated herself for taking advantage of that, but love made you horribly ruthless. And anyway, she told herself, her visits probably did more harm than good.

Meanwhile Helen and the children were spending a month with her parents in Wales while Neville remained in London, doing private coaching. Better still, Richard had gone away for the weekend and Paula would be in hospital till Tuesday. Neville would arrive in time for supper, and they would have the flat to themselves for three whole days . . .

Isabel got her new cap out of its little box and engaged in the squeamish but necessary business of inserting it, something she was always punctilious about. Toby was a walking advertisement for birth control. It wasn't his fault that he was spoilt, of course, but she couldn't help loathing him anyway, even though it seemed pathetic to loathe a child of five. Toby had served to confirm what she had always known – that she had absolutely no desire for children of her own. Better to fail at being an actress than fail at being a mother. Fay was living – if you could call it living – proof of that.

With the wretched object in place she turned her mind to more romantic preparations. Lighting the candles on the table, setting out the feast of hors d'oeuvres she had bought from the delicatessen – Isabel was quite unable to cook – putting a bottle of Chablis on ice and Bach's Double Violin on the sleek teak Swedish radiogram, bathing and dousing herself with L'Air du Temps, slipping naked into a diaphanous ivory-coloured négligé, falling headlong into the hackneyed role of mistress. Here there were no wailing kids, no weary wife, no bills to be paid; here there was sensuous luxury and privacy and peace. It gave her a sense of false virtue to soothe his troubled brow and minister to all his needs.

She released her hair from its ponytail and let it tumble in fiery, loose profusion, leaving her face bare of artifice, a form of vanity in her case, much vainer than poor old Paula with her battery of Rimmel and Outdoor Girl warpaint, her bottles of peroxide and Sta-blonde shampoo, the arsenal of ironmongery she slept in to maintain her Monroe coiffure. If Isabel had had to agonize over her looks as much as she did over her acting, she might have learned to value them. As it was, she saw her beauty as a handicap, detracting from the person inside, earning her praise for the wrong reasons. 'A beautiful Irena,' Daddy had said. She wished he had chosen a different word.

Hearing the doorbell, she drew the heavy lined watered silk silvery curtains against the bright summer evening light, her movements precise and graceful, as if responding to a stage direction; often, when she was alone, like now, she had a fantasy of being watched, of setting a scene. Leaving the room lit only by tall white candles, she ran to let Neville in.

The welcoming smile faded from her face.

'I've come round to collect a few things,' said Patrick. As usual he looked tousled and windblown. 'Paula wants all my stuff out before she gets back from the hospital.'

Isabel gathered the skimpy folds of lace and chiffon around her.

'It's not convenient at the moment.'

'Then you shouldn't have got out of bed to answer the door. Sorry if I interrupted anything. But I'll be in and out like a dose of salts, so I will. Have to be at the theatre in half an hour. I've got a taxi waiting.'

Patrick was prone to extravagances like taxis, perhaps because he was too disorganized to adapt to the vagaries of public transport. He would invariably be broke within forty-eight hours of payday and have to ask Richard for an advance on next week's wages.

'Please, Izzie. I'm running late as it is.'

Short of barring his way there was nothing she could do. He made straight for the living room, making her cringe with embarrassment at the candles, the drawn curtains, the soft lights and sweet music, all the trite accoutrements of lust. But he affected not to notice, rifling through the bookshelves and extracting the tattered volumes he had stored there – Raymond Chandler, James Joyce, Homer, Marcus Aurelius, a biography of Rocky Marciano, the collected plays of Sean O'Casey, an anthology of Gerard Manley Hopkins, all of them dog-eared, with the corners of the pages turned down, the spines bent back, and no doubt coffee stains and biscuit crumbs within.

'I've got a couple of records too,' he went on, making the needle jump on the second violin as he rifled through the radiogram and withdrew a catholic mixture of Gregorian chants, jazz, folk, Beethoven, Elvis Presley and – Isabel shuddered – Frank Sinatra.

'Don't mind me,' he said, not looking at her. 'Off with you back to the boudoir, you hussy.'

'Just hurry up, will you?'

'I could see it in your eyes, the other night. Eyes are a dead giveaway in a woman. Lucky bastard. Bet he's a high-class smoothie. Not a peasant like me.'

'I don't know why you're bothering with all that stuff,' said Isabel impatiently. 'You'll be back here by next week.'

'No I won't. Even if Paula climbed down, I'm not sharing a roof with your brother any more.' He stood up and took an envelope out of his pocket. 'Will you give him this when he gets back? It's my resignation. I'm leaving the show when we close next week. I'm not going with it to America.'

'What?'

'You and I will soon be colleagues. Your dad has offered me a line of parts at the Kean. Two small and one biggie. Roderigo in *Othello*, Montjoy in *Henry V* and – wait for it – John Tanner in *Man and Superman*. Now, I'd be a fool to turn them down, wouldn't I?'

'Don't kid yourself,' said Isabel coldly. 'I told you before, Daddy's only doing this to get at Richard. So much for never letting down a mate.' She began to wonder if he had planned this all along, jumped at the excuse of a row with Richard to salve his conscience, always supposing he had one.

'He's not a mate any longer. And don't kid yourself either. Daddy's doing it because I'm a good actor.'

'Good actors are two a penny.'

'And good actresses are ten a penny without Richard preying on a kid like Paula.'

'And you're not preying on her, I suppose?'

'I've been trying my best to protect her, actually.'

'Oh wonderful. I might have known you were doing her some kind of favour. The kind of favour you would never do that nice girl of yours back home.'

'Leave Terry out of this. You don't even know her.'

'No, but I know my father. I hope you get more from him than you bargained for. I hope you finally meet your match.'

'Oh, but she's sexy when she's angry . . .'

'Will you kindly take your garbage and go?'

He made a satirical bow, gathered up his possessions, and waited, laden, at the front door for her to open it for him, just as Neville was raising a hand to ring the bell. Isabel shut her eyes in mortification.

'Don't worry, I'm just leaving,' Patrick told him. 'She's all yours. Have a nice evening, won't you?' And then, as his parting shot, 'Till next week, then, Izzie. See you at the Kean.'

'I look bloody awful,' said Paula, as Richard arrived at the clinic to take her home. Her whole face was discoloured and swollen, not least the new nose, which was still twice the size of the old one. 'If this place wasn't dearer than Claridges I'd stay here and hide till I looked human again.'

The room was full of flowers – white lilies from Isabel, a riot of pink blooms from Richard, and a solitary hothouse orchid from Patrick in a cellophane case. She had wrapped up the first two bouquets in newspaper, to take home with her, having transferred the contents of the complimentary fruit basket to her suitcase along with two purloined towels.

Rather than leave the orchid behind, she removed it from its box and tried to flush it down the en-suite lavatory. Using its petals as water wings, it swam for its life and bobbed back reproachfully. Paula shut the lid on it.

She was furious with Patrick for running out on Richard. Another good reason for refusing to see him, not that she would have wanted him to see her looking like this. Nonetheless, she had allowed herself to contemplate his peace offering for several days before finally destroying it. There was no harm in eating, after all, as long as you didn't gain weight.

'We're going out to lunch,' announced Richard.

'I'm not hungry. I haven't stopped stuffing myself since I came in, just to get my money's worth.'

'You can watch me eat then.' He bundled her out of the building and into the car. After driving with his usual disregard for speed limits, the Highway Code, or the longevity of his brake linings, he parked, illegally, in Jermyn Street, right outside the Ecu de France.

'Everyone'll stare,' muttered Paula crossly, fazed by the poshness of the restaurant. 'They'll think I'm Frankenstein's monster.'

'Good practice,' he said, as the head waiter approached. 'The sooner you get used to people staring at you the better. Mr Parry's table, please.'

'Who's Mr Parry?' hissed Paula.

'Vincent. Vince. My new business partner. The guy who's backing *Bondage*.'

'You rat. You never said anyone else would be here. He'll take one look at me and say no deal.'

Vincent Parry rose to greet them, a fair-haired, fortyish City type in a pin-stripe suit, complete with starched handkerchief and snowy white cuffs studded with discreet gold links. A stuffed shirt, thought Paula.

'Vince, meet Paula Dorland.' Paula had elected this as her stage name, in memory of Bea. 'She doesn't normally look like this but she's just paid through the nose for a new one, God knows why.'

Vincent Parry extended a big square paw that didn't suit the rest of him. It should have been soft and limp and cool but it was hard and warm and strong.

'Pleased to meet you, Paula,' he said, not in the plummy voice she had expected but in a kind of damped-down cockney. Genuinely posh people were never pleased to meet you. They just asked how you did.

'Hope I don't put you off your food,' said Paula, as the waiter pulled back her chair. 'Don't worry, I look all right when I take my clothes off.'

Just. She was still seven pounds heavier than she should be. Seven pounds was equivalent to fourteen half-pound slabs of butter. No wonder, toting all that lot around with her, that she felt so damned tired all the time.

'No point in trying to shock Vince,' said Richard, reaching for the menu. 'You can be as outrageous as you like, he won't turn a hair. Grew up on the streets, did our Vince. Just like you, darling.'

Vincent Parry didn't smile, but his eyes did. Grey eyes the

colour of thunder. 'So what do you think of the play, Paula?' he asked.

'I think it's a load of arty-farty crap.'

'It's a brave protest against political and sexual repression,' said Richard solemnly. 'It attacks the misuse of power by the state and the church and speaks out against the subjugation of women. It –'

'It's a jumped-up peep show,' interrupted Paula. 'But I know the form. I tell the press that I only strip off when it's artistically valid. Have you cast the other parts yet?'

'We're auditioning as soon as I get back from the States,' said Richard. 'I have to be there at the try-outs, to do any tinkering. Then we'll have three weeks' rehearsal and an opening at our own little theatre club. After a big battle with the Lord Chamberlain, of course.'

'What theatre club?'

'The Renegade. Née the Rialto. An old fleapit Vince is converting, near the Elephant and Castle.'

'That must be costing you a packet,' said Paula.

'Not really. The Inland Revenue will end up paying for most of it.'

'So you're rich.'

'Filthy. Almost as filthy as the play. Are you ready to order?'

The menu was all in French. Rather than admit her ignorance Paula waved it aside and asked for a plate of smoked salmon with a side salad, no dressing. Richard and Vincent Parry had stuffed artichokes followed by fillet steaks swimming in a pool of blood. Paula had a bottle of white wine all to herself while they shared one of red.

'So who are you going to replace Delaney with?' Vince was saying. 'Do you reckon the show can survive without him?'

'Leo Marriot knows the part off pat, he can't wait to take over. It won't be the same, of course, but then that's no bad thing. Patrick was getting stale.'

Richard affected not to care about Patrick's defection, but Paula knew that he was hurt. Not so much because his former friend had jumped at a better offer but because his father had engineered it. Patrick would be a big success at the Kean, no doubt. No wonder he didn't want her to play Serafina. He was scared that she might turn out to be a big success as well.

116

And so she would. Not because she possessed Patrick's blazing talent, but because she knew exactly what she wanted out of life and intended to get it, which was more than could be said for him. Patrick was a mass of contradictions. He enjoyed being the centre of attention but affected to shun the limelight. He revelled in being a star, of sorts, but pretended not to be ambitious. He delighted in spending money but didn't seem to care about earning it. He liked the freedom of living in London but wallowed in bouts of maudlin homesickness. He had the morals of an alley cat and yet he had saddled himself with a squeaky-clean bride-to-be. He was utterly predictable, and yet you never knew where you were with him.

Patrick wanted it all ways. He was a hypocrite who thought that he was honest, a reactionary posing as a radical, a bully disguised as a benefactor. He'd give you the shirt off his back, his last crust of bread, he'd give you anything you asked of him except your freedom, or his. How could she have been stupid enough to let herself fall in love with him? The only solace was that he didn't know, that nobody knew. She was a better actress than anybody gave her credit for.

'Paula?'

'Sorry. I wasn't listening.'

'Vince just asked if you're having a holiday this year.'

'I've just had one, in the Cromwell Clinic.'

'You ought to convalesce before rehearsals start,' said Vince. 'Somewhere you can relax and learn your lines while you wait for the swelling to go down.'

'What a super idea. I'll beetle along to Cook's after we've eaten and book myself a cruise.'

'I've got a little place in Kent, if you're interested. Never have time to go there myself. A bit off the beaten track, but peaceful and quiet. You're welcome to use it. My housekeeper, Grace, would look after you.'

Paula was no lover of peace and quiet, but she was tempted nonetheless. All the while she was in London, Patrick might turn up on her. Do him good if she disappeared for a while. It might do her good too, come to that. She felt ill, exhausted. It was just the aftermath of the operation, of course, nothing to do with Patrick, nothing to do with being afraid of making a complete arsehole of herself and getting booed off the stage.

117

'No strings?' she demanded pertly.

'I wish there were,' he said mildly, 'but you've already got the part, remember? Let my secretary know if and when you want to go and she'll arrange a car.' He handed her a business card, giving an office address in Marylebone Road.

'Well, as long as it's a Roller, I won't say no,' said Paula, snapping it into her bag.

'A Roller it will be,' he said, poker-faced.

There would be strings all right, thought Paula, sooner or later. She might look like the back of a bus at the moment, but any actress prepared to take off her clothes on stage had to be a sex-mad little tart, now didn't she? Well, so she was. Or rather, so she tried to be. It wasn't the sex she was mad about, it was the things that went with it, if you were lucky. A cuddle or two, the odd endearment, something warm in the bed beside you, the satisfaction of knowing you were good at something, the relief of not being alone. Afterwards she always regretted it, like falling asleep in the sun, but at the time it made her feel better. The important thing was not to kid yourself, to realize that sex was just a transaction, not a contract, just small change, not the family silver.

'Well, if you've finished giving me the once-over,' she said, 'I may as well push off home. No, you two stay and talk. I'll get a cab.'

By this time she was feeling even worse than she looked, thanks to the wine. She wasn't supposed to drink with the painkillers they had given her. Mixed with booze they made you depressed. As if she wasn't depressed already.

It was a hot, heavy sort of day. The flat seemed unnaturally quiet, apart from the angry drone of a bluebottle hurtling itself against the living room window, trying to fly through the glass. There were gaps in the shelves where Patrick's books had been, but he had left several others behind, to give himself an excuse to come back. He still couldn't believe that she meant business, that it was over for good, that she wouldn't be there on tap for him when he had nothing better to do. How many times had she thrown him out, only to weaken a few days later? Patrick was like any other vice. Cutting down was no good, you had to stop altogether. Paula kicked off her shoes and lit a lonely cigarette.

Isabel had left a note saying 'Lots to eat in the fridge. See you tonight.' Paula wished that she were here now to make a fuss of her, to order her to bed and brew her a pot of her incorrigibly weak tea and reassure her that when the swelling went down her new nose would look absolutely fab.

This job of hers at the Kean was a patently rigged sinecure, and it had surprised Paula that she should have accepted it so readily, sensitive as she was to charges of nepotism. Unlike Paula she didn't have to grab any chance of work that came her way, for fear that she might never get another offer.

Paula had no illusions about her talent, or lack of it. She had none of Isabel's mellifluous gift for verse speaking, none of her physical grace, none of her painstaking attention to detail. Paula had no interest in researching the background of a play or putting it into its historical context. She lacked humility, application, patience, the ability to take criticism and the willingness to suffer for her art. She was impatient, superficial and easily bored.

But on the plus side, she was ambitious, unscrupulous and thick-skinned. She might not have beauty and charm and mystery, but she had a crude, unapologetic sex appeal and she intended to make the most of it. To this end she had slept with several FRIDA types she found frankly repulsive, just to prove to herself that she could do it, because if she wanted to get on in this business she couldn't afford to be picky. There was no shame in it, she told herself, just as long as you were the exploiter and not the exploitee. Which was why she had had to break things off with Patrick. With Patrick, no matter what games she played, he would always hold all the power. But for now she still needed something else to fill the void he had left behind him.

The fridge was indeed full of all Paula's favourites from the deli – chocolate gâteau, mortadella sausage, cream cheese, potted shrimps and potato salad. She arranged them on the kitchen floor in their cartons and wrappings without bothering with plates or cutlery, sat back on her heels and got stuck in. She ate very fast, picking the food up with her hands, cramming it into her mouth, smearing it over her face and on her clothes, heart beating wildly all the while, as if fearful of being caught in the act.

The phone rang while her mouth was full of cake and shrimps. She spat them out into the sink.

119

'Paula, it's Izzie. How are you feeling?'

'I'm fine,' lied Paula. 'Much better.'

'Oh good. The thing is, I won't be home tonight. I've been invited to stay with an old schoolfriend who lives near here. In fact she's asked me to stay a few days. It's such a trek back to town.'

She sounded evasive, excited, rushed. She sounded exactly as she had looked on her two brief visits to the hospital. A sick suspicion hovered, swooped and soared away again. It couldn't be Patrick. Isabel wouldn't have taken that job because of Patrick, or vice versa. Isabel wouldn't hold out on her. Or would she, in the name of tact, sensing how much it would hurt her? Every time Paula had pleaded with Izzie to for God's sake take Patrick off her hands, it had been like defying death. She could bear Patrick screwing the entire female population of the world, but not Izzie. Not her friend.

'Will you be all right on your own?'

'It's only my nose they've chopped off, not my arms and legs. In any case, I won't be here. Vincent Moneybags Parry's given me the run of some cottage in the country. I'm going to hole up there till my face looks normal again.'

'Oh good. You could do with a break. Well, have a nice time and let me know when you'll be back. Must go. 'Bye now.'

Paula got back to work at the trough till every morsel of food had disappeared and then got rid of it just as brutally as she had consumed it. To speed any residue on its way before it had time to settle she swallowed a couple of squares of Ex-Lax, washed down with a slug of scotch to settle her stomach. This done she stood on the bathroom scales, stripped naked and weighed herself again, did a hundred sit-ups, got out the tape measure, crawled into bed and wept as if her heart would break.

He hadn't been joking about the Rolls-Royce. It arrived next day with a uniformed chauffeur. Paula sat back on the leather seat, drinking champagne from the refrigerated cocktail cabinet while the miles slipped smoothly and soundlessly by.

The little place in the country turned out to be a five-bedroomed, two-bathroomed job with a thatched roof, polished stone floors and a big log fireplace. The furniture was all ye olde rustic and the curtains and upholstery resplendently chintzy. A glass-fronted cabinet in the living room displayed a huge collection of antique teapots and every surface was covered with itsy-bits of china. It wouldn't have appealed to Isabel with her no-frills taste in decor and her puritanical abhorrence of what she called clutter, but for Paula, who had grown up in sparsely equipped rooms devoid of adornment, this place hummed with the comfort and the security that came from acquisition.

The housekeeper, Grace, a cheerful cockney lady, appeared to be some kind of adopted aunt.

'Vince rang to say you weren't well and needed taking care of,' she said. 'Lord, but you're so skinny! You want building up.'

Paula was powerless to resist her ministrations, from the morning breakfast tray in bed till the cup of Ovaltine last thing at night. When she wasn't eating, she learned her lines and slept. Slept and slept, she just couldn't seem to get enough of it. Partly it was because of the painkillers, which made her feel dopey. Partly it was just a matter of being weak, of giving in to her own unacknowledged misery.

Grace was easy to talk to, or rather listen to, because Paula didn't feel much like talking. Grace had known Vince, bless his cotton socks, ever since he was a baby. She had once been a neighbour, back in Bethnal Green, and a good friend of his mother, who had been killed in a direct hit during the Blitz, while Vince was fighting in France. His younger sister Eileen had been buried alive in the rubble and horrifically injured.

'Vince was taken prisoner by the Germans, spent the rest of the war in a POW camp. His poor sister died of kidney failure soon after he got home, she'd been in and out of hospital since '41, and then he lost his father in an accident. Both my own boys were killed in the war, so we sort of adopted each other.'

Vince had invested his demob money in what Grace called 'a bit of this and a bit of that' – black marketeering, most like, thought Paula, though evidently with a great deal more success than Dad had done.

'He's in property, mostly, these days,' Grace told her proudly. 'He bought this house when my husband died, as a country place, he said, but it was really to set me up somewhere nice in my old age. If I see him once or twice a year I'm lucky. Work, work, work.

121

That's all he thinks of. Apart from the theatre, that is. It's his only hobby.'

'What about girlfriends?' asked Paula casually.

'Oh, I wouldn't know,' said Grace. 'Vince keeps his private life to himself. I keep hoping he'll marry and have children' – she gave Paula a quizzical look – 'but he tends to think women are just after his money.'

Like men were just after sex, thought Paula. She wondered when he would call in his debt for this little holiday, only to despise her for paying up. Whereas she would despise herself if she didn't. Paying up put things back on an equal footing. Why shouldn't she use her assets the same way he used his – to buy the things she wanted?

But two weeks went by and he didn't appear, didn't even phone. Perhaps he was waiting for her face to get back to normal. It did so, little by little, improving every day, until finally she looked in the mirror and saw what she had wanted to see. A neat, pert little snub nose that dramatically altered the proportions of her face, that made it look cute and kittenish, robbed it of character, destroyed a part of her for ever.

She was pretty now, yes. So why wasn't she satisfied? Hadn't she become an actress to escape the confines of the self? Hadn't she starved her body and bleached her hair to banish the fat, boring Paula she hated? Hadn't she submitted herself to the knife to make the camera love her? So what business did she have mourning the wretched jetsam?

The more the outward Paula changed, the more important it became to preserve the Paula inside. The Paula who would resist domination and dependence, who would keep herself apart and inviolate, who would harbour that core of identity, however imperfect and flawed, which belonged, indisputably, to her. No matter if she neither liked nor admired it, no matter if nobody else did, she would guard it ever more jealously, not let anyone touch or change it, cherish it like some poor lost child who relied on her for its home.

5

Autumn–Winter 1960

Ambition should be made of sterner stuff.

William Shakespeare – Julius Caesar

(The Times, *28 September 1960*)
After a long and well-chronicled battle with the Lord Chamberlain's office, Bondage, *by Felipe X, opened last night at the Renegade Theatre Club, Elephant & Castle, where members were able to view the unexpurgated version in all its tasteless, sensational glory.*

One can only pity the actors involved for wasting their talents on such turgid, pretentious material, especially Miss Paula Dorland whose own particular talents are exposed to public view for the greater part of the evening . . .

(The Guardian, *28 September 1960*)
. . . A paltry five shillings membership fee enables us to witness a play deemed unsuitable for those who choose not to pay it, illustrating the absurdity of our censorship laws . . . Bondage *has a serious point to make about the social, sexual and political faces of Fascism . . . Richard Mallory has rendered a spirited translation and drawn excellent perform- ances from his young and inexperienced cast (notably Paula Dorland, a newcomer to watch) . . . Good luck to him and to his brave little company, which has suffered more than its share of setbacks lately, not least the inevitable failure of the brilliantly satirical* Antidotage *to find favour with trans- atlantic audiences . . .*

30 October 1960

Dear Miss Baker
Following our recent discussions regarding your persistently

123

poor time-keeping, irregular attendance at classes, and non-payment of this term's fees, I have no option but to terminate your term of study at the Institute forthwith in accordance with paragraph 4(ii) of FRIDA's terms and conditions of acceptance, as signed by you.

Will you please ensure that you clear your locker and return the key without delay, together with any volumes on loan from the college library.

Yours regretfully
Julian Clavell

PS Best of luck.

Dear Serafina
I was out there watching you last night. I followed you home, whore. I know where you live, bitch. One day soon I'm going to fuck you, slut. I'm going to . . .

Paula forced herself to read her latest fan letter to the end, just to prove to herself that she wasn't scared. There had been at least a dozen similar threats, all anonymous but clearly from the same source, each more obscene and explicit than the last. Felipe X would have envied the writer his vivid imagination; too bad Richard couldn't sign him up to write the next Renegade play.

It had arrived by the second post, otherwise Isabel would have intercepted it as usual and forwarded it to the police. Her idea; Paula had known it would be a waste of time. The paper and envelope were standard Woolworth issue, the letters cut out of the *Daily Express*, and the varying postmarks red herrings. The detective who had questioned her had made it pretty clear that he thought she had brought the whole thing on herself.

Nonetheless, Vincent Parry had taken the threats seriously. Paula now travelled to and from the Elephant and Castle each day in the comfort of either a Merc or a Roller, whose chauffeurs were under strict instructions to see her safely indoors before they drove away. In addition two bouncers had been appointed, twins by the name of Trev and Ron on Vince's personal payroll, to deal with any suspicious characters lurking round the theatre. Certainly the publicity generated by the play had introduced the work of Felipe X to an ever widening and less cultured audience.

Paula had lost count of the interviews she had given. She soon discovered that it didn't much matter what you said to journalists because most of them were frustrated fiction-writers. But as long as they printed a nice big photo with her name underneath it, why worry if they misquoted her? She was doing well for a girl who had been sleeping rough less than two years ago. She ought to have been a lot happier than she was. But the fact was that she was tired, and scared, and still missing Patrick like hell.

Vincent Parry, meanwhile, continued to frustrate her expectations. So far he hadn't shown any inclination to mix business with pleasure, even though Richard insisted, with mock regret, that no, he wasn't queer. Not that she fancied him in any case. Paula preferred men dark and tall, and Vince was fair and stockily built and not particularly good-looking, and besides, he must be pushing forty, a great age. Presumably he didn't fancy her either because he treated her with unwavering eyeball-to-eyeball respect, inspiring a feeling even more threatening than the one she still harboured for Patrick: trust.

She rarely saw Richard these days; he was working all hours setting up *Kill Claudio*, a musical loosely based on *Much Ado About Nothing*, set in Mafia-torn Sicily and directed by Neville Seaton, a project in which Izzie had shown surprisingly little interest. Or rather, it wasn't surprising at all. Who else but Patrick could have cured her, overnight, of her infatuation? Until the summer she had talked about Neville all the time but these days she never mentioned his name. Only a fear of losing face had prevented Paula challenging her direct. Obviously Izzie thought she would be jealous – why else would she have kept it secret?

She was just getting ready to leave for the midweek matinée when she heard the front door slam below.

'Izzie?' she called, spying her from the landing. 'What are you doing home at this hour?' Her face was pale, her eyes red, as if she had been crying. 'Are you ill?'

'Yes. No. It's just a migraine.'

Izzie would never cut classes for a migraine. Paula felt a flutter of treacherous anticipation. Patrick had been bound to start playing around once she went back to college, most probably with Davina, his leading lady in *Man and Superman*. Or perhaps Izzie had finally put her foot down about the girl he kept on ice back home . . .

'It's man trouble, isn't it?' said Paula recklessly, unable to bear it any longer. Isabel didn't answer, but she didn't deny it either, which was confirmation in itself. 'And I don't need three guesses as to who he is.'

'I don't want to talk about it,' snapped Isabel. 'You'll only say I told you so. It's finished and that's all there is to it.'

With that she rushed past her and into her room, just as the chauffeur rang on the bell to take Paula to the theatre. She spent the drive trying to justify her relief that it was over, assuming it was really over. What a bastard. Izzie was better off without him . . . She mustn't think about it again till after the performance, it would wreck her concentration.

A down-at-heel picture palace jerry-built in the early thirties, the Rialto had been gutted and converted to a modern 450-seater theatre with an apron stage and steeply tiered banks of seats around three sides of it. No expense had been spared on acoustics or lighting and no money wasted on unnecessary frills. The backstage facilities, however, were vastly superior to those which lurked behind the genteel frontage of most decaying West End theatres. Vincent Parry was as sentimental about performers as he was cynical about audiences.

As the only female in the play, Paula had a large dressing room all to herself, well equipped with a day-bed, a shower and washbasin, and an electric kettle, its walls plastered with good-luck cards and first-night telegrams from the most unlikely people, solicited by Isabel, no doubt. Paula had all her 'slap' ritually arranged in an old cigar box of Richard's, each stick of greasepaint ranged from left to right in the order in which she would use it. She had become superstitious about her routine, doing everything in exactly the same order each night to placate the ever-vigilant furies.

She popped a chocolate caramel into her mouth while she removed her ordinary make-up and darkened her complexion with Leichner No. 5. And then another as she mixed deep red and dark green greasepaint to shape her cheekbones. And then another as she dusted her face with powder before outlining her eyes in black and shading them with a blend of red and blue. As the sugar entered her bloodstream it chased away her fatigue, mingling with the gradually rising adrenaline to produce an illusion of strength and energy.

126

Still chewing hungrily she darkened her brows with a black-tipped orange stick, applied three coats of mascara, and stained her lips with carmine, adding a dab of pink to the inner corner of each eye, to open them up. Her face complete, she pinned up her hair to make way for Serafina's long dark mane which would mercifully hide her own bleach-brittle, perm-frizzed hair, complete with split ends and fast-growing roots. Like every other part of her anatomy her hair was in constant revolt, protesting against the demands she made upon it.

The body make-up came next; fish-belly-white skin looked ghastly under the lights. It took almost an hour, with help from her dresser, to paint herself from top to bottom with brown dye. Then she donned her three items of costume – a low-cut blouse tack-stitched anew each day to rip apart during the quarrel scene, a peasant-style skirt, and beneath it, a torn, bloody post-rape replica of the same garment which exposed her legs to mid-thigh.

These preparations brought her up to the half, leaving time for a cup of very sweet tea, a KitKat, a furtive chapter of the latest Mills & Boon and a couple of soothing du Maurier, a brand she had remained loyal to in memory of Bea. Paula never allowed herself alcohol before a performance, however great the temptation. The one time she had broken this rule her timing had been way out. Never again.

By the time the stage manager called the five, she could hear the hum of a full house over the Tannoy, like a swarm of insects. Her heart began beating very fast and her panties to grow damp with a kind of sexual desire, except that waiting to go on was much more exciting than foreplay, just as applause was more satisfying than an orgasm. Whereas a successful performance had always fired Patrick's libido, it killed her own stone dead; by the time she came off stage she would want nothing more than to hurry home to bed and sleep.

Until she woke up in the small hours and wished that there was someone, anyone, there beside her in the dark to help chase away the bogeys of the night. She had been celibate now for nearly four months, from choice – there was little incentive to put herself about now that Patrick was safely out of her life and all her energies consumed by the play. Certainly she had taken a sullen delight in disappointing those members of the company who confused her with the insatiable Serafina, particularly her stage brother Alfonso, who, not content with fondling her breasts on stage, had tried it on once in the wings and found himself playing the ensuing scene with a voice a good octave above normal.

Tonight she threw him off his stroke by giving his hair a sharp, unexpected tug in the middle of the opening quarrel scene, producing a spontaneous yelp of pain and a retaliatory twisting of her arm behind her back, which forced her in turn to improvise a plea for mercy. After this kick-start it turned out to be a particularly good performance; it was often the way, at matinées, with everyone fresher and less tense than they were in the evening. She had just lain down for her customary nap between performances – another immutable habit – when she heard a tap at the door and yelled, 'Piss off! I'm asleep.'

The door opened and so did her eyes, to see Patrick standing there.

'Who let you in?' she demanded, hiding her fear and excitement behind a show of truculence.

'I slipped through the pass door without anyone noticing. I thought I'd drop by and see what all the fuss was about. I've got a free day.'

'Lucky you. Well, I haven't, and I've got to go on again in two hours' time, so will you please go away and let me get some kip?'

He produced a big bunch of amber-coloured chrysanths from behind his back and thrust them at her. Paula got up and dumped them in the washbasin.

'What do you want?'

'To tell you you were good. Even though the play's a load of rubbish.'

'I know I'm good. Is that all?'

'Don't be like that, Paula. Can't we be friends again?'

The sight of him still produced the same old futile longings. She pulled herself up sharply, thinking of Isabel. How typical of Patrick to have the gall to turn up here, uninvited, in search of a quick no-strings fuck, knowing that Paula wouldn't make any emotional demands on him or otherwise disrupt the carefree, careless pattern of his life.

'I'm fond of you, you know that,' he went on. 'I only stayed away this long because I wanted to stop being fond of you. But I can't help it.'

'All right, we're friends,' snapped Paula. 'You can invite me to your village wedding, okay?'

He had the grace to look sheepish.

'Look, I know it sounds daft, me being engaged, but it just sort of happened and now I can't very well get out of it without breaking the poor kid's heart. If I finished with her it wouldn't make any difference to you and you know it. If I asked you to marry me instead you'd laugh in my face. Terry loves me. You don't.'

You don't. It was a statement of fact, apparently devoid of guile; he believed it, thought Paula. Thank God for small mercies.

'And you knew about her right from the start,' he added. 'I never lied to you.'

This piece of honest-Joe self-congratulation was too much.

'I suppose you never lied to Izzie either? I suppose you told her, right from the start, that you didn't want to get serious? God, you make me sick.'

'Izzie? What are you talking about?'

'Oh don't give me that. Aren't there enough Paulas and Davinas in the world to keep you busy? I thought you kept your dirty hands off nice girls?'

'Look, I –'

'Oh, she never said a word. She knew I'd tear her off a strip for being a bloody fool. But I can tell. All those nights she was supposed to be staying with a friend, all those new undies, all the stupid, secret smiles on her face when she thought I wasn't looking . . . you rotten bastard! And now she's lying on her bed crying her eyes out and all because of you!' She wouldn't cash in on Izzie's misery. However great the temptation, she wouldn't give in . . .

'Will you just listen for a minute?'

'I don't want to hear your lies and excuses. I hate you for hurting her! You just can't leave well alone, can you? You just can't resist –'

'It's not me she's sleeping with!' he roared in counterpoint. 'It's bloody Neville Seaton!'

Paula shut up in mid-shout.

'Neville Seaton? But she never . . . How do you know?'

'Because I surprised the pair of them at the flat that night I went round to collect my stuff. I kept it quiet because Izzie asked me to. I'm not in the habit of breaking my word.'

'How very noble of you,' hissed Paula, feeling like an idiot. 'Men! You're all as bad as each other. You haven't done her any favours in keeping it quiet. You've done the favour to him!'

'You think I didn't know that? You think I enjoyed seeing her waste herself on a married man? All I had to do was leak just one word to Davina and she'd have been straight on the phone to the wife. But a promise is a promise.'

'I should have guessed,' muttered Paula, furious with herself. She had gone and given herself away completely. 'But I was so sure that you would try it on, sooner or later –'

'Relax. Izzie turns up her nose at the likes of me. Now that we've cleared the air about that . . .' – he took hold of both her hands – '. . . can we kiss and make up?'

Suddenly she felt too tired to fight him, too transparent to pretend. Numbly she let him slip off her dressing gown and push her back onto the couch and make long, lazy love to her, overcome by the sheer familiarity of it all, his hands, his mouth, the scratchy hair on his chest that always brought her breasts out in a rash, and most of all the feel of him inside her, reaching into that empty yearning space, sharpening the hunger it ought to have satisfied. Most of all overcome by the relief that she hadn't lost him to her best, her only friend . . .

'What time do you finish tonight?' he murmured afterwards, as she lay hunched and hostile with her back to him. 'We could go out to dinner, and then back to my place. I've got a bedsit near the Kean . . .'

She could just imagine it, full of used crockery and dirty washing, with some other woman's smell lingering on the sheets. Damn. The dye had rubbed off in patches, giving her a piebald effect. She would have to take a shower and put it on all over again. Just as well. It would wash him away.

'I'm not coming back to your place. You got what you came for. Now you can go.'

'What's got into you?' he demanded, thrown by the sudden change of mood.

'That,' she said dismissively, pointing. 'And I'll tell you

something. Once they're in they all feel the same. So don't flatter yourself yours is special.'

'Stop playing the hard-boiled whore. You know it's just a front. I'm on your side, can't you see? If only you'd let me get close to you –'

'If only I'd let you be the boss, you mean. Well, I'm my own boss and I always will be. Just because I let you fuck me for old time's sake –' His mouth tightened right on cue. Patrick hated women to use bad language, 'that doesn't mean anything's changed. Drop round again any time you're passing, and I'll see if I can fit you in. But that's as far as it goes.'

'You won't be happy, will you, till you turn into what you pretend to be.' He began throwing on his clothes, the usual crumpled assortment of ill-matched garments, the too-short trousers, the odd socks, the shirt with the laundry label still attached, the shoes worn down at the heel. She felt a wave of hopeless, angry affection for him.

'Don't try to change me, Patrick.'

'You're the one who's trying to change yourself. All I ever wanted to do was to find out what was really there. No wonder you didn't last the course at FRIDA. They were teaching you things about yourself you didn't want to know.'

'Just as well you never went there then. And stop trying to explain me!'

'Why does making love always have to end like this?'

'We weren't making love. We were having sex. That's all either of us is capable of.'

'Speak for yourself,' he said, suddenly cold. 'And don't expect me to come grovelling a second time. You've played hard to get once too often, Paula.'

'I *am* hard to get. Thanks for calling. Goodbye.'

She was glad he had seen the matinée; the evening performance never caught light somehow. Her own fault for letting him spoil her concentration. *Terry loves me. If I finished with her it wouldn't make any difference to you. If I asked you to marry me instead you'd laugh in my face. Terry loves me. You don't . . .*

She might be miserable without him, but she'd be much more

131

miserable with him, knowing that it wouldn't, couldn't last. Even if she stole him from this girl of his, it would just be a temporary solution. One day he would leave her a note, like Dad, saying 'Sorry love, you weren't to blame.' Or betray her, like Stan. Or even die on her, like Bea. She couldn't face going through all that again.

It took all her remaining energy to shower and remove her make-up after the performance. As she headed for the stage door, expecting the car to be waiting for her, one of Vince's twin bouncers intercepted her in the corridor. Trev or Ron, she couldn't tell them apart.

'There's a geezer been hanging round outside ever since the show finished,' he said. 'He sat through both the performances today and he was here last week as well.'

Paula disguised a shudder as a shrug.

'D'you think it might be him?' she said casually, apparently untroubled.

'We rang Vince and he says please will you go home by tube tonight. We'll be right behind you all the way. If this joker follows you, then we'll sort him out so he doesn't bother you again.'

Paula nodded, making light of it. This way, perhaps, the letters would stop and the fear that came with them. Striding out into the street with a cheery goodnight to the doorman, she walked briskly towards the tube station and descended to the Bakerloo line, running automatically as she heard a train pull in and jumping aboard a split second before they closed the doors.

She changed at Charing Cross, where she had to wait less than a minute for a Circle line train. There were several men standing nearby on the platform – a respectable-looking bloke wearing a hat and hornrimmed specs, two drunken Teddy boys effing and blinding at each other, and a bearded beatnik type in a duffel coat reading the *Daily Worker*. There was no sign of Trev or Ron and she realized belatedly that she shouldn't have been in such a hurry and risked leaving them behind.

With luck she had left the suspect behind as well. As the train rushed in on a blast of hot air, she debated briefly whether to wait for the twins to catch her up, but the urge to get home quickly was too strong for her. She got into a smoking carriage and sat down beside the only woman. Hat-and-glasses got on and seated himself opposite her. She was glad it wasn't the beatnik. The older man didn't look remotely like a pervert. He looked like a dull-as-dust family man with a semi in the suburbs. One of the exercises they gave you at FRIDA was to observe people on the tube, imagine their lives, file away gestures, expressions, ways of moving and walking, in an actor's notebook. No one building a picture of a sex maniac would draw any inspiration from him.

A lot of people got off at Victoria, leaving the carriage empty but for Paula, the bespectacled man and a ragged old vagrant, asleep in a corner seat, riding lap after lap of the Circle line to get out of the cold. The other man stared at his distorted reflection in the tunnel-black window opposite, and Paula followed his example, only for her eyes to close. God, but she was tired.

As the train drew in, she got up too fast, making her head swim. She hadn't had anything to eat all day, bar the caramels and KitKat; two performances plus Patrick had taken their toll. It wasn't far to the flat but once she heard the tattoo of following footsteps behind her, it seemed like miles. Not daring to turn round she began to run through the ill-lit mews that connected South Eaton Place with Elizabeth Street, until her high heel caught between the cobbles, sending her sprawling.

Before she could scramble to her feet a man was looming above her, kneeling over her, pinning her down, pressing a leather-gloved hand over her mouth and the blade of a knife against her cheek. 'Be quiet,' he hissed. 'Lie still or I'll kill you, bitch.'

He needn't have wasted his breath. She couldn't move, couldn't speak. It was like one of those dreams where you tried to scream and no sound would come out, tried to run and found all your limbs paralysed.

'Whore,' he said. 'Slut.'

Paula was a fighter by nature. She could never believe afterwards that she hadn't struggled, that she had allowed it to happen, that the fear of that blade had reduced her to dumb immobility. She lay rigid while his free hand burrowed beneath her skirt and tore at her panties and forced her legs apart, and all the time he kept hissing 'slag' and 'whore', and all she could think of was staying alive and not letting him slash her face. This couldn't be happening only yards from the flat, in a respectable part of London. Surely someone would look out through their heavy curtains, arrive home after a night out, surely someone would come to help her?

She clenched her teeth as he forced his way into her, chanting his litany of loathing, and tried to imagine that it was just another man she didn't even fancy, that the gesture of contempt was hers as well as his. She forced herself to open her eyes so that she would remember what he looked like, and shut them again, too late to cancel out the hideous image of the bespectacled man she had dismissed as harmless. She didn't want to remember. Afterwards she would forget it, forget him. She was good at forgetting things.

And then, just as the full force of his hate exploded inside her, she heard shouts, felt him fall away and saw him run off, pursued by Vince's two men. One of them felled him from behind; the other helped drag him back onto his feet and delivered a heavy blow to his belly and jaw, knocking him out cold. His head slumped forward, his hat falling off to reveal a balding head, his penis drooping flaccidly outside his flies like some monstrous dead slug.

'Are you all right, love?'

What a stupid question. She tried to speak and screamed instead, and screamed again and found that she couldn't stop. She was aware of being carried, aware of Izzie crying, 'God! What's happened to her?' but most of all aware of her own voice screaming and screaming and screaming, as if to prove that she was still alive, and her hands pawing blindly at her face, as if to prove that there wasn't any blood.

Isabel rang her own doctor straight away, or rather not straight away, because one of Vincent Parry's men got to the phone first while the other stood guard over the culprit outside. Having spoken to the guv'nor in a state of visible terror he passed the receiver to Isabel and went off to join his mate, saying that Vince was sending a car to fetch them.

'I'm on my way,' Vince told her. 'Don't contact the police. Wait till I get there.'

By this time Paula had recovered sufficiently to lock herself in the bathroom. Even when the doctor arrived she refused to come out, yelling at Isabel above the sound of running taps to leave her the fuck alone. They had no choice but to wait for her to emerge in her own good time, or rather in Vince's good time, because within seconds of hearing his voice on the other side of the door, Paula opened it a fraction and let him in. A few minutes later he led her out, huddled inside her dressing gown and reeking of Dettol, her exposed skin red and raw from prolonged scrubbing. In response to further soft-spoken directions, she let go of his arm with evident reluctance, and spent the next half hour closeted with Isabel's doctor, an old family friend.

'How could your men have slipped up like that?' Isabel challenged Vince furiously, having overheard the explanatory phone call.

'Do you think I haven't bollocked them for it? Even though it was down to me, not them. The whole thing is down to me.' It was a statement of fact, not an apology.

'We've got to call the police,' said Isabel, trying to sound authoritative. Vince gave her one of those deadpan looks of his. Once again she was aware of the sinister power of the man, a man who could reduce even a hysterical Paula to meek, co-operative docility. She had a sense that his bland public face and Savile Row suits were just a veneer, that underneath he was somehow dangerous. There was a whiff of gangland menace about him, a ruthless glint in those dark grey eyes of his; he very seldom smiled.

'You ever had any dealings with the police, with the courts, with lawyers?'

He spoke quietly, as always. Presumably he was angry and upset, but you'd never have known it to look at him. On the surface he seemed calm, unemotional, controlled, and yet he sent out invisible currents of a fury so formidable that the very air seemed to vibrate with it.

'No. But –'

'Well, let me give you some idea of what would happen if the police agreed to press charges and if Paula was prepared to give evidence. This joker's solicitor will claim that Paula invited him home with her and begged him to have sex with her right there in the street. After all, she's got no injuries, she didn't even struggle, which proves that she consented, doesn't it? Even if he's already a known rapist, the prosecution can't reveal his form in court or force him to give evidence. Paula, on the other hand, will be cross-examined and forced to admit what she does on stage every night. The jury will write her off there and then as a stripper, a whore, and a nymphomaniac. The upshot will be that the accused will be acquitted and probably sell his story to the Sunday papers as well. "My romp with sex bomb Paula", and so on. Now do you get the picture?'

Isabel got the picture.

'So . . . what will you do to him?'

'Don't ask me that, Isabel. You don't want to know. You never saw my boys here tonight and the rapist ran away. Or rather, nothing happened. Got that? You're not involved.'

He stood up to go.

'Tell Richard when he gets home that the play closed as of tonight,' he said. 'Ticket money to be refunded and everyone to get three months' pay in lieu.' And then, seeing the look on Isabel's face, 'I know. The point of *Bondage* was subversion, not perversion, you realize. It seemed like a good idea at the time. But that was before I knew her.'

'You don't know her,' said Isabel. 'Nobody knows Paula.'

'I know her better than you think,' he said, and left her.

'How are you feeling?' said Isabel, two mornings later, as she brought Paula breakfast in bed. To her relief Paula hadn't protested at the closure of the play, or perhaps the news hadn't sunk in yet, thanks to the sedatives. She had taken two phone calls from Vince, had a long tête-à-tête with a distraught Richard, and issued a strict embargo on anyone else knowing what had happened, including and especially Patrick.

The official story was that she was suffering from 'nervous exhaustion' – that well-worn showbiz cliché – and that she was deemed irreplaceable at short notice, much to the chagrin of her understudy. But thanks to the generous pay-off no one seemed inclined to pursue their grievances. Or perhaps Vincent Parry wasn't the kind of man people argued with.

'I'm all right,' insisted Paula. She still looked dopey and bloated with sleep. 'That tame quack of yours gave me penicillin, just in case I've caught the pox. And he says if my period's late he'll

136

arrange a D and C, no questions asked. I bet he charges a bomb, with a bedside manner like that.'

'Never mind how much he charges,' said Isabel. 'It was better than queuing up at casualty.'

'I wouldn't have gone to casualty. I told you, I wasn't hurt. I took it like a lamb.'

'Which was the sensible thing to do. Otherwise you might have been killed.'

'No loss if I had.' She scattered extra sugar over her frosted flakes and reached for her cigarettes. 'Is there anything in the papers about us closing?'

'There was a mention in last night's *Evening Standard*.' She went to fetch it and handed it to Paula. 'Somewhere near the middle, I think it was. I drew a ring round it.'

'Vince says he'll make sure I get another part right away,' said Paula, flicking through it. 'He's going to withdraw his backing for *Snowdrops in June* unless they give me the lead. He says the play is absolutely perfect for me. And I don't even have to take my clothes off.'

Snowdrops in June was a potboiler in which Vince had invested for purely commercial reasons; any profits he made on the deal would be ploughed back into Renegade. At least the prospect of a new part had helped to cheer her up, thought Isabel. But as if to disprove this optimistic assumption, Paula began trembling violently, dropping her lighted cigarette into the bowl of cereal where it hissed and swam briefly before sinking.

'I bloody asked for it, didn't I?' she muttered. 'I got what was coming to me. God, I feel so dirty. I can still smell him. However much perfume and talc I put on, I can still smell him . . .'

Isabel removed the tray and put an arm round her, hoping that she would cry. But as usual the smell of sympathy stanched the tears at source.

'It was no big deal,' said Paula irritably, shakily lighting a fresh fag. 'Not as if I was a good girl, like you.' There was a goading edge to her voice. 'I mean to say, what's one more fuck to a little slag like me?'

'You're not a slag,' said Isabel quietly. 'Any more than I'm a good girl.' What was the point in hiding it any longer? And in any case, Paula already knew, she had as good as told Isabel so the

137

other day. 'You were right, I've been having an affair with Neville.'

'Well, it couldn't be anyone else, could it?' said Paula. It seemed so obvious now, with hindsight. She would have guessed long ago if she hadn't been so blinded by jealousy and fear.

'And before you start laying into him,' continued Isabel, 'I was the one who started it, I more or less forced him into it. Because I wanted to be in love, because I thought that no one could possibly get hurt but myself. I used to think ahead to when he would break things off, and congratulate myself on how brave I'd be about it.'

'Well, thank your stars he has done,' muttered Paula. 'Better than him leaving his wife and making a mug out of you instead.'

'That's the whole trouble,' said Isabel, flushing. 'He *has* left her. He went and told her everything and moved out. He said he couldn't bear living a lie any longer. He asked me to marry him.'

'You're kidding,' said Paula, aghast.

'I wish I was.' Things had been so perfect as they were, thought Isabel. Love without responsibility. Why did he have to want more? Why did he have to go and spoil things for both of them?

'I didn't know anything about it until it was too late,' she went on, as if in mitigation. 'I never dreamed for one minute that he would ever do anything like that.'

Paula raised her eyes to heaven. Wait for it, thought Isabel. In a moment she would call her green as grass.

'You make me die, you do,' said Paula. 'What man in his right mind wouldn't want to leave a washed-out wife and a couple of screaming brats for a gorgeous piece of crumpet like you? He must have thought he'd died and gone to heaven. Any other woman would have seen it coming . . .'

'Well, I'm not any other woman,' snapped Isabel. 'I never wanted this to happen. I never wanted to *marry* him. I don't want to marry anyone. Not yet, anyway.'

'You mean you turned him down?' said Paula, impressed. 'Good for you.'

'Not good, no. I thought being good was not wanting to break up his home. I told myself I loved him too much for that. But the truth is, I didn't love him enough.'

'Then what the hell are you bleating about?' said Paula, exasperated. 'Trust you to make a tragedy out of it. Now you've given him the push he'll go crawling home to the wife, I guarantee it. And she'll take him back, more fool her.'

'That's what I thought. Hoped. That's why I broke things off.' At least if he went back to Helen she wouldn't feel so guilty. She would miss him terribly, but the pain would be part of her penance. 'I'm sorry I couldn't tell you before but I was scared it would leak out and he would get sacked. I was always so careful . . .'

Careful enough to stoop to asking Patrick for a favour. Patrick who had kept his promise to keep quiet. All through the summer at the Kean, their shared secret had been a bond between them. Having him know had been strangely satisfying, a way of rubbing his nose in his nice-girl taunts, a form of titillation. If Patrick hadn't known she might have revelled it in less, read the danger signs sooner. She had become so immersed in her chosen role that she had lost sight of reality . . .

'Christ,' breathed Paula. 'I don't believe it.'

'Well, it's true,' said Isabel. 'I told you, I –'

'Not that,' said Paula. 'Look. Look!' She pointed to the paper lying open on the bed.

The photograph showed a bald, middle-aged man with glasses, and the heading read EALING BANK CLERK MURDERED.

'It's him,' said Paula, with a kind of religious awe. 'It's him.'

10 December 1960

Dear Isabel

I'm sorry for all the things I said last time we met. You were right, I should have discussed it with you first, but I flattered myself that a fait accompli *was worth more than the kind of promises married men tend to make and break. If I misread the situation, it was wishful thinking on my part, not deception on yours. I was wrong to put you on the spot and I respect you for being honest with me.*

For God's sake don't blame yourself for Helen telling all and sundry what happened. Or for the divorce. You've become the scapegoat for something that would have happened long ago, if it hadn't been for that cursed car crash. I've resigned from FRIDA, but don't blame yourself for that either; Kill Claudio *won't leave enough time in my schedule for teaching next term, and I'm hoping it will lead to other work. I had a long talk with Julian Clavell and have his personal assurance that this business won't prejudice your diploma.*

I still love you and I'll always be here if you need me, personally or professionally. You have the makings of an extraordinary actress and I hope that one day we'll work together.

Neville

Heavy-hearted, Isabel decided to spend the Christmas vacation with Fay, partly to make up for her neglect the previous summer, partly to get away from the guilt and the gossip. Having unseated two wives in the course of acquiring her four husbands, Mummy was hardly in a position to sit in judgment. Not that Daddy or Davina were either, but that hadn't stopped Daddy lecturing her at interminable length, while Davina interceded for her with a poisonous 'Don't be too hard on her, darling. I know how persistent Neville can be. Those poor children . . .'

It was one of Fay's good days; Isabel could barely keep up with her restless nervous energy. They had spent the morning on Wilshire Boulevard, buying clothes that neither of them needed, and passed the afternoon being massaged and manicured and coiffed in readiness for that night's charity première of Marty's latest movie, a comedy thriller which Isabel knew she would find neither funny nor thrilling, Marty having already subjected her to a frame-by-frame résumé. And now they were 'relaxing' over iced tea before commencing the serious business of Getting Dressed.

'Cheer up, darling,' said Fay, noting her tense expression. 'I know what you're going through. People love a scandal. But they'll soon find someone else to talk about.'

Fay's own adventures made the Neville fiasco seem terribly suburban. Her first husband, a marquess, complete with decaying stately home, had caused a sensation by deserting the marchioness, a distant cousin of the King, in favour of an already notorious ex-deb-turned-actress with a string of lovers behind her. ('I did his wife a favour, darling. He turned out to be dreadfully boring in bed.') So boring that Mummy had left him three years later, after a whirlwind romance with a French racing driver whose

140

second wife had surprised them *in flagrante*. He had crashed his Bugatti at Le Mans within days of their wedding, leaving Fay with nothing but a mountain of debts and claims on his non-existent estate from two illegitimate children. Less than a month later she was sufficiently recovered to be playing opposite husband number three – an eligible bachelor for once – in a much acclaimed revival of *Private Lives*, the blueprint for a real-life tempestuous romance she had thought would last for ever. No one had ever fallen out of love with her, until Daddy.

'I thought I wouldn't have any problems this time, what with Marty being a widower,' continued Mummy, sighing. 'But his children all hate me, as you know. Even though I've tried so hard to make them like me. I'm the same as you, darling, sensitive and full of guilt. We're so alike, aren't we?'

The words sounded ominously prophetic. Could you hope to inherit the good genes without the bad ones? Was nature really that kind? Was mental illness hereditary, a sleeping dog that would one day wake up and bite her too?

Predictably, the good spell soon gave way to a panic attack, with a tearful, trembling Fay having to leave the première half way through, the prelude to a deep depression. A couple of days before Christmas, on her fourth consecutive day in bed, there was a telephone call from Paula.

'How's it going?'

'All right. You sound clear as a bell.'

'That's hardly surprising. I'm just up the road from you, at the Beverly Hills Hotel.'

'Are you pulling my leg?'

'Vince reckoned I'd earned a break, so here I am. It's dead flash here, you've never seen anything like it. Well, of course you have. But anyway. Can I come over and see you?'

'Of course you can!' said Isabel, too pleased at the thought of congenial company to consider how she would explain away Fay's indisposition. Neither she nor Richard ever spoke about her illness. 'Why didn't you phone to say that you were coming? I could have met you at the airport.'

'Oh, I felt like surprising you. And Vince's secretary booked the hotel along with the air ticket. I flew first class. They were grovelling all over me on the plane, I nearly bust a gut laughing.

First time I've ever flown in my life, or been further than bloody Southend, come to that. I still can't believe I'm really here.'

'Is Vince here with you?'

'No. He had things to do at home. I've just looked up Benedict Canyon Drive on the map. Which end are you at? Can I walk it?'

'Don't be silly. Nobody walks in Beverly Hills. We're about two minutes away by cab.'

'See you in two minutes then.'

She turned up in five, wearing a stunningly well-cut sheath dress in champagne-coloured jersey; not Paula's kind of thing at all. Her blonde bouffant hair was now light brown and coiffed in Jackie Kennedy-style flick-ups, complete with a little pillbox hat; she looked as if she had just stepped out of a beauty parlour, even though, or rather because she wasn't wearing half as much make-up as usual.

'What do you think?' she said, almost self-consciously, for her. 'I had it done just before I left and tinted its natural colour, only nicer. I'm packing in the perming and bleaching for a bit and getting it back in condition.'

'You look like the proverbial million dollars,' approved Isabel, twirling her round. She had little doubt that Vincent Parry was behind the transformation.

'I don't feel it. I'm dead nervous about meeting your mum.'

'No need,' said Isabel, hoping to God that Fay didn't show her up. The tentative mention of a visitor from England had roused her from her torpor, and she was now half way through the painstaking business of putting on her public face. 'I thought you were spending Christmas in London.'

'So I was. But then Richard got invited to some all-queers-together house party in the country. And Vince rang to say he had some bother to sort out and would have to work Christmas. He asked if I fancied going anywhere and I said yes, I'd like to visit you. I was only joking. Nearly died of shock when he came across.'

'Bother to do with the play?'

'Search me. With Vince you don't ask.'

Isabel thought again of the rapist's summary execution (caused by a blow on the head with a blunt instrument; too merciful, Paula had complained) and shivered. Not out of pity for him, but out of fear for Paula. What would happen to her if she ever crossed a man

142

like Vincent Parry, a man who seemed to have taken control of her life?

'I'll send a car to the hotel to collect your stuff,' said Isabel firmly. 'You must stay here with us, there's masses of room.' With Paula here, the rest of the holidays might even turn out to be fun.

The ersatz quality of Marty's house always made her cringe, but Paula obviously found it impressive, even though it was modest enough by local standards; Marty's former matrimonial home, a palace up in the hills on Mulholland Drive, high above the smog, had been in the name of his late wife and been left in her will to their eldest son by mutual consent. The new place was mock Tudor from the outside, like some monstrous erratic from the Kingston bypass (if you ignored the heart-shaped swimming pool); the interior, however, was vaguely Spanish colonial, heavy on marble and mirrors and mahogany, used to excess rather than effect. Huge framed portraits of Marty and Fay greeted guests on their way up the broad sweeping staircase, as if they were founders of some future dynasty.

'I didn't realize he was that old,' said Paula tactlessly.

'That was painted five years ago, and the artist flattered him.'

'What does she see in him?'

'He's kind. Which is more than Daddy ever was.'

'Richard said to watch him, he's a dirty old man.'

'Rubbish,' said Isabel, not wanting Paula to worry. Trust Richard to put the wind up her. She was nervous enough of men at the moment without him making things worse. And anyway, she told herself stubbornly, it wasn't true.

She changed the subject by giving Paula a tour of the guest accommodation, expecting her to choose the bordello suite, complete with sunken pink bathtub and mirrored ceiling. To be fair on Marty, most of the decor had been inherited from the previous owners and Mummy, never a home-maker, had shown little interest in changing it.

But Paula just said, 'I'd rather share with you, if you don't mind,' so Isabel had an extra bed moved into her sanctuary, a room stripped of its former furbelows, with oatmeal hessian walls, polished parquet floor and a clinical white bathroom.

'Can you put a lock on the door?' asked Paula sheepishly. 'I still can't sleep without one.'

'I'll get the handyman to fit a bolt. Will that do?'

'Top and bottom?'

'If you like. But you're quite safe here. Even if Marty *was* a dirty old man, he'd hardly take on the two of us.'

'I know,' Paula said, rather defensively. 'Just humour me, will you? I'm trying to snap out of it, honest.'

Isabel phoned down to the housekeeper and asked for it to be done right away. 'There's Marty now,' she said, seeing the gold Cadillac from the window as it swept up the palm-lined drive. 'Come and say hello. He's very nice.'

Paula said hello in her best BBC voice and smiled her cutest smile, reminding herself that she hadn't just come here to spend Christmas with Izzie. She had come here to try out the new improved Paula on people who didn't know her, who might turn out to be useful to her. And to prove she could manage without Vince, on whom she had allowed herself to become dangerously dependent, breaking her golden rule.

She ought to have picked a fight with him long ago, on principle, instead of letting him make her decisions, fight her battles, change her image, take advantage of the loss of confidence that had delivered her into his power, that kept her in thrall to the man he had killed, the man who was ruling her life from the grave.

If only Vince would take her to bed. Then she would feel less beholden. But for the rape she might have seduced him first, if only to devalue the relationship. But she hadn't the nerve, not any more, not with him, not even as a thank you for avenging her, not that he admitted to doing any such thing. 'Nothing to do with me,' he had said, in that steady voice of his. 'Or with you. Now forget it. It never happened, okay?'

But it had happened, it happened every night in her dreams and sometimes in her waking hours as well, in hideous flashback. The thought of having sex with anyone still filled her with nausea and dread. Which was all the more reason to expunge her fear by forcing herself to do it. Preferably with the anaesthetic of an incentive. Richard, unwittingly, had put the idea in her head. Marty, a dirty old man, was also a Hollywood producer. Might as well try to kill two birds with one stone.

Marty said hi and asked her how she was doing, rather than how she did. He was a big, heavy man with a paunch, his florid face drawn beneath the hearty smile, his handshake hot and clammy. Paula caught a flicker of sexual interest in his baggy eyes, a flicker that was enough to make her feel queasy. He was balding, with glasses, which didn't help.

They sat in the glass-covered sunroom which gave out onto the pool, waiting for Fay to come down. Isabel excused herself, saying that 'Mummy might need help with her hair.' Marty rattled a shaker and pressed Paula to join him in a Margarita. The tequila blazed an icy, fiery trail past her empty stomach and straight into her bloodstream, making her feel braver. She crossed her legs, showing a lot of thigh.

'So tell me about your career so far,' said Marty, shovelling a handful of nuts into his mouth. His double chin quivered as he chewed. Knowing that he was considered a pillar of Good Clean Family Entertainment, Paula glossed over *Bondage*, making it sound arty and intellectual, and moved on quickly to the lead in *Snowdrops*, a three-hanky weepy whose heroine, dying of a mystery illness in an Alpine resort, rehabilitates a dissolute society playboy by teaching him True Love.

Isabel thought it drivel, as did Richard, as did Paula herself. But Vince had declared it the ideal vehicle for cleaning up Paula's image.

'Sounds more like my kind of entertainment than that Spanish play,' commented Marty. 'I suppose Richard told you it was your big break, right?'

Paula nodded humbly. Marty sighed and picked up another fistful of nuts.

'You got yourself a decent agent?'

'I have a manager, Vincent Parry. He isn't a professional agent as such. But he knows about the business, he has a lot of contacts. I trust him absolutely. I mean to say, he's so much older and more experienced than I am.'

She assumed a look of earnest, arch *naïveté*.

Marty looked at her appraisingly for a moment, trying to decide, no doubt, if she was really stupid or just clever enough to play it dumb. Paula ventured a tilt of the head, leading him on just a fraction, but not enough to compromise herself. Treat it like a part, she reminded herself. Stop being so bloody wet. Go for it . . .

145

'Mummy, meet Paula,' said Isabel from the doorway, ushering in an older version of herself. Fay was shorter and smaller-boned than Isabel, but visually they were startlingly alike, with the same perfectly proportioned features and thick, coppery hair. She was wearing a full-skirted green shirtwaister, the same colour as her still vivid eyes. She would easily have passed for forty, her figure trim and her face unlined. Like Isabel, she radiated Class.

'Paula, darling. How lovely to meet you at last.' There was something rather stilted about her speech, as if she was unsure of her lines. The introductions made, she smiled a lot, in a fixed kind of way, but said very little, relying on her husband and daughter to do her talking for her. Paula noticed that Isabel watched her constantly, as did Marty, in the way one might keep an eye on a small child.

Eventually a meal was served in the mahogany-panelled dining room, the long polished table reflecting the glitter of the chandelier and the glow of the candelabra. They ate salad and seafood and gigantic steaks, of which nobody but Marty ate more than a fraction, while Marty strove to entertain their English guest with Hollywood anecdotes which his wife and stepdaughter had obviously heard a hundred times before. Paula didn't dare catch Isabel's eye for fear of dissolving into giggles; Marty had all the narrative flair of a speaking clock. Nonetheless she maintained an expression of fascinated attention, sticking demurely to one glass of wine, while Isabel and Fay looked on with identical vacuous smiles, their minds far away. As coffee and dessert were brought in Paula noticed that Fay's face was beginning to droop, as if its elastic had suddenly gone.

'You're looking tired, honey,' commented Marty, breaking off from his dissertation. For reply Fay slumped forward, banging her head on the table and bursting into tears with all the ferocious suddenness of a toddler. Marty helped her to her feet, and, with the briefest of apologies, said goodnight and bore her off to bed.

'I'm sorry,' said Isabel, embarrassed. 'I should have warned you she wasn't well. It's a virus. She should have stayed in bed but she insisted on getting up and coming down to meet you. I'm afraid she was just exhausted.'

'I ought to go back to the hotel. Trust me to turn up at a bad time.'

'Oh but it's not. It was bliss having you here tonight. You're so patient with Marty. He's a sweet man, I know, but terribly dull. Don't go, Paula. You've no idea how I've been dreading Christmas.'

To think that she had envied her her holidays in this house, with her dotty mother and her droning stepfather. There wasn't much to choose between the set-up here and the different but equally dire one in Windsor. There was no doubt about it, thought Paula, you were better off without a family. At least you could choose your friends.

Fay's 'virus' had taken a turn for the worse; two different doctors had come and gone in the course of the day and it looked as if the planned outing for Christmas Eve would have to be cancelled. They were supposed to be dining at some fish restaurant overlooking the ocean before opening their presents, which were already stacked around the base of the tree in gift-wrapped profusion.

Paula had come armed with a single malt scotch for Marty, a Hermes scarf for Fay, and a bottle of L'Air du Temps for Isabel, all purchased in haste from the duty-free shop at Heathrow. Isabel would put her to shame by presenting her with something brilliantly thoughtful and original and apt, but Paula had played it safe and unimaginative, knowing that she didn't have the good taste to reciprocate in kind.

She had already received Vince's Christmas present – a flying visit to Bond Street to buy her some new clothes, all chosen by him with ratatat speed and scant regard for the fawning recommendations of the upmarket Sharps and Norrises who had danced attendance on her. The outfits were not what she would have bought for herself – a cream linen tailored suit, a starkly plain little black dress, a navy blazer with gold buttons, the champagne-coloured jersey and a fitted coat in red bouclé wool with a fur trim, plus assorted accessories, all of them ridiculously expensive.

If she had been paying she would have bought twice as many items for a fraction of the price, never mind whether the skirts were lined or the hems hand-stitched. But she had to admit that they looked good on her. And if spending money on her helped Vince feel less guilty about what had happened, then why deny him that consolation? He could easily afford it, after all. And one day, soon, she would pay him back, evening up the score.

'Mummy doesn't feel well enough to get up,' announced Isabel that evening. Surprise, surprise, thought Paula. 'Look, it's silly to ruin your evening. I'll stay home with her and you go out with Marty as planned.'

'Are you sure?'

'I'd prefer it. Let's save our presents for the morning, shall we? She might be feeling better by then.'

Marty seemed reluctant to leave his wife, but given that she was doped up to the eyeballs and wouldn't have known if he was there or not, Isabel finally persuaded him to go. He was very quiet during the drive to the restaurant, suddenly erupting with 'What do you say we drive over to Malibu? I could show you the beach house we have there. We can send out for some seafood, go for a walk. I feel like some air.'

'That would be nice,' said Paula, nothing in her manner betraying the panic within. Here it comes, she thought. Richard was right. I'm not afraid. I'm not.

They drove in silence, in the dark, to the sound of the car radio, while Connie Francis and Bobby Darin and Pat Boone crooned of thwarted love. After half an hour or so Marty drew up outside a redwood-clad house built on stilts, right on the beach. Paula shivered, and not just because it was much too cold for a moonlight stroll.

She followed him into a room with one wall completely of glass, looking out over the invisible sand and sea. Marty pulled a cord and a heavy curtain swished over its blackness, shutting out the night. He disappeared briefly into the kitchen and returned with two glasses full of ice.

'This is all we seem to have in the house,' he said, picking up a bottle of Jack Daniels from the trolley. 'All right for you?'

Paula nodded, accepting a big slug, hoping that it would stop her shaking. Marty emptied his glass in one gulp and refilled it.

'I guess you want to get into the movies, do you?' He sat down on the other side of the coffee table. Paula found herself pressing her knees together.

'One day. Perhaps.'

'No perhaps about it. All actresses do. Apart from Isabel. I

148

can't understand her. With a face like hers . . . She looks so like her mother. Fay's still a beautiful woman.'

'Yes, isn't she,' acknowledged Paula.

'But she hasn't been too well, this past year or so. I expect Isabel's told you.'

'Er . . . yes.'

'I guess you wonder why she married a guy like me. I guess you think she married me for my money.' He polished off his second drink.

'Er . . . no, of course not.'

'Okay, so I'm not a poor man. But Fay's not a gold-digger either. I had to ask her to sign a pre-nuptial agreement, out of fairness to my family. And she did, without a murmur. If anything happens to me she only gets a sixth of my estate. The rest goes to my children and grandchildren.'

'Oh,' said Paula, surprised.

'I try to keep off the booze, you know,' he added, replenishing his glass yet again. 'Doctor's orders. But what the hell, it's Christmas. Merry Christmas, Paula.'

'Merry Christmas,' said Paula.

'You're a nice kid. Easy to talk to. I don't like to burden Isabel. She worries enough about her mother as it is. Fay's done her best to be a good wife to me. But for a long time, what with this . . . illness of hers, things have been kind of . . . well . . . platonic.'

'I see,' said Paula, trying not to believe him. The frigid wife had to be the oldest line in the book.

'Not that I'm complaining,' he said quickly, taking another big swallow. 'I promised to care for her in sickness and in health. And I would never do anything to hurt her. But I'm only a man. I've always been very . . . discreet. You understand what I'm saying?'

'I think so.'

She could smell that smell again, a pungent mixture of sweat and sex and bad breath, and the air around her was humming with whispered taunts, 'slut' and 'bitch' and 'whore', and opposite her she could see a balding man, with glasses . . .

You can't chicken out now, she told herself, as he got up and walked unsteadily towards her. Marty wasn't going to force her. It would all be over very quickly – she had ways of making sure of that – and then she would have overcome her fear, be firmly back

149

in charge of her life. And perhaps do her career a bit of good into the bargain.

'I'll make it up to you,' he said, his voice slightly slurred, pulling her to her feet. 'I know you don't get nothing for nothing in this town. Whatever you want, you have to pay for,' he added bitterly, as if to himself.

Swallowing hard, Paula let him lead her up the open-tread staircase to a galleried landing. The bedroom was evidently a guest room, not the one he shared with Fay, devoid of personal possessions. She was glad of that. He probably did this all the time. If it wasn't her it would be some other girl. Hollywood was full of would-be starlets with expert blow-jobs, the principal qualification, if Richard was to be believed, for getting into the movies. Her mouth went dry.

Marty took off his glasses and placed them carefully on the nightstand. His face looked naked without them. He began removing his cuff links while Paula fumbled for her zip. It was an oddly matrimonial scenario, with both of them undressing themselves without haste, or lust. Uncertainly, she got into the bed. He switched off the light before joining her and then he began to cry.

Paula had never known a man cry before. She had never credited men with having real feelings, the way women had feelings, she had envied them their insensitivity, tried to cultivate it in herself, seeing it as a sign of strength, the reason why men had things all their own way while women wept in vain.

He pressed his face into her shoulder and she put her hand on his head, shocked by the violence of his sobs. She had no idea what to do or say. The drink had made him maudlin, that was all. She had a sudden, surrealist vision of Marty as a little bespectacled boy, crying for his mother.

'It's all right,' she said helplessly, letting him burrow his face into her neck and send his tears coursing down her chest. 'You don't have to feel bad. You're not hurting Fay. It's not your fault she's ill.'

'I love her so much. I want her so much. Being old doesn't stop you wanting. You think I'm disgusting, don't you?'

'Of course I don't.' God. How had she got herself into this? 'You're a good person, Marty.'

'I've done my best.'

150

'I know you have.'

'I was hoping she'd feel better for Christmas. I wanted to make it s-special for her . . .'

She held him close while he rattled on and on and on, sharing his heartbreak, and Paula knew that it was the drink talking, that he had gone too far, that he would hate her tomorrow for having seen him in this pitiable state and no doubt turn against her. Which was no more than she deserved. But when his sobs subsided, and he began kissing her hungrily, messily, desperate for comfort, she didn't have the heart to refuse him. Not because of ambition, or some clenched-teeth experiment in overcoming fear, but because she understood pain and loss, because in comforting him, she was, against all expectation, comforting herself.

He pumped away for what seemed like forever, in a valiant attempt to satisfy her, while Paula moaned and writhed a bit in the hope of making him feel better. Poor Marty. Another living example of the destructive power of love. At this rate she would soon be crying too. She had just decided that it was high time she faked it when he let out a feeble groan and collapsed on top of her.

'That was terrific,' murmured Paula, relieved that it was over. And then, 'Marty, could you move just a little? You're terribly heavy.'

At first she thought he had fallen asleep. But when she finally managed to roll him onto his side and saw the grey, clammy face, heard the shallow breathing, and felt the feeble dying flutter in his chest, her only thought was to phone for help, and fast.

'Don't die,' she begged, holding his hand as she waited for the ambulance. 'Please don't die.' But he didn't hear her. And by the time the paramedics arrived, he had already gone.

'I'll be out of the flat by the time you get home,' said Paula.

Home, thought Isabel. Assuming she ever got there. Mummy was still prostrate with grief and begging her not to leave her all alone.

'That's up to you,' she said coldly. She had waited – no, wanted – for Paula to claim that Marty had forced himself on her, or that she had been drunk at the time, but she had offered no excuses. Quite the reverse.

'I thought if I screwed him it might get me a screen test,' she had told Isabel sullenly. 'I never bargained for him conking out on me.' Her only defence was that 'We never meant for it to hurt your mother.' But now it inevitably would. Short of keeping Fay in permanent isolation, Isabel couldn't keep the sordid truth from her for ever.

If it had happened at home, they could have covered it up. But thanks to Paula's frantic 911 call – 'I don't know the address, it's Marty Bauer's beach house in Malibu, please hurry' – the newshounds had been out in force before the body was cold. Paula had had to make a statement to the police, and within hours the media had identified her as the star of *Bondage*, variously described as 'banned play', 'nude review', 'London sex show' and worse. She was suddenly a minor celebrity, enjoying the kind of publicity that would otherwise have cost thousands of dollars. Bad publicity, in theory, but in practice there was no such thing. And now that the autopsy was over Paula was free to go. She wasn't trapped here, as Isabel was, by a suicidal mother . . .

Richard appeared at that moment, looking haggard from another session with Fay. He was booked to leave on the same flight as Paula, pleading pressure of work, the same excuse their father had used not to come at all.

'So when do you think you'll be back?' said Richard.

'I don't know.'

'You ought to hire a nurse to look after her. The longer you stay, the harder it'll be to leave. You've got your career to think of . . .'

'Oh yes,' snapped Isabel. 'My career. That's all we Mallorys care about, isn't it?' She flung him an accusatory look.

'I'd stay,' muttered Paula, 'if I thought I could do any good.' The olive branch came too late.

'Good?' echoed Isabel. 'You?' She flinched at the venom in her own voice, but taking it out on Paula was the only relief left to her, especially as Paula had snubbed her valiant attempts to be fair, and understanding, and sympathetic. Or rather selfish, she reminded herself bitterly. She hadn't wanted to lose a friend and ally. But now that Paula had rejected her, why shouldn't she do the same to her?

'Lay off her,' muttered Richard. To his mind, Marty was an old lech who had died the way he had lived; the easy way out of this was to speak ill of the dead, not blame the living.

'It's all right,' said Paula. 'I asked for it.'

'Yes, you always do, don't you?' said Isabel, flaring up. 'And you always get it. Another load of free publicity, another batch of interviews waiting for you at home. Just don't try to pass it off as a rape this time, okay?'

'Izzie!' remonstrated Richard, but Isabel couldn't stop the words coming, they poured out of her like a torrent of ice-cold acid.

'I'm not green as grass any more,' she hissed. 'And I'm through with making excuses for you. You're incapable of friendship, or love. All you care about is money and fame and success and you don't care how low you sink to get it!'

'That's enough!' began Richard, but Paula interrupted him with 'Let her say her piece. She's been thinking it for long enough. She's just been too polite to say it. I don't mind her hating me. At least it's honest.'

Isabel would have been putty in her hands, thought Paula, if she too had been honest, had let her see one fraction of what she was really feeling. But she didn't want to be forgiven. This was painful enough without coals of fire as well. Everything Isabel had said about her was true. She was a bad person. So she might as well make a good job of it.

'I'm feeling much better today, darling,' said Mummy, a week later. 'You're already late for the beginning of term. It's time you went back home.'

'Let's give it another week, Mummy. I can't leave you like this.'

'Like this' now embraced a state of constant paranoia, based on the conviction that Marty's offspring were planning to swindle her out of her share of his estate and turn her out, penniless, onto the street.

There were other delusions. One morning Isabel had gone to wake her to find her already washed and dressed, as excited as a child at the prospect of Daddy's imaginary arrival that day. Now that she was free again, Daddy would leave Davina, and soon they would all be together again (as if they had ever been 'together' in the past).

153

'I neglected you all so terribly,' she said, with bright-eyed penitence, 'but from now on I'm going to be a proper wife and mother. I'm going to stay home and look after you all. Oh darling, won't it be fun?'

'Nervous breakdown,' said the doctors. 'You can't cope with her here. She ought to be hospitalized.'

But Isabel was granted no such reprieve. Mummy refused point blank to leave the house, for the same reason she had refused to fly home. If she left the house, she would lose everything. Which was why Marty's family were in league with the doctors to have her committed. She refused to see her therapist, she refused to take her medication. They were all in the pay of her enemies. Isabel was the only person she could trust.

'Don't let them take me away, Izzie,' she had pleaded. 'Don't let them lock me up with a lot of crazy people.'

And now here she was, in one of her brief, lucid periods of remission, telling her calmly to go back home, she was quite all right.

'Oh, Izzie, you're such a good daughter to me. Just stay another week, then, until Daddy arrives . . .'

Isabel shut her eyes.

'All right. Till Daddy arrives. Now, be sensible and take one of these pills, otherwise you won't sleep again tonight . . .'

Having tucked Fay up, she locked her in, to prevent her going walkabout in the small hours; if she rattled the door of her cage, Isabel, who slept next door, would hear her. The previous week Fay had wandered out onto the patio in her sleep and walked into the deep end of the swimming pool. Luckily she had woken herself up and swum to safety, but Isabel wasn't taking any chances in future, for fear that she would drown next time, or fall downstairs and break her neck.

If only Daddy *would* fly out, just for a few days! Perhaps he would be able to persuade her to go home . . .

It had to be worth a try. Isabel looked at her watch. Nine thirty. Half past five in the morning at home. She went to bed with a book, intending to read for a couple of hours before ringing him. But exhausted by a series of sleepless nights, she dozed off and didn't surface till six next morning, two p.m. in England. She put through a call to Windsor straight away, only to be told by the latest au pair that Sir Adrian was at the teeter.

154

She had forgotten that it was a matinée day; the curtain went up at three. She dialled the operator again and gave the number of the Kean, stressing that her call was urgent, only to be told that all lines to England were suddenly busy and that they'd keep trying.

It was eight a.m., four in the afternoon GMT, when they finally connected her to the doorman.

'Sir Adrian's on stage at the moment, Miss Mallory. Can I take a message, ask him to ring you back?'

Isabel knew that you must never, ever disturb an actor in mid-performance, that news of death or disaster was traditionally withheld until the curtain came down, that the public took precedence over everybody and everything. And after years of accepting those priorities as holy writ, she mentally stamped her foot and said, 'No. I'll hold on for his next exit. Tell the SM to tell him it's about Lady Mallory and I have to speak to him right away.'

'Lady Mallory? She's on stage at the moment as well.' It must be an *Othello* day, with Davina as Desdemona, curse her.

'I'm talking about the real Lady Mallory,' seethed Isabel, all her frustration suddenly coming to the boil. 'The one who is seriously ill in Los Angeles. Send someone to fetch him as soon as he comes off. I'm calling long distance and I'm not hanging up.'

There was a click as she was put on hold. She could well imagine the commotion backstage. Daddy was famed for his trance-like concentration and his refusal to speak to anyone, even in the interval. Woe betide the brave soul who had the temerity to frighten away his muse.

She was just beginning to think that she must have been cut off when a voice said, 'Izzie, what's the matter? Are you all right?'

It was Patrick, who was playing Roderigo.

'Where's my father?'

'They gave him your message. He said he'd ring you back later. What's wrong?'

Isabel was too desperate to resort to euphemism.

'Tell him Mummy's having a breakdown and he's got to come out and help me. Does he have any free days coming up?'

'It's *Man and Superman* from tomorrow until Saturday. That gives him three days off, four including Sunday. I'm sure he'll be on the first plane out, Izzie.' He sounded infinitely reassuring. 'You poor love. You sound at the end of your tether.'

155

'I'm tired, that's all,' croaked Isabel. The sound of sympathy was horribly seductive; the sight of it would have reduced her to a gibbering wreck. Just as well there was six thousand miles of cable between them. 'Thanks, Patrick. Sorry to have disturbed you in the middle of the play.'

'You keep your chin up, now.' And then, sharply, to someone else, 'Sod my bloody cue.'

'You'd better go,' she said.

'Are you sure you're all right now?'

'Yes, I'm fine. Goodbye.'

Patrick's seemed like the first friendly voice she had heard since the storm broke. Isabel began to feel marginally less desperate.

It was three hours later before her father called her back.

'Isabel? What exactly is all this drama about?'

He sounded irritable, the way he always did when family matters intruded on his work. Isabel tried to relate Fay's symptoms without exaggeration, but with sufficient accuracy to convince him that this wasn't just one of the histrionic outbursts she had indulged in throughout their marriage.

'Couldn't this have waited? Did you have to discuss private business with an outsider? One who had the gall to try to lecture me?'

'Lecture you? But –'

'I told young Delaney, and I'm telling you, that it's out of the question for me to come rushing out there when there's nothing useful I can do. I have a meeting with the Arts Council tomorrow, and on Thursday we start rehearsing *Long Day's Journey into Night*. Your mother should be in a hospital, receiving proper care, and you should be back in London completing your studies.'

'But she won't go into a hospital!'

'Then she can be declared incompetent. I suggest you talk to Marty's attorney.'

'But Daddy –'

'They've just called the half, I can't talk any longer.'

He hung up. It was only then that Izzie heard a faint gasp and a second click, followed by a crash from the room above. She raced upstairs to find the extension lying in pieces on the floor of her mother's bedroom and Fay slicing savagely at her wrists with a pair of blunt nail scissors.

156

'Why don't you do what he tells you?' she screamed, as Isabel wrested them from her. 'Why don't you have them put me away, like they put away my mother? Why don't you run home to Daddy and leave me alone?'

Isabel passed an uncomfortable night sharing Fay's bed and letting her cuddle up close, and promising that of course she wouldn't put her away, that she would never leave her alone.

6

January–February 1961

We are all born mad. Some remain so.

> *Samuel Beckett* – Waiting for Godot

Marty had kept a safe in the house, to which Fay had the combination, containing jewellery and several thousand dollars in petty cash. The rest of his assets were temporarily beyond her reach pending the administration of the will, with his attorney making her a subsistence allowance, paying the domestic staff, and settling all incoming bills.

Fay saw this as proof that he was in league with the junior Bauers to defraud her and lost no time in engaging a second lawyer 'to protect our interests', despite Isabel's protests about incurring heavy, and quite unnecessary, legal fees. Meanwhile the telephone continued to ring, with journalists seeking interviews. Desperate to delay her mother finding out how and where Marty had died, Isabel screened all calls herself and issued standing orders to the domestics not to admit any visitors without her prior authorization.

Two mornings after Daddy's disastrous telephone call, Isabel rose later than usual, leaving her mother to sleep off the pills she had finally induced her to swallow at five a.m.

'What's going on out there?' she asked Etta, the black housekeeper, hearing an altercation at the front gate.

'Just some guy shooting a line to try to get into the house. Juan and Billy asked me to call the cops.'

The chauffeur and the gardener-cum-handyman seldom needed any assistance in repelling unwanted callers. But this latest intruder – another freelance hack, no doubt, laying claim to a bogus appointment – was evidently proving more persistent than most.

Isabel went to the window in time to see the policemen slapping a pair of handcuffs on a tall, scruffy young man who looked a bit like . . .

No. It couldn't possibly be. Isabel opened the door for a better look and began walking down the driveway, sure that her eyes must be playing tricks on her. But they weren't.

'Patrick!' she called, as she broke into a run.

He turned to look, still restrained by the two patrolmen, and shouted back, 'Izzie! Will you tell these bloody fools to lay off me?'

'It's all right,' panted Isabel, arriving on the scene, breathless with shock rather than exertion. What on earth was he doing here? 'He's a friend. Please let him go.'

With evident misgivings, they did so. Somehow Patrick managed to glare at them and smile at Isabel simultaneously.

'I never realized it was against the law to walk in this town. I was stopped three times on my way here.'

'You *walked*? Where from?'

'Wherever the airport bus put me down. I had to keep asking for directions. Didn't realize it was so far . . .'

'Sorry, ma'am,' muttered one of the cops, somewhat aggrieved. 'But your men here said you weren't expecting any visitors.'

More to the point, they couldn't believe that anyone quite so uncouth would have legitimate business at the Bauer residence. Patrick was wearing a Brandoesque ensemble of jeans, vest and leather jacket, with a very tattered haversack strapped to his back. A pair of sunglasses served only to make him look shady and sinister, as did the dark unshaven jaw and the subversive CND badge on his lapel.

'I would have got here earlier,' he said as she led him towards the house. 'But I had to waste a whole day hanging around the Embassy waiting for a US visa. Then I missed my connection to Los Angeles and the next flight was full so I had to come via San Francisco, but I got in so late I had to spend the night at the airport.'

'But . . . I don't understand. You said on the phone that *Man and Superman* was on for the rest of the week . . .'

'So it is. The show must go on. Without me.'

'You mean Daddy gave you leave of absence?'

'No. I asked and he wouldn't give it. So I said I was coming anyway and he sacked me.'

'Patrick! But you were doing so well . . .'

'I was getting bored. The Kean isn't really my style. All that fitting in and having to pretend to like people you can't stand, naming no names. And besides, you sounded like you could do with a bit of help.'

'But where on earth did you get the money to come all the way out here?'

He grinned. 'I got lucky on a horse.'

'I thought you didn't believe in betting?'

'I don't. But this time fate obviously meant for me to win.' He whipped off his glasses and treated a bemused Etta to a thousand-volt smile.

'Mr Delaney's very hungry, Etta,' said Isabel. 'Can you get Concha to rustle up something to eat?'

She ushered him into the breakfast room and poured him a glass of orange juice, her hand shaking so much that she spilt some over the cloth.

'It's all right,' said Patrick gently, taking the jug from her. 'I'm here now. You poor love, having to cope with this all on your own.'

'Patrick, I can't believe you've gone and lost your job because of me. What did my father say?'

'It's more a case of what I said to him. I'm afraid my big mouth got the better of me, as usual.'

Isabel wished she had been there to hear it.

'Davina did her best to persuade him to come,' he added, surprising her. 'It would suit her to have him out of the way for a bit, what with Desdemona having it off with Iago. An interesting new interpretation, don't you think?'

'Iago? You mean Brindsley Smythe? Does Daddy know?'

'No, but just about everyone else does. If he ever finds out, you never know your luck, he might just strangle her for real. Now, tell me everything.'

While Patrick tucked into bacon, eggs and pancakes, Isabel gave him an edited version of events, starting on the day after Marty's heart attack, still unable to believe that he was really here. Patrick had come all this way for her sake. Patrick had put her before his work, done what neither her father nor Richard had been prepared to do, people who were supposed to love her . . .

160

'You haven't told me the whole story, have you?' he said. 'You haven't told me the bit about Paula.'

Isabel hesitated. 'Has it been in the English papers?'

'Plastered all over the gutter press. Famous Hollywood producer dies in Malibu love-nest orgy. *Bondage* girl Paula questioned by the police. I rang her, in case she needed a shoulder to cry on, but Richard said she'd moved out.'

'That was her choice,' said Isabel, tight-lipped.

'He gave me another number to ring but Vincent Svengali Parry answered the phone and told me Paula didn't wish to speak to me. That bloke gives me the creeps.'

'I don't want to talk about Paula,' said Isabel uncomfortably. 'If it wasn't for her . . .'

'It takes two, remember,' said Patrick. Isabel scowled. She might have known he'd stick up for her. 'I don't suppose she was the first girl he took to that beach house.'

'None of the other girls he took there were supposed to be my friend, my guest.'

'Come on, Izzie. You would never have found out, if he hadn't gone and died on her. You didn't ought to take it personally. Knowing Paula, she was probably trying to prove something to herself, about what a tough, ambitious cookie she thinks she is. She's pretty cold-blooded when it comes to sex. Or so she likes to believe.'

So cold-blooded about sex that even being raped hadn't put her off it, thought Isabel. Not that she proposed to tell Patrick about the rape. She was glad now that Paula had sworn her to silence on the subject. She didn't want Patrick feeling sorry for Paula. If there was any sympathy going, she wanted it all for herself.

'If you've had enough to eat,' she said, changing the subject, 'I'll show you to your room.'

Unlike Paula, he seemed unimpressed by the grandeur of the house, or perhaps he was just determined not to be. Isabel was just pondering on whether to put him in the bordello suite when she heard a cry of 'Izzie! Izzie?'

She turned to see Fay at the door to her room, clad only in bra, roll-on and stockings, and minus her wig.

'I'll be with you in a minute, Mummy,' said Isabel, trying vainly to shield her *déshabillé* and shepherd her back into her room.

161

'Who's that?' demanded Fay, sidestepping her.

'A friend of Richard's from England. I'll introduce you after you've got dressed . . .'

But Fay brushed aside her restraining arm and advanced towards Patrick regally, evidently unaware that she was half naked, unmade-up, and all but bald.

'How do you do?' she intoned, extending her hand. 'I'm Lady Mallory.' Patrick took the hand and shook it gravely.

'I'm delighted to meet you, Lady Mallory. Patrick Delaney, at your service.'

'Patrick Delaney?' echoed Fay, with one of her unpredictable bursts of lucidity. 'You were in *Antidotage*, weren't you?'

'I had that honour.'

'I do wish I could have seen it,' lamented Fay. 'I was all set to fly to New York but I wasn't well, and then it closed. Izzie, Patrick must be tired and hungry after his journey. I expect he'd like a meal and a nap. Don't worry about me, I'll phone down for Etta to bring up a tray. I'll look forward to seeing you later then, Patrick.'

And with these hospitable overtures she drifted back into her room.

'I'm sorry,' began Isabel, embarrassed. 'You see, on the one hand she can be quite rational and on the other totally . . . bonkers,' she admitted, momentarily unable to think of a circumlocution. She showed him into a room as far away from Fay's as possible, whereupon he dropped his rucksack on the floor and put his arms around her while she wept the first tears she had shed since the nightmare began.

'That's better,' he murmured. 'Have a good cry.'

'You're going to wish you'd never come,' burbled Isabel, clinging to him, her normal barrier of reserve tumbling down. He felt so solid and warm and strong, she was glad of the excuse to touch him. 'It's not as if I can show you round. I daren't leave her alone, for fear of what she'll do next –'

'I didn't come here to go sightseeing. I want you to go back to bed, and sleep, and sleep, until you get rid of those circles under your eyes. Meanwhile leave your mother to me.'

Meekly, Isabel did as she was told, falling back into her bed and sleeping almost instantly, overwhelmed by sheer gratitude. By the time she woke again it was after three.

'Mrs Bauer and Mr Delaney went out,' Etta told her. 'He said you weren't to worry, they were just going for a drive.'

'My mother . . . went out?' Leaving her house vulnerable to invasion by Marty's children?

'It did my heart good to see it. She seems so much better today.'

Isabel showered and dressed, luxuriating in taking her time over it, in being selfish. After two weeks of non-stop babysitting she had already had enough, and that was with servants to cook and clean and launder. Some people devoted their lives to nursing elderly relatives single-handed, getting them dressed and bathing them and spoon-feeding them. Most women had children, from choice, and thought nothing of changing their smelly nappies, mopping up their endless dribble and enduring years of broken nights. She couldn't begin to imagine how they could bear it . . .

She looked out of the window as she heard a car draw up below and saw the chauffeur help her mother out while Patrick emerged from the other side, laden with parcels. Fay was exquisite in a pale yellow silk suit and a saffron-coloured broad-brimmed hat.

'Darling!' she greeted her, as Isabel ran downstairs to meet them. 'Are you feeling better now? We've had such a lovely time. Patrick said he was interested in boats, so we drove out to Marina del Rey and had lunch there and then we did some shopping on our way back . . .'

'Thank you,' she said to Patrick as Fay went upstairs to change for dinner. 'But it won't last. It never does.'

'One day at a time.' He indicated the pile of packages. 'I'm afraid she insisted on taking me to this fancy store and buying me some new clothes. I reckon they thought I was her gigolo.'

'Oh God. I'm sorry. How embarrassing.'

'I couldn't refuse without hurting her feelings.'

'Don't worry. She can afford it.'

'I don't want you to think I came here sponging.'

She realized that he was quite touchy on the subject, that allowing himself to be kitted out with clothes by Mummy had been harder for him by far than losing his job at the Kean.

'My mother loves spending money. If you can bear to wear your new things this evening, it would please her.' She couldn't imagine him looking smart, except in costume. It had been startling to see him as John Tanner in *Man and Superman*, 'carefully dressed' as Shaw had demanded in his stage directions, and wearing 'a frock coat that would befit a prime minister'. Any such garments worn off stage would have collapsed instantly into a thousand creases, but on it they sat as smoothly on him as skin.

'I warn you, you won't recognize me. She's bought me this white suit. I ask you. And a striped seersucker jacket. And a couple of Hawaiian shirts, with palm trees all over them. And a pair of Bermuda shorts. And two-tone shoes . . .'

Isabel laughed for the first time in weeks, just as the telephone began to ring. A moment later Etta appeared and announced that Sir Mallory, as she called him, was on the line from England.

'Tell him I'm busy,' Isabel heard herself saying airily. 'Tell him I'll phone him back some other time.'

'So tell me honestly,' said Isabel later that evening, after Fay, pleasantly exhausted by her outing, had been tucked up in bed. 'What do you think I should do?'

'No, you tell me honestly,' said Patrick. 'What do you want to do? What about your career?'

Isabel hesitated, reluctant to admit her rising panic on the subject of her diploma.

'What about yours? If you've just given up the rest of the season at the Kean, why shouldn't I miss the last two terms at FRIDA?'

Patrick took hold of both her hands, sending shooting sensations up her arms and beyond. She had always, instinctively, avoided touching him till now, even accidentally, as if knowing the effect it would have on her.

'Never mind about the last two terms just yet. Why not give it a few weeks, see how things work out? She might improve. She might agree to come back to England.'

'A few weeks?' And then what? 'Will you . . . that is, how long can you stay?'

'As long as you need me.'

It was the answer she had wanted, and yet it wasn't enough.

'Why?' said Isabel. 'Why are you doing this?'

She met his eyes, eyes which told her exactly why without actually admitting it, eyes that teased and challenged, playing peek-a-boo with the truth.

'I told you. I'd had it up to here with company life. And you know I've always had a soft spot for you, Izzie. Ever since the very first time you turned up your snooty little nose at me.'

'I haven't always been very civil to you, have I? You were right, you know, I'm usually nice to everyone. Even Davina, when I can manage it, just to annoy her.'

'I told you before, I didn't want you to be nice to me.'

'All right then,' said Isabel, steeling herself. 'In that case, what if Paula *had* needed that shoulder of yours to cry on? Would you still be here?'

Ridiculous to be competitive with Paula, over Patrick, and yet she was. For the first time she realized how peeved she had been that Paula had got to him first. Realized how much she had suffered, knowing they were making love in the bedroom next to hers. Realized that poor Neville had become an unwitting substitute for what she had really wanted . . .

'But she didn't need it, did she?' said Patrick. There was a distinct edge to his voice. 'She never has done. She's convinced herself that all I ever wanted her for was sex.' And then, flippantly, 'So naturally I risked a whole week's wages on a multiplier, slung in my job and flew six thousand miles on the off-chance of trying it on with you instead.'

'Even though I'm a nice girl?' He had used his eyes to tease her and now she did it back to him.

'Not any more, you're not. Neville Seaton did my dirty work for me. You can slap my face now, if you like. Not that it'll do much good. I'm as thick skinned as they come.'

Oh but he wasn't, thought Isabel. That swagger of his was like a cloak, hiding the insecurities beneath. In some ways he reminded her of Paula.

Vince hadn't asked for any explanations, hadn't delivered any sermons. Paula would have preferred him to turn against her, like Izzie, instead of standing by her. But the same techniques hadn't worked on him; so far she had courted his anger in vain.

'You've got to snap out of it,' Vince was saying, in that deceptively unemphatic way of his. 'You were bloody awful today at rehearsal.'

'It's not me that's awful, it's the character. I hate her. She's too

165

good to be true.' And yet, despite the saccharine script, the director's notes were always the same. 'Too insipid. More spirit. Remember how badly she wants to live.' But what was the point of wanting to live if you were doomed to die?

'So roughen up her edges a little. You're supposed to be an actress, aren't you? Though lately I've started to wonder.'

'Then replace me. I'm fed up with being pampered and patronized. For the last time, it wasn't your fault I got raped. In any case I'm over it now, otherwise I'd hardly have jumped into bed with Marty, now would I? You don't owe me a living and I don't want your charity.'

Nonetheless she had accepted it, yet again. They were in her new flat, in Cranley Gardens, South Ken, a chunk of which had been acquired and redeveloped by one of Vince's property companies. Paula had moved out of Elizabeth Street the day she got back to London, checked herself into a cheap but still ruinously expensive hotel, and been collected the same night by an implacable Vince, who had installed her, at a nominal rent, in the erstwhile show flat, expensively decorated and furnished to encourage would-be purchasers.

'I'm not in the charity business,' said Vince, helping himself to a drink from the trolley, a glass-and-chrome Italian contraption that Isabel would have loved, along with the shiny white venetian blinds and matt eau-de-nil walls. 'On the contrary, I expect a return on my investment.'

He handed her a straight tonic and sat back with a small glass of scotch. Paula got up and defiantly added a big slug of vodka, setting it down on the coffee table while she lit a cigarette. Vince reached over for her glass and poured its contents into the nearest pot plant.

'You'll kill it,' muttered Paula.

'Better than it killing you. Were you drunk when it happened?'

In the three weeks since her return, it was the first time he'd asked a direct question about that dreadful night.

'Would you rather I had been?'

'No. I think you treat sex and alcohol much the same way. I'm not sure which does you the greater harm. But I suppose it's best not to mix them.'

'Is that why you threw away my drink? So as not to mix them, I

166

mean?' She perched herself on the arm of his chair, letting her skirt ride up high. Damn his ice-cool superiority. How could a man she knew to be violent be so hard to provoke? She wanted to see his fury. She wanted him to punish her. Then she might feel better.

'I like you, Vince,' she murmured, running her hands through his slicked-down hair, the colour of tarnished brass. As usual he was dressed in a stiff pin-striped suit and she longed to see what he hid beneath the disguise. 'And you like me too, don't you?' She began rubbing her nose against his cheek and nuzzling into his neck, while he sat there rigid and unresponsive. She hoped that it was the calm before the storm. That any moment now he would snap, throw her down on the floor and screw the living daylights out of her. And then, at last, she would know where she was with him. And if she hated it, then so much the better. Sex had always left her cold, after all, long before the attack, but that hadn't stopped her doing it . . . except with Patrick. Because with Patrick she had liked it, and liking it was much, much harder to deal with than hating it.

'What do you take me for, Paula?' he said quietly. 'Another cradle-snatcher, like Stan?'

She had wanted him to frighten her and now he had, but not in the way she had expected.

'What the hell do you know about Stan?'

'Not as much as I know about Paula Butcher,' he said calmly. 'Correct me if I go wrong. Born in Stepney, 1943. First known to child welfare authorities at the age of thirteen months, referred by local casualty department following an alleged fall from her cot. Treated for multiple bruises, abrasions, broken ribs, and a dislocated shoulder.'

She couldn't remember any of it, and yet she felt as if she had always known, known long before Marje had told her in that final furious flow of parting poison.

'Mother disappeared after questioning, to avoid possible prosecution. Died the following year of a septic abortion. Child fostered until returned to care of father in 1945, following his discharge from the navy. Married one Marjorie Dean in 1950, deserted family in 1954. Mrs Butcher and Paula evicted for rent arrears and rehoused to Harlow. Case file re-opened following persistent truanting by Paula and an assault on a teacher. Paula readmitted into care in 1957 –'

'How did you find out, you bastard?'

'Finding things out isn't difficult. Confidential information just costs a bit extra, that's all.'

'What the hell do you think you're doing, checking up on me?' With a sudden bolt of fury she hit him hard with a clenched fist across the face. He didn't flinch.

'I was finding out if what your stepmother said about you was true.'

'Marje? You've been talking to that cow, about me?'

'That was the bother I had to sort out over Christmas. Seems that Marje is an avid reader of *Titbits*. She recognized you from that feature they did on you.'

Paula shut her eyes, cursing herself for a pea-brained exhibitionist. She had found herself telling the female reporter that she had lost five stone in weight, and after much persuasion she had shown her the one and only photograph she possessed of her old hideous self, taken by Bea on her box Brownie shortly before Paula had embarked on her diet and long before she had acquired her new nose. She had kept it as a constant reminder of what would happen to her if she ever let up, taken a pride in the journalist's incredulity that this revolting pudding of a girl could possibly be Paula sexpot Dorland. Lulled by flattery, she had allowed her to take the picture away, to be copied . . .

'Well, Marje is down on her luck, it seems,' continued Vince, dabbing his bleeding nose with a starched white handkerchief, 'and thought she'd try her hand at a spot of blackmail. She wrote to you care of Renegade. I'm afraid I was taking the precaution of intercepting all your post, just in case there were any more perverts gunning for you.'

He withdrew a letter from his pocket and handed it to her. It was ill-written on cheap lined paper in leaking ballpoint.

Dear Paula 'Dorland'
Well I suppose you think you're very clever making lots of money taking your clothes off in public and behaving like the cheap little scrubber you always were. I bet Titbits would be interested to know a bit more about you. If you'd prefer to buy my story instead of them you better let me know. Otherwise, you can look forward to reading plenty more about yourself in future.

'What . . .' She hardly dared ask the question. 'What did you do?'

'I went to see her. Flashed a wad of tenners at her and asked just what kind of information she had for sale and how much she wanted for it. She couldn't stop talking, thought she was going to get a big pay-off there and then.'

'Oh God,' said Paula.

'Don't worry, you won't be hearing from her again. I made her position very clear to her. By the time I left she was swearing blind that it had all been a little joke.'

Paula turned away, unable to meet his eye.

'What else did she say about me?'

'Suppose you tell me.'

It was a challenge, not a request. For a long time she didn't speak while he sat there patiently waiting, holding the blood-stained handkerchief to his nose. His blood was incredibly red. She wanted to lick it away, she wanted to taste it, to steal his strength and make it her own.

'I was thirteen when Stan moved in,' she began. 'He was supposed to be a lodger. Not that the neighbours were fooled, I mean we only had the two bedrooms. Stan did shifts. Sometimes he'd be home in the afternoons, when Marje was working and I was playing hookey. He was good to me. He'd buy me presents. Sweets, chocolate, books. I mean, magazines. You know, *True Confessions* and stuff. He'd say nice things to me, like what lovely big brown eyes I had. Pathetic, really.'

She poured herself another drink to give herself the courage to remember, and this time he didn't stop her.

'I didn't really want to do it, the first time, but I thought if I didn't he'd stop being nice to me. He said we had to keep it secret, because if anyone found out they'd put him in nick and lock me up in a children's home. What I'm saying is, he never forced me. I let him do it.'

She looked out of the window, keeping her back to him.

'Then Marje came home early one day and caught us on the job. She went for me like a mad thing, got hold of me by the hair and threw me down the stairs. I came to in the hospital, with concussion and a broken ankle and collar bone. And the next thing I know they're telling me I'm in the club. The baby was okay, on account of being so well padded, I suppose.

'Marje came to the hospital, to tell me she wasn't having me back. That's when she told me what happened when I was a baby, and about my mum dying of an abortion because she couldn't face having another one like me. Stan had scarpered by that time, to avoid getting had up. He was right about one thing though. They locked me up, in a mother and baby home, till it was born. And then they moved me to some other dump, and then I ran away.'

'I know,' said Vince. 'You don't have to tell me any more.'

'Yes I do. I wanted that baby. Because it was *mine*. But I was scared that I wouldn't be able to love it, that I'd treat it the way my mother treated me. Marje said that my mother hated me, that she'd knocked me about because I wouldn't stop whining. And I kept thinking, what if the same thing happened again? What if I ended up wanting to beat its brains out? So I let them take it off me, as soon as it was born. I never even saw it. Her. I didn't even give her a name. That's all and don't you remind me ever again.'

'I'm not going to. More importantly neither will anyone else.'

His voice was muffled by the handkerchief, his nose still leaking blood.

'God,' muttered Paula. 'Did I hurt you?'

'I don't hurt that easy.' He pulled her down beside him and kissed the top of her head, very lightly, making her scalp tingle, making her want to cry. 'And don't ever try to vamp me again, okay? Like I said, I only sleep with grown-ups. Inside you're still thirteen years old. And until you stop hating yourself you always will be.'

'What's the alternative? Liking myself? Do *you* like yourself?'

'Let's just say I know myself.'

'Is anyone else allowed to know you? What would I find out if I went digging up the dirt on you?'

'That I made my money on the black market, and then in illegal gambling clubs, and protection rackets. But that's all in the past. Everything I do now is legal. Well, almost everything.'

'I'd worked that out already. That you'd been a villain, I mean. What else would I find out about your murky past?'

'Nothing,' said Vince, giving her one of those rare smiles of his. 'So you'll just have to wait for me to tell you.'

*

170

Patrick had an almost magical ability to humour Fay out of the most capricious moods. It was as if he had been called upon to improvise in some incomprehensible avant-garde play and adapted himself instinctively to its surrealistic logic and staccato rhythms.

Certainly non-stop attention had done her more good than drugs. And as long as she was progressing with her imaginary lawsuit ('That attorney I found was just out to rook me, darling, Patrick's found me another one who's so much nicer') and instructing her new representative at length (Patrick on the downstairs extension talking jargon with a flawless West Coast accent) her paranoia remained manageable, offset by periods of apparent normality, when she became the old witty, acerbic Fay, a born raconteuse and indomitable performer, playing up to her new captive audience and basking happily in his applause.

Daddy hadn't phoned again – incensed, no doubt, at Patrick's interference in family affairs. Richard had rung once, sounding conciliatory at first, then defensive, then hostile.

'You're letting Fay manipulate you, as usual,' he had said. 'As for Patrick, he's getting a free holiday out of it and the chance to bed both of you, I shouldn't wonder, assuming he hasn't already . . .'

Whereupon Isabel had hung up on him and they hadn't spoken since.

Meanwhile the respite afforded by Patrick was proving to be two-edged. Isabel had begun to feel excluded, redundant, and most of all neglected. Fay monopolized all his attention. Sometimes, after one of her outings with Patrick, dressed to the nines and leaving Isabel to 'guard the house', she would return so glowing with manic *joie de vivre* that Isabel began to harbour gut-wrenching doubts, doubts she could never have brought herself to voice aloud, as Richard had so crudely done.

She looked at her watch for the third time in ten minutes; Patrick and her mother were late. Fay had insisted on spending the day at – horrors – the Malibu beach house, and as usual Isabel had been left behind on sentry duty. The chauffeur hadn't accompanied them on this occasion; Fay had given him the day off. Isabel had begun to worry that they had had an accident, but that didn't stop her worrying about something else altogether.

171

She had flattered herself that he had come here for her, that Fay was just an excuse. And resolved not to make things too easy for him, reluctant to end up as just another notch in his belt. She had steeled herself to make him sweat, never dreaming that he would make her sweat instead, that he might actually prefer the company of her mother . . .

They arrived home just before eleven, having stopped off for a leisurely dinner on the way home. Fay was bright-eyed but obviously worn out; her face was beginning to sag and her movements to become jerky.

'Goodnight, Patrick darling,' she cooed, kissing him on each cheek. 'Izzie, will you come up and help me undress? I'm so exhausted I can hardly move.'

Isabel didn't dare look at Patrick, for fear he would read her face.

'It's been such a beautiful day,' sighed Fay as Isabel unzipped her dress and helped her struggle out of her roll-on. 'Oh, I'm so looking forward to going home!'

'Going home? You mean –'

'Patrick spoke to that nice lawyer again. All the money side of things has been sorted out at last. So there's really nothing to keep me here any longer . . . Can you keep a secret?'

'Of course,' said Isabel automatically, too relieved at her mother's change of heart to smell what was coming next.

'I'm afraid Daddy has a shock coming to him.' She smiled a slow, satisfied smile. 'Patrick didn't want me to tell you till we got back home, but I can't keep it to myself any longer. He and I are getting married.'

All Isabel's thespian training deserted her.

'You and Patrick?'

'I know he's younger than me, but love transcends age.' And then, seeing Isabel's horrified expression, 'Oh dear. I might have known you'd disapprove. I suppose you think I'm old and ugly and that he's only after my money! And I did so want you to be happy for me . . .' Two large teardrops trembled jewel-like before trickling with glycerine gracefulness down her cheeks.

'Don't cry, Mummy,' said Isabel, struggling to control her features. 'I'm surprised, that's all.' It was just another absurd delusion . . . wasn't it?

'He's such a wonderful lover,' said Fay, dabbing her eyes with a tissue. It was as if she were playing a scene, every little bit of business executed with perfect co-ordination. 'Young men have so much stamina. To tell you the truth, darling, Marty couldn't really satisfy me. Not after a virile man like Daddy. But Patrick . . . oh, I've never known anything like it!' She lay back sensuously on the bed, in her slip, and stretched her arms above her head. 'He's taught me so many new things. Did you and Neville ever . . . oh, I have to whisper it! It's simply too wicked for words.'

Isabel sat trapped while Fay filled her ears with the purest pornography, unable to think of an excuse to flee. She had to endure ten solid minutes of girl-talk before Fay fell asleep in mid-sentence, by which time an excess of vivid detail had crowded out any self-indulgent doubts. It was hideous to hear her own most secret, shameful fantasies translated into another woman's reality . . .

She covered her mother with the quilt and took refuge in her bedroom where she lay down in her clothes, trembling with fury, jealousy, and worst of all the same crippling sexual desire which had been tormenting her for weeks now, hotter and more intense than ever . . .

'Izzie?' There was a gentle tap on her door. Isabel didn't respond. 'Izzie, are you asleep?'

'Go away.'

'What's the matter? Aren't you well? I thought you were coming back downstairs? Are you decent?' The door opened a fraction. 'Ready or not, here I come.' Isabel sat up and switched on the light.

'What do you want?' she demanded, repressing an urge to physically attack him.

Patrick pulled up a chair and sat down.

'I want to know what's biting you. For the last week or so you've hardly addressed a civil word to me. If I'm outstaying my welcome, just say so.'

'That's not my privilege. You're my mother's guest, not mine. She'd be devastated if you left,' she added icily, watching his face for a reaction.

He frowned. 'Do you think I've made her too dependent on me? That is, I was trying to make her dependent, but only so that when we went home she'd want to come too.'

173

'Well, you've succeeded. She's just told me about her plans to go back to England.'

'She told you what?' He whistled. 'Well, that's news to me.'

Not for the first time, Isabel felt as if she were the one who was going mad.

'You don't say. And now will you kindly let me get some sleep?'

He sighed and moved himself from the chair to the bed. Isabel stiffened.

'You silly girl,' he said softly, almost tauntingly. 'You're jealous.'

'Jealous? What would I have to be jealous about, exactly?'

'Look, I get embarrassed, same as you, the way your mother flirts with me. But there's no harm in it. It's good for her morale, she likes to have male attention. And it's all perfectly innocent. I've made it crystal clear to her that I'm involved with somebody else.'

Isabel gave a snort of derision.

'My mother's life is littered with discarded wives and mistresses. With all due respect to your fiancée, I doubt if Fay would regard her as serious competition.'

'Perhaps I should have told her the truth then. But I was scared of making a fool of myself. I still am. Isabel –' Incredibly, he blushed. She would never have believed Patrick capable of blushing. 'You must know very well that it's you I love. Why else would I have come out here? Why else would I have stayed this long?'

She looked into his eyes and they were so direct, so honest, so full of redeeming, reassuring hope that she blurted out, 'You mean it's not true?'

'Is what not true?'

'She said . . .' Now it was her turn to blush. 'She said that you and she were getting married and that you'd told her not to tell me. That you'd spent the whole day making love.'

Patrick didn't answer for a moment. He looked . . . amused.

'You seriously thought I was having an affair with Fay?' He threw back his head and laughed in delight. 'But Izzie, she's mad as a hatter! And even if she wasn't . . . she's your mother!'

'I'm sorry,' muttered Isabel, feeling ridiculous. 'But she's an actress, remember. She made it sound so horribly convincing . . .'

174

'It's all right,' he said, looking at her in something like triumph. 'I'm glad you were jealous, because now you know what it feels like. Now you know what I went through last summer, when you were with Neville Seaton.'

She didn't get time to wonder if he had planned it that way, used her mother as a pawn, because then he began kissing her, obliterating her power to think. First her fingers, one by one, and then the palms of her hands, then her eyes, then her cheeks, then her neck, before moving in on her mouth and swallowing her whole. It was like getting into a bath that was slightly too hot, first standing cautiously, then kneeling, then sitting, then lying, feeling its healing warmth penetrate blood and bone, and then finding that it wasn't quite warm enough, that you needed to run in more melting, soothing heat, bury your head beneath its bobbing surface, sink deep into its dark and roaring silence . . .

With Neville she had striven so hard to learn, to improve, to please. But with Patrick she didn't need to. This pleasure seemed inevitable, a force beyond her control. Where Neville had been precise, practised, skilful, Patrick was spontaneous, ebullient, unselfconscious. Where Neville had drained her dry, Patrick filled her full of life. Patrick had a way of making it all seem innocent, uncomplicated, joyful, all the things it had never been before, by choice. She had been happy, yes, but in an unreal, secret kind of way. That happiness had closed around her, limiting her. This happiness set her free . . .

'Say you love me too,' he whispered, holding her mercilessly at the very edge, torturing her, torturing himself. 'Say it.'

'Don't stop, Patrick, please don't stop . . .'

'Say it.' He withdrew slightly and kept very still, making her squirm with panic. 'Say it.'

And then she said it, said what she must surely have known from the very first moment she saw him.

'There's method in it, you know,' he murmured, much later, having forced her to say it twice more. 'If you say something often enough, you end up believing it. That's the secret of the Catechism. Constant repetition.'

'Faith not reason?'

175

'Oh, reason's got nothing to do wih it. Listen, about Teresa . . .'

'I know,' said Isabel, not wanting to think about her rival. 'Paula told me all about her. You don't have to give me the speech as well.'

'It's her I've got to make a speech to. I mean, none of the others mattered, they wouldn't have made any difference, but you . . .'

'Paula mattered, didn't she?'

'Yes. But she wasn't supposed to. And she doesn't any more. And besides, *I* never mattered to *her*. I'm going to write to Terry tomorrow . . .'

'There's no need,' said Isabel touchily, reluctant to admit how insanely jealous she was of Teresa, of Paula, of every woman he had ever known. 'I'm not a home-breaker, whatever it looked like with Neville.'

'Will you listen to me? I was never in love with her. I didn't know what love felt like until you. And now that I do –'

There was a sound of a door clicking open.

'That's Mummy,' hissed Isabel. 'Oh God. She must be sleep-walking again.' She had been in such a state when she left Fay that she had quite forgotten to lock her in.

'Izzie?' There was a perfunctory rap on the door and Fay walked in, still in her slip, too quickly for either of them to cover their nakedness. For a moment she stood, transfixed, staring at them, evidently wide awake, worse luck.

'Izzie,' repeated Fay faintly, as Isabel threw the sheet over Patrick and reached hastily for her dressing gown. 'Izzie, I don't feel very well.'

'It's all right, Mummy. Come on, let me take you back to bed.' She led her to her room like a blind person. Fay crawled between the covers and let Isabel tuck her up.

'I'm sorry about that, Mummy,' she said matter of factly, hoping that Fay would have forgotten her earlier fantasy. 'We didn't mean to embarrass you.'

'How stupid of me,' whimpered Fay, 'to think he would prefer me to you. I suppose it's all I deserve. I've been such a wicked woman, all my life . . .' She tailed off as Patrick, now fully dressed, appeared in the doorway.

'Patrick –' began Isabel, dreading a hideous scene. Undeterred, he sat down on the other side of the bed and took Fay's hand.

'Listen to me, Fay. I love Izzie. That's why I came here. And because I love Izzie, I love you too. You know that. But you also know that I never laid a hand on you, that there's never been anything like that between us. Now isn't that right?'

Fay looked away, ashamed. Then she said bleakly, 'I'm going mad, aren't I? Just like my mother.'

'Don't use that word, Mummy,' said Isabel. 'You're just ill, that's all. When we get home, everything will be all right, you'll see. We'll find you a lovely house and come to see you all the time . . .'

'Will you? Will you really? I wouldn't be a burden?'

'Of course not,' said Isabel, too eager to get back to England to think beyond it.

'I could go to see our old doctor, in Chelsea,' mused Fay. 'He was such a nice man, always so sympathetic. Perhaps he can help me get better. I will get better, won't I, once I'm home?'

'Of course you will, Mummy.'

Fay turned to Patrick. 'Did you mean what you said just now? Do you really and truly love her?'

'With all my heart,' said Patrick, unembarrassed.

'And you love him too, Izzie?' quavered Fay, like a vicar soliciting the marriage vows.

Isabel coloured, remembering the last time she had said it.

'Yes, Mummy,' she mumbled.

'I'm so glad. You make such a beautiful couple. Now run along. I'm quite all right now. Tomorrow we'll book our flight home, together. Everything will be all right, once we get home. Goodnight my darlings. Kiss kiss.'

They both bent to kiss her and she put both arms around them. Then they tucked her up like a child and left her to sleep, and this time Isabel remembered to lock the door.

Isabel awoke next morning to a mixture of hope and fear. Hope that the nightmare was nearly over, fear that Fay would either have changed her mind or retain no memory of what she had said last night.

She propped herself up on one elbow and looked at a still sleeping Patrick. It was scary, falling in love with someone like him. With Neville she had always felt in control, but Patrick dominated her absolutely, this time she wouldn't be calling the tune. That was part of the thrill of it. That and the attraction of opposites. Patrick was spur of the moment, irresponsible, care-free. She was a born planner, prudent and perfectionist and pessimistic. Objectively, she could see that they weren't remotely well suited, but for the moment she didn't want to be objective. She just wanted to carry on being happy . . .

He continued to sleep soundly while she showered and dressed and picked up his discarded clothes off the floor. She folded his new white trousers and jacket neatly over a chair, leaned across the bed and licked his face, making barking noises.

'What are you doing dressed?' he grumbled sleepily, pulling her down beside him. 'Come back to bed.'

'No. It's after ten already. I'm going down to fetch Mummy's tray. Let's both have breakfast with her, in her room, and try to carry on where we left off last night.'

'What, in front of her?'

'Be serious! Hurry up. Breakfast in ten minutes, okay?'

She tripped downstairs to fetch Fay's customary juice, coffee, and dry toast and asked for two cooked breakfasts for herself and Patrick to be brought up to Mrs Bauer's room. She laid the tray just so, with a starched white cloth and napkin, silver coffee pot, and the Royal Worcester china and Waterford crystal that Mummy had brought from home, and garnished it with a hothouse bloom from the flower arrangement in the living room, tweaking each item to the right and the left, as if the perfect order of her presentation could inspire a similar tidiness in her mother's muddled mind.

Setting down the tray on the table outside the bedroom, she knocked, turned the key and opened the door.

Fay was standing with her back to her, on the window ledge, both casements flung wide and the light lace curtains blowing around her, like a shroud, in the incoming breeze.

'Mummy!' shouted Isabel, thinking that she was about to jump. 'Mummy, don't!'

Fay turned, startled. Isabel ran towards her, arms outstretched,

178

realizing a fraction too late that she was asleep, not suicidal. Still locked in her dream, Fay screamed in sudden terror and took a single step backwards, into the void.

'Not a dry eye in the house,' commented Paula, dry-eyed, as the cast hugged and kissed each other to the sound of the last dying bravo. She fled to her dressing room, locked herself in, and took a big swallow of vodka. A moment later Vince knocked on the door. She put the bottle out of sight.

'Are you all right in there?'

'Of course I'm all right. Have you . . .' She gulped and cleared her throat. 'Have you heard any more?'

'Will you let me in?'

She did so, tearing off her stage clothes right in front of him, throwing on a wrap, and slapping Cremine all over her face prior to making up for the first-night party, waiting for him to tell her the worst.

'There's been no more news,' he said finally. 'The last we heard she was still in surgery. Richard's waiting by the telephone. I was with him in the flat for most of Act Two.'

Richard's first-night telegram was stuck to the mirror: 'I know you're "dying" for a big success. Much love, R.' He would have been here now, taking off her death scene with cynical glee. And instead he was sitting at home waiting for news of a real-life death, one which had happened, however indirectly, thanks to her.

She removed Richard's telegram and dropped it in the bin. Another friend gone, if he had any sense. Patrick's was already in there. 'May the Snowdrops keep blooming.' Did Isabel know he had sent it? Had they discussed it together? Or was Patrick simply hedging his bets against the day when Izzie dumped him, the way she had dumped Neville Seaton? She hoped for Izzie's sake that she would. She might have known that Patrick was just biding his time. It had been Izzie he had wanted all along . . .

Vince stood watching her while she applied her street make-up, lacquered her hair, and stepped into a plain, classy little black dress. The effect was demure, almost prim.

'Do you want to go round to Richard's place?'

'Better not. I might get my mucky fingerprints on Izzie's silk wallpaper. And besides, I'm queen of the party. Can't miss out on my moment of glory.'

She didn't have the courage to face Richard, couldn't bear for him to insist that it wasn't her fault. Knowing that, perhaps, Vince didn't press her.

'What's the word on the critics?' said Paula, dousing herself with duty-free Chanel No. 5.

'Harold Hobson had his hanky out.'

'Perhaps he was bored to tears.'

'I had my spies eavesdropping in the intervals. The consensus seems to be that the play is corny but that you were very affecting. They couldn't believe it was the same girl who played Serafina.'

'Ah, so I'm versatile. That's bad. Only character actresses are versatile. Stars always play themselves. Well, tell Richard how sorry I am and all that, won't you?'

'I'll catch you up later, take you home.'

'No need. Simon's already offered.'

Simon Fisk, the author of *Snowdrops*, was an outspoken critic of the kitchen-sink trend in theatre and cinema and a fervent fan of the old-fashioned well-made play. Thanks to his snobbish contempt for tabloid scandalmongering, he had taken Paula's part in the wake of the Marty Bauer affair, thinking, no doubt, that she would not be averse to showing her appreciation. So far he hadn't got lucky, but tonight, perhaps, she would reward him.

Vince looked at her stonily, but he didn't comment, other than to say, 'Don't drink too much, okay?' Meaning 'don't sleep with him', of course. Sod you, thought Paula defiantly. I'll drink as much as I like and I'll screw who I like and you're not going to stop me. She wasn't a kid, whatever he thought. Tonight she felt very, very old.

She arrived at the party late, on Simon's arm, after holding court in her dressing room to a stream of well-wishers, putting in her second performance of the evening. Now she embarked on her third, laughing and smiling to order, accepting fulsome compliments from people she knew despised her, and drinking one glass of champagne after another with scant regard for the filthy hangover she would have tomorrow morning. By the time the papers were brought in, she intended to be past caring. Nonetheless, when she saw them arrive she fled, in terror, to the Ladies',

180

where she threw up till the room had stopped revolving and sat dizzily in the privacy of a cubicle, crunching Polos until she felt better. Or rather, not quite so bad.

She was just trying to dredge up enough nerve to go out and face the music when she heard a chorus of voices on the other side of the door as a gaggle of women came in.

'Poor Simon. If it wasn't for him that little scrubber wouldn't have a part at all. And she gets all the credit!'

'Perhaps she sleeps with theatre critics as well as film producers.'

'Well, the way they're drooling about her it must have been a regular gang-bang.'

'Nothing would surprise me. Specially with an East End spiv like Vincent Parry for a pimp.'

'As for poor Fay Burnett . . .' Paula felt herself gagging again. The news must have broken. She could just imagine the headlines. *Grieving widow's death leap. Film star riddle – accident or suicide?* Either way, she felt as if she had pushed her.

She waited for the neighbouring cisterns to flush and the venomous voices to slither away. By the time she emerged nearly everyone had gone and an impatient Simon was waiting with her coat. His usual self-satisfied smirk had given way to a petulant scowl. The reviews had obviously rattled him. Ill-humouredly, he took her arm and hustled her into his car.

'Congratulations,' he growled. 'You're a star.'

'Same to you. It was your play.'

'A play of stunning banality, elevated to poetry by the sheer radiance of your performance. But for the gritty, spunky edge you gave to the part, the whole proceedings would have drowned in a mire of cheap sentimentality.'

Paula began to laugh. I wish you could have seen me tonight, Bea, she thought. I really proved I was a pro. I made death look artistic and uplifting and dignified. I lied. I lied and I knew I was lying and no one rumbled me . . .

'What's the joke?' demanded Simon, unamused.

'The joke? The joke is . . . that the audience loved it.'

'Loved you, you mean.'

'Oh no. Not me. It wasn't me up there tonight. I'm an actress, remember? I don't exist.'

'I'm the one who doesn't exist. I'm only the bloody playwright.'

'Oh, stop griping. As long as people talk about it, never mind what they say.'

'Talking of which, did you see the stop press, about Fay Burnett taking a running jump?'

If she hadn't known, this was hardly a tactful way to break the news.

'Richard Mallory rang Vince at the theatre and they put the call through to my dressing room. I picked up the phone.' Richard hadn't meant for her to know till after the performance, but he was in such a state of shock that it had been easy to worm it out of him. 'Just before I went on.'

'God. Well, it didn't show. You're a hard bitch, aren't you?'

'Reinforced concrete. Want to come in?' she added, as he drew up outside the flat.

'Vince isn't going to burst in on us, is he?'

'Why should he?'

'Come off it. Everyone knows about you and him.' Nonetheless he followed her inside.

'Well, everyone's wrong.'

'You don't say? I would never have put him down for a fairy. Are he and Richard Mallory. . . ?'

'No. And even if they were, you can take the sneer out of your voice. At least until you've proved you're not one yourself.'

She reinforced her challenge by kicking off her shoes and stepping out of her dress. He grabbed hold of her roughly and gave her a wet, boozy, bruising kiss. Paula closed her teeth around his tongue and bit it, making him yelp with pain.

'What did you do that for?'

'My, but you do scare easy. Don't tell me you make love the way you write plays.'

It probably wouldn't have worked if he'd been sober, or if he'd got the good reviews instead of her. But in his present mood it worked almost too well. He tore at the cheap chain-store underwear – Paula still couldn't bring herself to spend good money on things that didn't show – and pushed her down onto the floor, slipping his braces as he did so. Paula reached out a hand and felt him.

'Not exactly ready, are you?' she taunted. 'What was that word the critics used? Oh yes. Limp.' And then, thank God, he lost his temper and slapped her across the face. It didn't hurt much, unfortunately. But it was a start.

'Is that the best you can manage?' mocked Paula. 'That wasn't much harder than your cock, was it?'

He slapped her again. Strange how right it felt. Or rather, not strange at all. This was what she had been born to. Good children were rewarded, bad ones got themselves punished . . .

But Simon wasn't drunk enough, or quite angry enough, to give her what she thought she deserved. Seeing the strange glitter in her eyes, he pulled away from her, muttering, 'Christ. I have to get out of here.' He got unsteadily to his feet. 'You made me do that. You enjoyed it. You're bloody sick, that's what you are.'

Paula lay there in a posture of insolent abandon and watched him slam out of the flat. Then she rolled over and covered her face with her hands, overcome with self-disgust and self-knowledge. Inside you're still thirteen years old, Vince had said. Thirteen months, more like.

Never again. However strong the urge might be, never again would she play the victim. It was a matter of pride, rather than fear. Why ask someone else to punish her when she could do it so much better all by herself?

'Mummy? It's Izzie.'

Fay didn't respond. A dribble of saliva oozed out of the corner of her mouth.

'She can't hear you,' said the nurse gently. 'Don't distress yourself. She's not in any pain.'

For two weeks Isabel had done nothing but sit by her mother's bedside, holding her hand, talking to her, playing her favourite music, trying to bring her out of her coma. And eventually, miraculously, Fay's eyes had opened, against all expectation. But they hadn't recognized Isabel, any more than Isabel recognized her mother.

The living corpse that lay before her was unable to speak, or understand, or communicate. Fay would be an infant for the rest of her life. A life that might drag on well into old age. Her heart was strong and her broken body would heal as good as new. Only her brain was damaged beyond repair.

183

If only, thought Isabel. If only she hadn't locked her in that night. Had Fay rattled the door to her prison before choosing another exit? If only she had heard her. If only she had thought to lock the window too. If only she hadn't shouted and startled her, she would have been able to pull her to safety before she lost her balance. If only she hadn't signed that consent form, hadn't let them operate on her shattered skull. She remembered how Paula had given Bea that morphine, helped her choose her own dignified moment to die. And now she, Isabel, had effectively done the reverse, sentenced her mother to a living death. If only she had the guts to smother her with her pillow . . .

She had said as much to Patrick, hoping for his collusion, but he had gone all Catholic on her and said it was murder. 'No one's got the right to play God, whatever the reason. And besides, they'd do a post mortem and have you up for it.'

And since then he hadn't left her alone with her mother for a minute, he had watched her like a hawk.

All she could do for her now was take her back home, instal her in the best nursing home Marty's money could buy, visit every week to make sure they were looking after her properly. And try not to feel guilty that she was free, at last, to work again . . .

Work. She longed for it as never before. Patrick was doing his best for her, but Patrick wasn't enough, love wasn't enough. Love made you weak, work made you strong. Work was the only thing that could save her.

7

Spring–Autumn 1961

Marry'd in haste, we may repent at leisure.

William Congreve – The Old Bachelor

'I can't do it,' said Richard. 'I can't go in.'

'Yes you can,' said Paula, removing the cellophane-wrapped bouquet from the rear seat of her brand-new Mini. She had passed the test first time, thanks to Vince, who had sent his chauffeur to give her an intensive course of instruction. The car didn't belong to her; it was owned, taxed, insured and maintained by one of Vince's companies.

Taking Richard's hand firmly in hers she led the way up the shallow steps, flanked by stone balustrades, to the gleaming brass-embellished front door. Fay's home was now a Home, though it looked like a country house hotel, a gracious Regency building in mellow sandstone set amidst lawns and shrubberies and surrounded by parkland. Richard and Isabel had applied jointly to the Court of Protection to act as Fay's receivers and manage her estate, every penny of which was to be devoted to her care and comfort, for the rest of her unnatural life.

The lobby was carpeted in a thick soft green, springy as turf, and the hospital smell was deodorized by flowers, arranged everywhere in artful profusion. The receptionist summoned Fay's full-time minder by telephone; a few moments later she came out to greet them and made plummy small talk as she led the way to Fay's lavishly appointed suite.

Fay was seated in a wheelchair by an open french window, enjoying the warm spring day. Or perhaps not enjoying it, it was impossible to tell. She was wearing a loose-fitting shift in brilliant peacock blue, sheer stockings and spindly, high-heeled shoes; her make-up was immaculately applied and her wig carefully styled, as

185

per Isabel's strict instructions. Her expression was blank as the nurse showed her the flowers and told her, in cooing kiddispeak, that she had visitors. Richard held back, afraid to approach her. This was the first time he had seen his mother since the accident, despite repeated pleas from Isabel and holier-than-thou harangues from Patrick.

'I'll leave you to chat, then, while I put these in water,' said the sitter, as if Fay were capable of conversation. 'Press the bell if you need me.'

Responding to a look from Paula, Richard pulled up a chair.

'Hello Mummy,' he said. There was no response. He picked up a hand, recently manicured and much beringed, and kissed it awkwardly. But Fay just continued to stare, apparently fascinated by the billowing yellow blanket of daffodils clothing the grassy bank opposite her window.

'We had terrific reviews for *Kill Claudio*,' began Richard desperately. 'It's transferring to the West End next month, the Renegade isn't big enough to meet demand.'

Fay turned her head and looked at him, but with no sign of recognition. A trickle of saliva dribbled from the corner of her mouth. God, thought Paula, if it wasn't for me . . .

She blinked back the tears for Richard's sake, afraid she might set him off too. In private she could indulge as much as she liked in guilt and self-loathing, but when Richard was around her role was to cheer him up. It was her way of thanking him for refusing to blame her, for still treating her as a friend. After they left here they would go back to Cranley Gardens together and laugh themselves silly over nothing while they got very, very drunk.

Richard had sworn to stay fifteen minutes, but after five or so of valiant ad-libbing he dried.

'Mummy, I have to go now. But –'

His parting speech was interrupted by a perfunctory tap on the door. Without waiting for an answer, Isabel came in, closely followed by Patrick. Paula felt all the breath rush out of her lungs at the sight of him. He was wearing dark glasses and a raffish white suit, rather grubby round the cuffs and turn-ups, an outfit which made him look like a South American gangster.

'I didn't know you were going to be here,' said Isabel to Richard. 'It's silly both of us visiting the same day.'

'I phoned to tell you last night but there was no answer.' Oppressed by Patrick's unwelcome presence in the Elizabeth Street flat, Richard often stayed the night at Paula's place rather than go home.

'Hello, Paula love,' said Patrick. 'How are you?' He gave her a routine theatrical hug.

'All right.' And then, with an effort, 'Hello, Izzie.'

She looked pale and tired, unlike Patrick who had the sleek look of a jungle cat replete from a recent kill.

'Paula,' acknowledged Isabel stiffly, her good manners getting the better of her. They hadn't seen each other since Christmas. 'Show going well?'

'Better than it deserves to.'

Patrick crouched down in front of Fay.

'Hello darling,' he said softly. 'My, but you're looking beautiful today.' The effect was sudden and grotesque.

'Pa,' gurgled Fay, baby-like. Her face lit up and her features contorted into a twisted smile. 'Pa! Pa!'

This infantile display was infinitely more shocking than a blank lack of response. Richard turned away, appalled.

'How about a little walk?' said Patrick, unembarrassed, wiping the spittle from her chin with his handkerchief. It was easy for him, thought Paula. Fay wasn't his mother. 'Look what a lovely day it is! Let's have a spin.' He took hold of the wheelchair. 'Coming, Izzie?'

'No, I'll wait here.' A look passed between them, signifying an unspoken question on Patrick's part and an answer on Isabel's. Isabel held the door open wide; pivoting Fay round, Patrick wheeled her out of the room, her face frozen into an asinine rictus of pleasure.

'Patrick's very good with her,' said Isabel, almost apologetically. 'She seems to . . . Excuse me.'

She made a sudden bolt for the adjoining bathroom. There was a sound of taps running.

'She looks awful,' said Paula.

'She's just been given the lead in the July show,' said Richard dismissively. 'She's worrying herself sick about it already. You know what Izzie's like.'

No, thought Paula, I don't. Not any more. Not now that she's with Patrick. Perhaps I never did. But what she did know, from first-hand experience, was how possessive and possessing Patrick could be, and how hard she had had to fight to retain her independence. Was Izzie going through it too? Izzie, who was infinitely more private, more inaccessible, more unsuited to Patrick in every way?

'Are you all right?' said Paula, as Isabel emerged, whey-faced, from the bathroom.

Isabel fell to examination of her nails. 'You may as well know now as later,' she said. 'Patrick and I are getting married. I'm expecting a baby in October.'

There was a moment of statutory silence, as if to let some unseen audience absorb the impact of her revelation before the other characters picked up their cues. A baby, thought Paula with a pang. Izzie was having Patrick's baby.

'You can't be serious,' said Richard. 'You can't go having a baby now. Have you gone mad?'

'Amazingly enough, I haven't,' said Isabel coldly. 'No thanks to you, I might add.'

'The bastard. I ought to lay him out. How could you be so stupid? You hate babies, you know you do. You've always said you didn't want any.'

'Well, I've changed my mind.'

'Patrick's changed it for you, you mean, like the good Catholic he is. Have you told Adrian?'

'Not yet. I thought I'd treat this as a rehearsal, get some pointers. You two are so alike it isn't true.'

The insult hit home, but it didn't stop him reinforcing the comparison by saying, 'And what are you going to live on? Are you going to expect the old man to carry on supporting you? Or ask the Court of Protection for a handout from Fay? Or is Patrick actually going to deign to work for a change?'

Isabel's eyes flashed. Paula knew that this wasn't the first row they'd had on the subject of Patrick, rows that Patrick encouraged with that strangely innocent guile of his, casting Adrian and Richard as the villains of the piece, himself as the injured hero.

'Patrick's had several offers of work,' said Isabel icily. 'None of them has been right for him, that's all. Meanwhile, I've got some savings. We'll manage.'

'You won't manage once the money runs out! You've never cooked or done a stroke of housework in your life, and now you're planning to play mummies and daddies with an out-of-work actor and a screaming baby?'

'Patrick's not out of work! He's between jobs!'

Paula flung Richard a warning look. Izzie must surely be aware that Patrick's reputation went before him. Adrian Mallory had a wide sphere of influence, and according to Vince the word was well and truly out that Patrick was unprofessional, unreliable, uncooperative and generally insubordinate, all of which was perfectly true.

'If you want to come to the wedding,' continued Isabel, 'it's going to be on Saturday week, in Ireland. You won't have to put up with a baby in the flat, by the way. We've found a place of our own.'

'What about your diploma?' persisted Richard. 'What about your career? What about –'

'Lay off her, Richard,' interjected Paula. 'You're not helping.' Impulsively, she put a protective arm around Isabel and felt the answering shudder, which could have been a response or a rebuff. Unsure which, she withdrew it, and then, succumbing to a need to find out, said to Richard, 'Wait for me in the car, okay?'

Richard didn't flinch at this dismissal – glad, perhaps, of the excuse to storm out. For a moment neither woman spoke.

'He'll come round,' said Paula.

'No he won't. Nor Daddy either. Neither of them can forgive Patrick for showing them up.'

Just as Patrick had intended, thought Paula. Having taken the leading role in Isabel's life, he was busily acting everyone else off the stage.

'Nice place you've found, is it?'

'Not terribly. But it'll do for the moment. I suppose you think I won't be able to cope.'

'You'll cope a lot better than I would. If you can be happy with him, good luck to you. I mean it.' Unable to bear it any longer, she threw her arms around Isabel in an untypically demonstrative gesture, too afraid for her to be jealous. After a moment's hesitation Isabel returned the embrace, quite winding her.

'I'm sorry,' she said thickly. 'About . . . everything.'

189

'That's my line, not yours,' said Paula, embarrassed already, breaking free.

'You don't hate me? You don't mind?'

'About Patrick? You're kidding. If he gives you any trouble, just call on me and I'll black both his eyes for you any time you like.'

Isabel emitted a sound midway between a giggle and a sob.

'It wasn't his fault,' she said, blowing her nose. 'I was careless. Just once, the first time, but once was enough. It could only happen to me.'

'Don't flatter yourself. It happens all the time.'

'Richard's right, you know. I've never liked children. But Patrick adores them. You can see how patient he is with Mummy. So perhaps it'll be all right. It's just that . . . I never had a mother myself. Not in the way normal people have mothers. So it's hard to know what to do.'

I know the feeling, thought Paula.

'Are there any jobs on the horizon? For Patrick, I mean?' Perhaps she could twist Vince's arm into wangling a part for him somewhere.

'Not at the moment. But that's my fault, not his. He'd still be at the Kean if it wasn't for me, he was doing so well there. He's given up so much for me, why shouldn't I do the same for him?'

She isn't trying to convince me, thought Paula. She's trying to convince herself.

Thanks to Isabel's godless state the parish priest, back home in Kilmacross, was only prepared to solemnize their marriage if Isabel promised to take instruction in the One True Faith and bring all her children up as Good Catholics. Never having been inside a church other than to attend weddings, christenings and funerals, she was reluctant to feign any circumstantial interest in religion. But even more reluctant to say so; Patrick's family must have a low enough opinion of her already. To them she was the scheming Protestant hussy who had usurped the wholesome Teresa. (Well, C of E, nominally, but Isabel soon learned that Protestant was a generic term that embraced all brands of heathen.) She badly wanted them to like her for Patrick's sake.

190

'We would have got married anyway, wouldn't we?' Patrick had asked her, not content with her simple consent, not content with her decision to have the baby when she could have had an expensive if illegal abortion behind his back. 'You do love me?'

'Of course I love you.' Sometimes she wished she didn't. Whatever qualms she had about marrying him were swamped by her physical and emotional need of him. Passion didn't last, so people said, but as yet she couldn't think beyond it. Bed was an enchanted world where everything was simple, perfect, easy. In bed Patrick worked the same magic he worked on stage. But could he do the same in real life?

Neither Richard nor Adrian would be attending the wedding; Richard's reaction had been mild compared to his father's.

'You'll regret this, Isabel,' Daddy had roared. She had almost expected him to launch straight into Lear: '*How sharper than a serpent's tooth it is/ To have a thankless child!*' But instead he settled for a hackneyed 'After all I've done for you', which turned out to include canvassing Julian Clavell, not only for her place at FRIDA, but for all the roles she had been allocated so far, not to mention his personal intercession after the Neville Seaton affair, and his arrangement of next year's programme at the Kean to accommodate her Juliet and her Viola. Suddenly five terms of hard, punishing work counted for nothing; suddenly everything she had achieved was thanks to him, thanks to her name, thanks to favours being granted and called in, thanks to the stinking nepotism that corrupted the whole business from top to bottom.

'I never wanted to be an actress anyway!' she heard herself shouting. 'I only did it to please you! And from now on I'm going to please myself. I'm going to succeed where you and Mummy both failed. I'm going to be happy!'

No one could rig things for her on the path she had chosen; from now on the credit and the blame would be hers alone. If she had to get married, if she had to be a mother, no one would be able to fault her. She would be the best wife and the best mother in the world.

Meanwhile Patrick fussed over her and waited on her and made her feel pampered and grateful and, above all, loved. One morning she had fainted, after getting out of bed too quickly, and Patrick had been so concerned that he had stayed at home to look after her and missed an interview for a TV job. Still used to Mallory priorities, she found it infinitely flattering, if rather unnerving, to be put first.

'It was a lousy part anyway,' he had said. 'I'm glad of the excuse not to go for it. It might have stopped me taking something better.'

'Something better' was always just around the corner, Micawber style. The here and now was always temporary, and therefore not worth worrying about. The 'flat' in Parson's Green, for example, which was really a bedsitter, complete with a 'no children' clause in the agreement. But for the moment it was all they could afford, especially now that Adrian had cut off Isabel's allowance, not that Patrick would have allowed her to accept it anyway.

They travelled to Dublin by train and boat, a week before the wedding. Isabel was horribly sick throughout the voyage, even though the crossing was calm. As they disembarked, Patrick caught sight of a figure waving at them and ran towards it, leaving Isabel to catch him up.

'Izzie, this is Maureen,' said Patrick, breaking off from his embrace to introduce her to a plump, rosy, motherly-looking woman of about forty. She had learned all his siblings' names and stations off by heart, in readiness, and knew that Maureen was the eldest sister, married to Joe, who sold second-hand cars.

'Izzie!' Maureen gave her a no-nonsense hug. 'Well, I knew you'd be beautiful if nothing else. Da wasn't well enough to go out today and Ma didn't like to leave him. Otherwise I'd have brought them with me.'

Parked nearby was a dusty Jaguar with a large Alsatian barking and bounding around in the back seat. Isabel, never comfortable around canines, made an excuse to sit in the front while Patrick climbed in beside the ecstatic animal and allowed it to slaver all over him.

Maureen rattled away non-stop throughout the drive, frequently taking her hands off the wheel and her eyes off the road while Patrick plied her with questions. Isabel couldn't make head or tail of their conversation. So and so was getting married, and someone else had had a baby and someone else had died. It was like trying to follow a Russian novel, or listening to a language imperfectly understood.

They drove beyond the outskirts of the city, which gave way to fields and fences, hedgerows and ditches, and humps in the road as it crossed trickling streams. It was dark now, lights beginning to wink behind windows. It began to rain.

'You don't have to worry about running into Terry, by the way,' put in Maureen, rather tactlessly. 'She's taken herself off to her aunt's in Dublin . . .'

'Would you mind stopping the car?' said Isabel. 'I'm afraid I'm going to be sick.'

She retched and heaved by the roadside while Patrick held his jacket above her head and the dog barked loudly in encouragement. But it was nothing to do with being pregnant, or the aftermath of sea-sickness. Stage fright was nothing compared to this . . .

They drove on past the double parade of little shops which comprised downtown Kilmacross and drew up shortly after in front of a privet hedge and neatly regimented front garden, beyond which lay a large but ugly pebble-dashed house. As they walked up the crazy-paved front path a small, thin, white-haired woman opened the glazed front door and called to them to hurry up and get inside, they'd catch their death. The dog bounded ahead and went straight indoors with impunity, while the rest of them were required to wipe their muddy feet and shake out their wet coats in the porch.

No greetings were issued till they were in the front parlour, full of heavy dark old furniture and reeking of lavender polish. There was a large wooden crucifix hanging in the middle of the chimney breast which was flanked by two alcoves, one adorned by a picture of the Sacred Heart and the other by a crudely painted plaque inscribed: *Home – the place where we grumble the most and are treated the best*. There were framed photographs everywhere – on the mantelpiece, on the sideboard, on the upright piano, depicting innumerable weddings, baptisms and first communions.

'Well, sit down all of you,' said Mrs Delaney. Patrick pulled Isabel down beside him on the settee. Maureen sprawled back in one of the easy chairs while her mother sat on the edge of hers and the dog spread out languidly on the hearth.

'You've lost weight,' Mrs Delaney accused Patrick. 'Have you not been eating?'

'Nothing wrong with my appetite,' said Patrick. 'Izzie's the one who needs feeding up.'

'Well, let's be thankful she's on the skinny side,' sniffed his mother. 'You'll be wearing a white dress?'

Isabel nodded, thinking of the shroud of hypocritically virginal lace she had purchased at Patrick's insistence.

'You might at least bother to introduce Izzie first,' Maureen reproved Patrick. 'Before Ma starts giving her the third degree.'

'We know who each other is,' interjected Ma, before Patrick could answer. Isabel had never seen him so lost for words. 'Your father's not well enough to come down,' she went on. 'I just got him off before you arrived.' She made him sound like an infant in a cradle. 'I suppose you'll be wanting your tea. It's been ready this last half hour.'

'The boat was late in,' put in Maureen wearily, standing up. 'Come on, Isabel. Let me show you your room. I expect you'd like a wash before you eat.'

Glad of this reprieve, Isabel followed her into the hallway and up the stairs, each tread picked out by a gleaming brass rod. Although compulsively clean and tidy herself, she felt oppressed by the all-pervasive smell of elbow grease, afraid to touch the banister rail lest she leave an incriminating clammy fingerprint.

'She's extra cranky just now because of my father,' said Maureen, as they reached the landing. 'He hasn't been too well. Well, to tell you the truth, he's not long for this world.'

'Oh,' said Isabel. Patrick had mentioned that his father was ill, but not that it was serious. 'I'm sorry.'

'Don't you be minding her too much at first. All the husbands and wives have been through it. Took her all of five years to forgive my husband. I had a quick wedding like you. She blamed him and now she's blaming you. I'm only telling you this so you'll know.'

'I appreciate it,' said Isabel, heart sinking.

'Any problems, you just give me a ring. I'm the only one of the six of us who's not afraid to speak my mind. The rest of them, well you know how it is. Anything for a quiet life.'

'Thank you.'

'But in your case it's only for a week, after all. So not to worry.'

Yes, thought Isabel. Soon it would all be over, and then they could go back home.

Paula and Vince flew to Dublin first class, on Friday morning, and hired a car at the airport, arriving at the church in Kilmacross well in time for the ceremony, which had been moved forward a day at Isabel's request to accommodate Paula's Saturday matinée.

Patrick was already hanging round the vestry, looking unrecognizably spruce. Paula was assailed by a memory of her father all togged up for his wedding to Marje, a five-minute affair at the town hall with Paula as a kind of pretend-bridesmaid, bought off with a new dress and a Mars bar. He kissed Paula, shook Vince's hand and introduced his brother Michael, the best man. There was a bit of rather laborious banter, with Michael, a bluff, florid man of fifty-odd, patting all his pockets and affecting to have lost the ring.

Paula and Vince took their pews as the guests began to arrive, buxom matrons resplendent in their finery, wizened widows in black, pretty, fresh-faced young girls, together with assorted menfolk and well-scrubbed offspring, all of them crossing themselves and genuflecting and carrying well-worn missals.

Vince looked as out of place in a church as Paula felt. His bespoke suit and hand-made silk shirt sat too easily on him, denying him the starched and pressed humility of men in their Sunday best. She stared, curious as a tourist, at the saintly statues and the gilt-framed pictures depicting the Stations of the Cross, trying to imagine Patrick up there by the altar, dressed in priestly robes, chanting in Latin, holding his audience spellbound . . .

At last the organist switched to the Wedding March and all heads swivelled to the rear of the church as Isabel appeared in sacrificial white, on the arm of a tall but stooped old man who must once have looked like Patrick; he seemed to be clinging to her for support rather than the other way round. All eyes followed her slow progress towards the altar rail, attended by a tribe of little girls in pale pink. And then Paula caught sight of Patrick's face.

Thank God he had never looked at her like that. She wouldn't have known how to cope with it. She would rather be given worthless baubles than real jewellery, things she could afford to lose. Let Isabel bear the burden of those precious gems, let her worry about having them stolen or hocked and replaced with

195

fakes. She wouldn't have changed places with her at that moment for anything in the world.

Both parties made their vows quietly but audibly, their trained voices travelling to every corner of the church. It was soon over; thanks to Isabel not being a Catholic, they were denied a full-blown nuptial mass. The bridal pair turned to face the congregation. Patrick seemed dazed; Isabel was smiling stolidly, but she looked pale and drawn.

There was a mêlée outside the church while the photographer arranged various groupings and pleaded for nice big smiles. Children began scampering about and getting up to mischief while their parents stood gossiping in groups or sucking up to the priest. The pictures taken, Isabel came over to greet them, skirt hitched to stop herself tripping over her train.

'You were wonderful, darling,' teased Paula. 'Wasn't she, Vince?'

'You don't look well,' commented Vince.

'It's my interesting condition,' mouthed Isabel in a stage whisper. 'Everyone's got to pretend they don't know.' She pulled a comic face, but Vince was right, she looked ill. 'Let me introduce you to Patrick's mother.'

Mrs Delaney was holding court nearby to a gaggle of fellow-crones.

'Ma, meet my friends Paula and Vince.'

Paula was surprised at the familiar term of address, and at the way Isabel put an arm around her shoulder.

'How are you feeling now?' she demanded of Isabel, all motherly concern.

'Oh, I'm fine. It was just nerves.'

'Well, hurry up and get yourself into the car. Excuse us.' And with this she bore Isabel off towards a bestreamered Jaguar, where Patrick was waiting to help her into the back seat. Paula and Vince joined the long convoy of following cars to the Dublin hotel where the reception was being held.

After a long and ponderous grace, the guests fell upon the wedding breakfast like a pack of hungry wolves, making short work of the prawn cocktail, roast chicken and woolly imported strawberries served in tall glasses and topped with ice cream. There was silver service, and starched napery, and numerous if

196

inexpert waitresses rushing to and fro. And an elaborate five-tiered cake, with three shades of icing and a little plastic bride and groom on top and 'Patrick' and 'Isobel' (*sic*) scrolled in pink. Paula ate as little as possible, surreptitiously offloading her roast potatoes – one of her biggest weaknesses – onto Vince's plate. Despite heavy investment in slimming pills and diuretics and a punishing new diet she was putting on weight again. It was the booze that did it.

The speeches were robust and unoriginal, with brother Michael evidently well smitten by Isabel and paying her an embarrassing number of flowery compliments. The father, who looked on his last legs, poor man, waxed eloquent about his own idyllic marriage and wished the happy couple the same good fortune. Patrick seemed positively tongue-tied by comparison, reading a eulogy to the bridesmaids from a note beside his plate, and announcing simply that this was the happiest day of his life. It would have sounded corny if it wasn't so obviously true.

After the toasts the tables were pushed against the wall and the floor cleared for dancing, a three-piece band belting out an introductory 'Oh, How We Danced' But Isabel signalled fatigue and whispered something in Patrick's ear, whereupon he whisked his mother round the floor instead. This display was greeted with a round of applause, led by Isabel, who was working her way across the throng towards Paula.

'They've hired a room upstairs for me to change,' she hissed in her ear. 'Will you come with me and sit for a while? I don't feel very well and everyone else will fuss.'

Nodding, Paula followed. It wasn't until Isabel got ahead of her on the stairs that she saw the seeping bloodstain on the seat of her white dress.

Isabel had survived the first week knowing that it was just a week. She had fielded any number of snubs to win Patrick's mother over, asked her advice, accepted her reproofs, played the docile daughter for all she was worth, knowing that she would only have to keep it up for a week. And when finally Agnes Delaney had announced, on the eve of the wedding, that she was a good child, and said that she hadn't meant to be sharp with her, and invited her to call her Ma, when they had finally ended up embracing tearfully and vowing to love each other, 'for Patrick's sake', she had known that it wouldn't have happened so quickly, if at all, but for their imminent departure. And now, three days into their second, unscheduled, week, she was desperate to get away. She had agreed to a limited season, not a long run.

But she couldn't escape, she couldn't even move. Suddenly she didn't own her own body any more. She wasn't allowed to get out of bed, not even to go to the loo, for fear that any movement might dislodge her precious burden. The doctors had vetoed a journey back to London; the most she could hope for was to be discharged to the care of her mother-in-law. But Isabel hadn't protested at these restrictions. She felt wretchedly guilty for almost miscarrying, still convinced that she must have done something wrong, however much the doctors reassured her to the contrary. Henceforward she must do everything right. If her baby died, she would never forgive herself.

They were strict about visiting hours here. It seemed for ever until four o'clock came and Patrick arrived. Naturally, he wasn't alone.

'You're looking that much better today,' said Ma, all smiles.

She was glad, thought Isabel bleakly, to have her in her clutches. Glad that she was confined to bed and helpless and at her mercy. But she smiled back and said gaily, 'You haven't gone and brought me anything else to eat?' It was a fruit cake. The thought of it made her feel nauseous. 'Home made?' she inquired, with wide yum-yum eyes.

'You don't think I'd be bringing you a shop-bought cake, do you? Patrick, can't you see this poor girl wants a kiss?'

Patrick stooped and did as he was told while Ma looked on approvingly, ruining it.

'Any pain?' he said, his eyes bright with anxiety.

'No. I'm fine now, honestly.'

'But you'll only stay that way if you do as you're told,' put in Ma. 'You're not raising hand nor foot till my grandchild's safely born.'

'I rang Rex today,' said Patrick, picking up her hand and running his fingers up and down hers, making her long for him. Would that be forbidden too? After sleeping apart for so long she was feverish with need, she knew she would feel better instantly if

198

only they could be together, and alone. 'Told him I'm only prepared to work in Dublin for the moment.'

Thank God he wasn't going to leave her alone here, thought Isabel, appalled at her own selfishness.

'And if there's no work to be had acting,' added Ma, 'then Patrick's got a good degree, remember. They're crying out for a classics teacher at St Benedict's College . . .'

'No!' protested Isabel, before she could check herself. 'I don't want you to be a teacher. You're an actor!'

'Now there's no need to go upsetting yourself,' chided Ma. 'It's bad for the baby.'

'Ma, Izzie and I need to talk alone for a while.'

'Wasn't I just about to leave this very minute? I was a newly-wed once myself, you know.' She bent to kiss Isabel, her lips dry and papery. She smelt of mothballs and cheap hair lacquer. 'If it's money you two are worrying about, you know very well Da and I will help you out. So there's no need to be getting in a panic about a job just yet awhile.'

She waddled off, a shrunken old woman in a shabby coat. Isabel felt mean for not loving her.

'I've missed you,' murmured Patrick, leaning over her and giving her a long, longing kiss. Isabel responded hungrily, but it wasn't enough. Deprived of the drug of his lovemaking, she was as twitchy as an addict in need of a fix.

'I meant it about the teaching job,' she said, fearful of Ma's influence on him as always. 'Isn't it bad enough me having to give it all up without seeing the same thing happen to you?' She bit her lip, aware that she had said too much. She wasn't supposed to mind 'giving it up'. She would soon be a mother, after all. The most important, fulfilling career in the world . . . if you were normal.

'We can't live off my parents, Izzie. They're not well off. They passed the business on to Sean and Michael, remember. And Mary's husband's forever in debt, they've baled him out time and time again. And Maureen got a big screw out of them for that fancy house of hers. And they've just spent a fortune on the wedding. It's up to me to support you, not them.'

'Then take some casual work, something you can drop straight away if a real job comes along. See if there are any auditions going. Oh Patrick, please. You're so talented. I can't bear to see your talent go to waste, because of me!'

'Hush now. Something'll turn up. Didn't I tell you everything would be fine with Ma? And so it was. Well, just leave it to me to find work and that'll come right too. Who sent you those?' he asked, noticing the spray of white hothouse roses jostling for space on the table beside her bed. There had been so many flowers from Patrick's family that she had had to share them out with the rest of the ward.

'Richard. Paula told him what happened. He sent a telegram too.' She handed it to him.

DARLING IZZIE THINKING OF YOU SORRY I WAS SUCH A SWINE MUCH LOVE RICHARD.

'And Paula sent a message for me to ring and reverse the charges. They brought me the portable phone and we talked for ages.' It had been the one bright spot in a long day.

'Anything from your father?' said Patrick, handing the telegram back to her.

'No. He's not on speaking terms with Richard so he probably doesn't know.'

'He wouldn't care even if he did,' said Patrick. 'He'd be glad if you lost the baby. So would Richard, come to that, flowers or no flowers.'

Only then did it occur to her, belatedly, that Patrick was jealous of Richard, jealous of her father. Even Paula was a threat. He liked having her here, beyond their reach, forsaking all others, cleaving only unto him.

Paula had promised to visit Isabel again; that she didn't was out of concern, rather than a lack of it. Things sounded quite hard enough for her, living with her mother-in-law, without a third party stirring up the already muddy waters. Specially one noted for her quick temper and tactless tongue. Not that Isabel ever complained about anything. She even tried to make bad news seem good.

'Guess what!' she had carolled, with rather forced glee. 'It's going to be twins!'

'Twins? God.' Isabel would be a neurotic enough mother with

one child to care for, let alone two at once. Typically, she was devouring baby-care books by the score, researching her latest role with her usual perfectionist fervour. 'Are you pleased?'

'Well . . . it gets it all over with at once, doesn't it? It's no picnic, being pregnant. Specially when you're barely allowed to move.'

'So Ma's still got you tied to the bedpost?'

'Not quite. I'm allowed to pad around the house a bit, in my dressing gown. And even to put my clothes on, when the priest calls to give me instruction.'

'That sounds like a barrel of laughs. You don't believe all that stuff about birth control, do you?'

'I don't have to believe it, thank God. It's the children I'm worried about. I'm beginning to wonder what I've let them in for. Catholics get sent to Hell for the slightest thing.'

Trust Izzie to be fretting about their afterlife before they were even born.

'Da says it only seems that way to me because I take everything too seriously.' She seemed genuinely fond of the father, who was still soldiering on, despite his chronic emphysema. 'He's a lovely man. We spend a lot of time together, being as we're both confined to barracks.' (A situation which had at least served to spare her a chance encounter with the wronged Teresa, whose family were no longer on speaking terms with Patrick's.)

'His eyes are bad, he likes me to read the papers aloud to him, from cover to cover. I've become quite an expert on the Bay of Pigs and the war in Algeria, we talk for hours on end. Ma's always too busy washing her nets or sweeping under the rugs to sit still. Talk about a human dynamo. She's amazing for her age.'

'Well, just thank your stars you've got an excuse not to help her. At least this way she won't find out what a useless housewife you are.'

'God, yes.' Isabel dropped her voice to a whisper. 'She's always telling me how lazy Sean and Michael's wives are. She can't stand Maureen's husband either, he's supposed to have a fancy woman or something. And Kathleen went and married a drinker, and as for Mary, the farmer's wife, that man of hers beats her every day for breakfast, which he would do, being an O'Rourke, that family are nothing but trouble. So I suppose it's only a matter of time till the rot sets in with me . . .' And then she had laughed, as if it were

201

all a huge joke, as if she wasn't walking on eggs, trying to keep the old girl sweet. Unlike the rest of the family, she had to live with her.

After several months selling second-hand cars for his brother-in-law Patrick was finally treading the boards again, rehearsing Richard Dudgeon in a revival of Shaw's *The Devil's Disciple*, a barnstorming role ideally suited to his talents. Granted, it was only a fringe production in the forthcoming Dublin Festival, but it would mean two weeks' work and a chance to be seen by London managers, who were notorious for swooping on the city each year and poaching the cream of its talent. By the time the play opened, Paula would be repeating her *Snowdrops* rôle on Broadway, an event which had crept up on her with alarming speed, and one which she was secretly dreading, despite the jaunty tone of her parting letter to Isabel.

10 September 1961

Dear Izzie
Shorter than usual, because we're flying out tomorrow and I still haven't finished packing. We're going straight into four weeks of try-outs with extra rehearsals during the day because some American script doctor is on hand to rewrite all the bits that don't work. Vince is going to be there for the first night, but in the meantime he's trusting me to behave myself, silly man.

Not that she would have the courage or the energy to misbehave, terrified as she was of being panned by the critics, booed by the audience and exposed for the rotten untalented fraud she had always been. And besides, she was still off men, with the honourable exception of Richard, who was currently repeating his successful partnership with Neville Seaton by staging an all-male *Merry Wives of Windsor*, played as a high-camp drag show with a trio of outlandish pantomime dames. They were also collaborating on a dramatization of the life of Oscar Wilde, which provided an outlet for Richard's frustrated talents as a writer. Meanwhile *Kill Claudio* was still playing to packed houses in the West End, much to the delight of its investors, including Vince. Everything he touched seemed to turn to gold. Paula hoped he would have the same effect on her.

. . . Vince has already been to New York several times, making contacts and trying to whip up advance sales. That way, he said, even if the critics slate us, we might survive. It takes about six weeks for the public to forget bad reviews and for word of mouth to spread, so he's been canvassing the Broadway party ladies. They're women who block-book for fund-raisers and sell the tickets on at a profit so that the charity or whatever gets the difference. They earn their money on commission from the producer. Vince's paying them 10%, instead of the normal 7½, so they've been buying like the clappers. Luckily for us, party ladies aren't interested in quality – only in what they know they can sell. The audiences they're catering for are respectable midde-aged women and their husbands, the type of people who support good causes. So they buy comedies, musicals, and weepies, like Snowdrops. *I'm not sure if they've forgotten that I'm a scarlet woman, or whether that's a selling point. You know how two-faced people are.*

Richard is well and sends his love. Don't worry about Fay, they're taking good care of her, and so they should, the money they're charging. Send me a cable straight away when the sprogs are born. I'll be thinking of you.

Love, Paula.

She would be thinking of her all right. Envying her the right to hold her babies and keep them. Whenever Paula wondered about her daughter – something she tried not to do, in vain – she imagined a junior version of herself and worried that the adoptive parents would turn, Marje-like, against her. And now that she had a bit of money in the bank, she wished that she could go and get her back and tell her, 'I don't mind if you're fat and ugly. I'll love you anyway.' Just as well she couldn't. The child was entitled to spit in her face and say, 'Don't talk to me about love. If you'd loved me you wouldn't have given me away. It's too late.'

PS Hope the enclosed will keep the little buggers amused. I knew you already had bootees and stuff coming out of your ears.

She had got carried away in Hamley's and spent over fifty pounds on a Noah's ark of pram-sized bunny rabbits, giraffes, pandas and teddy bears, two of each. She could have got them to wrap and post them for her, but she had wanted the pleasure of doing it herself. She had never possessed such things in her own childhood and it gave her pleasure to handle and admire them, sublimating the wish to buy such cuddly comforters for herself.

At least Patrick couldn't veto such harmless gifts. She hated to think of Izzie and two small babies living on a shoestring and ending up in some ghastly poky flat – assuming they ever got away from Ma – but predictably Izzie had declined her offer of a loan, on Patrick's pig-headed instructions. Just as he had already shunned a similar overture from Richard, on the grounds that 'he'd only rub our noses in it later'. Probably he had said the same thing about her.

Odd what a misanthropist he could be behind that live-and-let-live façade. And yet once he decided to like or trust someone – the shifty Rex Jordan for example – he seemed to abandon all critical faculties. He avoided friendships within the profession (the theatre was full of phoneys, he said), but had a wide and indiscriminate acquaintanceship outside it – boxing cronies, fellow racing fanatics, sundry compatriots, all of whom he was willing to stand a drink or lend a few bob to, on the grounds that they were 'mates'. Hardly the kind of people Isabel would want to mix with, though no doubt she wouldn't be expected to. Her place would be at home, washing the nappies and warming Patrick's slippers, as Paula was quick to remind herself, to keep her own regrets at bay.

Vince arrived to take her out for a farewell dinner at the Mirabelle, just as she was wrapping the last few items.

'All packed?' he said, picking up a bear and making it squeak.

'Almost.'

'Looking forward to it?'

'Of course.'

'I'm going to miss you, you know.'

'I don't see how,' said Paula, gratified nonetheless. 'I hardly ever see you as it is.' She tried to keep the reproach out of her voice and failed.

'Your choice, not mine. You told me you didn't want me interfering in your personal life, remember?'

'I don't have a personal life.' He knew that, he must know. Nothing she did escaped his attention. He was all-seeing, all-powerful, impossible to lie to, impossible to fool. 'Drink?'

She poured herself her customary vodka and tonic, and a small whisky for him, no ice.

'Since when have you been buying half bottles?'

'It was all they had at the off-licence.'

'Only alcoholics buy half bottles.'

'I'm not an alcoholic. Have you ever seen me go on stage other than stone-cold sober?'

'No. But I know your hangovers last till lunch.' And then, with infuriating insight, 'I shouldn't have made you relive the past like that. I've never talked about mine, after all.'

He sat down beside her and took hold of her hand. His manner was remote and cool as always but his hand was warm. Warm hands, cold heart, she thought.

'I was beaten black and blue as a kid,' he began, without preamble; he could have been talking about the weather. 'By my father, in my case, not my mother. Once I got big enough to fight back, he kicked me out. Grace took me in, or I'd have been on the streets. I stopped going to school and took two jobs, so I could rent a place of my own and get my mother and sister away from him. That was before I learned that nobody makes money being honest. Before I learned that you've got to destroy your enemies before they destroy you. Or worse, the people you love.'

It was hard to imagine Vince loving anyone; it implied a loss of control. She wondered why he was telling her all this now.

'Then the war came. I was taken prisoner at Dunkerque. My little sister should have been evacuated, but Mum kept her at home, because she was lonely. Lonely enough to take a lover. My dad had been called up by then. Some busybody wrote to him at the training camp and told him that she was having it off with another man.'

His voice was expressionless, but the damped-down cockney had flared up again, gritty and harsh, and his slate-grey eyes were smouldering with rage, rage that was like a furnace, all the hotter for being confined.

'He came home one night on embarkation leave, knocked her senseless and then started kicking her head in with his army boots. Eileen kept screaming, but nobody came, all the neighbours knew what my dad was like and stayed well out of it. Then the air raid sirens went off and my father yelled at Eileen to get to the shelter. But Eileen wouldn't leave my mother, she was unconscious and too heavy for her to carry. So he left them to it.'

'And then there was a direct hit,' said Paula, watching his face. 'Grace told me.'

'My mother was killed. Eileen was badly injured. She was an invalid till she died.'

'And she never told anyone?'

'Only me, years later. Where I come from people don't talk to the police. My mother's body was so mangled no one could have proved anything, and who would believe the word of a kid against an adult? I fixed him my own way, after the war. Road accident. Hit and run. I've never told anyone this before. Not a soul.'

'So why are you telling me?'

'I learned about violence early on. Same as you, even though you were too young to remember. I understand why you're angry inside, because I am too, it never leaves you. But you ought to save your anger for your enemies, like I do. Not turn it on yourself. Last time you were hurt I was too late, same as I was too late for my mother, too late for my sister.'

'Oh for God's sake,' said Paula. He had opened a door, at last, but she was too scared to go in, or rather to venture out of her own space. 'Don't start on about the bloody rape again.'

'I'm not just talking about the rape. I'm talking about Simon Fisk.'

'Simon Fisk?' Oh shit.

'I knew something had happened between you and him. You were all over each other one minute and then suddenly it was all off. So I took him out and got him drunk and said I'd been trying to get you into bed for months and did he have any tips because I wasn't having any luck.'

Paula ground out her cigarette savagely, as if squashing a large insect.

'He said you were kinky, that you'd begged him to beat you up, and if I liked the old S and M I was welcome to you. I've had someone following you ever since, in case you got more than you bargained for. But there hasn't been anyone else. Why not? If he hurt you I swear to God I'll –'

'You've been having me followed?'

'Only for your own good. What did he do to you, Paula?'

'Nothing! We were both drunk. It was just a game. Sex is boring. I tried to liven it up, that's all. How dare you set your spies on me! What I do in private is none of your damned business!'

'I want it to be my business. I care about you, Paula.' And then, knocking her for six, 'I want to marry you.'

'What?'

'I don't expect an answer right away. I've had time to think about it. You haven't.'

'I don't need to think about it,' said Paula, panic-stricken. 'I don't love you. You don't love me. If you want to have sex with me, just say the word. God knows I owe you. You don't have to bloody marry me!'

'Yes I do. You scare me, Paula. With me, you'll be safe.'

'Safe? A prisoner, you mean. If you're having me watched now, you'll have me watched once we're married. And if I ever fancy a bit on the side, I'll end up dead meat like your mother . . .'

'Take that back,' he said quietly.

'. . . Except that you'd bump off the bloke as well!'

'I told you all that as a token of trust. Not so that you could throw it in my face. I was honest with you.'

But still he didn't say the words she longed to hear, the words she was incapable of saying herself.

'I'm sorry if I've intruded on your privacy,' he went on, in that curiously formal way of his. 'Like I said, it was only for your own good. But I would never try to keep you against your will. If you ever met anyone you really loved, someone who'd be good for you, I'd let you go. But I don't think you're capable of love. Not yet.'

'No more than you are. If you must know, I don't even fancy you. You leave me cold, you always have done.'

It was the second time she had tried to hurt him, with words this time rather than blows. But she knew even as she spoke that she was wasting her breath. She felt as powerless as a lone Lilliputian assailing a Gulliver, hammering and raging with her tiny fists, stamping her foot fruitlessly on the firm, floating platform of his palm . . .

Except that she didn't stamp her foot. As if hypnotized she let him kiss her, very gently, very expertly and very thoroughly, too stunned and too wary to offer more than a passive response. It seemed to go on for ever, with time standing still, and yet it all happened very fast within the stillness, like a spinning top. And then it stopped. Having lulled her into willing compliance, he drew back, leaving her cheated and confused.

'Time we had dinner,' he said. And for the rest of the evening he was the old impassive Vince, talking shop, swapping the latest theatre gossip, discussing what he should buy for Isabel's babies, while a troubled Paula found herself longing to muss up his sleek golden hair and tear off the armour of his city clothes and hear that quiet, steady voice erupt into a shout of ecstasy. No one watching them would have thought that he had just proposed to her, just demonstrated to her, with a simple, infinitely complex kiss, that there was nothing he couldn't do, including making her fall in love with him, if he had a mind. When Vince wanted something he got it. He wasn't offering her a choice, not really. He was just informing her of his intention. Won't you come into my parlour, said the spider to the fly . . .

He took her home and kissed her again, on the doorstep, and this time it was so explicit, so eloquent, so unbearably tantalizing that Paula weakened and said, 'Do you want to come in?' because she knew she would never rest until she knew how a man who kissed like that made love.

But he shook his head and said, 'No dice, Paula. I'm saving myself for my wedding night. The only way you'll get me is to marry me. Think about it while you're away.'

He softened his words with one of those rare, penetrating smiles of his.

'In the meantime, be good,' he said, raising a hand, and she knew what he meant, knew that he would be watching her from afar.

8

Autumn 1961–Autumn 1962

See how love and murder will out.

William Congreve – The Double Dealer

'For God's sake don't breathe a word to Ma,' warned Patrick. 'No point telling her unless I get the part. We'll just say I'm going to see Rex, and not mention the audition.'

A London producer, having seen him in *The Devil's Disciple*, had invited him to read for a supporting role in *Daggers Drawn*, a long-running West End thriller whose original cast were approaching the end of their contracts.

Isabel ought to have been delighted that her longed-for departure might, at last, be imminent. She tried to rationalize her diffidence by telling herself that Patrick would be wasted in a potboiler, but that wasn't the real reason. The real reason was her terror of being on her own, at home, with two infants, without Ma, with no one to turn to except the baby-care manuals (which, like recipe books, made it all sound much easier than it was), the district nurse (who would no doubt tick her off in some little black book as a nervous and incompetent mother), and Patrick. And doting father though Patrick might be, he knew even less about babies than she did.

The twins had been born two weeks early, after a long and excruciating labour terminating in a forceps delivery, an ordeal which Isabel had no intention of enduring ever again, even though she made light of it when questioned by the Delaney womenfolk, repelled by their interest in all the gory details. She had no wish to brag about the number of hours she had suffered, nor the number of stitches they had used to repair the damage. Such things were, to her mind, evidence that her body had malfunctioned, that she was a failure as a female. Fifty years ago she would assuredly have

209

died in childbirth, and the babies too, assuming she hadn't miscarried in the first place.

When she had held them in her arms for the first time, and marvelled that they were alive and well and perfect, her joy and relief were marred by the knowledge that it was no thanks to her. As for the fiercely maternal feelings that smote her with all the suddenness of a thunderbolt, they were even more frightening in their intensity than falling in love with Patrick had been. These helpless, trusting little creatures now relied on her absolutely, they had no idea how completely clueless she was . . .

And now, nearly six weeks after the birth, she still felt hopelessly inept, still took it personally when her babies cried, which they did with inexhaustible energy, reproaching her with the only vocabulary at their disposal.

Sophie and Sarah – she had got her own way about their names – were identical, with Patrick's dark hair and eyes so piercingly blue, just like his, that their colour must surely be permanent. She had prepared herself for them to be ugly, because newborn children invariably were, but they had been beautiful right from the start, and every day they grew bigger and bonnier, even as she herself grew more haggard, drained by the round-the-clock business of changing and bathing and feeding and winding and getting them back to sleep, a process which left her little time for anything else, least of all sleep of her own.

The anything else was all done by Ma, with effortless efficiency. Meals appeared as if by magic, the house was always spotless, baby clothes were laundered by hand, and nappies were ferociously boiled and lovingly ironed. Ironing nappies made them softer, Ma said. Sean's wife had never bothered, no wonder those poor little mites of hers had bawled night and day . . .

Unversed in the ways of the theatre, Ma was easily convinced that Patrick was routinely 'visiting his agent' as if any actor in his right mind would travel over three hundred miles on such a fatuous mission. The day after he left for London Ma went out with the twins, parading them proudly around Kilmacross, while Isabel, drained by another broken night, snatched a selfish hour or two of sleep, only to be cruelly awoken by the telephone ringing in the hall below. She got up quickly, shouting to Da that she would answer it. It was Patrick.

210

'I've got the part,' he said, triumphantly. 'Or rather not the part I read for, a better one. I was up for the murderer, but I hustled for the private eye instead. Twice as many lines and more money.'

'Oh, Patrick!' She tried to sound pleased, instead of panic-stricken.

'Rehearsals start the week after next. I'm going to stay another day or two and find us a flat. There's a mate whose floor I can sleep on.'

'There's no need to look for a flat just yet. Paula said we could use her place while she was away, remember?' And Paula looked likely to be away for several months. *Snowdrops* was playing, despite lukewarm reviews, to healthy pre-booked houses of blue-rinsed ladies whose word-of-mouth was spreading fast.

'I don't want to be beholden to Paula.'

'We wouldn't have to be. We can easily afford the rent.'

'Only because she's a kept woman.' Patrick had taken one of his instant dislikes to Vincent Parry, a feeling which Isabel suspected was mutual.

'Please, Patrick. Just to begin with. Till I find my feet.' A few months of living in relative luxury was just the kind of lifeline she needed.

'I wish you wouldn't say please like that. You know I can't say no to you. All right. I'll do a deal with you. We'll take up the offer of Paula's flat. And in return, you break the news to Ma for me, okay? She'll take it better, coming from you.' At that moment the operator intervened, telling Patrick his time was up and inviting him to insert further coins. 'I'm out of change,' he said. 'See you tomorrow.'

Ma came back from her expedition glowing with good humour.

'Did you get a little bit of a rest?' she said, removing her headscarf. 'Poor love, you still look dead beat. Why don't you go back to bed? I'll feed them and bath them and put them down for you . . .'

'Ma,' said Isabel, ignoring a hungry wail from Sophie, the more voracious and vociferous of the two. 'Patrick just phoned. He's got a part, in a West End play. We have to leave for London next week.' So much for breaking the news gently.

Ma sat down.

'Well then,' she said quietly. 'A West End part. That's grand.'

211

She looked up and saw Isabel's stricken expression. 'What's the matter? Are you not pleased for him?'

'I'll miss you, that's all,' said Isabel. 'We'll both miss you.' But even as she leant down to pick up her grizzling infant, her own selfish tears spurted out, tears that made her feel like a hypocrite. She would miss being looked after, that was all.

'There, there,' growled Ma. 'I'll miss you too. But you'll come again, won't you? And perhaps I can visit, once you're settled. If I wouldn't be in the way.'

'Of course you wouldn't,' sniffed Isabel, wishing she could love her properly, the way she loved Da, instead of just pretending to. 'You've been so good to us, I don't know how we'll cope without you.'

'Nonsense,' said Ma sturdily, if not quite convincingly. 'You'll cope just fine.'

Somehow she did cope. It was as if the upheaval had jerked her into a higher gear, drawn on the old reserves of masochistic energy that had fuelled her insatiable need for work. And being in Paula's well-appointed flat made things easier than they would otherwise have been. The new washing machine and heated drying cabinet had been installed by Vince in time for their arrival; Paula herself had sent everything to the laundry.

Nonetheless, every day was an assault course, a non-stop battle of order against chaos, a teeth-gritting exercise in pride and perfectionism. And if she felt as if her former life had been reduced to a prelude, as if her real self had gone into limbo and an automaton taken over, if sometimes she felt like screaming in frustration, if sometimes she sat weeping into the nappy pail, then she never let anyone know it, least of all Patrick. She was a professional to the core, and her profession was now that of wife and mother. Whatever happened, the show must go on.

Which was why she never said no to him, however unsexy she felt; it was hard to believe, in her present state of permanent exhaustion, that he had once teased her with being insatiable. Once she had actually fallen asleep in the middle of making love, and had managed to convince him that she had passed out from sheer pleasure. Better to deceive than disappoint.

212

Although Patrick declared himself eager to 'help out' and adored dandling his children, he turned out to be squeamish about nappies and once asleep remained deaf to the cries that woke Isabel instantly, almost before they were uttered. In the end it was easier and quicker to do things herself than spend time and effort training him up to her own implacably high standards.

'I guess men don't have the knack for these things,' he would say, glad that his avowedly good intentions would not be put to the test. As if to compensate, he handed over his wages in their entirety, just as his father had always done, keeping back only enough for fares, cigarettes, and the odd round of drinks in the pub. Even so, she was always down to her last few pennies by Patrick's payday, and the first time she got an electricity bill she nearly fainted from shock. She wouldn't have been able to pay it if Richard hadn't come to the rescue with a so-called Christmas present in cash.

Da died in the early spring. Patrick was granted one performance off to attend the funeral and flew back next day. Isabel had wanted to go with him, but both the twins were feverish at the time and not well enough to travel.

'Ma's taken it pretty bad,' he told her on his return. 'She's moved in with Maureen. Don't expect it'll last long. They'll be at each other's throat within the week.'

This loss inspired a guilty Isabel to make peace with her own father, at a time when an unusually subdued Patrick would be hard put to object. Adrian proved to be in low enough spirits to welcome a reconciliation, thanks to Davina having left him for Brindsley Smythe, something everyone else but him had been expecting for months. Glad though Isabel was to see the back of her at last, it pained her to see her father unhappy, though not as much as it frustrated her that he seemed inclined to give in to all Davina's demands.

She had filed for divorce, claiming mental cruelty, and was not only suing for the Windsor house, as part of a punitive financial settlement, but withholding access to Toby, who was now living with his mother in a rented cottage near the Kean. Meanwhile his warring parents continued to see each other, willy nilly, at the theatre, where they were still playing opposite each other in Ibsen's *The Master Builder* – appropriately, the story of an old man's obsession with a young and predatory woman.

It was unlike Adrian to be so defeatist. Isabel would have expected him to fight for Toby, at least, of whom he had always been passionately fond, especially in view of Davina's open adultery, which would surely have strengthened his hand in court.

'The little brat's had a lucky escape,' was Richard's only comment on the subject. 'I wish I'd managed to get away from the old bugger at the same age.'

'You honestly think he's better off with a mother like Davina?' said Isabel. She might have no love for Toby, but she was automatically on her father's side.

'Lesser of the two evils,' shrugged Richard. 'Don't go getting involved, for God's sake. Let them fight it out between them.'

Isabel couldn't have 'got involved' even if she had wanted to; she simply didn't have the time or surplus energy. But at least their rift gave her something non-domestic to tell Paula, who often rang for a chat from her Manhattan apartment with scant regard for the telephone bill. Isabel didn't like to bore her with talk of babies; Paula's news was always so much more interesting than her own. Especially the news about this new and unlikely man in her life.

'His name's Jess,' she said. 'He came to fix the shower and just sort of stayed.'

'You mean he's a plumber?'

'More of a general handyman. He cooks for me, runs my bath, irons my clothes, fixes my hair – you know what awful hair I have and he makes it look terrific. He does everything for me. It's a bit like . . . like having a wife.'

God almighty, thought Isabel, suppressing a pang of envy.

'So what does Vince think about it?'

'Oh, Vince doesn't know. Not officially anyway. Though I expect he's got his spies on me as usual. I hope they give him an earful. I'm fed up with him running my life.'

'Does that mean you've decided not to marry him?' Isabel had been quite alarmed to hear of Vincent Parry's proposal; for all his personal generosity to her, she still didn't trust him.

'I never had any intention of marrying him. It's bad enough having him as my manager without becoming his legal chattel. Anyway, I don't need him any more. I've had several agents visit me after the show and leave me their card. I'm in demand, would

214

you believe. This is where the opportunities are. And the money. Talking of which, when are you going to start looking for work?'

'Work?' What she did at the moment wasn't work, of course. 'Oh, God knows. Not until the girls are older.'

'You're not copping out, are you?'

'Having twins is hardly a cop-out. It makes FRIDA seem like a rest cure, I can tell you.'

'Why don't you get an au pair?'

'I've seen au pairs in action. Davina had half a dozen. All useless.' Her children were far too precious to entrust to some dozy girl who might not share her obsession with hygiene, who might allow them to poke their fingers into electric sockets or drink the Domestos, who might turn her back for the five seconds it took a baby to drown in the bath.

'Kids are much tougher than you think. You've always been over-conscientious. You'll end up spoiling them.'

'They're not spoiled. I'm very strict with them. I don't believe in all that Doctor Spock free-expression rubbish. Look what it's done to Toby.'

'Well, give them a cuddle for me. Must go, the cab's waiting.'

Waiting to take her to the theatre, thought Isabel. If only it was me . . .

It was a novelty for Paula, being the man. Jess was as biddable and docile as she imagined Patrick's Teresa to have been. No wonder men went for dumb blondes; now she had found the male equivalent she could understand the attraction. Except that Jess wasn't really dumb; he had the unnerving wisdom of a true innocent.

She had passed him once or twice in the corridor of her fancy apartment block on the Upper East Side, carrying his tools, eyes downcast. She had been struck straight away by his dark Latin-lover good looks, straight out of *West Side Story* – she had been to see the film three times – and wondered why he didn't have the strutting posture to go with it. A couple of months after moving in, she found out.

It had been a freezing cold day in February. New York had turned out in force to give a tickertape welcome to the astronaut

John Glenn, the first American to orbit the earth. Paula had joined the heaving throng, feeling like an extra in some vast crowd scene staged by Cecil B. de Mille, and shouted her bravos with the best of them, unable even to see the motorcade but finding release in being licensed to yell and yell and yell at the top of her voice. She hadn't realized until then how much pressure she had been under over the last three gruelling months. The show was now officially a success, but she still couldn't bring herself to relax and enjoy it.

On her return she had tried to take a shower, only for the tap to come off in her hand. She had rung down to the janitor, who had sent Jess to fix it, in the course of which he got accidentally soaked with cold water. Paula had insisted on lending him a dressing gown and brewing him coffee while his shirt steamed dry on the radiator. The poor man was shy to the point of being tongue-tied, and it wasn't long before she realized that he was a bit simple.

'So whereabouts do you live, Jess?' enquired Paula, amused and touched at the way he was bolting down chocolate chip cookies as if he hadn't eaten for a week. (She had just had six packets delivered with her grocery order, intending to have a private orgy of literally sick-making greed.)

'Gotta 'nother job, as a night watchman.'

'You mean you don't have a place to stay?'

'Not right now. Don't need one.'

'Don't you have any family?'

'No, ma'am. I was raised in a children's home in San Antonio, Texas.'

Paula's heart turned over. Some mother had given him up, or walked out on him, as she herself had been walked out on, as she herself had given up her child. It was as if, quite by chance, she had found something she had lost.

'That's a long way.'

'I like to keep movin'. Never stay any place for long.'

'So you work all day and all night?'

He shrugged. 'At night I sleep mostly.'

'Don't you get tired?'

'No, ma'am.'

'You look it.' His face was young, but his eyes were old. 'You can lie down on the couch and have a nap if you like.'

His eyes flew to the settee with its plump pink velvet cushions.

216

She wondered how long ago it was since he had last slept in a bed, remembering what it felt like to be poor and homeless and hungry, to have nothing and nobody, to be alone.

'Can't,' he said. 'Don't want to get into no trouble.'

'You won't. I'll sign your work sheet to say the job took longer than it did. I'll have to wake you up in an hour, in any case,' she added, as if to reassure him. 'Before I leave for the theatre.' He looked blank. 'I'm an actress. I'm playing in *Snowdrops in June*.' He looked even blanker. 'It's a play. Would you like to see it, tonight? For free?'

He shifted uneasily from foot to foot.

'Thank you, ma'am. But I gotta start work at eleven. In the Bronx.' He had a slow, soft, Southern drawl, distinct from the clipped speech of native New Yorkers. He belonged on horseback, with a stetson on his head and a blade of straw between his teeth, and a wide sky above his head, not doing odd jobs in a skyscraper block or minding some dingy warehouse.

'The show finishes at ten fifteen. Plenty of time for you to get to work. I think you'd enjoy it.' No brain power was needed to appreciate the sentimental excesses of *Snowdrops*; that was the secret of its success.

'Um . . . er . . . thank you, ma'am. That's real kind of you.' He didn't know how to refuse without appearing rude.

'Better catch yourself some sleep before we go, then,' she said. She left him alone and shut herself in her bedroom, half expecting him to seize his chance to flee. But she heard not the sound of the front door closing but the creak of the springs on the settee yielding under his weight.

Gratified, she lay down on the bed without bothering to undress or take a shower. Her pre-performance nap had become a ritual; even if she couldn't sleep she would lie there and empty her mind in preparation. But this time some instinct kept her watchful. She must be crazy, inviting a backward handyman to make himself at home on her couch. It made nonsense of the triple bolt on her door. Vince would go spare if he knew. Or rather, when he found out. Perhaps even now some private dick was patrolling the corridor outside, or spying on her through a telescope from the block opposite. Vince looked upon her as she looked upon Jess in there, as a victim. Love had nothing to do with it, just pity. And she didn't want his pity, wouldn't allow herself to be lured into loving a man who didn't love her back.

After an hour she got up and crept back into the living room. Jess was asleep, huddled up in a foetal ball. His worn tennis shoes were neatly arranged side by side on the floor. His bare feet were clean and he had evidently shaved that morning, in a public rest room perhaps, like a down and out. His dark, thick curly hair, still damp from his accidental shower, gave off a scent of cheap soap. His expression in sleep was anxious, his chocolate-brown wide-set eyes shuttered by heavy lids with long black lashes. His high cheekbones had a touch of Red Indian, but his olive complexion suggested Hispanic origins. He wasn't tall, but he was sturdily built, with broad shoulders and big, gentle-looking hands.

Just as she was about to rouse him he awoke of his own accord, alerted by some sixth sense, startled.

'Time to get up,' said Paula, handing him his dry shirt.

'Gotta be at work by eleven,' he repeated, as if afraid of forgetting. She wondered how much less than the going rate they paid him, and how much harder and longer he worked, on account of being a little slow.

'Don't worry. I won't let you be late. Now give me that work sheet so that you get your money.'

On the way to the theatre she told him the plot of the play, as if telling a child a bedtime story.

'What happens to the girl at the end?'

'Oh, you'll have to wait and see. I don't want to spoil the story for you. Do you have a girlfriend, Jess?'

'No,' he muttered awkwardly.

'But you're very good-looking. Did you know that?' The poor boy blushed scarlet. 'I bet women have told you that before, haven't they, when you went to mend their showers for them?' The building was full of idle wives not averse to a routine tumble with the hired help.

'Some,' he admitted miserably. 'But I don't like it. I don't like . . . being touched.' Paula could just imagine some painted middle-aged harpy pawing at his flies, shoving dollar bills in his pockets, trying to make a whore out of him. She wished she could protect him against it ever happening again.

She left Jess in the care of the front-of-house manager with instructions that he was to be given the best seat in the house and be escorted to her dressing room afterwards. There was a bouquet waiting for her with a card labelled 'Congratulations on your first hundred performances. Regards, Vince.' Regards indeed. He couldn't even write the word love, let alone say it, not that she would have believed him if he had. She plucked the card out and tore it up, trying to obliterate the memory of his kisses, the sensation of a door opening, she knew not where, except that it was another prison masquerading as a home. And yet the memory continued to tantalize, like a dare, lingering in her mouth like the taste of chocolate, like the taste of poison.

She drove Vince from her mind, drove Jess from her mind, prepared to do her job. She knew as soon as the curtain rose that it was a good house tonight. It was warm out there, they were begging for it. They were like sick people waiting for the doctor. Her job was to heal and soothe and restore, to send them away feeling better. No matter that it was a trashy play, a quack remedy, an illusion, there was still a kind of magic in it. This was still the only time she felt alive.

It was one of those performances when time seemed to gallop, when the play seemed to shrink to half its normal length. Always a good sign. Off-nights seemed interminable. This one was over in a trice. Five curtain calls and another batch of middle-aged ladies telling their friends that they had wept buckets, they simply must go see it. Simon Fisk might not be gifted or original, but he had written the dramatic equivalent of cheap, catchy music, the kind that was easy to hum. Just as she might not be a brilliant actress, but she understood how to manage an audience. She hadn't made them cry; she had merely given them permission. People were full of misery, chock full of tears, grateful for any pretext to shed them without shame.

Her dresser was waiting for her with a bourbon-laced cup of tea. Another washed-up actress, clinging to the wreckage, a warning of how she might end up one day. Paula gulped down the hot reviving liquid and was already in her street clothes by the time Jess tapped shyly on the door. His eyes were red; he had been crying.

'Thanks, Clarice,' said Paula, anxious to get rid of her. 'You can take those flowers home with you if you like.'

219

'You mean it?' said Clarice, fingering the expensive blooms.

'I mean it. See you tomorrow. Goodnight.'

Clarice took the hint, eyeing Jess curiously as she left the room.

'Well?' said Paula. 'Did you enjoy the play?'

He didn't answer for a moment, blinking furiously. Then he said, in a choked voice, 'No. She died. You never told me she died.'

'She didn't really die,' said Paula. 'It was only a story. Oh Jess. Don't cry. Don't cry.' She wanted to put an arm around him, but she didn't dare, in case he thought she was making a pass. She found herself remembering poor Marty, that dreadful night. Once again she felt disarmed, helpless, anxious to kiss it better. Perhaps men only became human when they cried. She couldn't imagine Vince in tears.

'It's all right,' she murmured. 'I'm still here. I'm alive. I'll go up there and die again, tomorrow night, and I'll still be alive. So there's no need to be sad.'

'I gotta go,' he mumbled, ashamed, wiping his eyes on the back of his sleeve. 'I gotta go to work.'

'Wait,' said Paula, on impulse. 'How would you like to work for me instead?'

'For you?' he echoed, surprised, though nowhere near as surprised as Paula herself. 'What kind of work?'

'I need . . . a bodyguard,' said Paula, improvising.

'You mean . . . you mean I'd have to fight people?' He shook his head. 'I don't like fighting.' She got the feeling he had done a lot of it, albeit against his inclination.

'You wouldn't have to fight. You'd just have to be there. So that people wouldn't bother me.'

'Dunno,' he said uncertainly.

'I'll pay you double what you're getting now. And you can sleep in my spare room, on a proper bed. How about that?'

He looked at her suspiciously.

'I'm not like those other women,' she said, reading his thoughts. 'I don't like to be touched either. If you don't like the job, you can quit and I'll find you another one. That's a promise.'

'Dunno,' he said again. 'I gotta think it over. I gotta go. Goodnight, ma'am.'

She cursed herself for a bungler all the way home, all through half a bottle of vodka. It was a crazy notion, taking him in like a lost animal, making a pet of him. No doubt he thought she was another rich broad lusting after his body. If only it were that simple.

Next morning she rang down to the janitor and said her shower was still giving her trouble. He turned up himself, ten minutes later.

'Where's Jess?'

'He didn't show up this morning. Can't find nothing wrong with this shower, lady,' he added reproachfully.

'Well it wasn't working when I tried it just now.'

'When Jess fixes something, he fixes it good.' He gave her a knowing sideways look. Paula shoved a couple of dollars at him, anxious to be rid of him, annoyed at his false assumption. She fetched a quart of maple-and-pecan ice cream from the freezer and started working her way through it in front of some mindless TV game show, breaking off guiltily as she heard a knock on the door.

It was Jess, carrying a battered carpet bag.

'Hi,' said Paula casually, wondering if it contained merely screwdrivers and spanners, or all his worldly goods.

'You really don't like being touched?'

'That's why I need a bodyguard.'

'Then I'll take the job.'

She tried not to look too pleased, for fear he would change his mind.

'Come in, then,' she said. 'You can start work right away.'

'It's not possible,' said Isabel, staring at the doctor. Not her bland, reassuring family doctor, whose fees she could no longer afford, but an overworked GP with a bulging waiting room, whose attentions she had anxiously awaited for the best part of an hour.

'I'm afraid it is,' he said wearily. 'I'll give you a letter for St Stephen's.'

'But I was so careful!'

'Accidents do happen.'

'I can't have another baby just yet,' protested Isabel, in a vain attempt to change his diagnosis. 'I mean, the twins are only eight months old. I just can't.'

221

'Well, I'm afraid you're going to have to. Best to get it all over with while you're young.'

'But it *was* all over with. I mean, I thought it was. Last time I spent half my pregnancy on my back. I can't go through all that again. I've got two other children to care for now . . .'

Weary of her burblings, he scribbled a note and handed it over his desk.

'I've mentioned your history in the letter. Make your first appointment as soon as possible, they'll want to keep a close eye on you.' He pressed his buzzer for the next patient. Accidental pregnancies were all in the day's work, no doubt he'd had half a dozen this week already.

Isabel walked home in a daze. Another baby. And it was all she could do to look after the two she had. She would never be able to cope . . .

She arrived home to find the girls sleeping like angels for Patrick's sole benefit. They could smell when she wasn't there, when it wasn't worth playing up; they made allowances for him, as if knowing that he was a mere male. He was sprawled on the settee with a dirty cup at his elbow, puffing away at an ill-made roll-up and chuckling happily over Aristophanes in the original Greek.

'Kids all right?' she greeted him automatically.

'Good as gold. Did you get what you wanted?' He thought she had gone out to buy a new kettle; he had let the old one boil dry and clogged the gas jets with molten metal. She hadn't wanted to worry him with what she thought – hoped – was a false alarm.

'No. I got what I didn't want.' She shut her eyes. 'I've just been to the doctor's. I'm pregnant.'

'I thought you –'

'I did. But it didn't work, obviously.'

'Izzie!' He jumped up and hugged her. 'Don't look like that. We might have a boy this time.' His face broke into a grin. 'I mean, the twins are gorgeous, but I'd like a son. Wouldn't you?'

A son. She might have known he'd want a son. Why couldn't she have had one of each to begin with? Not that that would have changed anything. She would still be pregnant.

'We might just as easily have another girl,' she pointed out, perversely annoyed that he was taking it so well. 'And besides, we can't afford another baby just yet.'

'We'll manage,' said Patrick, ever the optimist. 'Okay, so it wasn't planned, but neither were the twins, and now we'd be lost without them. I mean, you're such a terrific mother, Izzie, you've got a gift for it.'

Too late, she regretted trying too hard, being too good at it. The test of real art was that it looked easy. Patrick ought to know that. Patrick who pretended that acting was a piece of cake when he secretly sweated blood over it, who was sick before every performance, unbeknown to anyone else but herself. And yet he couldn't see that she too was sweating blood, he hadn't even noticed her throwing up the last three mornings. How could anyone with his intelligence be so damned insensitive?

'Can you imagine three kids in a one-bedroomed flat?' she persisted.

'Then we'll find somewhere bigger. I've been selling myself too cheap for too long. I'll go and see Rex first thing tomorrow.'

'For God's sake don't go picking a fight with the management by asking for a raise. You're on too many blacklists already.'

Patrick's good humour suddenly evaporated.

'Sometimes you make me feel like the world's worst failure.'

'What? I do nothing but encourage you. I'm always telling you how good you are. I –'

'You never miss a chance to make me feel that I don't deserve you.'

'How can you say that? Have I ever complained about anything?'

'I'd rather you complained than played the martyr. I've had enough of that to last me a lifetime, from Ma.'

It was the first time he had ever said a word against his mother.

'You're spoiled rotten,' accused Isabel. 'You always have been.'

'And you aren't, I suppose?'

That did it. Isabel picked up the Aristophanes and threw it at him. He ducked and it banged against the open venetian blinds and bounced off the window onto the table beneath it, knocking a vase of tulips onto the pile of clean, folded, newly ironed nappies.

'Now see what you've made me do!' exploded Isabel, inspecting the damaged slat and picking up the pile of sodden terry towelling. Hearing the commotion, both children woke up from their nap and set up a simultaneous wail for attention. Blinking back the tears Isabel stomped off to the bedroom.

'Don't cry, sweetheart,' she soothed. It was Sophie's turn to be picked up first. She heard the front door slam and began crying along, wondering all the while what dire psychological effect the tears and raised voices were having on her children. She mustn't let them hear them rowing again. Which meant not rowing at all, given that they were always within earshot. Patrick was right, she was spoiled. And besides, it was her own stupid fault she was pregnant, not his . . .

By the time he returned, an hour later, with a replacement bunch of flowers, a bottle of celebratory champagne, and that irresistible sorry-mum look on his face, she would have forgiven him anything. It was herself she couldn't forgive.

'I was wondering when you'd show up,' said Paula, her heart missing a beat as she emerged from her shower to find Vince filling half of her tiny dressing room. Thank God Jess was at his literacy classes this evening, instead of here, waiting to escort her home.

'Congratulations,' said Vince, with steely quietness, 'on landing the part in the *Snowdrops* movie.'

'Cut the sarcasm,' said Paula, sitting down to comb out her hair, addressing him in the mirror. 'I know perfectly well you only sold the film rights on condition they gave me the lead.' He had paid Simon Fisk a small fortune for them, no doubt with this in mind. 'Thank you once again. As always I'm very grateful.'

'Cut the sarcasm yourself. You could have told me yourself that you'd signed with Zach Goldberg, instead of getting him to write to me.'

'What's the point of telling you anything? You must have known already. I need someone who knows the movie business. You can't keep buying me parts. Or don't you think I'm a good enough actress to get work any other way?'

'Being a good actress isn't enough. Specially in Hollywood.'

Paula swung round to face him.

'Okay, so I'll have to gobble a few fat old producers. I've already proved I can do that, with Marty. But at least I won't have to marry them. From now on, I don't want any more handouts from you. That's why I moved out of the apartment.'

'To slum it with the beatniks in Greenwich Village?'

'At least I pay the rent myself. That really bugs you, doesn't it? Still, you can always buy up the block and have me evicted.'

Go on, thought Paula. Shout at me. Get angry. Show me how much you care . . .

'Have it your own way, then,' he said, his face like a mask. 'Just don't be too proud to ask for help if things go wrong.'

'You sound as if you hope they will.'

'I'm afraid for you, that's all. It's a jungle out there. Look what happened to Marilyn Monroe.' The ultimate screen sex symbol, and an idol of Paula's, had been found dead of a drug overdose the previous week. 'I don't want you to end up the same way. If you make it in Hollywood, everyone will want a piece of you. That half-witted gigolo of yours is just the beginning.'

Paula stood up and faced him, faced her biggest fear.

'Understand this. If anything ever happens to Jess, if anyone so much as touches a hair of his head, I swear to God I'll shop you. I'll tell the police what happened to the man who raped me, I'll tell them about your father. Even if they don't believe me, other people will. You like being one of the nobs, don't you, Vince? That's why you've cleaned up your act. You wouldn't like your new friends and business contacts knowing you were just a common murderer.'

His eyes didn't flicker; they just froze over, like black ice.

'Why have you turned against me like this? What did I do wrong?' His voice was cold, hard.

'You tried to make me dependent on you, to take away my freedom.'

'I asked you to marry me,' he reminded her. 'Most women would take that as proof of good faith.'

'All it proved to me is that you wanted to own me, instead of just renting me. Well, I'm not for sale.'

For a moment he didn't speak, still as a lion before the kill.

'Very well then,' he said tightly. 'I won't bother you again.' He turned to go, hesitated, and looked back at her. 'Or Jess either. On one condition. Does he hurt you? Do you let him hurt you?'

For reply Paula shucked her dressing gown off her shoulders, standing before him naked.

'Do you see any bruises?' she demanded, turning round slowly in front of him. 'Jess wouldn't hurt a fly.'

For a moment she thought – or rather hoped – that he was going to make a grab for her.

'Cover yourself up,' he said sharply, picking up her discarded wrap, just as she heard a perfunctory knock on the door.

'The teacher was sick,' announced Jess, walking in without waiting for an answer. 'We finished early –'

He broke off at the sight of Paula hastily drawing the garment around her.

'Jess, this is Vincent Parry. He's . . . he used to be my business manager.' She had told Jess a bit about him, but not too much. 'Vince, this is Jess Morales.'

'Hi,' said Jess truculently, uncowed by Vince's imposing presence, his unmistakable air of authority. He was getting more confident by the day, thanks to regular meals, decent clothes, a comfortable bed, and having Paula treat him as an equal. Learning to read had changed his life; the comic books he loved gave him even more pleasure now that he could decipher the little balloons. The sight of Jess laughing over a comic was a vision of perfect happiness that left Paula limp with delight.

'Vince was just leaving,' she continued. 'Well, goodbye then. It was nice to see you. Have a safe journey home.'

He looked at her for the last time, and for once the mask slipped, revealing not anger, not venom, not menace, but pain, pain that left no room for anything else, pain that shook her and shocked her. Pain he would have denied.

'Goodbye, Paula,' he said heavily. 'Goodbye, Jess. Look after her, won't you? She needs it.'

Jess watched as Vince left the room. Paula sat down and began putting on her street make-up, anxious to keep her hands busy so that Jess wouldn't notice them shaking.

'Why were you standing there with no clothes on?'

'I'd just had a shower. My robe slipped. Wait while I get dressed and we'll go home.'

She was uncomfortably aware of his presence on the other side of the screen. She had always been modest with him to the point of prudishness and now she felt she had lost his respect. But then, she had been bound to lose his respect, sooner or later. She had

226

allowed him to put her on a pedestal and it was only a matter of time till she fell off it.

She had lied to him. Lied about not wanting to be touched. Sex was just like booze, or food. However much you despised yourself for needing it, however much the thought of it repelled you, it always got the better of you in the end. She had wanted Vince to push her down onto the floor and make violent love to her. She had wanted it right from the start, and the bastard wouldn't do it, wouldn't have her on her terms, only his own. Well, now she was finally free of him. Good riddance.

'Ready?' she said. But for once Jess didn't return her smile. He was withdrawn and sulky in the cab going home and served up her steak and salad supper without a word. Since he had moved in she had been eating sensibly, drinking less, and not putting on any weight.

'Aren't you having any?'

'I ain't hungry.'

Paula wasn't hungry either, but she forced it down, chattering inanely all the while. Finally he cut across her prattle with a sudden 'You weren't expecting me. You thought I was going straight home from class.'

'So?'

'That man. You let him see you without any clothes on. You were going to let him touch you.'

'No, Jess, that's not true.'

'You think I'll believe anything,' he said, jumping up. 'You think because I'm a moron I'll believe anything you say.'

'How often do I have to tell you you're not a moron? I get so angry when you say things like that!'

'That man. He's rich. And clever. Not like me. If I hadn't come in you were going to . . . going to . . .' He couldn't get the word out.

'Jess, please –' She got up and put her arms around him, the first time she had dared to touch him, but he pushed her away.

'You told me you didn't like men. That's why I never – why I never –'

'What?' prompted Paula. Could he possibly feel the same way as she did? Sweet, innocent, wise, harmless, abused Jess. Jess with his beautiful face and perfect body, with his simple mind and

227

damaged soul. Jess who made her want to be good, for the first time in her life. Jess whom she hadn't dared to corrupt, whom she wanted only to protect. 'Why you never did what?'

'Forget it. I'm gonna move out. I'm gonna move in the morning. I can't stay here no more.'

Gently, desperately, she took his head between her hands.

'Don't go,' she said. 'Please don't leave me, Jess. I'd be so miserable without you. I . . . I love you.' There. She had finally said it, for the first time in her life. She wouldn't have dared to say it to anyone else but him. 'I love you better than anyone else in the whole world.'

He stared at her for a moment, with all that old streetwise mistrust she had tried so hard to overcome, the same mistrust she still couldn't overcome in herself.

'You're just saying that. You're just saying that because you feel sorry for me.'

Paula shut her eyes and took a deep breath.

'Jess,' she said. 'Will you marry me? Will you be my husband? Will you stay with me for ever and ever?'

But he just looked at her disbelievingly, as if this were some cruel, monstrous tease, until she had no choice but to put her arms round his neck and kiss him the way she had never kissed anyone before, putting her whole heart and soul into it, keeping nothing back, taking the biggest gamble of her life.

After a few agonizing seconds of no response, he took over, suddenly and spontaneously and ravenously while Paula strove to forget all she knew, all she had learned, because this was one thing she wouldn't, couldn't teach him, this was something she needed to learn from him, from scratch. With Jess she would be a virgin again.

He was clumsy and awkward and instinctive, he had no knowledge, no experience, no text-book tricks, no skill. But he said, 'I love you, Paula,' over and over again till she was drunk with it. Which made him the best, the most accomplished lover she had ever had.

'We can't possibly afford a place like this,' said Isabel. It was a ground-floor three-bedroomed mansion flat off the Exhibition

Road, with vast high-ceilinged centrally heated rooms, refurbished kitchen and bathroom, polished parquet floors and newly painted plain white walls. Patrick hadn't told her anything about it, except that it was 'bigger than Cranley Gardens'. She had braced herself for some damp, rat-infested basement, or a rickety mansarded attic with a leaking roof and umpteen stairs.

'Yes we can.' Patrick whipped an envelope out of his inside pocket and handed it to her.

'What's this?'

'A contract. *Harry Spencer Investigates*. Yet again. Remember that telly play I did, back in the summer?'

The author of *Daggers Drawn* had used the same private detective in a routine hour-long television whodunnit, in which Patrick was required only to repeat his stage character, thereby earning more in four days than he usually made in a month.

'You mean, there's going to be another one?'

'Not another one. Another twelve. A series. Rex managed to get me a terrific deal. I didn't want to tell you till it was all in the bag.'

'I don't want you to do it.'

'Are you crazy? It's money for old rope. Look at that bloke you used to be at FRIDA with, who picked up that part in *Z-Cars*. He's become a star overnight. All kinds of people are bound to spot me and offer me other work.'

'No they won't. You'll get type-cast, and so will he. These TV series are professional suicide unless you're already established.'

Patrick threw his hands up in the air.

'There's no pleasing you, is there? You said you wanted to move to a bigger place. Well, now we can, in time for the baby. It's not a dump, it's not in the sticks, it hasn't got floral wallpaper and the toilet doesn't smell.' Isabel winced at the word toilet. 'What more do you want? I thought you'd be pleased! And anyway, I've already signed the contract.'

'You mean you can't get out of it?'

'Why would I want to get out of it? Trust you to turn your nose up. Still a little snob at heart, aren't you?'

It was Patrick's favourite taunt, and it always hurt, perhaps because it was so undeniably true. She wanted him to play the kind

229

of parts she could be proud of, parts she could brag about to other snobs, like Daddy and Richard.

'Better than being an inverted one, like you,' countered Isabel. 'Your working-class-hero act gets pretty boring too. All those low-lifes you hang around with. Especially at that horrible gym.'

'Boxing keeps me fit. You wouldn't complain if I played squash or golf or went riding. Just because my friends aren't gushing thespians doesn't mean they're low-lifes. There is a world outside the bloody theatre, you know.'

'Don't swear in front of the children.' They always perked up at the merest whiff of a disagreement, sitting there in their double pushchair rapt and rosy and attentive, as if they were taking it all in.

'If you don't like the flat –'

'I never said I didn't like the flat!'

'– it's just too bad because I've signed the lease and paid the deposit. I got an advance from Rex.' He pulled a wad of notes out of his pocket. 'Here. That's to buy furniture and stuff with. I've got a mate who can get us a bed at cost. And Ma wants to buy us a fridge as a moving-in present.'

'You've already told Ma?'

'I was excited. I wanted to tell someone. It really bucked her up,' he added reproachfully, 'to know I was doing well.'

Conscience-stricken, Isabel threw her arms around him.

'I'm sorry. It's just that I hate you doing hack stuff, just to pay the bills. I didn't mean to be a bitch.'

'It's okay,' said Patrick nobly. 'You'll feel better when the baby's born,' he added, subtly reminding her that she was a slave to her hormones, hormones which would almost certainly make her feel worse after the baby was born, not better.

'I feel fine.' Having managed nearly seven months out of the nine without mishap, Isabel was ever loath to admit to feeling less than radiant; she didn't want Patrick thinking he had married a weakling. Or Ma either, who was due to come over from Ireland to look after the twins while she was in hospital.

The next week was spent in a hectic shopping spree. Isabel simply couldn't bring herself to buy anything cheap and nasty, and Rex's cash wouldn't run to the elegant Swedish and Italian imports she craved. Luckily the bank agreed to an overdraft, on the basis

230

of Patrick's contract, which, together with a spot of hire purchase and the 'borrowing' of several items from Elizabeth Street, enabled her to equip her new home to a reasonable, if not ideal, standard of taste and comfort. It was the first time in months she'd had any money to spend on anything other than essentials. Patrick knew nothing about the odd tenners Richard had slipped her, to help her pay the bills; he remained ultra-sensitive about being the poor relation, especially now that Richard was making pots of money.

Kill Claudio, billed as the thinking man's musical, was sold out until Easter 1963, while the all-male *Merry Wives* was still going strong at the Renegade; the Oscar Wilde play had just opened in the West End, following a triumphant regional tour, to unanimous critical acclaim. Backers were queuing up to finance Richard's next venture, entitled *Don't just sit there, do something* – an improvised, audience-participation 'adventure' directed yet again by Neville Seaton, who was fast establishing a reputation as a bold and innovative director.

'It's time you stopped avoiding Neville,' said Richard one day, minding the pushchair as Isabel fretted interminably over the lampshades in Heals. 'He's always asking after you, you know.'

'Well, give him my best regards.' She still felt unable to face Neville after having hurt him so badly. Especially as Patrick had never lost his insecurities on the subject of his former rival. She was regularly required to reassure him that of course she didn't still love Neville, she never had done, any more than he had loved Teresa.

'It's on the level, Izzie. He wants to help you, that's all. It drives him crazy that you're not working.'

'I can't work. I will shortly have three children under two.'

'If you worked, you could afford to get a girl in to mind them. Even if you couldn't you know I'd chip in. It's killing you being stuck at home all day. Anyone can see that. Everyone apart from bloody Patrick, that is . . .'

'Do you think this grey silk shade will show the dirt too much?'

'Having children never stopped Fay having a career,' persisted Richard. Or Davina,' he added, heedless that these two examples were not ones she cared to emulate. 'Talking of which, have you heard from the old bastard?'

'I took the twins over to Windsor the other day.'

She winced at the memory of it. The change in Adrian had been alarming, he seemed like a broken man.

'Cheer up, Daddy,' Isabel had said, almost impatiently. Both the girls had been playing up that day, wearing her patience to a frazzle. 'You're better off without her.'

'Better off without her. Better off without my home. Better off without my son. And how do I know she'll keep her word, once she's taken everything I have?' But the question wasn't addressed to her. It was as if he were talking to himself.

'What do you mean, Daddy? Keep her word about what?'

By way of an answer he had launched broodingly into a speech from *Othello*:

> *'Who steals my purse steals trash . . .*
> *. . . But he that filches from me my good name*
> *Robs me of that which not enriches him*
> *And makes me poor indeed . . .'*

'His good name, eh?' echoed Richard dryly, when Isabel recounted this exchange. 'What dirt do you reckon she's got on him?'

'God knows. I could hardly ask him, could I?' And then, seeing the knowing look on his face, 'Do you know something I don't?' Richard was always first with all the scandal.

Richard shrugged enigmatically. 'Just indulging my vile imagination, that's all. It must be something pretty sordid for him to be letting her bleed him white like this. Let's hope she blows the gaff on him anyway, once he's coughed up.'

'Richard! Whose side are you on?'

'Fay's, actually. It's high time the old bastard got his comeuppance, after what he did to her. Did he tell you he's been having trouble at the Kean?'

'What kind of trouble?' She hadn't stayed long enough to hear any more. Sophie had been spectacularly sick all over the carpet, causing a diversion, and by the time Isabel had cleaned up the mess and established that Sophie was running a temperature, Adrian had been due at the theatre and Isabel anxious to get her to the doctor's.

'It's common knowledge that he's been losing his grip. The rumour is that the board are planning to replace him as artistic director.'

'Replace him? But he built that place up from nothing! It was thanks to him they got the funding to build it in the first place. And he's had raves and full houses for everything he's done!' With the exception of the first production of the new Davina-less season, *The Tempest*, which had been universally panned. But then, Daddy was well overdue for a critical backlash.

'Neville went to see his Prospero last week. Said it was embarrassing. People were leaving in the interval.'

'He must have caught him on an off night,' said Isabel stubbornly, settling for the grey silk shade, impractical or not. 'I'll reserve judgment till I've seen it for myself.'

'Then go,' challenged Richard. 'I'll take the girls off your hands one afternoon so you can bunk off to a matinée.'

Richard was proving a surprisingly enthusiastic uncle. Thanks to his recently installed live-in housekeeper, a motherly theatrical widow, Isabel felt safer leaving the twins at Elizabeth Street than at home with Patrick.

The next couple of weeks, however, were fully taken up with the move, waiting for deliveries, scrubbing every crevice, and endlessly rearranging the furniture. Only after this tireless orgy of nest-building did she allow herself her promised half day. Not so much for her own benefit as for Daddy's.

He had phoned her twice in the last fortnight, evidently wanting a chat, but both calls had occurred at the worst possible moment. On the first occasion she had been slap in the middle of feeding time at the zoo, on the second the drainage hose from the washing machine had just leapt out of the sink of its own accord, flooding the kitchen with hot dirty suds. By the time she had phoned him back as promised, there was no reply, and repeated attempts had failed to find him in. Which might have worried her more had she not had so much else on her mind.

Just as Richard arrived to fetch the twins and drop her off at the station (Patrick was at the TV studio, recording episode one of *Harry Spencer*), Adrian phoned again.

'Are you ringing from the theatre, Daddy?' said Isabel, puzzled, looking at her watch.

'No. Rang them to say I couldn't go on today.'

Isabel had never known her father miss a performance. He had gone on stage no matter what, often against medical advice.

'Are you ill? Have you seen a doctor?' Richard put his ear up against the receiver.

'There's nothing a doctor can do for me. I want you to come to the house. Now. You're the only person I can trust.'

'Of course. I'll come right away . . .' Thank God she had already made arrangements for a sitter.

'Signed the papers yesterday. Gave the bitch everything she asked for. The house, the money, Toby, everything. I get to visit him one afternoon a month. One afternoon a month!'

'We'll talk about it when I get there, Daddy. Perhaps it's not too late to change the settlement. I'll ring your solicitor for you, if you like . . .'

'I thought that was the end of it. I thought, I've still got my work. But I got a letter this morning, from the board. They've sacked me, Izzie. They don't want me any more.'

'Oh Daddy . . .'

'Not only that, they want me to stand down as Prospero. And do you know who they've approached to take over the part? The same bastard who stole my wife and son! They've been planning this whole thing together right from the start . . .' His voice broke into a sob. 'I was a fool to give in to them. I thought I didn't have any choice. But now I have. Because without my work, I've nothing more to lose, except one thing. And I won't let her take that away from me. I won't let her!'

'Daddy, I want you to go to bed and lie down. I'm leaving now.'

'I can't live the rest of my life like this. I won't let them destroy me. I'd rather destroy myself.'

He rang off. Isabel looked at Richard.

'Did you hear all that?'

'Don't go off the deep end. He wouldn't have asked you to come over if he was really going to do himself in. He's obviously planning to pop a few pills for effect, and for you to find him in the nick of time. Stupid old bugger. I'd better come with you.'

The traffic was bad. It seemed to take for ever to get to Elizabeth Street, where they dropped off the girls, and then on to Windsor, with red traffic lights thwarting them all the way.

'Don't flap,' repeated Richard, squeezing her hand. 'He just wants a bit of attention.'

Attention. Everyone wanted her attention. Patrick, the twins, and soon the new baby would want it too. There simply wasn't enough of her to go round. She had cut her visits to Fay down to once a month, miserably aware that she was failing her. And now she was failing Daddy too. All these weeks he had been longing for someone to confide in and she had been too busy mopping up the floor and ironing nappies and wiping strained spinach off the walls to listen . . .

There was no answer when they rang the bell. But the back door had been left unlocked. They let themselves into the kitchen, Isabel calling out 'Daddy!' as they searched the house to no avail. On checking the garage they found the car gone. Isabel rang the theatre, but he wasn't there.

It was then that she noticed the white mark on the wall above the fireplace.

'Oh my God,' she said, pointing. 'It's gone. The Russian pistol the Moscow Arts Theatre gave him after *Uncle Vanya*. He must have taken it with him.'

'That old thing? It doesn't work, does it? I thought it was just a prop . . .'

Isabel started as she heard a car in the driveway and ran to the window.

'He's back!' she said, relieved. 'And he's got Toby with him . . .'

She hurried to the door and let them in. Toby was squirming in his father's arms and screaming blue murder. Oh no, she thought, he's gone and snatched him . . .

'Daddy!' said Isabel, alarmed at his stricken expression. 'What on earth's happened? I was so worried . . .'

Adrian walked past her into the living room and sat down heavily, as if all his strength was exhausted, still holding on to a resisting, sobbing Toby.

'Daddy, are you all right?'

'I am now,' said Adrian. And then, freezing her blood, 'I've done it, Izzie. I've killed her. I've killed them both.'

*

Late that same afternoon, Pacific Time, Paula was anxiously watching television with Jess in her trailer between shots. President Kennedy had just ordered a naval blockade against Soviet ships bound for Cuba and demanded the dismantling of missile bases on the island. Suddenly the world was on the brink of a nuclear war. Poor Izzie would go spare worrying about the kids when she read it in the papers tomorrow.

She channel-hopped impatiently to avoid the ads, pausing with interest as she spotted a shot of Isabel's father, and then listening, open-mouthed, to the newscaster.

'. . . *Sir Adrian Mallory, ex-husband of Fay Burnett, whose failed suicide bid shook Hollywood less than two years ago, has been charged with the double homicide of his estranged second wife, Davina Winter, and her fiancé, Brindsley Smythe, both well-known British Shakespearean actors. Other overseas news follows this message . . .*'

'What's the matter?' said Jess, just as the Second Assistant Director tapped on the door of the trailer to summon Paula for her final scene of the day.

'That man who did the murder,' said Paula, horrified. 'He's Izzie's father.'

'Izzie? The girl you used to share an apartment with? The one with the twins?' Jess never forgot a name, never forgot anything she told him.

'I'm coming!' shouted Paula, in response to the knock. The Cuban missile crisis paled into insignificance. She would get this scene over with and then get straight to a phone and check that Izzie was all right.

It was a non-speaking reaction shot, with Paula looking out of the hotel window – or rather, straight at the camera – watching as the hero arrives in the courtyard below. Ten seconds of love-at-first-sight, pathos, longing, and regret in the making, her face working hard, her self-discipline absolute, all thoughts of anything else banished from her mind. Having landed her first movie role, she was determined not to blow her big chance . . .

'I want to be rich and famous,' she had told the FRIDA interviewing panel, less than four years ago, an ambition they had sneered at. She would have liked that snooty trio to see her now.

236

The 'borderline case' from the wrong side of the tracks was about to show them she meant business.

A final primp from hair and make-up and wardrobe, a reminder from the cameraman about exactly how to hold her head. 'Stand by!' she heard, and then 'Roll camera', before the clapper-board snapped right in front of her face for the close-up. And then finally 'Action', though that was hardly the right word to describe it. Film acting was all about holding back rather than letting go. On the stage you had to show the audience what you were thinking, but on the screen you had to let the camera discover it, to ignore the watching crew, never forgetting that everything you did would be blown up to thirty-five times its normal size. No wonder it looked easy, understated, not like acting at all. No wonder everyone thought they could do it . . .

'Cut! That was great, Paula, honey.' She sighed in relief. 'But let's try it one more time, okay?'

The make-up girl wiped the sweat off her forehead and it all began again. It took four more takes before the director was satisfied, before Paula was free to call the new number Isabel had given her, heedless of it being nearly two a.m. in London. The phone was answered on the first ring.

'Hello?'

'Patrick? I just heard. How's Izzie?'

'Paula. Thank God it's only you. I just got back this minute from the hospital. I thought it was them.'

'The hospital?'

'The shock of it sent Izzie into labour. The baby's in an incubator, with breathing problems. She's six weeks premature, they say she might not make it . . .'

The story came out piecemeal, jumbled, with Patrick almost incoherent from anger and anxiety. Adrian had visited Davina's cottage, shot his wife through the heart at point-blank range, and then emptied the remaining five rounds into Brindsley Smythe. Othello had come to life with a vengeance.

'Adrian had threatened suicide over the phone, would you believe,' continued Patrick. 'And what does Richard do? He takes Izzie off to Windsor, in her condition, with the prospect of finding a dead body on the carpet. And then bloody Adrian turns up at the

237

house, hotfoot from the cottage, and asks Izzie to take care of Toby for him. Can you believe it? What a family.'

'Where are the kids?'

'The twins are with Richard's housekeeper, till my mother flies in tomorrow. Toby's in the care of the local authority.'

In a Home, thought Paula, with a pang.

'Oh God, Paula. I wish you were here.'

For the first time ever, Patrick needed her, and she was six thousand miles away.

'I wish I was too. Give Izzie my love. Tell her I'll write. When shooting's over, perhaps I can fit in a visit.'

'That would cheer her up. She misses you.' Quite an admission, coming from Patrick. 'I'd better get off the phone now, in case the hospital try to get through.' He sounded desolate, helpless. 'Thanks for calling. 'Bye, love.'

'You okay?' said Jess as Paula replaced the receiver.

'I'm fine. Let's go home now.'

They were living modestly in a bungalow in West Hollywood, eschewing the fashionable parties and watering holes where Jess would have felt unable to hold his own. While he drove her new Lincoln convertible, provided by the studio – Paula had taught him herself, and he was proving a careful and competent chauffeur – she told him, in brief, what had happened.

'So are you going to go to England?' he asked, his voice betraying the fear that she might not come back.

'No. No, I don't think so.'

The promise to visit had been hollow. There simply wouldn't be time. Zach, her agent, had already arranged for her to start another movie as soon as this one wrapped, assuming the world hadn't been blown to kingdom come by then. The rumours were spreading that the rushes were great, that *Snowdrops* was all set to be a smash, and producers were vying to sign her before her price went up.

She couldn't afford to rock the boat, not now she was aboard at last. Especially now that she wasn't working for herself any more. She was doing it for Jess. So that they could have a secure future together, so that never again would he have to sleep rough or mend showers or be molested by rich bored women. For the first time in her life she felt needed, loved, essential to another person's well-being, one who relied on her absolutely.

238

Which was in itself a worry, of course. *Snowdrops* might bomb at the box office. This next movie might be the last one she was ever offered; after that, she might never work again. A really successful film actress might survive ten years; most of them vanished without trace long before that . . .

She had to make the most of it while it lasted. Because it sure as hell wouldn't last for long.

9

Winter 1962–Autumn 1963

There is nothing either good or bad, but thinking makes it so.

William Shakespeare – Hamlet

'You're mad,' they all said, tactlessly using the word Isabel dreaded. Richard, Paula and Patrick were for once all in agreement. She had enough to cope with, they said, without taking on Toby too. Let the professionals take care of him; they knew what they were doing.

'How can you say that?' Isabel challenged Paula, who had rung long-distance almost daily ever since the crisis broke. 'You hated being in care so much you ran away.'

'I hated being with Marje as well,' Paula pointed out. 'I was never grateful to her for keeping me on after my dad disappeared. I took everything out on her. And Toby'll do the same to you, you'll see.'

Richard was equally brutal.

'I give it six months at the outside before he drives you to a nervous breakdown. You're a sucker for punishment, Izzie. You always were.'

'Your father's got a bloody nerve,' fumed Patrick. 'How can you give in to emotional blackmail like this? Hasn't the old sod done you enough harm already?'

But Isabel remained adamant. Not out of filial duty, self-delusion, or bloody-mindedness, or any of the selfless motives they ascribed to her, but because of the desperate deal she had done with God. Not the genial, easy-going C of E God, but the stern and implacable Catholic one, the one who didn't miss a trick, the one she had learned to fear. The sight of her precious infant lying in an incubator, fighting for every gasp of breath, had propelled her on her own personal road to Damascus. She had

240

realized in a blinding flash that this was her punishment, not only for not wanting this baby, but for refusing to embrace the faith.

'Let Emily live,' she had prayed, 'and I promise I'll take Toby. I'll take Toby and I'll love him like my own.'

And Emily had lived, thus obliging her to keep her side of the bargain. Patrick finally gave in, thinking, no doubt, that to let her try and fail was the only way to make her see sense. And it had helped that Ma, who had never met Toby, came down on Isabel's side.

During the long hours Isabel put in at the hospital, Ma held the fort in her absence, the only person she could have trusted to maintain her own high standards. Mercifully, Ma found no fault with Isabel's well-established routine. On the contrary, she congratulated her on how well the twins were doing and what a lovely home she had made.

'Careful,' Paula had said. 'Sounds to me like she's sucking up, hoping you'll ask her to move in for good.'

As Patrick had foretold Ma and Maureen had quickly fallen out. Ma had returned home to her big, empty house two weeks after Da's death, and none of the other siblings had so far invited the lonely widow to come and live with them.

'She wouldn't want to impose on us,' responded Isabel, too relieved to have her there to think that far ahead. Ma was a proud old bird, and surely wouldn't want to play second fiddle for the rest of her life in another woman's home.

Adrian had been denied bail, thanks to the prima facie evidence of guilt, and was being held in Wormwood Scrubs pending trial and psychiatric reports. A guilt-stricken Isabel had gone to see him as soon as Emily was out of danger. If only she had been more sympathetic and less wrapped up in her own affairs, perhaps he wouldn't have felt driven to commit such an appalling crime . . .

'How's Toby?' he had demanded, by way of greeting. He seemed calm, composed.

'All right.' Even though he was far from all right; it wouldn't help Daddy to know that. 'I visited him yesterday, in the children's home.' An initial foster placement had broken down, thanks to Toby's fiendish misbehaviour.

'You mean he isn't with you yet?'

'Daddy, the social services have to vet us first. And besides, I

241

shall be spending most of my time at St Stephen's, until the baby's well enough to come home.'

'You blame me for going into labour, I suppose.' It was more of a reproach than an apology.

'Of course I don't.' Even if everybody else did.

'I had to ring you. I needed you to take care of Toby for me, once I gave myself up to the police.'

'Oh Daddy! Oh Daddy, why did you have to do it?'

'It doesn't matter any more. I won't be the first husband to have killed a faithless wife, or her lover.'

But Isabel knew it had been more than *crime passionnel*. She remembered her father's fears about Davina stealing his good name, and Richard's theory that she had something on him and was using it to force his hand over the settlement. Had he taken a male lover, perhaps? But bisexuality was common enough in the theatre, after all, hardly a secret worth killing for. Or had he been embezzling funds from the Kean? If so, surely it would have come out by now . . .

'I considered killing myself, you know, instead of them,' said Adrian. 'I had nothing left to live for, after all. But they would only have spoken ill of the dead. And now they can't. Let them hang me, if they must. I'm not afraid.'

'Of course they're not going to hang you, Daddy,' said Isabel, shutting her mind to this fearful possibility. 'What does your solicitor say?'

'He's advised me to plead temporary insanity.' Insanity, thought Isabel, shuddering. 'Even though it was the sanest thing I ever did. You were right about her all along, Izzie. I should never have left your mother . . .'

Whereupon Isabel had burst into tears just as the guard announced that their time was up. Adrian had embraced her briefly and let them lead him away, head held high. It was as if the murder had had some cathartic effect, he seemed resigned, dignified, at peace. Unlike an anguished Isabel, who could only hope the solicitor knew his stuff.

The provisional go-ahead to bring Toby home came shortly after Emily's discharge from hospital. Over the coming months his progress would be closely monitored by social workers and child psychologists before there could be any question of the 'placement', as they called it, becoming permanent – an eventuality which neither Patrick nor Richard nor Paula regarded as remotely likely.

Patrick was currently working a fourteen-hour day, recording the TV series by day and performing on stage by night, so Richard drove Isabel to the children's home and waited outside in the car while she went in. Toby was having lunch. Or rather not having lunch. Having thrown his plate of mince onto the floor he was now sitting alone, in disgrace, watching while his fellow-inmates ate some revolting milk pudding.

'Hello, Toby,' said Isabel, squatting down beside him. 'What's the matter? Was the food horrible?'

'Dunno,' muttered Toby. 'Didn't have any.'

'Let's go home and have something to eat, then.' He didn't respond. 'Unless you'd prefer to stay here.' She stood up. 'Are you coming?'

He didn't take her proffered hand but after a show of indecision he followed her out of the room while the other detainees gaped enviously at the beautiful lady who had come to rescue him.

'Hi there, Toby,' said Richard casually, as Isabel flung his little suitcase in the back and seated him on her lap, much to his disgust. Toby didn't deign to answer, squirming silently and sullenly throughout the journey and shunning further valiant overtures from Richard, who dropped them off with some relief, declining Isabel's invitation to come in.

'Toby, this is Grandma,' said Isabel, as she opened the door. Ma merely nodded at him, sensing that a hug would be repelled. 'And this is Sophie and Sarah,' she went on, shepherding him into the kitchen, where the twins were enthroned on their high chairs, bibs streaked with the remains of their lunch. 'Girls, this is Toby, your uncle.'

Toby visibly grew a couple of inches with this new and unexpected rank; the girls stared at him briefly and fell to simultaneous chortling, sharing one of their mysterious private jokes. Toby scowled, but at this point Ma started quizzing him about what he would like to eat and he consented moodily to scrambled eggs on toast, which he devoured with immoderate haste while Isabel went to see to Emily.

'The poor child's half starved,' Ma told her, putting a head

243

around the door. Which was literally true. Toby's virtual hunger strike had helped cut through a lot of red tape. Having accepted and demolished a second helping while Ma put the twins down for their afternoon nap, he finally slunk into the living room, where Isabel was feeding the baby.

Isabel introduced him to Emily as if acquainting two strangers at a cocktail party, trying not to be fazed by his baleful stare. She could hardly expect him to view her offspring with anything other than hostility. After seven years of being a one-and-only, he would have to share the limelight with three other children, all of whom were ahead of him in the pecking order.

'She's awfully small,' he said scornfully.

'Yes, isn't she? Would you like to hold her?' She tried not to sound as anxious as she felt. The only way to counteract his destructive urges was to awaken his protective instincts, assuming he had any.

Toby shook his head. 'I might drop her,' he said, almost threateningly. 'And then you'll send me away.'

'You're much too big and strong to drop her,' said Isabel, setting aside the bottle and putting Emily over her shoulder. 'Let's wait for a big burp first.'

It finally arrived, producing a snort of derision from Toby. Isabel patted the settee next to her and passed over the precious bundle, showing him how to support her head. Emily, mercifully a placid child, wriggled warmly in pre-slumberous contentment, thawing the edges of Toby's anxious frown. But just as Isabel was congratulating herself on having handled him rather well, he chilled her with a sudden 'Is it true that worms eat dead bodies?'

'What?' said Isabel, startled. 'Who told you that?'

'Terry Pinks. His mum's dead too. He said the worms ate her. He said they eat the eyes first. I kicked him for telling lies.' And then, pleadingly this time, 'It's not true, is it?'

'No,' said Isabel. 'No, it's not true.' He knew far too much about death already without finding out any more . . .

Her heart began, inexorably, to melt. She and Toby had one important thing in common. A father who had destroyed both their mothers.

*

244

One bitter day in January, Ma tripped on the icy pavement on her way back from the grocer. In her attempt to safeguard a box of eggs, she fell awkwardly and broke her leg in two places. The accident left her encased in plaster from ankle to thigh and unable to move without the aid of crutches.

'Best if I go home,' she insisted, her face pinched with unacknowledged pain. 'I came here to help you, not be an extra burden.' But Isabel couldn't contemplate bundling her onto a plane in her present vulnerable state. Ma had waited on her hand and foot throughout her first pregnancy. Now it was time to repay her debt.

Isabel had to help her wash and dress and get in and out of the loo, services which she accepted rather tetchily. She insisted on making herself useful from her chair, knitting, sewing, peeling vegetables into a basin, and striking up an unexpected rapport with Toby, who turned out to have a redeeming soft spot for anyone he perceived as even more powerless and pathetic than himself – Emily on the one hand, on account of being so ridiculously small, and Grandma on the other, on account of being so unbelievably old. The twins he ignored – they always seemed to be laughing at him and he still hadn't developed a sense of humour. Patrick he was wary of, perhaps because Patrick, despite his bluff man-to-man manner, was so obviously wary of him.

And so it was Isabel who bore the brunt of Toby's bad behaviour, Isabel whom he tried and tested and tormented with his thousand and one food fads, his wilful bed-wetting and his outbursts of sexually explicit bad language which could only have been learned from his warring parents. Surprisingly, he could be cowed instantly by a word from Ma or Patrick, but even this was provocative, as if to make Isabel feel that she was the problem, no one else. Several times she came perilously close to striking him in anger; more than once she had to lock herself in the loo for a furtive weep. She had hated him, from the day he was born, and now here she was, in despair because he wouldn't love her. And yet, perversely, when his violent dreams woke him in the night, he refused to be comforted by anyone else but her, depriving her of what little sleep the new baby allowed her.

To make matters worse he didn't like his new school and regularly came home bearing evidence of yet another playground

245

fight. The teachers found him disruptive and aggressive, and their reports soon reached the ears of the social workers, one of whom arrived one day to take Toby away for 'assessment', thereby inducing such a violent screaming fit that the appointment had to be deferred to another day, at Isabel's insistence.

'It's all right,' she told him afterwards. 'You don't have to be afraid. They're not going to take you away from us. I promise.' A promise she was in no position to make, but he was frightened enough already, almost as frightened as she was. His fierce answering hug had wiped out his sins with all the dubious magic of the confessional.

Faced with the threat of official intervention, an already weakening Patrick closed ranks with Isabel, unable to bring himself to side with the bureaucrats, a breed for whom he had an innate and devastating contempt. Even though they provided a generous allowance for Toby's keep. An allowance on which Isabel had come to depend.

'Any sign of the rest of the TV money yet?' she asked Patrick in bed one night, not for the first time. The rent and the HP alone added up to more than Patrick was getting from the theatre.

'No,' said Patrick shortly.

'Why not?' persisted Isabel. 'Hasn't Rex chased it up for you?'

'Of course he has. But he says these delays are normal.'

'Then why not ring the TV people yourself?'

Patrick didn't answer. He found the whole subject of money distasteful; pleading poverty to his employers even more so.

'I'll get on to them for you, if you like,' ventured Isabel, picking up the hint, knowing that he would be only too glad for her to relieve him of this unpleasant duty. For the first time she noticed the lines of fatigue around his eyes, the unaccustomed furrow between his brows. Poor darling. He had been working so hard lately . . .

The secret of Patrick's success as Harry Spencer was the sheer sex appeal he brought to the part. The original character had been a seedy burned-out bum who was down on his luck; Patrick had transformed the role by making it much more upbeat, playing him as a maverick, cynical yet vulnerable, hard-bitten but soft-hearted, full of romantic contradictions. In other words, he played himself.

It was the new Harry Spencer who had inspired the TV series, not the stereotype the author had created. Patrick, unlike his better-known predecessor, was besieged at the stage door each night by breathless female fans of all ages who had seen the first few episodes of *Harry* on the box and were slavering to meet him in the flesh.

Isabel found this adulation threatening. How could she compete with all the women who would desire him, not just actresses but pert production assistants, make-up girls, bright, enthusiastic working women, women who were not permanently exhausted . . .

She reached out for him, but he picked up her hand and kissed it and said, 'I'm sorry, darling. I'm dead beat. It wouldn't be any good.'

It was the first time he had ever turned her down, not that she usually made the first move any more. Come to think of it, it must be nearly a week since they had last made love. Oh God, thought Isabel, he's going off me. I've been letting myself go . . .

Anyone else would have put his loss of libido down to overwork, money worries, the passion-killing likelihood of one or more of the children waking up before they had finished, the inhibiting effect of Ma on the other side of the wall. But Isabel had never been one to make excuses for herself.

Next morning she got up even earlier than usual to give herself time to do her hair and put on some make-up before the daily onslaught began. By the time Patrick appeared, bleary-eyed, at breakfast, she had already put in two hours' work, but she greeted him with a sunny smile and planted a kiss on the back of his neck as she dished up his bacon and eggs, hoping that her lavishly applied perfume would overpower the odour of frying.

But Patrick kept his nose buried in his script, mouthing his lines to himself as he chewed, cutting himself off from her, from all the din around him, with single-minded concentration. Taking a final gulp of tea, he kissed Emily and the twins, said goodbye to Ma and barked at Toby to hurry up. The highlight of Toby's day was being taken to school on the back of Patrick's second-hand Vespa, a far cry from the big bad bike he craved but which saved a small fortune in fares.

'What about me?' cooed Isabel. 'Don't I get a kiss too?'

He gave her a quick peck, looking at his watch over her shoulder.

'I'm late,' he said. 'See you.'

Annoyed that her efforts had gone unnoticed, Isabel settled down to open the mail. The electricity bill was higher than ever, thanks to the washing machine churning around non-stop, raising the ice-cold winter water to germ-killing boil. And the rent was well overdue. The sooner she rang the TV company's accounts department the better . . .

There was another official-looking buff envelope which Isabel opened with some trepidation, expecting another bill.

4 March 1963

Dear Mr and Mrs Delaney
Re: Toby Mallory
Further to a case conference held yesterday, grave concern has been expressed about Toby's recent performance in psychological tests, his anti-social behaviour at school, and his continuing inability to adjust to his new environment.

It is felt that a period in Shelby House, a residential centre for children with special problems, would be most beneficial to him. This decision in no way reflects on your competence as foster parents, but good intentions are regrettably not enough to repair the severe emotional damage this unfortunate child has suffered.

A vacancy at Shelby House is expected to arise shortly. Knowing that you have Toby's best interests at heart, we are confident of your full co-operation. However, we should point out, in fairness to you, that this decision has statutory force in accordance with the relevant legislation . . .

It took a few moments for the dry, official words to sink in. She had failed. They were going to take him away from her. Toby would think that she had broken her promise, he would never forgive her. She had not realized, till that moment, that she loved him.

'What's the matter?' said Ma, seeing her face blench in fear and then flush in fury. And then, when she had read the letter, 'How can they do this? Surely you've got more rights over him than they do? You're family, after all.'

'They've got all the rights. They can do what they like with him and we've got no say.'

'Sure, half of these social workers have never had any children themselves,' growled Ma, hauling herself onto her crutches and filling the kettle for tea, her cure-all in any crisis, while Isabel tried to phone the signatory of the letter, who proved to be permanently unavailable, leaving her no choice but to talk to one of his minions.

'Why wasn't I invited to this conference of yours?' she demanded. 'Don't I know Toby better than any of you?'

'With respect, these decisions have to be taken objectively. Naturally you're emotionally involved, and –'

'I see. Because I love him, my opinion doesn't count.'

'We did stress that the placement was only temporary –'

'Stop referring to me as a placement! This is Toby's home.'

'It's not normal practice to place such a disturbed child with someone as young and inexperienced as yourself. We realize that you've done your best, but –'

'Inexperienced? I have three children of my own!'

'Three very small children who must make enormous demands on your time and attention.'

'Are you saying I've been neglecting him?'

'Toby isn't making the progress we had hoped for. Ultimately, we are responsible for his welfare . . .'

In the end, Isabel hung up, well aware that she had done her case no good by flying off the handle. Sipping a cup of Ma's tongue-curlingly strong tea, she picked up the phone again, woke Richard from a deep sleep and ranted at him for a good ten minutes before he could get a word in edgeways.

'I'll have a word with Oliver Briggs,' he said wearily. 'Renegade's solicitor. I don't suppose he knows the first thing about childcare law, but he can always bone up on it. Don't worry about the bill, I can write it off as a business expense.'

'Thanks, Richard,' sighed Isabel, hoping she could square this subsidy with Patrick.

'He'll probably advise you not to fight it,' continued Richard discouragingly. 'Perhaps Toby could do with a spell in this kiddy-bin. He was a problem child long before all this happened.'

'Perhaps that was because he had a useless mother who couldn't

249

be bothered to look after him properly.' She sounded self-righteous, even to herself, but she needed to believe it, if only to make her own sacrifices seem worthwhile.

Oliver Briggs rang her later that morning and suggested a meeting at eleven thirty next day. Having arranged for Richard's housekeeper to come round and help Ma with the children, Isabel turned her attention to the TV company's accounts department. In fighting mood now, she delivered a blistering accusatory harangue, only to be told that payment had been made some time ago to Mr Delaney's agent.

'Are you sure? He hasn't received it.'

'The cheque has been cleared. I suggest you talk direct to Mr Jordan.'

Isabel rang. But Rex Jordan was away on a business trip and his secretary, who didn't deal 'with the money side', claimed not to know when he would be back.

Oliver Briggs occupied offices in Bruton Street, not the musty old-wood-and-leather variety but a suite of thickly carpeted hessian-clad rooms furnished with glass and chrome and fronted by a blonde with a bouffant hairdo. Old man Briggs, the firm's founder, had recently retired, and Oliver, described by Richard as a whizz-kid, was now the youthful senior partner with a flourishing theatrical practice.

Isabel sat in a stylish but uncomfortable tubular chair, flicking through a copy of *Life* magazine and trying hard to care about the civil rights marches in Alabama. After ten minutes or so the door leading to the back office swung open and a man showed himself out, unescorted, as if he were a regular visitor. It was Vincent Parry. As always he wore his impeccable business suit the way a soldier might wear camouflage, in order to blend unobserved into the surrounding jungle.

'Hello Isabel,' he said, with his usual deadpan courtesy, extending a hand and fixing her with those sinister grey eyes. 'What brings you here?'

'The social workers want to take Toby away. So I'm looking for some legal advice.' There seemed no point in keeping it a secret.

Richard, with his usual lack of discretion, would no doubt tell him anyway.

'I'm sorry to hear that. But I'm sure Oliver will sort things out. Have you . . .' He hesitated a moment. 'Have you heard from Paula lately?'

'Oh, she rings now and then. But she's terribly busy on this new film. She seems very well.'

'Well meaning happy?'

'Yes. Yes, I think she is.'

'Richard said the same thing. But you never know, with Paula. I hope you'd tell me if anything was . . . worrying her. She'd never come to me herself, you see.'

He's in love with her all right, thought Isabel, however much Paula chose to deny it. Paula had complained that he was a cold fish, callous and unfeeling and interested only in power and owning things. Isabel wondered why a man who conducted his business affairs with such ruthless skill should have lost Paula to a penniless drifter, without so much as a fight.

'I'm afraid she doesn't confide in me,' she said.

'And if she did, she wouldn't want you to tell me,' he observed, reading her face. 'I'm sorry. I didn't mean to put you on the spot. Good luck with your legal wrangle. If all else fails, remember not all judges are incorruptible. I'd be happy to help, if need be. Goodbye.'

Still reeling from this outrageous remark – was there anyone in the world Vincent Parry couldn't buy except Paula? – Isabel was ushered into Oliver Briggs's office, furnished in the same space-age style as the waiting room.

'Sorry to have kept you waiting,' he said, shaking her hand. Tall and fair, thirtyish, with a long straight nose, rather sunken cheeks and the beginnings of bags under his eyes, he had the jaunty, self-assured air of a cricket captain at a public school. Isabel handed him the letter, which he read with dismissive speed.

'Don't let them panic you,' he said briskly. 'The social services are used to dealing with penniless, uneducated people who won't or can't fight back. Now, if you'll just answer a couple of hundred boring questions . . .'

She found herself telling him everything, including the state of their bank balance and Patrick's unpaid fee.

251

'If they find out we're in debt, presumably they could use that against us?'

'It certainly wouldn't help your case. This agent of Patrick's is on the level, I take it?'

'Patrick seems to think so.' Rex was All Right. Rex was a former boxing promoter married to a girl from County Clare, Rex Jordan was a racing fan, a fellow-hetero, working class, not a phoney, Rex Jordan was a 'mate', beyond suspicion.

'Let's hope he's right. So you currently have – let's see – three adults and four children living in a three-bedroomed rented flat?'

'Yes. But they're big rooms. And three of the children are very small.'

'Does Toby have his own room?'

'Not at the moment. But he will when my mother-in-law goes back home.'

'Access to a garden?'

'There's a communal one, in the square. All the residents have a key.'

'And until Toby came to you, you'd never lived in the same household?'

'Only in the school holidays. I left home when he was four.'

'And you're only twenty-one?'

'I'm twenty-two next month. And the way I feel right now I'm sure I could pass for forty.'

'Nonsense. You look about eighteen. If you ever have to appear in court, I'd add on a few years courtesy of Leichner. What age is your husband?'

'He's twenty-five. But at the moment we have my mother-in-law staying with us. She's seventy. Would that help? She's got six children, eighteen grandchildren and four great-grandchildren. There's nothing she doesn't know about kids.'

'Seventy? In good health, is she?'

'Well, usually. At the moment, she's laid up with a broken leg.'

'So you're having to look after her as well?'

'Only till she's mobile again. Surely they can't hold that against us?'

'Forewarned is forearmed.'

Oliver was a merciless questioner. By the time he had finished cross-examining her, Isabel was beginning to see matters through a social worker's eyes – Toby, a severely damaged child, living in overcrowded accommodation with a feckless thespian family pursued by creditors, and having to share the available attention with too many other children. She had never felt more vulnerable in her life.

Finally Oliver put the cap on his pen and said, 'I think I've got enough information to be going on with. I'll come back to you once I've read up on the case law. Keep me informed of any developments. Meanwhile, try not to worry.'

Advice which proved impossible to follow, especially as there was worse to come.

The Rex Jordan bubble burst two weeks later, when his telephone line was cut off for non-payment, attracting a posse of clients to his Greek Street office, where they found his secretary clearing her desk and complaining that she hadn't been paid either and not to take it out on her. Rex had evidently left the country permanently, destination unknown, leaving the cupboard bare.

The police showed a weary lack of interest; under existing legislation, a theatrical agent was not obliged to hold client monies in a separate account. If he failed to pay them over, for whatever reason, this constituted a civil debt, not criminal misappropriation. Patrick was not the only actor left seriously out of pocket, but unfortunately it was his name that was mentioned in the newspaper reports as the least obscure of Rex Jordan's clients.

Missing Agent Leaves Actors Broke, read the headline, embellished by a photograph captioned, *Patrick Delaney, star of the hit TV series* Harry Spencer Investigates.

The unfortunate juxtaposition was not lost on their landlord, or their bank manager. Next day they were served with notice to quit for rent arrears, followed, within the week, by a terse letter requiring them to drastically reduce their overdraft within thirty days.

'Bastards,' hissed Patrick. 'Money-grabbing parasites.'

'Patrick, what are we going to do?' She remembered only too vividly Paula being locked out of Bea's flat, and all her belongings ending up on the street. And there had only been one of Paula, not seven. 'If we end up homeless, they might take our own children away, as well as Toby . . .'

253

'Don't panic. Just leave it to me, okay?'

Knowing better than to leave anything to Patrick, Isabel set about frantic flat-hunting, her daily forays taking her to the nethermost reaches of the tube and beyond. A dispiriting number of ads carried the proviso 'No Coloureds. No Irish. No Children', disqualifying the Delaneys on two counts out of the three. Those landlords prepared to take in large, impecunious families presided over appalling slums which would merely provide social services with further ammunition. Buying was out of the question. Even if they had been able to raise a deposit, no one would have given them a mortgage; acting was not regarded as secure employment.

Richard pressed them to accept a 'loan' and even offered to squeeze them all in at Elizabeth Street, not that that would have been a permanent solution. But Patrick wouldn't hear of it.

'I'll sort things out my own way,' he said irritably. 'Without any help from your family.' He was even reluctant to accept money from Ma, who had nonetheless tried to clear their rent arrears for them, only for the landlords, intent on recovering possession, to return her cheque.

Meanwhile Oliver Briggs, ironically enough, had done an excellent job for them. Independent expert witnesses had assessed Toby and were prepared to testify that a move at this time would be detrimental to his emotional and mental health. Counsel's opinion was that all other things being equal, their application to the court for guardianship stood a good chance of success.

But all other things were not, of course, equal. Isabel struggled daily to hide her despair from Toby, who had already been informed by a kindly social worker that he would shortly be moving. But luckily he had absolute faith in Patrick, if not in her. It was Patrick, the all-powerful, unconquerable male, who had convinced him that all would be well, Patrick who would rescue him single-handed from the clutches of the enemy. If they came through this ordeal, it would be Patrick who got all the credit. Harry Spencer, that latter-day knight errant, would have righted yet another wrong.

It was a part Paula would have killed for. *A Dark Sun Rising*, the movie of the bestselling novel of the same name, featured the best

254

female part since Scarlett O'Hara, a meaty, demanding role that could catapult her into the big time. And hopefully out of her rut, given that her current movie, *Fortune's Fool*, was another terminal-illness feature (she was dying of a brain tumour this time, which at least made a change from leukaemia) in which she played a rich orphan from Mayfair, England (*sic*) *who resolves to spend her last six months losing her fortune on the gaming tables of Las Vegas rather than leave it to her rapacious relatives. This being fantasy-land, she doubles her money instead while finding time to fall in love with a handsome doctor, to whom she bequeaths all her money to enable him to open a clinic for winsomely crippled children.*

The script was real fold-your-own-sickbag stuff. Bondage girl Paula had been further deodorized out of all recognition. Luckily people had short memories in this town for everything except grudges; she was now officially pigeonholed as a squeaky-clean virginal English type whose death scenes were a real class act.

Unfortunately, as Paula had recently discovered, only character actors made a career out of dying on screen. Big Stars were invariably still twinkling brightly when the final credits rolled. She didn't want to fall into the trap of safe, easy pickings, as Patrick was so clearly doing back in London. Trust Patrick to get himself ripped off into the bargain. She might have known he would be too proud to let her help him out.

And now, to her surprise, she was having similar problems with Jess. The more his confidence grew, the less content he was to be dependent on her.

'I gotta get a job,' he had insisted.

'You've got a job,' said Paula stubbornly. 'Looking after me.' Reluctant to see him pumping gas, unblocking lavatories, or labouring over holes in the road, she kept avoiding the issue, until one day he disappeared for an afternoon and returned with the announcement that he had got himself hired by a hairdressing salon on Wilshire Boulevard.

'You did what?' said Paula.

'I went in and asked for a job. I start tomorrow. I'll just be washing heads and sweeping up the hair to start with, but they'll train me to be a regular stylist.'

Paula wondered why she hadn't thought of hairdressing herself, given his obvious knack for it; a mental block, probably. She had liked having him there on tap, for her convenience, liked treating him as a husband might treat a wife. She couldn't help hoping that he would tire of being a dogsbody again, that the bored, rich women whose heads he washed would get fresh and frighten him off. Assuming he was still afraid of women, another fear she had helped him overcome.

Paula tried to resign herself to sharing him. Perhaps it was just as well he had other things to occupy his mind. She would have balked at deceiving the old all-seeing, ever-present Jess; the new, self-absorbed, work-centred Jess was infinitely easier to lie to.

Having sex, of a sort, with the producer of *Dark Sun* was a question of necessity, not choice. (Fortunately both the director and the leading man were fags.) A personal interview was a privilege confined to a short list of a dozen hopefuls and an essential part of the auditioning process. Paula had been warned what to expect.

Cy was fat and fifty and physically revolting in every possible way, from his huge, pendulous paunch to his rubbery lips to his obscenely large penis, of which he was inordinately and quite unjustifiably proud, given that it wasn't much bigger erect than it was when dangling between his legs, waiting to be blown up like a balloon – a common phenomenon with outsized specimens, Paula had discovered. Perhaps a lifetime of overuse had stretched it permanently, she thought, rinsing away the disgusting taste of him with neat bourbon.

It didn't count as cheating on Jess; she was doing it *for* Jess. And besides, what Jess didn't know couldn't possibly hurt him. None of which stopped her feeling dirty, degraded and as guilty as hell. Especially once she got the part and was required to demonstrate her gratitude. And even more so when Jess professed himself delighted for her, despite the separations the location work would involve. Separations which would once have appalled him.

'Perhaps I could get you a job on the movie,' she ventured, even though there was a studio embargo on male stylists. But Jess shook his head.

'I'm learning to cut, on model nights,' he said. 'Saul's planning to start his own salon. He says if I shape up, he'll offer me a job, at twice what I'm getting now.'

She nearly said, 'Never mind about Saul. What about me? I need you!' but the thought alone shocked her into silence. Jess was the one who was supposed to need her, not the other way round. Somewhere along the line he had turned the tables on her. She had nursed him back to health like a fledgling with a broken wing and now he was ready to fly while her feet remained firmly rooted, as always, to the ground. She envied him his wings.

14 Shrubbery Close, Burwell, Essex
15 August 1963

Dear Paula
Above our new address. Yes, I know I swore I'd never live in the suburbs, let alone the outer sticks, but after months of worry at last I can sleep again.

To cut a long story short, Ma sold her house in Ireland and bought this place in Patrick's name, where she'll be living with us from now on. Patrick wouldn't have agreed to let her do it, except that the house was due to come to him in her will in any case. All his siblings have had big hand-outs over the years and the rest of the family agreed that it was fair.

I'll bet they did, thought Paula, remembering their reluctance to take the old girl in themselves. They must have jumped at the chance to offload her.

Of course Kilmacross prices are light years away from London's so we had to move quite a long way out, given that we needed four bedrooms and had to buy outright (no one would lend us any money). It's a modern house and doesn't need any work doing to it, which was a major consideration. And of course it's nice for the kids having a garden and lots of little fellow-monsters close by.

Daddy is bearing up very well, considering. In the end he pleaded guilty to manslaughter with diminished responsibility, but he still got life, on account of the degree of premeditation and it being a double killing. But as his solicitor says, life doesn't mean life; there's always the chance that the Parole Board will recommend him for early release. He was repre-

sented at the guardianship hearing, and it's been ordered that I take Toby to visit him in prison four times a year, to maintain parental contact. Meanwhile we're still under the supervision of social services, because Daddy wouldn't give his consent to an adoption, and we didn't like to push our luck.

Patrick's signed up for another series of Harry Spencer. *A woman stopped him in the street the other day and tried to hire him to track down her missing husband, so he can always moonlight as a private eye if we run short of cash in future!*

Richard sends his love. I haven't seen very much of him lately as I can't get up to town and he regards Burwell as beyond the pale. As he's probably told you, he is heavily involved with Kevin Page, alias Lord Alfred Douglas in Oscar. *Needless to say, Patrick thinks he's just after Richard's money.*

I'm dying to meet Jess when you come to London this autumn for the Snowdrops *première. Many, many congrats on landing the lead in* Dark Sun. *I'm green with envy. You can just imagine what a cabbage I've become.*

All the children send their love, as do Ma and Patrick. The twins have really shot up, and Emily is thriving, as you can see from the attached photograph.

Much love as always
Izzie

The photograph showed a smiling Isabel with Emily on her lap, the twins giggling on one side of her and Ma beaming on the other, Patrick standing behind her with his hands on her shoulders, and Toby sitting cross-legged at her feet. A green-with-envy cabbage my arse, thought Paula. She looked the picture of contentment. Never mind that she had a mother rotting in an institution, a father doing time for murder, a severely disturbed sibling to look after, a rapidly ageing resident mother-in-law, and a husband who undoubtedly took her completely for granted. That frail exterior hid a will of iron, a heart of steel.

You'd never catch Izzie blowing off some old coot for the sake of a part, any part. Izzie had never compromised, in her life or in her art. Izzie, damn her, was the real thing.

*

258

'What do you mean, you're not coming with me?' said Paula, the night before she and Jess were due to fly to London for the *Snowdrops* UK première – a gala charity performance, attended by the Queen.

'I can't,' said Jess. 'I gotta be there for the new salon opening.'

'Can't they open the new salon without you?'

'This is my work,' said Jess, rather sullenly. 'I don't stop you working.'

'But someone else can do your work. Someone else can wash and sweep up the hair.' She could have said, more tactfully, 'Please, Jess. I need you to be there for me,' but that would have been too much of an admission.

'I told you, I do the bleaching and tinting now. Not anyone can do it. It goes wrong, they can sue you. I got appointments already. Customers ask for me specially.'

Paula didn't doubt it. His good looks were all the more seductive now that they were bolstered by self-respect. If I met him for the first time today, she thought, I wouldn't risk marrying him. Perhaps I wouldn't even want to . . .

She would be spending the next few days in her suite at the Savoy giving back-to-back interviews, protected by a studio press man to deflect any untoward questions; with the Queen attending the première, giving it the ultimate stamp of respectability, hopefully there would be no mention of *Bondage* or the Marty Bauer affair. Having done the same thing for the US opening – she would never forget the thrill of seeing her name on a billboard on Sunset Boulevard – she was now an old hand at projecting the right, false image of herself, at spouting complimentary scripted clichés about the director, the co-star, the writers, and everyone else who had participated in the film, and at enthusing about her perfect, happy, idyllic private life as epitomized by the touched-up publicity shots of herself and Jess, looking like the ultimate beautiful couple. Jess photographed extremely well and was now routinely described as 'hunky hairdresser to the stars'.

Isabel and Patrick, who had just finished the run of *Daggers Drawn*, would be attending the screening and the party at the White Elephant afterwards; Paula had arranged to put them up at her hotel for the night on expenses before going back to Essex with them the following day, to meet the kids. She phoned Isabel on

259

arrival, to find her bubbling over with excitement at the prospect of a night out in London. Richard was also coming, without Kevin Page, who was still appearing nightly in *Oscar*. Paula steeled herself for Vince to be there; he was on the board of the children's charity which would benefit from the event.

After a solid day of interviews, the most exhausting kind of acting there was, she rang Jess. He was already at the salon in readiness for the grand opening and was too busy to talk for more than a moment. She felt momentarily like a bored housewife phoning a harassed husband at the office. She rang him at home next morning, midnight in LA, but the line was permanently engaged; perhaps, she thought hopefully, he was trying to phone her. But no calls came through.

After another session of posing and prattling, Richard arrived to take her out to lunch.

'Izzie sounded well,' she ventured, in an attempt to change the subject away from Kevin.

'Izzie's good at putting a brave face on things. Can you imagine her stuck in the middle of nowhere, having to make small talk about her laundry over the fence and be nice to the ghastly neighbours when they pop in for a cuppa? And what's going to happen once Patrick's mother goes ga-ga? She'll end up having to wash her nappies as well.'

'Still full of the milk of human kindness, aren't you?'

'Bloody Patrick. He's got her just where he wants her. I said to her, at least you've got a live-in babysitter now, grab the chance to work while you can. I offered her a part on a plate. But she said the journey up to town would take too long because Patrick has the car and she'd have to use public transport, and besides Ma wasn't up to handling four kids, what with her arthritis, and Emily's inclined to be chesty and Toby's still terribly insecure, when what she really meant was that Patrick wouldn't like it. If there's one thing that terrifies him, it's Izzie stealing his thunder. Specially now that he's sold out to TV.'

'He needs the money,' pointed out Paula, remembering how the old Patrick had despised the stuff. A luxury he could no longer afford. 'He's got a family to support.'

'I might have known you'd stick up for him. You're not still in love with him, are you?'

'I was never in love with him. I happen to be in love with my husband.'

'Am I supposed to repeat that to Vince?'

'Why bother? He wouldn't believe it.'

Richard helped himself to another glass of champagne. He had put on quite a lot of weight, and looked every inch the successful impresario and bon viveur. 'I can't quite believe it either. You as a doting wife, I mean. Though I must say Jess looks gorgeous. If it wasn't for Kev, I could fancy him myself.'

Paula thought back wistfully to the pre-Kev days when Richard had been heart-whole and promiscuous, when he had spent long boozy evenings at her flat in Cranley Gardens, when they had cuddled up innocently in bed together. It had been too good to last. Sooner or later love always got in the way of friendship, same as it had done with Izzie.

She gave more interviews until five, after which she sent down to room service for two rounds of tuna salad sandwiches with mayonnaise, a wedge of sachertorte, a selection of Danish pastries, a strawberry ice cream sundae, a chocolate milkshake and a large bowl of assorted nuts.

After it was all disposed of, twice over, she washed her face, piled up the stack of empty plates on the tray and placed them furtively outside someone else's room. It was the first major binge she'd had since Jess, the first time she had forced herself to face the certain knowledge that sooner or later she would lose him.

She was no better than Stan. Like him she had seduced a child starved of affection, taken advantage of another's ignorance and lack of self-esteem. But unlike Stan, she had kidded herself about her motives. Without Jess, she thought bleakly, she would have no one. Unless she had his child, before it was too late. The trouble was, it was still too soon. She couldn't risk dropping out of circulation, even for a year, not yet.

By the time she had been coiffed and manicured and had changed into a shimmering beaded ivory dress, with a demure neckline but a plunging back, she looked plastic-perfect again. While she waited to be presented in the cinema foyer, grinning inanely about nothing for the benefit of the photographers, she braced herself to meet Izzie and Patrick, who would already be seated inside. Izzie would look serene and slim and aristocratic;

261

Patrick's dinner jacket would be crumpling inexorably around the smooth flesh beneath. If she hadn't loved them both so much, she would have hated them.

There was a hush as the royal party arrived. Her Majesty asked her graciously if she enjoyed working in America, and Paula must have mumbled something in reply, though she couldn't afterwards remember what it was. The bowing and scraping over, the royal party proceeded to their box while the presentees took their places. Paula had a bright long-time-no-see grin all ready on her face; it faded as she saw that the two seats next to hers were empty.

She caught Richard's eye on the other side of the aisle, but he just shrugged, none the wiser than she. There was no sign of Vince; obviously he was avoiding her, as Richard had warned her he would – not out of pique, he assured her, but because 'he thought you'd enjoy it more if he wasn't here'. Paula swallowed a pang of disappointment.

The film seemed interminable. There was nothing more cringe-making than seeing yourself up on the screen, especially when locked in an ardent clinch with a raging poof disguised as Hollywood's most eligible bachelor. As the handkerchiefs came out, she had to blink back tears of her own, weighed down by a dreadful, indistinct despair.

'What's happened to Izzie and Patrick?' she said, collaring Richard after the lights went up. 'Thank you,' she cooed at a dowager-duchess type, who caught her by the arm and murmured a tremulous tribute to her performance. 'Perhaps they've had an accident.'

'I'd better ring the old girl and find out,' said Richard gloomily. 'The car's a heap and Patrick's a bloody lethal driver.'

He went off to make his call, while Paula fielded more fans and scribbled her signature on souvenir programmes. After a few moments he rejoined her, grim-faced.

'Izzie collapsed just as they were getting ready to leave the house. Patrick drove her to casualty.'

'What's wrong with her?'

'Something called an ectopic pregnancy, whatever that means.'

'Is it serious? I never knew she was pregnant again.'

'Neither did I. Anyway, she's not any more, thank God. They

262

had to operate. There's nothing we can do tonight. I said we'd drive over there to see her tomorrow morning.'

Neither of them felt very partyish after that, though Paula put in her usual vivacious performance, dancing to the melancholy whine of 'Love Me Do' and even managing to smile sweetly at a drunken guest who asked her if she knew that she looked like Christine Keeler. On returning, exhausted, to her suite, she phoned the salon to find that Jess was doing a house-call in Bel Air and could they take a message? No, said Paula. No message. Having stuck to straight tonic all night – she never drank when she was working, and this was emphatically work – she made up for lost time with neat iced vodka laced with hot tears.

It took the best part of two hours to reach Burwell next day, with Richard grumbling all the way about how Izzie might as well be living on the moon. They drove straight to the hospital, where they were directed to a private room.

'There's posh,' said Richard, embracing a pale-faced Isabel. Her bright welcoming smile was belied by eyes that were red and swollen. 'I'm glad Patrick stumped up for a private bed.'

'Oh, we're not paying for it. Matron's an ardent *Harry Spencer* fan. She took one look at Patrick and rolled out the red carpet. How did the première go? I was so furious to have missed it. Where's Jess?'

Unlike the rest of the world, Isabel wasn't full of her own affairs. She brushed aside their enquiries about her health and demanded a blow-by-blow account of Paula's meeting with the monarch.

Paula's narrative was interrupted, however, by the arrival of Patrick, whereupon Isabel began asking urgently after the children and Richard made excuses to leave, saying that he had a meeting in London that afternoon. The hostility between him and Patrick was palpable.

'As there's obviously nothing the matter with Izzie, I'll leave you all to whoop it up without me,' he drawled. 'You don't mind getting the train back, do you, darling?'

'There's a fast service into Liverpool Street,' said Isabel apologetically, sounding like an estate agent.

'Or I can drive you,' offered Patrick, adding, 'Ma's made lunch for you,' as Isabel's arrived on a tray.

'Then you'd better hurry up and get home, before it spoils,' said Isabel. 'Come back and see me later, okay? Just Paula, this time, so we can have a good old gossip.'

'Don't believe a word she says about me,' said Patrick, trying to sound cheerful. Paula could tell by his face that he hadn't slept a wink all night. The way he looked at Isabel reminded her of all the things she had feared and fought against and failed at. However far she travelled she always seemed to end up at the point she had started off from: wanting to be Izzie.

Patrick drove her to the house in an old banger which was obviously burning oil; he had bought it cheap, from a 'mate' of his, he told her.

'How's married life treating you?' he asked, using the cliché to hide his curiosity.

'Better than I deserve. And you?'

'You took the words right out of my mouth.' What they deserved was each other, thought Paula. Then they'd both have plenty to complain about.

He drew up outside a semi-detached red-brick house in a close of identical dwellings, barely one notch up from the council estate Paula had once lived in, not so many miles away from here. The front doorstep of number 14 was gleaming with Cardinal polish, every window pane shone, the nets were Persil-white, and not a single weed marred the crew-cut precision of the minuscule front lawn. If the house had died it would have gone straight to Heaven.

Ma greeted Patrick with a flurry of queries, barely acknowledging Paula in her anxiety about Isabel. Inside, the house's mean proportions had been opened out by light colours and a ruthless lack of clutter. The furniture might be a bit battered, and the carpet a cheap grade of cord, but there was that indefinable stamp of class that Isabel gave to everything she touched.

Including her children. The twins were startlingly beautiful, impossible to tell apart, with Patrick's dark hair and riveting blue eyes. They responded to Paula's shy hello with sudden and inexplicable hilarity, as if she were the funniest thing they had ever seen. Emily was like a little plump Buddha, placidly allowing Paula to pick her up without protest and viewing her with a bored, lopsided yawn. Toby was at school.

The old girl served up a heavy three-course meal which was

punctuated every two minutes with offers of more bread, more stuffing, more gravy, more custard, while she limped to and fro between dining room and kitchen, where the children were being fed simultaneously, a process which generated an ear-splitting din which Patrick didn't seem to hear.

Having put the trio down for their afternoon nap – blessed peace and quiet at last, thought Paula – Ma rejoined them with her knitting, a miniature jumper for Emily in pink wool, a colour Isabel had always hated. Paula, who had been gobbling up the latest London theatre gossip, was forced to respond to questions about the weather and the prices in America, and to listen to comments about the weather and prices at home – it had rained every day for the last two weeks, it must be because of those satellites hurtling about in space, and the meat here cost twice what it did in Dublin, someone was making a big fat profit and why didn't the government do anything about it? Having exhausted this fascinating topic Ma used *Snowdrops* as a springboard to launch into detailed reminiscences of the films of Myrna Loy and Tyrone Power, and how they didn't make them like that any more, she hadn't been inside a cinema since *The Nun's Story*, that must be a good three years ago, now *there* was a lovely film . . .

She followed this up with lugubrious speculation about Izzie's operation and how worried she must be that it would stop her having more children, before subjecting Paula to a crash course in cottage obstetrics. God, how did Izzie stand it?

At last she took herself off to fetch Toby from school, whereupon Paula ventured, 'It must be a great help, having her here,' hoping wickedly that Patrick would roll his eyes and take the piss out of the old girl behind her back.

'We wouldn't be here at all, if it wasn't for her,' he snapped. 'Or anywhere else, come to that. So you can stop sniggering.'

'I'm not sniggering!'

'I was watching you while she was rattling on. I could hear you thinking, poor Izzie, having to share a rabbit hutch in the sticks with Patrick's ignorant boring chatterbox of a mother.'

'I never said –'

'She was trying too hard, that's all. Because you're Izzie's friend. Not a single one of my sisters or sisters-in-law could handle her, she drove them all up the wall, but Izzie's got her eating out of her hand. So it's not like you think. Sorry to disappoint you.'

At that point the telephone rang; it was one of the family calling from Ireland to ask after Isabel. Patrick stayed on the phone for a good twenty minutes, to punish her, by which time Ma had returned with Toby in tow, denying Paula the chance to answer back.

Paula wouldn't have recognized him. He still wasn't likely to win any charm contests, but he was no longer the malicious little brat she remembered from her Sunday visits to Windsor with Isabel; evidently she had worked her spell on him as well. He had grown into an undeniably good-looking child. With his mop of dark hair and blue eyes, a legacy from his mother, he would easily have passed for another junior Delaney, something he would no doubt have liked to be, judging by his evident hero worship of Patrick. After parroting a polite greeting at Paula he pounced on him excitedly, recounting some convoluted tale of his doings at school.

Meanwhile Ma gave Paula a guided tour of the house, complete with details of Izzie's home-decorating exploits. Patrick, she said, was no good with his hands (that's all you know, thought Paula), but Izzie had put those shelves up herself, and painted the walls, and stripped and varnished the floorboards upstairs, and run up all the curtains . . .

Unable to bear it any longer, Paula said she must be getting back to the hospital. Patrick, who was still sulking, had little to say for himself on the drive and didn't argue when Paula said not to bother to collect her afterwards, she would get a cab to the station. His parting embrace was perfunctory, his good wishes rang hollow. Paula felt hurt, but from long habit, she didn't show it. Which didn't stop Isabel seeing it.

'Don't tell me,' she sighed. 'Or rather do. What happened?'

Paula pulled a face.

'Why is Patrick so touchy about his mother?'

'I think he's touchy about you, actually. A big movie star like you visiting our humble abode.'

'Big movie star my fanny.' Paula prided herself on not believing her own publicity, an occupational hazard of sudden fame. 'Jumped-up nobodies like me are a dime a dozen out there. And since when has laughing boy cared for my good opinion?'

266

'You're one of the few people whose opinion matters to him, actually. He was bound to pick a quarrel with you about something.'

'So what's new? I'm your friend, aren't I? He's always been jealous of that.'

Isabel shrugged, not denying it, and dodged the issue with a bright 'Now tell me all about Jess.'

But Paula found she couldn't tell her much. Not because she didn't want to, but because she didn't really know him all that well. She knew only the child-husband she had created for herself, not the real emerging stranger beneath.

Izzie made things easy for her, of course, feeding her all the right cues; she wanted to believe that she was happy. Izzie had always been generous, bountifully endowed with natural good-will, but there was more to it than that. She was out there in the audience now, craving comforting fantasy, not the depressing truth. Paula quelled the urge to unburden herself and gave her what she wanted instead; one couldn't disappoint the fans.

And then, in the middle of the fairy tale, she noticed two symmetrical tears trickling down Isabel's cheeks, defying her determined smile. Paula pulled a Kleenex out of the pop-up box on the bedside table.

'Oh, Izzie. Here's me chattering away about nothing and forgetting that you must be feeling awful.'

'I'm fine.' Izzie hid her face behind the tissue. 'I suppose it's just a hormonal thing. I ought to be relieved. I didn't want another baby. And with luck I won't have any more, now I've lost one of my tubes. But I feel such a failure. Whenever I get pregnant, something always goes wrong. I can't do what any farmyard animal can do without screwing up.'

'How can you say that?' said Paula. 'You do everything right! Your children are gorgeous. Even Toby's become human, thanks to you. Why must you always be so hard on yourself?'

'I'm not brave enough to be a mother,' wailed Isabel, the tears falling free now. 'You can't imagine how terrifying it all is. I worry all the time about germs and traffic and the Bomb and . . . everything. I don't just worry about something happening to them, I worry about something happening to me, because Ma's getting old and Patrick's so helpless on his own. I just don't know

267

how I'm going to get through the next twenty years or so. I feel as if I'm bluffing, ad-libbing every line.'

'I bet everyone feels like that,' said Paula. If Izzie thought she couldn't cope, what hope was there for someone like her?

'No they don't. The other mothers round here are so sure of themselves. Next to them I feel such a freak.'

And so she was, thought Paula. Izzie hadn't been born to live in the real, mundane world. She belonged to the theatre, where everyone else was a freak as well, where no one expected you to be normal. However clean the laundry on the line, however neat her garden, Izzie would never fit in. She might be word perfect in the role life had dealt her, but she was cast against type.

'I wish now I hadn't become a Catholic,' she added gloomily. 'If I wasn't a Catholic I could get sterilized.'

'You mean you've converted?' said Paula, aghast. 'After all you said? What made you change your mind?' Isabel had told her time and again how glad she was not to have been born a Catholic.

'I can't explain,' said Isabel, embarrassed. 'I just had to, that's all. I knew that if I didn't something dreadful was bound to happen.'

'And then it would be all your fault,' sighed Paula. 'You always were a guilt-junkie. They must have seen you coming . . .'

Isabel shook her head, to close the subject, blew her nose and began apologizing for being feeble and self-pitying and a bore and ungrateful when she had so much to be thankful for.

'I wish I could be strong, like you,' she sniffed. 'You make choices. You're in control of your life. I just let things happen to me.'

But choosing and being in control were the tactics of a coward, as Paula knew to her cost. Just letting things happen called for courage.

ACT TWO
Spring 1966–Winter 1969

They are as sick that surfeit with too much
As they that starve with nothing.

William Shakespeare – The Merchant of Venice

10

Spring–Autumn 1966

Sigh no more, ladies, sigh no more
Men were deceivers ever.

William Shakespeare – Much Ado About Nothing

Paula felt the lights hot on her skin and looked through the shimmering screen that separated her from her audience, like a window. They were pointing at her and jeering; then, one by one, they got up and walked away.

Ashamed, she tried to run and hide. Relieved, she tried to stop and rest. But there was no escape. The projector trapped her in a treadmill that forced her through her paces, even though nobody was watching, even though nobody cared. She was forgotten, rejected, discarded, but nonetheless immortal, doomed to haunt herself for ever. She opened her mouth to scream 'Let me go!' but the words wouldn't come, because they weren't in the script. But still she struggled, until the effort wrenched her jaw apart and the pain woke her up.

She sat up in bed in a panic, thinking that she had missed her early call, wondering why Jess wasn't there beside her, groaning as her toothache reminded her that this was day one of a week-long break, her first in nearly two years.

She had squeezed it in between two back-to-back movies to accommodate the removal of her impacted wisdom teeth, one of which had been gnawing into her jawbone for the last three months, making it so painful to chew that she had lost nearly a stone without even trying. She might have kept the offending tooth as a handy appetite suppressant if she wasn't such a coward about pain.

Jess had left early this morning, without waking her. He was to have taken her to the clinic but work had intervened, in the shape

271

of a fashion shoot for a glossy magazine; the photographs would feature the much-prized credit 'Hair by Jess at *Way Ahead*'. No problem, Paula had assured him casually, feeling hard done by nonetheless. She was quite capable of driving herself. It was only her teeth, after all.

She knocked back a couple of uppers to kick-start her into the day. Just about everybody took them, and plenty else besides, though Paula herself had refused to dabble in more exotic drugs. This was about self-control, not self-indulgence. Junkies were weaklings, losers, who wound up throwing it all away. Paula intended to hold on to everything she'd got.

Which was quite a lot, she reminded herself, like a miser counting gold. All that hustling and grubbing for parts and sleeping with the right people had paid off, bolstered by her hard-won reputation as a word-perfect one-take Annie, a professional who could always be relied upon to deliver. Plus the small matter of her healthy box-office returns, which was all that mattered in the long run. Well aware of this, Paula had proved astute at choosing the right material.

And now she had a string of money-making movies to her credit, a chair on the set with her name on it, a face people recognized and money in the bank, though not nearly enough to make her feel secure – the whole object of the exercise – given the heavy overheads of success.

Vince had been right, everyone wanted a piece of her. First there was the ten per cent to her agent, then fifteen to her personal manager, five to her publicist, five to her business manager, and a minimum of twenty to the IRS, which at least was less than she would have paid to Harold Wilson back home. Which left her with less than half her income, out of which she had to pay a beauty parlour to keep the fine lines at bay and a masseur to pummel away the flab; she had to buy the kind of clothes that advertised her status and live in the kind of home that projected the right image.

She had moved out of the modest bungalow in West Hollywood to a five-bedroomed house on Hillcrest Drive, complete with a pool that cost a small fortune to maintain, where she gave occasional ruinously expensive parties in return for equally lavish hospitality she dared not refuse. Contacts were yet another thing that didn't come cheap. She had always dreamed of being rich, but being rich was all about having money to spend, rather than spending money. Spending it made you poor again, if you weren't careful. Which was why she was more than happy for Jess to spend his.

As the salon's top stylist he now earned more in a day than he had once made in a month. He delighted in buying Paula extravagant presents, not to mention the ones he had bought for himself – a walk-in closetful of dandified clothes, a gold Rolex wristwatch, a red sports convertible, the last word in hi-fi, and a speedboat moored at Marina del Rey. So that when Saul had offered him a partnership, to finance the expansion of the business, it was Paula who had put up the necessary capital, given that Jess himself was always broke. But she didn't begrudge the dent it made in her nest egg. All the while she owned part of the salon she owned a part of Jess, which made it seem like a good investment.

It's only my teeth, she reminded herself as she checked in at the hospital, ignoring the tight, heavy feeling in her chest. I'm not ill. If I was ill the movie insurance medicals would have picked it up. Medicals which were fairly routine for someone of her age, who had become adept at lying to doctors . . .

It had taken a dentist to rumble her. 'What have you been using as a mouthwash?' he had demanded, while Paula sat trapped, open-mouthed in the chair. It was her first visit since her schooldays; luckily her front teeth were even and white enough not to require the otherwise compulsory capping. 'Stomach acid, by the look of things.'

'I don't know what you mean.'

'I think you do. You'd be surprised how much of this I see, mostly from actresses, models, dancers, girls who need to stay thin. I have to warn you, the damage to your gums and tooth enamel is the tip of the iceberg . . .'

Paula felt as if she had been accused, quite rightly, of some gross perversion; he didn't seriously expect her to admit it, did he?

'Do you suffer at all from dizziness? Blackouts? Insomnia? Stomach pain? Menstrual problems? Loss of libido?'

'No,' Paula had lied, glad to have a simple explanation for her symptoms. Now she knew that they were just the result of hunger, and throwing up, she could stop worrying that she had some dread

273

disease. As for loss of libido, that was all to the good, given that Jess never seemed to want to do more than kiss and cuddle these days. Like her, he gave all his energy to his work. Or so she liked to think. She couldn't bear to admit to feeling jealous; it would have given him too much power.

'Relax,' Saul had told her once, catching her glaring at one of Jess's more flirtatious regulars. 'They leave him cold.' A rotund, florid, thirty-ish divorcee with two cute kids who came to stay weekends, Saul was the brains behind the business; it was in his interests to keep his principal asset on the straight and narrow. The last thing he would want was for Paula, with all the fury of a woman scorned, to withdraw her financial backing from the salon. On the other hand, that gave him an incentive to cover up for Jess if he went astray . . .

It's just my teeth, she repeated yet again as a Dr Kildare double peered into her mouth and put a spatula down her throat. There's nothing wrong with me except god-awful tooth-ache . . .

He began asking awkward questions; the bloody dentist had obviously shopped her. Paula lied and denied, but he wouldn't believe her, saying that he couldn't go ahead with the extraction unless she was honest with him, effectively torturing the truth out of her. If it wasn't done today, thought Paula, panicking, not only would she go out of her mind with the pain, but the swelling wouldn't have gone down in time for shooting next week . . .

By the time they finally wheeled her off she had agreed, in desperation, to undergo a battery of tests next day and discuss her problems with a therapist, fully intending to discharge herself when Jess came to visit that evening. Otherwise they were bound to find something wrong, if only to drum up business. As for seeing a shrink, that was the quickest known way to tear up hundred-dollar bills. When you'd taken the trouble to bury yourself good and deep, why invite a professional graverobber to dig up the corpse, let alone pay him for the privilege?

She came round to the sound of the telephone by her bed.

'Hi, honey. How do you feel?'

'Fine,' lied Paula. The anaesthetic had worn off and she felt, if that were possible, even worse than before. 'When are you going to be here?' Her face was swollen; it was hard to speak.

274

'Um . . . I dunno. The outdoor shoot was late starting, on account of the rain. And there's still the studio stuff to do. I won't get home till late. And they reckon it'll overrun into tomorrow . . . I'm sorry, honey.'

She could just see him primping the hair of some stunning Jean Shrimpton-lookalike, giving her the kind of attention that had once been reserved for her alone. But pride, as always, got the better of pique.

'It's okay. Don't worry about it.'

'You stay put and rest up,' said Jess, absolved. 'I'll see you tomorrow night. Love you.'

'Love you too.' More's the pity, thought Paula. When would she ever learn?

A nurse came in and administered a painkilling injection, together with a sleeping pill that knocked her out cold till morning. It was still dark outside when she awoke, and only the night staff were on duty. Paula heaved herself out of bed, groaning as she saw the puff-jawed monster facing her in the bathroom mirror. She threw on her clothes without bothering to wash or make up, and sneaked out of the side entrance into the parking lot, feeling much as she had felt when she had escaped from the Home, all those years ago.

Too late, she realized that she was in no fit state to drive. At one point she had to pull over, afraid that she was about to pass out at the wheel, and had to take the rest of the journey at a snail's pace, attracting angry hoots from other motorists. She arrived home just before six. Letting herself in very quietly, so as not to wake Jess, she crept upstairs and opened the door of the bedroom, like a wounded animal returning to the safety of its burrow . . .

She stood stricken for a moment while her blood bubbled and spluttered and came to a rapid rolling boil. Jess was lying curled up with a finger in his mouth, snuggling into the back of a figure covered by the bedclothes apart from the crown of dark curly hair.

'Bitch!' she screamed, taking off one of her shoes and belabouring the intruder with the steel-tipped stiletto heel. 'Whore! Get out of my bed, before I kill you!' She tore the covers aside, all the adrenaline draining away as she recognized her rival.

'Saul,' she said faintly.

'Paula,' began Jess, pulling on his robe. 'Don't get mad. Please don't get mad.' He placed himself protectively between them. 'Please, Paula. We never meant to hurt you . . .'

'Get out, both of you!' Her voice was all over the place. 'Get out of my house.' Not very original, but it would have to do. Once they had gone, she would sleep, and then wake up, and find she had dreamed the whole thing . . .

A terrified Saul grabbed his clothes and fled, but Jess stayed stubbornly put. Paula sat down weakly on the bed and then stood up again, as if fearing contamination.

'I'm sorry, Paula,' he mumbled. 'We weren't expecting you. We never meant for you to find out . . .'

'How long has this been going on?' Why had she asked that? She didn't want to know. And yet, suddenly, it was as if she had known all along. 'How long have you been cheating on me?'

'Not as long as you've been cheating on me,' said Jess.

Paula's head began spinning again. She leaned against the wall behind her for support.

'What's that supposed to mean?' she hissed. 'What the fuck has Saul been telling you?'

'He didn't tell me. I found out. Same way I found out about Marty Bauer. I meet a lotta movie people. I get to hear things. I'm not as dumb as you think.'

'Then you should have left me!'

'Paula, please, don't get mad at me,' he repeated, like a child pleading not to be spanked. 'I never got mad at you.'

Which said it all, thought Paula bitterly. Once upon a time he had been jealous. His jealousy of Vince had brought them together. And now she was the jealous one . . .

'Saul said it didn't mean you didn't love me. Saul said it was only business. Saul said –'

'I'll bet Saul said plenty. He didn't want us splitting up, in case I pulled out of the salon. He's no fool, even if you are.'

'I'm not a fool,' began Jess, as if to reassure himself.

'You've got a goddamned nerve, throwing things in my face that I only ever did for you, for us . . .' She sat down on the bed again, contaminated or not, with her head between her knees, fighting off the faintness.

'I never meant to hurt you, Paula,' he repeated. His voice

seemed to come from a long way off. 'I still love you. I don't want to leave you . . .'

'Nobody leaves me,' hissed Paula, standing up giddily. If she stayed here she would end up weeping, begging him to stay, she would lose what little self-respect she had left. 'Not any more. I'm the one who's doing the leaving. I'm the one who's leaving you.'

He ran after her as she stormed out, but she slammed the door in his face, hating him, hating herself. She had never felt more unattractive, more inadequate, more of a failure or a fool. She jumped into the car, put her foot down hard and shot off at high speed, across Sunset and into Santa Monica Boulevard, without any idea of where she was going other than towards an empty freedom.

A split second later she was back in bed, with Vince sitting by her side. Or rather two Vinces, shifting in and out of focus, the gold of his hair blurring into a halo. She hurt all over and she couldn't move her arms or legs. Panicking, she tried to wriggle her fingers and toes, moaning with relief as they obeyed her command.

'Relax,' said Vince, squeezing her hand. 'You're going to be all right.'

'Jess,' she said. 'Where's Jess?' And then, cruelly, her memory came flooding back.

'Outside, waiting to see you. You had an accident, on the freeway. You've been unconscious for three days.'

She remembered running, driving, speeding, but not crashing. Christ. She must have blacked out, at the wheel . . .

'Is my face all right?' She couldn't reach to feel it.

'It will be. You went through the windscreen, but your face will mend. All of you will mend. That's a promise.'

She found herself returning his strong, warm grip, as if to leech some of his strength.

'Was anyone else hurt?'

'Never mind about that. Everything's being taken care of.'

Vince would take care of everything. He always did. Thank God he was here . . .

'Do you want to see Jess now?' he said, when she surfaced again. It might have been hours later, or minutes, or seconds. She

277

had no way of telling. All that mattered was that he was still there. 'He didn't know if you'd want to speak to him. He blames himself for the accident. He thinks it was deliberate. Was it?'

'No.' She wasn't brave enough to kill herself, worse luck.

'He told me about you finding him with Saul,' continued Vince. 'He was pretty shaken up at the time. Still is.'

She could just picture Vince playing father confessor, the way he had once done with her. Perhaps he had known about Saul already, even before she did, the way Vince knew everything. Now that Vince knew, she wouldn't be able to take Jess back. As she might have done, given time. But not now that she knew Vince knew. Now it was too late.

'I want you to keep him away from me,' she said. 'I don't want him feeling guilty, and saying sorry, and crying all over me. I can't bear it. Tell him I'm not angry, that he can keep his share of the salon. I want you to get him a good attorney, to make sure Saul doesn't cheat him. He doesn't understand money.'

'I'll deal with it. And anything else you want doing. I'll be here for as long as you need me.'

And she did need him. She always had done. That was why she had run away from him . . .

'Isabel and Patrick send their love. And Richard. He wants you to convalesce at his place, once you're well enough to travel.'

Paula tried to shake her head and couldn't.

'No bloody fear,' she croaked. 'I've had it up to here with lousy queers. I can't stand to see him and Kevin pawing each other.'

'There's always the house in Kent. Grace would be glad to look after you.'

'The movie . . .' She had actually forgotten about the movie. The crash must have destroyed part of her brain.

'They'll have to replace you. You're going to be out of action for at least six months.'

Six months. Six whole months off work. Oh God . . .

Oh bliss.

Isabel was glad, at first, when *Harry Spencer* finally died a natural death. Three soft years had wasted Patrick's acting muscles; a paddling pool was no place for a channel swimmer. If he hadn't

278

had a family of six to support, he would surely have left the series long ago.

But alternative work proved depressingly hard to find. Not just because Patrick was type-cast, as she had predicted, but because he had relieved his boredom with the role by arguing with the long-suffering director at every opportunity, thus compounding his reputation as a troublemaker. Meanwhile the money was running out as fast as the bills came in.

It was with great reluctance, and in some desperation, that he went for an audition at the Hockleigh Community Playhouse, a brand-new municipal theatre in the North of England, dedicated to classical revivals and progressive new drama. It seemed like a chance to do some real, serious work again, a chance which Isabel welcomed, even if Patrick affected not to, covering himself against rejection by claiming that it was a bloody waste of time, everyone knew by now that he wasn't the kind of grovelling yes-man that made good company material.

Fortunately, however, Hockleigh's governing board saw Patrick's status as a TV star as a way of luring the locals, a largely working-class community, into the concrete monstrosity which had been paid for, willy-nilly, out of their rates and taxes, and which would continue to be subsidized at their expense. The line of parts he was offered – Petruchio in *The Shrew*, Henry V, and Jimmy Porter in a revival of *Look Back in Anger* – were all thundering look-at-me roles which gave him *carte blanche* to hog the stage with impunity. Or, as his ever-tactful wife preferred to put it, to make people sit up and take notice.

Patrick's departure coincided with the arrival of one of his numerous nieces from Ireland. Bridget, Maureen's youngest girl, was a none too bright sixteen-year-old who had just failed all her exams bar domestic science and didn't even have the saving grace of wanting to be a nun. To Maureen's mind, it would do her a power of good to spend some time away from Kilmacross before she started her shorthand and typing course. Would Isabel consider taking her in for a few months, in exchange for help around the house and with the kids? Perhaps she could help 'bring her out'.

Ma, who had always had a soft spot for Bridget, was strongly in favour, and Patrick raised no objection, displaying the vague *laissez faire* he applied to all matters domestic. But what seduced Isabel was Maureen's insistence on paying a generous sum for Bridget's keep, well aware, no doubt, that her kid brother was short of money yet again, and glad of an opportunity to help him without giving offence.

A lumpy, bashful girl who looked much younger than her years, Bridget adored the children, with Toby an unlikely if responsive favourite. Isabel hesitated to make a servant out of her, but Ma had no such compunction, and Bridget, who claimed to enjoy housework, seemed happy to be kept busy. So much so that for the first time in years Isabel didn't have enough to do. But she knew what Patrick's reaction would be if she suggested a part-time job. To the locals in Burwell he was a celebrity, whose wife couldn't be seen to be stamping books in the library or manning a supermarket checkout. She wasn't qualified for anything more exalted. All she had ever been trained to do was to act.

'Now that Bridget's there you can leave the kids and spend Sunday with me,' decreed Paula, ringing from Vince's cottage in Kent. 'I'm throwing a little party to celebrate coming out of plaster. Just you and me and Vince and Richard. Kevin's touring, thank God. Last time you came I was still doped up to the eyeballs. I'm almost human again now.'

Their previous visit, soon after Paula's return from America, had been a family affair, making a private conversation impossible. It would be nice to go on her own this time, to forget about being Patrick's wife and the children's mother and just be herself, however briefly. Herself, whoever she might be, seemed like a long-lost relative, one she had all but lost touch with.

'Patrick's taken the car,' said Isabel. 'But I'll work out how to get to you by train.'

'That'll take for ever. Vince is driving up from London. I'll get him to make a detour and pick you up.'

'Well, if it wouldn't be too far out of his way . . .'

'Don't be silly. Vince does what I tell him. If I told him to pick you up from Aberdeen he'd do it.'

He needn't expect any gratitude, thought Isabel. He was no doubt bearing the brunt of her bitterness and disillusion. Not that Paula admitted to feeling any. 'Five years isn't bad for a Hollywood marriage,' she had shrugged. 'I never expected it to last.'

Patrick rang from Hockleigh on the Sunday morning – they were rehearsing right through the weekend – just as Isabel was getting ready to leave, having been to early Mass.

'How's it going?' she asked, bracing herself.

'The rehearsal room's in a freezing basement with no natural light. Alan Shipton – the bloody stupid director – keeps banging on about the parallels between Henry V and Hitler. I don't know if I can stick it.'

'Still, *The Shrew* should be fun,' said Isabel soothingly, praying that Patrick wouldn't pick a fight with Shipton and walk out.

'Don't you believe it. We had the first read-through yesterday. Nora Herbert – Katharina – has got hold of this daft book by some American man-hater. She's full of bright ideas about Petruchio being impotent and Katharina's drive towards self-actualization being subverted and how the play is really a tragedy, not a comedy. Ugly bitch. I'd reckon she was a dyke if Shipton hadn't lapped all her ideas up like cream. It's obvious how *she* got the job.'

'Read-throughs are always a pain,' agreed Isabel, ignoring this misogynist diatribe. Patrick invariably claimed to loathe the actresses he worked with; they were always either slags or hags. Epithets she chose to take at face value rather than torture herself with suspicion.

'I suppose she'll want Jimmy Porter doing the ironing in Act One of *Anger* while Alison lounges in an armchair reading the paper. God, I wish you were playing her parts instead.'

What she wouldn't give to be doing just that! No. She hadn't meant to think that. She concentrated her mind on the pre-curtain terror, the backstage bitchery, the impossibility of ever being satisfied with her performance, the cruelty of critics, as if reciting the torments of Hell in an attempt to resist temptation.

'At least I'd know you weren't planning to upstage me all the time,' added Patrick, spoiling the compliment. 'What have you got planned for today?'

'Oh, Vincent Parry's picking me up and taking me to see Paula. I felt I ought to make the effort.'

She didn't mention that Richard would be there, or that she had been looking forward to it all week, for fear that Patrick would think she was having fun while he slaved away to pay the bills.

281

'Give her my love. Can I talk to the kids?'

'Ma's taken the girls to Mass. Toby's gone round to a friend's. But Bridie wants a word,' she added, seeing her hovering hopefully nearby.

Bridget came to the phone and blushed and giggled a lot while Patrick teased her about something; her abject crush on her favourite uncle was painful to behold. It never ceased to exasperate Isabel that Patrick wasted his capricious charm on his fans instead of using it to seduce his detractors. In a profession where arse-lickers flourished, he saved his silver tongue for sarcasm. Was it a weakness, or a strength?

'There's a car outside,' said Bridie, as she put down the telephone. 'But it's not a Rolls-Royce,' she added, disappointed.

Isabel looked out of the window to see a nondescript saloon, catching her breath as the driver emerged. It was Neville.

'Hello, Izzie,' he said, as she met him outside the house, having said a hasty goodbye to Bridie. She didn't want to have to introduce him, for fear that she would mention him to Patrick. 'Vince got stuck in Cardiff overnight, hatching some business deal. He asked me to pick you up instead.'

It was the first time they had met in over six years. The reddish-gold hair had more silver in it now, but otherwise he hadn't changed. The sight of him revived emotions she had striven to suppress – guilt for having hurt him so badly, and nostalgia for her vanished youth. It all seemed so long ago. And yet it seemed like yesterday. If she occasionally indulged, in her more self-pitying moments, in the odd what-might-have-been fantasy, it always concerned working with Neville, rather than sleeping with him.

'So you're driving again,' she said, as he opened the passenger door for her.

'Yes. It's an automatic, specially adapted, of course. How are you?'

'Very well, thanks,' said Isabel brightly. 'You?'

'Fine. How's Patrick getting on up in Hockleigh?'

Isabel drew breath to say something guarded and tactful and found herself quoting Patrick instead, whereupon Neville laughed and agreed that Shipton was a posturing prat. The ice broken, she began asking him about the latest Renegade project, a black comedy written by Richard, his first venture into solo playwriting since *Bondage*. He had proved very secretive about it, saying only that it was a modern-day Cinderella satirizing the British class system.

'Like you, Richard doubts his own talent,' said Neville. 'I had to twist his arm to let me put it on at all, he's convinced it's going to be a flop. So I might as well twist your arm as well, while I've got the chance. Now that you've got a nanny there's nothing to stop you picking up the threads of your career again, and –'

'Bridget's not a nanny,' Isabel interrupted him, quelling a flutter of excitement. 'She's just here on holiday.'

He pulled over, switched off the engine, and searched her eyes. Isabel looked away. Neville had always represented sin, but never more so than now.

'What are you afraid of, Izzie?' he said. 'Showing Patrick up?'

'Of course not,' protested Isabel. 'My children come first, that's all. I grew up playing second fiddle to my mother's career and I swore I'd never treat my own kids the same way.'

'It's always all or nothing with you, isn't it? There is such a thing as a happy medium. If you hide behind your children now, you'll only resent them for it in later life. And Patrick as well, assuming you don't already. What I was about to say was this. We're casting Richard's play at the moment and I'd like you to audition for the lead. Don't get too excited, it's just a club production for a limited season.'

Isabel shook her head, rejecting the offer as a sop.

'And if I got the part, what would that prove? Just that nepotism reigns supreme, as always.'

'Don't be so complacent. If you're not the best candidate, rest assured that you won't get the part. I've got my own reputation to think of.'

But if she *did* get the part . . . she could just imagine Patrick's reaction to her appearing on the London stage in a play written by Richard and directed by her ex-lover, while he was stuck up in Hockleigh in a job he had taken for lack of anything better.

'Thank you for thinking of me. But it's too soon. In a year or two, perhaps, once Emily is settled in school.'

'Very well,' he shrugged. 'I told Richard I was the wrong person to ask you. Naturally you suspect me of ulterior motives. But believe me, I've no intentions of making a fool of myself again.'

He started up the car a second time. Feeling suitably rebuked, Isabel fell silent, while Neville switched to determined small talk, thwarting her expectation that he would try to talk her into it. He was living in a flat in Battersea, he told her; Helen had remarried a chap from her home town, he drove down to Wales twice a month to see the children, they were eight and ten already. All of which she knew already, through Richard, though she affected not to. Just as he affected not to know all about her. Too late, she began to regret her haste in turning down his offer out of hand. 'What are you afraid of?' he had asked. She could have been honest and said, 'I'm afraid of failing. I don't know if I can do it any more.'

Vincent Parry's weekend cottage in Kent had been luxuriously refurbished, in typical overblown nouveau style. Isabel found Paula presiding over it like a châtelaine, with a studied, hard-boiled, get-this smugness. The facial scars had faded since Isabel had last seen her, but surprisingly she had left her broken nose alone, wearing it jauntily on the skew.

Leaving Vince and Richard to talk, Paula led Isabel upstairs to her room 'for a natter', leaning heavily on two sticks, her legs hidden in blue jeans.

'They're like two wizened little twigs,' she explained, pulling a face. 'I've got to do all these rotten exercises to build up my calf muscles. Still, I've always wanted skinny legs.'

She showed her into a frothy pink bedroom with swagged curtains, a frilly bedspread and the inevitable horticultural wallpaper. Vince had evidently had it redecorated to Paula's own specifications.

'Very nice,' teased Isabel.

'I knew you'd like it.' She flopped down on the bed and patted the space beside her. 'Now tell all. What happened with Neville?'

'Vince isn't in Cardiff at all, is he?'

'Er, no. But he's arriving by helicopter, to make it look as if he was. Don't blame him, it was my idea.'

'I'll bet it was.'

'Well? What happened?'

'I told him I'm not ready to go back to work,' said Isabel shortly. 'Or rather to go to work. I never did any work, as I recall. How many failed drama students get a chance like this? It isn't fair on other actresses, women who need a job.'

'Oh, don't be so holier-than-thou. You need a job more than anyone. God knows you've suffered enough for being a Mallory, so why not accept some of the perks? No, don't answer that, I'll tell you exactly why. You can't face having a row with Patrick about it, that's all. He's turning you into a clone of that little Irish mother of his. Getting you pregnant every five minutes, making you skivvy for him, robbing you of every ounce of confidence you ever had, not that you ever had much –'

'Belt up before I thump you,' growled Isabel, without rancour. Paula was the only person in the world who was allowed to lambast Patrick with impunity.

'You're a coward,' continued Paula mercilessly. 'Anything to be loved, that's your motto. You were fixated on being good, unselfish, generous and all the rest of it, even before those bloody Catholics got their claws into you . . .'

'How much have you had to drink this morning?' said Isabel, sniffing her breath.

'Don't you start. Vince'll give me a rocket, later on, when you've all gone home. Anyone would think we were married already.'

'You mean he's asked you again?'

'Not yet. But that's what all this is in aid of, isn't it? Sometimes I wonder if he planned the whole thing. He's been in his element ever since it happened, making sure I didn't get charged with dangerous driving, settling things out of court with the bloke I nearly killed, bullying the insurance people, hiring all these fancy rip-off doctors, you name it. Talk about Mr Fix-It. I'll bet it was him that leaked it to the press, about Jess being a fag. Just to make sure I couldn't go back to him without looking a bloody fool.'

'All it said in the papers over here was that you were getting divorced.' Which hadn't stopped the gossip behind the scenes. Everyone in the busines seemed to know the whole sorry story.

'That's only because British libel laws are tougher than they are in America. Over there the scandal sheets had a field day. Three-in-a-bed bisexual orgies, all the muck raked up about Marty and *Bondage*. Still, why should I care? If I marry Vince, I won't ever have to work again.'

'Don't you want to work? What about your precious independence?'

'Oh, I feel like a rest,' shrugged Paula. The accident must have taken its toll, thought Isabel. It was hard to imagine Paula opting for a life of leisure; she had always been so driven. 'And I'll still be independent. I've got a few dollars tucked away, back in the good old US of A, more than enough to fall back on if things don't work out.'

'Well, I think it's much too soon to go rushing into another marriage,' said Isabel. 'You ought to give yourself time to take stock.'

'Oh, I intend to keep him waiting a year or three. He's too used by half to having anything he wants, he only values what he has to pay through the nose for. I intend to be the most expensive thing he's ever bought . . .'

Hearing the sound of a helicopter in the field adjoining the house, she hauled herself onto her sticks again. 'There he is now.'

It was hard to work out what was really going on between them, given Paula's flippancy and Vince's usual impenetrable composure. They displayed no affection towards one another, both equally intent on hiding their feelings, at least as far as other people were concerned. But Isabel could sense a sexual tension in the air which made her doubt if they behaved the same way once they were alone. One thing, however, she was sure of. Whatever Paula's claims to the contrary, Vincent Parry was undoubtedly the boss. The fact that she didn't drink in his presence spoke for itself.

Neville paid Isabel very little attention all day, as if to demonstrate his bona fides, and neither he nor anyone else mentioned Richard's play again. He left early, saying that he had work to do and that Richard would drive her home. At eight o'clock Paula ran out of steam and fell asleep in her chair. Vince covered her with a quilt and showed them out, while they said their goodbyes in whispers, so as not to disturb her.

'So how did you find her?' said Richard, as they drove off.

'Hard to tell. The usual game of hide and seek. Now you see her, now you don't.'

Richard hesitated a moment before saying, 'Did she tell you she was ill?'

'What do you mean, ill? She's just broken half the bones in her body.'

'Then she didn't tell you. About her heart, I mean.'

'Her heart? What's wrong with it?'

'A congenital defect, the quacks say, made worse by excessive dieting, you know how fanatical she's always been about not getting fat. Plus she'd been taking amphetamines to speed up her metabolism and give her energy, which didn't help. Don't tell her I told you, for God's sake. She only told me because she was pissed.'

'But . . . she will get better, won't she?' said Isabel, refusing to understand.

'Not unless they operate. But there's only a fifty-fifty chance it would work and she might die on the table. Meanwhile they've told her to stop smoking and given her pills that don't mix with booze, so God only knows if she'll bother to take them.'

'But why didn't she tell me all this?' said Isabel, appalled to be getting such news second-hand.

'Because she doesn't want you pitying her, I suppose. The only other person who knows is Vince.'

'So that's why she's giving up work,' said Isabel, the pieces fitting into place.

'Doctor's orders. Vince isn't letting her take any chances. Still, if she marries him she can afford to retire. Not that one dares encourage her to marry him for fear she'll do the exact opposite. You two have more in common than you think.'

'Don't start,' muttered Isabel. 'I've already explained to Neville . . .'

'I told him you'd play hard to get. As a matter of fact, I wanted Paula for the part, not you. Offered to put it on ice till she was fit again. That's when she got sozzled and told me why she couldn't take it. At least *she's* got a real excuse.'

He withdrew a bound folder from the shelf beneath the glove compartment and tossed it at her. 'The audition passages are marked up. I hope for your sake that you hate it, it's bound to be a disaster.'

Isabel fell silent, her mind whirling with too much information. Paula's bad heart. Paula marrying Vince. Neville. Richard's play. The chance to be an actress again . . .

'Well?' Ma greeted her, after Richard had roared off into the night. 'Did you have a nice day?'

'Lovely, thanks. Was everything all right?'

'Toby woke up an hour ago with one of his nightmares.'

'I'd better go up to him.'

'No need. Bridie cuddled up beside him and got him back to sleep in no time. They're both dead to the world. What's that?' she added, indicating the folder.

'Richard asked me to read his new play.' She was about to lie, to invent some story about him wanting her opinion of it, but instead she blurted out, 'There's a part in it he wants me to audition for. I told him no, of course.'

Ma would be sure to endorse her decision. In Ma's world a woman's place was in the home.

'You said no? Before you'd even read it?'

'Even if I got the part – which I probably wouldn't – I can't go traipsing up to London six days a week.'

'Why not? Bridie and I are here to mind the children.'

'You don't mean to say you approve?'

'Why shouldn't I approve?'

'But . . . I was relying on you to talk me out of it!'

'Why would I be doing that? It would suit me fine if you started work. That way, I'd have a job as well. Or do you think that Bridie and I can't manage without you there to see we do everything just so?'

'No, of course not. But Patrick . . .'

'You just leave Patrick to me. I'm the one that spoiled him, after all. High time we women ganged up on him.'

And with that she gave Isabel a dry peck on the cheek and went up to bed, leaving her with nowhere to hide.

Isabel sat up late reading the script. The part of the heroine, a sassy social climber with a heart of gold, was tailor-made for Paula, Paula who was seriously ill, too ill to work, presenting Isabel with a painful reminder that life was short. Seeing Paula robbed of her health and strength made it seem urgent to exploit her own, to stave off a different kind of death . . .

The irony of it. All those fears she had once had about Ma trying to take over, and now she was relying on her to do just that. Perhaps, deep down, it was what she had wanted all along.

Two passages were marked for the audition, both of them tricky enough for an experienced actress, let alone a novice. After a couple of days of struggling alone Isabel rang Paula and asked for her help.

She arrived next morning by Rolls, just after Toby and the twins had gone to school, whereupon the chauffeur took Ma, Bridie, and Emily out for the day, so that Isabel could bellow her lines to her heart's content.

'You're gabbling,' Paula chided her. 'Have you forgotten how to breathe? Again.' And then, 'You're giving this line here too much weight, it's much better if you throw it away. Again.' And again and again and again.

'Not bad,' she said finally, as the car returned, having picked up the kids from school. 'But not good enough. I'd better come back tomorrow and yell at you some more.'

'Are you sure? You're not too tired?'

'Why should I be too tired? I sit around all day doing bugger all. Don't treat me like an invalid, okay? I'm not dead yet.'

Isabel opened her mouth to say something and shut it again.

'Richard told you, didn't he?' accused Paula. 'I knew as soon as I got here, it was written all over your face. Not much of an actress, are you?'

Isabel didn't answer, an answer in itself.

'That'll teach me to open my stupid gob. You haven't told laughing boy, have you?'

'No, of course not. Richard made me promise not to.'

'My own fault for getting pissed. One thing about these pills they gave me is that they save you a fortune on booze. A couple of doubles and you're high as a kite.'

'You look after yourself, do you hear me? I haven't slept a wink for thinking about it.'

Paula emitted her reassuringly dirty laugh.

'Fear not. Only the good die young. These posh paying doctors love to exaggerate so they can con you into spending oodles of money. Still, as long as Vince is paying, why worry?'

'Are you going to have that operation?'

'No bloody fear. Or rather, over my dead body, geddit?'

'Will you stop joking about it?'

'What do you want me to do? Start spouting speeches out of sodding *Snowdrops*? No, the death scene in *Fortune's Fool* was even funnier.' She clasped a hand to her heart and began burbling some immortal Hollywood prose until Isabel gave in and laughed. The alternative would have been to cry.

After another day of intensive coaching the car arrived, minus Paula, to take Isabel to London. The auditions were being held in a dingy rehearsal room above a greengrocer's shop in Vauxhall. Isabel was on last, theoretically an advantage. Inevitably, though, she arrived much too early and it proved impossible not to overhear her competitors through the partition wall. They all sounded much better than her. Oh God. Anything she wanted this badly had to be a sin . . .

'You've always been afraid to be as good as you can be,' Paula had said, echoing Patrick's words of long ago. 'You're like the brightest kid in the class who deliberately gets a few sums wrong so the other little snots won't hate you. Well, you're not at school now. This is war.'

War. As her name was called she pulled the cork on the anger and frustration and resentment and discontent that had cost her so many futile Hail Marys, so many faked orgasms. There were better ways to purge the soul than penance.

'Of course I'm pleased for you,' said Patrick irritably. Isabel smiled brightly at Ma, who tactfully left the room. Her twittering 'We've got some grand news for you, son. Isabel's done you proud' had wrong-footed him nicely.

'I wouldn't have considered it,' Isabel felt bound to say, 'if Ma had been on her own. But with Bridie here . . .'

'How are you going to get up to town?'

'Paula's lending me her car so I can get to the station. She can't drive at the moment.'

'What about the pre-run tour?'

'There isn't going to be one.'

'And who's directing? Neville Seaton, I suppose. Talk about an inside job.'

'I auditioned along with everyone else,' protested Isabel. 'It was perfectly fair.' Or as fair as things ever were, in the theatre.

'What about Equity?'

'It's not a West End production. I don't need to be a full member.'

'So what's it about? Ma didn't seem to know.'

'A girl from the wrong side of the tracks who marries the son of an earl. And then her past catches up with her. It's a good part.'

'Well, I'd hardly expect Richard to offer his own sister a bad part.'

'I'm being billed as Isabel Delaney.'

'Why? To hide the connection?'

'No! Because I'd rather use my husband's name than my father's, given that I haven't got one of my own. Any objections?'

'Why should I object? If you want to make life difficult for yourself, go ahead. My name's mud, after all. So how long have you been holding out on me?'

'Not long. I didn't get much notice. I wanted to surprise you.'

'I'm not surprised. It was bound to happen one day. Well, let's hope you become a big success. It should make up for me being such a bloody failure.'

'Darling, don't get depressed. Rehearsals are always miserable.'

'Specially when you're playing Henry V as a Nazi. Still, now I've got a wife to keep me I can always pack it in.'

Isabel shut her eyes.

'Patrick, I can't do this unless I know I've got your full support. Have you any idea how terrified I am? It doesn't come naturally to me the way it does to you. I've always had to work at it.'

'You think I don't work at it?'

'I was paying you a compliment!'

'Thanks a lot.' The pips went. 'I've no more change. 'Bye.'

Isabel replaced the receiver. Hearing the ping, Ma reappeared.

'Well? What did he say?'

'That he was pleased. That it sounded like a good part. That he was sure I'd be a big success.'

'There you are, then. No need to worry any more.'

But Isabel knew that her worries were only just beginning.

*

As the lights dimmed on the final act of Alan Shipton's *Henry V*, Paula joined in the uncertain first-night applause. *Henry V* as an anti-fascist tract featured Henry as a power-crazed madman, with the St Crispin's Day scene conducted à la Nuremberg Rally and the Agincourt speech as an incitement to mass murder. Patrick had looked uncomfortable in a blond wig, especially when wooing Katherine of France, also with flaxen curls, the only Aryan among the swarthy 'French', portrayed as an uneasy cross between victim and collaborator. Ideologically it was a total mess, but somehow Patrick managed to emerge from the fiasco as the kind of hero you loved to hate.

Thanks to the rehearsal schedule for *Cindy*, Isabel had been unable to attend, which gave her something else to feel guilty about, apart from being a Bad Mother. Guilt which was not alleviated by Patrick's sullen attitude of do-what-you-like-I'm-only-your-husband-after-all. Paula had come here intending to tear him off a strip, but having seen him battle bravely for three hours against insuperable odds, she was inclined to think that perhaps he had suffered enough for one evening.

She waited for the auditorium to empty before she made her way to his dressing room, via the stage door; it was still agony to be jostled in a crowd, as she had discovered in the bar in the interval. The doorman, recognizing her, asked her for her autograph and let her through without phoning up first. She held back in the corridor until his other visitors had emerged – mostly loud local worthies with Crimplene-clad wives – before she tapped on the open door.

'Shit,' said Patrick, catching sight of her in the mirror.

'That's a nice welcome, I must say.'

'Thank God I didn't know you were out there. Don't be polite about it, okay? I swear to God I'd have walked out by now if Izzie hadn't gone and got herself a job. I'm damned if I'm living off her . . .'

At that moment Nora Herbert, his leading lady, appeared at the door, a tall, thin, fey-looking girl with cropped Twiggy-style hair, spiky false eyelashes, very white pasty skin, and a wide thick-lipped mouth. She was dressed in a very short mini, thigh-length white boots, and a tight skinny-ribbed sweater.

'Hello,' she said, flashing Paula a brief on-off smile; she gave no sign of recognition. And then, in cooing, proprietorial tones, 'Hurry up and get changed, darling. We'll be late for the piss-awful party.' She put a hand on Patrick's shoulder and kissed the top of his head.

'You go on ahead,' said Patrick brusquely. 'I'll be along later.'

'Patrick and I have personal business to discuss,' said Paula sweetly. 'I'm an old friend of his wife's.'

'Paula Dorland,' said Patrick, by way of introduction. 'Nora Herbert.'

'Sorry I never managed to catch you in anything,' said Nora Herbert. 'I don't much care for American films. See you later then, Patrick.' She strolled off.

'Another little tart for your collection?' queried Paula.

'If Izzie sent you here to check up on me,' said Patrick warningly, 'you can start off by telling her that I'm giving the party a miss. That should freak her out. Got to suck up to the local bigwigs, you see. Good for my career. Got to get myself a reputation for being charming and co-operative and keen and above all grateful. I mean, I'm lucky to have a job at all, aren't I? Fancy a quick drink before closing time?'

'Not on an empty stomach, I don't. Where's the most expensive place to eat round here?'

'The restaurant at the Swan Hotel.'

'That's where I'm staying. Come on, then. I'll buy you dinner, so I can check up on you some more.'

Rather coyly, for Patrick, he disappeared behind a screen and reappeared in his civvies, looking mildly dishevelled as always, with the knot in his tie pinched and twisted from never being undone and a button missing from his cuff; evidently he hadn't cleaned his shoes since Isabel, or his mother, had last done it for him. Perhaps it was just as well, thought Paula, that he was bunking off from the party.

The Rolls was waiting outside.

'I'm not being flash,' said Paula, seeing his lip curl. 'I just can't walk all that far yet. Or even drive myself.'

'I gather you and Vincent Parry are getting married.'

'I haven't decided yet. No hurry.'

'Are you in love with him?'

'Of course not. You should never marry someone you love.'

293

'How true,' he said, as he helped her out of the car and led the way into the hotel dining room, looking as if he owned the place, despite his crumpled attire. Flashing his best Harry Spencer smile at the waitress, a fifty-ish matron who looked ready to swoon on the spot, he ordered soup and steak, and ignoring the coy menuspeak of 'French fried potatoes' asked for a double helping of chips. Paula asked for a bottle of the house red; it would look odd if she didn't drink. And having had that illicit double vodka in the interval she might as well go the whole hog.

'So how's Izzie?' he said casually while they waited for their order, pouring them both a glass of wine.

'Worrying about you as usual. She said that you were sending home too much money and not keeping back enough to live on. Do they feed you at your digs?' she added, as he helped himself to her neglected bread roll, having already polished off his own.

'Breakfast and one disgusting meal. Never mind. I can afford to eat out every night from now on, now that she's earning as well.'

'Why do you resent it so much?'

'Because I don't trust bloody Neville Seaton, that's why.'

'I'd trust Neville Seaton a lot more than I'd trust Nora Herbert.'

'That's different,' growled Patrick, by way of an admission.

'Sauce for the gander is sauce for the goose. It would serve you right if Izzie gave you a taste of your own medicine. Not that she ever would, more fool her.'

Damn, she had meant to be more subtle. Talk about a bull in a china shop.

'You'd like to see us split up, wouldn't you?' accused Patrick. 'Just because your own marriage went west, you can't bear for anyone else to be happy. Everything was fine between us till you started geeing her up.'

'Happy? Is that what you think she is? And leave my marriage out of it!'

'Then keep your bloody nose out of mine!'

And with that he threw down his napkin and stalked off. Cursing herself for having bungled things, Paula hobbled after him, but in her haste she sent herself sprawling, letting out a cry of pain. Hearing the commotion, Patrick turned and retraced his steps.

'Are you all right?' he said, bending over her.

'Of course I'm not all right. Help me up to my room, will you? I can't bear all these people gawping at me. Talk about a floor show.'

She felt faint, giddy, with that horrible hollow feeling in her chest and faint buzzing in her head – warning signs to lie flat immediately, with her feet above her head. She didn't want Patrick knowing she was ill. Enough people were treating her with kid gloves already.

It was an old-fashioned hotel without a lift. Patrick picked her up bodily and carried her up the stairs, Rhett Butler style, setting her down carefully and keeping a supporting arm around her while he used her key. Then he lifted her again and laid her down gently on the bed.

'I'm sorry I went off the deep end like that,' he said humbly. 'Are we friends again?'

'As much as we ever were,' shrugged Paula. 'But I'm Izzie's friend first and don't you forget it. I've always looked out for her, ever since we were at FRIDA, because she can't or won't look out for herself. She's so bloody soft it isn't true, with everyone except herself. Especially you. Why do you have to be so bloody mean to her?'

What the hell. Might as well give it to him straight. Patrick's conciliatory expression hardened into a scowl.

'Here we go again,' he muttered. 'Saint Isabel. Everyone worships her, even my mother. She has a different technique for everyone, you know. You, me, Toby. God help the people she doesn't bother with, or the people who don't respond. Anyone who hasn't got the sense to love Izzie might as well be dead and damned. Sometimes I hate her for making me love her so much. I do. Sometimes I hate her.'

Paula sat up on her elbows, appalled at the bitterness in his voice, if only because she knew exactly how he felt. However hard you tried, you could never quite deserve Izzie; her love was a token of her generosity rather than your own worth.

'I wouldn't mind her working if I wasn't so shit-scared of losing her altogether,' he blurted out, with heartbreaking candour. 'I know perfectly well that I ruined her life, that she would never have married me if she hadn't been pregnant, that she's regretted it ever since. Not that she'd ever risk a row by saying so. Her ambition is for the kids to grow up without ever hearing a voice raised in anger. Sometimes I'd give anything for a good row, like the ones I used to have with you.'

'Like the one we nearly had downstairs? So why did you walk out on it?'

'Because I knew I was going to lose.'

'Too right you are,' said Paula. 'I haven't finished with you yet. You're a selfish, insensitive, bloody-minded, inconsiderate, big-headed, pig-headed bastard. You're untidy, unpunctual, un-scrupulous, unprofessional and the worst stage-hog I have ever met in my life . . .'

'Go on. It's manna to my ears.'

'You have an ego the size of the Empire State Building, you're inconsistent and unreliable and spoilt rotten. I think you're bloody lucky to have a wife like Izzie who's good and beautiful and talented even if she's a pain in the neck sometimes, and three plus one healthy children, and a job. I think it's pathetic that you should feel so damned sorry for yourself. You know what you've got? Everything. And you're so greedy you're still not satisfied. Now clear off and leave me in peace. I'm tired.'

Tired. She would be giving that excuse, on and off, for the rest of her life, or what was left of it. But that wasn't the real reason she wanted him out of here.

'Do I have to go? Nora will be tapping at my door the minute she gets in. There's no avoiding her, we're in the same digs.'

'It was her that seduced you, I suppose.'

'More or less. I don't even like her. She was just . . . handy. I mean, it's only one peg up from wanking, screwing a slag like that.'

'And what was I? Two pegs up?'

'Don't mock how it was between us. I was always fond of you. Fonder than you were of me. You hurt me, you know.'

'Better than letting you hurt me.'

'I never would have hurt you. I wanted to stop you getting hurt, to protect you. I was afraid for you. I still am.'

'Don't worry about me. I'm as tough as old boots.'

'No you're not. You're just a very good actress. So good you don't even know when you're doing it. You didn't just come here to deliver a sermon about Izzie. You came here to take me out to

296

dinner, to do that little stage fall in the restaurant, to get me to carry you up to your room, to lie there looking frail and helpless and innocent and incredibly sexy . . .'

'Now wait a minute –'

'And now you're going to try to lie your way out of it, to pretend you didn't lure me up here with evil intent.'

His eyes glittered. It was impossible to tell if he was joking, fishing, or making a genuine pass. Impossible, given the sudden scrambling of her brains, to remember if his accusations were true or false.

'Stop pissing about,' said Paula. 'Go home and shag the slag like a good boy, so that I can get some sleep.'

'Don't I get a goodnight kiss first?'

'Just a peck. And if you dare try anything on, I'll knee you in the balls . . .'

He did. But she didn't. After a bit of half-hearted squeaking and squirming she let it happen, just as she must have known it would. It wasn't betraying Izzie, she told herself desperately. If he wasn't here, in her bed, he would be in Nora Herbert's, reassuring himself of the power Izzie had stolen from him with her patience, her self-control, her everlasting, intolerable forbearance. Izzie didn't love him the way she, Paula, loved him. Izzie worked at it, the way she worked at everything; Paula couldn't help it.

She was beyond being hurt now, by him, by anyone. She didn't want to take him away from Izzie. She just wanted to remind herself, however briefly, that she was still alive inside, that her damaged heart was still up to the challenge, just in case this was the last chance she ever got . . .

'I'm sorry,' he said, mortified, a few embarrassing minutes later. 'That's never happened to me before.'

'It's all right,' said Paula. Was she relieved or disappointed? 'We should have switched the light off. My legs are a real turn-off.'

'It's nothing to do with your legs. Don't start that I'm-ugly routine again, okay?'

Paula reached for her cigarettes.

'Okay, I'm gorgeous. Don't make a drama out of it. We would have felt shitty about it in the morning, in any case.'

'You know why I couldn't do it?' he challenged her, almost upbraidingly. 'Because it was you. Because I care about you, I

297

mean.' He hung his head. 'I've never been unfaithful to Izzie, not mentally, not emotionally. Do you see?'

Paula turned away so that he wouldn't see her face. It was the nicest thing he had ever said to her.

11

Winter 1966–March 1968

Children begin by loving their parents; after a time they judge them; rarely, if ever, do they forgive them.

Oscar Wilde – A Woman of No Importance

Success wasn't a triumphant thing, Isabel discovered. Just a huge relief.

'What did I tell you?' Paula had crowed when the first-night reviews came in. 'Mind you keep it up, or else. I've got a grand of my own money invested in this, remember.'

And she had kept it up. The limited run had been extended, and plans were in hand for a West End transfer. Isabel still couldn't quite believe it. It was an oddly schizophrenic existence, with her real self still a virtuous suburban housewife and her stage persona an emblem of the swinging sixties and the sexual revolution. *Cindy*'s dolly-bird heroine, with her mini-skirt and her long fringe, her big panda-eyes and her pale pouting lips, might be a fictional creation, but something of her character seemed to rub off on Isabel, giving her back something she had lost, returning her to the generation from which she had been exiled too soon. All through the rehearsals she had found herself vowing, I won't let Patrick spoil this. If he doesn't like me working that's just too bad.

But of course that was Cindy talking, not Isabel. Patrick could have spoiled things for Isabel with or without Cindy's permission. But in the end, to his credit, he didn't. After all the initial brooding and sulking he had come up trumps for the first night, sending her a huge bouquet and a long, loving good-luck telegram – so explicitly loving, in fact, that she couldn't put it up on her mirror with the rest of them. It wouldn't have cut any ice with the cynical Cindy, but it had spurred the soft-hearted Isabel to give her best performance ever.

But she hadn't just done it for Patrick, or even for herself. She had done it for Richard. After years of hiding, self-doubtingly, behind collaborators and adaptations – not to mention the non-existent Felipe X – he was at last being seen as a talent in his own right. And for Neville. Working with him had been everything she had hoped for. Not only had he kept his promise not to fan old flames, but he had gone one stage further, by showing an interest in Patrick.

'I went to see *Henry V*, up in Hockleigh,' he told her one day, taking her by surprise, 'to find out what all the ballyhoo was about.' The production had proved controversial if nothing else. 'It was like watching Houdini get out of a straitjacket. Patrick's still a director's nightmare, isn't he?' But he made it sound like a compliment.

'He doesn't always do what he's told, if that's what you mean,' said Isabel, feeling her way. 'But that's only because he cares so passionately about getting things right. He needs . . .' She hesitated, fearful of sounding too obvious. 'He needs to work in an environment that encourages originality and actor-participation.'

'Somewhere like Renegade, you mean?' smiled Neville.

'Somewhere like Renegade,' admitted Isabel. It was the ideal habitat for a maverick like Patrick, if only he and Richard would bury the hatchet . . .

'I said the same thing myself, to Richard.'

'Thank you,' said Isabel, flushing.

'Pure self-interest, I assure you. I enjoy a challenge. I'll talk to him nearer the end of the Hockleigh season.'

Isabel hugged this news to herself, not daring to say anything to Patrick, for fear of rocking the boat. If he could produce good work in spite of Alan Shipton, just think what he could do with help from Neville! It would be glorious to see him fulfilling his potential and getting the recognition he deserved. Her own success would be twice as sweet if only he could have a share of it . . .

With the introduction of the fourth play in Hockleigh's reper-toire, the only one in which Patrick did not appear, he was able to extend his Christmas break, driving down to London a day earlier than he had told Isabel to expect him and catching a performance of *Cindy* without her knowing he was in the audience.

300

'You were terrific,' he said afterwards, playing the confident, supportive husband in front of the fellow-actress who shared her dressing room. But Isabel, alert to every nuance of his mood, could tell what a big effort he was making. He might have reconciled himself to her getting a driving licence, but he didn't much care for her screeching round corners or exceeding the speed limit; that was his prerogative. If she'd known he was out there she would have felt compelled to stick to twenty-eight miles an hour and respect the Highway Code.

'I've booked us a table at the Savoy Grill,' he told her as he ushered her out of the stage door, waiting rather tetchily while two stage-struck schoolgirls sought and obtained her autograph. Evidently they weren't *Harry Spencer* fans because neither of them bothered to ask for his.

'The Savoy? Patrick! We can't afford it . . .'

'I had a little flutter. Won two hundred quid.'

'Two hundred? How much did you bet?'

'Not much. It was on an outsider. Come on.'

Over dinner he was at his most charming and seductive, reminding her of why she had fallen in love with him. Absence made the heart grow fonder, of course. And the champagne undoubtedly helped. But not as much as working helped. It was as if work had diverted all the dark, bad, destructive parts of her character, provided an outlet for her demons, left her purged and benevolent. Benevolent enough to find her husband attractive again. Better still, to *feel* attractive again . . .

For a long time now she had been going through the motions, pretending to a passion she no longer felt. Weary of an ever-diminishing safe period – trust a convert to take things too literally – Patrick had insisted on taking the precautions himself, thus depriving her of her god-given excuse to say no. Far from being grateful for his willingness to go to Hell in her stead, she had found herself resenting him for it. And now suddenly she wanted him again, the way she had wanted him at the beginning . . .

She had forgotten what an accomplished tease he was, how much he could do with his eyes, with his voice, with a hand clasped in hers across a table. She barely tasted the food on her plate, all she wanted to do was to get home, and quickly, before the mood evaporated. A pity that home was the best part of two hours' drive away.

'We ought to leave,' she said, when he suggested a dessert, rather piqued that he didn't seem to share her sense of urgency. 'Or Ma will worry.'

'Oh, I phoned her to let her know we'd be late. She said she'd wait up for us, she wants to hear all my news.'

What was he playing at? thought Isabel, confused now. This wasn't teasing, it was torture. Was he trying to punish her for something?

'But don't worry,' he said casually, not looking at her. 'We can always park in a lay-by somewhere, on the way. Unless you'd find this more comfortable.' He produced a key from his pocket and slid it across the table while he signalled for the bill.

'You've booked a room, here? Oh Patrick . . .'

By the time they reached it Isabel was past worrying about the extravagance of it all. It was all they could do not to grope each other in the lift, in front of the bellboy. They didn't even make it as far as the bed, tearing each other's clothes off and rolling around on the floor like a pair of sweaty adolescents. It reminded her of the very first time they had made love . . . The thought brought her up short.

'Patrick,' she panted, at the very last minute. 'Haven't you forgotten something?'

'Have a heart, Izzie. I can't bear to put one of those things on, not tonight. I want to feel you properly, don't you want to feel me?' But he didn't give her a chance to answer, suddenly she was full of him. 'Don't worry, I won't come inside you, I promise . . .'

It was as if he had turned her off at the mains. The gushing tap slowed to a trickle, then a drip, and dried up altogether. However 'careful' he was, one stray sperm would be enough to slam the prison door shut on her again . . .

And yet she couldn't bear for him to think her cold and unloving, not after so many weeks of separation, not at Christmas, not when he was being so nice to her. If she didn't reward him for good behaviour, what hope was there for the future? And so she put up a convincing show of lust, hating herself for not being able to feel it. She could almost feel herself getting pregnant . . .

By the time her fears proved to be unfounded, three nailbiting weeks later, the psychological damage was done. By then she had convinced herself, with the benefit of hindsight, that Patrick had cold-bloodedly set out to impregnate her, in order to restore the status quo. The removal of the threat did not remove its impact. That she had escaped unscathed was no thanks to him.

She found herself expressing as well as confessing her anger at her next confession, the inevitable long-winded soul-searching affair that left the waiting fellow-penitents outside wondering what on earth that woman must have done, to have been in there so long.

She had been looking for a stern talking-to from the reactionary old Father Dennihey. But the introductory blessing was given by a young, unfamiliar, sympathetic voice, which prompted a heretical outburst about how she was a person, not a baby-producing machine, she had a brain as well as a soul, she had four children to look after and that was enough, all the worry of it was wrecking her marriage . . .

'He said what?' said Paula.

'He said it would be all right for me to take the Pill, as long as it's prescribed for reasons other than to prevent conception. He said some doctors give it for period pains and menstrual irregularities, and in cases like that it wouldn't be a sin to take it, even if it stopped me getting pregnant.'

'There you go then,' said Paula, who found the dos and don'ts which Isabel lived by all but incomprehensible. 'You've always had a rotten time with the curse. Time you did something about it.'

'It sounds too good to be true. I think he must be one of those new rebel priests you keep reading about.'

'He's still a priest. So what he says must be right, right? Don't look a gift horse in the mouth.'

Isabel didn't. For the first time in years she felt in control of her body. She regretted being so crabby on the phone the last few times Patrick had rung. He had kept asking what was wrong and she hadn't dared tell him for fear of the torrent of home truths she might give vent to. To make up for it, she took advantage of Vince's offer of a helicopter ride to enable her to attend a matinée of *The Shrew* and get back in time for her own performance that evening.

Petruchio had been conceived by Alan Shipton as a villainous brute, Katharina as a symbol of female oppression. The play had been stripped of all its high spirits to become a kind of cautionary

303

tale with a bitter, downbeat ending. Which hadn't stopped Patrick subverting the director's intention by combining bad-boy sexual charisma with the most irresistible vulnerability, subtly soliciting not only sympathy but exoneration, leaving every woman in the audience convinced that all the poor man needed was lots of tender loving care and whatever was wrong with him it was all his mother's fault.

'How long have you got?' demanded Patrick straight away, when she appeared in his dressing room, forestalling her intended eulogy on his performance.

'Hardly any. I've got to get back to the heliport straight away. Darling, you were brilliant. It was like watching Houdini get out of a straitjacket,' she added, passing off Neville's simile as her own. Now that she had seen the phenomenon for herself she could see how apt it was.

'Then I shouldn't find it too hard to get my own wife out of her clothes, now should I?'

'Patrick, there isn't time,' Isabel protested, as he locked the door, slipped her coat off her shoulders, slid the zip of her dress, peeled down her tights (a newfangled garment which Patrick abhorred) and panties and opened his flies. 'I've only got five minutes.'

'It won't take that long,' Patrick assured her. 'God, I've been thinking about this all day . . .'

He lifted her off her feet and pinned her against the wall, and this time she didn't even have time to remind him to be careful, which he wasn't, machiavellian bastard. She found herself relishing the deception, enjoying the shift of power, thinking of all those troublesome tadpoles getting their evil little tails chopped off . . .

'Half a minute to spare,' he said, as they collapsed in a heap on the floor. 'Um . . . it was safe, wasn't it? I mean, you didn't say it wasn't.'

'It was safe,' said Isabel slyly. Let him enjoy his little macho fantasy of knocking her up – or rather down – again . . .

'You haven't taken a lover, have you?' he demanded, taking her by surprise. The odd thing was, she felt as if she had; she felt herself colouring guiltily.

'What makes you think that?'

'You seem different, that's all.'

'Better or worse?'

'Better, I suppose. As long as it's not thanks to Neville Seaton.'

'I'm sure he'd be flattered to know he was under suspicion.'

'That's not an answer.'

'If you weren't so insecure, you wouldn't need an answer. Or be so scared of him. Specially as he's one of the few directors who isn't scared of you.'

'Have you been trying to pull strings?' snarled Patrick, rattled now. 'I don't need any help from bloody Renegade, okay?'

Oh God, thought Isabel, why did I open my big trap?

'Neville came to see your Henry,' she said, trying to retrieve the situation. 'He was terribly impressed.'

'And he'll fix me up with a part if you sleep with him, I suppose?'

'Take that back!'

'That's what other people will think, whether it's true or not. That's what I hate about this business. All the whoring and pimping that goes on. All the back-scratching and cliquery and nepotism. You were brought up on it, of course, it comes naturally to you, but I –'

'Are you saying I didn't get the part fair and square?'

'If you want to believe that, far be it from me to contradict you.'

Isabel slammed the door behind her. Damn him. He would ring her tomorrow and apologize, say he hadn't meant it, but even if he hadn't that wouldn't take away the reason he had said it – to undermine her fragile self-esteem. Well, she wouldn't let him. She would get her next job without any help from anyone. She would show him. She would show them all.

'Do I look all right?' said Paula anxiously, adjusting her veil. After all her bravado about keeping Vince on a string the wedding had been fixed, quickly and quietly, for the spring of 1967.

'You look lovely.'

'Liar. I feel bloody ridiculous all done up in white like a frigging virgin.'

Even though she felt like one. Vince had kept to his promise. Nothing doing till the wedding night. Not even Isabel knew that. Paula had been too embarrassed to tell her. There had been

305

nothing but those infuriatingly titillating kisses. They were like one tiny square of chocolate. They left you wanting more.

It was to be a church wedding, allegedly at Vince's insistence, rather than her own. Marrying Jess had taken all of two minutes in front of a judge who pronounced them man and wife as if he were sentencing them to a jail term. This time she had wanted the works – a cake, bouquets and buttonholes, a knock-out of a dress, lots of people watching, and a vicar with a quavering voice making a meal of it. And Vince had been happy to oblige her. A hefty donation to the parish building fund had miraculously softened the local padre's hard line on divorcées, and even the glorious May sunshine outside seemed by special arrangement, as if he had managed to pull off a similar deal with God.

The dress was a ravishing, romantic, frothy confection which Paula liked to pretend that Isabel had bullied her into buying. Likewise the girls' bridesmaids' outfits – Dresden shepherdess ensembles in pale primrose. Isabel hoped that the twins wouldn't start giggling madly half way through the service; at least Emily, a naturally self-contained child, as Isabel herself had been, could be relied upon to behave with a decorum well beyond her five and a half years.

Paula had never been so nervous in her life, even though she had a role to hide behind as always, that of a gold-digger this time – a false assumption which she wouldn't have deigned to deny, least of all to Vince himself. He still hadn't told her that he loved her. Which at least relieved her of the need to reciprocate. Not that she would have done so. She still cringed at the memory of telling Jess she loved him. What a hostage to fortune that was. Never again.

'I'll marry you,' she had told Vince. 'But I can't promise you anything.' Except that it wouldn't be for long. The doctors had told her she had five years at the most, if they didn't open her up. But even five years was better than none, in Paula's view. Let them find some other guinea pig to sharpen their scalpels on.

'Don't promise me anything,' Vince had said. 'Except not to lie to me.' But what was the point of lying? The object of lies was deceit and there was no deceiving Vince, there never had been. He seemed to know her better than she knew herself. He probably knew that she was having second thoughts at this very moment . . .

There was the sound of the car drawing up outside, swathed in white ribbons. Paula thought of Vince waiting at the church, together with Richard, his best man, and a hundred guests, nearly all invited by him. She thought of Sophie and Sarah and Emily, beautiful as angels, waiting to carry her train. She thought of Patrick downstairs, waiting to give her away, weary after an overnight drive from Hockleigh, wearing the same suit he had worn to marry Izzie. Vince had been at that wedding too, helping her to bear it. She couldn't humiliate him in front of all those people. And yet this was her last chance to escape. Or rather, to let him go.

'Tell me I'm doing the sensible thing, for once in my life,' she challenged Isabel, who was snipping at a loose thread on her hem. 'Tell me I won't do better.'

'I think you're being sensible,' said Isabel. 'You won't do better than Vince.' Knowing Paula's taste in men, that was probably true. Whatever doubts Isabel had about the wisdom of this marriage, she had come to regard it as inevitable. In a shipwreck any landfall was better than none. She couldn't bear to see Paula adrift again.

'I suppose I'd better go through with it, then. My wedding, his funeral. Poor sod. Think how much it'll cost him to divorce me.'

'Beginners please,' shouted Patrick's voice from the hallway. 'Hurry up, you two!'

Paula pulled her veil over her face. 'Well, what are we waiting for?' she said. 'It's show time!'

The flight to Nice was turbulent and Vince wouldn't let her drink any of the free champagne to settle her stomach; she had to make do with a barley sugar instead. By the time the taxi arrived outside their honeymoon villa, owned by one of Vince's business associates, Paula felt physically ill with first-night nerves.

'You don't look well,' he commented, as she pecked at a cold supper laid out in the marble-floored dining room overlooking the pool. The setting was pure Hollywood. 'Do you need a doctor?' He was trying to sound off-hand, the way he always did when he was worried.

'Of course not. I'm just tired, that's all. Can we go to bed and get it over with, so I can get some sleep?'

'Get some sleep first. There's no hurry.'

He led the way up the curved stairway, overlooked by a gallery hung with hideous modern paintings. One depicted a huge eyeball and a disembodied ear, another was a mess of spattered paint, clinging to the canvas in warty lumps. They were probably worth a packet, thought Paula. Some people had more money than sense.

'This is all very flash,' she said, viewing the canopied bed, the elaborate *belle époque* ormolu furniture, the heavy gilt-framed mirrors, the antique chiming clock which greeted their entry into the bedroom. 'Can you shut that thing up?' she said irritably. 'I won't get a wink otherwise.'

She locked herself into the gold-plated bathroom and began undressing. She felt absurdly shy, even though her legs were almost normal again, newly waxed and a nice wholesome brown, like the rest of her, thanks to liberal applications of Tanfastic. She could hear the pitter-patter of a shower on the other side of the wall; Vince must be using another bathroom. Very American, all this pre-coital hygiene. Jess had become very fussy that way, so that she wouldn't smell Saul on him, no doubt. And she had sluiced away similar sins, with no more hope of success than Lady Macbeth trying to wash the blood from her hands.

She got into bed quickly, before Vince reappeared. Izzie had given her an ivory silk nightie and négligé as a wedding present; the fact that she had chosen it seemed to imbue it with cleanliness and class. Paula would never have wasted good money on silk that didn't show. The sheets were crisp and chilly to the touch. She began trembling with more than cold.

He came in wearing a towelling dressing gown, slid it off and hung it up. It had been hard to imagine Vince naked. Like most people, he was defined by his costume and the way he wore it; she had never seen him other than smartly dressed. You'd never catch Vince with his flies undone or his shoes down at heel or wearing odd socks, all regular aberrations of Patrick's. Vince's clothes seemed to grow out of him like a pelt. Stripped of his Jermyn Street shirts and pin-stripe suits he seemed defenceless.

She forced herself to look at him, hoping to see slack muscles, flab, skinny arms, a hairy back or nobbly knees. But no such luck. He wasn't physically beautiful, the way Patrick or Jess had been, but neither was he physically repellent, the way most men were.

Even his prick wasn't threatening. It cowered sleepily in its still-damp nest, not bothering even to look at her.

'Relax,' he said. 'I'm not about to do anything, as you can see. I had a cold shower specially, and I never wear anything in bed.'

'I said I wanted to get it over with, didn't I?'

'You say a lot of things you don't mean.' He got in beside her and pulled her into the crook of his arm. Heat radiated from him like a furnace. A moment ago she had been shivering; now she began to sweat. 'Think of all the whoppers you told in church today.'

Speak for yourself, she thought. She had wanted to hear him make those vows. You didn't have to promise anything in a registry office. And the price of hearing him say all those pretty words had been to say them herself, words someone else had written for her, as always. A church wedding was the ultimate *pièce de théâtre*, after all, most women's only chance to be a star, and in her case the last leading role she would ever play.

'I meant the bit about for richer, for poorer,' said Paula. 'You're rich now, but I'll soon make you poor, so be warned.'

'Who are you trying to impress? Nobody can hear you, only me.' He removed a stray lock of hair from her eye.

'In sickness and in health,' persisted Paula. 'Till death do us part. At least you're in with a chance there.'

'I'm not going to let you die.'

'Come off it. You know what they said. That the damage is permanent, and progressive. That I'll be lucky to make it to thirty unless I let them have a go with their knives and forks. Who wants to be thirty anyway?'

'Sometimes I wonder if I ought to talk you into taking a chance. It's just that I'm so scared of losing you.'

'Nobody talks me into anything. So if you're hoping I'm going to take to my bathchair and do exactly what I'm told, you're wrong. I may have promised to obey you, but I lied.'

He didn't argue, didn't lay down the law. He knew that her own cowardice would do the job for him. Any rebellious fantasies she might have had about going back to work had been scotched by debilitating fatigue, fatigue which would have made it impossible for her to pull her weight and ruined her reputation as a pro. But at least no one would know that. Everyone would think that she had found herself a rich bloke and retired.

'Go to sleep now,' he said, switching off the light. 'You've had a long day.'

'You're scared to make love to me, aren't you?' said Paula, who couldn't have slept even if she'd wanted to. 'You're scared I'll croak on the job, like Marty did.'

'Rubbish,' he said, less than convincingly. 'I checked with the doctors that it would be all right. As long as I do all the work,' he added, trying to make a joke of it. 'Sex isn't important, Paula. I didn't marry you for that. I married you because I care about you.' Still he wouldn't say the word love.

'But you do fancy me?' said Paula, almost plaintively, feeling fat again. It didn't take much to make her feel fat.

'I always did. The first time I saw you. Even though you looked like you'd just done ten rounds with Cassius Clay.'

Paula fingered the bump in her nose, the only visible relic of the accident. But she would leave well alone this time. Perfection didn't suit her.

'So exactly how much do you fancy me?' She felt for him under the bedclothes. So much for that cold shower. He was huge and hard as a rock. Oh God. Why did she have to fancy him back? This would be so much easier if she didn't . . .

'It must be a real nuisance, having one of those,' she said pertly. 'Come on, let's get rid of it. Anything you'd like particularly? I know all kinds of tricks.'

'Why don't you just leave it all to me? I've got a few of my own.'

'You won't mind if I doze off, will you?'

'In your case, I'd take it as a compliment.'

There was a big damp patch on her new silk nightie where it had bunched between her legs. 'That's better,' he murmured, pulling it free. 'That's the truth for a change. No more lies, okay?'

He seemed to fill her full of life and hope. All the while he was inside her she felt immortal, as if he were inoculating her against death. She could feel her heart beating louder, faster, feel it getting stronger, better. Perhaps her heart was like her shrivelled legs, in need of exercise. Not the kind you got from sex, the kind you got from love . . .

'There now,' he said. 'We've got it over with.'

'Smug bastard,' muttered Paula, putting a hand up to his smile and tracing it with her fingers. 'How do you know I wasn't faking it?'

'Because you're not as good an actress as you think,' he said.
'Thank God.'

At last things were looking up for Patrick, much to Isabel's relief.
With only another month at Hockleigh to go, not only had he been
offered a season at Stratford by a young new-broom director, but
Neville had tempted him with the chance to play Hamlet, a role
expressly calculated to overcome his prejudice against Renegade.
Isabel had no doubt he would choose the latter, thanks to his
mistrust of big hierarchical companies, his desire to work from the
comfort of his own home again, and his lifelong ambition to play
the part, one which could seal his reputation.

Unfortunately a third option presented itself at the eleventh
hour. Impressed by Patrick's show-stopping Jimmy Porter, a
visiting TV casting director invited him to read for a new twice-
weekly soap, set on a fictional Fleet Street tabloid. Patrick's part
was that of a foot-in-the-door scoop-seeking reporter, a hard-
bitten, hard-drinking stereotype forever in trouble with his editor,
whose wife he was knocking off on the side. To add charm to this
dubious list of attributes, they had decided to make him Irish.
(The Scots and the Welsh were also to be represented, as in old
British war films.) Recording would clash with rehearsal dates for
Hamlet, making it impossible for him to do both.

'I'll get a shot at *Hamlet* another time,' Patrick told Isabel airily,
when he phoned her from Hockleigh with the news. 'And don't
start bleating about me getting type-cast again. The programme
probably won't survive the six-week trial run. And then I'd still
have the Stratford season to fall back on.'

'But surely you have to sign something saying that you're willing
to stay with the series if they extend it?'

'Yes,' admitted Patrick. 'But only for a year.'

'*Only* a year?'

'It's regular work. And the money's good.'

'I don't care about the money! We'll manage. I'll be working
too, remember . . .'

'I was waiting for you to rub it in.'

'Patrick! It's taken you all this time to get people to forget Harry
Spencer. That's why you went up to Hockleigh, remember? To

prove that you're a serious actor, not a hack.'

'I came to Hockleigh to feed my family. Because that was the only work I could get. And now I've got the chance to earn what I'm worth, I intend to take it. Nobody's stopping *you* working for the pin money Renegade pay.' He made it sound as if she spent it on fripperies. 'If this series takes off, we could afford to move nearer town. You know how you hate living in bloody Burwell.'

'I've got used to it,' said Isabel. The house had come to represent security. 'And the children are settled in school.'

'They're young enough to adjust. As it is, the travelling leaves you hardly any time with the kids,' he added, going straight for her Achilles' heel. Never mind that they seemed to be thriving perfectly well without her, that made her feel worse, in a way. It had been quite a shock to discover that she wasn't as indispensable as she thought.

'I promised you I'd get you back to London one day,' Patrick reminded her. 'And this is the only way we'll be able to afford it.'

'We won't be able to afford it anyway,' Isabel pointed out. 'You know how expensive houses are nearer town . . .'

'Why do you always have to pour cold water on everything I say?'

'I just don't want us to get into debt again.'

'For God's sake. I can't do anything any more without getting your permission first. Can't take a job, can't move house, can't decide what's best for my kids. Whereas you do anything you want to do, without even bothering to consult me . . .'

He had a point there, thought Isabel uncomfortably. *Cindy* had just reached the end of its nine-month run, and she had jumped at the chance to join the cast of a smash-hit revival of Noël Coward's *Hay Fever*, replacing an actress who was leaving to have a baby. (It's an ill wind, she had thought, with a certain smugness.) *Cindy* had established her as having a flair for comedy, and attracted gratifying comparisons with Maggie Smith, with the result that this part had fallen into her lap, almost too easily. But at least Patrick couldn't write it off as another put-up job.

'Sorry to embarrass you in front of Seaton,' he said, as his parting shot. 'But like you, I prefer to get work on my own merits.' Whereupon Isabel shut up, miserably aware that she was beaten.

Patrick's return from Hockleigh was followed by a two-week family holiday in Ireland. It was their third since their wedding and followed a now established pattern. So as not to give offence, they spent a couple of days with each of Patrick's brothers and sisters, shifting around from house to house, calling on innumerable friends and relatives, never eating a meal at the same table twice, and allowing Toby and the girls to be spoiled out of their wits.

Isabel could see the tautness leave Patrick's face as soon as they arrived. On home territory he was safely the centre of attention again, everybody's favourite brother/nephew/uncle/cousin/mate, the local boy made good. He spent most of his time catching up with various cronies while Isabel drank gallons of tea with the family womenfolk, vainly trying to keep track of the latest births, marriages and deaths. It was like listening to Genesis, read at top speed, with no hope of remembering who begat whom. She was repeatedly asked by well-meaning matrons when she was going to 'try for a boy', as if four kids weren't quite enough to cope with already. As for her recent return to the stage, this was viewed as a glorified hobby, as if she had started selling Tupperware on the side or set up a little home dressmaking business.

Everyone commented approvingly on how Bridie had 'come out' under Isabel's influence, she was quite the young lady these days. To prove it, she was soon walking out with a boy called Michael, a distant cousin-by-marriage who had recently joined her father's business as a trainee second-hand car salesman. Bridie took to spending her days at the showroom, 'helping out with the paperwork', and was seldom seen without a faraway look in her eye.

Meanwhile Isabel's normally well-disciplined children ran wild. Egged on by their tearaway cousins they climbed trees and three-bar gates, ate unwashed sour gooseberries and sticks of rhubarb straight from the bush, frolicked with large, savage-looking dogs, squirted each other with ice-cold water from garden hoses, hid in barns and shed and lay awake talking half the night with their newfound partners in crime. When Toby wasn't busy masterminding the misdemeanours of the younger children he would disappear for a day at a time with older ones, riding borrowed bikes at daredevil speed, tearing his clothes and smoking illicit cigarettes, which Isabel could smell on him, despite the peppermint chews he used to clear his breath, one of which removed a filling.

She expected daily to hear that one of the children had drowned in a muddy river, run in front of a car, eaten poisonous berries, fallen off a roof or been mauled by a demented Alsatian, a breed of which the Delaney clan was inordinately fond. Ma seemed to have no difficulty suspending all the rules she enforced – or claimed to enforce – at home, leading Isabel to wonder what she and Bridie turned a blind eye to while she was at work. Often she had to sit on her hands and feign deafness rather than appear a neurotic killjoy mother. As always, she found herself counting the days till they could go home again.

'You know,' said Patrick in bed one night, 'for the price of that box in Burwell, we could buy a big place over here, with a few acres of land.'

He couldn't be serious, thought Isabel.

'I thought you wanted to move back to London?'

'Only because of the TV job. But God knows if that will work out or not.' He kissed the top of her head. 'I'm just thinking ahead, that's all.'

And with that he rolled over and went to sleep, leaving a wakeful Isabel to add another worry to her collection. She pictured an unemployed Patrick – never mind if she was in work or not – moving the family to Kilmacross and then leaving her there as soon as another job came up. ('It's no worse than when I was at Hockleigh,' he would remind her.) Never mind about her burgeoning career on the London stage or her own selfish ambitions. The kids would be all for it; to them Delaney territory was one big playground. And Ma would be delighted. Not to mention Bridie, who was in the throes of first love, weeping into her pillow at the thought of leaving next week and swearing to write to Michael every day. Isabel's holiday had been blighted by the fear that she would decide to stay put. And then what? Ma wasn't physically capable of managing the kids on her own . . .

One puff and her carefully stacked house of cards would collapse around her ears. It had been a mistake to start work because now it would be agony to give it up. It was like a shameful addiction to some dangerous, mind-altering drug. So much for her putting her husband and children first.

314

Actresses always claimed, in magazine interviews, that their careers would never take precedence over marriage and mother-hood. (Though of course they usually did, given half a chance, however much they believed their own PR to the contrary.) The subject was always blissfully married, if married, however many times she or her husband had been married before, in which case she would be depicted in a glowing family photograph, complete with stepchildren if appropriate, by her first marriage, or his second, as the case might be. And then, in the fullness of time, you would read or hear somewhere else that the happy couple had agreed to part and the reason for the break-up was always the same: pressures of work, long separations, and so on.

Isabel had sworn to herself that she would not tread this well-worn furrow. Her family really and truly *would* come first. But when it came to it, the choices weren't that simple. She wanted to have her cake and eat it too . . .

'There is such a thing as a happy medium,' Neville had said. But there wasn't, not really. Just an unhappy one.

Paula saw little of Isabel over the next few weeks. Like her, she was busy looking for a house in London, and given the difference in their budgets, it would have been tactless, even by Paula's standards, to go on viewing expeditions together. Paula hated to think of Izzie ending up in some dilapidated house in Tulse Hill or Crouch End while she herself queened it with the nobs in a listed Georgian pile in St John's Wood.

They could easily have made do with Vince's flat in Portland Place, instead of buying a house that was much too big for two people. But doing it up would keep her busy for a while, if you could call it being busy, sitting there like Lady Muck while an interior decorator brought swatches and samples for her approval. Paula's first priority was to cover up the Peter Rabbit wallpaper in the smallest bedroom. That wallpaper had almost stopped her buying the place at all.

The quack had put the frighteners on Vince, warning that a pregnancy would put too much strain on her heart. They had taken her off the Pill on account of it raising her blood pressure and inserted a coil instead. As Vince said, they could always

315

adopt. But it didn't seem fair to get some poor unsuspecting kid to love her, only to desert it a few years later. Paula knew what it felt like when someone you loved went and died on you.

'I'll get a daily woman in,' Paula told Vince, when he suggested a full-time housekeeper. 'I don't need a babysitter, okay?' They compromised with a multi-extension hot line to Vince's office in Marylebone Road; if she felt ill she had only to pick up the receiver, without even dialling, and help would be there within minutes.

The domestic agency sent along a Mrs Beasley, a surly middle-aged woman wearing curlers and an overall incongruously set off by a pair of sunglasses, which she kept on while she worked, ignoring the non-stop background blast of Paula's new *Sergeant Pepper* album.

'Something wrong with your eyes?' queried Paula.

'Conjunctivitis,' she said shortly. 'Don't worry, I can see what I'm doing, even if I can't hear it.'

Mrs Beasley obviously wasn't impressed by the house or by Paula herself; if she recognized her, she didn't say so, but more likely she hadn't been to the pictures since Mr Beasley had last groped her in the back stalls, twenty-five-odd years ago. She never volunteered any information about herself, and responded to Paula's nosey-parker promptings with mind-your-own business terseness. Her first name was Marian, no, she didn't mind if she called her that, it was all the same to her. She lived with her husband Ted in a council flat in Kilburn. She had two boys, one in the navy and one who'd married a girl from Hull and moved up north.

If she'd been polite and friendly, Paula would have shown little interest in her. Friendly, polite people were two a penny, when you were rich. Inured to fawning flunkeys, Paula respected her for not bothering to ingratiate herself, even though she was obviously hard up and needed the job.

'Miserable cow,' commented Richard, a week later, as Paula poured him a sherry before lunch and a tonic for herself. Marian had let him in while Paula was on the phone, with her usual truculent lack of charm. He was stoned as usual, and his hair was longer than ever; Kevin's influence. Paula only ever saw him these days when Kevin was otherwise engaged.

'What's with the film star shades?' he went on, without bothering to lower his voice. 'Is she afraid of being mobbed by her fans? And dig those crazy curlers. She looks like an escapee from *Coronation Street*.'

'Ssh. She'll hear you. She's a bloody hard worker, I don't want to lose her. And a good cook too. I'm paying her overtime to feed your fat face, so shut up.'

'Do I smell roast duck?' approved Richard, sniffing the air, Bisto-style.

'Your fave. So be good or you'll get steamed fish instead . . .'

She broke off as they heard a crash and a scream from the kitchen next door, where they found Marian standing, white-faced, in a pool of boiling fat with the duck, roast potatoes and baking tin lying scattered all around her on the floor.

'It just slipped out of my hands . . .' she began.

'Did you burn yourself?' For an answer Marian fainted, slipping on the puddle of grease and banging her head as she fell on the open oven door.

'Help me lift her onto the settee,' said Paula, alarmed. 'Then pick up the red phone' – she indicated the hot line – 'and tell them to send a doctor. And fetch my dressing gown from the bathroom, will you? She's splashed herself all over. I'd better get her clothes off, before they stick to her skin.'

She did so, uncovering not just burned and blistering flesh but a mass of bruises, some old, some new. Paula removed the dark glasses to reveal the remains of a spectacular black eye. Marian moaned.

'It's all right,' said Paula quietly. 'You're safe now. You're safe.' There but for the grace of God, she thought, go I.

'This is terrific,' applauded Paula, one morning in December, inspecting Isabel's new abode. Patrick must be earning a bigger screw than she thought, to be buying a place like this. 'Masses of room.'

It was a large three-storeyed terraced house in Hammersmith, close to the river, with white walls, sanded floors and high ceilings. The street had a certain raffish chic; the neighbouring windows, unlike those in Shrubbery Close, displayed a studied lack of net curtains and the front gardens tended to be overgrown.

'Oh, there's room all right. Six bedrooms and two bathrooms. But it's only on lease, till the owners come back from abroad.'

'I thought you were planning to buy?'

'We were. But no one would give us a mortgage, except a loan shark, on account of Patrick's contract only being for a year. We were lucky to find this place. Most landlords won't allow children, and I was starting to get desperate, especially as we'd already sold the house.'

'You could always come to stay with me, in an emergency,' said Paula, well aware of Isabel's fear of being exported with the kids to Kilmacross. 'Marian adores kids.'

After yet another savage beating, Paula had finally persuaded her to leave her husband, as she might have done long ago, had she had anywhere else to go. Vince had been all in favour of the plan, given that he was getting his own way, as usual, in the shape of a live-in minder, for all that Marian knew nothing about Paula's illness, at her insistence; she couldn't bear to be treated like an invalid. She was careful never to take her pills in Marian's presence and had told her that the hot line to Vince's office was for urgent business use.

'Oh, I wouldn't inflict my brood on you,' said Isabel. 'The twins are crazy about ballet, they start thumping around doing jetés at seven every morning. Emily's learning piano, you can just imagine the din. And Toby's developed this thing about reptiles. He's got a lizard and a snake.'

'Eek! That settles it then. Invitation hereby cancelled.'

'I took him to see his father again last week,' said Isabel anxiously, going off on a tangent. 'Daddy always insists that I leave the visiting room so that he can talk to him in private. I don't know what he says to him, because Toby won't tell me, but I'm sure it's bad stuff about Davina, because afterwards he starts having nightmares again. Bridie is the only one who can calm him down.'

'Then stop taking him,' shrugged Paula.

'If I did, I'd be in breach of the order, and Daddy wouldn't take that lying down. I don't want to put Toby through another court case or invite social services interference.'

318

'Have you talked to your father about it?'

'I tried. He got quite irate, denied even mentioning Davina and said that something else must be worrying Toby, as if it was all my fault . . .'

She broke off as the front door opened and Toby and Bridie came in, carrying a box with holes in the top.

'Put it straight in the shed, Toby,' said Isabel, averting her eyes.

'What have you got in there?' said Paula.

'Lucifer's dinner.' He lifted the lid, revealing a dozen baby mice heaving about like maggots. Paula peered at them bravely.

'Poor little things,' she mused.

'It's just like eating sausages, for a human,' Toby informed her gravely. 'If I didn't feed him, he'd have to slither around the house catching them for himself.'

'That might not be a bad idea,' put in Bridie. 'This place is running alive with mice.'

'We caught three last night,' shuddered Isabel. 'Toby empties the traps for me.'

'Lucifer wouldn't touch them,' went on Toby knowledgeably. 'He only eats live stuff so he knows it's fresh.'

'I wouldn't fancy eating a live sausage,' commented Paula.

'An oyster, then,' said Toby. 'Want to watch me feed him?'

Isabel pulled a face and left them to it, while Paula stolidly observed an unfortunate rodent disappearing down Lucifer's elegant neck like an orange working its way down a Christmas stocking. Toby fazed her less than Izzie's own children, perhaps because he wasn't Patrick's, didn't make her wonder how things might have been if Patrick had got her pregnant instead of Izzie. She remained in awe of the girls, for all that they were only five and six. They were already more self-assured than she would ever be, confident without being cocky. They had that indefinable classiness you had to learn young.

'You can hold him, if you like,' said Toby. 'He's very friendly.'

Unwilling to funk a dare, Paula allowed Toby to drape Lucifer round her like a stole, swallowing her distaste by pretending that she was in a play. 'What lovely smooth skin he's got,' she said, smiling.

*

319

Stop Press had worked its way steadily up the ratings. Fan mail for Patrick arrived by the sackful, which only went to prove that women loved a bastard. His character was a copybook Irish hell-raiser and part-time sentimentalist, to whom his numerous girlfriends were for ever saying things like, 'That's enough of your blarney, Mick O'Mara,' a line which reoccurred with the frequency of a running gag.

Patrick had behaved himself immaculately until his first year's contract was safely signed and sealed, after which he started taking his usual liberties with the script and arguing that his character wouldn't *do* that. Isabel wearily agreed that the scriptwriters were a bunch of illiterates and the director a bloody fool. Now that Patrick was back in a paddling pool again, he was bound to make waves to create an illusion of challenge.

But so what? Patrick would have said. He was famous, wasn't he? More people saw him in one evening than visited the entire London theatre in a year. And as he kept reminding Isabel, the money was good. After sweating blood over *Henry V* et al he deserved a bit of jam. And thanks to him she could afford to indulge her artistic pretensions. Just as her father had indulged his, thought Isabel, subsidized by the fortune Fay had earned churning out entertainment for the masses. She hated to think she was like her father. She hated to think she was a snob. She hated to think that she had forced Patrick to compete with her, albeit on his own terms rather than hers. And so she held her peace.

On the morning of the next scheduled prison visit, Emily woke up with a temperature and a rash.

'Would you mind taking Toby to see his father for me?' Isabel asked Bridie, anxious to take Emily to the doctor herself. 'I'll ring Paula and ask if she'll lend us her chauffeur for the day.'

Having turned out to be one of those model inmates so beloved of penal reformers, Adrian had been moved to an open prison in Leicestershire, where he had formed a drama group, become an education orderly, made an ally of the chaplain, and started work on his autobiography. Now that he had served five years of his life sentence he had high hopes of getting an early parole.

'No problem,' said Paula, in response to Isabel's request. 'I may as well go along for the ride.'

'Want to come with me?' she teased Marian, as she prepared to leave, knowing full well that she had had a bellyful of prison visiting. Her husband, a small-time crook, had been in and out of nick all their married life.

'What, and miss the chance of a skive?' growled Marian. 'Glad to have you out from under my feet for a bit.'

She would probably seize the chance, thought Paula, to sneak off and visit her old man. In spite of Paula's lectures, Marian still cooked and cleaned and laundered for him, and gave him money. And no doubt slept with him as well. There was no accounting for taste. Paula had seen a dog-eared photograph of Ted, who had no obvious charms. He looked exactly what he was, a cut-price, third-rate, washed-up villain, the kind who wasn't bright enough not to get caught.

Sure enough, Marian began removing her ever-present curlers and shoving them into the pocket of her overall. What a giveaway, thought Paula.

'That's right,' she mocked. 'Tart yourself up. Want to borrow a feather boa and a pair of fishnet tights while you're at it?'

'That's enough of your lip,' countered Marian, with a glare that would have sent anyone else running for cover. But Paula knew she was all bark and no bite. 'You may be the guv'nor but I'm still old enough to be your mother.'

'And I've still been around a lot longer than you.' Green as grass, Marian was. 'Remind him what I said, won't you?'

Paula had told Marian to tell Ted that if he dared lay a finger on her ever again one of Vince's men would work him over. If Marian had passed the message on it was probably to protect him rather than herself.

Toby had been granted the day off school by a standing special arrangement; the other children would be told that he was sick. He looked it. Paula let him sit in the front while she chatted in the back with Bridie. Or rather tried to. Bridie seemed to have been infected by Toby's gloom. No doubt she was missing the car-salesman boyfriend.

The chauffeur, Bert, an avuncular retired bruiser, seemed to be making some headway with Toby, enumerating all the switches on the dashboard and letting him move the gearstick under his guiding hand. Weary of Bridie's non-response, Paula eventually dozed off – her pills left her permanently sluggish – waking to find

321

that they were parked in some anonymous Midlands high street, near one of those underground municipal lavatories. Toby and Bridie had evidently gone to have a pee; Bert was placidly reading the *Daily Mirror*.

Paula yawned.

'How much further?'

'About another half hour.'

The minutes ticked by. Perhaps Toby had the runs and who could blame him. This was hardly a fun day out. If she were in Isabel's shoes she would get the order varied and let the old bastard do his worst . . .

'Where's Toby?' said Bridie, getting back into the car. Paula caught the sour smell of vomit on her breath.

'Still in the Gents',' said Paula. 'Bert, you'd better go and see if he's okay. Are you all right?' she added, noting Bridie's pallor. 'You look awful.'

'I get car sick.'

'Have some chewing gum,' said Paula, offering her a stick. She masticated all the time, American-style, to try to keep herself from smoking. Bridie shook her head and opened the window. A moment later, Bert reappeared.

'He's not there,' he said. 'I'll check the newsagents, over the road. Most likely he went to buy sweets.'

Half an hour later, having checked every shop in the parade, they still hadn't found him and Paula was beginning to panic. What the hell was she going to tell Izzie?

'We'd better go to the police,' she said finally, having sent Bert to trawl the shops one more time. Bridie had shown no interest in joining in the search, sitting there with a stricken look on her face and being less than useless while Paula accosted passers-by, asking them if they had seen a thirteen-year-old-boy with dark hair, wearing brown cords and a green anorak. Nobody had.

'Perhaps someone's abducted him,' she added, if only to shake Bridie out of her torpor. 'All kinds of perverts hang round public lavs waiting for kids.'

'There's only one pervert waiting for Toby,' blurted out Bridie, suddenly erupting out of her silence. 'No wonder he's run away!' She clapped a hand to her mouth and burst into tears.

'What are you talking about?' demanded Paula.

'Nothing,' mumbled Bridie, through her sobs. 'It's a secret. Toby made me promise not to tell. He doesn't want Izzie to know.' Her naturally ruddy complexion darkened from salmon to lobster.

'Well, you're going to have to tell me. Because if you don't I'll make you tell the police instead.'

Bridie hesitated, torn between her childish promise to keep quiet and her obvious need to talk.

'Toby asked me one day if it was true that a priest couldn't tell what he heard in confession,' she began, unhappily. 'So I said, yes it was. Then he asked if he could come to confession with me. And I said he couldn't, because he's not a Catholic. And he asked if he became a Catholic, would the priest forgive him for all the bad things he'd done. And I said yes, but as he wasn't a Catholic, all he had to do was say a little prayer that he was sorry and that would be enough. But he said he'd tried that and it didn't work. And I said I didn't believe he could have done anything that bad, and if he liked he could confess it to me and I'd forgive him instead. I was only trying to make him feel better, because he seemed so upset . . .'

There was a pause while Paula dispensed tissues, already several jumps ahead of her.

'Every time Toby goes to visit his father,' resumed Bridie, 'he tells him that he'll soon be out of prison. He talks about them being together again, like they used to be. He tells Toby how much he loves him and makes Toby say he loves him back. And that's the awful thing! He does love him! In spite of . . . what he did to him.' She faltered. 'But he hates him too. He has terrible dreams about killing him.'

'So what exactly *did* his father do to him?' said Paula. And then, following another agonized, tongue-tied, tissue-twisting silence, 'Come on, out with it. Did he just fiddle with his willie, or did he poke him up the bum?'

Bridie gave an all-purpose nod, going several shades redder, glad not to have to find the words herself. 'He told Toby that it was their secret, that he mustn't breathe a word to anyone, but in the end Toby told his mother, and she said not to worry any more, he would never have to live with his father ever again.'

So that was the dirt Davina had had on Adrian, thought Paula, remembering what Isabel had told her. That was what she had used to bleed him white . . .

'Toby thinks that's why his father killed his mother,' continued Bridie. 'Because he told her, I mean. So he never dared tell anyone else, until me. He thought if the social workers found out they would put him in a home, like they did before. He thinks everything that happened was all his f-fault.'

No wonder he had been a disturbed child, thought Paula. She knew what it felt like to feel bad, really rotten, inside. Children were programmed to think themselves responsible for adult monstrosities – you could batter them, abandon them, abuse and degrade them and they would always think that somehow they deserved it. Parents, like gods, were deemed to move in a mysterious way, whatever thunderbolts they rained down upon you were punishment for some unwitting crime . . .

Having reported Toby missing at the local police station, Paula left Bert sitting in the car, still parked in the last place Toby would have seen it, and hired a local cab to drive her and Bridie home, in case he had found his own way back to London. Bridie was sick all over the back seat, much to the disgust of the driver.

On arrival in Hammersmith Paula drew Isabel to one side, watching alarm turn to shock turn to horror.

'You've got to see a solicitor,' said Paula, 'to make sure that if and when he gets parole, they don't give Toby back to him.'

Isabel nodded numbly and fell to beating herself up as usual. 'I was so anxious not to turn him against his father, I suppose I must have seemed part of the conspiracy. What if he doesn't come home? What if he's run away for good?'

'What, and leave his snake behind? Don't be daft. He'll turn up when he's hungry.'

He did. At half past five Bert telephoned to say that Toby had reappeared, claiming to have 'got lost'. (It later transpired that he had done a bold dash from the Gents' to the Ladies', where he had spent the day locked in a cubicle until the prison visiting hours were safely over.)

But long before that, to compound Isabel's troubles, another drama had unfurled. Ma had told Bridie what was wrong with Emily. Whereupon Bridie had broken down and confessed what had happened during her Christmas visit to Ireland, two months before.

*

324

Never having had German measles, and fearful for her unborn child, Bridie spent the night at Paula's house while Isabel broke the news to Maureen. Next morning there was a telephone call from Bridie's irate mother, who spent a good half hour squawking at her before passing the phone to the guilty youth, who proposed marriage without further ado. Bridie packed her bags and left the same day, in the hope of rescuing her reputation with a seven-month baby.

'Don't panic,' Paula advised a distraught Isabel. 'Marian and I will help Patrick's mother out with the kids, until you find someone else.'

A someone else would have to live in, given that Isabel was seldom home before midnight. With Ma getting ever more frail, Isabel was no longer happy to leave her in sole charge, even though – or rather because – the children were getting older, and therefore more adept at outwitting her. Without Bridie as an able adjutant, Ma was no match for their combined capacity for mischief.

She knew better, however, than to ask Patrick to spend his evenings babysitting, nor did he volunteer his services. He might adore the children, but they were his recreation, not his job. After a busy day at the TV studio he couldn't be expected to stay at home, forsaking his mates at the pub, while his wife played at being an actress.

Unfortunately there was no obvious successor to Bridie back in Ireland. Although Marian, like Richard's housekeeper, could help out in an emergency, neither presented a permanent solution, and Isabel remained deeply mistrustful of au pairs; Davina's had all been dippy, lazy girls who spilt nail polish on the carpet, ran up huge phone bills and left Toby locked in his room while they fornicated with their boyfriends.

'Then you'd better hire a nanny,' said Patrick, thus exonerating himself from further responsibility. 'Someone with a diploma, and references. To hell with the expense. I don't want you taking any chances with the kids.' The implication being that she was doing just that already.

A trained nanny, allowing for national insurance payments, cost nearly double Isabel's salary, making her work seem more of a self-indulgence than ever. Luckily the dubious glamour of working for Mick O'Mara attracted a good crop of applicants, and Isabel finally chose an impressively, not to say dauntingly, qualified girl with an immaculate record. Debbie was twenty-five, a big, loud, horsy type of girl who exuded well-bred confidence. The girls responded well to her brisk, jolly-hockey-sticks manner, Toby was deeply, if furtively, impressed by the size of her well-upholstered bosom, Patrick was charming to her face while taking off her plummy accent behind her back, and Ma thought her snooty.

'That's a sinful amount of money you're paying her, Izzie,' she fretted. 'It's not as if she does a stroke of housework. And the children are at school all day.'

'It's not her job to do housework, Ma. And the children get sick, and have half terms, and holidays. I need someone here all the time.'

'I'm here all the time, aren't I?'

'Ma, you're seventy-five. Running around after four children is exhausting enough when you're young.'

Isabel looked at her watch. She was already running late for her appointment with Oliver Briggs. The last thing she needed was Ma complaining yet again that 'you don't need me any more'.

'You don't need me any more,' lamented Ma, right on cue. 'Now that girl's here I'll just be in the way, so I will.'

'Of course you won't, Ma. You're family. You belong here . . .'

Lately she had had to cope with five children, not four. Or rather six, counting Patrick. Patrick, whose idea of offering her moral support was to remind her daily that her father was a disgusting old paedophile who ought to be hung, drawn and quartered, preferably in public. Richard had likewise been no help, withdrawing from the topic altogether; he had never been any use in a family crisis. Ma hadn't been told, at Patrick's insistence, not that Isabel would have wanted her to know. The only person she had had to lean on lately was Paula.

It was Paula who had had a long talk with Toby – he had refused to discuss it with Isabel – and prepared him for the ordeal of visiting the solicitors, assuring him that he would never have to live with his father again and of course he wouldn't kill Izzie when he got out of prison. Above all she had assured him, repeatedly if fruitlessly, that he wasn't to blame for his mother's death.

326

Grateful though she was for Paula's intervention, Isabel was mortified that Toby hadn't confided in her long ago, that he had carried all that fear and guilt around with him for so many years and even considered embracing a faith he didn't understand for the sake of sharing his burden with a priest.

Looking back, she should have made the connection between Davina withholding access to Toby and Adrian's veiled references to blackmail. Perhaps she hadn't wanted to, perhaps she had deliberately blocked her mind to the unthinkable. She could only assume that the marriage to Davina had wrought some monstrous change in her father's sexuality. The father she had known as a child would surely never have done anything like that.

It was almost a relief to talk it over with Oliver Briggs, an uninvolved, dispassionate outsider, while Toby sat outside in the waiting room guzzling Coca-Cola.

'So what do I do now?'

'You could apply for an order specifically denying your father unsupervised access to Toby on his release from prison. Naturally you'd have to give your reasons and Toby would have to give evidence. But your father may well contest the action, claiming that you coached Toby to tell lies. Child abusers are adept at denying their crimes, even to themselves. Toby may be thirteen now, but he's relating events that happened when he was very much younger. There's always a credibility problem with juvenile witnesses. Shall I have a word with him now, man to man? Best if you wait outside, I think.'

Toby was in there for what seemed like hours. Eventually Oliver called Isabel back in. Toby was sitting with his head hung so low his chin was on his chest.

'Toby's just asked me several very intelligent questions,' said Oliver. 'The central problem, as he sees it, is that he doesn't want to get his old man into any more trouble . . .'

'I'm not a nark,' interjected Toby sullenly. 'And I'm bigger now. I won't let him do it any more. Patrick's taught me how to box. I'll be all right.'

Oliver raised an eyebrow.

'We understand how you feel, Toby,' said Isabel. 'But –'

'No you don't. Nobody does. I wish I'd never told Bridie. And I'm bloody well not telling anyone else!'

He marched out of the room, slamming the door behind him.

'This isn't my field, as you know,' sighed Oliver. 'But now you know why there are so few convictions for this type of crime. Children are desperately loyal to their parents. I hate to say it, but there are social workers trained to deal with this kind of thing. I know you've had bad experiences with them in the past, but –'

'I'll talk to him.' But she knew, from the look on Toby's face when she rejoined him, that he didn't want to talk to her.

'Let's drop in on Paula, for tea,' she said casually. 'Then I can go straight on to the theatre and Bert can drive you home.'

Paula wouldn't mind her turning up uninvited. If anyone could bring Toby round, it was her.

'Hi gang,' Paula greeted them, opening the door, releasing the sickly-sweet smell of marijuana, a sure sign that Richard was present. 'Toby, Marian's making meringues in the kitchen,' she added, reading Isabel's face. 'You're just in time to lick the bowl.' She ushered Isabel into the living room and shut the door.

'How did it go?' said Richard casually. He seemed too stoned to care.

'Toby's playing up. He doesn't want to shop his father. Says he's big enough to fight him off. He's angry with all of us, and even angrier with himself.'

'How about if I have a word with Vince,' suggested Paula, 'and arrange to have Adrian bumped off? As my old man says, if it's justice you're after, don't waste your time looking to the law.'

'It's no joking matter,' said Isabel, shuddering. 'Actually I was hoping you'd have a word with Toby. He takes a lot more notice of you than he does of me.'

'Stands to reason,' drawled Richard, taking another puff. 'She's the glam auntie with the Roller. You're just the resident ratbag who makes him wash behind his ears. Want a hit? It's good stuff. Acapulco gold.'

'No thanks,' scowled Isabel. 'Some of us have got to work tonight.'

'Tea then,' said Paula, getting up to fetch it. 'But don't hold your breath that I can talk Toby into anything. He probably thinks I've conned him once too often already.'

'Can I ask you something?' demanded Richard suddenly, as soon as they were alone.

'Depends what it is,' said Isabel moodily, her mind far away.

Richard inspected his nails for a moment. Then he took another drag on his joint and said through a cloud of smoke, 'Did he ever try it on with you?'

'What? Who?'

'Adrian. Did he ever try to get inside your knickers?'

'No!'

'Thank God for that,' said Richard. 'I used to worry myself sick about you, on the quiet. Not that I had the guts to do anything about it. Looks like I needn't have lost any sleep. He obviously prefers little boys.'

'You don't mean . . . oh no. Oh Richard . . .'

Suddenly everything made sense, from Richard's moody, disruptive behaviour as a boy to his cryptic remarks about Toby being better off with Davina. And like Toby, he hadn't told her, he'd kept it all to himself, out of shame . . . Isabel slumped to the floor, put her head in his lap, and sobbed.

'You can lay off Toby,' said Richard gently, stroking her hair. 'I'll fix the old sod for good and all. I'll go and see him in prison. I'll tell him that if he dares give you any trouble, I'll be the one in the witness box, not Toby. I'll threaten to tell the whole world his grubby little secret, same as Davina did, poor bitch. Will that do?'

Isabel nodded through her tears.

'Thank you,' she said.

12

Spring–Winter 1969

Misery acquaints a man with strange bedfellows.

William Shakespeare – The Tempest

'Mrs Delaney? I'm sorry to bother you, but . . .'

Debbie had a knack for posing a problem just as Isabel was about to leave for the theatre. Not that she could possibly have understood how unsettling it was. Being a non-theatrical she thought the job started when the curtain went up, knew nothing of the mental gearing-up that started several hours beforehand.

'It's Mrs Delaney senior. She still isn't back from the chiropodist.'

'Weren't you taking her there and bringing her back?'

Isabel usually did it herself but today she had stayed in bed, dosed up with linctus and antibiotics, coddling the sore throat which had dogged her all week, threatening the precious vocal cords on which her current role – Joan of Arc in Jean Anouilh's *The Lark* – made particularly heavy demands, given that she was on stage for most of the play, delivering a performance which had been acclaimed as 'luminous', 'heart-stopping' and 'spellbinding', plaudits which increased the pressure she put upon herself to excel each night. She had been so thoroughly overpraised that she was surely riding for a fall.

'I did drive her there,' said Debbie. 'But she insisted that she didn't want me to wait for her and that she'd get the bus home. That was at two o'clock and now it's four thirty. I didn't like to disturb you, knowing you weren't feeling well. I thought perhaps she'd just gone shopping.'

It was typical of Ma to give Debbie the runaround. Still sulking at having been usurped by an outsider, she was hell bent, in Isabel's view, on forcing her resignation.

330

'I rang the chiropodist,' continued Debbie efficiently. 'And they say she left on time, at half past two.'

'Well, I can't go out looking for her now,' said Isabel, shutting her mind to images of Ma collapsing in the street or lying crushed under the wheels of a bus. If she'd had an accident, they would surely have heard by now.

This wasn't the first time she'd gone walkabout in a fit of pique, thought Isabel. She might have known that delegating the chiropodist run to Debbie would spark off another Toby-style tantrum, not that Toby indulged in tantrums any more, thank God, secure in the knowledge that now he had been legally adopted (with Adrian's consent, thanks to Richard), no one could put him in a home or return him to his father ever again. Ma had long since become the problem child of the family.

'You'd better get a message to my husband at the TV studio,' continued Isabel, willing herself to be strong, 'and ask if he'd come straight home from work and find her. I'll leave the car for him and take the tube to the theatre.'

Patrick's preferred mode of transport was a vintage Harley-Davidson, hardly a suitable vehicle for locating and bringing home his errant mother. Let Patrick do the rounds of the local shops and cafés, the public library and cinema and park benches. If Ma got hold of the idea that Isabel would miss a performance in response to a disappearing act, where would it ever end? And besides, it would do Patrick good to desert his mates in the pub for an evening and spend some time with the children. His increasing absenteeism was, she knew, an unspoken reproach at her not being at home, waiting for him, like a good wife should.

Isabel tried as always to leave her domestic problems behind her. But as usual they followed her onto the stage, sabotaging her precious concentration. Pathetic. A real pro wouldn't let anything get in the way of her performance. Whereas she, Isabel, allowed the slightest upset to distract her. Or rather one of the many and increasingly frequent slight upsets that threatened the fragile order of her life, that reminded her daily that her freedom was built on sand.

Mercifully her voice held out till the final curtain, denying her ever-hopeful understudy the chance to outshine her. She was just clattering down the narrow metal steps from the dressing rooms when she bumped into Neville on his way up.

'Hello, Izzie. I was just coming to see you. Obviously it's a bad time.'

'I'm sorry,' said Isabel, mortified that he had seen her on an off-night. 'But I'm in a bit of a hurry to get home.'

'Can I give you a lift? It's pouring with rain out there.'

'Well . . . thanks. I usually bring the car, but . . .'

She found herself blurting out the whole story on the drive home.

'I know I must seem a monster,' she muttered. 'She might really be ill, or hurt. But in the last few months she's cried wolf so often, just to get attention –'

'You did the sensible thing, telling Patrick. He wasn't working this evening. You were. And besides, you'll get home to find you've been worrying over nothing as usual.'

His voice was wonderfully calm and soothing. She could smell his aftershave and those French cigarettes he smoked. Suddenly she found herself thinking, treacherously: if only I'd married Neville instead of Patrick . . .

'Here will do fine, thanks,' she said, a few yards before they got to the house. Things would be tricky enough when she got in without Patrick knowing that Neville had driven her home.

'Listen, why don't we have dinner, after the show one night?' said Neville. 'It's a long time since we talked. And you seem like you need to talk to someone. No strings. I promise. I'm just worried about you, that's all.'

'Was my performance that bad?'

'You're incapable of giving a bad performance,' he said tactfully. 'How about tomorrow?'

'Tomorrow? Er . . . yes, why not.' At least with Neville she could talk about her work to her heart's content. And besides, why shouldn't she have a social life of her own, as Patrick did?

'See you tomorrow night, then.'

The house was in darkness. Having checked on the children, and established from the snores emanating from Ma's bedroom that she was safely home, thank God, Isabel found Patrick sitting up in bed, learning his lines for next day. He barely looked up to acknowledge her arrival.

'Where did you find her?' said Isabel.

'In church,' growled Patrick, not taking his eyes from the page. 'If you'd stopped to think you might have remembered that it's Da's birthday. He would have been eighty years old today.'

'Oh,' said Isabel, chastened.

'When you think of all she's done for us . . . can't you be a bit kinder to her?'

'I'm always kind to her! You don't realize how awkward she can be. Ever since Debbie came . . .'

'If Debbie's the problem, get rid of her.'

Which was exactly what Ma wanted, of course. And Patrick too, no doubt, if for different reasons . . .

But Isabel forbore to say so, knowing that Patrick would simply accuse her of paranoia. Anything was better than being forced into a row. Especially one she was bound to lose. And one which Patrick would be quick to make up the easy way, in bed. Easy for him, that is. Isabel found making love after an unresolved quarrel akin to going swimming on a full stomach. Half way through it she would get emotional cramps, and feel herself drowning in the murky depths of her resentment.

'Debbie isn't to blame,' she said, keeping her voice level. 'The children like her, and she's very patient with Ma. And besides . . . where are you going?'

'To sleep on the couch,' growled Patrick, helping himself to the quilt. 'I'd hate to disturb your beauty sleep. I gather you spent most of the day in bed.'

'I wasn't well!'

'You were well enough to get yourself to the theatre, even though Ma could have had an accident. You're just like your father at heart. If the whole bloody lot of us went down in a plane you wouldn't want to be told until after curtain. Isabel Delaney my arse. You're a Mallory through and through. You always will be.'

And with that he strode out of the room, leaving Isabel to weep silently, furiously into her pillow while she fought the compulsion to run after him and admit that yes, she was a terrible wife, a terrible mother, interested in no one but herself . . .

She was just on the point of giving in, unable to bear it any longer, when she felt something sharp and hard press into her

333

back. She sat up and switched on the bedside lamp, inspecting the gold chain with its small pearl pendant; the clasp had broken. It certainly hadn't been there when she had made the bed, that afternoon. It didn't even belong to her. And it certainly didn't belong in the bed she shared with Patrick.

It belonged to Debbie.

All her married life she had fought against the cancer of suspicion and jealousy, shut her mind to the numerous opportunities Patrick had to be unfaithful, even told herself that it didn't matter if he had the odd fling with an actress, an occupational hazard of long hours and claustrophobic working conditions . . . *as long as she didn't know.* But now she did know, now the evidence was in her hands, less than twenty-four hours after she and Patrick had last made love in this very bed . . .

She resisted the urge to have it out with him there and then. Any confession she wrung from him would be underpinned with subtle accusations. When a husband strayed it was always the wife's fault. And once she admitted that she knew, pride would demand that she sack Debbie. And then what? How many prospective nannies would be prepared to stay in six evenings a week, to put up with Ma's eternal carping, to share a roof with roving reptiles, rodents and snakes?

Only ones who fancied Patrick, of course. It seemed obvious now why Debbie had been such a willing worker. A situation, thought Isabel grimly, that she might as well continue to exploit. Why should she risk her career at the altar of her outrage? Why should her children's routine be disrupted? Why should she suffer any more than she was suffering already?

By morning she had made a thorough job of dressing up cowardice as self-interest. Patrick came skulking into the room in search of his clothes as she was getting dressed.

'I'm sorry,' he said.

'It's all right.'

'I know Ma can be a pain, but when you think what we've had to put up with from *your* family . . .'

He crossed over to where she stood and put his arms around her.

'We don't see enough of each other,' he murmured into her hair. 'I can feel you slipping away from me. I get scared sometimes. Scared of losing you.' He kissed her neck, his stubble scratching her skin. 'Let's go back to bed,' he said. 'It's still early.'

'Not now,' said Isabel, breaking away. 'My throat's still sore. And I've got a splitting headache.'

'You've had headaches ever since you started taking the Pill.' He had found out in the end, come across the packet in a drawer while searching for something. 'I told you before, I don't like you taking it. I'm afraid it'll give you cancer.'

You don't like me taking it because you can't get me pregnant any more, thought Isabel. Come to think of it, neither could anyone else . . .

'I'm having supper with Richard and Kevin, after the show tonight,' she said. 'You're invited as well,' she added, knowing that he wouldn't want to come.

'You ought to put them off if you're not well.'

'I've put them off once already,' said Isabel, taking a chilly satisfaction in deceiving him, as he had deceived her. 'You know how sensitive Richard is about people cold-shouldering Kevin.'

'I'd rather cold-shoulder him than risk giving him an earful.' Patrick, like Paula, thought Kevin a shameless sponger, one who had turned Richard on to drugs and away from his work. These days Richard took less and less interest in the management of Renegade, on the grounds that he wanted to devote more time to his writing, despite which he hadn't completed another play since *Cindy*. 'Make some excuse for me, will you? And don't stay too long,' he added, all husbandly solicitude. 'You're already run down as it is.'

There would still be plenty of time, thought Isabel sourly, for him to fit in another bunk-up with Debbie after the children were safely tucked up in bed. Perhaps he would desert his mates early for once, to make the most of the opportunity. No doubt he had told the poor bitch that his wife didn't understand him . . .

She carried her anger around with her all day, carried it onto the stage with her that night. Anger that was directed at herself, as well as him. What kind of wife was she to care more about keeping her job than keeping her husband? What kind of mother would rather he slept with her children's nanny than risk not having a

335

nanny at all? Why did her work matter so much? It wasn't essential, or useful, or even profitable. On the contrary, it was a luxury, another household expense, a drain on the family budget. As a wife and mother, at least she had earned her keep; as an actress she was a financial liability, a bored housewife in the grip of a self-indulgent hobby, one which she put before her family's welfare, one which was driving her husband away . . .

Damn. She was doing it again. As always, she was blaming herself, instead of him. Why should she feel guilty when he so obviously didn't? She was the one who had been betrayed, and deceived, and made a fool of. She was the one who had been wronged. He was the one who deserved to be punished . . .

'You don't look well,' commented Neville when he picked her up. 'Would you rather we left it till another night?'

'No, really. I'm fine.' The antibiotics seemed to be working, thank God; pity there wasn't an equivalent remedy for an infected mind.

'What do you fancy to eat?' The thought of a meal made her gag. She wouldn't be able to swallow a single mouthful.

'I'm afraid I'm not very hungry.'

'Shall we make do with a snack at my place, then?' His tone was devoid of innuendo.

'If you like.' To have refused would have sounded coy.

They drove separately to his flat in Battersea, not far from the Renegade Theatre, Isabel thinking all the while of Patrick in bed with Debbie. Jealousy coursed through every vein in her body, multiplying itself like some deadly parasite, making her sweat and shiver at once. Were they doing it even at this moment? How were they doing it? Did she have her legs wrapped around his neck or had he taken her from behind, or were they having a stand-up quickie, fully clothed, or did she have his prick in her mouth, or was she sitting on his face? 'I don't trust that girl,' Ma had said, and yet she, Isabel, had trusted her, because it suited her to do so . . .

'Sorry about the mess,' said Neville as he let her in. The place was indeed untidy, proving that he had not planned to bring her here. He moved a heap of playscripts off a chair so that she could sit down. 'What can I offer you? Soup? A sandwich? Or there's a Chinese takeaway on the corner . . .'

'Just coffee for me, thanks. Don't let me stop you.'

'Izzie, what's wrong?'

'Were you out there tonight as well?'

'Yes.'

'Did it show?'

'Only to me. Is it something to do with Patrick?'

Isabel didn't answer.

'I thought so. It must be hard for an actor in his position, having such a talented wife.'

'A talented actress, perhaps,' said Isabel. 'But I'm hardly a talented wife.'

'I don't suppose Patrick's a particularly talented husband,' said Neville. 'And I speak as a dismally untalented husband myself. You were right, you know, to turn me down.'

'We must have hurt Helen terribly,' muttered Isabel. She hadn't realized how much, until now. Hadn't realized how much Daddy had hurt Mummy. How much Jess had hurt Paula. Like any pain, it was impossible to imagine adequately, until you'd felt it for yourself.

'That was a long time ago. And it all turned out for the best in the end. She's much happier now, and so am I. It was a bad marriage, long before you came along. Trying to keep it going for the sake of the kids just prolonged the agony.'

Perhaps she ought to make a clean break, as Helen had done. But then Helen hadn't had a career to worry about, and even if she had done, she had only two children to consider, not four. Whether she left Patrick, or threw him out, she couldn't very well expect him to continue to subsidize her desire to work. She was trapped by her own cold-blooded ambition . . .

'You don't have to talk to me, if you'd rather not,' said Neville. 'But you've got to talk to someone. Paula, Richard . . .'

She would rather tell Neville than go crying to Paula, Paula whose problems made her own seem trivial. And Richard would only say I told you so.

'I thought I'd be so much happier once I started working again,' she began. 'And I was, at first, but now I feel more miserable than ever . . .'

Once she started talking she couldn't stop. She ended up telling him everything, her fear and frustration and fury flooding out of her like lava. She must sound like a madwoman. She felt like one.

'You poor darling,' he said finally, immobilizing one of her trembling hands in his. He still had that little callus on his middle finger, from gripping his pen too hard. It felt familiar, reassuring, like an old toy. 'Of course it's not your fault.' He pulled her close and let her sob into his chest. 'If Patrick feels threatened by your success, that's his problem, not yours. And if he's having an affair, of course that doesn't mean you're not a good wife.'

Of course, of course, of course. Two little words that dispensed with the need for proof, that ignored all the evidence to the contrary. A good wife. She had spent her whole marriage trying to be a good wife. In eight years she had never so much as looked at another man. And what good had being good done her? Suddenly she needed very badly to be bad . . .

'Kiss me,' she said.

'No, Izzie,' he said gently. 'You don't mean that. I don't want to take advantage of . . .'

Determined now, she wound her arms around his neck and pressed her mouth against his. The thirst for revenge was the ultimate aphrodisiac, more potent by far than lust. Lust didn't come into it. She knew she wasn't being fair to Neville. She knew that she would regret this tomorrow. But it was still tonight. Tonight was unstoppable . . .

'I've never stopped loving you,' he murmured, poor darling, unable to resist her. 'Not for a single minute . . .'

Just as she had never stopped loving Patrick, damn him to hell. And the worst of it was, she still did.

It was ironic that Paula should have learned to be happy just when it could stop at any time. Happy in a quiet, understated way, a way which had nothing to do with having everything that money could buy, even though she bought plenty, reinforcing the public image of herself as a fortune-hunting little tart.

Mostly she bought things for other people – Vince, Marian, Izzie, the kids. It was a lot more fun than spending it on herself. Her softest spot was for Toby, who came every weekend on his bike to see his cats. Isabel, racked by constant sneezing, had finally had to banish his growing collection of strays, who now inhabited a specially built cattery at the bottom of Paula's garden.

At the last count there had been twenty-four vagrants housed in their luxurious dosshouse. Paula spent almost as much on vet's fees as Vince spent on doctors.

It was very hot that June. Paula felt more than usually breathless and bloated. But apart from that, life was good, for as long as life lasted. You never appreciated anything until you stood to lose it.

Perhaps that was why her marriage seemed to be working, because she knew she was living on borrowed time. Perhaps that was why she was too damn scared to risk the operation that might make her well again, despite the recent advances in heart surgery. Not just out of fear that she might die under the knife, but fear that she would survive, be faced with the burden of a future, a future she was bound to fuck up, the way she had fucked up her past. At the moment she was making a decent job of her present, and that was all she could cope with right now. She was content to take one precious day at a time.

Unlike Izzie. Just lately she had been living on her nerves more than ever, which Paula put down to the lease on the Hammersmith house running out and the difficulty of finding an alternative large enough to accommodate eight people.

'Still no luck?' Paula asked her when they met for lunch one day. Isabel had hardly eaten a thing.

'It's not the move. That's the least of my worries at the moment.' She added a spoonful of sugar to her coffee. Usually she drank it without. 'I've been invited to join the National at the Old Vic.'

Paula stifled the automatic congratulations, sensing that there was a problem, knowing very well what the problem must be.

'So why aren't you grinning all over your face? Is laughing boy playing up?'

'I haven't told him.'

'I'll do it for you if you like. Tell him he can't have it both ways. If you were the TV soap star and he was the serious actor, he'd have a complex about you earning more than him.'

'There's no point in telling him anything. Because I'm not going to do it. Or rather, I can't do it.'

'Why not? Because you can't face a routine little put-down about Larry owing his old mate Adrian a favour?'

Isabel laughed. It wasn't a happy sound.

'I should have such problems. You won't believe this. I didn't, at first. I'm pregnant. Again.'

'How the bloody hell did you manage that? I thought you were on the Pill?'

'I'm a walking accident black spot, remember? Apparently antibiotics can stop it working. Not that anyone bothered to warn me beforehand.'

'I suppose you're going to go ahead and have it?' Silly question, in Izzie's case, even though abortion had been legal for nearly two years now, all you had to do was to simulate incipient nervous breakdown, easy enough for an actress. You could even get one on the NHS, in theory, if you didn't mind the nine-month waiting list.

'I'd get rid of it like a shot,' blurted out Isabel, 'and go to Hell for it, if only . . . if only I knew for sure that it wasn't Patrick's baby.'

It took a minute for her words to make sense.

'Whose else could it be?' demanded Paula incredulously.

'Don't ask. I shouldn't have told you at all.'

'Spoilsport. And here's me dying to spread it around to anyone who'll listen.'

'You know that's not the reason.'

'You always were a secretive little cow. I remember that time you were humping Neville, on the quiet . . .' Isabel went very red. 'Don't tell me. Not the one-armed bandit again. He never gives up, does he?'

'It was my doing, not his,' muttered Isabel. 'I wanted to get my own back on Patrick. Not that Patrick knows anything about it, which made it all pretty pointless, I suppose.'

'To get your own back?'

'For Debbie. He's been having an affair with Debbie. He still is, for all I know.'

'The nanny?' Surely he wasn't that desperate? Debbie was *fat*, dammit.

'I don't suppose she was the first, either. So I thought to myself, now it's my turn.'

Good for you, thought Paula. Or it would have been good for her, if she hadn't got caught.

340

'And meanwhile the bitch is still working for you?'

'Why not? Why cut off my nose to spite my face? The children are used to her, I couldn't work if it wasn't for her. Not that I'll be able to now, in any case. Poetic justice, isn't it?'

'Have you told Neville?'

'No. I haven't seen him since . . . that night. It only happened the once. It should never have happened at all. I don't know which of us felt worse afterwards, him or me. Trust me to ruin a perfectly good friendship. If he ever asks about the baby, I'll tell him I was already pregnant. Which might just be true. Not that I deserve it to be.'

Paula wondered what would happen to Isabel's articulacy if certain words and phrases were denied her. Like Never Forgive Myself and My Own Stupid Fault, and Sorry, the endless recurring litany of guilt and responsibility. No wonder she had become a Catholic. And now she would cherish and nurture this latest piece of bad luck, bad luck she would mistake for divine retribution.

'Paula . . . I'm right not to tell Patrick, aren't I?'

'You'd be off your rocker if you did.'

'I knew you'd say that. That's why I told you. If I'd told you about Debbie that night, instead of Neville, I might not be in this mess. But if the baby isn't Patrick's . . . oh, God, Paula, I think I'd kill myself.'

'Don't talk daft. One, you'll have no way of knowing whose it is, and neither will he. And two, you've got four other kids to think about.'

'Sometimes I think they'd be better off without me. I've trained them not to need me, after all. And Patrick would soon find some other woman to take them on.'

Not for the first time, Paula felt afraid for Isabel, afraid of all the violent emotion she buried beneath the surface calm, emotion that only found release through her work. Without that release it would burrow ever deeper inside her, destroying her from within . . .

'Go ahead and kill yourself, then,' shrugged Paula. 'But not until after I've popped my clogs, okay? I'm first in the queue and I'm buggered if I'm going to let you steal my thunder.'

'If that was supposed to make me feel ashamed of myself,' sniffed Isabel, 'it bloody well worked.'

Paula hoped that it would keep on working.

Patrick, according to Isabel, was 'pleased about the baby', not that that made her feel any better, of course. Paula didn't get a chance to speak to him alone until one Saturday morning in August, when Vince was away on business. It was Toby's regular time for calling to see his cats, and this time he arrived on the back of Patrick's motorbike.

'How's it going?' asked Patrick, over a can of lager, while Toby ministered to his charges.

'Never better.' Patrick had no reason to believe otherwise. Like most people, he thought she was a lazy cow who was living the life of Riley at her husband's expense. 'How's Mick O'Mara?'

'Just about paying the bills,' said Patrick shortly.

'I hear you got rid of the nanny.' She watched his face for a tell-tale flicker. But Patrick didn't oblige her.

'Yes. She upset my mother once too often so Izzie gave her her cards. Now she's packed up work she reckons we can do without one for a bit.'

'I'm glad you're going to be near me. Much easier for Toby and the cats.' The family had just decamped to a rambling Victorian house in Maida Vale. The rent was astronomic and a huge deposit had been levied against fixtures and fittings, which had made further inroads on the nest egg left from the sale of the Essex house. But Isabel had been too relieved to find a safe haven to quibble about the cost.

'We're being ripped off, of course,' said Patrick glumly. 'That's the trouble with being on telly. Everyone thinks you must be rolling in it, including the Inland Revenue. I've just had to hire a shark of an accountant to appeal against my tax demand, it's even more ridiculous than the last one. Catch me voting Labour again.'

It was unlike Patrick to talk about money, let alone appear to worry about it.

'I went along for an interview at Pinewood the other week,' he went on. 'A remake of *Lady Chatterley's Lover*. I did a good audition. They admitted it. But they said my face was too well known. That I was too strongly defined in the public mind as Mick O'Bloody Mara.'

342

Paula sighed in commiseration. But what had he expected?

'Like I told them,' he went on, 'if I grew a beard, no one would recognize me. I ought to go to America, like you did. No one's heard of Mick O'Mara there.'

'No one's heard of Patrick Delaney either,' pointed out Paula. 'You wouldn't like Hollywood. You don't just have to act in front of the camera, you realize. You have to act all the time. The entire place is one big movie set. You wouldn't be able to keep it up. You're too shy.'

Surprisingly, he didn't deny it. Perhaps he knew himself better than she gave him credit for. Patrick had never fitted in backstage. He was even less likely to fit in in the infinitely falser, even more artificial world of Tinseltown. He was too proud to ingratiate himself with the right people, too thin-skinned to court and survive the inevitable rejection. He thought that being a good actor ought to be enough, and so it ought, but it wasn't and it never would be.

'It doesn't matter what I'm like inside,' he said. 'All that matters is what people think you are. I earn my living pretending to be something I'm not. What makes you so sure I'd fail?' It wasn't so much a challenge as a plea for reassurance.

'I didn't say that. But it's not as easy as you think. There's no point waiting for Hollywood to come to you, you'd have to go to Hollywood. You'd have to take a gamble, quit *Stop Press*, fly to LA on a tourist visa, shell out for an apartment, get yourself a set of wheels, find an American agent, bombard casting directors with mug shots and résumés, and be prepared to sit it out for months, if necessary, until something comes up. And all that's before you try and con your way into one of the unions or start hassling over a work permit. Which you won't get unless the studio wants you enough to pull strings with the immigration people. I know it looked as if I got work without even trying, because of *Snowdrops*. But I was always hustling, making contacts, selling myself.'

'And it paid off. Five good years out there, like you had, and I could afford to pack it in.'

'Not unless you found yourself a rich husband,' said Paula, keeping up the charade. 'And anyway, actors never pack it in. They just stop getting work.'

'I hate acting. I hate it more and more.'

343

'You mean you hate Mick O'Mara.'

'I always did. But we needed the money. We still do. I only ever meant to do it for a year or two. I was all set to pull out, you know, when Izzie got pregnant again.'

So the baby had upset his plans as well as Isabel's, curtailed his freedom too. Paula hadn't stopped to consider his point of view, other than to credit him with smug satisfaction at having got his wife back where he wanted her. But he seemed neither smug nor satisfied. He seemed tired, depressed, anxious.

Part of him, no doubt, wanted to shed his responsibilities, escape the bonds of duty and domesticity. But the other part of him needed the security of a wife and family. There had always been that duality about him, that mixture of conformity and rebelliousness. It mirrored the perverse combination of self-control and spontaneity, detachment and passion, that made an actor.

Marian was becoming quite a theatre buff, under Paula's guidance. Every Wednesday or Thursday they went to a matinée together – Paula couldn't keep awake long enough these days to sit through an evening performance – with Paula supervising her dramatic education in much the same way Bea had supervised hers – delivering throwaway summaries of classical plots, dishing the available dirt on the performers, taking her backstage, watching her growing interest with all the satisfaction of a missionary converting a lifelong heathen.

She had hoped to include Izzie in her outings, now that she had stopped work, but she rarely had the time to join them, having thrown herself back into full-time domesticity with a will. When she wasn't decorating, running up curtains, baking her own wholemeal bread or cultivating her garden, she was ferrying the girls from school to piano and ballet classes, or Toby to football practice, or Ma to the Legion of Mary. She claimed always to be 'up to her eyes', her way of denying that she was bored, of not giving herself time to be.

'I can't come with you today,' Marian announced, following a phone call from her husband, one Wednesday afternoon in November.

'Oh, for God's sake,' said Paula. 'If he's run out of money, I'll get Bert to deliver a tenner, after he's dropped us off. You can't keep running every time he whistles.'

'It isn't money,' said Marian stubbornly. 'I told him we had tickets for *Hadrian the Seventh*, he knew I'd been looking forward to it. He said it was urgent.'

'Well, I'm going anyway,' said Paula, annoyed, even though, truth to tell, she felt pretty ropy and wouldn't have minded staying at home. She was damned if she was giving in to her illness the way Marian gave in to her husband.

'She'll end up going back to him,' Vince had predicted wearily. 'She reminds me of my mother. So don't get too involved. You're soft on lame ducks, that's your trouble.'

She had badly wanted to rescue Marian, the way Bea had rescued her. To restore the self-esteem her husband had beaten out of her, to develop her abilities, to give her some ambition. But Marian was thirty years further down the road than she had been and that much harder to save.

'I'm too old to train for a job,' Marian had shrugged, in response to Paula's exhortations. 'All I know about is cooking, cleaning and kids.'

'Then do a catering course. Or get a diploma as a nursery nurse. I'll pay the fees, give you time off to study.' Offers which had fallen on deaf ears.

'Want me to wait for you?' said Bert dutifully, dropping Paula off outside the Haymarket.

'No need.' He had got used to having her matinées as time off. 'Be outside from about five, you can push off till then.'

She began to feel very odd during the first act, faint and breathless. As the curtain came down for the interval, she delved in her bag for her pills, intending to swallow one dry rather than fight her way to the bar for a soft drink.

'Attention please.' Paula unscrewed the cap as the Tannoy crackled into life. 'Would Mrs Vincent Parry go to the box office please. We have an urgent message for Mrs Vincent Parry.'

Had Izzie's baby started early? thought Paula, momentarily forgetting the heavy feeling in her head, the hollow feeling in her chest. She leapt to her feet and began elbowing her way towards the exit. Something must be wrong. Otherwise the news could surely have waited until she got home . . .

'Mrs Parry?' A middle-aged man approached her as she entered the foyer. Evidently he recognized her; he looked vaguely familiar but she couldn't quite place him.

'Yes. What's wrong?'

'It's about your husband. He was taken ill at the office, this afternoon, and rushed to hospital. There's a car waiting outside, to take you there.'

'Ill? What's wrong with him?' Vince couldn't be ill. She was the one who was ill, not him.

'I'm sorry, luv, that's all I know. I was just told to fetch you, like.'

Perhaps it was just appendicitis, she thought, as she followed him out into the street. It couldn't be anything serious. Vince was immortal . . .

The man shepherded her into a car, whose driver was waiting right outside the theatre, and got into the back beside her. Only then did she notice that the car was old, its upholstery torn and the windscreen dirty. And Vince would never let one of his men sit in the back, or call his wife luv, come to that . . .

'What's going on?' she managed to say, just as he produced a sweet-smelling rag and pressed it over her mouth. She tried to scream, but nothing happened. And then she knew, as her strength ebbed away from her, what it would feel like to die.

Once the news of Isabel's pregnancy reached Neville, via an unsuspecting Richard, he had phoned her straight away to ask if the baby was his, an event which she had foreseen and prepared for. Neville wasn't the type to duck his responsibilities.

Once again she had used him, once again she had got more than she bargained for. But at least this time she could spare him the consequences. He had been only too ready, poor man, to believe her well-rehearsed assurances; this time he was the one who didn't want to come between man and wife. Isabel wished she could convince herself as easily. Oh for the absolution of giving birth to a miniature replica of Patrick! If her prayers were granted she would never complain about anything ever again . . .

The telephone rang just as she was slapping yellow paint on the nursery wall. The only way to chase away the bogeys was to keep herself busy from morning to night.

'I'll get it,' she shouted to Ma, putting down her paintbrush. Debbie's sacking, and the prospect of a new grandchild, had rejuvenated her. These days she was in a constant good humour.

'Hello?' she said, picking up the extension in the bedroom.

'Izzie, it's me, Paula.'

'Where are you phoning from? I rang you earlier today and Vince said you'd gone away for a few days.' She had been surprised to find him at home on a weekday morning. He hadn't said where Paula had gone, just that she was 'visiting friends'.

'I want you to give a message to Vince.' Her voice was flat, robotic.

'A message? Why don't you call him yourself? Have you two had a tiff, or what?'

'Listen.'

She began speaking in that odd, toneless voice again, and the words she used were obviously not her own. Isabel listened with mounting horror, waiting for her to break into a dirty laugh and crow, 'Fooled you!'

'Paula, tell me this is a joke.'

'I'm sorry, Izzie.' Suddenly she sounded like the real Paula again, as if she had come out of a trance. 'I didn't want you involved. They made me do it.' She began speaking very fast. 'Tell him not to pay it. Tell him I'm not worth it. Tell him I –'

A man's voice came on the line, rough and rasping.

'You heard,' it said. 'You can tell Parry she's alive. He does what he's told and nothing will happen to her. He goes to the filth and she's dead. Don't speak to anyone but Parry. In person. Not if you want to see your friend again. You'll get another call same time tomorrow. Be there.'

The line went dead.

'Paula wants to borrow a book,' Isabel told Ma, flinging a coat over her paint-spattered smock. 'I'll drop it over to her now.'

Grabbing the first book that came to hand Isabel leapt into the car and drove to St John's Wood, her mind still too numb to grasp the enormity of what she had been told. Marian answered the door. She looked frightened.

'Is Vince in?' said Isabel. 'I've got a message for him. From Paula.'

'They've rung you too? Did you speak to her? Is she all right. . . ?'

Vince appeared at that moment and dismissed Marian curtly, ushering Isabel into the living room. He hadn't shaved and there were dark circles under his eyes. He listened while she relayed the message, stressing the warning about not going to the police.

'The police?' he barked. 'Do me a favour.'

'Can you raise that much money?'

'Not without hocking pretty well everything. I reckon they just thought of a number and doubled it. Not that I'm proposing to haggle.' He punched his palm with his fist. 'I should have protected her better. I thought I was safe from this kind of thing. No villain with a brain in his head would mess with me. But this one obviously doesn't have a brain. Or won't have, once I've got her back.'

'You know who it is?'

'It didn't take much working out. Every week Marian goes to a matinée, with Paula. This week, would you believe, her husband asks to see her urgently, and then stands her up. Meanwhile Paula disappears.'

'But that doesn't prove . . .'

'Marian took the first phone call, yesterday evening, before I got home. If it wasn't him on the line, it was one of his mates, someone whose voice she recognized. She won't admit it, of course, because she's shit scared of what I'll do to him, once this is over. Rightly so.'

Isabel could almost hear the bomb ticking away inside him. He would keep his icy calm till Paula was safely home, having followed the kidnappers' orders to the letter, and then he would take a dreadful revenge. Vince wouldn't delegate the power to punish to the police, or the courts, any more than he had done with the rapist.

'I'm sorry you were dragged into this,' he said. 'He must have seen it as a way of upping the pressure. If I turned out to love my money more than my wife, I'd have you as my guilty conscience. The cold, calculating husband, the loyal, soft-hearted best friend. Seems like Marian's been giving him plenty of pillow talk.'

'Does he know that Paula's ill?'

'No, she never told Marian. If I thought he had a shred of common decency I'd tell you to mention it, but chances are he'd just use it as more ammunition. I don't want him threatening to take her pills off her, to tighten the screws.'

'She's got them with her?'

'She never goes anywhere without them. They're all that's been keeping her alive.' He got up. 'Excuse me, Isabel. I've got a lot of calls to make.'

'I'll come again tomorrow,' said Isabel, 'as soon as I hear from them again.'

'Are you sure you're up to it?'

'I feel fine.' This child seemed as firmly lodged as a limpet.

'I appreciate this. Thank you.' He saw her out with his usual courtesy, rigidly controlled as always. She wished for his sake that he could shout, weep, smash something, release some of that fearful, murderous rage. She was almost as afraid for him as she was for Paula.

Paula had no idea where she was, or how long she had been there. She had woken in the dark, her eyes blindfolded and her hands tied together behind her back, lying on an evil-smelling mattress, on a bare wooden floor. Her brain wasn't working; she felt drugged. Someone had put a glass of water to her lips; she had drunk from it thirstily. It tasted bitter and a few minutes later she had fallen asleep again.

The next day – was it the next day? – they had untied her hands and let her use the loo, where she had rummaged in her bag for her pills, only to find that they weren't there. At first she thought she must have left them at home, till she remembered taking one in the theatre. They must have fallen off her lap when she rushed off to the foyer . . .

Then they took her to a phone and made her talk to Izzie and read out their demands from a piece of paper. She remembered telling Izzie to tell Vince not to pay, even though she knew he would, even if he didn't have it, even if he had to steal it first. 'Vince only values things he has to pay for,' she had told Izzie

once. 'I intend to be the most expensive thing he's ever bought.'
And now those flippant words had come hideously true.

She forced herself to eat the food they brought her – stale ham
sandwiches, a meat pie, a bag of crisps – to keep her strength up,
dry, stale, salty fare that made her terribly thirsty, too thirsty not
to drink the doctored water, the only liquid on offer. But at least
when she was asleep she couldn't feel the cramping sensations in
her chest, or the fear that went with them. She mustn't die, not
now. If she died Vince would have bankrupted himself for
nothing.

She dreamed. She dreamed that she was swimming, her breath
coming in gasps, her body being buffeted by the waves, and woke
to find herself suspended between the two men, one holding her
by the shoulders, the other by her legs, her body jolting and
swaying as they trundled her out into the open air and into the
back of a van. It was very cold.

But the coldness was coming from somewhere inside her,
chilling her blood, numbing her limbs. She hadn't been swimming
at all, but drowning. It was already too late. She would never see
Vince again. Never hear him say he loved her. And he did. She
knew that now. Perhaps she had always known it. It was her own
lovability she had doubted, not his ability to love . . .

She waited for her life to flash before her, the way it was
supposed to do. Her mother pleading with her not to cry, in vain.
Her father tying her to the bed to stop her wandering. Being
hungry all the time. Dad disappearing in the night. Taking her
misery out on Marje and Marje doing the same to her. Stan saying
she had lovely eyes. The Home. A baby's cry. Babies didn't know
how to laugh, until you taught them. Crying came naturally. They
were born protesting. No! they screamed, not this! They never
told me it would be like this! And death would be the same, no
doubt. One long, primeval scream of terror . . .

There was Bea, in the queue, with her Thermos, Izzie and
Richard in Neville's dressing room, Patrick, shirtless, at the door
of Elizabeth Street, FRIDA and *Bondage* and Vince and Fay and
Marty and *Snowdrops* and Jess and Vince and Vince and Vince
. . . She had never told him she loved him either. Too late for that
too. Too late for everything.

The lights were fading, for the last time. There was no audience to applaud and bring them on again. There was only Izzie. Izzie would tell her how well she had done, pretend that her life hadn't been a flop. Izzie, her scourge and her inspiration, Izzie, her other self, Izzie her friend . . .

Izzie was shouting Paula, Paula, Paula, her voice getting nearer and nearer, louder and louder. She wasn't in the audience at all. She was in the play with her, bending over her, trying to bring her back to life so the show could go on. A pro didn't die half way through a performance. She had let her public down . . .

'Paula! Can you walk? I can't carry you. There's only me. Oh God. Paula, please don't die.'

There was a light shining through the blindfold, fingers groping behind her head to remove it, to untie her hands. She saw two large round eyes looking at her. No, not eyes. The headlamps of a car.

'I don't feel well,' she said. The words were thick and slurred in her mouth. 'Can't breathe.'

Izzie began running towards the lights. Paula wanted to shout, don't leave me, but she couldn't project her voice, it was like a bird with its wings torn off, writhing uselessly in her throat. The car moved towards her. For a moment she thought it was going to run her over. What had happened to the play? What was she doing, lying by the side of the road?

'Help me, Paula,' said Isabel. 'Help me get you into the car.' It was parked just a few inches from where she lay. Gritting her teeth, Paula rolled over and dragged herself towards it, clambering aboard it like a raft as Isabel pulled from the inside. Exhausted, she collapsed, face down, onto the back seat.

'Vince,' she moaned. 'I want Vince.'

'They wouldn't let him come. They said just me, alone. Because I'm a woman, and pregnant. You're safe now. Don't try to talk.'

She was aware of the engine roaring and the road sliding away beneath her. And then she was back in the audience, watching a film this time. That crumpled heap in the back of the car was nothing to do with her. How small and pathetic it looked! She was glad to be free of it at last.

'Where the hell have you been?' demanded Patrick when Isabel

351

got home, late that night. ' "I'm spending the evening with Paula," '
he mimicked savagely. ' "I might be late." You weren't there at all. I
rang and rang and there was no answer. So where were you?'

'It's a long story.' Bone-tired, she sat down and related it from
the beginning, ending with, 'Paula's in a bad way. They're having
to do an emergency operation. They say it's her only chance . . .'

Belatedly, her own words came home to her. She had been so
calm until now. She had been calm all through the last five
harrowing days, while Vince borrowed frantically, at punitive
rates, against all his assets. She had been calm throughout the
negotiations and instructions, calm during the drive to a country
lane in the wilds of Sussex, calm on the way to the nearest hospital,
speeding all the way. Her role as intermediary had required her to
be brave and strong and capable. It was luxury now to come out of
character, to be her own weak and weary self again.

'I can't believe it,' said Patrick, appalled. 'How could Vince use
you as a courier like this? You could have lost the baby . . .'

'I could have lost my best friend. I still might lose her. And
Vince didn't have any choice. That's why I couldn't tell you
before. I knew you wouldn't have let me do it.'

'Nobody stops you doing anything you want to do,' said Patrick,
torn between his obvious concern for Paula and anger that Isabel
had kept him in the dark. 'Least of all me.'

'Patrick, please don't start. I'm tired.'

'This just goes to show how far apart we've grown. I never know
what you're thinking any more. When I found that you'd lied to
me tonight, I thought . . . I thought you must be having an affair,
with Paula covering up for you. It's just the sort of thing she would
do. You've always been closer to her than you are to me.'

'Me, having an affair?' said Isabel weakly. Or rather strongly.
The weak thing to do would be to break down and confess. 'In my
condition? Chance would be a fine thing.'

'You've been so distant these last few months. At first I just
thought you were angry with me for getting you pregnant again.
But then I started wondering if there was someone else.' And
then, pleadingly, tearing her guts out, 'Tell me there isn't, Izzie.'

Isabel couldn't look him in the eye. Feeling the tell-tale colour
rush to her cheeks, she went on the attack. Let him think she was
angry rather than ashamed.

'It would serve you right if there was,' she snapped. 'It's not as if you've been faithful to me!'

'What are you talking about?' he said, affronted. Oh, what a brilliant actor he was.

'I found Debbie's pendant, in our bed,' said Isabel, wishing now that she hadn't started this. 'And don't tell me it got there by accident!'

Patrick rubbed his eyes, hiding his face, giving himself time to think.

'No,' he said, finally. 'No, I don't suppose it did.'

'You admit it then?'

'I admit she made a perfect pest of herself, trying to get off with me. She had a crush on me, I suppose. Or on Mick O'Mara, more like. You know I get all kinds of crazy women writing to me, wanting to marry me, sending me nude photos. That's one of the things I hate about the part. But you were so neurotic about losing the girl that I couldn't very well suggest getting rid of her. So I just told her, very nicely, that she was a sweet kid but there was nothing doing. She must have put the necklace there for spite, to cause trouble between us.'

Isabel's head began to spin. If Patrick had been innocent all along . . . She didn't want him to be innocent. She wanted him to be guilty, as she was.

'Why didn't you ask me about it at the time?' said Patrick. It was an accusation, not a question. 'Because you didn't care? Or because it wasn't important enough to fight over?'

'Keep your voice down! You'll wake the children!'

'You know why you hate rows, Izzie? Because when people get angry the truth comes out. Well, the truth is I've always loved you more than you love me, always wanted you more than you wanted me.'

'That's not true!'

'The only reason you stay with me is because of the kids. And if you were ever able to support them yourself, I'll bet I wouldn't see you for dust . . .'

'Stop it! I can't bear it! How can you say such h-hurtful things to me?'

Cravenly, she resorted to tears, knowing they would shut him up. Patrick couldn't bear to see her cry. But it didn't help when he softened and said sorry and reminded her how tender and loving he could be. It only made things worse.

'I can always sell my story to the papers,' said Paula jauntily, squeezing Vince's hand. He hadn't stirred from her side for the best part of a week. And that was the way she wanted things to stay. 'That should raise a few bob. My ordeal with kidnap gang. Then my brave battle for life and all that rubbish.'

Brave indeed. Survival was a natural instinct. It was letting go of life that took guts. People stayed alive because they were afraid of dying, not because they were brave. And now the death sentence had been lifted at last, now that the leaking pump had been repaired, she had to start thinking beyond tomorrow, for the first time in over three years.

'And there's all that jewellery you bought me,' she added. 'You didn't flog that as well, did you?'

'No. I didn't touch anything of yours. And the cottage is in Grace's name. So at least we'll have a roof over our heads.'

'You should have called their bluff.'

'I intended to get back every penny. And I would have done, too, if your friend Marian hadn't stuck her oar in.'

Marian had gone to the police while Paula was still in surgery, before a distraught Vince had time to set his own formidable forces on the trail of her husband. Thanks to her, Ted was now safely in custody, along with his accomplice, beyond reach of Vince's avenging arm.

'She still loves the bastard,' shrugged Paula. 'That's why she did it. To save his life.'

'She did it for a share of the loot, more like.'

'I don't believe that. If she knew where it was she'd have turned it in, same as she turned him in. Vince . . . you're not going to take it out on her, are you? It won't make him talk, he doesn't give a damn about her, you could tear her limb from limb and it wouldn't make any difference. Same with her two sons, and the grandchildren . . .'

'Do you seriously think I'd stoop that low?'

'No,' said Paula uncertainly. 'It's just that you frighten me sometimes.'

'There's nothing to be frightened of any more,' said Vince

354

bitterly. 'Power comes expensive. Favours have to be paid for. Without money, I'm nothing. Harmless.'

Thanks to Marian, the ransom would never be recovered. The police were not authorized to use the strong-arm tactics Vince would have employed to force the culprits to reveal its whereabouts. They would rather serve their time and come out rich than trade their ill-gotten gains for a shorter sentence. What was ten or fifteen years in clink against more money than they could earn in as many lifetimes?

'But don't worry,' said Vince. 'I won't be poor for long. There are plenty of people who can finance me, help me get back on my feet.'

Paula could just imagine the kind of people who were waiting to exploit his sudden penury, to harness his hunger, to lure him back into the dirt and danger.

'I don't want to be a gangster's moll, thank you very much. I don't want to wonder every time you're late home if you've been arrested or knifed or had to go into hiding. You've moved on from that world. You've spent the last fifteen years cleaning up your act, you told me so yourself. I won't let you –'

'Calm down. You're supposed to be taking it easy.'

'I can't take it easy all the while I'm worrying about you!'

'What the hell do you want me to do, Paula? Get a nice steady job with the gas board?'

'Listen. I've still got all my movie money stashed away in a savings account in LA. I left it there . . . in case we split up.' She squirmed at the admission. 'So I wouldn't have to ask you to keep me. I got citizenship when I married Jess, in time I can pass it on to you. We can live simply, I can take the odd part. We'll manage. We'll be together.' Away from all Vince's old cronies. Away from temptation.

'You want me to let you support me?'

'How can you say that, after I just cost you everything you have?'

'Cheap at the price. Perhaps now you'll believe how much I care about you.'

'Care about me? Can't you do better than that?'

A short, agonizing pause.

'Love you, then.' At last. The word sounded odd in his mouth.

'Can you repeat that, please?' said Paula, feigning puzzlement. 'I think I must have misheard.'

'I said, I love you,' said Vince, looking her straight in the eye. It was as if the shutters had gone up, revealing what had been there all along. 'I love you more than everything I possess. At least this way I got a chance to prove it. There was no point in saying it before. You wouldn't have believed me.'

And now that he had, she was free to say it too.

'You know, I used to try and kid myself that I'd married you for your money,' she began. 'I even let you think it. It made me feel in control. But now you've lost it there's no point in pretending any more. I love you too, Vincent Parry. I love you so much that if you won't come to the States with me, I swear to God I'll go on my own. And I won't come back. I mean it. So which is it to be? Or rather, how much do you really love me?'

He didn't answer. Paula winced and screwed up her face, hoping he wouldn't recognize an old bit of business from *Snowdrops*.

'What's the matter?' he said, panicking, right on cue.

'Just a little pain,' said Paula. 'It happens when I get anxious. You know what they said about taking it slow, at first.'

'This is blackmail, Paula.'

'We could go for six months, to start with, while I convalesce. We could take a little beach house. Please.' Please was even harder to say than love. 'Prove that you love me as much as I love you.'

Another agonizing pause. A long one, this time.

'All right,' he said finally. 'You win. But only for six months. Only while you convalesce.'

He would be bored within six weeks, thought Paula. Bored enough to smell out some business opportunity, bored enough to allow her to set him up in an office with a couple of phones, and then his Midas touch would do the rest, six thousand miles away from the stench of his past. America was a wheeler-dealer's paradise, once he started making money out there he wouldn't want or need to come back . . .

She would miss Izzie, and Toby, and the kids, and Richard, and even poor old Marian. She would miss watching Mick O'Mara every Tuesday and Thursday night. But that was a small price for peace of mind. She had been given a second chance at a future. A future which wouldn't be worth a damn without the man she loved.

ACT THREE
1971–1976

To be wise and love exceeds man's might.

William Shakespeare – Troilus and Cressida

13

1971–1972

It is a wise father that knows his own child.

William Shakespeare – The Merchant of Venice

They had called the baby Patrick junior, PJ for short. Isabel couldn't very well object to the name. Even though she knew he had no right to it. She had known it from the very first moment she had held him in her arms, the moment when all her worst fears had come true.

Family resemblance, however, proved to be in the eye of the beholder. Both Ma and Patrick claimed that PJ was the image of Izzie, the only one of the children to have her red hair, Neville's red hair. Patrick's delight in having a son at last was painful to behold. Ma and the girls spoiled him shamelessly. Toby added him to his collection of overindulged pets. Like the baby of any large household, he ruled it like a little sultan. And all because nobody knew.

'You don't know either,' Paula had told her, long-distance. 'You're just seeing what you don't want to see, like the raving masochist you always were. The sooner you stop brooding and get back to work the better.'

But how could she allow Patrick to fork out for another Debbie to look after a baby that wasn't even his? Why should she do a job she enjoyed while he slaved away at one he hated? She had wronged him enough already.

In any case, they couldn't have afforded a nanny. Even without one they were flat broke by the end of every month. Not only had the rent gone up twice since they had moved in but the twins now took ballet lessons four times a week with a view to trying for full-time ballet school once they were sixteen; it all mounted up. As did the cost of feeding Toby's animals. And on top of that they had Emily's school fees to find.

Despite her precocious reading ability, her musical talent, and an IQ of 165, Emily had turned out to be the dunce of her class, deemed by her teachers to be lazy, inattentive, lacking in team spirit (no doubt whose child *she* was, thought Isabel wryly) and poorly motivated to learn. All symptoms, in Isabel's view, of terminal boredom. In the end they had enrolled her, at vast expense, at a special school for gifted children, where she was now flourishing happily in a small class of misfits like herself.

'Worth every penny,' Patrick had said, proud of her rapid progress. Even though the decision would trap him in *Stop Press* for the foreseeable future. Isabel kept expenditure down by growing and freezing her own vegetables, cooking everything from scratch, and shopping around for bargains. At least she was paying her way now, she told herself, which was more than she had done when she was working.

Meanwhile Patrick still managed to afford to spend his evenings in the pub. Not that Isabel ever complained. He earned all the money, after all. She wouldn't even have complained if she had found that his evenings with the boys involved another woman. These days she welcomed any bad behaviour, encouraged it, even; it helped exonerate her own.

'Are you ever going to tell me what's biting you?' demanded Patrick suddenly in bed one night.

'Nothing's biting me.'

'Even when we make love I can't get close to you any more. You seemed miles away as usual.'

'I'm sorry if I wasn't any good. I was just a bit tired tonight, that's all.'

'You're scared of the Pill letting you down again, aren't you? I've a good mind to get myself snipped.'

'Don't be silly,' said Isabel quickly. 'It wouldn't be the end of the world if we had another baby.' Perhaps it would make her feel better. At least the next one would definitely be Patrick's.

'Wouldn't it just. You're always dead beat as it is. Ever since PJ was born, you've been different . . .'

He was beginning to smell a rat, thought Isabel. It was like a game of hunt the thimble. He was getting warmer and warmer. And in the end, inevitably, he would find it.

'If you want to go back to work . . .'

'. . . Richard could always find me a part, I know.'

'I wouldn't count on it. At the rate he's going he'll soon be out of business.'

Patrick couldn't resist a certain satisfaction in the demise of Renegade's fortunes. Vince had had to withdraw his financial backing, in order to honour the loans he had raised against capital. Since then Richard had embarked on a series of ill-advised moneyspinning ventures, all of which had flopped. A hugely ambitious and much publicized 'psychedelic opera' had incurred heavy losses, as had *Flower Power*, a *Hair*-inspired hippy review. Two further plays, including one dashed off in haste by Richard himself, had also failed, making future finance even harder to come by, especially now that Neville had left the company, in the wake of insoluble 'artistic differences' with a permanently spaced-out Richard.

'What I was actually about to say,' went on Patrick, 'was that I could get you a few episodes of *Stop Press*. You could just do it for a laugh. It might buck you up.'

'No. I can't leave PJ with Ma.' She couldn't leave Ma, come to that.

'You could leave him with a childminder. Lots of working women do.'

Why was he being so nice to her? Couldn't he see that it made her feel worse? Not working was part of her penance, dammit. She reined in the ever-present, suicidal urge to confess, squeezed his hand and said, 'It's sweet of you to suggest it. But I don't know if I could cope at the moment. If I'm a bit preoccupied, it's because of Daddy coming up for parole again. He's bound to get it this time.'

'So? We're Toby's legal parents now. If we'd known he would stay inside till Toby was sixteen, we could have saved ourselves a lot of worry. Not that anything would stop you worrying. You always were the world's worst pessimist.'

And perhaps she was. But in Isabel's experience, one could never be quite pessimistic enough.

'You mean it's impossible?' said Paula, cutting across all the jargon. 'There's nothing at all you can do?'

She was shocked but not surprised. She had known that there

must be something wrong with her, after two futile years of trying. Sod's bloody law. Women who didn't want babies, like Izzie, got pregnant at the drop of a hat.

'The condition should have been picked up and treated after the birth of your first child.' She had told them it was stillborn. 'Whoever gave you your post-natal exam was almost certainly negligent.'

She hadn't had a post-natal, of course. She had scarpered before they could give her one. Perhaps it was just as well. If she'd had another child it might have taken after her, as the first one had probably done.

She left the clinic quickly and began driving home, not that there was anything to go home to. Vince was away on business yet again. There were now three Serendipity Food stores, two in LA and one in San Francisco, with plans to open several more, and expand, in time, into a franchise operation. Vince had been quick to exploit the growing West Coast mania for organic food, herbal products, health supplements, vitamin pills, and other aids to immortality. All a big scam, in Paula's view. But that hadn't stopped her placing all her capital at his disposal and taking any crummy TV part that came her way to help make ends meet.

TV was a retrograde move, career-wise. But with the movie industry in deep recession, dozens of sound stages standing empty, and more than half of all film union members currently unemployed, she knew that she was lucky to get work at all. Especially now that she was pushing thirty. And besides, she had learned the hard way that fame and fortune didn't make you happy. She was wrong to want more. Wrong to feel there was something missing. She had got a second chance at life, and this time she had promised herself that she wouldn't blow it. When would she ever learn not to be greedy?

And yet the urge to drown her sorrows was hideously strong. She'd stuck to a no-drinking, no-smoking, no-bingeing régime all the while she was hoping for a baby. And now that hope was gone. Now she would never be able to replace the child – or rather the two children – she had lost . . .

She would never know what had become of her first baby, but she could find out what had happened to her second. A temptation she had resisted until now, fearful of opening up old wounds. She had never enquired after Jess since returning to LA, never tapped into the grapevine; tactfully, no one who had known them as a couple ever mentioned him in her presence. But now she had to see him again, had to salvage something from the wreckage of the past.

The salon was still there, at the junction of Santa Monica Boulevard and Rodeo Drive, the name emblazoned on the smoked plate-glass window: *Way Ahead*. Feeling like an intruder, Paula walked in, her high heels buckling on the thick soft carpet. A jungle of giant pot plants obscured her view of the interior. A Thunderbird-style receptionist smiled a hygienic smile.

'I'd like a word with Jess, please.'

'Jess? I'm sorry, we don't have a stylist of that name. Do you mean Jake?'

Leave, she told herself. Leave now, before you hear any more bad news.

'In that case can you tell Saul that Paula Dorland would like to see him? It's personal.'

The girl disappeared behind the potted palms. Paula sat down on the white leather banquette, next to a synthetic woman of indeterminate age, somewhere between her first face-lift and her second. She tilted her head girlishly and echoed, 'Paula Dorland? You and Jess used to be married, didn't you?' Bitch, thought Paula. 'Such a nice boy. He always used to do my hair.'

'I was just passing by and thought I'd say hello,' said Paula coolly. 'We've kind of lost touch. Do you happen to know where he's working these days?'

'My dear, I asked the same question myself. Last fall, it must have been. They said he'd gone East, but then salons always say that when they don't want to lose a customer.'

'Miss Dorland?' cooed the receptionist, returning. 'Will you step this way please?'

Perhaps he really had gone East, thought Paula. Sold his interest and started up on his own. She hoped the attorney Vince had found him had done a decent job. It would have been all too easy for Saul to rook him . . .

She was shown up to a plush, over-furnished office above the shop, complete with a day bed. Perhaps it was a casting couch, of sorts. Saul stood up to greet her.

'Hi, Paula.' His florid features tensed into an anxious smile. 'How can I help you?'

'Where's Jess?' demanded Paula. 'What's happened to his share in the business?'

Saul raised his hands in a self-protective gesture.

'I bought him out. Fair and square. I can show you the paperwork.' He rummaged in a filing cabinet and produced a document, complete with Jess's ill-formed signature at the bottom. The figure he had sold for was higher than Paula would have expected. It all seemed on the level.

'So what happened?' she said, accepting a placatory cigarette. Saul sat back in his chair and sighed.

'Believe me, I never meant to come between you two. Hell, you were like a mother to him.'

It didn't help to have him rub it in.

'Jess really loved you,' he went on. 'With me it was just sex. After you left him he was never the same, he went kind of moody and depressed. Then last fall he starts hanging out with these weirdos. The Children of the New Tomorrow.'

The name rang a bell. 'You mean, like the Moonies?'

'Similar outfit. They picked him up in the street one day, took him along to a meeting, convinced him he had to hand over all his worldly goods to the movement and go and live in some commune. I tried to talk him out of it, but it was like they'd brainwashed him. Then one day he comes in with a sharp lawyer – not the one you found for him, some other guy – who does all the talking and says either I can buy his share or he'll sell it to someone else. I didn't want some outsider coming in. So I made him an offer. This shyster drove a hard bargain, I reckon he was on the Children's payroll. I never saw Jess again.'

It was too elaborate to be a lie. And it figured. Jess was a natural-born sucker. He'd married her, hadn't he?

'Where is this commune?'

'Don't waste your time, Paula. There was a programme about it, on the TV. Parents trying to get their kids to come home. Husbands looking for their wives. No one ever leaves. All kinds of drop-outs and fruits wind up there, they turn them into fanatics. Some Reverend or other runs the joint, lives like a sheik, so they say. Do yourself a favour and forget him, like I had to do. He's gone.'

364

Gone. Lost. Stolen. Even if she went and got him back, what would she do with him then? Adopt him?

'I knew something would happen to him,' muttered Paula, dragging jerkily on her cigarette. 'I knew he'd end up in trouble without me to look out for him.'

'You didn't ought to blame yourself. I guess he's happy enough, in his way. Can I get you something to drink? You look kinda pale.'

He poured her a generous measure of Jack Daniels. It made her feel better. She called in at the liquor store on her way home, so she could pour herself another.

And another. She had been stupid to set herself up for a crisis, for two crises, while Vince was away. At home there would have been Izzie, or Richard, or Marian to pour it all out to. But here there was no one she could call a friend, no one she could trust not to sell her secrets to the *National Enquirer*. She had never been any good at making friends, only contacts. Contacts were something you found for yourself; friendships happened to you by accident, like love.

She picked up the telephone and put it down again. 'No, of course it's not a bad time,' Izzie would say, but she was always busy, too busy, these days, to talk for long. You'd never catch Izzie sitting round at a loose end, getting smashed and feeling sorry for herself. Not with five kids, Patrick's mother and a dozen pets to cater for, which now included Princess, an enormous Alsatian bitch rescued by Toby from Battersea Dogs' home, compensation for the loss of his cattery after Paula's move. Poor Izzie. Cats had only made her sneeze; she had always been terrified of dogs, especially big ones. But this one had no doubt been trained to wipe its paws on the doormat and not to bark with its mouth full. A pet crocodile wouldn't have disrupted the perfect order of her home.

No point in phoning Richard either. He would probably be high, as usual. As for Marian, she had long since taken Paula's advice and got herself a proper job, as an aide in a shelter for battered wives – work for which she was eminently well qualified – where there was always an unholy racket going on in the background and someone else wanting her attention. God, but she was so damned lonely . . .

The phone rang. She braced herself for a lecture. Vince would know straight away from her voice that she had been drinking.

'Paula? It's me, Patrick.'

'Patrick?' Patrick never rang her. 'Is something wrong? Are Izzie and the kids okay?'

'Yes, they're fine. I've got a favour to ask you. I need your help.'

'It's been on the cards for months that the show would be scrapped,' Patrick told an impassive Isabel. 'I didn't mention it before because I didn't want to worry you. I've been trying for a long time now to line up other work. Nothing doing. Nothing that would pay enough, I mean. Once you go backwards, word soon gets round that you're desperate and all you get offered is shit.'

'And now the train's going into the tunnel,' said Isabel. She made chugging noises as the forkful of neglected spinach approached PJ's mouth. Reluctantly it opened and closed round the green mess while the hooter whistled.

'You think I'm right to try my luck in the States? The alternative is to give up acting altogether.'

'Of course you're right,' said Isabel, loading up another mouthful. 'Over there you're not type-cast. There will be more opportunities.'

'It's a gamble, you realize. It'll eat into what's left of our savings. That's why I went cap in hand to Paula. She's got a spare room, she's agreed to put me up till I find work. That should save a few quid.'

He must have hated asking, thought Isabel. At one time such an unpalatable task would have been delegated to her. Presumably asking her would have been even harder. Evidence of the growing distance between them. Her fault, not his. He had even gone and had that vasectomy, without telling her, in an attempt to rekindle the spark between them. But it had done the reverse. He thought, in his ignorance, that he already had the son he had longed for. And now she couldn't even bear him another one, to redeem her lie . . .

'She's going to put me in touch with her agent, and an immigration lawyer, and introduce me to a few people. If things work out, I can send for you and the kids.'

366

Isabel preferred not to think that far ahead. She dreaded any upheaval, any disruption to her meticulous, mind-numbing routine. Every day was an assault course of self-imposed tasks, her life was ruled by ever-growing lists of Things To Do. They made up for all the things she couldn't do, things she would never do again, things she should never have tried to do in the first place.

She couldn't even bear to go to the theatre any more, couldn't bear to sit there, trapped in the auditorium, wishing she were up on the stage. And besides, she still nurtured a phobia about running into Neville. He had phoned several times, when Patrick was at work, to ask how she was, repeating that he was sorry about 'what had happened' – not that he knew what had really happened – and reminding her that he was still her friend, he would always be there if she needed him. But Isabel had kept him firmly at arm's length. Whatever happened, he must never see PJ, lest he see himself.

'Another train coming! Quick! Open up before it crashes!'

'He doesn't like spinach,' put in Patrick. 'Any more than I do. Why do you make him eat it?'

'Don't like it,' said PJ, hopefully. 'Don't want it.'

'It's full of iron. It'll make you strong like Popeye.'

'No.'

'Right then,' said Isabel firmly, putting down the fork. 'No spinach, no ice cream.'

She flung Patrick a warning look. She had always put her children's welfare before her own popularity. No wonder they all preferred him to her . . .

'PJ, I'm disappointed in you,' said Patrick, backpedalling. 'You'll never make a boxer at this rate. Come on. Eat the horrible stuff. Mum had a bet with me you couldn't do it.'

PJ promptly scooped up the last vestiges of the hated vegetable and swallowed it.

'That's my boy,' said Patrick fondly, ruffling his hair. 'That's Patrick Delaney junior.'

If only he was, thought Isabel.

21 July 1972

Dear Paula
I'm sorry I couldn't talk for long when you phoned the other

day. My father had just called round to see Toby. It was pretty heavy going, because Toby just ignored him, but then Toby's at the horrible age when he ignores pretty well everyone. These days he communicates with me solely by way of grunts – normal behaviour, so I'm told, for seventeen-year-old boys.

Daddy has now left the probation hostel and moved to a flat in Chalk Farm. An old crony of his has given him the run of it while he's away on tour, which is just as well as he's broke at the moment. People invited him to lots of parties, just after he got out, as a kind of performing bear, and gave him what Patrick would call 'the usual theatrical gush', but so far there have been no offers of work, apart from a voiceover for dogfood which he regarded as beneath him. But he's almost finished his autobiography (I'm two-finger typing it for him) which he's hoping will fetch a big advance, even though I can't believe that anyone will risk publishing it in its present form. He's dished the dirt on absolutely everyone you can think of, including some amazing stuff about Larry. But at least he's been nice about Mummy.

I can't help feeling sorry for him, in spite of everything. Yes, I know I'm green as grass; Patrick thinks so too. But I honestly think he's sorry for what he did and wants to make amends. He's never once mentioned Richard forcing his hand over the adoption, which he likes to pretend he agreed to voluntarily, perhaps because it's too painful for him to admit otherwise.

Richard sends his love. He's decided to wind up Renegade – he had to surrender the lease on the theatre in any case – and travel for a bit. He and Kevin are off next week, heading overland for Kathmandu. I told him he's much too old to be a wandering hippy, but it was like talking to a wall.

Anyway, I must finish now, before the kids get home from school. The only reason you're getting such a long (and probably boring) letter is because I left PJ with Patrick while I went shopping and then hid out in the local reference library on my way back. It's impossible to do anything at home without being interrupted. I'm going to post this rather than give it to Patrick to hand to you when he arrives tomorrow. He'll only lose it or forget about it. So by the time you read this he will probably be driving you to distraction, leaving his dirty laundry all over the place and making you wish you hadn't been so hospitable. My apologies in advance.

Remember me to Vince. I'm glad the shops are doing well. Kisses from the kids. Ma sends her best.

Love, Izzie.

Afterwards she thought, it must have been happening, while I was posting that letter to Paula, while I was walking back home. There I was, thinking about stupid things like what to cook for dinner, and I didn't have the slightest premonition, I didn't even hurry back . . .

The first she knew of it was the sight of the ambulance, parked outside the house, its light flashing. She ran inside, assuming that it must be for Ma, until she encountered her in the hallway, weeping hysterically and pointing dumbly towards the living room.

Two men were lifting PJ onto a stretcher, leaving behind a big red stain on the carpet. His leg was bleeding through a bandage, his clothes torn and soaked in blood. He's dead, she thought numbly, as she shouted his name to no response. My baby is dead . . .

She was barely aware of Patrick's arms closing around her and his voice saying, over and over again, 'It was the dog. He was playing in the garden with the dog.' Too stunned to speak, she got into the ambulance and held PJ's hand as they put an oxygen mask over his face and set up a drip. There was blood all over Patrick's shirt.

'She went berserk,' he was saying. 'PJ must have startled her in some way. I tried to drag her off him but she wouldn't let go of his leg. In the end I managed to knock her out with a spade . . .'

At the hospital she watched them wheel him away, cowering on a bench while Patrick went to talk to the doctor. It had happened at last. Her punishment. She prayed. She would do anything, promise anything, suffer *anything*, to save him . . .

She jumped up, white-faced, as Patrick rejoined her, expecting the worst.

'They have to operate on the leg,' he said. 'He'll need a transfusion. But it turns out he's a rare blood group and they've none in stock, so they want to test both of us right away.'

She followed Patrick into a little room where a nurse was waiting to take samples of their blood. This is a waste of time, she thought, as the needle plunged into Patrick's arm, as she rolled up her own sleeve in readiness. It won't be the right kind. My child is bleeding to death when his real father could save him . . . It was a moment of pure, blind panic.

'Patrick,' she heard herself saying. 'You've got to get hold of Neville.'

'Neville?'

'For the blood. Neville's blood will match PJ's.'

'What?'

'Hurry up! Phone him! Tell him to get here right away!'

'Jesus Christ. What the hell are you saying?'

Afterwards she realized that she should have waited. Waited on the off chance, however remote it seemed at the time, that Patrick's blood, or hers, would match. And even if it didn't, she discovered later, they would have used a compatible group, as a compromise, or drawn on some other source of supply. Hospitals had contingency plans to deal with such emergencies.

But she didn't wait. She ran straight into the burning building to rescue her baby, without waiting for the fire brigade. For a moment Patrick stared at her, speechless.

'Phone him where?' His voice was hard and cold as ice.

'Try him at home.' She fumbled in her bag. She still had his number in her address book. 'If he's not in, try the Royal Court.' She had read in the *Guardian* the other day that he was directing a play for them.

'You ring him,' said Patrick stonily.

'But –'

'I said, you bloody ring him!' He turned away from her in disgust.

They let her use the phone in a neighbouring office. There was no answer from Neville's flat and she had to get the Royal Court's number from directory enquiries. The doorman transferred her to someone else, who informed her that Mr Seaton was at a rehearsal room in Paddington and could he take a message; after Isabel shrieking at him that this was an emergency, he gave her the number.

'Can he phone you back?' said a haughty-sounding girl, after twenty-five rings. 'We're in the middle of rehearsals.'

370

'Tell him it's Isabel. Tell him it's a matter of life and death.'

He came to the phone within seconds.

'Oh God,' he said, when she had told him. 'Oh God, Izzie, I wish I could help. But the thing is, I'm group O, the commonest kind there is. Or so I was told, after that car crash. But of course I'll come straight away, just in case . . .'

By which time the tests had already confirmed that Patrick's blood was a perfect match for his son's.

Patrick postponed his departure for the States until PJ came out of hospital. In the interim he slept in the spare room. No one realized; he had always been the last to go up to bed. And now he made a point of being first up as well.

Isabel tried to explain, but he wouldn't listen. Never mind that PJ had been proved, indisputably, to be his son. His wife had spent the last three years believing otherwise, deceiving him, letting him support, as she thought, another man's child, letting him deny himself the chance of another. Neville had only made things worse, by attempting to tell him the truth of what had happened. Patrick didn't recognize the truth, any more than she had done herself. Like her, he chose to believe the worst.

'Would you like me to try talking to him again?' asked Neville when Isabel phoned him, as promised, from a call box.

'No. He's likely to break your jaw.' As he would have done already, had Neville had two arms with which to defend himself.

'I feel so responsible. If there's anything at all I can do to help –'

'There is. And that's to forget this ever happened. It's easier for me if we don't see or even speak to each other in future. I don't want to have to lie to Patrick about it.'

Not that it would make any difference. Patrick would never trust her again . . .

The whole house seemed unnaturally silent. Toby had withdrawn into his shell, blaming himself for having rescued a highly strung dog with a history of ill-treatment; it had since been destroyed by a man from the RSPCA. Ma took to her bed, suffering from delayed shock. The girls crept around the house like mice, doing all the chores unbidden and offering up umpteen rosaries for their little brother's recovery. And Patrick said not a

371

word. It wasn't until the eve of his departure that he deigned to address her on the subject, tapping on her door after the rest of the household had gone to bed.

'I don't want Seaton coming to the house once I'm gone,' he said. 'Do your whoring at his place, okay?'

'I tried to tell you, I haven't seen him for years. It only happened the one time . . .'

'It's over, Isabel. I can't live with you any more. If I wasn't going to America, I'd have to move out, somewhere else. This way, at least, the kids don't have to know why, not yet. But they will, believe me, if you start cooking up any schemes with your pal Oliver Briggs to take them away from me. I'm damned if I'll let Seaton take my place.'

'Patrick –'

'If I have to, I'm warning you, I'll tell them everything, I'll take them away from *you*.'

'You can't do that,' said Isabel. 'I'm their mother.'

'A mother who never wanted children in the first place. Who never once got pregnant except by accident. Who'd rather be prancing about on a stage than looking after them. Who sleeps with other men. You don't deserve to have kids!'

She didn't cry. She didn't beg. Let him insult her all he liked, she wouldn't take the bait. She would stay calm. She wouldn't give in to the mad Mallory genes. If she lost her grip now, if she gave way to the despair that threatened to overwhelm her, she risked losing her children as well as Patrick. And without them, she might as well be dead . . .

Paula's drunken offer of hospitality had provoked a decidedly cool response from Vince, who was less than delighted at the prospect of having his wife's old flame as a house guest.

'I'm doing it as a favour to Izzie,' said Paula sullenly, having failed to pass off her hangover as a headache. 'And God knows we owe her one. She just about saved my life, remember?'

But that wasn't the real reason. The real reason was that she was lonely, and that Patrick was a breath of home. If she'd been less selfish she would have discouraged him from coming, warned him just how tough things were likely to be, with Hollywood facing its worst year in living memory. But his call had caught her at a vulnerable moment, and afterwards she couldn't have put him off without giving offence.

Two days after Patrick's arrival Paula got home from the TV studios (she was guesting in a late-night cop show as the victim of a serial killer) to find him repacking his suitcase.

'Your husband drove me out to see an apartment in Van Nuys,' he informed her shortly. 'I'm moving in tonight.'

'But . . . why?' As if she didn't know.

'Why do you think? Not that I'm blaming Vince. Any husband who trusts his wife is a fool. I know that better than anyone.'

Paula caught the smell of scotch on his breath. He had never been averse to a few pints of Guinness, in the public bar, with his mates. But she had never known him drink spirits, never known him drink alone, until now. He had been pissed on arrival, otherwise he would surely not have poured his heart out to her on the drive home from the airport. By the time Vince had got home that night, he had already passed out on the couch in a drunken stupor – hardly a good start to his stay.

'You shouldn't have come over here, not now,' said Paula helplessly. 'You ought to be at home, trying to work things out with Izzie, not running away from her.' Trust Izzie to act as her own judge, jury and executioner. It would be farcical if it wasn't so bloody tragic.

'I didn't run away from her. I walked out on her. I couldn't bear to look at her. I couldn't look at her without thinking of her with him.' He sat down on the bed. 'And now I'm here, I can't sleep for thinking of her with him.'

'She isn't with him. How often do I have to tell you? She had a one-night stand because she thought you were screwing whatsername, the nanny. She only did it to get even.'

'Well I wasn't screwing the nanny!' said Patrick hotly. Paula knew from the way his eyes flickered that he was lying. He might fool Izzie, but he didn't fool her.

'God, what a hypocrite you are. Anyone would think you'd never cheated on her. You even tried it on with me, once, remember?' And to her shame, she had let him.

'I'm a man!' pointed out Patrick, aggrieved. 'I don't get pregnant. If she'd told me at the time that PJ might not be mine, I might have come to terms with it.' Like hell he would, thought Paula. 'But she lied to me.'

'She lied to herself, fathead. Now you both know he's yours –'

'I could never believe my luck, you know. The most beautiful girl in the world and she's married to me, she's mine. Except that she was never mine. She's never loved me, not the way I love – loved her.'

Paula sat down beside him on the bed and took his hand.

'Of course she loves you, idiot. And you still love her. You have to go home and make things up . . .'

'I don't want to make things up. And in any case, I can't go back empty-handed. I haven't forked out all that money on the air fare for nothing. I keep telling you, there's no work for me at home. Nothing that would pay the kind of expenses I've got. I won't have her saying I'm a failure who can't provide for my kids!'

'Izzie would never say any such thing.'

'No. Izzie never says what she thinks.' He stood up unsteadily. 'There's my cab. I've got to go.'

'Call me, okay? Let me know how you get on with Zach. And mind you're sober when you see him, he's TT.'

'Thanks for fixing up the appointment. 'Bye.' He pulled her towards him and kissed her hard, full on the mouth, quite winding her. But he'd been drinking, after all. No point in protesting too much. It didn't mean anything. Not to him.

'You didn't have to throw him out like that,' Paula challenged Vince that night.

'He's been half cut ever since he arrived here. He'd have had you back on the booze in no time flat.'

'That wasn't why you did it.'

Vince gave an infuriating deadpan shrug. But his eyes were hard; he meant business.

'If he can be jealous, I suppose I've got the right to be as well. It would never surprise me if he tried to pay Izzie out by coming on to her best friend.'

'And you think I'd let him?' challenged Paula hotly, remembering that kiss, remembering that night up in Hockleigh, remembering too many things she had tried to forget.

374

'It's not you I don't trust,' said Vince. 'It's him.'

'Oh, I get it. Now that we're trying for a baby, you want to be absolutely sure it's yours.' She still hadn't got round to telling him that she couldn't have one.

'If you want to put it like that. I've always thought of Isabel as a paragon of wifely virtue. It made me wonder if I was being complacent.'

'Well, you don't have to worry,' snapped Paula. 'It turns out my insides are all buggered up. So I don't need to be a paragon of wifely virtue, now do I?'

She blew her nose noisily, turning away from him.

'How long have you known?' he said quietly.

'A few months. But it was getting to be obvious, wasn't it? All that thrashing about for nothing.' Fear of pregnancy might, by Izzie's account, be the ultimate passion killer, but making love to order was even worse.

'Why didn't you tell me before?'

'Because I didn't want to believe it. I wanted to believe those soppy stories you read in magazines, about women who managed to prove the doctors wrong. I went for a second opinion, and then a third. They all said the same thing.'

'It doesn't matter. We'll –'

'Stand in line for some little scrubber's cast-off?'

'Do you have to put it like that?'

'If it's not yours, I don't want it!'

She had suffered enough heartbreak without courting any more. She didn't want to have to convince some smug do-gooder that she was a deserving case, only to be found wanting. And besides, if she adopted everyone would know that there was something wrong with her. Better to be thought childless by choice, better to be labelled 'selfish' and 'cold' and 'hard', than to be pitied and patronized.

'I suspected something was bothering you,' said Vince, putting his arms around her. 'But I thought it was me. I know I've been neglecting you lately, working long hours, but –'

'It isn't you. It's me. It's always me. Everything I touch turns to shit. Including my career. Think of it. A has-been at twenty-nine.'

'You're not a has-been.'

'Only because I was never anything to start with. It's not as if

375

I'm talented, like Izzie. You bought me the part in *Snowdrops* and that led to everything else. And now you can't afford to buy me parts any more. So I'm back where I belong. On the scrap-heap.'

One day she would look back on that little tirade of self-pity and remember it with anguish. She should have known Vince would take it personally. He couldn't bear not to be able to give her anything she wanted. He had always loved her too much.

Los Angeles, 12 December 1972
Dear Sophie, Sarah, Emily, Toby and Patrick junior
I'm going to miss you all terribly over Christmas, but I want you to share the enclosed between you to buy whatever you want. Yes, your old Dad's in the money, or will be soon. The picture is about a mad scientist who breeds monster killer fish with robot brains. He releases them into the ocean in a bid to take over the world. Then one day a ship goes down off the coast of his private island and a group of survivors swim to the shore. I play the ship's engineer who thwarts his evil plan. We start shooting early in the new year . . .

The letter was crumpled and dog-eared by the time the children had devoured it and passed it on to Isabel and Ma. Patrick was learning to sell himself, Paula claimed. With her help, thought Isabel. She had got him into the Screen Actors Guild via the back door, taking him with her to the TV studio and arranging with her producer for him to have a last-minute unscripted line in a crowd scene. (Scripted lines went to Union members only.) Having spouted three words, Patrick had automatically acquired the right to join the Guild, the passport to other work.

This done, she had dragged him off to a party, where he had made a big hit with a casting director – female, no doubt – who had asked him to interview for a part at short notice, someone else having dropped out. The director had been impressed enough for the studio to file a special petition with the immigration people, on the grounds that Patrick would be playing an Irish national.

As Paula said, it was a start. A start which wouldn't in fact begin till early spring – the 'new year' had simply been an excuse for not coming home for Christmas. In the meantime Paula had arranged

376

inserts in the Castings columns of Daily Variety and The Holly-wood Reporter, a routine form of self-advertisement Patrick would surely never have stooped to on his own, and was busy introducing him to all her contacts.

Half a dozen times Isabel had got up in the night and sat down to write a long, please-forgive-me letter. But she always tore it up next morning, fearful of inviting further rejection. It seemed safer to take Paula's advice and wait for him to make the first move. Assuming he ever did.

'Give him time to cool off,' Paula had counselled. 'Don't panic.'

Don't panic. Isabel repeated it constantly to herself, like a mantra. Don't panic. Keep busy and keep calm. Whatever you do, don't go to pieces, don't let him paint you as mentally unstable, like your mother. Every time she went to visit Fay, frozen into eternal babyhood, she was reminded of the curse that was waiting to claim her.

Christmas came. Isabel bought the biggest tree she could find, laid on a terrific spread and spent far too much money on presents. But it wasn't a success. Patrick's phone call, at midnight LA time, eight a.m. in London, was the highlight of the day; after that it fell flat, despite all her efforts to be jolly. It had been a mistake, looking back, to take pity on her father and invite him to join them for Christmas lunch. He showed zero interest in anyone else, droning on interminably about his theatrical exploits of long ago, boring the kids witless and straining their well-drilled manners to the limit. Ma was the only one who managed to get a word in edgeways, interrupting his flow with the wistful refrain 'I wonder what Patrick is doing at this moment', even though, as Isabel kept pointing out, they were eight hours behind out there and he would be fast asleep, in bed. In bed with whom?

A few days later the whole family, apart from Toby, made a seasonal expedition to the Palladium, to see a matinée of *Babes in the Wood*. PJ, now fully mobile again, soon began getting restless; Isabel let him eat her peppermint creams – a Christmas present from Ma – on top of his own tube of Smarties, anything to keep him quiet and stop him disturbing other people. Queuing for ices in the interval she heard a voice behind her say, 'Izzie? How are you, love?'

It was Marian Beasley. Isabel didn't recognize her at first. Gone were the customary curlers and the Mrs Mop floral overall. She had cropped her hair short and straight, knocking several years off her age, and was dressed in a blue denim boiler suit encrusted with button badges, among them, 'When God made man, She was only joking', and 'US forces OUT of Vietnam'.

'Hello,' said Isabel. Marian seemed like someone she had met in a former life. 'What are you doing here?'

'I brought a load of kids from the refuge. To give the mums a break. How's it going? Have you heard from Paula lately? The lazy cow hasn't written to me in months.'

'She's fine. She's been getting quite a few TV parts. And Vince's business is doing well, apparently.'

'I'll bet. Conning overfed Yanks into paying through the nose for beans and brown rice, exported by starving third world countries. There's capitalism for you.'

Isabel agreed politely, startled. She had never heard Marian utter a political opinion before. As the queue made its slow progress Marian rattled on about her work, about how the law about domestic violence needed changing, about how she had divorced her old man, and not before time, she would never forgive him for using her to get at Paula. It wasn't just her appearance that had changed in the last three years, thought Isabel, bemused. The old downtrodden Marian had metamorphosed into what Patrick would have called 'one of those bloody women's libbers'.

'And what about you?' said Marian finally.

'I'm fine. Patrick's filming in America at the moment.'

'I was glad to see the back of Mick O'Mara,' said Marian. 'The original male chauvinist pig. It used to make me sick to see the women at the shelter lapping up all that sexist rubbish . . .'

Isabel was spared the need to comment by the sudden appearance of Sophie.

'Mum, PJ's just been sick.'

'I'll get your ice creams,' said Marian, as Isabel groaned. She returned to her seat to find Ma's dress sodden with vomit and PJ a delicate shade of green, indicating that he hadn't yet shed all his load.

'We'll have to go home,' said Ma. 'Look at the state of me. People will complain about the smell.'

'We don't *all* have to leave, do we?' grumbled Sarah, fearing a general exodus.

378

'Well, you're certainly not coming home in the dark on your own,' decreed Isabel, mopping up with a tissue while the girls began muttering mutinously. Damn. If Toby were here, she could have left him in charge. But he was engaged in an elaborate all-day toilette, prior to some ghastly teenage party where he hoped, by his own admission, to 'pull a few birds'.

'Whew,' said Marian, wrinkling her nose, as she distributed the ices. 'If you want to take him home, I'll run the girls back to your place for you after the show. We've borrowed a mini-bus.'

'You're sure it won't take you too far out of your way?'

'Miles. But don't worry. I'll drop our mob off first. They'll be clamouring for their tea. Then you can give me mine, okay? You kids stay here and wait for me after curtain.'

It was sleeting outside. Isabel left Ma waiting with PJ in the foyer while she went to collect the car from its parking place. Just recently it had started making sinister knocking noises and she dreaded to think how much it would cost to repair. The minute a garage got sight of a lone female, they would rob her blind . . .

Succumbing to a wave of despair she sat there, stupidly, in the car, for several minutes, crying, crying for the first time since Patrick had left her. He would never come back, except to take the children away from her. She was starting to crack up. She couldn't cope . . .

By the time she collected Ma and PJ, she had regained her usual composure. It didn't falter again till they were both safely in bed and the girls sprawled in front of the television in the living room, watching some magic show, while she drank tea with Marian in the kitchen.

'Home-made?' queried Marian, helping herself to a second slice of Christmas cake. Isabel nodded. Nobody else had eaten any, Patrick was the only one who liked it.

A crumbly bit fell off onto the floor on its way between plate and mouth. Isabel immediately scooped it up with dustpan and brush and deposited it in the pedal bin, wishing that Marian would hurry up and leave so that she could do the dishes and wash Ma's and PJ's dirty clothes and make rissoles for tomorrow from the final remains of the turkey and finish her ironing and . . . just look at those dirty fingermarks on the kitchen door! She couldn't restrain herself from attacking them with a damp J-cloth there and then.

'You've lost a hell of a lot of weight since I last saw you,' said Marian, lighting a cheroot. 'God knows you were skinny enough to start with.'

'Oh, I eat like a horse,' said Isabel, handing her an ashtray. 'I just burn it up quickly.'

'No wonder,' commented Marian, looking round. 'First sign of madness, you know.'

'What?' said Isabel, starting at the sound of the dreaded M-word.

'This place is too spotless to be healthy, what with five kids stomping about, not to mention Toby's pets.'

'Oh, it's usually a dreadful mess,' lied Isabel; her war on germs and dirt had become an obsession, her way of kidding herself that she was on top of things.

'I'll bet you even clean behind the cooker,' continued Marian, with heartless insight. She parked her cheroot and scribbled something in her Welfare Rights Diary. 'Do you good to get out of the house for a bit,' she said, tearing out the page. 'Keep this address to yourself, okay? Come along on Tuesday, at two. Bring PJ with you, there are plenty of other kids for him to play with. Granny too, if you like. We've got a woman in at the moment who's sixty-eight.'

'You mean . . . you need volunteers?' said Isabel, wondering how she could get out of it. She didn't have time for voluntary work. She had far too much to do . . .

'We've just started up a drama group. Improvisations. It's an American idea. To help the women verbalize and enact their feelings. Trouble is, they've learned the hard way, most of them, to keep their traps shut. A professional like you could help bring down their inhibitions. We couldn't pay you anything, of course.'

'It's very nice of you to ask me,' began Isabel, panic-stricken, 'but the thing is –'

'They're not all downmarket types like me,' interrupted Marian. 'You'd be amazed how many doctors and vicars and solicitors knock their wives about. People of your own class,' she added slyly.

'Class has got nothing to do with it,' protested Isabel, caught on the raw. Patrick had accused her time and again of being a snob; she couldn't bear for Marian to think the same. 'I've just never taught drama before, that's all. But . . . if you really think I can help you . . . I'm willing to give it a try.' God. What had she let herself in for?

'More to the point,' said Marian, tipping her ash into her saucer, 'perhaps *we* can help *you*.'

14

Spring–Summer 1973

Those have most power to hurt us that we love.

Francis Beaumont – The Maid's Tragedy

Paula hadn't the heart to discourage Patrick by telling him all the things that could go wrong. That his part might end up on the cutting-room floor. That the movie might prove so dire that it was never released. That a studio coup – a frequent occurrence – might scupper the project before, or after, completion. Or that it might simply lose money, tainting everyone in it with its failure. He was getting quite discouraged enough already.

Used to the fast pace of a TV soap, or the nerve-racking ordeal of live theatre, the constant hanging about and short, unsatisfying takes reduced him to a permanent state of coitus interruptus, a condition which he rectified off-set, relieving his frustrations on make-up and continuity girls, production assistants, film extras, and the leading lady's stand-in, while perversely ignoring the leading lady herself, an established and well-connected actress who didn't take kindly to having her advances spurned.

'Don't you think you've had enough booze for one evening?' said Paula as Patrick called for two cognacs with the coffee. 'You've got an early call tomorrow, remember.'

He had been drinking solidly all through dinner while she stuck primly to Coke. It wasn't the first time they'd eaten out together while Vince was out of town and without his knowledge. But this time, sensitive to subsidy as always, Patrick had insisted on paying, thus giving himself the right to get smashed at his own expense.

Thank God Isabel couldn't see him like this; she would be bound to blame herself. Paula's letters had stressed how hard Patrick was working, with no mention of his womanizing or heavy drinking, or the night he had spent in a police lock-up after a punch-up in some low-class bar. The ensuing black eye had defeated the make-up artists and several scenes had had to be rescheduled. Established stars could just about get away with that kind of behaviour. Aspiring ones most emphatically couldn't.

Luckily he had already been signed up for another movie, but the contract could still be broken. Especially as there were even more unemployed actors about than usual, ready and willing to take his place. All that stood between him and disaster was his undeniable star quality and the buzz it generated both on the set and on the grapevine; once the camera started rolling no one could fault him. But talent, as always, wasn't enough.

'I hate drinking alone,' said Patrick irritably. 'One little swallow of brandy won't kill you –'

He broke off as a blonde crept up behind him, put her hands over his eyes and warbled, 'Guess who?'

Hardly a fair question, in Paula's view, given the number of possibilities. Patrick reached up and removed the human blind-fold, turning round as he did so.

'Hi there, darling,' he said.

'Aren't you going to introduce us?' She bared her perfect, carnivorous teeth in the semblance of a smile.

'Paula Dorland,' mumbled Patrick. 'This is . . .' The woman's smile set into a rictus.

'Don't tell me you've forgotten me already?' she cooed.

'How could I? Listen, honey, I'll give you a call tomorrow, okay?'

'Now where have I heard that before? I'll leave you two lovebirds to your meal, then.'

She drifted back to her table.

'I take it you haven't a clue who she is?' said Paula.

'I just don't remember her name, that's all. I picked her up at some party or other. Couple of weeks ago.'

'And then you said you'd call her, and you didn't.'

'Something like that. I don't remember.'

'You're a bastard, Patrick.'

'Carry on. I love it when you insult me. At least I've always known where I am with you. Unlike my soon-to-be-ex-wife.'

He reached for her hand. Paula withdrew it quickly.

'You haven't told me anything about this new movie,' she said, changing the subject.

'There's nothing to tell,' he said dismissively. 'Except that the script is crap and they're paying me peanuts. But as Zach keeps reminding me, I'm hardly in a position to turn work down.' He switched his accent to perfect Humphrey Bogart. 'The working title's *The Spin of the Wheel*. It's about this heist on a casino, see. I play a crooked croupier.' And then, reverting to his normal voice, 'I get three weeks' location in Las Vegas. At least it ups the expenses.'

'I worked there once. That film about the dying heiress who tries to lose her fortune and doubles her money instead.'

Paula remembered the lonely hours she had spent in her hotel, missing Jess and getting sloshed every night. Las Vegas was a boozer's paradise. Casino bars practically gave the stuff away to attract the punters. It was the worst possible place for Patrick to be alone.

'When does shooting start?'

'Not till September,' he said moodily. 'So it looks like I'll be out of work for most of the summer.'

'Then go home and see the kids.'

'No. I'm sending out air tickets and buying extra beds, so they can spend the school holidays here with me.'

His scale-plus-ten fee for *Curse of the Killer Fish* surely didn't run to such extravagance, thought Paula. Presumably he would have to draw further on what was left of the family nest egg – but the whole point of coming here had been to convert dollars into pounds, not the other way round.

Still, at least while the kids were here he wouldn't be out boozing every night. Perhaps they would succeed where she had failed in jolting him out of his self-pity. She watched despairingly while he knocked back her neglected cognac as well as his own. It proved to be one drink too many. While they were waiting for the check he slumped forwards, sending both glasses crashing to the floor. People turned to look, including the nameless blonde.

Embarrassed, Paula paid the bill and got a waiter to help her heave him out to his car, where they loaded him into the passenger seat like some unwieldy parcel and Paula rifled his pockets for his keys. After several abortive attempts the engine stuttered into life; Patrick had bought himself a boy racer of a second-hand sports convertible which was permanently on the blink. Having sold used cars himself, he ought to have smelt when he was being conned, but he had congratulated himself on getting a bargain, the same as he had done with that dreadful old heap Izzie was stuck with at home. In some ways Patrick was as green as grass . . .

'Come on,' said Paula, as she drew up outside his apartment building. 'Move.' She shook him awake, pulled him out of the car and into the elevator, pushed him out onto the third-floor landing and used his keys to unlock the door. The place was a tip, littered with empty bottles, dirty glasses and overflowing ashtrays. Evidently his budget didn't run to a cleaning woman.

'You're a pal, Paula,' hiccupped Patrick as she shepherded him into his bedroom. 'A real mate.' And then, as he collapsed onto the rumpled sheets, 'Don't go. Stay. I'm so fucking miserable, you've no idea . . .' He reached for her hand. 'I won't try anything on, I promise. I'm too pissed to get it up in any case. Vince is away, you told me so yourself. He doesn't need to know. Just don't leave me.'

Paula hesitated. If Vince rang the house and got no answer, she could say she had unplugged the phone so as to have an early night. Patrick needed her. She had always been a sucker for being needed.

'All right,' she said. 'I'll stay. But on one condition. That you promise to go on the wagon, starting tomorrow.' So far her pleas had gone unheeded; it was time to stop being soft and sympathetic and get tough instead, even if he hated her for it. 'Otherwise you're going to get kicked off the picture. And once word gets round that you're an alcoholic, no one will hire you again, you'll be finished.'

'I'm not an alcoholic.'

'You're heading that way. I've been there, remember? I can help you. But if you won't let me then I don't want anything more to do with you. Watching you drink makes it harder than ever for me to stay dry. So do we have a deal?'

'Women,' growled Patrick, rolling over onto his stomach. 'This is a real home from home. Next thing I know you'll have me eating bloody spinach.'

'Spinach?' echoed Paula, mystified by the allusion.

'And now the train's going into the tunnel. But there's no light at the end of it. It's going to crash . . .' He began laughing mirthlessly, laughter that was perilously near to tears. Paula helped him undress, covered him up, and lay down beside him, still fully clothed, on top of the covers.

'It's all right,' she said, laying a protective arm across him, wanting only to take the hurt away. 'I'm here. I'll look after you. Try to sleep now.' And in the end he did, and so did she.

She was awakened by the shrill bleat of the bedside telephone. Patrick was already up; she could hear the sound of the shower in the bathroom next door. Yawning, she looked at her watch. Five thirty a.m. It must be Patrick's alarm call.

'Hello,' she said sleepily.

'Hello Paula. I thought you might be there.'

Shit.

'Vince. Listen. I –'

'You'd better start getting dressed. I'm coming over there to collect you.' He hung up.

'Patrick!' yelled Paula, knocking on the bathroom door. He opened it, wearing nothing but a towel round his waist, surrounded by steam, like an angel emerging from a cloud.

'Morning,' he said blearily, kissing her on the cheek. 'I've been awake since four, couldn't get back to sleep.'

'Vince just rang. He must have come home early. He's on his way here now. You'd better go . . .'

'And leave you to face him alone? Forget it. I'll just tell him the truth. That nothing happened. Worse luck.'

'The truth? That we had dinner, that we spent the night together, and that you didn't try to lay me? You think he's going to believe that?' Paula thought rapidly for a moment. 'Listen . . . we'll say you invited me to a party at your place. I got pissed and passed out and didn't wake up till morning. I'd never tell him I'd been drinking if it wasn't true, now would I?'

'You're scared of him, aren't you? If he dares raise a finger to you, I'll . . .'

'Cut the macho crap, will you? You're the one I'm worried about, not me. Just do what I tell you, okay?'

386

Retrieving several empty bottles from the garbage, Paula added them, along with some extra cloudy glasses from the cupboard, to the collection scattered about the apartment. By the time Vince's car drew up outside, half an hour later, the place was in an even worse state than she had found it.

'Am I glad to see you,' Patrick greeted Vince, man to man. 'I'm afraid Paula's a bit under the weather. My fault. I had a little party last night, as you can see, and she had a bit too much to drink.'

'I feel awful,' added Paula, in a small voice. That much was true enough.

'I can believe that,' said Vince, his voice chillingly quiet. He looked round the room in disgust. 'Get in the car.' And then, to Patrick, 'If you ever give my wife drink again I'll break the bottle over your head and ram it down your throat. Is that understood?'

'Absolutely,' said Patrick humbly. He could only ever be humble when he was putting it on. 'You have my solemn word it won't happen again.' He embellished this pledge with a mock bow, spicing it with just a touch of insolence.

Paula got into the car. She mustn't play it too penitent. That would only make him more suspicious.

'You might have told me you were coming home early,' she flew at him, as he drove off. 'Or were you trying to catch me out?'

'You sounded so fed up on the phone that I decided to cut the trip short and surprise you. I waited up all night, even called the police and the hospitals. Trying his number was a hunch, I despised myself for it. Did you sleep with him?'

'Don't be ridiculous. There were loads of other people there, you saw all the bottles and glasses. I fell asleep on the couch and the next thing I knew it was morning.'

She couldn't tell if he believed her or not; his silence was more unnerving than angry words would have been. He didn't speak again till he drew up in the driveway of the new house; they had recently moved to a bigger place, in Santa Monica, big enough to raise a family in, as part of his attempt to wear her down on the issue of adoption.

'I don't want you to see him again,' he said, in that steely, deceptively cool voice of his.

'Vince, he needs help. He's got a serious drink problem, much worse than mine ever was. I never let it jeopardize my career. And

387

I never drank when I couldn't afford it. You helped me stop, and now I want to do the same for him . . .'

'So that he can start you off again, the way he did last night?'

Oh, what a tangled web, thought Paula. By lying she had painted herself as weak-willed. Even though she had resisted more temptation than he knew . . .

'It's not just his drinking, is it?' she countered. 'You don't trust me. Once a slut, always a slut, is that it?'

'I've never called you a slut, Paula.'

'No, you just make me feel like one! It would serve you bloody well right if I did have an affair, the amount of time you leave me alone! It would never surprise me if you'd got another woman!'

A hollow accusation; his work was a much more formidable rival than a mistress would have been.

'All right,' he sighed, weakening. 'You've made your point. I'm sorry I doubted you. And I know I've been away a lot lately. But I'm working for us, for our future. You know that.'

'Then can't I come with you sometimes?' said Paula, not for the first time. 'It's hardly as if I'm in full-time work.'

'You'd be bored.'

'You always find some excuse not to take me. Are you ashamed of me or what?'

'I've told you before, you're too much of a distraction. I can't think about business when you're around.'

He muzzled further argument by giving her one of those delicious, lingering kisses, which turned out to be the prelude to a day in bed, to seal their truce. No one made love like Vince, not even Patrick, because Vince loved her and Patrick never had done, loved her so much it frightened her, making her wonder, as always, what on earth he saw in her, how he had subverted her perverse compulsion to drive him away, to test him to destruction, to prove both to him and herself that she didn't deserve to be loved . . .

'Don't leave me,' she murmured, echoing Patrick. 'Don't ever leave me.'

He didn't leave her for the rest of the weekend. They slept late, went for long walks on the beach, let the telephone ring. His way of saying he was sorry, proof that he blamed himself, not her, for her lapse. Patrick wasn't mentioned again, but that didn't stop her worrying about him. Next time she saw him she would make sure Vince was there, try to cultivate a friendship between them . . .

She woke on the Monday morning, replete with sleep and sex, and knew straight away that the honeymoon was over, that he was about to revert to the other Vince, preoccupied, secretive, work-obsessed. He was dressed for business, standing by the window, with his back to her. A tray laid for two stood on the nightstand.

'Come and have some breakfast before you go,' she said, reaching for the coffee pot. It was cold. So was the toast. It was then that she saw the weekly supermarket tabloid lying on the bed. An avid follower of movie gossip, Paula had it delivered with her grocery order. It was lying open at the incriminating page.

> . . . *Paula Dorland, best known for the 1962 tearjerker* Snowdrops in June, *made a hasty exit from Chasen's on Thursday night following a very public tiff with Irish actor Patrick Delaney. Onlookers report that smiles and kisses ended in loud recriminations over his relationship with 22-year-old starlet Candy Milson (see pic).*

The photograph alongside showed the anonymous blonde in the restaurant falling out of a low-cut dress.

> . . . *Delaney, still unknown to US audiences, is fast carving himself a reputation as a hard-drinking hell-raiser. Miss Dorland, teetotal since her second marriage to English businessman Victor Parrish, 52 (her first, to bisexual crimper Jess Morales, was dissolved in 1966), recently bailed Delaney out of jail following a nightclub brawl. Said Candy, 'Paula has no reason to be sore at me. Patrick and I are just good friends. He's a married man, after all . . .'*

'Don't bother to deny it,' said Vince. 'I rang the restaurant, asked if you could book the same table for this evening. Yessir, they said, table number five.'

'I can explain. Candy Milson was there that night. She had it in for Patrick, for dumping her. She must have rung the paper, to give herself a plug. The story's completely distorted. They even got your name wrong . . .'

'How often have you been seeing him behind my back?' His voice was quiet but his eyes were deafening. 'The truth, this time.'

'About once a week,' admitted Paula. 'Just to keep an eye on him.'

'Why didn't you tell me?'

'Because I knew you'd get the wrong idea. You threw him out of the house, after all. It's not true about the kisses. Or that I bailed him out of jail. Or that we argued about Candy. It was all completely innocent.'

'So innocent that you lied about it. Lied so well that I believed you, like a fool.'

'But –'

'You're going to write him a letter, now, telling him you never want to see him again.'

'No.'

'If you don't, I'll make sure *he* never sees *you* again. Don't think I can't do my own dirty work. A drunk like him could easily have a nasty accident. He could crash his car, or fall down and hit his head.'

'You wouldn't. You wouldn't do that.'

'I did once before, remember?'

'But that man raped me!'

'He's raping you too. Emotionally. Mentally. He won't be happy till he's destroyed you, the way he's destroying himself. He won't be happy till your marriage is over, same as his. If you don't want his blood on your head, you'll do as I say. And if you ever deceive me again, believe me, I'll find out. I'll know.'

He meant it. Vince never said anything he didn't mean. She had known that when she married him. Known that she was marrying a man who neither respected nor feared the law. A man who had killed his own father to avenge his mother, and got away with it, who made Adrian Mallory look like the bungling amateur he was. Hadn't she brought him here to ensure that there wouldn't be any more deaths, not least his own? And yet there was a death, deep inside her. She would comply, but out of fear. She would comply out of love for Patrick, not for Vince.

*

390

Isabel waved the girls off cheerily as an airline official escorted them to the plane, a courtesy which they accepted rather gracelessly. At nearly twelve and ten and a half years old they were already adults in their own eyes. Big enough, even in hers, to make certain decisions, as she herself had done at the age of thirteen, when she had opted to stay with her father.

She had spent many gloomy hours worrying that they wouldn't want to come back. But how could she refuse them this long-awaited treat without having to explain the reason why? She didn't want Patrick to know she was afraid, or to think she was laying down the gauntlet. Like it or not, he had a right to see his children, and they had a right to see him. She would risk more by keeping them here than by letting them go.

Toby, having got a summer job at London Zoo, was staying behind, as was PJ, who was deemed too young to spend a whole summer away from home. There was no question of Ma making the trip. Her health made her uninsurable; one emergency hospital admission would bankrupt them. She kept asking querulously why Patrick couldn't come home, just for a week or two; Isabel repeated that he had to be on the spot, in case an offer of work came up. Mercifully neither she nor the children seemed to smell a rat – proof, perhaps, that Isabel's performance had broken through the pain barrier, acquired a life of its own.

She wasn't aware when the turning point came. The process was gradual, like getting over a bereavement. At first her grief was constant, like a gnawing toothache. Then it was more like a sudden, shooting pain in response to specific stimuli – the agony of Christmas, the reruns of *Harry Spencer*, the discovery of one of Patrick's socks when she was pruning the climbing roses. It must have blown off the washing line and impaled itself, spent the long hard winter flapping and shivering among the naked thorns.

And then, somewhere along the line, it had stopped hurting for a whole day at a time. Usually one of the days she spent at the refuge, leading the improvisation sessions, bringing stunted, repressed emotions to the surface, including her own, watching them bubble and gush like hot springs out of cold, packed earth.

The shelter, a large, condemned house, was squalid and overcrowded, the women guarded and hostile. She had to win their trust by making a complete idiot of herself, the way they had taught her to do at FRIDA. She let them fire impossible tasks at her – she was an elephant riding a bicycle, a bluebottle playing a guitar, a fish trying on a pair of jeans. She made them laugh. She made them want to do it too. Everyone wanted to do it, deep down. Everyone wanted to be an actor. Everyone had once been a child.

She moved on to role-playing exercises, persuading one of the women to play a stony-faced housing official while Isabel, as a disgruntled tenant, assailed her with problems about her leaking roof and her noisy neighbours.

'Tell her you need a transfer!' yelled one of the audience, impatient with her poor grasp of the situation. 'Tell her you're in arrears because your old man spends it all at the boozer. Tell her the walls are damp and your kid's got asthma!'

'No,' said Isabel, dragging her to the front. 'You tell her.'

And so she did, the words flowing out of her like pus out of a septic wound. Then Isabel press-ganged another volunteer, who played the part of her husband with a conviction that could only have come from long experience.

'You lazy cow!' he/she bellowed. 'Look at the state of this place! You need sorting out, you do!' And as she pushed her victim onto the ground and made as if to kick her, three other women leapt forward, spontaneously, to rescue her, turning reality on its head, discovering another kind of truth.

At first Isabel wondered, almost impatiently, why they had put up with brutal treatment for so long. Until, with a jolt, she found the answer inside herself, realized that she too had been a victim, of sorts. Or, to be fair to Patrick, more of a willing martyr. Like them she had allowed herself to be bullied and demoralized, like them she had blamed herself and accepted punishment as her due. In her case the bruises didn't show, but that didn't make them any less real. It was all too easy to become addicted to suffering, to the extent that you started inflicting it on yourself . . .

Her pupils changed from week to week. Some were rehoused, most went back home to their husbands. But many said they wanted to carry on with the drama group. Isabel persuaded the local Catholic priest to lend them the church hall, where she held classes two afternoons a week, complete with crèche. Soon they were rehearsing a whole play, based on a sequence of improvisations, illustrating the need for more women's shelters, the object being a public performance, not only to raise funds but to attract the attention of the media.

Isabel took Ma along, as Marian had suggested. Surprisingly, she enjoyed herself thoroughly, helping to mind the kids, making the tea, and telling anyone who would listen about the short-comings of her daughters' spouses. Isabel was lucky, she reminded her, to have a good husband like Patrick.

And so she was, or rather had been, when you saw what other women had to put up with. On the other hand, there was a lot to be said for not having a husband at all. Guiltily at first, and then triumphantly, she was finding that she was happier without one.

Paula couldn't very well tell Isabel that Vince had forbidden her to see Patrick. So she had to say things like 'I haven't heard from him lately', and 'Last time I saw him he was fine'. Fortunately, however, Isabel had other things on her mind. Her letters were full of her doings at the shelter and peppered with snippets of feminist jargon, obviously picked up from Marian. Paula had always pooh-poohed women's lib, on the grounds that she had never been oppressed by men and always made her own decisions. Whereas Izzie, like the Marian of old, was a natural-born doormat. And now, insidiously, their roles seemed to have reversed. Paula found herself envying them both their newfound independence.

The summer holidays arrived. Izzie would no doubt think it odd that she made no effort to see the girls, but she could always plead pressure of work. Not that her work, what there was of it, put her under any pressure, other than to make her wonder why she was doing it at all.

It wasn't as if she needed the money, now that the shops were beginning to take off. She could have afforded to work for nothing, or next to nothing, in the theatre, which would at least have given her access to decent roles again. But it had been so long since she had faced a live audience that she had lost her nerve.

At least if she blew her lines on set the scene could be shot again. She had got used to relaxing between takes, rather than staying at high doh for three hours at a stretch. She no longer had the mental stamina to endure long gruelling rehearsals or the stresses of a first night or the hostility of a bad audience. These days she preferred to play it safe.

In more ways than one. Patrick had taken her rejection very badly, as she had intended him to. 'I'm not going to risk all the progress I've made by spending time with a drunk,' she had written, reneging on her offer of help. 'For God's sake get in touch with AA.'

But she knew he wouldn't. He was too proud. She had deserted him in his hour of need and she couldn't forgive Vince for making her do it. She had been in a prolonged sulk ever since, while Vince stubbornly stood his ground, with the rift widening between them every day.

She was asleep when the phone call came, in the early hours of the morning.

'It's Sophie Delaney for you,' said Vince impassively, passing her the receiver, rendering her instantly alert.

'Sophie? It's Paula. What's the matter?'

'Mum gave us your number before we left home. She said to ring you if there was ever an emergency.' She sounded calm but anxious.

'What's the emergency, darling?'

'Dad went out to buy some cigarettes, at about eleven o'clock. He let us sit up to watch a film on television. He said he'd only be a few minutes and he's still not back. He took the car, so we're worried that he's had an accident.' Paula looked at the bedside clock. Two a.m. 'Ought I to call the police?'

'No, don't do that,' said Paula hurriedly. Another brush with the police was the last thing Patrick needed. 'Look, I'll come straight over and wait with you till he gets back. He probably ran into someone he knew and forgot the time. Don't worry. We'll be with you in less than half an hour.'

She looked at Vince. 'Patrick's gone out and left the kids alone. You're not going to object to me going over there, are you?'

'I'll take you,' said Vince, throwing on his shirt. 'Then I'll check out the local bars. I don't suppose he's gone far.'

They found the girls still dressed, in their Levis and Mickey Mouse teeshirts. Paula had to stop herself uttering the ultimate groan-making cliché, 'Haven't you grown?' She would only have recognized them by their resemblance to their parents, even more

394

pronounced now that the childish chubbiness had left their features. All three had Patrick's black hair – the twins wore it half way down their backs, while Emily's was short and layered – and his innocent blue eyes – Emily's hidden behind a pair of spectacles – but everything else about them was pure Isabel. Sophie and Sarah were still indistinguishable, apart from the tiny identifying scar on Sophie's forehead, the relic of a childhood fall.

She wouldn't have recognized the apartment either. It was clean and only slightly untidy. But it was terribly hot and stuffy, despite the windows being open, thanks to the lack of air conditioning, which was more essential in the smog-sodden Valley than the cooler and more expensive parts of town.

'Vince is going out to look for your dad,' said Paula jauntily, as if hunting for missing fathers was his favourite nocturnal pursuit. 'Are you hungry?'

They said no, but feeding them seemed like a motherly kind of thing to do. The fridge was empty, however, apart from a six-pack of Coke and there wasn't a scrap of food in the place apart from some stale bread. Paula opened four of the bottles, taking one for herself, to break the ice. At first they seemed reluctant to answer her questions, but gradually, following some mutual signalling, they began to open up.

It transpired they had had a Chinese takeaway for dinner, which must at least have made a change from the burgers, Kentucky Fried Chicken and french fries that seemed to form the mainstay of their diet.

'Mum keeps asking if we're eating plenty of fruit and vegetables,' giggled Sophie. 'She keeps asking if we're having a nice time.'

'And aren't you?'

Silence, followed by a loyal 'Disneyland was great' from Emily, supported by vigorous nods from her sisters. 'And the beach. Dad tried to teach us to surfboard. But it was awfully hot that day and we all got burned.'

'Em had a temperature and was sick,' put in Sarah. 'And all the skin came off Sophie's back. And I came out in a rash.'

'And then Dad wasn't well,' added Sophie. 'He was in bed all last week with the flu, so we didn't like to go out and leave him alone. We phoned out for pizzas and stuff.'

'What about the lady who comes to clean the apartment? Couldn't she have fixed your meals for you?'

The girls exchanged glances.

'Dad hasn't got a cleaning lady,' said Sophie.

'He's absolutely *hopeless* around the house,' sighed Emily, her intonation uncannily like Isabel's. 'You should have *seen* the place when we arrived. Mum would have thrown a *fit!*'

'He doesn't even have a *Hoover*,' chimed in Sophie, as if it were a huge joke. 'We had to sweep the carpet with a broom!'

'And tear up an old shirt for dusters.' More giggles from the twins, but their mirth seemed rather strained. Emily, the most serious and thoughtful of the three, didn't join in.

'What did your mother say when she heard your dad wasn't well?' said Paula, addressing the question to her. Despite being the youngest she seemed more mature than her sisters.

'Oh, Dad said not to tell her,' explained Emily gravely. 'He said if she knew he was ill we'd have to go home.'

'And you don't want to do that, do you?'

Another sheepish silence, followed by a chorus of unconvincing nos and more half-hearted comments about how great the beach was, when it wasn't too hot, and how Dad let them stay up till all hours watching horror films and eating popcorn.

'Has he ever been home this late before?' said Paula, looking at her watch, trying to sound casual.

'Sometimes,' said Sophie guardedly. 'Sometimes he has to meet producers and people like that. But usually he phones and says not to wait up for him.'

Poor darlings, thought Paula. And they still had another month of this to go. Obviously they had already had enough, but were too loyal to their father to admit it. Perhaps this would teach them to appreciate boring, reliable old Mum.

While they were getting ready for bed she had a quick snoop, discovering a cache of empty bottles at the bottom of Patrick's wardrobe. He probably thought he was fooling them by drinking in bars and in his bedroom, by telling them not to wait up for him when he knew he was going to come home plastered, by saying he'd got the flu when he had a filthy hangover or simply wanted to be left alone to work his way through a bottle. But they knew. Kids always knew more than you gave them credit for. Specially kids who had inherited the family talent for dissimulation, who had learned from their mother to say that everything was fine when it wasn't. They were like three little players performing on an adult stage, troopers at the ripe old age of . . . how old were they now? It didn't seem possible . . .

The phone rang. Paula ran to answer it before one of the girls beat her to it, hoping it wasn't bad news.

'I've found him,' said Vince.

'Thank God for that. Where was he?'

'Lying in a puddle, in the parking lot outside Harry's Bar. Apparently two guys mugged him and took his wallet. He's had quite a bang on the head, I'm taking him to the nearest emergency room. So it might be a couple of hours before we get back. I didn't want you to worry.'

'Vince . . . thank you.'

'I did it for the kids, not for him.'

He rang off. Paula tapped on the door of the children's room. They were sitting in their pyjamas on one of the beds, with the light on, as if holding a council of war.

'That was Vince on the phone,' she said. 'Your dad had a slight accident with the car. He's not badly hurt, just a few cuts and bruises. Vince is taking him to get patched up.'

'Are you sure he's all right?' demanded Sophie, looking at her sisters, sensing that she was holding out on them.

'Absolutely. He would have been home earlier, but the car wouldn't start again and he had to wait for the Auto Club. So go to sleep now. You'll see him for yourselves in the morning.'

A silent, coded exchange.

'Um . . . perhaps we'd better not let Mum know,' said Sophie, always the spokeswoman. 'About Dad's accident, I mean. She'd only worry.'

And already they preferred to do her worrying for her, thought Paula, her heart turning over.

'I won't breathe a word,' she said, giving them all a big goodnight hug, wishing that they were hers.

'Think yourself lucky,' said Paula, when Patrick returned with Vince and the dawn. 'I very nearly rang Izzie and arranged to put the children on the first plane home.'

He was very sober now, chastened by an anti-tetanus shot and a god-awful headache. Vince stood with his hands in his pockets, letting Paula do all the talking.

'And if you ever threaten her again with taking the children away from her, she can count on me to give evidence in her favour. No court in its right mind is going to award custody to a drunk who leaves them alone nights, who doesn't feed them properly, who doesn't even think to protect them against sunburn. You don't even know how to look after yourself, let alone your kids. You're no better than a big baby yourself.' Which was what made him so irresistible.

Patrick didn't comment, his expression half way between sheepish and sullen.

'I'm going to take them home with us,' continued Paula, 'while you check into a clinic, at our expense, and get yourself properly dried out. We'll tell them you've had to go away on location. And if you don't play ball, I swear to God I'll tell Izzie everything.'

'I'm sorry,' mumbled Patrick. 'I didn't mean to drink while they were here. It's just that every time I look at them, I see Izzie. They smile exactly the same way she does, they've got the same laugh. Having them here makes it worse, not better . . . Oh God!' He put his head in his hands. 'I want her back!'

Paula sat down and put an arm around him, defying Vince to object. He clung to her tightly, burying his face in her shoulder. 'It's going to be all right,' she murmured, looking her husband straight in the eye, hoping that it was true, knowing that if his marriage broke up, so would hers.

The children brought Vince and Paula together again, bridging the gulf Patrick had opened between them. It was a relief, after weeks of strain, to laugh together, to have an interest in common. Rarely had she seen Vince so relaxed and intent on enjoying himself.

He cancelled appointments to take the girls sailing and arranged surfing and water-skiing lessons. They went to the ballet and the theatre, drove out for picnics and laid on behind-the-scenes visits to the studios. As Isabel kept protesting, they were spoiling the girls to death.

'I can't thank you enough,' she repeated on the telephone. 'What with Patrick suddenly getting this job, I don't know how he would have coped without you.'

'Oh, we haven't had so much fun in ages,' said Paula airily, already dreading their departure. 'How are things with you?'

'Hectic. We're putting on our first public show in a couple of weeks. *Time Out* did a piece about us, so it's already sold out and we're having to put on extra performances. And guess what? I've got a job!'

'A job? You mean a part?'

'Heavens no. Teaching, part time. Drama classes for disturbed children. A social worker who visits the shelter saw one of my sessions and we got chatting. She's keen for me to study for a special diploma. Gave me all these books to read. God, and I thought I came from a problem family. It's helped put things in perspective.'

'How's Toby?' It was hard to imagine Toby as a hulking great youth of eighteen, despite the photo Isabel had sent her, showing him in jaw-length sideburns and bell-bottomed jeans. Paula felt another pang of homesickness.

'Loving his job at the zoo. They've said they'll take him on next vacation as well. And there's another piece of good news. Daddy's found a publisher for his book. An expurgated version, of course. So the advance will get him off supplementary benefit at last . . .'

Paula had to bite her tongue to stop herself saying 'How's this for some more good news? Patrick's come to his senses at last. He wants to forgive and forget . . .' But she didn't want to spoil the impact of his unexpected homecoming, either for him or for Isabel.

'You'll miss the girls, won't you?' said Vince one night, after they had gone to bed. The house seemed terribly quiet, but not half as quiet as it would seem when they had gone.

'Of course I will.'

'Enough to reconsider adopting one of our own?'

As if she didn't consider it every day of her life.

'I told you, I just can't bear the thought of getting my hopes up and then being turned down. You're fifty-two, remember. Well over the age limit.'

'Just leave all that to me. Money talks even louder over here than it does at home. And we've got enough of it now to bend any rule in the book.'

Of course. They were rich again. She had almost forgotten. It had all happened so quickly. Not that she should have been surprised. Vince had always had a genius for making money.

'Kids don't have to be your own for you to love them,' he said, taking her silence for consent. 'The girls prove that.'

Perhaps, if you didn't much love yourself, it was easier to love a child that wasn't yours. Not that loving was ever easy. It hurt too much.

Adrian had declined Isabel's dutiful invitation to attend the first night of *Till My Death Do Us Part*, an unapologetic shocker exposing the laws which condoned marital violence. The first-night audience would include several heavily cultivated do-gooders and local politicians, all anxious to demonstrate how concerned and caring they were. Isabel hoped no one would have the neck to put less than five pounds in the kitty.

'I know you mean to help these poor wretches, darling,' Daddy had drawled. 'I did the same sort of thing myself, in prison. But producing amdram is one thing, watching it is quite another. And besides, I'm having dinner with my agent.'

Isabel found herself mimicking this response to Toby, eliciting a gratifying bark of laughter. In Patrick's absence he had been promoted to the man of the house, a role which had done wonders for his self-confidence, as had getting his driving licence. In return for use of the car, he willingly washed it, topped up the radiator, maintained the tyre pressure and changed the oil. When its numerous ailments defeated his amateur tinkering he took it to the garage for her and fooled the mechanics, by a suitable show of macho truculence, into charging him half what they would have charged a woman.

'You didn't seriously think the tight-fisted old sod would risk being touched for money, did you?' grunted Toby, in the same cynical tones Richard would have used. Isabel hadn't heard from her brother since his departure, bar the odd postcard from Bangkok, Singapore and Manila. Toby had done much to fill the gap; it was nice to have a big brother again. She would miss him when he went off to veterinary college in Liverpool next term.

'I thought it was worth a try,' said Isabel, 'now that he's had the first part of his advance. I've become quite brazen about touting for funds.'

'Pity you're not so brazen about reminding him how much he owes you.'

'Oh, it isn't that much.'

'Isn't it just. I found the pawn tickets the other day, in the biscuit tin.'

'Well, you had no business to go snooping,' said Isabel, colouring.

'I was only snooping for biscuits. I never realized things were that bad. I feel like packing up the idea of college and getting a permanent job.'

'You'll do no such thing! I only hocked a few bits of jewellery Mummy had given me. And now I'm earning, I can start redeeming them.'

'You ought to ask Patrick for more money. If he knew you were having a struggle –'

'No. He's probably having a struggle as well. He must have spent a fortune on the girls this summer, on top of what they cost him in air fares. I won't have him saying I can't manage money. Which he will do if you don't take up your place.'

Toby brooded for a moment before blurting out, 'Are you and Patrick splitting up?'

'Why do you ask?' said Isabel, caught on the hop.

He didn't answer straight away.

'I was listening at the door,' he muttered reluctantly, 'the night before he went away. I heard him shouting, and I thought he was having a go at you because of me. Because of Princess mauling PJ. And then I heard him laying into you, about Neville Seaton.'

Isabel turned away, mortified.

'I'm sorry you had to overhear something like that. You didn't let on to . . . anyone else, did you?'

'What do you take me for?' said Toby, affronted. 'I know when to keep my trap shut. After all, I never split on Patrick when *he* . . .' He replaced the rest of the sentence with a shrug.

'When he what?'

Toby hesitated for a moment before mumbling, 'He made me promise not to tell. But I nearly blew the whistle on him, after what he said to you that night. I thought he was a lousy hypocrite.'

It was unlike the laconic Toby to utter more than one sentence at a time. A sure sign that he was actually dying to talk, that he had been bottling this up too long, silenced by some masculine code of *omerta*. Whatever he had discovered must have happened here, in this house . . .

'If it's about Debbie,' prompted Isabel, taking a chance, 'then I already know.'

'You do?' he said, falling headlong into the trap. Isabel nodded, feeling a surge of something like elation.

'How did you find out?' she asked casually, as if it were a matter of no importance.

'I caught them in bed one night,' admitted Toby, embarrassed, 'when you were at the theatre. Grandma sent me upstairs to see if Patrick had any Rennies and I walked in on them. Debbie came to me afterwards and said she never meant for it to happen, she liked you too much to do anything to hurt you. She was in a hell of a state. Then Patrick took me to one side, made out it was all Debbie's doing and said you'd be terribly upset if you knew, that you might even leave him. He was in a hell of a state as well.'

So he had been guilty after all, thought Isabel, relieved. It was like an absolution. Even though she had already forgiven herself for Neville, a process which had given her far more relief than anything she had felt in the confessional. These days her faith was a comfort rather than a stick to beat herself with, not because the Church had changed, but because she had.

'So are you two getting divorced?' repeated Toby, troubled. 'Because if I've got to take sides, I'm on yours.'

Not an easy decision, thought Isabel, moved by his gruff support. Toby had always hero-worshipped Patrick. So much so that she had been quite jealous.

'Thank you, Toby. That means a lot to me. But I hope it won't come to taking sides. As for us getting divorced . . . well I suppose it might come to a legal separation, one day. But I don't want to say anything to the kids just yet. Not till I've had a chance to talk things over with Patrick.' Assuming he ever came home.

She had come to accept that her marriage was over. In all the months Patrick had been away, he had never once written to her, never spoken to her on the phone for more than a moment before asking to speak to the children. It hurt, of course it did, but the wound was no longer raw, the scar tissue had thickened with every week that passed.

'You've changed, you know,' said Toby. 'Since Patrick went, I mean.'

'In what way?'

'I don't know. It's as if . . . as if you were in black and white before. And now you're in colour.'

'Well, I'll take that as a compliment,' said Isabel, bemused.

'Now I've buttered you up, can I have the car tonight?'

Isabel sighed and threw the keys at him. He was off to some disco again, on the pick-up. The Mallory charm might be late-flowering, in Toby's case, and rarely displayed inside the home, but it was beginning to get results outside it.

As soon as Jan had arrived to sit with PJ and Ma – an ex-inmate of the shelter who had been rehoused nearby – Isabel donned her crash helmet – a ton-up job which completely swallowed her face – and roared off to rehearsals on Patrick's precious motorbike, recently liberated from its polythene shroud in the garden.

She had taught herself to ride it, not without trepidation, thinking that it might save her money on petrol and prolong the life of the car, only to discover that it was fun. In the past, when she had ridden pillion with Patrick she had kept her eyes shut and her head pressed into his back while she hung on miserably, fearing for her life. Now that she was in the driving seat she found herself enjoying the sense of speed and freedom and . . . power.

She had been afraid that she wouldn't be able to cope alone. And perhaps she wouldn't have done, except that she wasn't as alone as she thought. She had grown closer to Toby. She had met other single parents, formed what Marian would call a 'support network'. She had made new friends, people who had never known her as half of a couple. And there was someone else she was learning to rely on, to trust and respect, someone who had a vested interest in not letting her down. Herself.

'I'll get it,' called Isabel to Ma, running to answer the bell a few days later. Jan was late; she should have left for the church hall five minutes ago . . .

'Surprise!' yelled a chorus of voices, as she opened the door and three bodies hurled themselves at her at once. A wave of sheer delight knocked her flat. She had never known her daughters so pleased to see her.

'How on earth did you get here all on your own?' remonstrated Isabel, between kisses. 'Why didn't you tell me you were coming? I wasn't expecting you till next week . . .'

They turned and pointed, grinning, as the taxi drove off, revealing Patrick and the luggage, standing in the middle of the road.

'Run inside and say hello to Ma and PJ,' said Isabel hurriedly. 'They've missed you terribly. Go on.'

She walked down the front path, meeting Patrick at the gate. He looked thinner, older. The sight of him gave her a sharp pain beneath her ribs.

'Hello,' she said inadequately. They exchanged an uncertain embrace. 'I wish you'd phoned,' she added, picking up two of the suitcases.

'The girls wanted to surprise you. I have to be back by next week, to start the new picture. So I thought I'd come home and see Ma while I had the chance.'

'How are you? You don't look well.'

'You do. You look . . . younger. You –'

He broke off as Jan arrived, panting, with her baby in its pushchair. Isabel did the introductions while Jan gaped, open-mouthed, at Mick O'Mara in the flesh and mumbled a shy hello. Patrick made short work of returning it, and taking the hint, she hurried inside.

'Look . . . I hate to dash off like this,' said Isabel, 'but I'm already running late. I'm producing a play.' Paula or the girls must surely have told him all about it. 'The first night is tonight and . . .'

'So? It's only two o'clock.'

'We're having the dress rehearsal first. And there are a million other things to do. People are expecting me.' She forced herself to ignore the answering frown, a frown which said clearly enough, 'Still a Mallory, aren't you? Your children come home after six weeks away and all you can think about is your rotten first night . . .'

But before he could put the accusation into words Ma came hobbling out of the house and pinioned him in a tearful embrace. 'Come inside this minute and have something to eat,' she fussed.

404

'You look half starved. You won't believe how much Patrick junior has grown . . .'

The house was already filled with the gloriously familiar sound of Emily at the piano. Sophie and Sarah were also playing a duet on their own favourite instrument – the telephone.

'Mum, can we go round to Sue's?'

'What, now? You've only just got home!'

'Please. We've got simply heaps to talk about! Can we stay for tea?'

'Oh, all right then. As long as you wash and change first. And I want you back in time for an early night . . .'

'See what a big boy he is?' said Ma. Patrick lifted PJ up into his arms and kissed him.

'Do you remember me?' he asked softly. 'Do you remember your old dad?'

'I really must go,' repeated Isabel, grabbing her things and swallowing the lump in her throat.

'What's that for?' demanded Patrick, noticing the crash helmet under her arm. 'Have you got yourself a scooter?'

'No. I'm riding the bike.'

'*My* bike?'

'Yes.'

'What happened to the car?'

'Toby's taken it to work today. He's bringing Ma to the play tonight. He can bring you too, if you like.'

'You're crazy. You'll get yourself killed. Ring up for a cab instead.'

'I don't need a cab!' said Isabel, rattled. 'I'm perfectly safe, I passed the test first time. I'm a much better driver than you.'

Exchanging glances with Isabel, Ma ushered PJ into the living room while Isabel, pursued by Patrick, exited by the back door, where the bike was tethered to a drainpipe. Ignoring his protests, she began releasing the padlock while he rooted around in the garden shed, displacing tools, wellington boots, flowerpots and a leaking bag of Growmore, until he located his helmet.

'I'll drive,' he said grimly, shaking out a family of woodlice. 'You can ride pillion.'

'What is it you're really worried about? Me or your precious bike?'

405

'Both! Now will you move?'

Isabel took a deep breath. 'No,' she said, starting up the engine. 'If you want to come with me, hop on the back.' She began expertly manoeuvring the heavy machine out of the side entrance and into the street. Exasperated, Patrick leapt aboard, yelling instructions in her ear all the way.

'I suppose all your butch lesbian friends are very impressed by the Easy Rider act,' he accused her as they dismounted. 'Talk about penis envy.'

'When it comes to something hot and throbbing between my legs,' said Isabel coolly, 'I much prefer the bike.'

'Well, that's a nice welcome, I must say. I come home, ready to forgive you and start all over again, and . . .'

Paula had been predicting it from day one. But Isabel had never believed her. At first to avoid tempting fate. And later because she simply didn't want to.

'I never asked you to forgive me,' she heard herself saying. 'We can call it quits, if you like, and that's being generous, on my part. But as for starting all over again . . . I don't know if that would work. I'm not the same person any more, Patrick. I've changed. I've got a life of my own now.'

'A life of your own? You mean with Seaton, I suppose?'

'You can't accept, can you, that I could possibly survive without a man to tell me what to do. Look, I really haven't got time to discuss this now. If you want to take the bike home, go ahead. Toby can drive me back tonight.'

And with that she strode into the hall, even more amazed, if that were possible, than Patrick. A moment later she heard an angry roar as the bike sped off.

Just as well she hadn't had prior notice of his arrival. If she'd had too much time to think about it, she might have regressed to her old passive self. Hadn't she just spent the last few months extolling the merits of improvisation? 'Don't think, just feel,' she had instructed her pupils. And for once she had applied the same formula off-stage. After years of being what Patrick wanted her to be, she had finally managed to be herself, whoever that was, a creature who was changing and growing every day, taking her constantly by surprise, as she had done just now . . .

She didn't allow herself to think about Patrick again until that night's performance was safely over, when she made her appeal from the stage for funds to a second robust round of applause, and saw, as the lights went up, that Ma and Toby were sitting alone.

'Patrick went to bed early,' Ma explained later, after the donations had been collected. 'He said perhaps he'd come another night. Didn't it go well?' And then, *sotto voce*, 'What a mood he was in, about you using his bike! I told him if he didn't like it, then it's high time he bought you a new car, the other one is falling to bits.'

'I don't know if he can afford a new car, Ma.'

'Sure he can. He was telling me how well he was doing over there, specially with this new film in the pipeline. So I mentioned about you needing a new washing machine while I was about it.'

'Ma . . .'

'Think how much money you've been wasting at that launderette ever since the old one broke down. And you never know whose clothes have been in there before yours. He said he'd see to it right away.'

'Ma, I know you mean well, but –'

'I've always been better at getting round him than you. Men are all the same. They need a prod now and again. One thing about Patrick, he's never been mean. He just doesn't notice things, that's all . . .'

'What did he say to you?' hissed Toby, once they were inside.

'That he was ready to forgive me.'

'That was big of him. Well, if he starts getting heavy with you again, I'm here, okay?'

Isabel smiled, recognizing the belligerent toddler of long ago.

'Thanks, Toby. But I can handle him. Goodnight.'

She saw Jan out, and looked in on the children. The twins, like PJ, were fast asleep; Emily was awake, reading, still on LA time.

'How did the play go?' she said, putting aside her book.

'Very well.' Isabel sat down on the bed. 'You can come along to see it tomorrow night, if you like. I expect it feels a bit flat, coming home, doesn't it?'

'I'd had enough,' shrugged Emily. 'Paula and Vince were terribly nice, but they were so worried we'd be bored they never gave us a minute to ourselves. I missed my piano. And the twins missed their dippy friends. And we missed Toby and PJ and . . .'

and you, I suppose,' she added artlessly, as if surprised at her own admission. Emily had always been the most self-sufficient of her children.

'Well, thanks very much. I'll give myself a gold star.'

'I don't think Dad likes living there much. Pity he's got to go back straight away. Mum . . .'

'Yes?' prompted Isabel, bracing herself. She met her daughter's eyes full on. Emily looked away first.

'I think I'll go to sleep now,' she said, sliding under the covers. ''Night, Mum.'

Had the children guessed that there was more to Patrick's protracted absence than work? The old Isabel wouldn't have hesitated to patch things up with him, for their sake if not for her own. Even the new one wondered if she ought to let him 'forgive' her, go back to being the kind of wife he wanted, give up her so-called 'butch lesbian friends' and make propping up his fragile ego her number one concern. But if she did, she would have sacrificed all her hard-won progress, she would end up back at square one. And yet she didn't want to slam the door on a possible reconciliation. There had to be some half-way house, some way of starting from scratch, on equal terms . . .

She found Patrick already occupying his side of the bed.

'Come here,' he said, holding out his arms. Isabel returned his embrace cautiously, only to find herself pulled down and rolled onto her back. He was naked. She shut her eyes, held her breath against the achingly familiar smell of him.

'Patrick . . .'

'There's only one way to solve this. We can talk till the cows come home and all it'll do is open up old wounds. Let's just forget the past and start again.'

Isabel struggled to sit up but he pinned her down and began kissing her, undoing the buttons of her blouse as he did so, his lips moving onto her breasts.

'God, I've missed you so much,' he murmured. 'I want you so much . . .'

It would be so easy to give in. And that was exactly what it would be. Giving in. The way she had always done.

'Patrick, no.' She wriggled free.

'Why not?' He seemed genuinely puzzled, damn him.

'Do you really need to ask? I'm not ready for this. You've been gone for over a year, you never even bothered to write to me, the last time we spoke you were threatening to take the children away from me and calling me a whore, and now you turn up out of the blue and expect me to jump straight into bed with you!'

He drew back.

'Oh I get it. I'm supposed to say sorry. You want me to grovel and beg you to take me back. All right, I apologize. I grovel. Will that do?'

'I don't want you to apologize.' She got up and began rebuttoning her blouse. 'And you don't have to grovel. This is your home, and the children need you. But we need some new ground rules. We can't go back to the way we were before.'

'What new ground rules?'

'My right to have my own interests, my own career, my own friends. And my own room. I need to carry on being myself for a bit. To get back some of the years I lost. We both married far too young.'

'What do you mean, be yourself for a bit? Those fucking women's libbers have brainwashed you. Have you started fancying girls now? Is that it?'

'When am I going to make you understand that this isn't about sex? Just because I don't want to sleep with you doesn't mean I'm frigid, or a lesbian, or that I've got another man!'

Patrick ran his hands through his hair. She could tell that he wasn't getting the point. Patrick had never listened to her, not properly. He had a genius for only hearing what he wanted to hear, and distorting the rest, and misquoting her. So that in the end she had given up talking altogether.

'Of course it's to do with sex,' he said bitterly. 'You're still trying to punish me for Debbie, aren't you?'

'It's nothing to do with Debbie . . .' began Isabel, surprised that he should have owned up.

'Why do you think it happened? Not because I loved her, not because I didn't love you. It was because you didn't love me!'

'I did love you,' said Isabel. 'I still do. But love isn't enough, Patrick. I need respect as well. Not just from you, from myself.'

Relenting, she sat down on the bed and took his hand.

'You said yourself you have to go back to LA next week, to do

409

this new picture. That'll give us both a bit more breathing space. Perhaps you need to find yourself as well . . .'

'Find myself? Don't credit me with your own hang-ups. Don't add insult to injury.'

'Will you let me finish? I know it hasn't been easy for you either. Being responsible for such a large family, having to take whatever work you could get, worrying about money all the time. I know you've tried to do your best for us, I know I'm partly to blame for all this.' Which was different from blaming herself. 'If you'd married a different kind of woman, you'd have had a much easier time of it.'

'You were the one who married the wrong man. You've always been ashamed of me. Because I don't fit in with the classical set, because I'm not even trendy working class, just a naff lower-middle, because I'm not a rotten prancing pseud . . .'

'You know that's not true.'

'It was bad enough worrying about letting you down, without you and Ma ganging up on me! She's just been and given me a whole shopping list of all the things I've failed to provide for my family.'

'She didn't mean it like that! I told her not to –'

'Not to worry me? Oh, that's you all over. You'd always rather complain about me behind my back.'

'Will you stop trying to dodge the real issue here? If you love me, you'll meet me half way. You'll accept me for what I am, not for what I've pretended to be. And I want to do the same for you. Because you've been pretending too. You've been living a lie every bit as much as me.'

'A lie? Is that all our marriage has been?'

'We only lied out of love. And now it's time to tell the truth, out of love.'

He fell silent for a moment. It seemed, at last, as if her words were sinking in.

'The truth,' he said bitterly. 'You'd love me better if I told you the truth, would you? Somehow I don't think so.'

'What do you mean?'

For a moment he seemed about to enlighten her. But all he said was 'So where do you want me to sleep?'

'You stay here. I'll use the spare room.'

410

He looked so desolate, lying there, that she almost weakened. Anything to see him smile again. But give Patrick an inch and he would always take a mile.

'Sleep well,' she murmured. 'I love you.'

'Not enough,' he said, as if to himself, turning away from her. 'Not enough.'

Paula's sympathies should have been with Isabel. At last she was toughening up and putting her own interests first, something Paula had constantly, if vainly, encouraged her to do, ever since they had first met. But Izzie was six thousand miles away and Patrick was here, in LA, and the sight of his suffering was more than she could bear.

'You should have told Izzie you had a drink problem,' she said, exchanging glances with Vince. 'If she knew . . .'

'If she knew she'd feel sorry for me, that's all. I don't want her taking me back on sufferance. I've eaten enough humble pie already.'

Vince didn't comment. His only interest in this meeting, before Patrick went off to Las Vegas on location, was in maintaining his new status as his rival's 'friend' – a much more powerful player than his enemy, as he should have realized long ago.

'So now you'll go back on the bottle, I suppose,' said Paula, by way of a caveat. 'Drink yourself to death. And then Izzie will blame me for keeping her in the dark.'

Too bad the girls were so loyal to him. They would no more sneak on him than on each other. And now she, Paula, was part of the conspiracy. Having helped cure him, she was expected to preside over his relapse.

'You don't have a very high opinion of me, do you?' said Patrick. 'Any more than she does. Talking of which' – he fished out his wallet – 'that's what I owe you, for the clinic.' He handed Vince a wad of dollar bills.

'You don't have to pay us back just yet,' began Paula.

'Yes I do! Will you stop making a lame duck out of me? You two have been good to me, but from now on I've got to manage on my own.'

He stood up to go, pre-empting further protests. 'Good luck

with the adoption.'

He shook hands with Vince and gave Paula a quick kiss on each cheek. And then he was gone.

'Izzie must have had a brainstorm,' muttered Paula. 'This is just so unlike her.'

'Your friend Marian's influence,' shrugged Vince, not without malice. 'Seems like she's taught the worm to turn at last. You ought to approve of that.'

'I just feel sorry for the kids, that's all,' said Paula, trying to rationalize her feelings.

'Be honest, Paula. You never bargained on her not taking him back. You wanted them to patch things up so that you'd feel safe again. So you wouldn't be tempted.'

Paula looked away, not denying it.

'Okay, so I still love him a little, I always will.' Not so long ago she would have denied it, even to herself. But there was no point in lying to Vince, he had known all along. 'But not the way I love you. You were the one who turned him into a threat, by throwing him out and then forbidding me to see him.'

'Perhaps. But I didn't want him to hurt you. I was afraid of losing you. And now I'm more afraid than ever.' Quite an admission, coming from Vince.

'There's no need. If Izzie can resist him, I daresay I can as well.'

'Are you sure about that? Because if we're going to adopt a child . . .'

'If we're going to adopt a child, you've got to stop doubting me,' said Paula, kissing his doubts away, and her own. She mustn't let thoughts of Patrick jeopardize her future happiness. She would put him out of her mind, leave him to mess up his own life rather than hers, or Vince's, or the life of the child to whom they would give a home.

15

1974

There's no scandal like rags, nor any crime so shameful as poverty.

George Farquhar – The Beaux' Stratagem

15 January 1974

Dear Patrick
I hate to worry you, but the monthly transfer hasn't been credited yet, which resulted in one of those nasty letters telling me I was overdrawn. Can you chase up the bank at your end?

Isabel chewed the top of her pen, wishing, not for the first time, that she earned enough to pay all the bills herself. She hated having to pester Patrick for money. Especially after he had spent a fortune on the items on Ma's 'shopping list', including a second-hand Cortina estate with a suspiciously low mileage. If he could afford the outlay, she would much rather have had the cash, but it would have sounded horribly mercenary to say so.

He must be due to wrap *The Spin of the Wheel* any day now. So far there had been no mention of any more work. Would he stay out there indefinitely, till something else turned up? Had she made it more difficult for him to come home? Would her new 'ground rules' work, even if he did?

She found herself endlessly re-evaluating the week he had spent at home, back in September. For the first time in years he had spent his evenings *en famille* instead of propping up some low-class bar or working out his frustrations at the gym. One night he had even gone so far as to help with the washing up, much to Ma's consternation. There had been no midnight taps on her door, no more outbursts about her using his bike or mixing with a bunch of dykes, no objection to her nightly attendances at the play. He had even come to see it and put a couple of tenners in the hat, and generally shown a degree of consideration bordering on the provocative.

'You see?' he seemed to be saying. 'I'm not such a lousy husband after all. You don't know when you're well off.'

But well off was the last thing she felt at the moment. Two weeks later the money had still not materialized, making it impossible for Isabel to pay the rent or meet three final demands or respond to a reminder about Emily's school fees. Repeated attempts to ring Patrick had produced the unobtainable tone and the information that the number had been disconnected. In desperation, she rang Paula, saying simply that there was a fault on Patrick's line and could she please get a message to him to call her back.

'Is it urgent?' said Paula. 'Is anything wrong?'

'No, no. It's just . . . decisions about the children. Things like that.'

Patrick would never forgive her if she confided in Paula. He had always been ultra-sensitive about money. And by the look of things, he was short of it at the moment. So why hadn't he told her? Why had he spent all that money on things they could have done without?

'How are you?' she added, trying to sound normal. 'How's the adoption going?'

'All right, touch wood. We're waiting for one to be born, it's due in April.'

'Oh Paula! That's wonderful.'

'I'm trying not to think about it, in case anything goes wrong. I feel sorry for the poor little bastard, having a mother like me. I shall probably be on the blower all hours of the day and night, asking you what to do. Talking of which, this call must be costing you a bomb. I'll drive over to Patrick's place now and shove a note in his mailbox.'

Two days later Isabel still hadn't heard from Patrick, although she did have a visit from a couple of grim-faced men who had come to repossess the car. Patrick hadn't even told her that he had bought it on hire purchase. To make matters worse she got back from taking her class that afternoon to find the house as cold as a tomb.

414

At first she thought it was just the result of yet another power cut, courtesy of the miners' strike and the three-day week. The house always took ages to warm up again. But it turned out that the ancient central heating boiler had finally packed up, with the temperature outside well below zero.

On phoning the landlord's agents she was reminded curtly that the rent was overdue and that no repairs could be put in hand until it was paid. By evening the temperature inside had cooled to forty-six degrees, the high ceilings and ill-fitting windows mocking a borrowed two-bar electric fire. Isabel packed her shivering children off to bed with hot-water bottles, assuring a querulous Ma that a man would be along to fix the heating next day.

There was only one way to make that happen. She had been toying for several days now with the idea of asking her father for help. Not only did he owe her the best part of two hundred pounds, but his book had recently been auctioned in America, fetching a handsome advance, enabling him to take a lease on a mews house in Cheyne Walk.

His phone was engaged, indicating that he was in. Impatiently Isabel donned boots and an ancient ski suit and set off for Chelsea on the bike, reasoning that she would have had to go there later in any case; her problem was too urgent to wait for a cheque to arrive in the post.

Her arrival outside the house coincided with that of a party of guests, who beat her to the door, carolling effusive greetings and braying about what perfectly vile weather it was, darling. Now that Adrian was in a position to return hospitality, his social life had miraculously revived, so much so that Isabel seldom heard from him these days, an inadmissible relief. He boomed a jovial welcome at his visitors, his smile fading as Isabel removed her helmet.

'I'm sorry if this is a bad time, Daddy,' she said, embarrassed. 'But can I see you for a moment? It's urgent.'

Without bothering to introduce her, he pointed her wordlessly towards his study and ushered his visitors into the living room. Isabel sat nervously awaiting him, admiring his antique writing desk and button-back swivel chair, new acquisitions since the weekend she had spent helping him move into the house and cleaning the place from top to bottom.

It was almost fifteen minutes before he rejoined her, with a glass of sherry in his hand, which he sipped reflectively while Isabel explained her problem. She did her best to blame it all on a mix-up at the bank, but she could tell from the look on his face he wasn't fooled.

'In other words, your wonderfully successful hack of a husband is failing to maintain you,' he said, with undisguised satisfaction.

'Patrick doesn't even know,' protested Isabel. Old loyalties died hard. 'Otherwise he'd have sorted it out by now. He's away on location and I can't reach him.'

'Don't lie to me, Isabel. If you want a loan, I expect you to be honest with me.'

Old grudges died hard as well, thought Isabel, squirming. He wanted her to say that he had been right about Patrick all along, to trade her pride and privacy for his patronage. How utterly degrading all this was!

So much for her so-called independence. So much for her newfound self-respect. Not that a mother could afford such a luxury. From the beginning of time women had endured any humiliation, rather than see their children suffer. And yet she rebelled; refusing to be bullied had become a habit.

'I'm being honest,' she said stubbornly.

'Come, come. Do you think I don't realize what's going on? He's left you for another woman, hasn't he?'

'As a matter of fact, he hasn't,' snapped Isabel. 'Though if he had, you're hardly in a position to cast the first stone.'

'That remark was unworthy of you, Isabel. Whatever mistakes I've made in my life, I've paid for them. As you are now having to do.'

He was back to his old self with a vengeance, thought Isabel. And now he was trying to turn her into her old self as well, a craven, dutiful daughter submitting humbly to yet another 'private talk' calculated to put her in the wrong.

'It isn't fair of you to make me sing for my supper like this,' she said. 'I never sent you away empty-handed.'

'I don't recall ever asking you for money,' Adrian reminded her. He was firmly on his dignity now, as impossible to unseat as a horseman carved in stone. 'You insisted that I take it.'

And so she had, in an attempt to purge her own hostile feelings towards him.

'Never mind about a loan, then,' she said, struggling to keep her temper. 'Just pay me back what you owe me.'

Adrian raised an infinitely expressive eyebrow.

'What *I* owe *you*? It appears that I completely misread the nature of your offer. I thought you were repaying a debt, not creating one. I thought, in my naïveté, that you were signalling your regret for having given credence to all those wicked lies Richard told you about me, lies he persuaded Toby to repeat until the poor child ended up believing them.'

Isabel stared at him, dumbstruck. Had he really convinced himself of his own innocence? Or was this the only way he could cope with his guilt?

'And now you tell me that you want paying back?' he hissed. The venom in his voice was like a slap in the face. 'Paying back for having blackmailed me into giving up my son, the way his cursed mother tried to do? Very well, then.'

His withdrew his cheque book from his desk drawer, scratched at it briefly with a gold fountain pen, and regally extended a cheque for ten pounds. 'There,' he said. 'Now I've paid you back.' He paused for a moment to let the words sink in. 'And now, if you'll excuse me, I have guests to attend to.'

Isabel sat stunned for a moment. So this was his revenge. It was as if he had been waiting, patiently, for just such a chance as this. It was almost a relief. At least neither of them had to pretend any more.

Slowly, deliberately, she tore the cheque into tiny pieces, glad now that it hadn't been for more. Never again would she put herself in this position. Never again would she throw herself on the mercy of a man, any man, including Patrick. If he couldn't support her, for whatever reason, she would have to find a way to support herself. One way or another, she would make her independence real . . .

She arrived home to find Ma on the telephone in the hall, wearing an overcoat over her dressing gown.

'Here she is now,' she said, gesturing at Isabel. 'Well, I'll say cheerio, then, son. You look after yourself now and don't work too hard.'

Trembling with more than the cold, Isabel took over the receiver, her mind suddenly as numb as her hands and feet.

'Hello,' she said woodenly. 'I've been trying to get hold of you for ages.'

'I've only just got your letter and the note Paula put through my door, I've been out of town and my phone was out of order. The problem was at this end. I've sorted it out now. There's an urgent transfer on its way.'

'Have you been short of money?' demanded Isabel, in a frozen voice.

'Of course not. The bank in LA mislaid my instructions.'

She tried to feel relief and couldn't. This was only a reprieve, not a solution. The solution wouldn't come from Patrick, only from herself.

'Isabel . . . I'm sorry. I –'

'It's all right,' she said, not wanting to hear any lies. 'Don't worry about it. Goodnight.'

'Goodnight,' said Patrick, replacing the receiver. And then, turning to Paula, 'She more or less hung up on me.'

'I don't blame her. She must have been at her wits' end. And she doesn't know the half of it. Why didn't you come to me before, instead of leaving her to struggle like that?'

Patrick ran his hands through his hair.

'I didn't want to sponge off you. I kept putting it off, hoping my luck would change. All the while I was winning, it seemed like a chance to get straight again and pay off all my debts. And it worked, at first. If I'd told Izzie, back in the summer, that we were nearly broke she'd have gone to pieces.'

Patrick had never been any good, thought Paula, at quitting when he was ahead. All the luck he'd had in his life had been frittered away against the promise of something better, something extra, something for nothing. He'd kept off the booze in Las Vegas all right, traded in that gain, like all his other gains, for yet another loss.

'And now you're completely broke. And unemployed, what-ever lies you've told Izzie. And likely to stay that way, by the sound of it.' No wonder he had been avoiding her lately. 'You had your chance over here and you blew it. The way you always have done, in your marriage as well as your career. And don't try to blame it on Izzie, either. You've used her as a scapegoat long enough.'

If only, Paula found herself thinking. If only she hadn't run away from Patrick, all those years ago. She wouldn't have pampered and weakened him, the way Izzie had done. She wouldn't have been afraid to fight him. She would have bawled him out and brought him to heel. And in the end, inevitably, he would have outgrown her, asserted himself, moved on. But by then she would have raised him up to be a man . . .

'I know you've stuck your neck out for me,' said Patrick. 'I know I've embarrassed you and let you down. That's why I've decided to pack up acting for good, get a proper job for once in my life. I'm going to go home, on Izzie's terms, as the lodger. What else can I do?'

He couldn't keep the bitterness out of his voice. Giving up acting was his way of punishing Izzie, as well as himself. Perhaps it would do him good to spend some time in the wilderness. Denied the use of his talent, he might learn to value it more . . .

She was spared the need to tell him so by a ring at the doorbell. Two men were standing there. One of them flashed a badge at her.

'Mrs Parry? Los Angeles police department. It's about your husband. Can we come in?'

Their voices seemed to echo, the way they did in an empty theatre.

'What's happened to him? Has he had an accident?'

'Mrs Parry, I have to tell you that your husband is under arrest. We'd like to ask you a few questions.'

26 May 1974

Dear Izzie
Thank you for your lovely long letter. I'm sorry it's taken me so long to reply. And sorry you had to hear about what happened in the newspapers – I was hoping the trial wouldn't make the English press – but I just wasn't up to telling you before. I suppose I didn't want to believe it was happening.

Stupid of me not to realize, I suppose, that we were getting too rich too quick. I don't know how much you already know, but the health shops were basically just a front, Vince's way of laundering and investing the drug money so as to fool me,

419

along with everyone else. He did it for my sake, of course. So that he could buy me a baby, buy me parts, give me back everything we'd lost. He's never been able to accept that I love him for himself, without his lousy money.

Anyhow, Vince isn't the type of mug who ends up taking the fall, which is why he agreed to grass on some bigger fish in return for immunity and a new identity somewhere they can't find us. Which means leading a blameless unobtrusive life on what's left of our ill-gotten gains. (Quite a lot, as it happens. Vince had already sewn things up so that I'd be well provided for if anything happened to him.) Naturally my acting career is over – no great loss to the world, I know – because I'll have to maintain 'low visibility' in future (as if it wasn't low enough already), but I'll probably have another nose job and dye my hair, to avoid being recognized. So it's an ill wind as far as the long-suffering public is concerned.

Naturally the adoption went down the pan as well. That was the worst part of it for both of us. But once we get our new blameless honest-Joe IDs we're going to try again.

So don't worry about me, okay? And many, many congrats about the fish finger commercial. Talk about a family concern. The old girl must be wetting herself at the thought of seeing all of you on the box at once. I'm not surprised you walked the audition, collectively you're so photogenic it isn't true. As you say, it ain't Shakespeare, but as long as they pay you lots of lovely lolly what the hell.

Don't know when you'll next hear from me. The trial starts tomorrow and then as soon as it's over Vince will be released from protective custody – even I don't know where they're hiding him – and then we do our disappearing act God knows where. It'll be a relief to leave the house after all this time. I've been more or less confined to barracks ever since this thing started, with two plain-clothes cops as house guests, in case someone tries to get at Vince through me. Better than a movie, isn't it?

Oodles of love to you and all the kids.
Paula

It would all be over soon, thought Paula. And then Patrick, who had stuck by her since this nightmare began, would be free to leave, having wrapped the non-existent TV movie Isabel thought he was making (never to be seen, of course, in the UK). Had he really hung around all this time for her sake? Or had he just lost his nerve about going home? Or was it simply a quid pro quo, in exchange for her topping up Izzie's bank balance each month? Not that it mattered. She had been too relieved to have him here to quibble about his motives. No one else wanted to know her right now, and she couldn't have borne the fear and isolation without the security of a friendly face, the face of someone who owed her, to whom she didn't need to feel too grateful.

She woke up next morning feeling almost euphoric that Vince's day in court had arrived at last. The local TV news was covering the trial, which she would view from a safe distance. She switched the set on while she drank her morning coffee. Pictures of the accused were flashed up on the screen, men with lawyers as sharp as their suits, men who relied on other people to take the rap upon pain of something worse than prison.

'I'm not afraid of them,' Vince had said stubbornly. 'I'm much more afraid of spending what's left of my life in gaol, without you.'

There had been no remorse, other than at his own stupidity at getting caught out by some undercover cop, thereby exposing Paula to suspicion and, later, danger. He had scant sympathy for the luckless junkies at the end of the trading chain; they would always find someone to supply them, he said. The only way to put the dealers out of business was to make the stuff legal and tax it, like fags and booze, lethally addictive drugs by any other name, sanctified by social and commercial acceptability. To his mind the law was as two-faced as the society it claimed to protect. Paula didn't care about the ethics of it all; she just wanted him back.

Patrick arrived earlier than usual, letting himself in with his own key and submitting to the routine frisking even he had to endure.

'Did you get any sleep?' he asked, bending to kiss the top of her head. He seemed preoccupied.

'Thanks to mother's little helpers.'

'Have you had any breakfast?'

'I'm not hungry. Stop fussing, will you? I'll be glad to see the back of you, honest I will.' Odd how they had swapped roles. Patrick looking after her, instead of the other way round. She turned round as she spoke and saw immediately from his face that something was wrong, something that had nothing to do with the trial.

'What's the matter?'

'Nothing.'

'Tell me.'

He made a show of reluctance before blurting out, 'I spoke to Izzie last night, to tell her I'd be home soon. I told her she could have things her own way, separate rooms and the rest, until we saw how things worked out, like she said she wanted, last time I was home.'

'And?' prompted Paula.

'She said she'd been doing a lot of thinking since then. She wants me to move out as soon as I can find somewhere else. She wants a legal separation.'

Paula was less surprised than he evidently was. Nothing Izzie did would surprise her any more. Poor bloody Patrick. This would either be the end of him or the making of him.

'So did she say why she had changed her mind?' said Paula, flicking her lighter.

'She didn't need to. I've become surplus to requirements, haven't I, now that she's started earning her own living. Or rather getting the kids to earn their own living. This commercial is pure exploitation. I ought to put a stop to it.'

'Don't be such a killjoy,' snorted Paula. 'They're all having the time of their lives.'

'Money's all she thinks about these days. She even boned up on the law – or so she says, I expect it was Oliver Briggs again, giving her free advice – and applied to have the rent reduced, ended up paying less than when we first moved in. The landlord threatened to evict her, of course, but it turns out that there's some legal loophole and she's become a protected tenant. And meanwhile he's got to do a great long list of repairs, by order of the public health department.'

'Clever girl.'

'Not only that, she went and blackmailed that fancy school of Emily's into reducing the fees, by threatening to take her away. Apparently they don't want to lose the credit for getting her into Oxford at fifteen.'

'Good for her. So what has she told the kids? And your mother?'

'She wants us to break the news to them together. She wants me to find a place nearby and, quote, "make an effort to see a lot more of them than you did when you were living at home". And she doesn't want any maintenance either. She's told me to put whatever I can afford into a savings account for the kids. So I may as well take it easy from now on.'

In other words, he would lose all incentive to get his act together, embark on a downward spiral of self-indulgence and self-pity. And there wasn't a damn thing she could do about it . . .

She wrenched her attention back to the screen. The defence attorney was giving an impromptu press conference, saying that the case against his client relied on the evidence of one unreliable witness who would be quickly discredited under cross-examination. Paula blew a raspberry at him. Vince was not among the arrivals outside the courthouse; he would be smuggled in, heavily guarded, via a back or side entrance. She imagined him in the witness box, poker-faced. He had always been ice cold under pressure . . .

The camera cut the defence off in mid-sentence. For a moment the screen went blank. And then the anchor-man, in the studio, appeared with a news flash.

'We've just received reports of an explosion involving the key witness for the prosecution . . .' Paula tried to cry out, and couldn't. '. . . Vincent Parry. Parry and two police officers were killed instantly by a car bomb, which went off as an armoured police van made its way towards the courthouse. Several other vehicles were damaged by the blast, and nearby windows were blown out. An estimated twenty people are believed injured . . .'

She didn't burst into tears or shriek 'Oh no!' the way it always happened in the movies. She remained rigid, dry-eyed, dumb, numb, unaware of Patrick pressing her face into his chest or the tears that nestled like warm drewdrops in her hair.

'There they are,' said Grace, Vince's elderly housekeeper, as Patrick and Paula approached the barrier. She ran forward to greet them while Isabel held back, shocked at the ravages grief had wrought on Paula's face.

423

Patrick acknowledged Isabel stiffly with a quick peck on the cheek. Paula exchanged Grace's embrace for Isabel's, making short work of it. 'You shouldn't have come,' she said thickly. 'Still, at least nobody else has, thank God.' They had travelled under false names, to avoid the press.

'Toby's outside in the car.' Thanks to the fish finger contract, the family was mobile again. 'Would you like to come back to our place first?'

Paula shook her head. 'Best go straight to the cottage. I'm not very good company at the moment. I might start hurling your china around or something. I've already smashed all my own.'

Toby was parked outside in a no-waiting zone; he had hitched home from college specially, to lend his support. He got out and kissed Paula awkwardly before helping her and Grace into the back, next to Isabel, while Patrick took the passenger seat, all of them unnaturally quiet.

'If you'd like me to stay with you for a while . . .' began Isabel.

'I'm staying with her,' put in Patrick. 'Sorry to spring this on you, Toby. But Izzie's asked me to move out.'

'She already told me,' said Toby gruffly. 'But the kids don't know yet.'

Isabel reached for Paula's hand and held it during the drive. It felt very small and cold and limp. Paula had always vibrated with life, not least when she had thought that she was dying, but now all the spirit seemed to have gone out of her, even her determined wisecracks sounded stilted.

'If you fancy a fun day out for the kids,' she said, freeing her hand to light a Marlborough, 'I'm throwing a funeral bash, once the body clears customs. Or rather, what's left of it. The cops are hanging on to it for the moment, still trying to find all the pieces, I guess.'

'Why don't you close your eyes and try to get some rest?' put in Grace. 'Did the doctor give you anything to help you sleep?'

'To help me die, more like. None of your NHS stinginess over there. I've got enough in my bag to bump off a convention of sumo wrestlers. Pity I'm such a frigging coward.'

'Just in case she's not,' said Patrick, turning round, 'I confiscated them on the plane, while she was asleep. So don't worry.' He caught Isabel's eye briefly, as if to say 'I won't let her do

424

anything stupid. I'll look after her the way I looked after you, remember?'

It seemed a long time ago since his mercy dash to Beverly Hills. He had come to Paula's rescue as he had once come to Isabel's, like some wayward guardian angel. And that, of course, was when her troubles had really begun . . .

The cottage smelt of flowers and home baking. It was here that Paula had recuperated from her nose job, from her car accident, from her divorce, here that she had held her coming-out-of-plaster party, here that she had donned her wedding dress, here that she and Vince had retreated, briefly, after his financial ruin before leaving the country. And here that she had come to recover from the latest blow life had dealt her. Isabel followed her up to her room, leaving Grace to serve tea to the men down below. She knew better than to say something trite like 'I'm so dreadfully sorry about Vince'. She just put her arms around her wordlessly, but Paula didn't, or rather couldn't, respond. She had never been able to handle sympathy.

'It was nice of you to come and fetch me,' she said briskly, extricating herself, 'but I'm in a filthy mood so I won't ask you to stay.' And then, with typical flippancy, 'If it freaks you out, Patrick staying here, I can easily tell him to piss off.'

'Don't be silly.'

'I thought to myself, might as well use him as a punchbag for a bit, if Izzie doesn't object. I can always sock him a few for her while I'm at it.'

'I think I've socked him quite enough already.'

'And yourself, I'll bet.'

'Yes. But it had to be done.' And then, whether this was the right time to tell her or not, 'Specially once I found out about the money.'

'What?'

'I sensed that he was lying to me, that night he phoned. It was all too glib. Then the next few payments came in regular as clockwork, always for the same amount, and always bang on time. So I got my bank to check the name and branch of the American bank that had transferred it. Then I rang them, and said I was Paula Dorland, alias Mrs Paula Parry, and had they made the payment I'd requested to a Mrs Isabel Delaney in London, England. And they said, "Yes, ma'am." '

Paula attempted to shrug it off. 'So I helped him out. It was no big deal.'

'Not for you, perhaps. But it must have been, for him. He'd never have come to you unless things were really desperate. What happened?'

'He had a few bad breaks. Jobs that didn't come off. He didn't want to worry you.'

'He didn't think I could cope with it, you mean. He's always underestimated me, he's never learned to treat me as an equal. Well, now he's going to have to. I'm not going to be a burden on him any longer. Or rather on you.'

'But –'

'I just wanted to say thank you, that's all. And to let you know that I don't want Patrick to come between us. Whatever happens, I want us to stay friends.'

'Whatever happens?'

'Whatever happens,' repeated Isabel, not without difficulty. She had told herself that she didn't mind if he found somebody else, that she would welcome it, even. Somebody else, anybody else, but not Paula . . .

'It hasn't, yet, in case you're wondering. But you know me. The original sex-mad little tart. Silly to pretend he won't try his luck, sooner or later.'

'Paula . . . don't let him hurt you, will you?'

'You flatter him. Nothing can hurt me ever again, not after this. If he tries to use me to make you jealous, that'll only hurt you. You're the one who loves him, not me.'

Isabel didn't believe her. A part of her had always known that Paula still loved Patrick, that she always had done, Vince or no Vince.

'Now bugger off, like a good girl,' said Paula, 'so that I can get some shuteye. I'll ring you.'

Isabel left her, hoping that she wanted the privacy to cry. Toby and Grace made themselves scarce as soon as she appeared, leaving her uneasily alone with Patrick.

'We need to talk to the children,' she began.

'I'm sure you're more than capable of doing it without me. They don't need me any more, according to you.'

This was proving to be even harder than she had expected. But if she weakened now, all the agony would have been for nothing, they would all suffer more in the end.

'They've always needed you,' she said. 'They still do. But you were never there, even when you lived at home. You were never more than a weekend father, Patrick.'

'I had to earn a living, dammit!'

'That wasn't it. You've always preferred to spend money on them rather than time. Now I want you to do the opposite. And you can start off by letting them know that none of this is their fault.'

'No, it's all mine, I suppose.'

'I never said that. For God's sake don't do what I did. Don't blame yourself. Guilt gets to be a vice, believe me. We'll never be at peace with each other until we're at peace with ourselves.'

It was easy to say, hard to do. Like every skill it required practice, and time, and motivation. She was still struggling to master it herself.

'Very philosophical,' muttered Patrick, stubbing out his cigarette. 'All right, we'll tell them together, tomorrow. Make out we're the best of friends, okay?'

Isabel nodded, relieved. They were both at their best when they were performing.

'Just one more thing,' she said. 'You'll be getting a solicitor's letter, about the separation . . .'

'You didn't waste much time, did you?'

'I know it hurts, Patrick. It hurts me too.' More than he would ever believe. But he would never accept that she meant business unless she made things official. This way he would be free to start a new life, as she had done. 'But you've got to promise me one thing. However much it hurts, don't take it out on Paula. Hit back at me all you like, I can take it. But leave her alone.'

She left the room quickly, before he could respond, and waited for Toby in the car, furtively wiping her eyes.

'I never thought you'd go through with it, you know,' he said, rejoining her. 'And neither did he, I'll bet.'

Isabel blew her nose.

'Did he say anything when I was upstairs with Paula?'

Toby didn't answer for a moment.

'He just asked me to look after you,' he said.

427

The first few months were one long blur of pain interrupted only by sleep, the sticky, foggy, chemical sleep that left her thick-headed and unrefreshed. Patrick rationed the pills ruthlessly, gradually cutting them down until she finally managed her first night without them. A night that ended prematurely at dawn, when she woke, dry-mouthed and panic-stricken as always, consumed with a craving for the most powerful and addictive drug of all: work.

A craving underlaid by a crippling lethargy. She was like a stroke victim, struggling to move her paralysed limbs, her will exceeding her capability. It was Patrick who translated her feeble twitchings into action, who put the advertisement in *The Stage* stating simply, *New theatre company seeks strong contemporary plays*, provoking an instant deluge of dog-eared much-rejected scripts. Established playwrights had no interest in entrusting their work to some upstart company with no track record, and new, talented ones were, as ever, thin on the ground.

In the end they settled for a revival, a small studio production of Strindberg's *Miss Julie*, a part Paula had always longed to play, with Patrick in the sinister role of Jean, the valet, whose affair with his employer's daughter leads to her suicide. Paula might have been tempted to follow her example by now, if it hadn't been for Patrick – not just because he had eased her pain, but because she seemed to ease his.

The play was out of copyright, which spared them the need to pay royalties, and there was only one other small speaking part, bar their own, which all helped to keep down overheads. Likewise the hire of one of the small fringe theatres which were mushrooming all over London. Patrick volunteered to direct himself, allegedly as an economy measure, but in reality because he had his own firm ideas on how it should be done. Working to a budget was a psychological, rather than a financial, necessity; Paula couldn't bear to be written off as a more-money-than-sense dilettante who could afford to fail. And as a proportion of any profits would go to charity, it made sense to maximize them, to launder the dirty money Vince had left her into something clean again, given that she wasn't soft-headed enough simply to give it all away.

Or to look any gift horses in the mouth. People she had never seen before had turned up at the funeral. Shady-looking men in camel coats with astrakhan collars, their blowsy wives dripping jewellery and furs. And faceless types who didn't quite fit, who might well have been CID masquerading as mourners, watching to see what came out of the woodwork. All of them oozed sympathy and hushed assurances of support. Strangers pressed respectable business cards into her black-gloved palm, strangers whom Patrick now telephoned, asking if they would like to invest, say a thousand, in the grieving widow's recuperative venture. They nearly all responded; to them it was small change after all. However they had made the stuff, perhaps this way it would end up doing some good.

Neville Seaton, following an approach from Isabel, at Paula's request, allowed them to use his name as an 'associate director' to give the project artistic credibility, a measure to which Patrick, much to Paula's surprise, had raised no objection.

'It might help people take us seriously,' he conceded. 'Given that I'm best known as a hack, and the press won't be able to resist raking up your sordid life story yet again. Talking of which, no one's ever going to believe that we're just good friends.'

The truth sounded so unlikely – that Patrick hadn't laid a finger on her, nor on anyone else, for that matter, that he spent long virtuous evenings closeted with a pile of reference books, annotating the text in his illegible scholar's handwriting. She had always assumed Patrick to be a gut-reaction actor, like herself, not one of those types who researched the part and analysed the meaning of every line, like Izzie. She had forgotten how brainy he was supposed to be.

'I do wish you'd leave off,' she said. 'There's no point giving a thickie like me any long-winded intellectual theories about the play.'

'I don't intend to. I've been on the receiving end of those, remember? This isn't an ego trip, quite the reverse. I'm even more scared than you are. I've spent my entire career slagging off directors, so it would be poetic justice, wouldn't it, if I made a hash of doing the job myself.'

'You should have worked with Neville when you had the chance,' said Paula heartlessly. 'He's brilliant.'

'I know. That's the real reason I funked doing *Hamlet*. In case I didn't measure up.'

His profound lack of self-confidence, masked by an apparent surfeit of it, had always been his undoing. But now it was as if he had finally reached his professional coming of age. Rehearsals were a revelation, with Patrick, that most selfish of actors, far less concerned with his own performance than hers, as was apparent to everyone involved in the project. The backstage staff might be young and inexperienced, deliberately so, the better to mould them to Patrick's way of working, but they learned quickly, responding well to his hands-on democratic style. As did Paula. She was used to winging it, getting through any part with a mixture of bluff and instinct, a technique which had worked, after a fashion, without ever making her feel that she was doing it right. But now she was forced to dig deep inside herself, to plumb her own pain, to use it as fuel and convert it into energy.

'Julie's afraid of her own sexuality,' Patrick had told her, as they spewed scripted desire and venom at each other, day after arduous day. 'She despises herself for being female.'

Paula understood that, only too well. Vince hadn't been dead six months, she didn't ought to be lusting after Patrick. If only he would leap on her, at least she could blame him for her own weakness. But he was treating her exactly as Vince had done at the beginning, with infuriating, infinitely titillating respect . . .

'I don't have the depth for a part like this,' she said, exhausted, after dinner one night, struggling against the longing for a stiff brandy, for a whole chocolate gâteau, for instant artificial sleep, most of all for Patrick. 'We should have got hold of a proper actress, like Izzie.'

'I would never have the nerve to direct Izzie, not that she'd deign to let me. And besides, you're going to be dynamite.'

'Don't know why I should be finding it so hard. I've seduced enough men in real life, after all. Including you.'

'I seem to remember it being the other way round.'

'Rubbish. No one bothers to seduce a pushover like me. Why peel the spuds yourself when you can pick up a bag of chips?'

'Is that what I made you feel like? A bag of chips?'

'Every man I ever had made me feel like that, sooner or later.

430

Cheap and easy. All except Vince. With him I was expensive and bloody hard work. Right up to the end.'

He put an arm round her, sending a tremor hurtling jaggedly round her body, as if trapped inside a pinball machine.

'I was never taken in by that act of yours,' he said. 'I knew you were pretending, same as me. You know the real reason I made a play for you? Because I liked you. The sex was just an excuse. In those days I didn't know how to get close to a woman without going to bed with her. And now I do. You're the best friend I ever had, Paula. And I want to be yours. I don't intend to spoil it this time the way I did before.'

She searched his eyes for a moment. She had ascribed his immaculate behaviour to decency, restraint, the good manners to bide his time. Not to a total lack of desire. Not to a kind of love . . .

A love she didn't want to lose. As she surely would if he realized how she felt. She smiled and nodded, pretending like mad. From now on she would have to pretend as never before.

16

Summer 1975–Spring 1976

Love sought is good, but given unsought is better.

William Shakespeare – Twelfth Night

Isabel was getting used to being stopped in the street. Nobody knew her real name of course. They just recognized her as that fish finger woman on the telly. Often they would commiserate, knowingly, on the shortcomings of her screen husband, who was invariably depicted bodging the DIY, or tinkering ineffectually with the car, or being unable to help the kids with their homework, in sharp contrast to the easy-peasy omnipotence of Mum. Female consumers, according to market research, loved to see men portrayed as inept buffoons and identified strongly with Isabel's air of amused feminine superiority.

Steven Ratchett, alias Mr Fish Finger, with whom Isabel conducted a tepid off-screen romance, was a lightweight jobbing actor by his own admission. He was sociable, sophisticated, and a perfect gentleman. He was attentive, considerate, undemanding, and unthreatening. He was unlike Patrick in every possible way.

Clothes hung on him immaculately. He could keep a crease in a pair of jeans and never lost one half of a pair of cuff links. He shaved every day, even on Sundays. When he cooked for her in his Gloucester Road bachelor flat – imagine Patrick cooking! – he weighed and measured his ingredients with care and washed up as he went along. An informed, fussy shopper, he would sniff melons and inspect the gills of fish and require the butcher to do complicated surgery on hand-picked joints. Like Isabel, he knew exactly what everything should cost. Like Isabel he preferred wine to beer and coffee to tea. Unlike Patrick, he would never have dreamed of eating grapes without washing them or demanding a bacon sandwich after making love, not that Isabel had put the latter assumption to the test. Despite his battery of nice-guy virtues, Steven didn't turn her on, which was one of the reasons she liked him.

Paula, with a certain mischief, had personally invited him to the first-night party of the second Encore Theatre Group revival, *A Streetcar named Desire*, thus ensuring that Patrick got to meet him, something Isabel had strenuously avoided until now – not that she could admit that to Steven. She could hardly say 'My husband will write you off as a prattling theatrical phoney. He's bound to be rude and sarcastic. I'd much rather you didn't come with me.' Trust Paula to put her on the spot.

Poor Steven had gone out of his way to praise the production (which he would have done anyway, regardless of its merits), employing any number of hyperbolic clichés while Isabel waited, embarrassed by him, for Patrick to embarrass her as well. But he had accepted Steven's tribute with uncharacteristic graciousness, either to thwart her expectations or because his newfound confidence had mellowed him, or both. If he was jealous, he was too clever, or too proud, to let it show; after all, they were legally separated, he had no rights over her any more. Ironically, they got on better now than they had ever done in the past. As Emily had remarked approvingly, with her usual solemn candour, Dad seemed much more grown up these days.

After years of boredom and frustration and disillusionment he was enjoying his work again. After years of being ordered about by autocratic directors or pandered to by weak ones, he took a pride in doing the job properly. He might not be earning much, yet, but the recent sale of *Stop Press* to Australia and New Zealand brought in a healthy quarterly cheque which he endorsed over to Isabel, to spend on or save for the children. He had lost his self-defensive swagger and begun walking tall instead.

Isabel, likewise, had come into her own. She was financially independent, thanks to the commercials, which paid more per hour than she had earned in a month in the theatre. Her teaching schedule was flexible enough to fit in with her family commitments, especially now that the girls were old enough to be left in charge if necessary. She had more freedom than she had had since she was single. And still she wasn't satisfied. She wanted more.

Which was why she hadn't bothered to prevaricate when Patrick

433

had asked her, with studious formality, to play Yelena opposite his Astrov in *Uncle Vanya*, the next Encore production, which was due to go into rehearsal as soon as *Streetcar* finished its post-London provincial tour. It was the toughest challenge she could have set herself. Much tougher than accepting a lucrative part in a TV sitcom or a tempting offer from Neville, both of which would have given her a good excuse to say no. But neither would have exorcized the demons that still troubled her. She needed to prove, to herself and to Patrick, that she wasn't afraid to work with him, even though – or rather because – she was.

On-stage chemistry was an unpredictable thing. People who got on well in real life often failed to connect professionally, and the reverse was also true. Was she capable of playing a love scene with Patrick without her real feelings, whatever they were, coming to the surface? Did she have enough self-discipline and self-knowledge to separate life from art? Seeing him with Paula in *Streetcar*, you would have sworn that they were lovers; the public certainly thought so. As she would have done herself, if Paula hadn't taken pains to deny it, albeit in the most off-hand fashion.

'If we started all that nonsense up again, it wouldn't last five minutes before we started killing each other, the way we did before. Encore is too important to me to risk falling out with my biggest asset. If we don't deny the gossip it's because he's good cover. This way I don't get pestered by anyone else, which I would do, what with me being a rich widow.'

Paula's much-acclaimed performance as Blanche Du Bois was, however, infinitely less draining than the one she was obliged to give in real life, unbeknown to either Isabel or Patrick, one which would be mirrored by her role as Sonia, nursing her unrequited love for Patrick's Astrov.

She knew now what Patrick was working towards, not that he ever admitted it. Not just critical acclaim, not just the respect of his peers, not just artistic satisfaction. More than all those things, he wanted Izzie back. He had set out to prove to her that he was stronger, braver, tougher, more mature than the man she had married. Sufficiently so not to be fazed by the likes of Steven Ratchett. (Paula had little doubt that Izzie was trying to make Patrick jealous, whether she realized it or not.) He was clever enough to keep her guessing, to woo her from a distance, to watch and wait till the time was ripe, however long it took.

And meanwhile Paula made it her business to help things along, feeding them little snippets about each other, passing on un-acknowledged messages, acting as a party to the slow, subtle foreplay that would lead to their eventual reunion. A project that was close to her heart, however much she dreaded its conclusion. Once Patrick was gone . . . it was like contemplating death. Meanwhile living was quite hard enough to be going on with.

'Mum!' bellowed Sophie, always first to the phone. 'It's some man for you.'

'Ask who it is,' called Isabel from the kitchen, 'and tell him I'll ring him back.'

'Mrs Delaney's busy at the moment,' she heard Sophie drawl, anxious to despatch the caller and leave the line free for some spotty youth from St Mary Magdalene's youth club. 'What? Oh. Just a minute.'

'He says he's the Foreign Office,' she announced, putting her head round the door. 'It's about Uncle Richard.'

Isabel abandoned a pile of chopped onions, wiping her eyes on her apron.

'Hello? This is Isabel Delaney. Is my brother in some kind of trouble?' She hadn't heard from Richard in over a year.

'He's presented himself as indigent to the consul in Bangkok, applying for a passage home. I've been asked that we inform you of his arrival . . .'

Isabel scribbled quickly on the pad by the phone.

'Is he all right?'

'I assume so. That is the only information I have.'

'I'll be at the airport to meet him. Thank you for letting me know. Goodbye.'

Richard would be home, tomorrow! Paula would be over the moon . . .

Excited, Isabel dialled the cottage in Kent straight away, glad to have got the news before *Streetcar* went up to Birmingham the following day. Paula ought to have time to come to the airport with her before the company hit the road.

Patrick answered the phone.

'Guess what?' blurted out Isabel. 'Richard's on his way home . . .'

He listened in silence before saying, 'That's all we need. Don't tell Paula, for God's sake. Not yet, anyway.'

'What? Why not? It's good news, isn't it?'

'Since when has Richard been good news?' He kept his voice low. 'If he's finally rejoined the human race, which I doubt, well and good. But the last thing Paula needs at the moment is a washed-up junkie touting for sympathy and wrecking her concentration. Don't be taken in by the brave face she puts on for her public, including you. She going through a bad patch. And don't you dare tell her I told you.'

'What kind of bad patch?' She felt diminished by having to ask. Once upon a time she, Isabel, had been Paula's sole confidante; now she was one of her 'public'.

'Remember how Toby used to be? One minute you'd think he was making headway, and then he'd start playing up again? I thought she was getting over Vince, but in the last few weeks she's deteriorated. She's been losing her temper a lot. Trying to make me lose mine. Having a lot of bad dreams. So check Richard out first, will you, before you get her all worked up? Please, Izzie.' He kept his voice calm, reasonable, shifting all the responsibility on to her. 'Touring's always a strain and I don't want any upsets.'

'Oh, all right,' conceded Isabel crossly. 'We mustn't take any risks with the play, now must we. I hereby declare you an honorary Mallory.'

It was unlike her to be so provocative. But Patrick let the jibe pass.

'Where is he going to stay?' he asked levelly.

'With us, of course. Where else?'

'I don't want him bringing any drugs into the house.'

'And I do, I suppose? What do you take me for? Besides, if he's broke, he won't have the money to buy any drugs.'

'Until he asks you for some, and you give it to him.'

'Will you kindly stop telling me what I will and won't and can and can't do?' These days she had no compunction about arguing with him.

'I wish I could yell back at you,' he said softly. 'But Paula might hear.'

'I'm not yelling!'

'Don't stop, I rather like it . . . Here she is now,' he added, raising his voice to its normal level. 'Remember what I said, won't you?'

'Remember what?' said Paula, taking over the phone. 'What have you two been whispering about?'

'Whispering?'

'He was keeping his voice down, so I couldn't hear from the living room. Are you holding out on me about something?'

'Of course not,' said Isabel evasively, confirming Paula's suspicions. The wrong ones, as it happened, but that didn't stop them being right.

Having waved goodbye, three years before, to a long-haired, bearded, would-be hippy, Isabel was relieved to see a smart, clean-shaven Richard saunter through the barrier, dressed in a white tropical suit. Until she noticed that it hung on him loosely, that his face was gaunt and pale, his eyes deeply lined and his once vivid red hair dull and streaked with grey. Close to, he looked nearer fifty than thirty-seven.

'Izzie darling!' he greeted her urbanely, as if she were meeting him off a pleasure trip. She hugged him, blinking back the tears. Her arms went round much further than in the past; the old Richard had always inclined to tubbiness.

'You're so thin.'

'That's what these nasty tropical bugs do to you. Hope the FO didn't put the wind up you.'

'They just said you were destitute.'

'Well, so I am. Flat stony. But don't worry. A pretty boy like me never starves.' He made a camp gesture. 'So how's tricks? How are the kids? And what about Patrick? Have you left the miserable bastard yet?'

Isabel smiled. He was still the same old waspish, bitchy Richard.

'I asked him to leave, actually. A couple of years ago now.'

'Thank God for that. Does that mean I can crash out *chez toi* for a bit?'

'Of course.' And then, remembering her resolution, 'As long as

437

. . . Richard, you're not still on LSD or anything, are you? I've got the kids to think of.'

'Poor Izzie. Acid's so horribly *passé*. Fear not, your sweet innocent sproglings have nothing to fear from me. So are you working?'

'Never mind about my news. I want yours first. You never wrote me a single letter. Just those stupid postcards once in a blue moon, without even an address to write back to.'

'Darling, I wrote screeds and screeds. But you know how dreadful the post is in foreign parts . . .'

His responses to her questions were infuriatingly vague. Kevin and he had parted company a year after leaving home, or it might have been two, when Kevin had found himself a sugar daddy in Singapore. Since then Richard claimed to have made ends meet by working in 'bars and hotels'. Isabel couldn't imagine him waiting tables or carrying suitcases or doing anything that didn't involve the theatre.

'Oh the theatre,' he said dismissively. 'After Renegade failed I lost heart for it. Talking of which, how's Paula?'

'Not too good. Vince was killed in America, last year, she took it very badly. He was mixed up in drug dealing.'

'Drug dealing?' He looked suitably shocked. 'Trust Vince to make money out of the lousy stuff. So is she still out there?'

'No. She's touring at the moment. Actually . . . she's living with Patrick now.'

'Ah,' said Richard knowingly. 'That figures.'

Isabel swallowed the urge to explain; Richard would never believe that they weren't lovers. In a way it was easier if he thought they were, same as everybody else.

The children were still at school when they got home. Luckily Ma's sight was too poor to notice the change in Richard's appearance. He declined the meal Isabel had prepared, saying that all he wanted to do was sleep.

'I take it Fay hasn't croaked,' he asked as she showed him upstairs, 'and left us lots of loot?'

'No. She's still soldiering on, poor thing. Daddy's out of jail, by the way. He's written a book.'

'I know. I had a flick through it, in a bookshop in Bangkok. How is the old bastard?'

'All right, as far as I know,' shrugged Isabel. 'I haven't seen him in over a year.'

'I'm surprised at you, Cordelia,' said Richard, impressed. 'What's happened to you? You've toughened up.'

'You bet I have. And I'll be tough with you too, if I catch you misbehaving. Any exotic substances and you're out on your ear.'

'Frisk me,' said Richard, raising his arms. 'And don't forget my crotch. It's simply ages since anyone touched me up.' He shuddered in mock ecstasy.

'I expect that's full of dirty washing,' said Isabel, still suspicious, picking up his battered suitcase. 'And that suit could do with dry cleaning. Hand it over.'

He removed it without demur, pirouetting and throwing both halves of it over his shoulder *à la* Gypsy Rose Lee, while she unpacked for him, reassuring herself that he hadn't smuggled anything illegal through customs.

'I'll keep this shirt till you've washed the others,' he said vaguely when Isabel asked for that as well. 'It's the only clean one I've got left. Izzie . . . I hate to ask, but can you lend me a tenner?'

'Have twenty. More if you need it. And don't worry about repaying it just yet. Oh, it's so nice to have you back!'

'Still the same old soft-hearted Izzie,' he murmured, returning her embrace fondly and sounding quite emotional, for him. Too bad if Patrick didn't want him here, thought Isabel stubbornly. Richard was her brother, he was ill and he was skint. She thought of all the cash he had slipped her when the children were small, of the time he had offered to take them all in when they were facing eviction, of the way Renegade had footed the bill for the legal battle over Toby. He might have let her down in other ways, but would never have turned her away when she was in trouble.

'Get some rest now. Is there anything I can fetch you?'

'Er . . . you haven't got anything for constipation, have you? I took too much stuff for the old Montezuma's.'

'There's syrup of figs in the bathroom cabinet, if you can bear it. The key's on top, so Patrick junior can't reach. Help yourself.'

She thought no more about it. She was too pleased to have him home.

Patrick rang that night, from a telephone box in Birmingham.

'So, how did you find him?'

'He's lost a lot of weight and he looks pretty rough, thanks to some tropical bug he picked up. So perhaps you were right about not telling Paula yet,' she conceded, before he said it first. 'By the time the tour is over I'll have fattened him up a bit.'

'And you're absolutely sure he's clean?'

Isabel suppressed a twinge of doubt. 'I went through his clothes and his luggage. There was nothing there.'

'I expect he was pleased as punch that we'd split up.'

'He thought it was mildly hilarious, yes. I hope you're going to try and be civil to him, for Paula's sake.'

'For yours,' he said quietly. 'Isabel . . .'

A long pause. A tingle that travelled down the telephone line and up her arm and onward.

'Yes?'

'I'll call you again tomorrow.'

He did, and every day thereafter, in the same clandestine manner, though they talked about a lot more than Richard. Paula, meanwhile, called her from the pay phone in a succession of digs and cheap hotels – she was slumming it with the rest of the company, in the interests of group morale – sounding her usual flip self and demanding to know who on earth she had been rabbiting to, her phone had been engaged for *hours* . . . a situation which Isabel blamed on the garrulous twins.

She had easily persuaded Richard not to contact Paula till she got back to London; sociable as ever, he seemed to have any number of other people on his visiting list. He slept till late, not emerging until he had dressed with his usual dandyish care, after which he would go out for the rest of the day, not returning till the early hours of the following morning.

'How are you managing for money?' said Isabel. He had repaid her twenty pounds almost straight away and declined all offers of a further loan.

'People owe me. I've been calling in my debts.'

440

'But they won't keep owing you for ever. Perhaps you should sign on, or something.'

'Sign on? God forbid. Look, if you must know, I've wangled an allowance out of the old man.'

'Daddy gave you money? How on earth did you manage that?'

'How do you think?'

'Richard! You didn't!'

'Why not? It worked before, didn't it? Here, have some of it, in lieu of rent. He can afford it.'

Surreptitiously Isabel searched his room several times but found nothing incriminating, enabling her to report to Patrick, truthfully if not quite honestly, that there was 'no problem'. Certainly Richard looked less haggard now that he had visited his old doctor and got a prescription; their agreed plan was for Isabel to take him to the house in Kent, the weekend after the tour, as a surprise for Paula.

By then she had got used – no, addicted – to Patrick's daily illicit calls, more illicit by far than they purported to be. Richard was just a pretext, not just to talk, really talk, for the first time in years, but to talk without Paula's knowledge, Paula who hovered like a ghost between them, Paula who was closer to both of them than they had ever been to each other, until now. No matter that Paula had always encouraged them to kiss and make up, that only made things more difficult. They both knew that she would be lost without Patrick, just as Patrick would once have been lost without her, that what she had with him was a kind of marriage, one which could not be severed without pain.

And so, for Paula's sake – or that was their excuse – they learned to make love without touching, in a way they would never have dared to do face to face. It was all perfectly innocent, and almost unbearably erotic . . .

Patrick had always been able to do incredible things with his voice, to explore and caress and arouse with it, to make every word, every pause, every sigh sing with meaning. Even his silences were seductive. He had learned how to listen. Like her he could hear all the things it was still too soon to say, both of them preparing for a distant first night that grew a little bit nearer every day.

Paula was glad to be home. Inconvenient though the cottage had been for daily commutes into London, it represented permanence; when Patrick eventually moved on, Grace, at least, would still be there.

Patrick had gone up to town first thing that morning, to prepare for the first rehearsals of *Vanya* (and to visit Maida Vale, no doubt, but she wouldn't ask him about that). Izzie had been most peculiar on the phone lately, something was brewing for sure, and not before time.

There was a letter from yet another adoption society in the morning post, telling her what she knew already, that unmarried women were not deemed worthy recipients of other people's discarded babies but thanking her for her interest, yours very truly, etc. Perhaps she should find herself a husband of convenience, some solid citizen whom she could pay off as soon as the kid was legally hers. Time was running out. Soon she would be thirty-five, too old to be considered at all. Old enough to be a grandmother, in her particular case . . .

Grace was out in the garden hanging out washing when the telephone rang. Paula answered it.

'Paula? It's me, Richard.' And then, when she didn't respond, 'Paula, is that you?'

'Richard?' she echoed weakly. 'Where the hell are you ringing from?'

'Bow Street Magistrates' Court. They've set bail at two hundred quid and I don't have it. Can you come and get me?'

'Bail? What are you up for? Possession?'

'I'll tell you when I see you. Hurry, will you? And for God's sake don't say anything to Izzie.'

Paula set off immediately, telling Grace simply that she was spending the day in town. How long had Richard been in London? Why hadn't he contacted her before?

She broke the speed limit all the way. An hour later she found Richard twitchily awaiting her arrival and looking a good fifteen years older than the last time she had seen him. He was unshaven, sporting a swollen jaw and nose, and obviously in dire need of a fix. He greeted her as if they had just seen each other yesterday.

'Can you get me out of here quick?' he said, without preamble. 'They've had me in a holding cell all night, I've been climbing the walls.'

Paula steeled herself not to be sympathetic. As soon as she paid up he would be off in search of fresh supplies.

'What are you on? Heroin, by the look of you.' She pulled back his sleeve, displaying the puncture marks.

'Izzie doesn't know,' he said, by way of confirmation. 'That's why I rang you and not her. She said Vince had been dealing drugs. So I thought you wouldn't have the nerve to sit in judgment.'

'Izzie knows you're back?'

'I've been staying with her. I had to have somewhere to crash, and you were on tour. But she doesn't know . . . what I've been doing. I told her I'd screwed some money out of the old man. I would have done, too, but the bastard wasn't there, turns out he's in America, promoting his stinking book. Paula, I haven't had a fix since last night . . .'

'So how much stuff did they find on you?' persisted Paula, determined to get the whole story out of him while she had the whip hand.

'None. I was trying to earn the money to pay for it, wasn't I?' Paula, who didn't shock easily, had to make a conscious effort not to look shocked. 'Officially I resisted arrest and assaulted a policeman. Their excuse for duffing me up. That's why the beak was so hard on me. They all hate queers like poison.' And then, 'Can we go now?'

'Not yet. How long have you been on the game?'

Richard blew his nose. He was shaking.

'A year or so, I can't remember. I got involved with this pimp in Bangkok. That is, I didn't know he was a pimp, not at first. At first he just gave me the shit, as much as I wanted, then he made me work for it. It was high-class trade, businessmen and tourists. But then I got ill, with hepatitis. I ended up in this vile public hospital, and the guy I'd been working for wouldn't have me back, said I'd lost my looks. I freelanced for a bit, but it got scary. So I came home.'

'Did you bring anything in with you?'

'Of course. Swallowed it in a rubber with a couple of cement pills. But it didn't last long.' He stood up. 'Come on, Paula. Don't keep me hanging about.' And then, when she didn't respond, 'What's the matter? You are going to get me out of here, aren't you?'

Paula hesitated, reading the agony in his eyes. A different kind of pain from poor Bea's, but just as terminal.

'Not unless you agree to treatment, no. And you'll get the same answer from Izzie, if you try it on with her. I'll make sure of that, believe me.'

'Treatment?' said Richard, angry now. 'You've got to be kidding. I'm not letting them lock me up with a bunch of junkies. I'd rather die.'

'Fine. In that case I'll leave them to lock you up with a bunch of criminals instead. They'll probably send you down anyway, once your case comes up. As you said, the courts hate queers. But not as much as the lags do. Cheerio, then.' She began walking away.

'Paula!' he yelled after her. 'Don't go. For God's sake don't leave me here!'

'Does that mean you agree?'

He looked at her shiftily.

'If I do . . . we'll go get some stuff right away, won't we, to tide me over? I've just got to make a phone call. They'll want cash.'

'If you agree I'll hold you to it. Don't think you can bullshit me the way you did Izzie.' She put her arms around him and held him very tight, feeling his fear. 'I'll get you a good lawyer. And I won't lock you up with any junkies. I promise I'll be there with you, all the way.'

'Oh God,' he said, in a cracked voice. 'Oh Jesus, Paula. I'm in Hell.'

'Welcome to your tour guide,' said Paula. 'I know Hell like the back of my hand. So stick with me and you won't get lost.'

'It's a crazy idea,' said Patrick. 'I won't let you do it.'

'I'm not asking your permission,' said Paula. 'I'm telling you.'

'He's my brother,' put in Isabel. 'If anyone takes responsibility for him, it ought to be me.'

'Absolutely not,' said Patrick. 'You've got the kids to think of. And he's fooled you once too often already. How could you be so

444

blind? I told you at the start, I didn't want any drugs in the house.'

'I never saw any drugs in the house! He never even asked me for money. I'd have given him the money rather than let him sell himself!'

'I'll bet you would! If I'd been there I'd have . . .'

'You've never been there!' exploded Isabel. 'You've always left me to deal with everything, from the very first day we were married. And now you've got the gall to –'

'I did not leave you to deal with everything! I was there for you when bloody Richard didn't want to know! What about your mother?'

'My mother? What about yours?'

'Don't drag my mother into this!'

'Will you shut up, you two?' bellowed Paula, fearful that Richard would overhear. She had warned him to stay in his room till they had gone. 'It doesn't matter what either of you think. I'm not breaking my word. I'm laying on all the professional help he needs, right here in this house.'

'But you're in no position to be a nursemaid!' said Patrick. 'You've got the company to consider. We start rehearsals for *Vanya* next week, remember?'

'Then you'll have to replace me,' said Paula calmly. 'This is more important.'

'You can't leave us in the lurch like this. It's . . . it's un-professional.'

'That's great, coming from you. As you just reminded Izzie, you walked out on the Kean in mid-season when she needed help. And Richard's in a lot more trouble than she ever was. Don't you dare talk to me about being unprofessional. I've been too damn professional all my life. And what have I got to show for it? Just a pile of money that Vince made out of the filthy stuff that's killing Richard. This is my chance to put that right.'

Let them think she was doing this out of guilt, rather than for purely selfish motives. She had someone to look after again, an antidote to her own self-pity.

'Oh and by the way, you'll have to find somewhere else to stay for a bit,' she told Patrick, seizing her chance. 'I can't risk you interfering and upsetting Richard. In fact, I don't want either of you seeing him until he starts to improve.'

445

Patrick looked at Isabel and Isabel looked at Patrick.

'I suppose you can have the spare room in the meantime,' she murmured, in answer to his unspoken question.

'Thank you,' he said.

Paula Dorland, founder of the much-praised Encore Theatre Group, has withdrawn from the forthcoming production of Uncle Vanya *following a rift with live-in partner Patrick Delaney, the company's flamboyant actor/manager, better known as TV heartthrob Mick O'Mara of the late lamented* Stop Press.

Miss Dorland, whose drug-dealer husband Vincent Parry was murdered by US mobsters last year, is claimed to be suffering from 'nervous exhaustion' – provoked, according to those in the know, by a showdown over Delaney's secret trysts with ex-wife Isabel, engaged against Dorland's wishes to play Yelena opposite his Astrov. Banned from Dorland's luxury home in Kent, Delaney is reported to have moved back into the family home in Maida Vale.

Leggy redhead Isabel, 34-year-old mother of five, recently shot to fame as the Fish Finger Mum in the award-winning TV commercials. Says screen husband and former escort, Steven Ratchett, 'This has been on the cards for months. It was obvious to everyone who knew them that Izzie and Patrick would get back together one day . . .'

'Who invents all this stuff?' muttered Isabel, flushing.

'You know what Paula says,' shrugged Patrick. 'Pay attention to what you read about yourself in the papers. It might just come true one day.' And then, softly, 'It's started to come true already, hasn't it?'

'I don't know,' said Isabel, twitching like an iron filing trying to resist a magnet. This was what she had dreamed of, for months now, for longer than she cared to admit. And now the moment had come she was scared stiff. Patrick had been home for two days now, and she had picked one needless row after another, frazzled with the strain of wanting him.

'I don't know if it would work,' she went on. 'I'm harder to live with now. I'm used to answering back and getting my own way.'

'So I've noticed. But it suits you. And it suits me too.' He folded his arms, as if restraining the urge to touch her. 'I loved the old Izzie, but I like the new one better. It used to drive me mad, you know, the way you gave in to me all the time. And then I got to depend on it. You were so careful not to spoil the kids, why did you spoil me?'

The reason seemed obvious in retrospect.

'To compensate for feeling so angry with you all the time. To hide how choked with frustration and resentment I was, either because I wasn't working, or because I felt as if I shouldn't be.'

'I made you feel like that,' said Patrick, catching the ball she had thrown at him. 'I tried not to, but I couldn't help it. Tit for tat, I suppose. You made me feel so damned inferior . . .'

'I know I did,' said Isabel, unapologetically. This wasn't about saying sorry, or forgiving each other. It was about forgiving themselves. 'Even when I seemed to be encouraging you I was subtly undermining your confidence. That was tit for tat as well. It was all quite deliberate, except that I didn't realize I was doing it, if that makes sense.'

'To me it does. Once you've got under the skin of a part, you forget that you're acting, even though you're acting like mad. I know. I did it too. I did it with everyone, until Paula.'

Paula. Paula who had set this whole thing up, with their connivance.

'I know you're worried that she won't be able to manage without me, once Richard's off her hands. But she'll have more than me. She'll have us.'

'Us?'

He caught hold of her wrists and pulled her towards him. The relief of it made her catch her breath. 'You and me. Together. Properly together. Don't think about how it was. Think about how it could be, how it's going to be, from now on.'

Isabel hid her face against his chest. 'That's enough of your blarney, Mick O'Mara,' she muttered, wanting more of it.

'Every night I'm going to have to kiss you, just once, on stage. You knew that when you took the part. Did you honestly think just once, on stage, was going to be enough?'

'No,' she said quietly. 'And it terrified me. It still does.'

447

'Not as much as it terrifies me.' He took her face between his hands and forced her to tread water in the deep blue of his eyes. 'I knew I was losing you, you know, long before it happened. And now I've found you, the real you. Haven't I?'

Isabel nodded. She had found the real Patrick as well. He bent to kiss her. It was a long time since they had kissed like this, and yet it couldn't have happened any sooner. It was like reaching a common destination, after a long hard journey, taking in several stops on the way. They had travelled separately, by different routes, but at last they had arrived.

It seemed deliciously sinful and furtive, creeping upstairs in the middle of the morning, locking the door in case Ma went wandering, falling onto the bed where she had spent so many nights without him. And then . . .

It was still the same, and yet different. Unexpectedly, inevitably, different. The great thing about a revival was the charm of familiarity, and yet every move, every line, held hidden secrets, spiced with the challenge of rediscovery. A classic was solid stuff, it thrived on reinterpretation. But only as long as you respected what was there in the first place. Some things couldn't be changed, she had to accept that. Give Patrick an inch and he would always take a mile. But if she gave the mile willingly, she could ask the same from him. And now she knew that he would give it too.

Paula understood Richard's fury, of which she bore the brunt in the next few months. She knew from her spell in council care what it felt like to be deprived of your freedom, to hate your warders, to dream of escape. And because she knew, she didn't make the mistake of trusting him. The régime she imposed – with the help of a doctor and two strapping male nurses, who administered the prescribed drugs – was more rigorous than any he would have encountered in a clinic. Meanwhile his progress, slow and painful as it was, was the pacemaker for her own. By the time he was cured, Paula told herself, so would she be.

They passed a quiet Christmas on their own, having missed a Dickensian feast *chez* Delaney thanks to a timely blizzard. Or rather a minor snowfall which Paula had exploited. Christmas made her feel weepy at the best of times.

'You didn't miss a thing,' Isabel had assured her. 'Ma overcooked the turkey and Patrick made his usual fist of carving it and Toby threatened to report them both to the RSPCA. The kids have all got to the stage where they think Christmas is a bore, specially when the clapped-out parents fall asleep in front of the box straight after lunch. PJ and Ma are the only ones who still enjoy it.'

This was Izzie being tactful, of course. No flaunting happy families to a widowed, childless friend, no tempting fate, no self-congratulation. Just a cautious 'We're taking it one day at a time.' But when Paula next saw them together, she could see the enormity of the understatement. There was a relaxed warmth between them she had never seen before; they had learned to be friends as well as lovers. One day at a time was a crossed-fingers way of saying for ever.

She and Richard finally went to see *Vanya* one evening in the early spring, his first outing up to town, after which they were taking Izzie and Patrick out to dinner near the theatre – a converted warehouse in Covent Garden which had housed all three Encore productions. It was the first time Paula had seen them share a stage, pooling their talent, sublimating their mutual envy, united by a common purpose. She would have felt excluded, watching them, if she hadn't helped make it happen. As it was she simply felt outclassed, regretting, too late, the promise she had made to Richard, the secret she had shared with Izzie, but it was too late to back out now . . .

Having put on over a stone in weight and dyed away the grey in his hair, Richard looked much more like his old, raffish self. More importantly, he had begun to show an interest in the theatre again, having spent his confinement, as part of his therapy, in writing another play.

'It's high time I got back to work,' said Paula over dinner, trying to sound more confident than she felt. 'So I've bullied this lazy slob into writing a part for me. And for you too, Izzie.'

'Really?' said Isabel, feigning surprise, as if she wasn't in on the whole thing.

'After all, I couldn't have you girls fighting over the lead as well as over Patrick, now could I?' said Richard. 'I thought casting you together would give the jolly old gossip columnists something new to sharpen their fangs on. Specially now that Paula's gone and shacked up with another queer.'

'Still a hype-merchant at heart, I see,' commented Patrick.

'Too right he is,' said Paula. And then, crossing her fingers under the table, 'As it happens, I've asked him to join the company, as our press officer, and he's accepted.'

'I need a day job, in case the play bombs,' explained Richard self-mockingly, his flippant tone masking his usual insecurities. 'Unless Patrick objects, of course.'

'Of course he doesn't object,' said Paula, giving Patrick a don't-you-dare look. 'Do you, darling?'

Patrick looked from Isabel to Paula and back again.

'I seem to be outnumbered,' he said. 'So no, I won't object. As long as it doesn't commit us to putting on Richard's play.'

'Absolutely not,' Paula assured him, removing a folder from her tote bag and handing it across the table. 'Don't feel under any pressure, will you,' she added sweetly. 'This is just a courtesy, really. Neville Seaton's already made an offer.'

'You showed it to him first?' said Patrick, unable to hide his annoyance. He looked accusingly at Isabel, who shrugged innocently, blatantly enjoying his discomfiture.

'Oh, we knew you'd have a down on it,' said Paula. 'Whereas Neville simply loved it.' She met Patrick's scowl with a sunny smile. 'Any excuse to work with Izzie again.' Unable to bear it any longer, Isabel corpsed. 'And of course, Neville's never been afraid to take a risk.'

'You're a machiavellian bitch, Paula,' said Patrick without rancour, fishing a pair of half-moon glasses out of his breast pocket, ignoring the congealing food on his plate and swatting away Isabel's attempts to peek over his shoulder as he read, with ferocious concentration and mounting, visible interest.

This would be a new beginning, for all of them, thought Paula hopefully. For the first time since Vince's death, the future held more than fear. She was over the worst. And so was Richard. Things were looking up at last.

17

Summer–Winter 1976

If only one had the courage, life might be liveable in spite of everything.

Henrik Ibsen – Hedda Gabler

'Here she goes,' sighed Paula as Isabel made straight for the telephone in the hotel lobby while Patrick checked in. The last three try-outs for *Alter Ego* had been within striking distance of London. But the final one, in Nottingham, necessitated a week away, Jan having moved into the house for the duration.

They had left London all of three hours ago, and already PJ had succumbed to meningitis, been run over, and gone mysteriously missing. By the time they returned home, at the end of the week, the girls would have lost their collective virginity, Ma would finally get round to breaking a hip and Toby (who was away at college in any case) would have crashed the second-hand Honda he had bought with his share of the fish finger money. And all because Isabel was away on tour. No amount of women's lib would ever stop her worrying.

'. . . I'm sure he's all right, Sophie darling, but would you just look in on him now, while I hold on? And can I have a word with Jan, while you do that? Thanks. Jan? There were a couple of things I forgot to tell you . . .'

'Well?' said Patrick, joining them a few minutes later and handing Paula her key. 'Has the house burned down yet?'

'Don't joke about it,' shuddered Isabel.

'They're the ones who should be worrying about us,' said Paula. 'What a hole.' It was the usual no-star boarding house. 'If you've quite finished with the phone, I might as well call Richard. Too bad Jan can't babysit him as well.'

451

Richard had been sporadically present during the try-outs, working on last-minute rewrites, but this week he was back in London, devoting his full attention to publicizing the opening. Or rather, not devoting his attention to it, a growing source of strife between him and Patrick.

Patrick wouldn't have minded, he said, if Richard was working on another play. But Richard, whose visits from the muse had always been erratic, was spending more and more of his working hours campaigning for GAP – Gays Against Prejudice – a pressure group he had joined as part of his return to the land of the living. He had quickly been elected to the committee as Public Relations Officer, a role which inspired a much greater commitment than the similar one he held at Encore.

But Paula remained stubbornly deaf and blind as far as Richard was concerned. Having him in the company enabled her to keep an eye on him while providing him with a job, an income, and an illusion, at least, of independence. She had leased adjoining his-and-her flats in a service block in Holland Park – Richard shared Izzie's dislike of country living – to give him a place and a life of his own, a life which increasingly excluded her.

'Richard? It's me.'

'Hello you. Checking up on me, are you? Can you hold on, while I shoot up? I've got hold of some really great shit.' He began making orgasmic noises down the phone.

'Where are you off to tonight?' asked Paula, ignoring this routine wind-up.

'Meeting of the group. I've invited this hack from *Time Out*. So a couple of us will probably take him out to dinner afterwards. And then I might invite a few people back for a nightcap.'

'Don't forget about that suspended sentence, will you?' Paula felt bound to say. She lived in constant fear of Richard being lured back onto drugs.

'No chance of that with you around, you old ratbag. Oh, and mind you buy the *Guardian* tomorrow. They're printing that interview I did last week. 'Bye, my darling.'

Paula picked at an indigestible dinner and met up with the rest of the company in the pub afterwards, being the life and soul on lemonade as usual. Nearly everyone involved in *Alter Ego* had worked on one or all of the last three Encore productions, with

452

Patrick gathering around him a core of kindred spirits, the basis, it was hoped, of a permanent troupe of performers and technicians. No longer the anti-social outsider, condemning all and sundry as pseuds and posers, he was now the captain of a hand-picked crew, all of whom he had chosen himself . . . except Richard.

She passed a restless night in a lumpy bed, plagued by dreams. She dreamt that Vince was there beside her, warm and solid and reassuring. But when she reached out to touch him he was gone, and Richard was there in his place, no bigger than an infant. She cradled him to her breast to find a needle embedded in his arm, and when she tried to pull it out, blood gushed out and spurted all over her, hurtling her into wakefulness and towards the wash-basin, damp and sticky, desperate to rinse it away. But it was only sweat, sweat that had left the thin sheets moist and cold, as welcoming as a shroud.

She lay there shivering, with the light on, waiting for the relief of day, only to drop off at dawn and sleep densely through a morning cacophony of slamming doors, hammering pipes, loud voices, and her alarm clock, hearing nothing till the knock on her door. It was Patrick.

'Are you all right? Izzie looked in earlier but she didn't like to wake you.'

'I'm fine,' yawned Paula, stretching languorously, in the manner of one who has slept like a top.

'I wanted to talk to you, in private.' He pulled up a chair and handed her the newspaper. 'Richard got himself quite a spread. Everyone was talking about it over breakfast. Particularly about his failure to mention Encore, let alone his own play. As usual.'

The half-page article was headlined 'Still angry after all these years' and dealt exclusively with Richard's role as spokesman for GAP. As in the last three published interviews, he was attacking 'institutionalized homophobia' in the police, the judiciary, Parliament and the press, and promoting a forthcoming gay rights rally.

'So?' said Paula, reaching for her cigarettes. 'You surely don't disagree with the things he says here, do you?'

'Don't dodge the issue, Paula, or try to paint me as some kind of anti-gay bigot. I don't disagree with what he says, I've told him so myself. But I've had just about enough of GAP hijacking our publicity drive. If we were talking about anyone else but Richard, you'd agree with me. You're letting him get away with it because you're scared that if you don't he won't love you any more. You're not doing him any favours, Paula. You're turning him into a sponger.'

'Look who's calling who a sponger!'

She regretted the words as soon as she had uttered them. Patrick had repaid his debt to her, over and over again, not in money but in the brains and talent and energy that had got the company off the ground, that had made a proper actress out of her at last.

'It takes one to know one,' he said, refusing to take offence. 'I've had personal experience of just how over-generous you can be. If you want to support GAP, send them a donation. Or take Richard off the payroll and give him an allowance to spend as he chooses. But you can't let him carry on like this.'

'I'm not taking him off the payroll. I gave you a job, why shouldn't I do the same for him?' Damn. She had done it again. This time his eyes flickered.

'You may as well know that I've had several offers in the last few months. Offers I've turned down, because Izzie and I both see Encore as a long-term project, because we're both committed to you, and the rest of the company, and all the things we're trying to achieve together. You know the policies we agreed. To work as a collective, to make decisions democratically, to give everyone a share of any profits. Richard is rocking the boat. People see him as a hanger-on, indirectly subsidized by them. So, do you want to talk to him, or shall I?'

He was using that reasonable-but-implacable director's voice of his, inviting you to argue as much as you pleased, until you saw fit to admit that he was right.

'I'll do it,' muttered Paula sullenly. 'But I'm not firing him, okay? I'll lay it on the line to him and give him another chance.'

'As long as it's a last chance.' He tried to take her hand but she snatched it away. 'You don't look well. You've had one of your bad nights, haven't you?'

There was a tap on the door, pre-empting her intended denial.

'Patrick,' called Isabel. 'You're wanted on the phone.'

'Come on in,' said Paula, glad of this reprieve. She glared at

Patrick's departing back. 'I suppose you know what all that was about?'

'We discussed it, yes. Don't look at me like that. Richard's my brother and I love him. And I know how responsible you feel for him, God knows I'm the same with the kids. But –'

'But I'm not Richard's mother,' snapped Paula. 'I'm not even his sister, or his wife. Or anyone else, come to that. Do you know who's down as next of kin on my passport? You.'

Isabel sat down on the bed and put an arm around her. Paula stiffened.

'You're *my* sister,' said Isabel.

'You don't need one,' countered Paula. 'You've got a husband and four children and two brothers and a couple of hundred in-laws. What the hell do you want with a sodding sister? Haven't . . . you got . . . enough problems . . . already?' Her voice hovered on the edge of collapse.

'Go on,' said Isabel. 'Cry. You haven't cried properly since Vince died. You've lost your temper, you've made sick jokes, you've worked yourself to a standstill, but you've never taken the time to grieve. You were too busy sorting out Patrick and then Richard . . .'

'I'm so bloody angry with him!' Paula heard herself shouting, through a sob. 'I'm so angry with him for getting himself killed! He never stopped trying to buy my love, right up to the end. Even though I stuck by him when he had nothing, he still had to make me feel that I'd driven him to it. I'll never forgive him for that! I'll never stop hating him for it!'

'It's all right to hate him,' said Isabel. 'It doesn't mean you don't love him.'

'If he'd got caught just a few weeks later,' went on Paula, unappeased, 'I would have had the baby they promised us. But he left me with nothing but money. And now I'm doing what he did. Trying to buy love with it, and dependence, and loyalty. Richard's, yours, Patrick's . . .'

'Then learn from his mistakes. We all loved you when you didn't have a bean, remember? And we always will . . .'

It wasn't the same, thought Paula. It wasn't the same as having someone who belonged to you, as of right. She was sorely tempted to spill the beans about her long-lost baby. But Izzie felt sorry

455

enough for her already. And secrets were best kept where they belonged, in the dark. Switching on the light was supposed to dispel the shapes lurking in the shadows. But it didn't work if they were real. If they were real you just saw them more clearly than ever.

Paula rang Richard as soon as she had dressed. He never got up before lunch if he could help it.

'I saw that article,' she began resolutely. And then, going off on a tangent, 'I do wish you'd be more careful what you say. You're going to make yourself a target for every queer-basher in London.'

'Queer-bashers can't read. Specially not the *Guardian*.'

'That doesn't stop the tabloids picking up the story and making out that you're advocating homosexual orgies in Hyde Park on Sunday afternoons.'

'What a perfectly super idea. Sounds much more fun than a boring old rally. That reporter from *Time Out* is going to give it a big plug.'

'Can he possibly manage a plug for the play while he's at it?' She tried to sound sarcastic rather than anxious. 'You're supposed to be working for Encore, remember?'

'Um . . . I was coming to that.' Paula braced herself for more excuses, willing herself to be stern. 'The thing is . . . I've been offered another job.'

'What?'

'I just heard. We've managed to get a grant from the GLC. Enough for two paid workers and a walk-in advice centre staffed by volunteers. They've asked me to be a full time co-ordinator. I'd be working from home to begin with, till we get premises.'

'Shit,' said Paula.

'Sorry, darling. But I've already accepted. Not just because I want the job, but because I can take a hint. Patrick's a bloody good director but I'm just too old and cynical to fit in with his little band of acolytes. And Izzie seems so happy these days I don't want to spoil things for her by falling out with him again. You'll soon find somebody else. And this matters to me. A lot. You're not going to make me feel ungrateful, are you?'

'You know me better than that,' said Paula. She ought to be relieved. Richard's new job had got her off the hook. But she felt more anxious than ever.

'Don't think you've got rid of me, will you? I'm only leaving

456

Encore, not my favourite girl. You're stuck with me for life, for your sins.'

'For yours, more like,' said Paula, making light of it. Remembering that she wasn't his mother, she muzzled her misgivings. It was time to let him go.

ALTER EGO – ACT THREE, SCENE FOUR
Eve's bedroom. Eve One is lying on the bed, crying quietly to herself. Eve Two is pacing to and fro.

EVE TWO

Just look at her. Look at her wallowing in her own self-pity. I told her what would happen. Over and over again. And now she expects me to feel sorry for her! (*She walks across to* EVE ONE *and shakes her*.) You're well shot of him. Stop whining.

EVE ONE

Leave me alone, bitch. This is all your fault. You were the one who told me to give him an ultimatum. If I'd been more patient, more understanding . . .

EVE TWO

. . . He'd still be making a fool of you.

EVE ONE

You're the one who made a fool of me, not him. I've had enough of you being smug and objective and sensible. It's easy for you. You don't have any feelings.

EVE TWO

And you don't have any brains! I've let your heart rule my head for long enough. You can live without him, I promise you . . .

EVE ONE

Correction. You can live without him. I can't. (*She opens the bedside drawer and takes out a bottle of sleeping pills*.) And this time you're not talking me out of it.

457

I never talked you out of it. You were too chicken to go through with it. You still are. You won't take enough to kill yourself. Just enough to make him sorry. You're pathetic.

EVE ONE

Watch me. (*She exits to the bathroom and returns with a glass of water.*) And just remember one thing. It won't just be me. It'll be you as well. (*She begins swallowing the pills.*)

EVE TWO grabs the glass, throws it to the ground, and scatters the pills onto the floor. EVE ONE lunges at her.

EVE ONE

All right. If that's the way you want it, it'll be you first!

(The two women struggle. EVE ONE eventually gets the better of her alter ego, grabs her by the throat and throttles her until she loses consciousness.)

EVE ONE

That's her shut up for a bit. (*She kneels and puts her head to her chest.*) Still alive, though. No getting rid of her without getting rid of me. As long as I'm around, there she'll be, telling me what to do, what I should have done. Well, this time she isn't getting a look-in. This time I'll have no one to blame but myself.

Fetches more water. Retrieves the pills from the floor, shovelling them into her mouth as she does so. Then she goes back to the bed and lies down. Slowly, EVE TWO begins to come round. The bedside telephone begins to ring. EVE ONE is now unconscious. EVE TWO heaves herself towards it and manages to pick up the receiver.

JACK'S VOICE

Eve? Eve, is that you? Listen. I've told her it's all over. I'm glad you made me choose. It's you I love. Eve? Please talk to me. I didn't mean all those things I said tonight. Can we forget what happened and start again?

EVE ONE, *revived by his words, begins to come round. She struggles to move.* EVE TWO *is holding the telephone just out of her reach.*

EVE ONE

For God's sake. Tell him. Tell him to get round here quickly. Tell him I've done something stupid.

EVE TWO

I did try to stop you. But you wouldn't listen.

EVE ONE

You tried to stop me for the wrong reasons. It's me he loves, not her.

EVE TWO

Idiot! She's given him the elbow, can't you see? If you're going to let him ruin your life, you're better off dead.

JACK'S VOICE

Eve? Eve, are you all right? Eve, please speak to me. Otherwise I'm going to come straight over.

EVE ONE

(*Relieved.*) He's coming. No need to do anything. All we have to do is wait for him. I don't want to die. Not any more . . .

EVE TWO

(*Into the telephone, with a supreme effort, very loud and clear.*) Don't come over, Jack. Don't come near me ever again. The thing is, you see . . . (*She turns to look at* EVE ONE *and smiles.*) . . . I'm not alone.

She replaces the receiver and slumps to the floor, all strength exhausted. The telephone begins to ring again. EVE ONE *begins to reach towards it, feebly, as the curtain falls.*

Darkness. Lights. Applause. Relief. A heady mixture of energy

459

and fatigue, like a wound-down clockwork toy that had suddenly sprouted wings. No separate bows. Company policy. Just the six players, hands linked, taking collective credit. Isabel caught sight of Marian in the newly illuminated audience, together with a contingent of her ex-students, and next to them Ma, the twins, Emily, and Toby, who had come down from college to attend with his latest girlfriend, all of them clapping wildly.

Richard's seat was still empty. Patrick had taken a phone call, just before they went on, saying that he had been delayed. Cold feet, most probably. Despite his outward bravado and their good reception out of town, he was secretly terrified, as always, that his play would be a huge flop. If previous form was anything to go by, he would remain in hiding till he had seen the reviews.

After four long curtain calls they filed off breathlessly, weightless with the aftermath of tension.

'I have to talk to you both,' came Patrick's voice behind them, ushering them both into their shared dressing room and following them inside.

'What's the matter?' said Isabel, seeing the vein throbbing in his temple and the tension lines around his mouth, anticipating yet more rehearsals tomorrow, until they had ironed out the remaining wrinkles, including the ones in his own performance. Patrick's timing had been slightly out and he had dried – most unusual for him – in the very first scene, with Paula feeding him his missing line with her usual aplomb.

Patrick hesitated a moment. 'I don't know any way of breaking this to you gently. Richard was attacked on his way to the theatre tonight.'

Paula sat down, transfixed by his eyes, which said far more than his words, said things she couldn't bear to hear.

'Is he badly hurt?' demanded Isabel. 'Where is he?'

'They took him to St Mary's. Paula . . . Izzie . . . I'm so terribly sorry . . .'

'He's dead,' said Paula. Her voice was expressionless. Patrick bowed his head. Isabel shook hers in a dumbshow of denial, refusing to understand.

'What are you talking about?' she demanded. 'He can't be dead. He –'

'I warned him,' said Paula. Her voice was cold, unnatural,

matter of fact. 'I warned him they were out to get him. I warned him not to put his home address on that poster, not to put that sticker in his car. The stupid bastard!'

'They?' echoed Isabel faintly. 'You mean –'

'The caretaker found his body in the car park, under the flats,' said Patrick. 'They'd daubed anti-gay graffiti all over the windscreen.'

Keep calm, Isabel told herself, suppressing a wave of raw hysteria. Paula's about to freak out, so you've got to keep calm. First Vince, and now Richard. She was more aware, initially, of Paula's pain than of her own. First Vince, and now Richard . . .

'You knew before we went on, didn't you?' rasped Paula, her voice harsh and hollow. 'That was what that phone call was about. Wasn't it?'

'If he'd still been alive, I'd have called off the performance,' said Patrick, 'and rushed you both to the hospital to see him. But he was dead on arrival. There was nothing we could have done for him.'

'You let me go on, not knowing. So as not to spoil your lousy first night!'

'It was Richard's first night too. I decided it was best. I was afraid that you would have forced yourself to go on anyway. I thought it would make it easier for you. How do you think it was for me?'

'Damn you!' howled Paula. 'He only took that job with GAP because you wanted him out. That's how he ended up addressing that rally, that's what got him killed!'

'Paula, don't,' pleaded Isabel, putting her arms around her. 'He wanted to do it, no one could have stopped him . . .'

'I'd better go,' said Patrick woodenly. 'Head off visitors, cancel the party. Then I have to go and identify him . . .'

'No you won't,' spat Paula, still dry-eyed. 'I'll do it. You were never his friend. You don't care that he's dead.'

Isabel returned Patrick's anguished look, knowing that he wanted to comfort her, comfort both of them, that he couldn't find the platitudes to do so, inhibited by Paula's rage, by his own distress. He left the room without another word. There was a sound of approaching footsteps, Patrick speaking in a low voice, a collective murmur, a general retreat, doors being knocked on,

461

Patrick's voice again, everyone creeping about and speaking quietly. Isabel found herself thinking, if I start crying, perhaps she will as well, but the tears wouldn't come. They just sat there, holding each other, speechless, shaking, sharing, while the theatre cooled and grew silent, the news spreading like some deadly virus stripping it of joy.

'Will you . . . will you come with me?' said Paula.

'Are you sure you want to see him?'

'If I don't, I'll only imagine something worse.'

'I'll phone for a cab. Get changed now, or you'll catch cold.'

She found Patrick waiting for her to emerge, smoking a cigarette. He ground it out and reached out for her. Isabel slumped against him.

'I'm sorry, Izzie,' he kept saying. 'I'm so sorry.'

'She didn't mean those things she said. She needs someone to blame, that's all.'

'Should I have told you before we went on?'

'No. No, you did right. You go home now, talk the kids through it. I'll stay with her tonight.'

'Do you want me to cancel tomorrow's performance?'

'Not unless Paula pulls out. But I know her. She won't. She'll go on so as not to let Richard down. We've got to do the same for her.'

The sensation of Richard's violent death ('Gay activist slain by queer-bashers') made *Alter Ego* front-page news. Features were run in the press, some on the lines of 'The Mallory curse strikes again', dredging up the stories of Fay's allegedly bungled suicide and Adrian's conviction for murder, and others headlined 'Paula's new heartbreak', rehashing the numerous blows fate had dealt her, not that they knew the half of it.

The demand for tickets rocketed in the wake of all the publicity, resulting in a hasty West End transfer. London's gay community flocked to the play as a gesture of support. A benefit performance was announced in aid of GAP. The newly published paperback of the Mallory autobiography went into immediate reprint. Paula moved to a hotel to avoid the paparazzi laying siege to her flat, and because she couldn't bear to use the car park any more.

The Delaney phone was kept off the hook, with not a whisper of complaint from the twins. Toby turned the garden hose on a reporter from the *News of the World*. Emily, that most ladylike of children, sustained a broken finger in a fight with a classmate who referred to her uncle as a bum-bandit. PJ kept asking unanswerable questions, Ma spent a great deal of time in church, and Isabel cried herself to sleep every night in Patrick's arms.

And yet somehow they both went to the theatre every night and strutted their stuff. As did Paula, for whom the play had become a haven from the torment of her thoughts, the only thing that kept her going. But off-stage she became ever more remote and inaccessible. Despite patching things up with Patrick in her usual forget-it style, she withdrew emotionally from both him and Isabel, repeating that she was all right, and rejecting all palliatives except nicotine and work.

Hotel living suited her. Here there were no memories, good or bad, nothing personal at all. Here she could have been anyone, anywhere, an anonymous being in transit between one place and another. She could leave her former life to gather dust, she could cease to exist except under cover of her role.

She tried to snap out of her depression, impatient with herself as always, only for it to deepen with every day, every week, every interminable month that passed, as Richard's play continued to play to packed houses. Cry, Isabel had said. And so she had, in private. But like any habit, it was proving hard to break. The slightest thing set her off. Seeing *Snowdrops* on the telly, which normally made her roar with laughter. The hand-painted birthday card she received from PJ. The smell of Vince's aftershave on a stranger in the hotel lift. And most of all sympathy. Hence her desire to be alone.

She wasn't just mourning Richard; she was mourning all the losses in her life. It was as if his death had toppled her off the tightrope she had been walking since the day she was born; she no longer had the nerve or the strength to risk yet another fall. It was instinctive to distance herself from the remaining people she dared to love – Patrick, Izzie, the kids – lest she somehow endanger them as well. They kept inviting her to spend Sundays with them, but after a few superficially successful attempts to be her normal, laugh-a-minute self, if only to stop Izzie fussing, Paula had become adept at inventing excuses. The effort of pretending to be cheerful left her even more depleted than before.

She liked to think that it didn't show, but the physical effects did. After a lifetime of waging war against her appetite, she was losing weight with no effort at all. Which would have been fine in itself, except that Izzie, who saw her strip for a quick-change in the course of the play each night, didn't miss a thing.

'So are you coming home with us tomorrow night?' she asked Paula, two days before Christmas. Christmas was on a Saturday this year; with Boxing Day deferred till Monday, the company would enjoy the luxury of two consecutive performance-free days. 'Or would you rather Patrick picked you up on Christmas morning?'

Paula could tell that she wasn't about to be fobbed off again.

'Actually, I've made other plans,' said Paula. She couldn't face all that seasonal merriment, couldn't risk throwing a wobbler and spoiling things for everyone else.

'I don't believe you,' said Isabel shortly. 'No more excuses, okay? If you think I'm going to let you spend Christmas day in bed . . .'

'That's exactly where I'm going to spend it,' said Paula, improvising. 'I'm off for a dirty weekend.'

'A dirty weekend? Who with?'

'Wouldn't you like to know.'

'Tell me! It's not Gregory Sherborne, is it?'

Gregory Sherborne was a friend of Oliver Briggs, one of the angels who had backed *Alter Ego*. He had asked Paula out, and been duly spurned, several times.

'Do me a favour. Too posh by half. More your type than mine.'

'Who then?'

'Mind your own business. Suffice it to say, I intend to spend Christmas screwing myself silly.'

Brilliant. That way she could hole up in her room until Monday, leaving Izzie with a clear conscience.

'You're not having me on, are you?'

'Why should I? Is it that incredible that someone might still want to hump me?'

'No, of course not,' said Isabel, wrong-footed. 'The kids will be disappointed, though.'

464

To them, even now, she was still the outrageous, wisecracking, what-the-hell aunt, the deliciously Bad Influence who fed them unmentionable theatrical gossip behind their parents' back. They had never seen the mask drop, not even at Richard's funeral, following which she had seen fit to take off the warbling queen of a vicar – as Richard would undoubtedly have done himself. But she couldn't keep up the big brave act for two whole days. The kids would rumble her for the miserable cow she really was and start being tactful and sympathetic, like Patrick and Izzie. Things would never be the same again.

'Dream up a cover story for me, will you? An ailing granny or something. I'll give you their presents tomorrow, before I leave.'

Although still not quite convinced, Isabel let the subject drop. Perhaps Patrick was right, she thought. The time to worry, he said, was when her work fell below par, and everyone agreed that her performance as Eve One was the best thing she had ever done. For Patrick, doing good work was the great cure-all. It would have saved him even if Isabel hadn't taken him back.

And now she was doing good work too, unapologetically, without guilt. Work, previously a source of strife, had forged a new and powerful bond between them, but a bond which allowed them room to move and grow as individuals. The love that had always been there was now underpinned by respect and free of resentment. Isabel would have been happier, despite Richard's death, than she had ever been in her life, if only Paula could have been happy too . . .

Christmas Eve. Paula got to the theatre early as usual, arriving at five for an eight o'clock kick-off, well before Isabel and Patrick. Her pre-performance ritual hadn't changed since *Bondage* and left ample time for a cup of very sweet tea, a bar of fruit-and-nut, a quiet read of a romantic novel (which she devoured with all the furtiveness of a schoolboy wanking over a porno-mag), and a flick through any mail that had come to the theatre. And then a good, slow hour to put on her make-up and wig and stage clothes, to transform herself, with huge relief, into somebody else, to leave the real Paula hanging on a peg like an empty coat.

She had brought a suitcase with her tonight, to lend verisimilitude to her story. And because she had booked herself into a different hotel, just in case Izzie checked up on her. As a

Christmas treat she had packed her sleeping pills, which she never took when she was working, because for the next couple of days it wouldn't matter if she was thick-headed, and the quickest way to get through the weekend would be to sleep it away.

The doorman had handed her a wad of post, mostly Christmas cards. Whereas Isabel took hers home, to join up with silver twine and hang from the picture rails, Paula scanned hers, as usual, without interest and consigned them, including one from Gregory Sherborne, to the waste-paper bin, till she came to the last two items, a letter and a large square card in a pink envelope, addressed in large, childish capitals that looked like PJ's. Smiling, she withdrew it, a home-made effort with a drawing in coloured crayons on the front, which she viewed, for the first time, upside-down, still smiling, knowing it would make her want to cry . . .

She turned it the right way up. It depicted a naked man, hideously mutilated in crude, explicit detail, and inside was written, in the same ill-formed capitals, *DID THEY LET YOU SEE WHAT WE DID TO YOUR BENT FRIEND? YOU SHOUD HAVE HEARD HIM SQEAL. WISHING YOU A GAY XMAS AND A QUEER NEW YEAR.*

Paula made a bolt for the lavatory, where she retched painfully for several minutes. Sobbing with rage, she tore the card into pieces and tried to flush it away, but it was too thick and heavy, bits of it still floated gloatingly in the pan. She sank to the floor, clutching herself, seeing Richard's face contort in agony, hearing his screams for mercy, all her anguish returning as if it had happened yesterday. They had only let her see his face, of course, a bruised, bloody mess, and the inquest had merely referred to 'extensive injuries', not to castration. The police had never caught the culprits, not that she had expected them to. They were still out there, glorying in their crime. Dear God, let it not be true. Let it just be a piece of unrelated malice, not the confirmation of all her worst nightmares . . .

Trembling, she weighed down the remaining debris with loo paper, waiting the age it took for the cistern to fill, thanking God Izzie hadn't been around when she opened the envelope. She must act normal, so that she didn't guess that anything was wrong . . .

Or rather, that everything was wrong. She simply couldn't bear this final blow, not on top of everything else. Every time she managed to crawl out of the pit, something happened to send her hurtling back where she belonged. She had been fighting a losing battle all her life, one she had lost all heart for. She sat hunched on the hard, cold cubicle floor, rocking to and fro, while the pain burned deep inside her, trying to draw strength from it. The strength to do what she should have done long ago.

Her novel remained unread, her chocolate uneaten, her tea undrunk. Isabel found her, an hour later, already changed and made up, looking calm and composed, calmer, in fact, than she had seen her in ages. That nervy, abrasive edge had gone.

'I've brought your presents,' said Isabel, depositing two bulging carrier bags. 'You're under strict instructions not to open them till tomorrow.'

'Likewise,' said Paula, indicating a stack of parcels.

'I expect you've spent far too much money on us as usual.'

'Money doesn't cost me anything. I've been pretty mean in other ways lately.'

'Nonsense. You've –'

'Listen. I've got to say this, however soppy it sounds. I want you to know how much I love you all, even if I haven't been very good at showing it. I want you to know that you've been a good friend, the best. But I don't want you to feel responsible for me any more. I don't want you to feel guilty about me, ever again. Will you promise me that? Please?'

In an untypically demonstrative gesture, Paula threw her arms around her and hugged her tight. Isabel was surprised and touched. There had always been, throughout their long friendship, an unspoken taboo against the show of too much affection. Whenever she herself had broken it, Paula had made her feel absurd, sentimental, patronizing.

'Promise,' said Paula.

'I promise. Sorry if I've been overdoing the mother hen bit recently.'

'You have to stop making me feel that I mustn't let you down.'

'Oh God. Is that what I do? Patrick said the same thing, once.'

'So do I have your permission to be bad? Being good is making me so vile-tempered.'

'Bad? With this mystery man, you mean?'

'Just tell me that you won't feel you should have stopped me,

467

and above all that you won't think it's somehow your fault. You may as well play ball, because I'm going to do it anyway.'

'What are you talking about? Is he married?'

'Like Neville was, you mean?' said Paula sweetly.

Isabel sighed. 'Oh all right. Point taken. Do what you like and on your own head be it.'

'Thank you,' said Paula. 'Thank you for everything.'

One more performance, she thought. And then, at last, she would be free.

Act Three, Scene Four. The final performance. The last ten minutes of my career.

It's a full house tonight. Five hundred people sitting in the dark, watching us. Two women on a spotlit stage, playing two halves of the same person. But this time only one of us is acting. The other one's doing it for real.

We look alike, thanks to the wigs and make-up. One night we swapped parts in the second act, for a lark, and nobody out there noticed. Are we playing the same character, different roles? Or the same role, different characters? If there are two people inside everyone, that means there are four of us up here. And at the moment, it feels like three against one. I'm outnumbered, but I won't let that stop me.

This will be the last time I die, or live, on stage, the last time I share the limelight with my rival, my best friend. In the heat of performance, she won't notice that the tablets are slightly smaller than usual. I swapped them for the dummy ones on the props table, in the interval, when no one was looking. I'm a great believer in improvisation. Specially during a long run. It helps to keep things fresh.

It would be simpler, of course, to take them later, in private. But not easier. An audience forces you to overcome fear, a role gives you something to hide behind, the strength to do things your real self could never do. And besides, what more fitting exit for an actress than to make her final bow on stage?

The fight scene. Carefully rehearsed so that we don't really hurt each other. If only life could be choreographed as neatly.

Kick, scratch, bite, throttle. And Eve Two is out for the count, leaving Eve One free to destroy herself, to quell the pain once and for all.

Mustn't take too many. Don't want them working too soon, don't want sirens and stomach pumps and shrinks and everyone saying it was just a cry for help, poor thing. No. A handful now, here on stage, as my fond farewell to the theatre. And a top-up once I'm safely in bed, ready to sleep for ever . . .

The phone rings. Suspense in the auditorium. Will Eve Two manage to answer it and summon aid in time? Then the twist in the tail, to keep you all guessing. Then the applause, the only send-off I need or want.

Soon it will all be over.

'Paula!' called Isabel, just as she was making her getaway. 'You forgot this.'

'Thanks,' said Paula abstractedly, taking the still unopened letter. 'Have a good Christmas now.'

'And have a wicked one, if you must,' said Isabel, pulling a disapproving face, imagining all kinds of sinful goings on. She had been well fooled by that little speech, thank God. But later Izzie would remember what she had said with her usual immaculate recall – that she was going to do something bad and that she wasn't to blame herself. A pity Izzie didn't have it in her to see the funny side: death scenes had always been her forte, after all.

'You're not running away without saying goodbye, are you?' said Patrick, accosting her in the corridor.

'Goodbye,' muttered Paula, in a hurry now. She had wanted to avoid this. Saying goodbye to Izzie had drained her dry. She forced herself to look at him for the last time.

'Shall we imagine some mistletoe?' said Patrick, putting his arms around her and kissing her. 'Don't wear yourself out over Christmas, now will you?'

'Not as much as Izzie will, running round after you lot. Look after her for me.'

'And you look after yourself.'

Don't worry, thought Paula. I already have done.

She began to feel very woozy in the taxi. They were stuck in a traffic jam, and the ten-minute journey seemed to be taking forever. It would be disastrous if she passed out in the back of the cab. She must, must, must keep awake till she got to the hotel, till she had told the desk not to put through any calls and hung the 'Do not disturb sign' on her door. That way, by the time they found her, Christmas, along with her life, would be safely over.

Her head nodded, the jolt of it waking her up. God, those things worked fast. How many had she taken? She couldn't remember. The script had her gobbling the whole bottle, perhaps she had got carried away. She tried running through her lines in her head, to keep herself conscious, but she knew them too well, they didn't demand any effort. She shook herself, noticed the envelope still in her gloved hand, and tore it open, switching on the overhead light. Reading it might concentrate her mind for long enough to get her through the drive and into the safety of her room.

It contained a sheet of thick headed notepaper, written in a stylish, educated hand, and a photograph of a slim, rather pretty young girl, who looked vaguely familiar. Some would-be actress, no doubt, soliciting advice and introductions.

Dear Paula Dorland
This letter may be unwelcome, in which case there's no need to answer it.
  My name is Susan Philmore. You won't have heard of me, but I was born on 28th December, 1957, a date I think you will remember, and adopted shortly afterwards.

Paula's heart began hammering, as if to wake her up. She looked at the photograph again. No wonder the face was familiar. She was looking at a younger version of herself . . .

  So now you know who I am. But I thought I would never know who you *were, until they changed the law last year, allowing adopted children over eighteen access to their birth certificates. All my life I've wondered where I came from. I never really fitted in at home, somehow. Which isn't meant as a criticism of my adopted parents. I couldn't have wished for better.*

Paula's eye flew to the embossed letterhead. The Grange, Pewitt Lane, Little Addlesfield, Bucks. A posh, home-counties set-up, by the sound of it. No wonder she didn't fit in . . .

All I had to go on at first was your maiden name and the hospital where I was born. From their records I found out you'd been admitted from a children's home, which eventually, after a lot of persistence, yielded your original address in Harlow. The tenant, Mrs Butcher – I thought at first she must be my grandmother – had been rehoused elsewhere but when I eventually found her, she was very helpful.

I'll bet she was, thought Paula, cringing. Bloody Marje.

It came as quite a shock to know that Paula Butcher was Paula Dorland, because of course I'd heard of and read about you.

Oh God. Richard's death had brought all the old skeletons out of the cupboard – *Bondage*, Marty, Fay, Jess, Vince's drug-dealing . . . Talk about your sins finding you out. Talk about judgment day. And she wasn't even dead yet . . . or was she?

Since then I've been to see you in Alter Ego *about a dozen times. I waited at the stage door for you to come out, but I never managed to pluck up the courage to speak to you. You've had enough to cope with in your life, I know, without me turning up out of the blue and expecting you to be pleased to see me. So I took the coward's way out and wrote instead.*

The poor kid must be soft in the head. She had discovered that her long-lost mother was none other than the notorious Paula Dorland and she still wanted to know her? She was like a junior version of Izzie, with her anxious, apologetic tone, her painfully good manners. Why didn't she hate her for giving her away? Why wasn't she angry with her? Perhaps she was, and was too well bred to show it. No, not well bred. Well brought up. Not the same thing at all.

I haven't told my parents who you are yet, in case you don't want to take this any further. And I'm deliberately not telling you anything about myself, other than to enclose this photo, in the hope that you'll be curious enough to make contact.
Holding my breath
Yours sincerely
Susan Philmore née Butcher

It was all nonsense, of course. It was the damn pills. She was having hallucinations. People did, when they were dying. They babbled of green fields, like Falstaff. Still she might as well make the most of the dream while it lasted . . .

Had her daughter been out there tonight, watching? She must have walked past her, several times, blindly, locked in her world of grief and regret. She knew nothing of this change in the law, she never read a newspaper, except when she was in it. If she'd known, she would have dreaded the prospect of this ever happening, dreaded the confrontation, the accusations, the explanations, the rejection, the renewed, savage sense of guilt . . .

All her life she had been looking for love, running away from it, finding it, losing it, giving it up. And now this girl she didn't even know, a stranger, was ready to give it to her gratis, for no other reason except biology, whether she deserved it or not . . .

She was so young. So naïve. So romantic. She needed someone to put her straight, before she got herself hurt. The poor kid was as green as grass. Assuming that she really existed, outside her imagination . . .

There was only one way to find out. Paula leaned forward, head swimming, and tapped on the driver's window, hoping it wasn't already too late. The traffic was clearing, they were beginning to move again. Her arm was as heavy as lead.

'Can you take me to the nearest hospital?' she said. The words came out slurred; he would think she was drunk. 'Hurry. It's urgent.'

'What's up, miss? You ill?'

'I'm . . . I think I'm going to . . . have a baby. So step on it, will you?'

The cab sped obligingly forwards into the future, backwards into the past. Paula smiled and sighed. And slept.